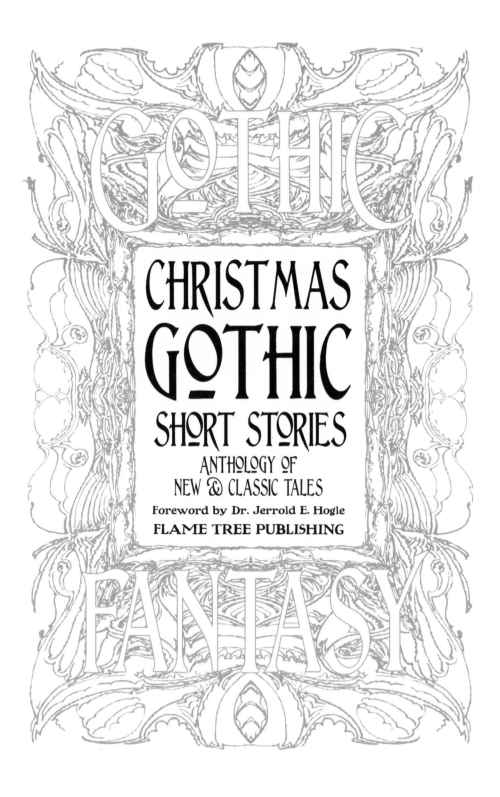

CHRISTMAS GOTHIC

SHORT STORIES

ANTHOLOGY OF NEW & CLASSIC TALES

Foreword by Dr. Jerrold E. Hogle

FLAME TREE PUBLISHING

This is a FLAME TREE Book

Publisher & Creative Director: Nick Wells
Editorial Director: Catherine Taylor
Editorial Board: Catherine Taylor, Gillian Whitaker, Josie Karani and
Taylor Bentley.

Publisher's Note: Due to the historical nature of classic fiction, we're aware that there may be some language used which has the potential to cause offence to the modern reader. However, wishing overall to preserve the integrity of the text, rather than imposing contemporary sensibilities, we have left it unaltered.

FLAME TREE PUBLISHING
6 Melbray Mews, Fulham,
London SW6 3NS, United Kingdom
www.flametreepublishing.com

First published 2022
Copyright © 2022 Flame Tree Publishing Ltd

22 24 26 25 23
1 3 5 7 9 10 8 6 4 2

ISBN: 978-1-80417-164-6
Special ISBN: 978-1-80417-165-3

The cover image is created by Flame Tree Studio based on artwork courtesy of Shutterstock.com.

A copy of the CIP data for this book is available from the British Library.

Printed and bound in China

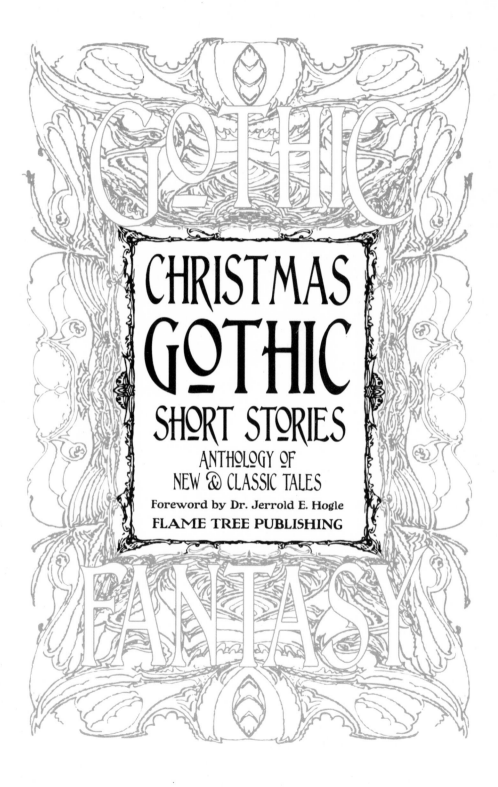

CHRISTMAS GOTHIC

SHORT STORIES

ANTHOLOGY OF NEW & CLASSIC TALES

Foreword by Dr. Jerrold E. Hogle

FLAME TREE PUBLISHING

Contents

CONTENTS

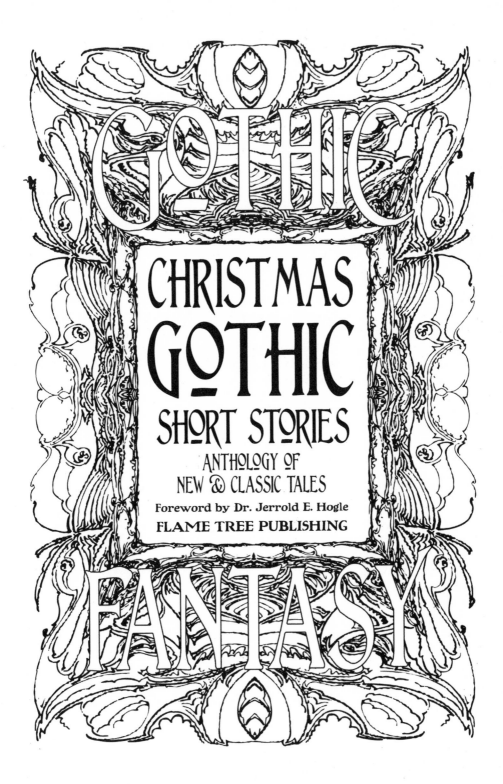

GOTHIC

CHRISTMAS GOTHIC SHORT STORIES

ANTHOLOGY OF
NEW & CLASSIC TALES

Foreword by Dr. Jerrold E. Hogle

FLAME TREE PUBLISHING

FANTASY

Foreword: Christmas Gothic Short Stories

THE CHRISTMAS SHORT TALE with ghosts in a Gothic mode in print really started to coalesce as its own entity in the 1830s in England amid the rapid growth of periodicals and story collections. It then took such hold of the reading public from the 1840s on that it has lasted nearly two hundred years; hence this collection of scintillating examples, twelve of them quite new and published here for the first time, ranging from the dawn of Queen Victoria's reign right through to 2022. The parts of this powerful combination, however – the Winter Solstice ghost tale, the association of ghosts with Christmas, the borrowing of settings and terrors from longer Gothic fictions – each had disparate points of origin in time before they came together. The oldest of these elements are European Yuletide spirit legends prior even to medieval times before the Yule season became Christianized. These stories were told orally as 'winter's tales' at the end of the old and the start of the new year, a transitional period when the portals separating the living and the dead were thought to open (as in the much later Christian All Hallows Eve) and shades of the departed were welcomed into narratives told aloud before fires during ancient Yule celebrations. As Christianity swept through Europe and the Middle east, Christmas, once it became the most crucial part of the end of the calendar year, gradually subsumed this Winter Solstice custom, among many. One medieval result was the now-classic Sir Gawain and the Green Knight (c. 1375-1400), where a ghost-like, magical apparition invades a Christmas celebration in King Arthur's court and ultimately reveals what such gatherings have forgotten and ought to remember.

Christmas ghost tales told around the fire thus grew into a European, and certainly an English, custom. This compounding of a story and a setting first came into print, from what we can tell, during the eighteenth century in such collections as the anonymous *Round about our Coal Fire* (1734), though only some of its tales featured ghosts. The inextricable link between Christmas and the ghost story was most fully codified in a printed text when Thomas K. Hervey in 1836 published *The Book of Christmas*, where 'impressions of the wild and shadowy and insubstantial' were called 'especially welcome food' around the 'winter hearth'. It was therefore in December of that year that Charles Dickens included 'The Story of the Goblins who Stole a Sexton' – the oldest work in this collection – as an inset tale recounted before a Christmas fire in the tenth monthly issue of *The Pickwick Papers*. This piece, as you will see, centers on a self-involved 'grave-digger' in a Gothically 'old churchyard' where he encounters an 'unearthly figure' on a 'tombstone' who leads the sexton into an underground 'cavern' that reveals images of a truer, communal Christmas behind a dark 'fog'. There could hardly be a more anticipatory preview of what became the novella *A Christmas Carol* in an expanded 1843 periodical issue (too widely available to be included here), and the symbolic suggestions and Gothic imagery in both works were extended by 1848 in Dickens' *The Haunted Man and the Ghost's Bargain*, also included here, with its aging professor confronting a look-alike specter who emerges from the walls of his 'solitary and vault-like' chamber.

This succession of Dickens stories had two big effects: it launched an immense effulgence of Christmas ghost stories that manifestly continues through today *and* it firmly united the 'Gothic Story' tradition begun in Horace Walpole's *The Castle of Otranto* (1764) – antiquated, near-death settings haunted by specters (including *Doppelgängers*) harboring buried secrets – with the Christmas ghost story in a fashion hardly ever used so consistently before. Now that these three elements were so tightly interwoven, they became consistently inseparable in a host of *Gothic* Christmas ghost stories that have followed out of Dickens, are always at least slightly reminiscent of him, and have kept these three elements together despite the many different approaches to narrative we see in the following treasure-trove of stories. One reason for this longevity is the lasting appeal of the Gothic, which began, in Walpole's words of 1765, as a deliberately uneasy 'blend' of 'ancient' and 'modern' belief-systems that oscillates between older myths of supernatural intervention and post-Enlightenment doubts about those very notions. Consequently, the stories in this book that develop, and sometimes radically adapt, these beginnings shift back and forth, between and within themselves, from seeing specters as truly apparitions from another level of being to wondering how much – and what it means that – such figures are projections of the human mind. They even oscillate, as the Gothic always has, between different definitions of what the figure of the ghost encompasses and quite disparate beliefs about what they signify, in these cases about Christmas. I therefore invite our readers to enjoy these variations across two centuries as they combine the old winter's tale and the Christmas ghost with the Gothic conflict among new and old beliefs, all of which, like that conflict, are still all too with us.

Dr. Jerrold E. Hogle

Publisher's Note

Dating back to the pagan festivals of old, gathering together on cosy winter evenings to share chilling stories is an enduring Christmas tradition. It is perhaps the warmth and merriment of the season that gives us all a bit more courage, as we take delight in the thrill and suspense of tales of ghosts and the supernatural. Collected here is a selection of Christmas tales new and old, from classic Victorian tales of Gothic horror to exciting new voices with fresh interpretations of the theme. The stories to follow range from the subtly uncanny to wilder tales of spirits and reimagined creatures and characters from Christmas legends, as well as more light-hearted fare. In order to preserve the variety of content and writing style, we have retained the US and UK spellings used originally by the authors. We hope this proves an engaging and satisfying read, to be read with friends and family for years to come.

Wolverden Tower

Grant Allen

I

MAISIE LLEWELYN had never been asked to Wolverden before; therefore, she was not a little elated at Mrs. West's invitation. For Wolverden Hall, one of the loveliest Elizabethan manorhouses in the Weald of Kent, had been bought and fitted up in appropriate style (the phrase is the upholsterer's) by Colonel West, the famous millionaire from South Australia. The Colonel had lavished upon it untold wealth, fleeced from the backs of ten thousand sheep and an equal number of his fellow-countrymen; and Wolverden was now, if not the most beautiful, at least the most opulent country-house within easy reach of London.

Mrs. West was waiting at the station to meet Maisie. The house was full of Christmas guests already, it is true; but Mrs. West was a model of stately, old-fashioned courtesy: she would not have omitted meeting one among the number on any less excuse than a royal command to appear at Windsor. She kissed Maisie on both cheeks – she had always been fond of Maisie – and, leaving two haughty young aristocrats (in powdered hair and blue-and-gold livery) to hunt up her luggage by the light of nature, sailed forth with her through the door to the obsequious carriage.

The drive up the avenue to Wolverden Hall Maisie found quite delicious. Even in their leafless winter condition the great limes looked so noble; and the ivy-covered hall at the end, with its mullioned windows, its Inigo Jones porch, and its creeper-clad gables, was as picturesque a building as the ideals one sees in Mr. Abbey's sketches. If only Arthur Hume had been one of the party now, Maisie's joy would have been complete. But what was the use of thinking so much about Arthur Hume, when she didn't even know whether Arthur Hume cared for her?

A tall, slim girl, Maisie Llewelyn, with rich black hair, and ethereal features, as became a descendant of Llewelyn ap Iorwerth. The sort of girl we none of us would have called anything more than "interesting" till Rossetti and Burne-Jones found eyes for us to see that the type is beautiful with a deeper beauty than that of your obvious pink-and-white prettiness. Her eyes, in particular, had a lustrous depth that was almost superhuman, and her fingers and nails were strangely transparent in their waxen softness.

"You won't mind my having put you in a ground-floor room in the new wing, my dear, will you?" Mrs West inquired, as she led Maisie personally to the quarters chosen for her. "You see, we 're so unusually full, because of these tableaux!"

Maisie gazed round the ground-floor room in the new wing with eyes of mute wonder. If this was the kind of lodging for which Mrs. West thought it necessary to apologise, Maisie wondered of what sort were those better rooms which she gave to the guests she delighted to honour. It was a large and exquisitely decorated chamber, with the softest and deepest Oriental carpet Maisie's feet had ever felt, and the daintiest curtains her eyes had ever lighted upon. True, it opened by French windows on to what was nominally the ground in front; but as the Italian terrace, with its formal balustrade and its great stone balls, was raised several feet above the level of the sloping garden below, the room was really on the first floor for all practical purposes. Indeed, Maisie rather liked the unwonted sense of space and freedom which was given by this easy access to the world without; and, as the windows were secured by great shutters and fasteners, she had no counterbalancing fear lest a nightly burglar should attempt to carry off her little pearl necklet or her amethyst brooch, instead of directing his whole attention to Mrs. West's famous diamond tiara.

She moved naturally to the window. She was fond of nature. The view it disclosed over the Weald at her feet was wide and varied. Misty range lay behind misty range, in a faint December haze, receding and receding, till away to the south, half hidden by vapour, the Sussex downs loomed vague in the distance. The village church, as happens so often in the case of old lordly manors, stood within the grounds of the Hall, and close by the house. It had been built, her hostess said, in the days of the Edwards, but had portions of an older Saxon edifice still enclosed in the chancel. The one eyesore in the view was its new white tower, recently restored (or rather, rebuilt), which contrasted most painfully with the mellow grey stone and mouldering corbels of the nave and transept.

"What a pity it's been so spoiled!" Maisie exclaimed, looking across at the tower. Coming straight as she did from a Merioneth rectory, she took an ancestral interest in all that concerned churches.

"Oh, my dear!" Mrs. West cried, "please don't say that, I beg of you, to the Colonel. If you were to murmur 'spoiled' to him you'd wreck his digestion. He's spent ever so much money over securing the foundations and reproducing the sculpture on the old tower we took down, and it breaks his dear heart when anybody disapproves of it. For some people, you know, are so absurdly opposed to reasonable restoration."

"Oh, but this isn't even restoration, you know," Maisie said, with the frankness of twenty, and the specialist interest of an antiquary's daughter. "This is pure reconstruction."

"Perhaps so," Mrs. West answered. "But if you think so, my dear, don't breathe it at Wolverden."

A fire, of ostentatiously wealthy dimensions, and of the best glowing coal burned bright on the hearth, but the day was mild, and hardly more than autumnal. Maisie found the room quite unpleasantly hot. She opened the windows and stepped out on the terrace. Mrs. West followed her. They paced up and down the broad gravelled platform for a while – Maisie had not yet taken off her travelling-cloak and hat? and then strolled half consciously towards the gate of the church. The churchyard, to hide the tombstones of which the parapet had been erected, was full of quaint old monuments, with broken-nosed cherubs, some of them dating from a comparatively early period. The porch, with its sculptured niches deprived of their saints by puritan hands, was still rich and beautiful in its carved detail. On the seat inside an old woman was sitting. She did not rise as the lady of the manor approached, but went on mumbling and muttering inarticulately to herself in a sulky undertone. Still, Maisie was aware, none the less, that the moment she came near a strange light gleamed suddenly in the old woman's eyes, and that her glance was fixed upon her. A faint thrill of recognition seemed to pass like a flash through her palsied body. Maisie knew not why, but she was dimly afraid of the old woman's gaze upon her.

"It's a lovely old church!" Maisie said, looking up at the trefoil finials on the porch – "all, except the tower."

"We had to reconstruct it," Mrs. West answered apologetically. Mrs. West's general attitude in life was apologetic, as though she felt she had no right to so much more money than her fellow-creatures. "It would have fallen if we hadn't done something to buttress it up. It was really in a most dangerous and critical condition."

"Lies! lies! lies!" the old woman burst out suddenly, though in a strange, low tone, as if speaking to herself. "It would not have fallen – they knew it would not. It could not have fallen. It would never have fallen if they had not destroyed it. And even then – I was there when they pulled it down – each stone clung to each, with arms and legs and hands and claws, till they burst them asunder by main force with their new-fangled stuff – I don't know what they call it – dynamite, or something. It was all of it done for one man's vainglory!"

"Come away, dear," Mrs. West whispered. But Maisie loitered.

"Wolverden Tower was fasted thrice," the old woman continued, in a sing-song quaver. "It was fasted thrice with souls of maids against every assault of man or devil. It was fasted at the foundation against earthquake and ruin. It was fasted at the top against thunder and lightning. It was fasted in the middle against storm and battle. And there it would have stood for a thousand years if a wicked man had not raised a vainglorious hand against it. For that's what the rhyme says?

"Fasted thrice with souls of men. Stands the tower of Wolverden; Fasted thrice with maidens' blood. A thousand years of fire and flood Shall see it stand as erst it stood."

She paused a moment, then, raising one skinny hand towards the brand-new stone, she went on in the same voice, but with malignant fervour?

"A thousand years the tower shall stand Till ill assailed by evil hand; By evil hand in evil hour. Fasted thrice with warlock's power. Shall fall the stanes of Wulfhere's tower."

She tottered off as she ended, and took her seat on the edge of a depressed vault in the churchyard close by, still eyeing Maisie Llewellyn with a weird and curious glance, almost like the look which a famishing man casts upon the food in a shop-window.

"Who is she?" Maisie asked, shrinking away in undefined terror.

"Oh, old Bessie," Mrs. West answered, looking more apologetic (for the parish) than ever. "She's always hanging about here. She has nothing else to do, and she's an outdoor pauper. You see, that's the worst of having the church in one's grounds, which is otherwise picturesque and romantic and baronial; the road to it's public; you must admit all the world; and old Bessie will come here. The servants are afraid of her. They say she's a witch. She has the evil eye, and she drives girls to suicide. But they cross her hand with silver all the same, and she tells them their fortunes – gives them each a butler. She's full of dreadful stories about Wolverden Church? stories to make your blood run cold, my dear, compact with old superstitions and murders, and so forth. And they're true, too, that's the worst of them. She's quite a character. Mr. Blaydes, the antiquary, is really attached to her; he says she's now the sole living repository of the traditional folklore and history of the parish. But I don't care for it myself. It 'gars one greet,' as we say in Scotland. Too much burying alive in it, don't you know, my dear, to quite suit my fancy."

They turned back as she spoke towards the carved wooden lych-gate, one of the oldest and most exquisite of its class in England. When they reached the vault by whose doors old Bessie was seated, Maisie turned once more to gaze at the pointed lancet windows of the Early English choir, and the still more ancient dog-tooth ornament of the ruined Norman Lady Chapel.

"How solidly it's built!" she exclaimed, looking up at the arches which alone survived the fury of the Puritan. "It really looks as if it would last for ever."

Old Bessie had bent her head, and seemed to be whispering something at the door of the vault. But at the sound she raised her eyes, and, turning her wizened face towards the lady of the manor, mumbled through her few remaining fang-like teeth an old local saying, "Bradbury for length, Wolverden for strength, and Church Hatton for beauty!"

"Three brothers builded churches three; And fasted thrice each church shall be: Fasted thrice with maidens' blood. To make them safe from fire and flood; Fasted thrice with souls of men. Hatton, Bradbury, Wolverden!"

"Come away," Maisie said, shuddering. "I'm afraid of that woman. Why was she whispering at the doors of the vault down there? I don't like the look of her."

"My dear," Mrs. West answered, in no less terrified a tone, "I will confess I don't like the look of her myself. I wish she'd leave the place. I've tried to make her. The Colonel offered her fifty pounds down and a nice cottage in Surrey if only she'd go – she frightens me so much; but she wouldn't hear of it. She said she must stop by the bodies of her dead – that's her style, don't you see: a sort of modern ghoul, a degenerate vampire – and from the bodies of her dead in Wolverden Church no living soul should ever move her."

II

For dinner Maisie wore her white satin Empire dress, high-waisted, low-necked, and cut in the bodice with a certain baby-like simplicity of style which exactly suited her strange and uncanny type of beauty. She was very much admired. She felt it, and it pleased her. The young man who took her in, a subaltern of engineers, had no eyes for any one else; while old Admiral Wade, who sat opposite her with a plain and skinny dowager, made her positively uncomfortable by the persistent way in which he stared at her simple pearl necklet.

After dinner, the tableaux. They had been designed and managed by a famous Royal Academician, and were mostly got up by the members of the house-party. But two or three actresses from London had been specially invited to help in a few of the more mythological scenes; for, indeed, Mrs. West had prepared the entire entertainment with that topsy-turvy conscientiousness and scrupulous sense of responsibility to society which pervaded her view of millionaire morality. Having once decided to offer the county a set of tableaux, she felt that millionaire morality absolutely demanded of her the sacrifice of three weeks' time and several hundred pounds' money in order to discharge her obligations to the county with becoming magnificence.

The first tableau, Maisie learned from the gorgeous programme, was "Jephthah's Daughter." The subject was represented at the pathetic moment when the doomed virgin goes forth from her father's house with her attendant maidens to bewail her virginity for two months upon the mountains, before the fulfilment of the awful vow which bound her father to offer her up for a burnt offering. Maisie thought it too solemn and tragic a scene for a festive occasion. But the famous R.A. had a taste for such themes, and his grouping was certainly most effectively dramatic.

"A perfect symphony in white and grey," said Mr. Wills, the art critic.

"How awfully affecting!" said most of the young girls.

"Reminds me a little too much, my dear, of old Bessie's stories," Mrs. West whispered low, leaning from her seat across two rows to Maisie.

A piano stood a little on one side of the platform, just in front of the curtain. The intervals between the pieces were filled up with songs, which, however, had been evidently arranged in keeping with the solemn and half-mystical tone of the tableaux. It is the habit of amateurs to take a long time in getting their scenes in order, so the interposition of the music was a happy thought as far as its prime intention went. But Maisie wondered they could not have chosen some livelier song for Christmas Eve than "Oh, Mary, go and call the cattle home, and call the cattle home, and call the cattle home, across the sands of Dee." Her own name was Mary when she signed it officially, and the sad lilt of the last line, "But never home came she," rang unpleasantly in her ear through the rest of the evening.

The second tableau was the "Sacrifice of Iphigenia." It was admirably rendered. The cold and dignified father, standing, apparently unmoved, by the pyre; the cruel faces of the attendant priests; the shrinking form of the immolated princess; the mere blank curiosity and inquiring interest of the helmeted heroes looking on, to whom this slaughter of a virgin victim was but an ordinary incident of the Achean religion. All these had been arranged by the Academical director with consummate skill and pictorial cleverness. But the group that attracted Maisie most among the components of the scene was that of the attendant maidens, more conspicuous here in their flowing white chitons than even they had been when posed as companions of the beautiful and ill-fated Hebrew victim. Two in particular excited her close attention – two very graceful and spiritual-looking girls, in long white robes of no particular age or country, who stood at the very end near the right edge of the picture. "How lovely they are, the two last on the right!" Maisie whispered to her neighbour – an Oxford undergraduate with a budding moustache. "I do so admire them!"

"Do you?" he answered, fondling the moustache with one dubious finger. "Well, now, do you know, I don't think I do. They're rather coarse-looking. And besides, I don't quite like the way they've got their hair done up in bunches; too fashionable, isn't it? – too much of the present day – I don't care to see a girl in a Greek costume, with her coiffure so evidently turned out by Truefitt's!"

"Oh, I don't mean those two," Maisie answered, a little shocked he should think she had picked out such meretricious faces; "I mean the two beyond them again – the two with their hair so simply and sweetly done – the ethereal-looking dark girls."

The undergraduate opened his mouth, and stared at her in blank amazement for a moment. "Well, I don't see??" he began, and broke off suddenly. Something in Maisie's eye seemed to give him pause. He fondled his moustache, hesitated and was silent.

"How nice to have read the Greek and know what it all means!" Maisie went on, after a minute. "It's a human sacrifice, of course; but, please, what is the story?"

The undergraduate hummed and hawed. "Well, it's in Euripides, you know," he said, trying to look impressive, "and – er – and I haven't taken up Euripides for my next examination. But I think it's like this. Iphigenia was a daughter of Agamemnon's, don't you know, and he had offended Artemis or somebody – some other Goddess; and he vowed to offer up to her the most beautiful thing that should be born that year, by way of reparation – just like Jephthah. Well, Iphigenia was considered the most beautiful product of the particular twelvemonth? don't look at me like that, please! you – you make me nervous – and so, when the young woman grew up – well, I don't quite recollect the ins and outs of the details, but it's a human sacrifice business, don't you see; and they're just going to kill her, though I believe a hind was finally substituted for the girl, like the ram for Isaac; but I must confess I've a very vague recollection of it." He rose from his seat uneasily. "I'm afraid," he went on, shuffling about for an excuse to move, "these chairs are too close. I seem to be incommoding you."

He moved away with a furtive air. At the end of the tableau one or two of the characters who were not needed in succeeding pieces came down from the stage and joined the body of spectators, as they often do, in their character-dresses – a good opportunity, in point of fact, for retaining through the evening the advantages conferred by theatrical costume, rouge, and pearl-powder. Among them the two girls Maisie had admired so much glided quietly toward her and took the two vacant seats on either side, one of which had just been quitted by the awkward undergraduate. They were not only beautiful in face and figure, on a closer view, but Maisie found them from the first extremely sympathetic. They burst into talk with her, frankly and at once, with charming ease and grace of manner. They were ladies in the grain, in instinct and breeding. The taller of the two, whom the other addressed as Yolande, seemed particularly pleasing. The very name charmed Maisie. She was friends with them at once. They both possessed a certain nameless attraction that constitutes in itself the best possible introduction. Maisie hesitated to ask them whence they came, but it was clear from their talk they knew Wolverden intimately.

After a minute the piano struck up once more. A famous Scotch vocalist, in a diamond necklet and a dress to match, took her place on the stage, just in front of the footlights. As chance would have it, she began singing the song Maisie most of all hated. It was Scott's ballad of "Proud Maisie," set to music by Carlo Ludovici?

"Proud Maisie is in the wood. Walking so early; Sweet Robin sits on the bush. Singing so rarely. 'Tell me, thou bonny bird. When shall I marry me?' 'When six braw gentlemen Kirkward shall carry ye.' 'Who makes the bridal bed. Birdie, say truly?' 'The grey-headed sexton That delves the grave duly. 'The glow-worm o'er grave and stone Shall light thee steady; 'The owl from the steeple sing. Welcome, Proud lady.'"

Maisie listened to the song with grave discomfort. She had never liked it, and tonight it appalled her. She did not know that just at that moment Mrs. West was whispering in a perfect fever of apology to a lady by her side, "Oh dear! oh dear! what a dreadful thing of me ever to have permitted that song to be sung here tonight! It was horribly thoughtless! Why, now I remember, Miss Llewelyn's name, you know, is Maisie! And there she is listening to it with a face like a sheet! I shall never forgive myself!"

The tall, dark girl by Maisie's side, whom the other called Yolande, leaned across to her sympathetically. "You don't like that song?" she said, with just a tinge of reproach in her voice as she said it.

"I hate it!" Maisie answered, trying hard to compose herself.

"Why so?" the tall, dark girl asked, in a tone of calm and singular sweetness. "It is sad, perhaps; but it's lovely – and natural!"

"My own name is Maisie," her new friend replied, with an ill-repressed shudder. "And somehow that song pursues me through life I seem always to hear the horrid ring of the words, 'When six braw gentlemen kirkward shall carry ye.' I wish to Heaven my people had never called me Maisie!"

"And yet why?" the tall, dark girl asked again, with a sad, mysterious air. "Why this clinging to life – this terror of death? this inexplicable attachment to a world of misery? And with such eyes as yours, too! Your eyes are like mine!" which was a compliment, certainly, for the dark girl's own pair were strangely deep and lustrous. "People with eyes such as those, that can look into futurity, ought not surely to shrink from a mere gate like death! For death is but a gate – the gate of life in its fullest beauty. It is written over the door, 'Mors janua vit.'"

"What door?" Maisie asked, for she remembered having read those selfsame words, and tried in vain to translate them, that very day, though the meaning was now clear to her.

The answer electrified her: "The gate of the vault in Wolverden churchyard."

She said it very low, but with pregnant expression.

"Oh, how dreadful!" Maisie exclaimed, drawing back. The tall, dark girl half frightened her.

"Not at all," the girl answered. "This life is so short, so vain, so transitory! And beyond it is peace – eternal peace – the calm of rest – the joy of the spirit."

"You come to anchor at last," her companion added.

"But if – one has somebody one would not wish to leave behind?" Maisie suggested timidly.

"He will follow before long," the dark girl replied with quiet decision, interpreting rightly the sex of the indefinite substantive. "Time passes so quickly. And if time passes quickly in time, how much more, then, in eternity!"

"Hush, Yolande," the other dark girl put in, with a warning glance; "there's a new tableau coming. Let me see, is this 'The Death of Ophelia'? No, that's number four; this is number three, 'The Martyrdom of St. Agnes.'"

III

"My dear," Mrs. West said, positively oozing apology, when she met Maisie in the supper-room, "I'm afraid you've been left in a corner by yourself almost all the evening!"

"Oh dear, no," Maisie answered with a quiet smile. "I had that Oxford undergraduate at my elbow at first; and afterwards those two nice girls, with the flowing white dresses and the beautiful eyes, came and sat beside me. What's their name, I wonder?"

"Which girls?" Mrs. West asked, with a little surprise in her tone, for her impression was rather that Maisie had been sitting between two empty chairs for the greater part of the evening, muttering at times to herself in the most uncanny way, but not talking to anybody.

Maisie glanced round the room in search of her new friends, and for some time could not see them. At last, she observed them in a remote alcove, drinking red wine by themselves out of Venetian-glass beakers. "Those two," she said, pointing towards them. "They 're such charming girls! Can you tell me who they are? I've quite taken a fancy to them."

Mrs. West gazed at them for a second – or rather, at the recess towards which Maisie pointed – and then turned to Maisie with much the same oddly embarrassed look and manner as the undergraduate's. "Oh, those!" she said slowly, peering through and through her, Maisie thought. "Those – must be some of the professionals from London. At any rate? – I'm not sure which you mean – over there by the curtain, in the Moorish nook, you say – well, I can't tell you their names! So they must be professionals."

She went off with a singularly frightened manner. Maisie noticed it and wondered at it. But it made no great or lasting impression.

When the party broke up, about midnight or a little later, Maisie went along the corridor to her own bedroom. At the end, by the door, the two other girls happened to be standing, apparently gossiping.

"Oh, you've not gone home yet?" Maisie said, as she passed, to Yolande.

"No, we're stopping here," the dark girl with the speaking eyes answered.

Maisie paused for a second. Then an impulse burst over her. "Will you come and see my room?" she asked, a little timidly.

"Shall we go, Hedda?" Yolande said, with an inquiring glance at her companion.

Her friend nodded assent. Maisie opened the door, and ushered them into her bedroom.

The ostentatiously opulent fire was still burning brightly, the electric light flooded the room with its brilliancy, the curtains were drawn, and the shutters fastened. For a while the three girls sat together by the hearth and gossiped quietly. Maisie liked her new friends – their voices were so gentle, soft, and sympathetic, while for face and figure they might have sat as models to Burne-Jones or Botticelli. Their dresses, too, took her delicate Welsh fancy; they were so dainty, yet so simple. The soft silk fell in natural folds and dimples. The only ornaments they wore were two curious brooches of very antique workmanship – as Maisie supposed – somewhat Celtic in design, and enamelled in blood-red on a gold background. Each carried a flower laid loosely in her bosom. Yolande's was an orchid with long, floating streamers, in colour and shape recalling some Southern lizard; dark purple spots dappled its lip and petals. Hedda's was a flower of a sort Maisie had never before seen – the stem spotted like a viper's skin, green flecked with russet-brown, and uncanny to look upon; on either side, great twisted spirals of red-and-blue blossoms, each curled after the fashion of a scorpion's tail, very strange and lurid. Something weird and witch-like about flowers and dresses rather attracted Maisie; they affected her with the half-repellent fascination of a snake for a bird; she felt such blossoms were fit for incantations and sorceries. But a lily-of-the-valley in Yolande's dark hair gave a sense of purity which assorted better with the girl's exquisitely calm and nun-like beauty.

After a while Hedda rose. "This air is close," she said. "It ought to be warm outside tonight, if one may judge by the sunset. May I open the window?"

"Oh, certainly, if you like," Maisie answered, a vague foreboding now struggling within her against innate politeness.

Hedda drew back the curtains and unfastened the shutters. It was a moonlit evening. The breeze hardly stirred the bare boughs of the silver birches. A sprinkling of soft snow on the terrace and the hills just whitened the ground. The moon lighted it up, falling full upon the Hall; the church and tower below stood silhouetted in dark against a cloudless expanse of starry sky in the background. Hedda opened the window. Cool, fresh air blew in, very soft and genial, in spite of the snow and the lateness of the season. "What a glorious night!" she said, looking up at Orion overhead. "Shall we stroll out for a while in it?"

If the suggestion had not thus been thrust upon her from outside, it would never have occurred to Maisie to walk abroad in a strange place, in evening dress, on a winter's night, with snow whitening the ground; but Hedda's voice sounded so sweetly persuasive, and the idea itself seemed so natural now she had once proposed it, that Maisie followed her two new friends on to the moonlit terrace without a moment's hesitation.

They paced once or twice up and down the gravelled walks. Strange to say, though a sprinkling of dry snow powdered the ground under foot, the air itself was soft and balmy. Stranger still, Maisie noticed, almost without noticing it, that though they walked three abreast, only one pair of footprints – her own – lay impressed on the snow in a long trail when they turned at either end and re-paced the platform. Yolande and Hedda must step lightly indeed; or perhaps her own feet might be warmer or thinner shod, so as to melt the light layer of snow more readily.

The girls slipped their arms through hers. A little thrill coursed through her. Then, after three or four turns up and down the terrace, Yolande led the way quietly down the broad flight of steps in the direction of the church on the lower level. In that bright, broad moonlight Maisie went with them undeterred; the Hall was still alive with the glare of electric lights in bedroom windows; and the presence of the other girls, both wholly free from any signs of fear, took off all sense of terror or loneliness. They strolled on into the churchyard. Maisie's eyes were now fixed on the new white tower, which merged in the silhouette against the starry sky into much the same grey and indefinite hue as the older parts of the building. Before she quite knew where she was, she found herself at the head of the worn stone steps which led into the vault by whose doors she had seen old Bessie sitting. In the pallid moonlight, with the aid of the greenish reflection from the snow, she could just read the words inscribed over the portal, the words that Yolande had repeated in the drawing-room, "Mors janua vit."

Yolande moved down one step. Maisie drew back for the first time with a faint access of alarm. "You're – you're not going down there!" she exclaimed, catching her breath for a second.

"Yes, I am," her new friend answered in a calmly quiet voice. "Why not? We live here."

"You live here?" Maisie echoed, freeing her arms by a sudden movement and standing away from her mysterious friends with a tremulous shudder.

"Yes, we live here," Hedda broke in, without the slightest emotion. She said it in a voice of perfect calm, as one might say it of any house in a street in London.

Maisie was far less terrified than she might have imagined beforehand would be the case under such unexpected conditions. The two girls were so simple, so natural, so strangely like herself, that she could not say she was really afraid of them. She shrank, it is true, from the nature of the door at which they stood, but she received the unearthly announcement that they lived there with scarcely more than a slight tremor of surprise and astonishment.

"You will come in with us?" Hedda said in a gently enticing tone. "We went into your bedroom."

Maisie hardly liked to say no. They seemed so anxious to show her their home. With trembling feet she moved down the first step, and then the second. Yolande kept ever one pace in front of her. As Maisie reached the third step, the two girls, as if moved by one design, took her wrists in their hands, not unkindly, but coaxingly. They reached the actual doors of the vault itself – two heavy bronze valves, meeting in the centre. Each bore a ring for a handle, pierced through a Gorgon's head embossed upon the surface. Yolande pushed them with her hand. They yielded instantly to her light touch, and opened inward. Yolande, still in front, passed from the glow of the moon to the gloom of the vault, which a ray of moonlight just descended obliquely. As she passed, for a second, a weird sight met Maisie's eyes. Her face and hands and dress became momentarily self-luminous – but through them, as they glowed, she could descry within every bone and joint of her living skeleton, dimly shadowed in dark through the luminous haze that marked her body.

Maisie drew back once more, terrified. Yet her terror was not quite what one could describe as fear: it was rather a vague sense of the profoundly mystical. "I can't! I can't!" she cried, with an appealing glance. "Hedda! Yolande! I cannot go with you."

Hedda held her hand tight, and almost seemed to force her. But Yolande, in front, like a mother with her child, turned round with a grave smile. "No, no," she said reprovingly. "Let her come if she will, Hedda, of her own accord, not otherwise. The tower demands a willing victim."

Her hand on Maisie's wrist was strong but persuasive. It drew her without exercising the faintest compulsion. "Will you come with us, dear?" she said, in that winning silvery tone which had captivated Maisie's fancy from the very first moment they spoke together. Maisie gazed into her eyes. They were deep and tender. A strange resolution seemed to nerve her for the effort. "Yes, yes—I—will—come—with you," she answered slowly.

Hedda on one side, Yolande on the other, now went before her, holding her wrists in their grasp, but rather enticing than drawing her. As each reached the gloom, the same luminous appearance which Maisie had noticed before spread over their bodies, and the same weird skeleton shape showed faintly through their limbs in darker shadow. Maisie crossed the threshold with a convulsive gasp. As she crossed it she looked down at her own dress and body. They were semi-transparent, like the others', though not quite so self-luminous; the framework of her limbs appeared within in less certain outline, yet quite dark and distinguishable.

The doors swung to of themselves behind her. Those three stood alone in the vault of Wolverden.

Alone, for a minute or two; and then, as her eyes grew accustomed to the grey dusk of the interior, Maisie began to perceive that the vault opened out into a large and beautiful hall or crypt, dimly lighted at first, but becoming each moment more vaguely clear and more dreamily definite. Gradually she could make out great rock-hewn pillars, Romanesque in their outline or dimly Oriental, like the sculptured columns in the caves of Ellora, supporting a roof of vague and uncertain dimensions, more or less strangely dome-shaped. The effect on the whole was like that of the second impression produced by some dim cathedral, such as Chartres or Milan, after the eyes have grown accustomed to the mellow light from the stained-glass windows, and have recovered from the blinding glare of the outer sunlight. But the architecture, if one may call it so, was more mosque-like and magical. She turned to her companions. Yolande and Hedda stood still by her side; their bodies were now self-luminous to a greater degree than even at the threshold; but the terrible transparency had disappeared altogether; they were once more but beautiful though strangely transfigured and more than mortal women.

Then Maisie understood in her own soul, dimly, the meaning of those mystic words written over the portal. "Mors janua vit." Death is the gate of life; and also the interpretation of that awful vision of death dwelling within them as they crossed the threshold; for through that gate they had passed to this underground palace.

Her two guides still held her hands, one on either side. But they seemed rather to lead her on now, seductively and resistlessly, than to draw or compel her. As she moved in through the hall, with its endless vistas of shadowy pillars, seen now behind, now in dim perspective, she was gradually aware that many other people crowded its aisles and corridors. Slowly they took shape as forms more or less clad, mysterious, varied, and of many ages. Some of them wore flowing robes, half mediaeval in shape, like the two friends who had brought her there. They looked like the saints on a stained-glass window. Others were girt merely with a light and floating Coan sash; while some stood dimly nude in the darker recesses of the temple or palace. All leaned eagerly forward with one mind as she approached, and regarded her with deep and sympathetic interest. A few of them murmured words – mere cabalistic sounds which at first she could not understand; but as she moved further into the hall, and saw at each step more clearly into the gloom, they began to have a meaning for her. Before long, she was aware that she understood the mute tumult of voices at once by some internal instinct. The Shades addressed her; she answered them. She knew by intuition what tongue they spoke; it was the Language of the Dead; and, by passing that portal with her two companions, she had herself become enabled both to speak and understand it.

A soft and flowing tongue, this speech of the Nether World – all vowels it seemed, without distinguishable consonants; yet dimly recalling every other tongue, and compounded, as it were, of what was common to all of them. It flowed from those shadowy lips as clouds issue inchoate from a mountain valley; it was formless, uncertain, vague, but yet beautiful. She hardly knew, indeed, as it fell upon her senses, if it were sound or perfume.

Through this tenuous world Maisie moved as in a dream, her two companions still cheering and guiding her. When they reached an inner shrine or chantry of the temple she was dimly conscious of more terrible forms pervading the background than any of those that had yet appeared to her. This was a more austere and antique apartment than the rest; a shadowy cloister, prehistoric in its severity; it recalled to her mind something indefinitely inter'ate between the huge unwrought trilithons of Stonehenge and the massive granite pillars of Philaend Luxor. At the further end of the sanctuary a sort of Sphinx looked down on her, smiling mysteriously. At its base, on a rude megalithic throne, in solitary state, a High Priest was seated. He bore in his hand a wand or sceptre. All round, a strange court of half-unseen acolytes and shadowy hierophants stood attentive They were girt, as she fancied, in what looked like leopards' skins, or in the fells of some earlier prehistoric lion. These wore sabre-shaped teeth suspended by a string round their dusky necks; others had ornaments of uncut amber, or hatchets of jade threaded as collars on a cord of sinew. A few, more barbaric than savage in type, flaunted torques of gold as armlets and necklets.

The High Priest rose slowly and held out his two hands, just level with his head, the palms turned outward. "You have brought a willing victim as Guardian of the Tower?" he asked, in that mystic tongue, of Yolande and Hedda.

"We have brought a willing victim," the two girls answered.

The High Priest gazed at her. His glance was piercing. Maisie trembled less with fear than with a sense of strangeness, such as a neophyte might feel on being first presented at some courtly pageant. "You come of your own accord?" the Priest inquired of her in solemn accents.

"I come of my own accord," Maisie answered, with an inner consciousness that she was bearing her part in some immemorial ritual. Ancestral memories seemed to stir within her.

"It is well," the Priest murmured. Then he turned to her guides. "She is of royal lineage?" he inquired, taking his wand in his hand again.

"She is a Llewelyn," Yolande answered, "of royal lineage, and of the race that, after your own, earliest bore sway in this land of Britain. She has in her veins the blood of Arthur, of Ambrosius, and of Vortigern."

"It is well," the Priest said again. "I know these princes." Then he turned to Maisie. "This is the ritual of those who build," he said, in a very deep voice. "It has been the ritual of those who build from the days of the builders of Lokmariaker and Avebury. Every building man makes shall have its human soul, the soul of a virgin to guard and protect it. Three souls it requires as a living talisman against chance and change. One soul is the soul of the human victim slain beneath the foundation-stone; she is the guardian spirit against earthquake and ruin. One soul is the soul of the human victim slain when the building is half built up; she is the guardian spirit against battle and tempest. One soul is the soul of the human victim who flings herself of her own free will off tower or gable when the building is complete; she is the guardian spirit against thunder and lightning. Unless a building be duly fasted with these three, how can it hope to stand against the hostile powers of fire and flood and storm and earthquake?"

An assessor at his side, unnoticed till then, took up the parable. He had a stern Roman face, and bore a shadowy suit of Roman armour. "In times of old," he said, with iron austerity, "all men knew well these rules of building. They built in solid stone to endure for ever: the works they erected have lasted to this day, in this land and others. So built we the amphitheatres of Rome and Verona; so built we the walls of Lincoln, York, and London. In the blood of a king's son laid we the foundation-stone: in the blood of a king's son laid we the coping-stone: in the blood of a maiden of royal line fasted we the bastions against fire and lightning. But in these latter days, since faith grows dim, men build with burnt brick and rubble of plaster; no foundation spirit or guardian soul do they give to their bridges, their walls, or their towers: so bridges break, and walls fall in, and towers crumble, and the art and mystery of building aright have perished from among you."

He ceased. The High Priest held out his wand and spoke again. "We are the Assembly of Dead Builders and Dead Victims," he said, "for this mark of Wolverden; all of whom have built or been built upon in this holy site of immemorial sanctity. We are the stones of a living fabric. Before this place was a Christian church, it was a temple of Woden. And before it was a temple of Woden, it was a shrine of Hercules. And before it was a shrine of Hercules, it was a grove of Nodens. And before it was a grove of Nodens, it was a Stone Circle of the Host of Heaven. And before it was a Stone Circle of the Host of Heaven, it was the grave and tumulus and underground palace of Me, who am the earliest builder of all in this place; and my name in my ancient tongue is Wolf, and I laid and hallowed it. And after me, Wolf, and my namesake Wulfhere, was this barrow called Ad Lupum and Wolverden. And all these that are here with me have built and been built upon in this holy site for all generations. And you are the last who come to join us."

Maisie felt a cold thrill course down her spine as he spoke these words; but courage did not fail her. She was dimly aware that those who offer themselves as victims for service must offer themselves willingly; for the gods demand a voluntary victim; no beast can be slain unless it nod assent; and none can be made a guardian spirit who takes not the post upon him of his own free will. She turned meekly to Hedda. "Who are you?" she asked, trembling.

"I am Hedda," the girl answered, in the same soft sweet voice and winning tone as before; "Hedda, the daughter of Gorm, the chief of the Northmen who settled in East Anglia. And I was a worshipper of Thor and Odin. And when my father, Gorm, fought against Alfred, King of Wessex, was I taken prisoner. And Wulfhere, the Kenting, was then building the first church and tower of Wolverden. And they baptized me, and shrived me, and I consented of my own free will to be built under the foundation-stone. And there my body lies built up to this day; and I am the guardian spirit against earthquake and ruin."

"And who are you?" Maisie asked, turning again to Yolande.

"I am Yolande Fitz-Aylwin," the tall dark girl answered; "a royal maiden too, sprung from the blood of Henry Plantagenet. And when Roland Fitz-Stephen was building anew the choir and chancel of Wulfhere's minster, I chose to be immured in the fabric of the wall, for love of the Church and all holy saints; and there my body lies built up to this day; and I am the guardian against battle and tempest."

Maisie held her friend's hand tight. Her voice hardly trembled. "And I?" she asked once more. "What fate for me? Tell me!"

"Your task is easier far," Yolande answered gently. "For you shall be the guardian of the new tower against thunder and lightning. Now, those who guard against earthquake and battle are buried alive under the foundation-stone or in the wall of the building; there they die a slow death of starvation and choking. But those who guard against thunder and lightning cast themselves alive of their own free will from the battlements of the tower, and die in the air before they reach the ground; so their fate is the easiest and the lightest of all who would serve mankind; and thenceforth they live with us here in our palace."

Maisie clung to her hand still tighter. "Must I do it?" she asked, pleading.

"It is not must," Yolande replied in the same caressing tone, yet with a calmness as of one in whom earthly desires and earthly passions are quenched for ever. "It is as you choose yourself. None but a willing victim may be a guardian spirit. This glorious privilege comes but to the purest and best amongst us. Yet what better end can you ask for your soul than to dwell here in our midst as our comrade for ever, where all is peace, and to preserve the tower whose guardian you are from evil assaults of lightning and thunderbolt?"

Maisie flung her arms round her friend's neck. "But – I am afraid," she murmured. Why she should even wish to consent she knew not, yet the strange serene peace in these strange girls' eyes made her mysteriously in love with them and with the fate they offered her. They seemed to move like the stars in their orbits. "How shall I leap from the top?" she cried. "How shall I have courage to mount the stairs alone, and fling myself off from the lonely battlement?"

Yolande unwound her arms with a gentle forbearance. She coaxed her as one coaxes an unwilling child. "You will not be alone," she said, with a tender pressure. "We will all go with you. We will help you and encourage you. We will sing our sweet songs of life-in-death to you. Why should you draw back? All we have faced it in ten thousand ages, and we tell you with one voice, you need not fear it. 'Tis life you should fear – life, with its dangers, its toils, its heartbreakings. Here we dwell for ever in unbroken peace. Come, come, and join us!"

She held out her arms with an enticing gesture. Maisie sprang into them, sobbing. "Yes, I will come," she cried in an access of hysterical fervour. "These are the arms of Death – I embrace them. These are the lips of Death – I kiss them. Yolande, Yolande, I will do as you ask me!"

The tall dark girl in the luminous white robe stooped down and kissed her twice on the forehead in return. Then she looked at the High Priest. "We are ready," she murmured in a low, grave voice. "The Victim consents. The Virgin will die. Lead on to the tower. We are ready! We are ready!"

IV

From the recesses of the temple – if temple it were – from the inmost shrines of the shrouded cavern, unearthly music began to sound of itself; with wild modulation, on strange reeds and tabors. It swept through the aisles like a rushing wind on an aeolian harp; at times it wailed with a voice like a woman's; at times it rose loud in an organ-note of triumph; at times it sank low into a pensive and melancholy flute-like symphony. It waxed and waned; it swelled and died away again; but no man saw how or whence it proceeded. Wizard echoes issued from the crannies and vents in the invisible walls; they sighed from the ghostly interspaces of the pillars; they keened and moaned from the vast overhanging dome of the palace. Gradually the song shaped itself by weird stages into a processional measure. At its sound the High Priest rose slowly from his immemorial seat on the mighty cromlech which formed his throne. The Shades in leopards' skins ranged themselves in bodiless rows on either hand; the ghostly wearers of the sabre-toothed lions' fangs followed like ministrants in the footsteps of their hierarch.

Hedda and Yolande took their places in the procession. Maisie stood between the two, with hair floating on the air; she looked like a novice who goes up to take the veil, accompanied and cheered by two elder sisters.

The ghostly pageant began to move. Unseen music followed it with fitful gusts of melody. They passed down the main corridor, between shadowy Doric or Ionic pillars which grew dimmer and ever dimmer again in the distance as they approached, with slow steps, the earthward portal.

At the gate, the High Priest pushed against the valves with his hand. They opened outward.

He passed into the moonlight. The attendants thronged after him. As each wild figure crossed the threshold the same strange sight as before met Maisie's eyes. For a second of time each ghostly body became self-luminous, as with some curious phosphorescence; and through each, at the moment of passing the portal, the dim outline of a skeleton loomed briefly visible. Next instant it had clothed itself as with earthly members.

Maisie reached the outer air. As she did so, she gasped. For a second, its chilliness and freshness almost choked her. She was conscious now that the atmosphere of the vault, though pleasant in its way, and warm and dry, had been loaded with fumes as of burning incense, and with somnolent vapours of poppy and mandragora. Its drowsy ether had cast her into a lethargy. But after the first minute in the outer world, the keen night air revived her. Snow lay still on the ground a little deeper than when she first came out, and the moon rode lower; otherwise, all was as before, save that only one or two lights still burned here and there in the great house on the terrace. Among them she could recognise her own room, on the ground floor in the new wing, by its open window.

The procession made its way across the churchyard towards the tower. As it wound among the graves an owl hooted. All at once Maisie remembered the lines that had so chilled her a few short hours before in the drawing-room?

"The glow-worm o'er grave and stone Shall light thee steady; The owl from the steeple sing. 'Welcome, proud lady!'"

But, marvellous to relate, they no longer alarmed her. She felt rather that a friend was welcoming her home; she clung to Yolande's hand with a gentle pressure.

As they passed in front of the porch, with its ancient yew-tree, a stealthy figure glided out like a ghost from the darkling shadow. It was a woman, bent and bowed, with quivering limbs that shook half palsied. Maisie recognised old Bessie. "I knew she would come!" the old hag muttered between her toothless jaws. "I knew Wolverden Tower would yet be duly fasted!"

She put herself, as of right, at the head of the procession. They moved on to the tower, rather gliding than walking. Old Bessie drew a rusty key from her pocket, and fitted it with a twist into the brand-new lock. "What turned the old will turn the new," she murmured, looking round and grinning. Maisie shrank from her as she shrank from not one of the Dead; but she followed on still into the ringers' room at the base of the tower.

Thence a staircase in the corner led up to the summit. The High Priest mounted the stair, chanting a mystic refrain, whose runic sounds were no longer intelligible to Maisie. As she reached the outer air, the Tongue of the Dead seemed to have become a mere blank of mingled odours and murmurs to her. It was like a summer breeze, sighing through warm and resinous pinewoods. But Yolande and Hedda spoke to her yet, to cheer her, in the language of the living. She recognised that as revenants they were still in touch with the upper air and the world of the embodied.

They tempted her up the stair with encouraging fingers. Maisie followed them like a child, in implicit confidence. The steps wound round and round, spirally, and the staircase was dim; but a supernatural light seemed to fill the tower, diffused from the bodies or souls of its occupants. At the head of all, the High Priest still chanted as he went his unearthly litany; magic sounds of chimes seemed to swim in unison with his tune as they mounted. Were those floating notes material or spiritual? They passed the belfry; no tongue of metal wagged; but the rims of the great bells resounded and reverberated to the ghostly symphony with sympathetic music. Still they passed on and on, upward and upward. They reached the ladder that alone gave access to the final story. Dust and cobwebs already clung to it. Once more Maisie drew back. It was dark overhead and the luminous haze began to fail them. Her friends held her hands with the same kindly persuasive touch as ever. "I cannot!" she cried, shrinking away from the tall, steep ladder. "Oh, Yolande, I cannot!"

"Yes, dear," Yolande whispered in a soothing voice. "You can. It is but ten steps, and I will hold your hand tight. Be brave and mount them!"

The sweet voice encouraged her. It was like heavenly music. She knew not why she should submit, or, rather, consent; but none the less she consented. Some spell seemed cast over her. With tremulous feet, scarcely realising what she did, she mounted the ladder and went up four steps of it.

Then she turned and looked down again. Old Bessie's wrinkled face met her frightened eyes. It was smiling horribly. She shrank back once more, terrified. "I can't do it," she cried, "if that woman comes up! "I'm not afraid of you, dear," she pressed Yolande's hand, "but she, she is too terrible!"

Hedda looked back and raised a warning finger. "Let the woman stop below," she said; "she savours too much of the evil world. We must do nothing to frighten the willing victim."

The High Priest by this time, with his ghostly fingers, had opened the trap-door that gave access to the summit. A ray of moonlight slanted through the aperture. The breeze blew down with it. Once more Maisie felt the stimulating and reviving effect of the open air. Vivified by its freshness, she struggled up to the top, passed out through the trap, and found herself standing on the open platform at the summit of the tower.

The moon had not yet quite set. The light on the snow shone pale green and mysterious. For miles and miles around she could just make out, by its aid, the dim contour of the downs, with their thin white mantle, in the solemn silence. Range behind range rose faintly shimmering. The chant had now ceased; the High Priest and his acolytes were mingling strange herbs in a mazar-bowl or chalice. Stray perfumes of myrrh and of cardamoms were wafted towards her. The men in leopards' skins burnt smouldering sticks of spikenard. Then Yolande led the postulant forward again, and placed her close up to the new white parapet. Stone heads of virgins smiled on her from the angles. "She must front the east," Hedda said in a tone of authority: and Yolande turned her face towards the rising sun accordingly. Then she opened her lips and spoke in a very solemn voice. "From this new-built tower you fling yourself," she said, or rather intoned, "that you may serve mankind, and all the powers that be, as its guardian spirit against thunder and lightning. Judged a virgin, pure and unsullied in deed and word and thought, of royal race and ancient lineage – a Cymry of the Cymry – you are found worthy to be intrusted with this charge and this honour. Take care that never shall dart or thunderbolt assault this tower, as She that is below you takes care to preserve it from earthquake and ruin, and She that is midway takes care to preserve it from battle and tempest. This is your charge. See well that you keep it."

She took her by both hands. "Mary Llewelyn," she said, "you willing victim, step on to the battlement."

Maisie knew not why, but with very little shrinking she stepped as she was told, by the aid of a wooden footstool, on to the eastward-looking parapet. There, in her loose white robe, with her arms spread abroad, and her hair flying free, she poised herself for a second, as if about to shake out some unseen wings and throw herself on the air like a swift or a swallow.

"Mary Llewelyn," Yolande said once more, in a still deeper tone, with ineffable earnestness, "cast yourself down, a willing sacrifice, for the service of man, and the security of this tower against thunderbolt and lightning."

Maisie stretched her arms wider, and leaned forward in act to leap, from the edge of the parapet, on to the snow-clad churchyard.

V

One second more and the sacrifice would have been complete. But before she could launch herself from the tower, she felt suddenly a hand laid upon her shoulder from behind to restrain her. Even in her existing state of nervous exaltation she was aware at once that it was the hand of a living and solid mortal, not that of a soul or guardian spirit. It lay heavier upon her than Hedda's or Yolande's. It seemed to clog and burden her. With a violent effort she strove to shake herself free, and carry out her now fixed intention of self-immolation, for the safety of the tower. But the hand was too strong for her. She could not shake it off. It gripped and held her.

She yielded, and, reeling, fell back with a gasp on to the platform of the tower. At the selfsame moment a strange terror and commotion seemed to seize all at once on the assembled spirits. A weird cry rang voiceless through the shadowy company. Maisie heard it as in a dream, very dim and distant. It was thin as a bat's note; almost inaudible to the ear, yet perceived by the brain or at least by the spirit. It was a cry of alarm, of fright, of warning. With one accord, all the host of phantoms rushed hurriedly forward to the battlements and pinnacles. The ghostly High Priest went first, with his wand held downward; the men in leopards' skins and other assistants followed in confusion. Theirs was a reckless rout. They flung themselves from the top, like fugitives from a cliff, and floated fast through the air on invisible pinions. Hedda and Yolande, ambassadresses and intermediaries with the upper air, were the last to fly from the living presence. They clasped her hand silently, and looked deep into her eyes. There was something in that calm yet regretful look that seemed to say, "Farewell! We have tried in vain to save you, sister, from the terrors of living."

The horde of spirits floated away on the air, as in a witches' Sabbath, to the vault whence it issued. The doors swung on their rusty hinges, and closed behind them. Maisie stood alone with the hand that grasped her on the tower.

The shock of the grasp, and the sudden departure of the ghostly band in such wild dismay, threw Maisie for a while into a state of semi-unconsciousness. Her head reeled round; her brain swam faintly. She clutched for support at the parapet of the tower. But the hand that held her sustained her still. She felt herself gently drawn down with quiet mastery, and laid on the stone floor close by the trap-door that led to the ladder.

The next thing of which she could feel sure was the voice of the Oxford undergraduate. He was distinctly frightened and not a little tremulous. "I think," he said very softly, laying her head on his lap, "you had better rest a while, Miss Llewelyn, before you try to get down again. I hope I didn't catch you and disturb you too hastily. But one step more, and you would have been over the edge. I really couldn't help it."

"Let me go," Maisie moaned, trying to raise herself again, but feeling too faint and ill to make the necessary effort to recover the power of motion. "I want to go with them! I want to join them!"

"Some of the others will be up before long," the undergraduate said, supporting her head in his hands; "and they'll help me to get you down again. Mr. Yates is in the belfry. Meanwhile, if I were you, I'd lie quite still, and take a drop or two of this brandy."

He held it to her lips. Maisie drank a mouthful, hardly knowing what she did. Then she lay quiet where he placed her for some minutes. How they lifted her down and conveyed her to her bed she scarcely knew. She was dazed and terrified. She could only remember afterward that three or four gentlemen in roughly huddled clothes had carried or handed her down the ladder between them. The spiral stair and all the rest were a blank to her.

VI

When she next awoke she was lying in her bed in the same room at the Hall, with Mrs. West by her side, leaning over her tenderly.

Maisie looked up through her closed eyes and just saw the motherly face and grey hair bending above her. Then voices came to her from the mist, vaguely: "Yesterday was so hot for the time of year, you see!" "Very unusual weather, of course, for Christmas." "But a thunderstorm! So strange! I put it down to that. The electrical disturbance must have affected the poor child's head." Then it dawned upon her that the conversation she heard was passing between Mrs. West and a doctor.

She raised herself suddenly and wildly on her arms. The bed faced the windows. She looked out and beheld – the tower of Wolverden church, rent from top to bottom with a mighty rent, while half its height lay tossed in fragments on the ground in the churchyard.

"What is it?" she cried wildly, with a flush as of shame.

"Hush, hush!" the doctor said. "Don't trouble! Don't look at it!"

"Was it? after I came down?" Maisie moaned in vague terror.

The doctor nodded. "An hour after you were brought down," he said, "a thunderstorm broke over it. The lightning struck and shattered the tower. They had not yet put up the lightning-conductor. It was to have been done on Boxing Day."

A weird remorse possessed Maisie's soul. "My fault!" she cried, starting up. "My fault, my fault! I have neglected my duty!"

"Don't talk," the doctor answered, looking hard at her. "It is always dangerous to be too suddenly aroused from these curious overwrought sleeps and trances."

"And old Bessie?" Maisie exclaimed, trembling with an eerie presentiment.

The doctor glanced at Mrs. West. "How did she know?" he whispered. Then he turned to Maisie. "You may as well be told the truth as suspect it," he said slowly. "Old Bessie must have been watching there. She was crushed and half buried beneath the falling tower."

"One more question, Mrs. West," Maisie murmured, growing faint with an access of supernatural fear. "Those two nice girls who sat on the chairs at each side of me through the tableaux, are they hurt? Were they in it?"

Mrs. West soothed her hand. "My dear child," she said gravely, with quiet emphasis, "there were no other girls. This is mere hallucination. You sat alone by yourself through the whole of the evening."

Ghosts That Have Haunted Me
A Few Spirit Reminiscences
John Kendrick Bangs

IF WE COULD only get used to the idea that ghosts are perfectly harmless creatures, who are powerless to affect our well-being unless we assist them by giving way to our fears, we should enjoy the supernatural exceedingly, it seems to me. Coleridge, I think it was, was once asked by a lady if he believed in ghosts, and he replied, "No, madame; I have seen too many of them." Which is my case exactly. I have seen so many horrid visitants from other worlds that they hardly affect me at all, so far as the mere inspiration of terror is concerned. On the other hand, they interest me hugely; and while I must admit that I do experience all the purely physical sensations that come from horrific encounters of this nature, I can truly add in my own behalf that mentally I can rise above the physical impulse to run away, and, invariably standing my ground, I have gained much useful information concerning them. I am prepared to assert that if a thing with flashing green eyes, and clammy hands, and long, dripping strips of sea-weed in place of hair, should rise up out of the floor before me at this moment, 2 A.M., and nobody in the house but myself, with a fearful, nerve-destroying storm raging outside, I should without hesitation ask it to sit down and light a cigar and state its business – or, if it were of the female persuasion, to join me in a bottle of sarsaparilla – although every physical manifestation of fear of which my poor body is capable would be present. I have had experiences in this line which, if I could get you to believe them, would convince you that I speak the truth. Knowing weak, suspicious human nature as I do, however, I do not hope ever to convince you – though it is none the less true – that on one occasion, in the spring of 1895, there was a spiritual manifestation in my library which nearly prostrated me physically, but which mentally I hugely enjoyed, because I was mentally strong enough to subdue my physical repugnance for the thing which suddenly and without any apparent reason materialized in my arm-chair.

I'm going to tell you about it briefly, though I warn you in advance that you will find it a great strain upon your confidence in my veracity. It may even shatter that confidence beyond repair; but I cannot help that. I hold that it is a man's duty in this life to give to the world the benefit of his experience. All that he sees he should set down exactly as he sees it, and so simply, withal, that to the dullest comprehension the moral involved shall be perfectly obvious. If he is a painter, and an auburn-haired maiden appears to him to have blue hair, he should paint her hair blue, and just so long as he sticks by his principles and is true to himself, he need not bother about what you may think of him. So it is with me. My scheme of living is based upon being true to myself. You may class me with Baron Munchausen if you choose; I shall not mind so long as I have the consolation of feeling, deep down in my heart, that I am a true realist, and diverge not from the paths of truth as truth manifests itself to me.

This intruder of whom I was just speaking, the one that took possession of my arm-chair in the spring of 1895, was about as horrible a spectre as I have ever had the pleasure to have haunt me. It was worse than grotesque. It grated on every nerve. Alongside of it the ordinary poster of the present day would seem to be as accurate in drawing as a bicycle map, and in its coloring it simply shrieked with discord.

If color had tones which struck the ear, instead of appealing to the eye, the thing would have deafened me. It was about midnight when the manifestation first took shape. My family had long before retired, and I had just finished smoking a cigar – which was one of a thousand which my wife had bought for me at a Monday sale at one of the big department stores in New York. I don't remember the brand, but that is just as well – it was not a cigar to be advertised in a civilized piece of literature – but I do remember that they came in bundles of fifty, tied about with blue ribbon. The one I had been smoking tasted and burned as if it had been rolled by a Cuban insurrectionist while fleeing from a Spanish regiment through a morass, gathering its component parts as he ran. It had two distinct merits, however. No man could possibly smoke too many of them, and they were economical, which is how the ever-helpful little madame came to get them for me, and I have no doubt they will some day prove very useful in removing insects from the rose-bushes. They cost $3.99 a thousand on five days a week, but at the Monday sale they were marked down to $1.75, which is why my wife, to whom I had recently read a little lecture on economy, purchased them for me. Upon the evening in question I had been at work on this cigar for about two hours, and had smoked one side of it three-quarters of the way down to the end, when I concluded that I had smoked enough – for one day – so I rose up to cast the other side into the fire, which was flickering fitfully in my spacious fireplace. This done, I turned about, and there, fearful to see, sat this thing grinning at me from the depths of my chair. My hair not only stood on end, but tugged madly in an effort to get away. Four hairs – I can prove the statement if it be desired – did pull themselves loose from my scalp in their insane desire to rise above the terrors of the situation, and, flying upward, stuck like nails into the oak ceiling directly over my head, whence they had to be pulled the next morning with nippers by our hired man, who would no doubt testify to the truth of the occurrence as I have asserted it if he were still living, which, unfortunately, he is not. Like most hired men, he was subject to attacks of lethargy, from one of which he died last summer. He sank into a rest about weed-time, last June, and lingered quietly along for two months, and after several futile efforts to wake him up, we finally disposed of him to our town crematory for experimental purposes. I am told he burned very actively, and I believe it, for to my certain knowledge he was very dry, and not so green as some persons who had previously employed him affected to think. A cold chill came over me as my eye rested upon the horrid visitor and noted the greenish depths of his eyes and the claw-like formation of his fingers, and my flesh began to creep like an inch-worm. At one time I was conscious of eight separate corrugations on my back, and my arms goose-fleshed until they looked like one of those miniature plaster casts of the Alps which are so popular in Swiss summer resorts; but mentally I was not disturbed at all. My repugnance was entirely physical, and, to come to the point at once, I calmly offered the spectre a cigar, which it accepted, and demanded a light. I gave it, nonchalantly lighting the match upon the goose -fleshing of my wrist.

Now I admit that this was extraordinary and hardly credible, yet it happened exactly as I have set it down, and, furthermore, I enjoyed the experience. For three hours the thing and I conversed, and not once during that time did my hair stop pulling away at my scalp, or the repugnance cease to run in great rolling waves up and down my back. If I wished to deceive you, I might add that pin-feathers began to grow from the goose-flesh, but that would be a lie, and lying and I are not friends, and, furthermore, this paper is not written to amaze, but to instruct.

Except for its personal appearance, this particular ghost was not very remarkable, and I do not at this time recall any of the details of our conversation beyond the point that my share of it was not particularly coherent, because of the discomfort attendant upon the fearful hair-pulling process I was going through. I merely cite its coming to prove that, with all the outward visible signs of fear manifesting themselves in no uncertain manner, mentally I was cool enough to cope with the visitant, and sufficiently calm and at ease to light the match upon my wrist, perceiving for the first time, with an Edison-like ingenuity, one of the uses to which goose-flesh might be put, and knowing full well that if I tried to light it on the sole of my shoe I should have fallen to the ground, my knees being too shaky to admit of my standing on one leg even for an instant. Had I been mentally overcome, I should have tried to light the match on my foot, and fallen ignominiously to the floor then and there.

There was another ghost that I recall to prove my point, who was of very great use to me in the summer immediately following the spring of which I have just told you. You will possibly remember how that the summer of 1895 had rather more than its fair share of heat, and that the lovely New Jersey town in which I have the happiness to dwell appeared to be the headquarters of the temperature. The thermometers of the nation really seemed to take orders from Beachdale, and properly enough, for our town is a born leader in respect to heat. Having no property to sell, I candidly admit that Beachdale is not of an arctic nature in summer, except socially, perhaps. Socially, it is the coolest town in the State; but we are at this moment not discussing cordiality, fraternal love, or the question raised by the Declaration of Independence as to whether all men are born equal. The warmth we have in hand is what the old lady called "Fahrenheat," and, from a thermometric point of view, Beachdale, if I may be a trifle slangy, as I sometimes am, has heat to burn. There are mitigations of this heat, it is true, but they generally come along in winter.

I must claim, in behalf of my town, that never in all my experience have I known a summer so hot that it was not, sooner or later – by January, anyhow – followed by a cool spell. But in the summer of 1895 even the real-estate agents confessed that the cold wave announced by the weather bureau at Washington summered elsewhere – in the tropics, perhaps, but not at Beachdale. One hardly dared take a bath in the morning for fear of being scalded by the fluid that flowed from the cold-water faucet – our reservoir is entirely unprotected by shade-trees, and in summer a favorite spot for young Waltons who like to catch bass already boiled – my neighbors and myself lived on cracked ice, ice-cream, and destructive cold drinks. I do not myself mind hot weather in the daytime, but hot nights are killing. I can't sleep. I toss about for hours, and then, for the sake of variety, I flop, but sleep cometh not. My debts double, and my income seems to sizzle away under the influence of a hot, sleepless night; and it was just here that a certain awful thing saved me from the insanity which is a certain result of parboiled insomnia.

It was about the 16th of July, which, as I remember reading in an extra edition of the *Evening Bun*, got out to mention the fact, was the hottest 16th of July known in thirty-eight years. I had retired at half-past seven, after dining lightly upon a cold salmon and a gallon of iced tea – not because I was tired, but because I wanted to get down to first principles at once, and remove my clothing, and sort of spread myself over all the territory I could, which is a thing you can't do in a library, or even in a white-and-gold parlor. If man were constructed like a machine, as he really ought to be, to be strictly comfortable – a machine that could be taken apart like an eight-day clock – I should have taken myself apart, putting one section of myself on the roof, another part in the spare room, hanging a third on the clothes-line in the yard, and so on, leaving my head in the ice-box; but unfortunately we have to keep ourselves together in this life, hence I did the only thing one can do, and retired, and incidentally spread myself over some freshly baked bedclothing. There was some relief from the heat, but not much. I had been roasting, and while my sensations were somewhat like those which I imagine come to a planked shad when he first finds himself spread out over the plank, there was a mitigation. My temperature fell off from 167 to about 163, which is not quite enough to make a man absolutely content. Suddenly, however, I began to shiver. There was no breeze, but I began to shiver.

"It is getting cooler," I thought, as the chill came on, and I rose and looked at the thermometer. It still registered the highest possible point, and the mercury was rebelliously trying to break through the top of the glass tube and take a stroll on the roof.

"That's queer," I said to myself. "It's as hot as ever, and yet I'm shivering. I wonder if my goose is cooked? I've certainly got a chill."

I jumped back into bed and pulled the sheet up over me; but still I shivered. Then I pulled the blanket up, but the chill continued. I couldn't seem to get warm again. Then came the counterpane, and finally I had to put on my bath-robe – a fuzzy woollen affair, which in midwinter I had sometimes found too warm for comfort. Even then I was not sufficiently bundled up, so I called for an extra blanket, two afghans, and the hot-water bag.

Everybody in the house thought I had gone mad, and I wondered myself if perhaps I hadn't, when all of a sudden I perceived, off in the corner, the Awful Thing, and perceiving it, I knew all.

I was being haunted, and the physical repugnance of which I have spoken was on. The cold shiver, the invariable accompaniment of the ghostly visitant, had come, and I assure you I never was so glad of anything in my life. It has always been said of me by my critics that I am raw; I was afraid that after that night they would say I was half baked, and I would far rather be the one than the other; and it was the Awful Thing that saved me. Realizing this, I spoke to it gratefully.

"You are a heaven-born gift on a night like this," said I, rising up and walking to its side.

"I am glad to be of service to you," the Awful Thing replied, smiling at me so yellowly that I almost wished the author of the *Blue-Button of Cowardice* could have seen it.

"It's very good of you," I put in.

"Not at all," replied the Thing; "you are the only man I know who doesn't think it necessary to prevaricate about ghosts every time he gets an order for a Christmas story. There have been more lies told about us than about any other class of things in existence, and we are getting a trifle tired of it. We may have lost our corporeal existence, but some of our sensitiveness still remains."

"Well," said I, rising and lighting the gas-logs – for I was on the very verge of congealment – "I am sure I am pleased if you like my stories."

"Oh, as for that, I don't think much of them," said the Awful Thing, with a purple display of candor which amused me, although I cannot say that I relished it; "but you never lie about us. You are not at all interesting, but you are truthful, and we spooks hate libellers. Just because one happens to be a thing is no reason why writers should libel it, and that's why I have always respected you. We regard you as a sort of spook Boswell. You may be dull and stupid, but you tell the truth, and when I saw you in imminent danger of becoming a mere grease spot, owing to the fearful heat, I decided to help you through. That's why I'm here. Go to sleep now. I'll stay here and keep you shivering until daylight anyhow. I'd stay longer, but we are always laid at sunrise."

"Like an egg," I said, sleepily.

"Tutt!" said the ghost. "Go to sleep, If you talk I'll have to go."

And so I dropped off to sleep as softly and as sweetly as a tired child. In the morning I awoke refreshed. The rest of my family were prostrated, but I was fresh. The Awful Thing was gone, and the room was warming up again; and if it had not been for the tinkling ice in my water-pitcher, I should have suspected it was all a dream. And so throughout the whole sizzling summer the friendly spectre stood by me and kept me cool, and I haven't a doubt that it was because of his good offices in keeping me shivering on those fearful August nights that I survived the season, and came to my work in the autumn as fit as a fiddle – so fit, indeed, that I have not written a poem since that has not struck me as being the very best of its kind, and if I can find a publisher who will take the risk of putting those poems out, I shall unequivocally and without hesitation acknowledge, as I do here, my debt of gratitude to my friends in the spirit world.

Manifestations of this nature, then, are harmful, as I have already observed, only when the person who is haunted yields to his physical impulses. Fought stubbornly inch by inch with the will, they can be subdued, and often they are a boon. I think I have proved both these points. It took me a long time to discover the facts, however, and my discovery came about in this way. It may perhaps interest you to know how I made it. I encountered at the English home of a wealthy friend at one time a "presence" of an insulting turn of mind. It was at my friend Jarley's little baronial hall, which he had rented from the Earl of Brokedale the year Mrs. Jarley was presented at court. The Countess of Brokedale's social influence went with the château for a slightly increased rental, which was why the Jarleys took it. I was invited to spend a month with them, not so much because Jarley is fond of me as because Mrs. Jarley had a sort of an idea that, as a writer, I might say something about their newly acquired glory in some American Sunday newspaper; and Jarley laughingly assigned to me the "haunted chamber," without at least one of which no baronial hall in the old country is considered worthy of the name.

"It will interest you more than any other," Jarley said; "and if it has a ghost, I imagine you will be able to subdue him."

I gladly accepted the hospitality of my friend, and was delighted at his consideration in giving me the haunted chamber, where I might pursue my investigations into the subject of phantoms undisturbed. Deserting London, then, for a time, I ran down to Brokedale Hall, and took up my abode there with a half-dozen other guests. Jarley, as usual since his sudden "gold-fall," as Wilkins called it, did everything with a lavish hand. I believe a man could have got diamonds on toast if he had chosen to ask for them. However, this is apart from my story.

I had occupied the haunted chamber about two weeks before anything of importance occurred, and then it came – and a more unpleasant, ill-mannered spook never floated in the ether. He materialized about 3 A.M. and was unpleasantly sulphurous to one's perceptions. He sat upon the divan in my room, holding his knees in his hands, leering and scowling upon me as though I were the intruder, and not he.

"Who are you?" I asked, excitedly, as in the dying light of the log fire he loomed grimly up before me.

"None of your business," he replied, insolently, showing his teeth as he spoke. "On the other hand, who are you? This is my room, and not yours, and it is I who have the right to question. If you have any business here, well and good. If not, you will oblige me by removing yourself, for your presence is offensive to me."

"I am a guest in the house," I answered, restraining my impulse to throw the inkstand at him for his impudence. "And this room has been set apart for my use by my host."

"One of the servant's guests, I presume?" he said, insultingly, his lividly lavender-like lip upcurling into a haughty sneer, which was maddening to a self-respecting worm like myself.

I rose up from my bed, and picked up the poker to bat him over the head, but again I restrained myself. It will not do to quarrel, I thought. I will be courteous if he is not, thus giving a dead Englishman a lesson which wouldn't hurt some of the living.

"No," I said, my voice tremulous with wrath – "no; I am the guest of my friend Mr. Jarley, an American, who—"

"Same thing," observed the intruder, with a yellow sneer. "Race of low-class animals, those Americans – only fit for gentlemen's stables, you know."

This was too much. A ghost may insult me with impunity, but when he tackles my people he must look out for himself. I sprang forward with an ejaculation of wrath, and with all my strength struck at him with the poker, which I still held in my hand. If he had been anything but a ghost, he would have been split vertically from top to toe; but as it was, the poker passed harmlessly through his misty make-up, and rent a great gash two feet long in Jarley's divan. The yellow sneer faded from his lips, and a maddening blue smile took its place.

"Humph!" he observed, nonchalantly. "What a useless ebullition, and what a vulgar display of temper! Really you are the most humorous insect I have yet encountered. From what part of the States do you come? I am truly interested to know in what kind of soil exotics of your peculiar kind are cultivated. Are you part of the fauna or the flora of your tropical States – or what?"

And then I realized the truth. There is no physical method of combating a ghost which can result in his discomfiture, so I resolved to try the intellectual. It was a mind-tomind contest, and he was easy prey after I got going. I joined him in his blue smile, and began to talk about the English aristocracy; for I doubted not, from the spectre's manner, that he was or had been one of that class. He had about him that haughty lack of manners which bespoke the aristocrat. I waxed very eloquent when, as I say, I got my mind really going. I spoke of kings and queens and their uses in no uncertain phrases, of divine right, of dukes, earls, marquises – of all the pompous establishments of British royalty and nobility – with that contemptuously humorous tolerance of a necessary and somewhat amusing evil which we find in American comic papers. We had a battle royal for about one hour, and I must confess he was a foeman worthy of any man's steel, so long as I was reasonable in my arguments; but when I finally observed that it wouldn't be ten years before Barnum and Bailey's Greatest Show on Earth had the whole lot engaged for the New York circus season, stalking about the Madison Square Garden arena, with the Prince of Wales at the head beating a tomtom, he grew iridescent with wrath, and fled madly through the wainscoting of the room. It was purely a mental victory. All the physical possibilities of my being would have exhausted themselves futilely before him; but when I turned upon him the resources of my fancy, my imagination unrestrained, and held back by no sense of responsibility, he was as a child in my hands, obstreperous but certain to be subdued. If it were not for Mrs. Jarley's wrath – which, I admit, she tried to conceal – over the damage to her divan, I should now look back upon that visitation as the most agreeable haunting experience of my life; at any rate, it was at that time that I first learned how to handle ghosts, and since that time I have been able to overcome them without trouble – save in one instance, with which I shall close this chapter of my reminiscences, and which I give only to prove the necessity of observing strictly one point in dealing with spectres.

It happened last Christmas, in my own home. I had provided as a little surprise for my wife a complete new solid silver service marked with her initials. The tree had been prepared for the children, and all had retired save myself. I had lingered later than the others to put the silver service under the tree, where its happy recipient would find it when she went to the tree with the little ones the next morning. It made a magnificent display: the two dozen of each kind of spoon, the forks, the knives, the coffee-pot, water -urn, and all; the salvers, the vegetable-dishes, olive-forks, cheese-scoops, and other dazzling attributes of a complete service, not to go into details, presented a fairly scintillating picture which would have made me gasp if I had not, at the moment when my own breath began to catch, heard another gasp in the corner immediately behind me. Turning about quickly to see whence it came, I observed a dark figure in the pale light of the moon which streamed in through the window.

"Who are you?" I cried, starting back, the physical symptoms of a ghostly presence manifesting themselves as usual.

"I am the ghost of one long gone before," was the reply, in sepulchral tones.

I breathed a sigh of relief, for I had for a moment feared it was a burglar.

"Oh!" I said. "You gave me a start at first. I was afraid you were a material thing come to rob me." Then turning towards the tree, I observed, with a wave of the hand, "Fine lay out, eh?"

"Beautiful," he said, hollowly. "Yet not so beautiful as things I've seen in realms beyond your ken."

And then he set about telling me of the beautiful gold and silver ware they used in the Elysian Fields, and I must confess Monte Cristo would have had a hard time, with Sindbad the Sailor to help, to surpass the picture of royal magnificence the spectre drew. I stood inthralled until, even as he was talking, the clock struck three, when he rose up, and moving slowly across the floor, barely visible, murmured regretfully that he must be off, with which he faded away down the back stairs. I pulled my nerves, which were getting rather strained, together again, and went to bed.

Next morning every bit of that silver-ware was gone; and, what is more, three weeks later I found the ghost's picture in the Rogues' Gallery in New York as that of the cleverest sneak-thief in the country.

All of which, let me say to you, dear reader, in conclusion, proves that when you are dealing with ghosts you mustn't give up all your physical resources until you have definitely ascertained that the thing by which you are confronted, horrid or otherwise, is a ghost, and not an all too material rogue with a light step, and a commodious jute bag for plunder concealed beneath his coat.

"How to tell a ghost?" you ask.

Well, as an eminent master of fiction frequently observes in his writings, "that is another story," which I shall hope some day to tell for your instruction and my own aggrandizement.

The Mystery of My Grandmother's Hair Sofa

John Kendrick Bangs

IT HAPPENED last Christmas Eve, and precisely as I am about to set it forth. It has been said by critics that I am a romancer of the wildest sort, but that is where my critics are wrong. I grant that the experiences through which I have passed, some of which have contributed to the gray matter in my hair, however little they may have augmented that within my cranium – experiences which I have from time to time set forth to the best of my poor abilities in the columns of such periodicals as I have at my mercy – have been of an order so excessively supernatural as to give my critics a basis for their aspersions; but they do not know, as I do, that that basis is as uncertain as the shifting sands of the sea, inasmuch as in the setting forth of these episodes I have narrated them as faithfully as the most conscientious realist could wish, and am therefore myself a true and faithful follower of the realistic school. I cannot be blamed because these things happen to me. If I sat down in my study to imagine the strange incidents to which I have in the past called attention, with no other object in view than to make my readers unwilling to retire for the night, to destroy the peace of mind of those who are good enough to purchase my literary wares, or to titillate till tense the nerve tissue of the timid who come to smile and who depart unstrung, then should I deserve the severest condemnation; but these things I do not do. I have a mission in life which I hold as sacred as my good friend Mr. Howells holds his. Such phases of life as I see I put down faithfully, and if the Fates in their wisdom have chosen to make of me the Balzac of the Supernatural, the Shakespeare of the Midnight Visitation, while elevating Mr. Howells to the high office of the Fielding of Massachusetts and its adjacent States, the Smollett of Boston, and the Sterne of Altruria, I can only regret that the powers have dealt more graciously with him than with me, and walk my little way as gracefully as I know how. The slings and arrows of outrageous fortune I am prepared to suffer in all meekness of spirit; I accept them because it seems to me to be nobler in the mind so to do rather than by opposing to end them. And so to my story. I have prefaced it at such length for but one reason, and that is that I am aware that there will be those who will doubt the veracity of my tale, and I am anxious at the outset to impress upon all the unquestioned fact that what I am about to tell is the plain, unvarnished truth, and, as I have already said, it happened last Christmas Eve.

I regret to have to say so, for it sounds so much like the description given to other Christmas Eves by writers with a less conscientious regard for the truth than I possess, but the facts must be told, and I must therefore state that it was a wild and stormy night. The winds howled and moaned and made all sorts of curious noises, soughing through the bare limbs of the trees, whistling through the chimneys, and, with reckless disregard of my children's need of rest, slamming doors until my house seemed to be the centre of a bombardment of no mean order. It is also necessary to state that the snow, which had been falling all day, had clothed the lawns and house-tops in a dazzling drapery of white, and, not content with having done this to the satisfaction of all, was still falling, and, happily enough, as silently as usual. Were I the "wild romancer" that I have been called, I might have had the snow fall with a thunderous roar, but I cannot go to any such length. I love my fellow-beings, but there is a limit to my philanthropy, and I shall not have my snow fall noisily just to make a critic happy. I might do it to save his life, for I should hate to have a man die for the want of what I could give him with a stroke of my pen, and without any special effort, but until that emergency arises I shall not yield a jot in the manner of the falling of my snow.

Occasionally a belated home-comer would pass my house, the sleigh-bells strung about the ample proportions of his steed jingling loud above the roaring of the winds. My family had retired, and I sat alone in the glow of the blazing log – a very satisfactory gas affair – on the hearth. The flashing jet flames cast the usual grotesque shadows about the room, and my mind had thereby been reduced to that sensitive state which had hitherto betokened the coming of a visitor from other realms – a fact which I greatly regretted, for I was in no mood to be haunted. My first impulse, when I recognized the on-coming of that mental state which is evidenced by the goosing of one's flesh, if I may be allowed the expression, was to turn out the fire and go to bed. I have always found this the easiest method of ridding myself of unwelcome ghosts, and, conversely, I have observed that others who have been haunted unpleasantly have suffered in proportion to their failure to take what has always seemed to me to be the most natural course in the world – to hide their heads beneath the bed-covering. Brutus, when Caesar's ghost appeared beside his couch, before the battle of Philippi, sat up and stared upon the horrid apparition, and suffered correspondingly, when it would have been much easier and more natural to put his head under his pillow, and so shut out the unpleasant spectacle. That is the course I have invariably pursued, and it has never failed me. The most luminous ghost man ever saw is utterly powerless to shine through a comfortably stuffed pillow, or the usual Christmas-time quota of woollen blankets. But upon this occasion I preferred to await developments. The real truth is that I was about written out in the matter of visitations, and needed a reinforcement of my uncanny vein, which, far from being varicose, had become sclerotic, so dry had it been pumped by the demands to which it had been subjected by a clamorous, mystery-loving public. I had, I may as well confess it, run out of ghosts, and had come down to the writing of tales full of the horror of suggestion, leaving my readers unsatisfied through my failure to describe in detail just what kind of looking thing it was that had so aroused their apprehension; and one editor had gone so far as to reject my last ghost-story because I had worked him up to a fearful pitch of excitement, and left him there without any reasonable way out. I was face to face with a condition – which, briefly, was that hereafter that desirable market was closed to the products of my pen unless my contributions were accompanied by a diagram which should make my mysteries so plain that a little child could understand how it all came to pass. Hence it was that, instead of following my own convenience and taking refuge in my spectre-proof couch, I stayed where I was. I had not long to wait. The dial in my fuel-meter below-stairs had hardly had time to register the consumption of three thousand feet of gas before the faint sound of a bell reached my straining ears – which, by-the-way, is an expression I profoundly hate, but must introduce because the public demands it, and a ghost -story without straining ears having therefore no chance of acceptance by a discriminating editor. I started from my chair and listened intently, but the ringing had stopped, and I settled back to the delights of a nervous chill, when again the deathly silence of the night – the wind had quieted in time to allow me the use of this faithful, overworked phrase – was broken by the tintinnabulation of the bell. This time I recognized it as the electric bell operated by a push-button upon the right side of my front door. To rise and rush to the door was the work of a moment. It always is. In another instant I had flung it wide. This operation was singularly easy, considering that it was but a narrow door, and width was the last thing it could ever be suspected of, however forcible the fling. However, I did as I have said, and gazed out into the inky blackness of the night. As I had suspected, there was no one there, and I was at once convinced that the dreaded moment had come. I was certain that at the instant of my turning to re-enter my library I should see something which would make my brain throb madly and my pulses start. I did not therefore instantly turn, but let the wind blow the door to with a loud clatter, while I walked quickly into my dining -room and drained a glass of cooking-sherry to the dregs. I do not introduce the cooking-sherry here for the purpose of eliciting a laugh from the reader, but in order to be faithful to life as we live it. All our other sherry had been used by the queen of the kitchen for cooking purposes, and this was all we had left for the table. It is always so in real life, let critics say what they will.

This done, I returned to the library, and sustained my first shock. The unexpected had happened. There was still no one there. Surely this ghost was an original, and I began to be interested.

"Perhaps he is a modest ghost," I thought, "and is a little shy about manifesting his presence. That, indeed, would be original, seeing how bold the spectres of commerce usually are, intruding themselves always upon the privacy of those who are not at all minded to receive them."

Confident that something would happen, and speedily at that, I sat down to wait, lighting a cigar for company; for burning gas-logs are not as sociable as their hissing, spluttering originals, the genuine logs, in a state of ignition. Several times I started up nervously, feeling as if there was something standing behind me about to place a clammy hand upon my shoulder, and as many times did I resume my attitude of comfort, disappointed. Once I seemed to see a minute spirit floating in the air before me, but investigation showed that it was nothing more than the fanciful curling of the clouds of smoke I had blown from my lips. An hour passed and nothing occurred, save that my heart from throbbing took to leaping in a fashion which filled me with concern. A few minutes later, however, I heard a strange sound at the window, and my leaping heart stood still. The strain upon my tense nerves was becoming unbearable.

"At last!" I whispered to myself, hoarsely, drawing a deep breath, and pushing with all my force into the soft upholstered back of my chair. Then I leaned forward and watched the window, momentarily expecting to see it raised by unseen hands; but it never budged. Then I watched the glass anxiously, half hoping, half fearing to see something pass through it; but nothing came, and I began to get irritable.

I looked at my watch, and saw that it was half-past one o'clock.

"Hang you!" I cried, "whatever you are, why don't you appear, and be done with it? The idea of keeping a man up until this hour of the night!"

Then I listened for a reply; but there was none.

"What do you take me for?" I continued, querulously. "Do you suppose I have nothing else to do but to wait upon your majesty's pleasure? Surely, with all the time you've taken to make your début, you must be something of unusual horror."

Again there was no answer, and I decided that petulance was of no avail. Some other tack was necessary, and I decided to appeal to his sympathies – granting that ghosts have sympathies to appeal to, and I have met some who were so human in this respect that I have found it hard to believe that they were truly ghosts.

"I say, old chap," I said, as genially as I could, considering the situation – I was nervous, and the amount of gas consumed by the logs was beginning to bring up visions of bankruptcy before my eyes – "hurry up and begin your haunting – there's a good fellow. I'm a father – please remember that – and this is Christmas Eve. The children will be up in about three hours, and if you've ever been a parent yourself you know what that means. I must have some rest, so come along and show yourself, like the good spectre you are, and let me go to bed."

I think myself it was a very moving address, but it helped me not a jot. The thing must have had a heart of stone, for it never made answer.

"What?" said I, pretending to think it had spoken and I had not heard distinctly; but the visitant was not to be caught napping, even though I had good reason to believe that he had fallen asleep. He, she, or it, whatever it was, maintained a silence as deep as it was aggravating. I smoked furiously on to restrain my growing wrath. Then it occurred to me that the thing might have some pride, and I resolved to work on that.

"Of course I should like to write you up," I said, with a sly wink at myself. "I imagine you'd attract a good deal of attention in the literary world. Judging from the time it takes you to get ready, you ought to make a good magazine story – not one of those comic ghost -tales that can be dashed off in a minute, and ultimately get published in a book at the author's expense. You stir so little that, as things go by contraries, you'll make a stirring tale. You're long enough, I might say, for a three-volume novel – but—ah— I can't do you unless I see you. You must be seen to be appreciated. I can't imagine you, you know. Let's see, now, if I can guess what kind of a ghost you are. Um! You must be terrifying in the extreme – you'd make a man shiver in mid-August in mid-Africa. Your eyes are unfathomably green. Your smile would drive the sanest mad. Your hands are cold and clammy as a—ah—as a hot-water bag four hours after."

And so I went on for ten minutes, praising him up to the skies, and ending up with a pathetic appeal that he should manifest his presence. It may be that I puffed him up so that he burst, but, however that may be, he would not condescend to reply, and I grew angry in earnest.

"Very well," I said, savagely, jumping up from my chair and turning off the gas-log. "Don't! Nobody asked you to come in the first place, and nobody's going to complain if you sulk in your tent like Achilles. I don't want to see you. I could fake up a better ghost than you are anyhow – in fact, I fancy that's what's the matter with you. You know what a miserable specimen you are – couldn't frighten a mouse if you were ten times as horrible. You're ashamed to show yourself – and I don't blame you. I'd be that way too if I were you."

I walked half-way to the door, momentarily expecting to have him call me back; but he didn't. I had to give him a parting shot.

"You probably belong to a ghost union – don't you? That's your secret? Ordered out on strike, and won't do any haunting after sundown unless some other employer of unskilled ghosts pays his spooks skilled wages."

I had half a notion that the word "spook" would draw him out, for I have noticed that ghosts do not like to be called spooks any more than negroes like to be called "niggers." They consider it vulgar. He never yielded in his reserve, however, and after locking up I went to bed.

For a time I could not sleep, and I began to wonder if I had been just, after all. Possibly there was no spirit within miles of me. The symptoms were all there, but might not that have been due to my depressed condition – for it does depress a writer to have one of his best veins become sclerotic – I asked myself, and finally, as I went off to sleep, I concluded that I had been in the wrong all through, and had imagined there was something there when there really was not.

"Very likely the ringing of the bell was due to the wind," I said, as I dozed off. "Of course it would take a very heavy wind to blow the button in, but then—" and then I fell asleep, convinced that no ghost had ventured within a mile of me that night. But when morning came I was undeceived. Something must have visited us that Christmas Eve, and something very terrible; for while I was dressing for breakfast I heard my wife calling loudly from below.

"Henry!" she cried. "Please come down here at once."

"I can't. I'm only half shaved," I answered.

"Never mind that," she returned. "Come at once."

So, with the lather on one cheek and a cut on the other, I went below.

"What's the matter?" I asked.

"Look at that!" she said, pointing to my grandmother's hair-sofa, which stood in the hall just outside of my library door.

It had been black when we last saw it, but as I looked I saw that a great change had come over it. *It had turned white in a single night!*

Now I can't account for this strange incident, nor can any one else, and I do not intend to try. It is too awful a mystery for me to attempt to penetrate, but the sofa is there in proof of all that I have said concerning it, and any one who desires can call and see it at any time. It is not necessary for them to see me; they need only ask to see the sofa, and it will be shown.

We have had it removed from the hall to the white-and-gold parlor, for we cannot bear to have it stand in any of the rooms we use.

Thurlow's Christmas Story

John Kendrick Bangs

I

(Being the Statement of Henry Thurlow Author, to George Currier, Editor of the "Idler," a Weekly Journal of Human Interest.)

I HAVE ALWAYS maintained, my dear Currier, that if a man wishes to be considered sane, and has any particular regard for his reputation as a truth-teller, he would better keep silent as to the singular experiences that enter into his life. I have had many such experiences myself; but I have rarely confided them in detail, or otherwise, to those about me, because I know that even the most trustful of my friends would regard them merely as the outcome of an imagination unrestrained by conscience, or of a gradually weakening mind subject to hallucinations. I know them to be true, but until Mr. Edison or some other modern wizard has invented a search-light strong enough to lay bare the secrets of the mind and conscience of man, I cannot prove to others that they are not pure fabrications, or at least the conjurings of a diseased fancy. For instance, no man would believe me if I were to state to him the plain and indisputable fact that one night last month, on my way up to bed shortly after midnight, having been neither smoking nor drinking, I saw confronting me upon the stairs, with the moonlight streaming through the windows back of me, lighting up its face, a figure in which I recognized my very self in every form and feature. I might describe the chill of terror that struck to the very marrow of my bones, and wellnigh forced me to stagger backward down the stairs, as I noticed in the face of this confronting figure every indication of all the bad qualities which I know myself to possess, of every evil instinct which by no easy effort I have repressed heretofore, and realized that that *thing* was, as far as I knew, entirely independent of my true self, in which I hope at least the moral has made an honest fight against the immoral always. I might describe this chill, I say, as vividly as I felt it at that moment, but it would be of no use to do so, because, however realistic it might prove as a bit of description, no man would believe that the incident really happened; and yet it did happen as truly as I write, and it has happened a dozen times since, and I am certain that it will happen many times again, though I would give all that I possess to be assured that never again should that disquieting creation of mind or matter, whichever it may be, cross my path. The experience has made me afraid almost to be alone, and I have found myself unconsciously and uneasily glancing at my face in mirrors, in the plate-glass of show-windows on the shopping streets of the city, fearful lest I should find some of those evil traits which I have struggled to keep under, and have kept under so far, cropping out there where all the world, all *my* world, can see and wonder at, having known me always as a man of right doing and right feeling. Many a time in the night the thought has come to me with prostrating force, what if that thing were to be seen and recognized by others, myself and yet not my whole self, my unworthy self unrestrained and yet recognizable as Henry Thurlow.

I have also kept silent as to that strange condition of affairs which has tortured me in my sleep for the past year and a half; no one but myself has until this writing known that for that period of time I have had a continuous, logical dream-life; a life so vivid and so dreadfully real to me that I have found myself at times wondering which of the two lives I was living and which I was dreaming; a life in which that other wicked self has dominated, and forced me to a career of shame and horror; a life which, being taken up every time I sleep where it ceased with the awakening from a previous sleep, has made me fear to close my eyes in forgetfulness when others are near at hand, lest, sleeping, I shall let fall some speech that, striking on their ears, shall lead them to believe that in secret there is some wicked mystery connected with my life. It would be of no use for me to tell these things. It would merely serve to make my family and my friends uneasy about me if they were told in their awful detail, and so I have kept silent about them. To you alone, and now for the first time, have I hinted as to the troubles which have oppressed me for many days, and to you they are confided only because of the demand you have made that I explain to you the extraordinary complication in which the Christmas story sent you last week has involved me. You know that I am a man of dignity; that I am not a school-boy and a lover of childish tricks; and knowing that, your friendship, at least, should have restrained your tongue and pen when, through the former, on Wednesday, you accused me of perpetrating a trifling, and to you excessively embarrassing, practical joke – a charge which, at the moment, I was too overcome to refute; and through the latter, on Thursday, you reiterated the accusation, coupled with a demand for an explanation of my conduct satisfactory to yourself, or my immediate resignation from the staff of the *Idler*. To explain is difficult, for I am certain that you will find the explanation too improbable for credence, but explain I must. The alternative, that of resigning from your staff, affects not only my own welfare, but that of my children, who must be provided for; and if my post with you is taken from me, then are all resources gone. I have not the courage to face dismissal, for I have not sufficient confidence in my powers to please elsewhere to make me easy in my mind, or, if I could please elsewhere, the certainty of finding the immediate employment of my talents which is necessary to me, in view of the at present overcrowded condition of the literary field.

To explain, then, my seeming jest at your expense, hopeless as it appears to be, is my task; and to do so as completely as I can, let me go back to the very beginning.

In August you informed me that you would expect me to provide, as I have heretofore been in the habit of doing, a story for the Christmas issue of the *Idler*; that a certain position in the make-up was reserved for me, and that you had already taken steps to advertise the fact that the story would appear. I undertook the commission, and upon seven different occasions set about putting the narrative into shape. I found great difficulty, however, in doing so. For some reason or other I could not concentrate my mind upon the work. No sooner would I start in on one story than a better one, in my estimation, would suggest itself to me; and all the labor expended on the story already begun would be cast aside, and the new story set in motion. Ideas were plenty enough, but to put them properly upon paper seemed beyond my powers. One story, however, I did finish; but after it had come back to me from my typewriter I read it, and was filled with consternation to discover that it was nothing more nor less than a mass of jumbled sentences, conveying no idea to the mind – a story which had seemed to me in the writing to be coherent had returned to me as a mere bit of incoherence – formless, without ideas – a bit of raving. It was then that I went to you and told you, as you remember, that I was worn out, and needed a month of absolute rest, which you granted. I left my work wholly, and went into the wilderness, where I could be entirely free from everything suggesting labor, and where no summons back to town could reach me. I fished and hunted. I slept; and although, as I have already said, in my sleep I found myself leading a life that was not only not to my taste, but horrible to me in many particulars, I was able at the end of my vacation to come back to town greatly refreshed, and, as far as my feelings went, ready to undertake any amount of work. For two or three days after my return I was busy with other things. On the fourth day after my arrival you came to me, and said that the story must be finished at the very latest by October 15th, and I assured you that you should have it by that time. That night I set about it. I mapped it out, incident by incident, and before starting up to bed had actually written some twelve or fifteen hundred words of the opening chapter – it was to be told in four chapters. When I had gone thus far I experienced a slight return of one of my nervous chills, and, on consulting my watch, discovered that it was after midnight, which was a sufficient explanation of my nervousness: I was merely tired. I arranged my manuscripts on my table so that I might easily take up the work the following morning. I locked up the windows and doors, turned out the lights, and proceeded up-stairs to my room.

It was then that I first came face to face with myself – that other self, in which I recognized, developed to the full, every bit of my capacity for an evil life.

Conceive of the situation if you can. Imagine the horror of it, and then ask yourself if it was likely that when next morning came I could by any possibility bring myself to my work-table in fit condition to prepare for you anything at all worthy of publication in the *Idler*. I tried. I implore you to believe that I did not hold lightly the responsibilities of the commission you had intrusted to my hands. You must know that if any of your writers has a full appreciation of the difficulties which are strewn along the path of an editor, *I*, who have myself had an editorial experience, have it, and so would not, in the nature of things, do anything to add to your troubles. You cannot but believe that I have made an honest effort to fulfil my promise to you. But it was useless, and for a week after that visitation was it useless for me to attempt the work. At the end of the week I felt better, and again I started in, and the story developed satisfactorily until – *it* came again. That figure which was my own figure, that face which was the evil counterpart of my own countenance, again rose up before me, and once more was I plunged into hopelessness.

Thus matters went on until the 14th day of October, when I received your peremptory message that the story must be forthcoming the following day. Needless to tell you that it was not forthcoming; but what I must tell you, since you do not know it, is that on the evening of the 15th day of October a strange thing happened to me, and in the narration of that incident, which I almost despair of your believing, lies my explanation of the discovery of October 16th, which has placed my position with you in peril.

At half-past seven o'clock on the evening of October 15th I was sitting in my library trying to write. I was alone. My wife and children had gone away on a visit to Massachusetts for a week. I had just finished my cigar, and had taken my pen in hand, when my front -door bell rang. Our maid, who is usually prompt in answering summonses of this nature, apparently did not hear the bell, for she did not respond to its clanging. Again the bell rang, and still did it remain unanswered, until finally, at the third ringing, I went to the door myself. On opening it I saw standing before me a man of, I should say, fifty odd years of age, tall, slender, pale-faced, and clad in sombre black. He was entirely unknown to me. I had never seen him before, but he had about him such an air of pleasantness and wholesomeness that I instinctively felt glad to see him, without knowing why or whence he had come.

"Does Mr. Thurlow live here?" he asked.

You must excuse me for going into what may seem to you to be petty details, but by a perfectly circumstantial account of all that happened that evening alone can I hope to give a semblance of truth to my story, and that it must be truthful I realize as painfully as you do.

"I am Mr. Thurlow," I replied.

"Henry Thurlow, the author?" he said, with a surprised look upon his face.

"Yes," said I; and then, impelled by the strange appearance of surprise on the man's countenance, I added, "don't I look like an author?"

He laughed, and candidly admitted that I was not the kind of looking man he had expected to find from reading my books, and then he entered the house in response to my invitation that he do so. I ushered him into my library, and, after asking him to be seated, inquired as to his business with me.

His answer was gratifying at least He replied that he had been a reader of my writings for a number of years, and that for some time past he had had a great desire, not to say curiosity, to meet me and tell me how much he had enjoyed certain of my stories.

"I'm a great devourer of books, Mr. Thurlow," he said, "and I have taken the keenest delight in reading your verses and humorous sketches. I may go further, and say to you that you have helped me over many a hard place in my life by your work. At times when I have felt myself worn out with my business, or face to face with some knotty problem in my career, I have found much relief in picking up and reading your books at random. They have helped me to forget my weariness or my knotty problems for the time being; and today, finding myself in this town, I resolved to call upon you this evening and thank you for all that you have done for me."

Thereupon we became involved in a general discussion of literary men and their works, and I found that my visitor certainly did have a pretty thorough knowledge of what has been produced by the writers of today. I was quite won over to him by his simplicity, as well as attracted to him by his kindly opinion of my own efforts, and I did my best to entertain him, showing him a few of my little literary treasures in the way of autograph letters, photographs, and presentation copies of well-known books from the authors themselves. From this we drifted naturally and easily into a talk on the methods of work adopted by literary men. He asked me many questions as to my own methods; and when I had in a measure outlined to him the manner of life which I had adopted, telling him of my days at home, how little detail office-work I had, he seemed much interested with the picture – indeed, I painted the picture of my daily routine in almost too perfect colors, for, when I had finished, he observed quietly that I appeared to him to lead the ideal life, and added that he supposed I knew very little unhappiness.

The remark recalled to me the dreadful reality, that through some perversity of fate I was doomed to visitations of an uncanny order which were practically destroying my usefulness in my profession and my sole financial resource.

"Well," I replied, as my mind reverted to the unpleasant predicament in which I found myself, "I can't say that I know little unhappiness. As a matter of fact, I know a great deal of that undesirable thing. At the present moment I am very much embarrassed through my absolute inability to fulfil a contract into which I have entered, and which should have been filled this morning. I was due today with a Christmas story. The presses are waiting for it, and I am utterly unable to write it."

He appeared deeply concerned at the confession. I had hoped, indeed, that he might be sufficiently concerned to take his departure, that I might make one more effort to write the promised story. His solicitude, however, showed itself in another way. Instead of leaving me, he ventured the hope that he might aid me.

"What kind of a story is it to be?" he asked.

"Oh, the usual ghostly tale," I said, "with a dash of the Christmas flavor thrown in here and there to make it suitable to the season."

"Ah," he observed. "And you find your vein worked out?"

It was a direct and perhaps an impertinent question; but I thought it best to answer it, and to answer it as well without giving him any clew as to the real facts. I could not very well take an entire stranger into my confidence, and describe to him the extraordinary encounters I was having with an uncanny other self. He would not have believed the truth, hence I told him an untruth, and assented to his proposition.

"Yes," I replied, "the vein is worked out. I have written ghost stories for years now, serious and comic, and I am today at the end of my tether – compelled to move forward and yet held back."

"That accounts for it," he said, simply. "When I first saw you to -night at the door I could not believe that the author who had provided me with so much merriment could be so pale and worn and seemingly mirthless. Pardon me, Mr. Thurlow, for my lack of consideration when I told you that you did not appear as I had expected to find you."

I smiled my forgiveness, and he continued:

"It may be," he said, with a show of hesitation – "it may be that I have come not altogether inopportunely. Perhaps I can help you."

I smiled again. "I should be most grateful if you could," I said.

"But you doubt my ability to do so?" he put in. "Oh – well – yes – of course you do; and why shouldn't you? Nevertheless, I have noticed this: At times when I have been baffled in my work a mere hint from another, from one who knew nothing of my work, has carried me on to a solution of my problem. I have read most of your writings, and I have thought over some of them many a time, and I have even had ideas for stories, which, in my own conceit, I have imagined were good enough for you, and I·have wished that I possessed your facility with the pen that I might make of them myself what I thought you would make of them had they been ideas of your own."

The old gentleman's pallid face reddened as he said this, and while I was hopeless as to anything of value resulting from his ideas, I could not resist the temptation to hear what he had to say further, his manner was so deliciously simple, and his desire to aid me so manifest. He rattled on with suggestions for a half-hour. Some of them were good, but none were new. Some were irresistibly funny, and did me good because they made me laugh, and I hadn't laughed naturally for a period so long that it made me shudder to think of it, fearing lest I should forget how to be mirthful. Finally I grew tired of his persistence, and, with a very ill-concealed impatience, told him plainly that I could do nothing with his suggestions, thanking him, however, for the spirit of kindliness which had prompted him to offer them. He appeared somewhat hurt, but immediately desisted, and when nine o'clock came he rose up to go. As he walked to the door he seemed to be undergoing some mental struggle, to which, with a sudden resolve, he finally succumbed, for, after having picked up his hat and stick and donned his overcoat, he turned to me and said:

"Mr. Thurlow, I don't want to offend you. On the contrary, it is my dearest wish to assist you. You have helped me, as I have told you. Why may I not help you?"

"I assure you, sir—" I began, when he interrupted me.

"One moment, please," he said, putting his hand into the inside pocket of his black coat and extracting from it an envelope addressed to me. "Let me finish: it is the whim of one who has an affection for you. For ten years I have secretly been at work myself on a story. It is a short one, but it has seemed good to me. I had a double object in seeking you out tonight. I wanted not only to see you, but to read my story to you. No one knows that I have written it; I had intended it as a surprise to my—to my friends. I had hoped to have it published somewhere, and I had come here to seek your advice in the matter. It is a story which I have written and rewritten and rewritten time and time again in my leisure moments during the ten years past, as I have told you. It is not likely that I shall ever write another. I am proud of having done it, but I should be prouder yet if it—if it could in some way help you. I leave it with you, sir, to print or to destroy; and if you print it, to see it in type will be enough for me; to see your name signed to it will be a matter of pride to me. No one will ever be the wiser, for, as I say, no one knows I have written it, and I promise you that no one shall know of it if you decide to do as I not only suggest but ask you to do. No one would believe me after it has appeared as *yours,* even if I should forget my promise and claim it as my own. Take it. It is yours. You are entitled to it as a slight measure of repayment for the debt of gratitude I owe you."

He pressed the manuscript into my hands, and before I could reply had opened the door and disappeared into the darkness of the street. I rushed to the sidewalk and shouted out to him to return, but I might as well have saved my breath and spared the neighborhood, for there was no answer. Holding his story in my hand, I re-entered the house and walked back into my library, where, sitting and reflecting upon the curious interview, I realized for the first time that I was in entire ignorance as to my visitor's name and address.

I opened the envelope hoping to find them, but they were not there. The envelope contained merely a finely written manuscript of thirty odd pages, unsigned.

And then I read the story. When I began it was with a half-smile upon my lips, and with a feeling that I was wasting my time. The smile soon faded, however; after reading the first paragraph there was no question of wasted time. The story was a masterpiece. It is needless to say to you that I am not a man of enthusiasms. It is difficult to arouse that emotion in my breast, but upon this occasion I yielded to a force too great for me to resist. I have read the tales of Hoffmann and of Poe, the wondrous romances of De La Motte Fouque, the unfortunately little-known tales of the lamented Fitz-James O'Brien, the weird tales of writers of all tongues have been thoroughly sifted by me in the course of my reading, and I say to you now that in the whole of my life I never read one story, one paragraph, one line, that could approach in vivid delineation, in weirdness of conception, in anything, in any quality which goes to make up the truly great story, that story which came into my hands as I have told you. I read it once and was amazed. I read it a second time and was—tempted. It was mine. The writer himself had authorized me to treat it as if it were my own; had voluntarily sacrificed his own claim to its authorship that he might relieve me of my very pressing embarrassment. Not only this; he had almost intimated that in putting my name to his work I should be doing him a favor. Why not do so, then, I asked myself; and immediately my better self rejected the idea as impossible. How could I put out as my own another man's work and retain my self -respect? I resolved on another and better course – to send you the story in lieu of my own with a full statement of the circumstances under which it had come into my possession, when that demon rose up out of the floor at my side, this time more evil of aspect than before, more commanding in its manner. With a groan I shrank back into the cushions of my chair, and by passing my hands over my eyes tried to obliterate forever the offending sight; but it was useless. The uncanny thing approached me, and as truly as I write sat upon the edge of my couch, where for the first time it addressed me.

"Fool!" it said, "how can you hesitate? Here is your position: you have made a contract which must be filled; you are already behind, and in a hopeless mental state. Even granting that between this and tomorrow morning you could put together the necessary number of words to fill the space allotted to you, what kind of a thing do you think that story would make? It would be a mere raving like that other precious effort of August. The public, if by some odd chance it ever reached them, would think your mind was utterly gone; your reputation would go with that verdict. On the other hand, if you do not have the story ready by tomorrow, your hold on the *Idler* will be destroyed. They have their announcements printed, and your name and portrait appear among those of the prominent contributors. Do you suppose the editor and publisher will look leniently upon your failure?"

"Considering my past record, yes," I replied. "I have never yet broken a promise to them."

"Which is precisely the reason why they will be severe with you. You, who have been regarded as one of the few men who can do almost any kind of literary work at will – you, of whom it is said that your 'brains are on tap' – will they be lenient with *you?* Bah! Can't you see that the very fact of your invariable readiness heretofore is going to make your present unreadiness a thing incomprehensible?"

"Then what shall I do?" I asked. "If I can't, I can't, that is all."

"You can. There is the story in your hands. Think what it will do for you. It is one of the immortal stories—"

"You have read it, then?" I asked.

"Haven't you?"

"Yes—but—"

"It is the same," it said, with a leer and a contemptuous shrug. "You and I are inseparable. Aren't you glad?" it added, with a laugh that grated on every fibre of my being. I was too overwhelmed to reply, and it resumed: "It is one of the immortal stories. We agree to that. Published over your name, your name will live. The stuff you write yourself will give you present glory; but when you have been dead ten years people won't remember your name even – unless I get control of you, and in that case there is a very pretty though hardly a literary record in store for you."

Again it laughed harshly, and I buried my face in the pillows of my couch, hoping to find relief there from this dreadful vision.

"Curious," it said. "What you call your decent self doesn't dare look me in the eye! What a mistake people make who say that the man who won't look you in the eye is not to be trusted! As if mere brazenness were a sign of honesty; really, the theory of decency is the most amusing thing in the world. But come, time is growing short. Take that story. The writer gave it to you. Begged you to use it as your own. It is yours. It will make your reputation, and save you with your publishers. How can you hesitate?"

"I shall not use it!" I cried, desperately.

"You must – consider your children. Suppose you lose your connection with these publishers of yours?"

"But it would be a crime."

"Not a bit of it. Whom do you rob? A man who voluntarily came to you, and gave you that of which you rob him. Think of it as it is – and act, only act quickly. It is now midnight."

The tempter rose up and walked to the other end of the room, whence, while he pretended to be looking over a few of my books and pictures, I was aware he was eyeing me closely, and gradually compelling me by sheer force of will to do a thing which I abhorred. And I—I struggled weakly against the temptation, but gradually, little by little, I yielded, and finally succumbed altogether. Springing to my feet, I rushed to the table, seized my pen, and signed my name to the story.

"There!" I said. "It is done. I have saved my position and made my reputation, and am now a thief!"

"As well as a fool," said the other, calmly. "You don't mean to say you are going to send that manuscript in as it is?"

"Good Lord!" I cried. "What under heaven have you been trying to make me do for the last half hour?"

"Act like a sane being," said the demon. "If you send that manuscript to Currier he'll know in a minute it isn't yours. He knows you haven't an amanuensis, and that handwriting isn't yours. Copy it."

"True!" I answered. "I haven't much of a mind for details tonight. I will do as you say."

I did so. I got out my pad and pen and ink, and for three hours diligently applied myself to the task of copying the story. When it was finished I went over it carefully, made a few minor corrections, signed it, put it in an envelope, addressed it to you, stamped it, and went out to the mail-box on the corner, where I dropped it into the slot, and returned home. When I had returned to my library my visitor was still there.

"Well," it said, "I wish you'd hurry and complete this affair. I am tired, and wish to go."

"You can't go too soon to please me," said I, gathering up the original manuscripts of the story and preparing to put them away in my desk.

"Probably not," it sneered. "I'll be glad to go too, but I can't go until that manuscript is destroyed. As long as it exists there is evidence of your having appropriated the work of another. Why, can't you see that? Burn it!"

"I can't see my way clear in crime!" I retorted. "It is not in my line."

Nevertheless, realizing the value of his advice, I thrust the pages one by one into the blazing log fire, and watched them as they flared and flamed and grew to ashes. As the last page disappeared in the embers the demon vanished. I was alone, and throwing myself down for a moment's reflection upon my couch, was soon lost in sleep.

It was noon when I again opened my eyes, and, ten minutes after I awakened, your telegraphic summons reached me.

"Come down at once," was what you said, and I went; and then came the terrible *dénouement,* and yet a *dénouement* which was pleasing to me since it relieved my conscience. You handed me the envelope containing the story.

"Did you send that?" was your question.

"I did – last night, or rather early this morning. I mailed it about three o'clock," I replied.

"I demand an explanation of your conduct," said you.

"Of what?" I asked.

"Look at your so-called story and see. If this is a practical joke, Thurlow, it's a damned poor one."

I opened the envelope and took from it the sheets I had sent you – twenty-four of them.

They were every one of them as blank as when they left the paper -mill!

You know the rest. You know that I tried to speak; that my utterance failed me; and that, finding myself unable at the time to control my emotions, I turned and rushed madly from the office, leaving the mystery unexplained. You know that you wrote demanding a satisfactory explanation of the situation or my resignation from your staff.

This, Currier, is my explanation. It is all I have. It is absolute truth. I beg you to believe it, for if you do not, then is my condition a hopeless one. You will ask me perhaps for a *résumé* of the story which I thought I had sent you.

It is my crowning misfortune that upon that point my mind is an absolute blank. I cannot remember it in form or in substance. I have racked my brains for some recollection of some small portion of it to help to make my explanation more credible, but, alas! it will not come back to me. If I were dishonest I might fake up a story to suit the purpose, but I am not dishonest. I came near to doing an unworthy act; I did do an unworthy thing, but by some mysterious provision of fate my conscience is cleared of that.

Be sympathetic Currier, or, if you cannot, be lenient with me this time. *Believe, believe, believe,* I implore you. Pray let me hear from you at once.

(Signed) HENRY THURLOW.

II

(Being a Note from George Currier, Editor of the "Idler" to Henry Thurlow, Author.)

Your explanation has come to hand. As an explanation it isn't worth the paper
it is written on, but we are all agreed here that it is probably the best bit of fiction you

ever wrote. It is accepted for the Christmas issue. Enclosed please find check for one hundred dollars.

Dawson suggests that you take another month up in the Adirondacks. You might put in your time writing up some account of that dream -life you are leading while you are there. It seems to me there are possibilities in the idea. The concern will pay all expenses. What do you say?

(Signed) Yours ever, G. C. THE DAMPMERE MYSTERY

Dawson wished to be alone; he had a tremendous bit of writing to do, which could not be done in New York, where his friends were constantly interrupting him, and that is why he had taken the little cottage at Dampmere for the early spring months. The cottage just suited him. It was remote from the village of Dampmere, and the rental was suspiciously reasonable; he could have had a ninety-nine years' lease of it for nothing, had he chosen to ask for it, and would promise to keep the premises in repair; but he was not aware of that fact when he made his arrangements with the agent. Indeed, there was a great deal that Dawson was not aware of when he took the place. If there hadn't been he never would have thought of going there, and this story would not have been written.

It was late in March when, with his Chinese servant and his mastiff, he entered into possession and began the writing of the story he had in mind. It was to be the effort of his life. People reading it would forget Thackeray and everybody else, and would, furthermore, never wish to see another book. It was to be the literature of all time – past and present and future; in it all previous work was to be forgotten, all future work was to be rendered unnecessary.

For three weeks everything went smoothly enough, and the work upon the great story progressed to the author's satisfaction; but as Easter approached something queer seemed to develop in the Dampmere cottage. It was undefinable, intangible, invisible, but it was there. Dawson's hair would not stay down. When he rose up in the morning he would find every single hair on his head standing erect, and plaster it as he would with his brushes dipped in water, it could not be induced to lie down again. More inconvenient than this, his silken mustache was affected in the same way, so that instead of drooping in a soft fascinating curl over his lip, it also rose up like a row of bayonets and lay flat against either side of his nose; and with this singular hirsute affliction there came into Dawson's heart a feeling of apprehension over something, he knew not what, that speedily developed into an uncontrollable terror that pervaded his whole being, and more thoroughly destroyed his ability to work upon his immortal story than ten inconsiderate New York friends dropping in on him in his busy hours could possibly have done.

"What the dickens is the matter with me?" he said to himself, as for the sixteenth time he brushed his rebellious locks. "What has come over my hair? And what under the sun am I afraid of? The idea of a man of my size looking under the bed every night for – for something – burglar, spook, or what I don't know. Waking at midnight shivering with fear, walking in the broad light of day filled with terror; by Jove! I almost wish I was Chung Lee down in the kitchen, who goes about his business undisturbed."

Having said this, Dawson looked about him nervously. If he had expected a dagger to be plunged into his back by an unseen foe he could not have looked around more anxiously; and then he fled, actually fled in terror into the kitchen, where Chung Lee was preparing his dinner. Chung was only a Chinaman, but he was a living creature, and Dawson was afraid to be alone.

"Well, Chung," he said, as affably as he could, "this is a pleasant change from New York, eh?"

"Plutty good," replied Chung, with a vacant stare at the pantry door. "Me likes Noo Lork allee same. Dampeemere kind of flunny, Mister Dawson."

"Funny, Chung?" queried Dawson, observing for the first time that the Chinaman's queue stood up as straight as a garden stake, and almost scraped the ceiling as its owner moved about. "Funny?"

"Yeppee, flunny," returned Chung, with a shiver. "Me no likee. Me flightened."

"Oh, come!" said Dawson, with an affected lightness. "What are you afraid of?"

"Slumting," said Chung. "Do' know what. Go to bled; no sleepee; pigtail no stay down; heart go thump allee night."

"By Jove !" thought Dawson; "he's got it too!"

"Evlyting flunny here," resumed Chung.

"Jack he no likee too."

Jack was the mastiff.

"What's the matter with Jack?" queried Dawson. "You don't mean to say Jack's afraid?"

"Do' know if he 'flaid," said Chung, "He growl most time."

Clearly there was no comfort for Dawson here. To rid him of his fears it was evident that Chung could be of no assistance, and Chung's feeling that even Jack was affected by the uncanny something was by no means reassuring. Dawson went out into the yard and whistled for the dog, and in a moment the magnificent animal came bounding up. Dawson patted him on the back, but Jack, instead of rejoicing as was his wont over this token of his master's affection, gave a yelp of pain, which was quite in accord with Dawson's own feelings, for gentle though the pat was, his hand after it felt as though he had pressed it upon a bunch of needles.

"What's the matter, old fellow?" said Dawson, ruefully rubbing the palm of his hand. "Did I hurt you?"

The dog tried to wag his tail, but unavailingly, and Dawson was again filled with consternation to observe that even as Chung's queue stood high, even as his own hair would not lie down, so it was with Jack's soft furry skin. Every hair on it was erect, from the tip of the poor beast's nose to the end of his tail, and so stiff withal that when it was pressed from without it pricked the dog within.

"There seems to be some starch in the air of Dampmere," said Dawson, thoughtfully, as he turned and walked slowly into the house. "I wonder what the deuce it all means?"

And then he sought his desk and tried to write, but he soon found that he could not possibly concentrate his mind upon his work. He was continually oppressed by the feeling that he was not alone. At one moment it seemed as if there were a pair of eyes peering at him from the northeast corner of the room, but as soon as he turned his own anxious gaze in that direction the difficulty seemed to lie in the southwest corner.

"Bah!" he cried, starting up and stamping his foot angrily upon the floor. "The idea! I, Charles Dawson, a man of the world, scared by—by – well, by nothing. I don't believe in ghosts – and yet – at times I do believe that this house is haunted. My hair seems to feel the same way. It stands up like stubble in a wheat-field, and one might as well try to brush the one as the other. At this rate nothing'll get done. I'll go to town and see Dr. Bronson. There's something the matter with me."

So off Dawson went to town.

"I suppose Bronson will think I'm a fool, but I can prove all I say by my hair," he said, as he rang the doctor's bell. He was instantly admitted, and shortly after describing his symptoms he called the doctor's attention to his hair.

If he had pinned his faith to this, he showed that his faith was misplaced, for when the doctor came to examine it, Dawson's hair was lying down as softly as it ever had. The doctor looked at Dawson for a moment, and then, with a dry cough, he said:

"Dawson, I can conclude one of two things from what you tell me. Either Dampmere is haunted, which you and I as sane men can't believe in these days, or else you are playing a practical joke on me. Now I don't mind a practical joke at the club, my dear fellow, but here, in my office hours, I can't afford the time to like anything of the sort. I speak frankly with you, old fellow. I have to. I hate to do it, but, after all, you've brought it on yourself."

"Doctor," Dawson rejoined, "I believe I'm a sick man, else this thing wouldn't have happened. I solemnly assure you that I've come to you because I wanted a prescription, and because I believe myself badly off."

"You carry it off well, Dawson," said the doctor, severely, "but I'll prescribe. Go back to Dampmere right away, and when you've seen the ghost, telegraph me and I'll come down."

With this Bronson bowed Dawson out, and the latter, poor fellow, soon found himself on the street utterly disconsolate. He could not blame Bronson. He could understand how Bronson could come to believe that, with his hair as the only witness to his woes, and a witness that failed him at the crucial moment, Bronson should regard his visit as the outcome of some club wager, in many of which he had been involved previously.

"I guess his advice is good," said he, as he walked along. "I'll go back right away – but meanwhile I'll get Billie Perkins to come out and spend the night with me, and we'll try it on him. I'll ask him out for a few days."

Suffice it to say that Perkins accepted, and that night found the two eating supper together outwardly serene. Perkins was quite interested when Chung brought in the supper.

"Wears his queue Pompadour, I see," he said, as he glanced at Chung's extraordinary head-dress.

"Yes," said Dawson, shortly.

"You wear your hair that way yourself," he added, for he was pleased as well as astonished to note that Perkins's hair was manifesting an upward tendency.

"Nonsense," said Perkins. "It's flat as a comic paper."

"Look at yourself in the glass," said Dawson.

Perkins obeyed. There was no doubt about it. His hair was rising! He started back uneasily.

"Dawson," he cried, "what is it? I've felt queer ever since I entered your front door, and I assure you I've been wondering why you wore your mustache like a pirate all the evening."

"I can't account for it. I've got the creeps myself," said Dawson, and then he told Perkins all that I have told you.

"Let's—let's go back to New York," said Perkins.

"Can't," replied Dawson. "No train."

"Then," said Perkins, with a shiver, "let's go to bed."

The two men retired, Dawson to the room directly over the parlor, Perkins to the apartment back of it. For company they left the gas burning, and in a short time were fast asleep. An hour later Dawson awakened with a start. Two things oppressed him to the very core of his being. First, the gas was out; and second, Perkins had unmistakably groaned.

He leaped from his bed and hastened into the next room.

"Perkins," he cried, "are you ill?"

"Is that you, Dawson?" came a voice from the darkness.

"Yes. Did—did you put out the gas?"

"No."

"Are you ill?"

"No; but I'm deuced uncomfortable What's this mattress stuffed with – needles?"

"Needles? No. It's a hair mattress. Isn't it all right?"

"Not by a great deal. I feel as if I had been sleeping on a porcupine. Light up the gas and let's see what the trouble is."

Dawson did as he was told, wondering meanwhile why the gas had gone out. No one had turned it out, and yet the key was unmistakably turned; and, what was worse, on ripping open Perkins's mattress, a most disquieting state of affairs was disclosed.

Every single hair in it was standing on end!

A half-hour later four figures were to be seen wending their way northward through the darkness – two men, a huge mastiff, and a Chinaman. The group was made up of Dawson, his guest, his servant, and his dog. Dampmere was impossible; there was no train until morning, but not one of them was willing to remain a moment longer at Dampmere, and so they had to walk.

"What do you suppose it was?" asked Perkins, as they left the third mile behind them.

"I don't know," said Dawson; "but it must be something terrible. I don't mind a ghost that will make the hair of living beings stand on end, but a nameless invisible something that affects a mattress that way has a terrible potency that I have no desire to combat. It's a mystery, and, as a rule, I like mysteries, but the mystery of Dampmere I'd rather let alone."

"Don't say a word about the – ah – the mattress, Charlie," said Perkins, after awhile. "The fellows'll never believe it."

"No. I was thinking that very same thing," said Dawson.

And they were both true to Dawson's resolve, which is possibly why the mystery of Dampmere has never been solved.

If any of my readers can furnish a solution, I wish they would do so, for I am very much interested in the case, and I truly hate to leave a story of this kind in so unsatisfactory a condition.

A ghost story without any solution strikes me as being about as useful as a house without a roof.

Mustapha

S. Baring-Gould

I

AMONG THE MANY hangers-on at the Hotel de l'Europe at Luxor – donkey-boys, porters, guides, antiquity dealers – was one, a young man named Mustapha, who proved a general favourite.

I spent three winters at Luxor, partly for my health, partly for pleasure, mainly to make artistic studies, as I am by profession a painter. So I came to know Mustapha fairly well in three stages, during those three winters.

When first I made his acquaintance he was in the transition condition from boyhood to manhood. He had an intelligent face, with bright eyes, a skin soft as brown silk, with a velvety hue on it. His features were regular, and if his face was a little too round to quite satisfy an English artistic eye, yet this was a peculiarity to which one soon became accustomed. He was unflaggingly good-natured and obliging. A mongrel, no doubt, he was; Arab and native Egyptian blood were mingled in his veins. But the result was happy; he combined the patience and gentleness of the child of Mizraim with the energy and pluck of the son of the desert.

Mustapha had been a donkey-boy, but had risen a stage higher, and looked, as the object of his supreme ambition, to become some day a dragoman, and blaze like one of these gilded beetles in lace and chains, rings and weapons. To become a dragoman – one of the most obsequious of men till engaged, one of the veriest tyrants when engaged – to what higher could an Egyptian boy aspire?

To become a dragoman means to go in broadcloth and with gold chains when his fellows are half naked; to lounge and twist the moustache when his kinsfolk are toiling under the water-buckets; to be able to extort backsheesh from all the tradesmen to whom he can introduce a master; to do nothing himself and make others work for him; to be able to look to purchase two, three, even four wives when his father contented himself with one; to soar out of the region of native virtues into that of foreign vices; to be superior to all instilled prejudices against spirits and wine – that is the ideal set before young Egypt through contact with the English and the American tourist.

We all liked Mustapha. No one had a bad word to say of him. Some pious individuals rejoiced to see that he had broken with the Koran, as if this were a first step towards taking up with the Bible. A free-thinking professor was glad to find that Mustapha had emancipated himself from some of those shackles which religion places on august, divine humanity, and that by getting drunk he gave pledge that he had risen into a sphere of pure emancipation, which eventuates in ideal perfection.

As I made my studies I engaged Mustapha to carry my easel and canvas, or camp-stool. I was glad to have him as a study, to make him stand by a wall or sit on a pillar that was prostrate, as artistic exigencies required. He was always ready to accompany me. There was an understanding between us that when a drove of tourists came to Luxor he might leave me for the day to pick up what he could then from the natural prey; but I found him not always keen to be off duty to me.

Though he could get more from the occasional visitor than from me, he was above the ravenous appetite for backsheesh which consumed his fellows.

He who has much to do with the native Egyptian will have discovered that there are in him a fund of kindliness and a treasure of good qualities. He is delighted to be treated with humanity, pleased to be noticed, and ready to repay attention with touching gratitude. He is by no means as

rapacious for backsheesh as the passing traveller supposes; he is shrewd to distinguish between man and man; likes this one, and will do anything for him unrewarded, and will do naught for another for any bribe.

The Egyptian is now in a transitional state. If it be quite true that the touch of England is restoring life to his crippled limbs, and the voice of England bidding him rise up and walk, there are occasions on which association with Englishmen is a disadvantage to him. Such an instance is that of poor, good Mustapha.

It was not my place to caution Mustapha against the pernicious influences to which he was subjected, and, to speak plainly, I did not know what line to adopt, on what ground to take my stand, if I did. He was breaking with the old life, and taking up with what was new, retaining of the old only what was bad in it, and acquiring of the new none of its good parts. Civilisation – European civilisation – is excellent, but cannot be swallowed at a gulp, nor does it wholly suit the oriental digestion.

That which impelled Mustapha still further in his course was the attitude assumed towards him by his own relatives and the natives of his own village. They were strict Moslems, and they regarded him as one on the highway to becoming a renegade. They treated him with mistrust, showed him aversion, and loaded him with reproaches. Mustapha had a high spirit, and he resented rebuke. Let his fellows grumble and objurgate, said he; they would cringe to him when he became a dragoman, with his pockets stuffed with piastres.

There was in our hotel, the second winter, a young fellow of the name of Jameson, a man with plenty of money, superficial good nature, little intellect, very conceited and egotistic, and this fellow was Mustapha's evil genius. It was Jameson's delight to encourage Mustapha in drinking and gambling. Time hung heavy on his hands. He cared nothing for hieroglyphics, scenery bored him, antiquities, art, had no charm for him. Natural history presented to him no attraction, and the only amusement level with his mental faculties was that of hoaxing natives, or breaking down their religious prejudices.

Matters were in this condition as regarded Mustapha, when an incident occurred during my second winter at Luxor that completely altered the tenor of Mustapha's life.

One night a fire broke out in the nearest village. It originated in a mud hovel belonging to a fellah; his wife had spilled some oil on the hearth, and the flames leaping up had caught the low thatch, which immediately burst into a blaze. A wind was blowing from the direction of the Arabian desert, and it carried the flames and ignited the thatch before it on other roofs; the conflagration spread, and the whole village was menaced with destruction. The greatest excitement and alarm prevailed. The inhabitants lost their heads. Men ran about rescuing from their hovels their only treasures – old sardine tins and empty marmalade pots; women wailed, children sobbed; no one made any attempt to stay the fire; and, above all, were heard the screams of the woman whose incaution had caused the mischief, and who was being beaten unmercifully by her husband.

The few English in the hotel came on the scene, and with their instinctive energy and system set to work to organise a corps and subdue the flames. The women and girls who were rescued from the menaced hovels, or plucked out of those already on fire, were in many cases unveiled, and so it came to pass that Mustapha, who, under English direction, was ablest and most vigorous in his efforts to stop the conflagration, met his fate in the shape of the daughter of Ibraim the Earner.

By the light of the flames he saw her, and at once resolved to make that fair girl his wife.

No reasonable obstacle intervened, so thought Mustapha. He had amassed a sufficient sum to entitle him to buy a wife and set up a household of his own. A house consists of four mud walls and a low thatch, and housekeeping in an Egyptian house is as elementary and economical as the domestic architecture. The maintenance of a wife and family is not costly after the first outlay, which consists in indemnifying the father for the expense to which he has been put in rearing a daughter.

The ceremony of courting is also elementary, and the addresses of the suitor are not paid to the bride, but to her father, and not in person by the candidate, but by an intermediary.

Mustapha negotiated with a friend, a fellow hanger-on at the hotel, to open proceedings with the farrier. He was to represent to the worthy man that the suitor entertained the most ardent admiration for the virtues of Ibraim personally, that he was inspired with but one ambition, which was alliance with so distinguished a family as his. He was to assure the father of the damsel that Mustapha undertook to proclaim through Upper and Lower Egypt, in the ears of Egyptians, Arabs, and Europeans, that Ibraim was the most remarkable man that ever existed for solidity of judgment, excellence of parts, uprightness of dealing, nobility of sentiment, strictness in observance of the precepts of the Koran, and that finally Mustapha was anxious to indemnify this same paragon of genius and virtue for his condescension in having cared to breed and clothe and feed for several years a certain girl, his daughter, if Mustapha might have that daughter as his wife. Not that he cared for the daughter in herself, but as a means whereby he might have the honour of entering into alliance with one so distinguished and so esteemed of Allah as Ibraim the Farrier.

To the infinite surprise of the intermediary, and to the no less surprise and mortification of the suitor, Mustapha was refused. He was a bad Moslem. Ibraim would have no alliance with one who had turned his back on the Prophet and drunk bottled beer.

Till this moment Mustapha had not realised how great was the alienation between his fellows and himself – what a barrier he had set up between himself and the men of his own blood. The refusal of his suit struck the young man to the quick. He had known and played with the farrier's daughter in childhood, till she had come of age to veil her face; now that he had seen her in her ripe charms, his heart was deeply stirred and engaged. He entered into himself, and going to the mosque he there made a solemn vow that if he ever touched wine, ale, or spirits again he would cut his throat, and he sent word to Ibraim that he had done so, and begged that he would not dispose of his daughter and finally reject him till he had seen how that he who had turned in thought and manner of life from the Prophet would return with firm resolution to the right way.

II

From this time Mustapha changed his conduct. He was obliging and attentive as before, ready to exert himself to do for me what I wanted, ready also to extort money from the ordinary tourist for doing nothing, to go with me and carry my tools when I went forth painting, and to joke and laugh with Jameson; but, unless he were unavoidably detained, he said his prayers five times daily in the mosque, and no inducement whatever would make him touch anything save sherbet, milk, or water.

Mustapha had no easy time of it. The strict Mohammedans mistrusted this sudden conversion, and believed that he was playing a part. Ibraim gave him no encouragement. His relatives maintained their reserve and stiffness towards him.

His companions, moreover, who were in the transitional stage, and those who had completely shaken off all faith in Allah and trust in the Prophet and respect for the Koran, were incensed at his desertion. He was ridiculed, insulted; he was waylaid and beaten. The young fellows mimicked him, the elder scoffed at him.

Jameson took his change to heart, and laid himself out to bring him out of his pot of scruples.

"Mustapha ain't any sport at all now," said he. "I'm hanged if he has another para from me." He offered him bribes in gold, he united with the others in ridicule, he turned his back on him, and refused to employ him. Nothing availed. Mustapha was respectful, courteous, obliging as before, but he had returned, he said, to the faith and rule of life in which he had been brought up, and he would never again leave it.

"I have sworn," said he, "that if I do I will cut my throat." I had been, perhaps, negligent in cautioning the young fellow the first winter that I knew him against the harm likely to be done him by taking up with European habits contrary to his law and the feelings and prejudices of his people. Now, however, I had no hesitation in expressing to him the satisfaction I felt at the courageous and determined manner in which he had broken with acquired habits that could do him no good. For one thing, we were now better acquaintances, and I felt that as one who had known him for more than a few months in the winter, I had a good right to speak. And, again, it is always easier or pleasanter to praise than to reprimand.

One day when sketching I cut my pencil with a pruning-knife I happened to have in my pocket; my proper knife of many blades had been left behind by misadventure.

Mustapha noticed the knife and admired it, and asked if it had cost a great sum.

"Not at all," I answered. "I did not even buy it. It was given me. I ordered some flower seeds from a seeds-man, and when he sent me the consignment he included this knife in the case as a present. It is not worth more than a shilling in England."

He turned it about, with looks of admiration.

"It is just the sort that would suit me," he said. "I know your other knife with many blades. It is very fine, but it is too small. I do not want it to cut pencils. It has other things in it, a hook for taking stones from a horse's hoof, a pair of tweezers for removing hairs. I do not want such, but a knife such as this, with such a curve, is just the thing."

"Then you shall have it," said I. "You are welcome. It was for rough work only that I brought the knife to Egypt with me."

I finished a painting that winter that gave me real satisfaction. It was of the great court of the temple of Luxor by evening light, with the last red glare of the sun over the distant desert hills, and the eastern sky above of a purple depth. What colours I used! the intensest on my palette, and yet fell short of the effect.

The picture was in the Academy, was well hung, abominably represented in one of the illustrated guides to the galleries, as a blotch, by some sort of photographic process on gelatine; my picture sold, which concerned me most of all, and not only did it sell at a respectable figure, but it also brought me two or three orders for Egyptian pictures. So many English and Americans go up the Nile, and carry away with them pleasant reminiscences of the Land of the Pharaohs, that when in England they are fain to buy pictures which shall remind them of scenes in that land.

I returned to my hotel at Luxor in November, to spend there a third winter. The fellaheen about there saluted me as a friend with an affectionate delight, which I am quite certain was not assumed, as they got nothing out of me save kindly salutations. I had the Egyptian fever on me, which, when once acquired, is not to be shaken off – an enthusiasm for everything Egyptian, the antiquities, the history of the Pharaohs, the very desert, the brown Nile, the desolate hill ranges, the ever blue sky, the marvellous colorations at rise and set of sun, and last, but not least, the prosperity of the poor peasants.

I am quite certain that the very warmest welcome accorded to me was from Mustapha, and almost the first words he said to me on my meeting him again were:

"I have been very good. I say my prayers. I drink no wine, and Ibraim will give me his daughter in the second Iomada – what you call January."

"Not before, Mustapha?"

"No, sir; he says I must be tried for one whole year, and he is right."

"Then soon after Christmas you will be happy!"

"I have got a house and made it ready. Yes. After Christmas there will be one very happy man – one very, very happy man in Egypt, and that will be your humble servant, Mustapha."

III

We were a pleasant party at Luxor, this third winter, not numerous, but for the most part of congenial tastes. For the most part we were keen on hieroglyphics, we admired Queen Hatasou and we hated Rameses II. We could distinguish the artistic work of one dynasty from that of another. We were learned on cartouches, and flourished our knowledge before the tourists dropping in.

One of those staying in the hotel was an Oxford don, very good company, interested in everything, and able to talk well on everything – I mean everything more or less remotely connected with Egypt. Another was a young fellow who had been an attaché at Berlin, but was out of health – nothing organic the matter with his lungs, but they were weak. He was keen on the political situation, and very anti-Gallican, as every man who has been in Egypt naturally is, who is not a Frenchman.

There was also staying in the hotel an American lady, fresh and delightful, whose mind and conversation twinkled like frost crystals in the sun, a woman full of good-humour, of the most generous sympathies, and so droll that she kept us ever amused.

And, alas! Jameson was back again, not entering into any of our pursuits, not understanding our little jokes, not at all content to be there. He grumbled at the food – and, indeed, that might have been better; at the monotony of the life at Luxor, at his London doctor for putting the veto on Cairo because of its drainage, or rather the absence of all drainage. I really think we did our utmost to draw Jameson into our circle, to amuse him, to interest him in something; but one by one we gave him up, and the last to do this was the little American lady.

From the outset he had attacked Mustapha, and endeavoured to persuade him to shake off his "squeamish nonsense," as Jameson called his resolve. "I'll tell you what it is, old fellow," he said, "life isn't worth living without good liquor, and as for that blessed Prophet of yours, he showed he was a fool when he put a bar on drinks."

But as Mustapha was not pliable he gave him up. "He's become just as great a bore as that old Rameses," said he. "I'm sick of the whole concern, and I don't think anything of fresh dates, that you fellows make such a fuss about. As for that stupid old Nile – there ain't a fish worth eating comes out of it. And those old Egyptains were arrant humbugs. I haven't seen a lotus since I came here, and they made such a fuss about them too."

The little American lady was not weary of asking questions relative to English home life, and especially to country-house living and amusements.

"Oh, my dear!" said she, "I would give my ears to spend a Christmas in the fine old fashion in a good ancient manor-house in the country."

"There is nothing remarkable in that," said an English lady.

"Not to you, maybe; but there would be to us. What we read of and make pictures of in our fancies, that is what you live. Your facts are our fairy tales. Look at your hunting."

"That, if you like, is fun," threw in Jameson. "But I don't myself think anything save Luxor can be a bigger bore than country-house life at Christmas time – when all the boys are back from school."

"With us," said the little American, "our sportsmen dress in pink like yours – the whole thing – and canter after a bag of anise seed that is trailed before them."

"Why do they not import foxes?"

"Because a fox would not keep to the road. Our farmers object pretty freely to trespass; so the hunting must of necessity be done on the highway, and the game is but a bag of anise seed. I would like to see an English meet and a run."

This subject was thrashed out after having been prolonged unduly for the sake of Jameson.

"Oh, dear me!" said the Yankee lady. "If but that chef could be persuaded to give us plum-puddings for Christmas, I would try to think I was in England."

"Plum-pudding is exploded," said Jameson. "Only children ask for it now. A good trifle or a tipsy-cake is much more to my taste; but this hanged cook here can give us nothing but his blooming custard pudding and burnt sugar."

"I do not think it would be wise to let him attempt a plum-pudding," said the English lady. "But if we can persuade him to permit me I will mix and make the pudding, and then he cannot go far wrong in the boiling and dishing up."

"That is the only thing wanting to make me perfectly happy," said the American. "I'll confront monsieur. I am sure I can talk him into a good humour, and we shall have our plum-pudding."

No one has yet been found, I do believe, who could resist that little woman. She carried everything before her. The cook placed himself and all his culinary apparatus at her feet. We took part in the stoning of the raisins, and the washing of the currants, even the chopping of the suet; we stirred the pudding, threw in sixpence apiece, and a ring, and then it was tied up in a cloth, and set aside to be boiled. Christmas Day came, and the English chaplain preached us a practical sermon on "Goodwill towards men." That was his text, and his sermon was but a swelling out of the words just as rice is swelled to thrice its size by boiling.

We dined. There was an attempt at roast beef – it was more like baked leather. The event of the dinner was to be the bringing in and eating of the plum-pudding.

Surely all would be perfect. We could answer for the materials and the mixing. The English lady could guarantee the boiling. She had seen the plum-pudding on the boil," and had given strict injunctions as to the length of time during which it was to boil.

But, alas! the pudding was not right when brought on the table. It was not enveloped in lambent blue flame – it was not crackling in the burning brandy. It was sent in dry, and the brandy arrived separate in a white sauceboat, hot indeed, and sugared, but not on fire.

There ensued outcries of disappointment. Attempts were made to redress the mistake by setting fire to the brandy in a spoon, but the spoon was cold. The flame would not catch, and finally, with a sigh, we had to take our plum-pudding as served.

"I say, chaplain!" exclaimed Jameson, "practice is better than precept, is it not?"

"To be sure it is."

"You gave us a deuced good sermon. It was short, as it ought to be; but I'll go better on it, I'll practise where you preached, and have larks, too!"

Then Jameson started from table with a plate of plum-pudding in one hand and the sauce-boat in the other. "By Jove!" he said, "I'll teach these fellows to open their eyes. I'll show them that we know how to feed. We can't turn out scarabs and cartouches in England, that are no good to anyone, but we can produce the finest roast beef in the world, and do a thing or two in puddings."

And he left the room.

We paid no heed to anything Jameson said or did. We were rather relieved that he was out of the room, and did not concern ourselves about the "larks" he promised himself, and which we were quite certain would be as insipid as were the quails of the Israelites.

In ten minutes he was back, laughing and red in the face. "I've had splitting fun," he said. "You should have been there."

"Where, Jameson?"

"Why, outside. There were a lot of old moolahs and other hoky-pokies sitting and contemplating the setting sun and all that sort of thing, and I gave Mustapha the pudding. I told him I wished him to try our great national English dish, on which her Majesty the Queen dines daily. Well, he ate and enjoyed it, by George. Then I said, 'Old fellow, it's uncommonly dry, so you must take the sauce to it.' He asked if it was only sauce – flour and water. 'It's sauce, by Jove,' said I, 'a little sugar to it; no bar on the sugar, Musty.' So I put the boat to his lips and gave him a pull. By George, you should have seen his face! It was just thundering fun. 'I've done you at last, old Musty,' I said. 'It is best cognac.' He gave me such a look! He'd have eaten me, I believe – and he walked away. It was just splitting fun. I wish you had been there to see it."

I went out after dinner, to take my usual stroll along the river-bank, and to watch the evening lights die away on the columns and obelisk. On my return I saw at once that something had happened which had produced commotion among the servants of the hotel. I had reached the salon before I inquired what was the matter.

The boy who was taking the coffee round said: "Mustapha is dead. He cut his throat at the door of the mosque. He could not help himself. He had broken his vow."

I looked at Jameson without a word. Indeed, I could not speak; I was choking. The little American lady was trembling, the English lady crying. The gentlemen stood silent in the windows, not speaking a word.

Jameson's colour changed. He was honestly distressed, uneasy, and tried to cover his confusion with bravado and a jest.

"After all," he said, "it is only a nigger the less."

"Nigger!" said the American lady. "He was no nigger, but an Egyptian."

"Oh! I don't pretend to distinguish between your blacks and whity-browns any more than I do between your cartouches," returned Jameson.

"He was no black," said the American lady, standing up. "But I do mean to say that I consider you an utterly unredeemed black

"My dear, don't," said the Englishwoman, drawing the other down. "It's no good. The thing is done. He meant no harm."

IV

I could not sleep. My blood was in a boil. I felt that I could not speak to Jameson again. He would have to leave Luxor. That was tacitly understood among us. Coventry was the place to which he would be consigned.

I tried to finish in a little sketch I had made in my notebook when I was in my room, but my hand shook, and I was constrained to lay my pencil aside. Then I took up an Egyptian grammar, but could not fix my mind on study. The hotel was very still. Everyone had gone to bed at an early hour that night, disinclined for conversation. No one was moving. There was a lamp in the passage; it was partly turned down. Jameson's room was next to mine. I heard him stir as he undressed, and talk to himself. Then he was quiet. I wound up my watch, and emptying my pocket, put my purse under the pillow. I was not in the least heavy with sleep. If I did go to bed I should not be able to close my eyes. But then – if I sat up I could do nothing.

I was about leisurely to undress, when I heard a sharp cry, or exclamation of mingled pain and alarm, from the adjoining room. In another moment there was a rap at my door. I opened, and Jameson came in. He was in his nightshirt, and looking agitated and frightened.

"Look here, old fellow," said he in a shaking voice, "there is Musty in my room. He has been hiding there, and just as I dropped asleep he ran that – knife of yours into my throat."

"My knife?"

"Yes – that pruning-knife you gave him, you know. Look here – I must have the place sewn up. Do go for a doctor, there's a good chap,"

"Where is the place?"

"Here on my right gill."

Jameson turned his head to the left, and I raised the lamp. There was no wound of any sort there.

I told him so.

"Oh, yes! That's fine – I tell you I felt his knife go in."

"Nonsense, you were dreaming."

"Dreaming! Not I. I saw Musty as distinctly as I now see you."

"This is a delusion, Jameson," I replied. "The poor fellow is dead."

"Oh, that's very fine," said Jameson. "It is not the first of April, and I don't believe the yarns that you've been spinning. You tried to make believe he was dead, but I know he is not. He has got into my room, and he made a dig at my throat with your pruning-knife."

"I'll go into your room with you."

"Do so. But he's gone by this time. Trust him to cut and run." I followed Jameson, and looked about. There was no trace of anyone beside himself having been in the room. Moreover, there was no place but the nut-wood wardrobe in the bedroom in which anyone could have secreted himself I opened this and showed that it was empty.

After a while I pacified Jameson, and induced him to go to bed again, and then I left his room. I did not now attempt to court sleep. I wrote letters with a hand not the steadiest, and did my accounts.

As the hour approached midnight I was again startled by a cry from the adjoining room, and in another moment Jameson was at my door.

"That blooming fellow Musty is in my room still," said he. "He has been at my throat again."

"Nonsense," I said. "You are labouring under hallucinations. You locked your door."

"Oh, by Jove, yes – of course I did; but, hang it, in this hole, neither doors nor windows fit, and the locks are no good, and the bolts nowhere. He got in again somehow, and if I had not started up the moment I felt the knife, he'd have done for me. He would, by George. I wish I had a revolver."

I went into Jameson's room. Again he insisted on my looking at his throat.

"It's very good of you to say there is no wound," said he. "But you won't gull me with words. I felt his knife in my windpipe, and if I had not jumped out of bed—"

"You locked your door. No one could enter. Look in the glass, there is not even a scratch. This is pure imagination."

"I'll tell you what, old fellow, I won't sleep in that room again. Change with me, there's a charitable buffer. If you don't believe in Musty, Musty won't hurt you, maybe – anyhow you can try if he's solid or a phantom. Blow me if the knife felt like a phantom."

"I do not quite see my way to changing rooms," I replied; "but this I will do for you. If you like to go to bed again in your own apartment, I will sit up with you till morning."

"All right," answered Jameson. "And if Musty comes in again, let out at him and do not spare him. Swear that."

I accompanied Jameson once more to his bedroom. Little as I liked the man, I could not deny him my presence and assistance at this time. It was obvious that his nerves were shaken by what had occurred, and he felt his relation to Mustapha much more than he cared to show. The thought that he had been the cause of the poor fellow's death preyed on his mind, never strong, and now it was upset with imaginary terrors.

I gave up letter writing, and brought my Baedeker's Upper Egypt into Jameson's room, one of the best of all guide-books, and one crammed with information. I seated myself near the light, and with my back to the bed, on which the young man had once more flung himself

"I say," said Jameson, raising his head, "is it too late for a brandy-and-soda?"

"Everyone is in bed."

"What lazy dogs they are. One never can get anything one wants here."

"Well, try to go to sleep."

He tossed from side to side for some time, but after a while, either he was quiet, or I was engrossed in my Baedeker, and I heard nothing till a clock struck twelve. At the last stroke I heard a snort and then a gasp and a cry from the bed. I started up, and looked round. Jameson was slipping out with his feet onto the floor.

"Confound you!" said he angrily, "you are a fine watch, you are, to let Mustapha steal in on tiptoe whilst you are cartouching and all that sort of rubbish. He was at me again, and if I had not been sharp he'd have cut my throat. I won't go to bed any more!"

"Well, sit up. But I assure you no one has been here."

"That's fine. How can you tell? You had your back to me, and these devils of fellows steal about like cats. You can't hear them till they are at you."

It was of no use arguing with Jameson, so I let him have his way.

"I can feel all the three places in my throat where he ran the knife in," said he. "And – don't you notice? – I speak with difficulty."

So we sat up together the rest of the night. He became more reasonable as dawn came on, and inclined to admit that he had been a prey to fancies. The day passed very much as did others – Jameson was dull and sulky. After déjeuner he sat on at table when the ladies had risen and retired, and the gentlemen had formed in knots at the window, discussing what was to be done in the afternoon. Suddenly Jameson, whose head had begun to nod, started up with an oath and threw down his chair.

"You fellows!" he said, "you are all in league against me. You let that Mustapha come in without a word, and try to stick his knife into me."

"He has not been here."

"It's a plant. You are combined to bully me and drive me away. You don't like me. You have engaged Mustapha to murder me. This is the fourth time he has tried to cut my throat, and in the sale à manger, too, with you all standing round. You ought to be ashamed to call yourselves Englishmen. I'll go to Cairo. I'll complain."

It really seemed that the feeble brain of Jameson was affected. The Oxford don undertook to sit up in the room the following night.

The young man was fagged and sleep-weary, but no sooner did his eyes close, and clouds form about his head, than he was brought to wakefulness again by the same fancy or dream. The Oxford don had more trouble with him on the second night than I had on the first, for his lapses into sleep were more frequent, and each such lapse was succeeded by a start and a panic.

The next day he was worse, and we felt that he could no longer be left alone. The third night the attaché sat up to watch him.

Jameson had now sunk into a sullen mood. He would not speak, except to himself, and then only to grumble.

During the night, without being aware of it, the young attaché, who had taken a couple of magazines with him to read, fell asleep. When he went off he did not know. He woke just before dawn, and in a spasm of terror and self-reproach saw that Jameson's chair was empty.

Jameson was not on his bed. He could not be found in the hotel. At dawn he was found – dead, at the door of the mosque, with his throat cut.

The Ghost of Christmas Eve

J.M. Barrie

A FEW YEARS ago, as some may remember, a startling ghost-paper appeared in the monthly organ of the Society for Haunting Houses. The writer guaranteed the truth of his statement, and even gave the name of the Yorkshire manor-house in which the affair took place. The article and the discussion to which it gave rise agitated me a good deal, and I consulted Pettigrew about the advisability of clearing up the mystery. The writer wrote that he "distinctly saw his arm pass through the apparition and come out at the other side," and indeed I still remember his saying so next morning. He had a scared face, but I had presence of mind to continue eating my rolls and marmalade as if my briar had nothing to do with the miraculous affair.

Seeing that he made a "paper" of it, I suppose he is justified in touching up the incidental details. He says, for instance, that we were told the story of the ghost which is said to haunt the house, just before going to bed. As far as I remember, it was only mentioned at luncheon, and then skeptically. Instead of there being snow falling outside and an eerie wind wailing through the skeleton trees, the night was still and muggy. Lastly, I did not know, until the journal reached my hands, that he was put into the room known as the Haunted Chamber, nor that in that room the fire is noted for casting weird shadows upon the walls. This, however, may be so. The legend of the manor-house ghost he tells precisely as it is known to me. The tragedy dates back to the time of Charles I., and is led up to by a pathetic love-story, which I need not give. Suffice it that for seven days and nights the old steward had been anxiously awaiting the return of his young master and mistress from their honeymoon. On Christmas eve, after he had gone to bed, there was a great clanging of the door-bell. Flinging on a dressing-gown, he hastened downstairs. According to the story, a number of servants watched him, and saw by the light of his candle that his face was an ashy white. He took off the chains of the door, unbolted it, and pulled it open. What he saw no human being knows; but it must have been something awful, for, without a cry, the old steward fell dead in the hall. Perhaps the strangest part of the story is this: that the shadow of a burly man, holding a pistol in his hand, entered by the open door, stepped over the steward's body, and, gliding up the stairs, disappeared, no one could say where. Such is the legend. I shall not tell the many ingenious explanations of it that have been offered. Every Christmas eve, however, the silent scene is said to be gone through again; and tradition declares that no person lives for twelve months at whom the ghostly intruder points his pistol.

On Christmas Day the gentleman who tells the tale in a scientific journal created some sensation at the breakfast table by solemnly asserting that he had seen the ghost. Most of the men present scouted his story, which may be condensed into a few words. He had retired to his bedroom at a fairly early hour, and as he opened the door his candle-light was blown out. He tried to get a light from the fire, but it was too low, and eventually he went to bed in the semi-darkness. He was wakened – he did not know at what hour – by the clanging of a bell. He sat up in bed, and the ghost-story came in a rush to his mind. His fire was dead, and the room was consequently dark; yet by and by he knew, though he heard no sound, that his door had opened. He cried out, "Who is that?" but got no answer. By an effort he jumped up and went to the door, which was ajar. His bedroom was on the first floor, and looking up the stairs he could see nothing. He felt a cold sensation at his heart, however, when he looked the other way. Going slowly and without a sound down the stairs, was an old man in a dressing-gown. He carried a candle. From the top of the stairs only part of the hall is visible, but as the apparition disappeared the watcher had the courage to go down a few steps after him. At first nothing was to be seen, for the candle-light had vanished. A dim light, however, entered by the long, narrow windows which flank the hall door, and after a moment the on-looker could see that the hall was empty. He was marveling at this sudden disappearance of the steward, when, to his horror, he saw a body fall upon the hall-floor within a few feet of the door. The watcher cannot say whether he cried out, nor how long he stood there trembling. He came to himself with a start as he realized that something was coming up the stairs. Fear prevented his taking flight, and in a moment the thing was at his side. Then he saw indistinctly that it was not the figure he had seen descend. He saw a younger man, in a heavy overcoat, but with no hat on his head. He wore on his face a look of extravagant triumph. The guest boldly put out his hand toward the figure. To his amazement his arm went through it. The ghost paused for a moment and looked behind it. It was then the watcher realized that it carried a pistol in its right hand. He was by this time in a highly strung condition, and he stood trembling lest the pistol should be pointed at him. The apparition, however, rapidly glided up the stairs and was soon lost to sight. Such are the main facts of the story, none of which I contradicted at the time.

I cannot say absolutely that I can clear up this mystery, but my suspicions are confirmed by a good deal of circumstantial evidence. This will not be understood unless I explain my strange infirmity. Wherever I went I used to be troubled with a presentiment that I had left my pipe behind. Often, even at the dinner-table, I paused in the middle of a sentence as if stricken with sudden pain. Then my hand went down to my pocket. Sometimes even after I felt my pipe, I had a conviction that it was stopped, and only by a desperate effort did I keep myself from producing it and blowing down it. I distinctly remember once dreaming three nights in succession that I was on the Scotch express without it. More than once, I know, I have wandered in my sleep, looking for it in all sorts of places, and after I went to bed I generally jumped out, just to make sure of it. My strong belief, then, is that I was the ghost seen by the writer of the paper. I fancy that I rose in my sleep, lighted a candle, and wandered down to the hall to feel if my pipe was safe in my coat, which was hanging there. The light had gone out when I was in the hall. Probably the body seen to fall on the hall floor was some other coat which I had flung there to get more easily at my own. I cannot account for the bell; but perhaps the gentleman in the Haunted Chamber dreamed that part of the affair. I had put on the overcoat before reascending; indeed I may say that next morning I was surprised to find it on a chair in my bedroom, also to notice that there were several long streaks of candle-grease on my dressing-gown. I conclude that the pistol, which gave my face such a look of triumph, was my briar, which I found in the morning beneath my pillow. The strangest thing of all, perhaps, is that when I awoke there was a smell of tobacco-smoke in the bedroom.

Between the Lights

E.F. Benson

THE DAY HAD been one unceasing fall of snow from sunrise until the gradual withdrawal of the vague white light outside indicated that the sun had set again. But as usual at this hospitable and delightful house of Everard Chandler where I often spent Christmas, and was spending it now, there had been no lack of entertainment, and the hours had passed with a rapidity that had surprised us. A short billiard tournament had filled up the time between breakfast and lunch, with Badminton and the morning papers for those who were temporarily not engaged, while afterwards, the interval till tea-time had been occupied by the majority of the party in a huge game of hide-and-seek all over the house, barring the billiard-room, which was sanctuary for any who desired peace. But few had done that; the enchantment of Christmas, I must suppose, had, like some spell, made children of us again, and it was with palsied terror and trembling misgivings that we had tip-toed up and down the dim passages, from any corner of which some wild screaming form might dart out on us. Then, wearied with exercise and emotion, we had assembled again for tea in the hall, a room of shadows and panels on which the light from the wide open fireplace, where there burned a divine mixture of peat and logs, flickered and grew bright again on the walls. Then, as was proper, ghost-stories, for the narration of which the electric light was put out, so that the listeners might conjecture anything they pleased to be lurking in the corners, succeeded, and we vied with each other in blood, bones, skeletons, armour and shrieks. I had, just given my contribution, and was reflecting with some complacency that probably the worst was now known, when Everard, who had not yet administered to the horror of his guests, spoke. He was sitting opposite me in the full blaze of the fire, looking, after the illness he had gone through during the autumn, still rather pale and delicate. All the same he had been among the boldest and best in the exploration of dark places that afternoon, and the look on his face now rather startled me.

"No, I don't mind that sort of thing," he said. "The paraphernalia of ghosts has become somehow rather hackneyed, and when I hear of screams and skeletons I feel I am on familiar ground, and can at least hide my head under the bed-clothes."

"Ah, but the bed-clothes were twitched away by my skeleton," said I, in self-defence.

"I know, but I don't even mind that. Why, there are seven, eight skeletons in this room now, covered with blood and skin and other horrors. No, the nightmares of one's childhood were the really frightening things, because they were vague. There was the true atmosphere of horror about them because one didn't know what one feared. Now if one could recapture that—"

Mrs. Chandler got quickly out of her seat.

"Oh, Everard," she said, "surely you don't wish to recapture it again. I should have thought once was enough."

This was enchanting. A chorus of invitation asked him to proceed: the real true ghost-story first-hand, which was what seemed to be indicated, was too precious a thing to lose.

Everard laughed. "No, dear, I don't want to recapture it again at all," he said to his wife.

Then to us: "But really the – well, the nightmare perhaps, to which I was referring, is of the vaguest and most unsatisfactory kind. It has no apparatus about it at all. You will probably all say that it was nothing, and wonder why I was frightened. But I was; it frightened me out of my wits. And I only just saw something, without being able to swear what it was, and heard something which might have been a falling stone."

"Anyhow, tell us about the falling stone," said I.

There was a stir of movement about the circle round the fire, and the movement was not of purely physical order. It was as if – this is only what I personally felt – it was as if the childish gaiety of the hours we had passed that day was suddenly withdrawn; we had jested on certain subjects, we had played hide-and-seek with all the power of earnestness that was in us. But now – so it seemed to me – there was going to be real hide-and-seek, real terrors were going to lurk in dark corners, or if not real terrors, terrors so convincing as to assume the garb of reality, were going to pounce on us. And Mrs. Chandler's exclamation as she sat down again, "Oh, Everard, won't it excite you?" tended in any case to excite us. The room still remained in dubious darkness except for the sudden lights disclosed on the walls by the leaping flames on the hearth, and there was wide field for conjecture as to what might lurk in the dim corners. Everard, moreover, who had been sitting in bright light before, was banished by the extinction of some flaming log into the shadows. A voice alone spoke to us, as he sat back in his low chair, a voice rather slow but very distinct.

"Last year," he said, "on the twenty-fourth of December, we were down here, as usual, Amy and I, for Christmas. Several of you who are here now were here then. Three or four of you at least."

I was one of these, but like the others kept silence, for the identification, so it seemed to me, was not asked for. And he went on again without a pause.

"Those of you who were here then," he said, "and are here now, will remember how very warm it was this day year. You will remember, too, that we played croquet that day on the lawn. It was perhaps a little cold for croquet, and we played it rather in order to be able to say – with sound evidence to back the statement – that we had done so."

Then he turned and addressed the whole little circle.

"We played ties of half-games," he said, "just as we have played billiards today, and it was certainly as warm on the lawn then as it was in the billiard-room this morning directly after breakfast, while today I should not wonder if there was three feet of snow outside. More, probably; listen."

A sudden draught fluted in the chimney, and the fire flared up as the current of air caught it.

The wind also drove the snow against the windows, and as he said, "Listen," we heard a soft scurry of the falling flakes against the panes, like the soft tread of many little people who stepped lightly, but with the persistence of multitudes who were flocking to some rendezvous. Hundreds of little feet seemed to be gathering outside; only the glass kept them out. And of the eight skeletons present four or five, anyhow, turned and looked at the windows. These were small-paned, with leaden bars. On the leaden bars little heaps of snow had accumulated, but there was nothing else to be seen.

"Yes, last Christmas Eve was very warm and sunny," went on Everard. "We had had no frost that autumn, and a temerarious dahlia was still in flower. I have always thought that it must have been mad."

He paused a moment.

"And I wonder if I were not mad too," he added.

No one interrupted him; there was something arresting, I must suppose, in what he was saying; it chimed in anyhow with the hide-and-seek, with the suggestions of the lonely snow.

Mrs. Chandler had sat down again, but I heard her stir in her chair. But never was there a gay party so reduced as we had been in the last five minutes. Instead of laughing at ourselves for playing silly games, we were all taking a serious game seriously.

"Anyhow, I was sitting out," he said to me, "while you and my wife played your half-game of croquet. Then it struck me that it was not so warm as I had supposed, because quite suddenly I shivered. And shivering I looked up. But I did not see you and her playing croquet at all. I saw something which had no relation to you and her – at least I hope not."

Now the angler lands his fish, the stalker kills his stag, and the speaker holds his audience.

And as the fish is gaffed, and as the stag is shot, so were we held. There was no getting away till he had finished with us.

"You all know the croquet lawn," he said, "and how it is bounded all round by a flower border with a brick wall behind it, through which, you will remember, there is only one gate.

"Well, I looked up and saw that the lawn – I could for one moment see it was still a lawn – was shrinking, and the walls closing in upon it. As they closed in too, they grew higher, and simultaneously the light began to fade and be sucked from the sky, till it grew quite dark overhead and only a glimmer of light came in through the gate.

"There was, as I told you, a dahlia in flower that day, and as this dreadful darkness and bewilderment came over me, I remember that my eyes sought it in a kind of despair, holding on, as it were, to any familiar object. But it was no longer a dahlia, and for the red of its petals I saw only the red of some feeble firelight. And at that moment the hallucination was complete. I was no longer sitting on the lawn watching croquet, but I was in a low-roofed room, something like a cattle-shed, but round. Close above my head, though I was sitting down, ran rafters from wall to wall. It was nearly dark, but a little light came in from the door opposite to me, which seemed to lead into a passage that communicated with the exterior of the place. Little, however, of the wholesome air came into this dreadful den; the atmosphere was oppressive and foul beyond all telling, it was as if for years it had been the place of some human menagerie, and for those years had been uncleaned and unsweetened by the winds of heaven. Yet that oppressiveness was nothing to the awful horror of the place from the view of the spirit. Some dreadful atmosphere of crime and abomination dwelt heavy in it, its denizens, whoever they were, were scarce human, so it seemed to me, and though men and women, were akin more to the beasts of the field. And in addition there was present to me some sense of the weight of years; I had been taken and thrust down into some epoch of dim antiquity."

He paused a moment, and the fire on the hearth leaped up for a second and then died down again. But in that gleam I saw that all faces were turned to Everard, and that all wore some look of dreadful expectancy. Certainly I felt it myself, and waited in a sort of shrinking horror for what was coming.

"As I told you," he continued, "where there had been that unseasonable dahlia, there now burned a dim firelight, and my eyes were drawn there. Shapes were gathered round it; what they were I could not at first see. Then perhaps my eyes got more accustomed to the dusk, or the fire burned better, for I perceived that they were of human form, but very small, for when one rose with a horrible chattering, to his feet, his head was still some inches off the low roof. He was dressed in a sort of shirt that came to his knees, but his arms were bare and covered with hair.

"Then the gesticulation and chattering increased, and I knew that they were talking about me, for they kept pointing in my direction. At that my horror suddenly deepened, for I became aware that I was powerless and could not move hand or foot; a helpless, nightmare impotence had possession of me. I could not lift a finger or turn my head. And in the paralysis of that fear I tried to scream, but not a sound could I utter.

"All this I suppose took place with the instantaneousness of a dream, for at once, and without transition, the whole thing had vanished, and I was back on the lawn again, while the stroke for which my wife was aiming was still unplayed. But my face was dripping with perspiration, and I was trembling all over.

"Now you may all say that I had fallen asleep, and had a sudden nightmare. That may be so; but I was conscious of no sense of sleepiness before, and I was conscious of none afterwards. It was as if someone had held a book before me, whisked the pages open for a second and closed them again."

Somebody, I don't know who, got up from his chair with a sudden movement that made me start, and turned on the electric light. I do not mind confessing that I was rather glad of this.

Everard laughed.

"Really I feel like Hamlet in the play-scene," he said, "and as if there was a guilty uncle present. Shall I go on?"

I don't think anyone replied, and he went on.

"Well, let us say for the moment that it was not a dream exactly, but a hallucination.

"Whichever it was, in any case it haunted me; for months, I think, it was never quite out of my mind, but lingered somewhere in the dusk of consciousness, sometimes sleeping quietly, so to speak, but sometimes stirring in its sleep. It was no good my telling myself that I was disquieting myself in vain, for it was as if something had actually entered into my very soul, as if some seed of horror had been planted there. And as the weeks went on the seed began to sprout, so that I could no longer even tell myself that that vision had been a moment's disorderment only. I can't say that it actually affected my health. I did not, as far as I know, sleep or eat insufficiently, but morning after morning I used to wake, not gradually and through pleasant dozings into full consciousness, but with absolute suddenness, and find myself plunged in an abyss of despair.

"Often too, eating or drinking, I used to pause and wonder if it was worth while.

"Eventually, I told two people about my trouble, hoping that perhaps the mere communication would help matters, hoping also, but very distantly, that though I could not believe at present that digestion or the obscurities of the nervous system were at fault, a doctor by some simple dose might convince me of it. In other words I told my wife, who laughed at me, and my doctor, who laughed also, and assured me that my health was quite unnecessarily robust.

"At the same time he suggested that change of air and scene does wonders for the delusions that exist merely in the imagination. He also told me, in answer to a direct question, that he would stake his reputation on the certainty that I was not going mad.

"Well, we went up to London as usual for the season, and though nothing whatever occurred to remind me in any way of that single moment on Christmas Eve, the reminding was seen to all right, the moment itself took care of that, for instead of fading as is the way of sleeping or waking dreams, it grew every day more vivid, and ate, so to speak, like some corrosive acid into my mind, etching itself there. And to London succeeded Scotland.

"I took last year for the first time a small forest up in Sutherland, called Glen Callan, very remote and wild, but affording excellent stalking. It was not far from the sea, and the gillies used always to warn me to carry a compass on the hill, because sea-mists were liable to come up with frightful rapidity, and there was always a danger of being caught by one, and of having perhaps to wait hours till it cleared again. This at first I always used to do, but, as everyone knows, any precaution that one takes which continues to be unjustified gets gradually relaxed, and at the end of a few weeks, since the weather had been uniformly clear, it was natural that, as often as not, my compass remained at home.

"One day the stalk took me on to a part of my ground that I had seldom been on before, a very high table-land on the limit of my forest, which went down very steeply on one side to a loch that lay below it, and on the other, by gentler gradations, to the river that came from the loch, six miles below which stood the lodge. The wind had necessitated our climbing up – or so my stalker had insisted – not by the easier way, but up the crags from the loch. I had argued the point with him for it seemed to me that it was impossible that the deer could get our scent if we went by the more natural path, but he still held to his opinion; and therefore, since after all this was his part of the job, I yielded. A dreadful climb we had of it, over big boulders with deep holes in between, masked by clumps of heather, so that a wary eye and a prodding stick were necessary for each step if one wished to avoid broken bones. Adders also literally swarmed in the heather; we must have seen a dozen at least on our way up, and adders are a beast for which I have no manner of use. But a couple of hours saw us to the top, only to find that the stalker had been utterly at fault, and that the deer must quite infallibly have got wind of us, if they had remained in the place where we last saw them. That, when we could spy the ground again, we saw had happened; in any case they had gone. The man insisted the wind had changed, a palpably stupid excuse, and I wondered at that moment what other reason he had – for reason I felt sure there must be – for not wishing to take what would clearly now have been a better route. But this piece of bad management did not spoil our luck, for within an hour we had spied more deer, and about two o'clock I got a shot, killing a heavy stag. Then sitting on the heather I ate lunch, and enjoyed a well-earned bask and smoke in the sun. The pony meantime had been saddled with the stag, and was plodding homewards.

"The morning had been extraordinarily warm, with a little wind blowing off the sea, which lay a few miles off sparkling beneath a blue haze, and all morning in spite of our abominable climb I had had an extreme sense of peace, so much so that several times I had probed my mind, so to speak, to find if the horror still lingered there. But I could scarcely get any response from it.

"Never since Christmas had I been so free of fear, and it was with a great sense of repose, both physical and spiritual, that I lay looking up into the blue sky, watching my smoke-whorls curl slowly away into nothingness. But I was not allowed to take my ease long, for Sandy came and begged that I would move. The weather had changed, he said, the wind had shifted again, and he wanted me to be off this high ground and on the path again as soon as possible, because it looked to him as if a sea-mist would presently come up."

"'And yon's a bad place to get down in the mist,' he added, nodding towards the crags we had come up.

"I looked at the man in amazement, for to our right lay a gentle slope down on to the river, and there was now no possible reason for again tackling those hideous rocks up which we had climbed this morning. More than ever I was sure he had some secret reason for not wishing to go the obvious way. But about one thing he was certainly right, the mist was coming up from the sea, and I felt in my pocket for the compass, and found I had forgotten to bring it.

"Then there followed a curious scene which lost us time that we could really ill afford to waste, I insisting on going down by the way that common sense directed, he imploring me to take his word for it that the crags were the better way. Eventually, I marched off to the easier descent, and told him not to argue any more but follow. What annoyed me about him was that he would only give the most senseless reasons for preferring the crags. There were mossy places, he said, on the way I wished to go, a thing patently false, since the summer had been one spell of unbroken weather; or it was longer, also obviously untrue; or there were so many vipers about.

"But seeing that none of these arguments produced any effect, at last he desisted, and came after me in silence.

"We were not yet half down when the mist was upon us, shooting up from the valley like the broken water of a wave, and in three minutes we were enveloped in a cloud of fog so thick that we could barely see a dozen yards in front of us. It was therefore another cause for self-congratulation that we were not now, as we should otherwise have been, precariously clambering on the face of those crags up which we had come with such difficulty in the morning, and as I rather prided myself on my powers of generalship in the matter of direction, I continued leading, feeling sure that before long we should strike the track by the river. More than all, the absolute freedom from fear elated me; since Christmas I had not known the instinctive joy of that; I felt like a schoolboy home for the holidays. But the mist grew thicker and thicker, and whether it was that real rain-clouds had formed above it, or that it was of an extraordinary density itself, I got wetter in the next hour than I have ever been before or since. The wet seemed to penetrate the skin, and chill the very bones. And still there was no sign of the track for which I was making.

"Behind me, muttering to himself, followed the stalker, but his arguments and protestations were dumb, and it seemed as if he kept close to me, as if afraid.

"Now there are many unpleasant companions in this world; I would not, for instance, care to be on the hill with a drunkard or a maniac, but worse than either, I think, is a frightened man, because his trouble is infectious, and, insensibly. I began to be afraid of being frightened too.

"From that it is but a short step to fear. Other perplexities too beset us. At one time we seemed to be walking on flat ground, at another I felt sure we were climbing again, whereas all the time we ought to have been descending, unless we had missed the way very badly indeed. Also, for the month was October, it was beginning to get dark, and it was with a sense of relief that I remembered that the full moon would rise soon after sunset. But it had grown very much colder, and soon, instead of rain, we found we were walking through a steady fall of snow.

"Things were pretty bad, but then for the moment they seemed to mend, for, far away to the left, I suddenly heard the brawling of the river. It should, it is true, have been straight in front of me and we were perhaps a mile out of our way, but this was better than the blind wandering of the last hour, and turning to the left, I walked towards it. But before I had gone a hundred yards, I heard a sudden choked cry behind me, and just saw Sandy's form flying as if in terror of pursuit, into the mists. I called to him, but got no reply, and heard only the spurned stones of his running.

"What had frightened him I had no idea, but certainly with his disappearance, the infection of his fear disappeared also, and I went on, I may almost say, with gaiety. On the moment, however, I saw a sudden well-defined blackness in front of me, and before I knew what I was doing I was half stumbling, half walking up a very steep grass slope.

"During the last few minutes the wind had got up, and the driving snow was peculiarly uncomfortable, but there had been a certain consolation in thinking that the wind would soon disperse these mists, and I had nothing more than a moonlight walk home. But as I paused on this slope, I became aware of two things, one, that the blackness in front of me was very close, the other that, whatever it was, it sheltered me from the snow. So I climbed on a dozen yards into its friendly shelter, for it seemed to me to be friendly.

"A wall some twelve feet high crowned the slope, and exactly where I struck it there was a hole in it, or door rather, through which a little light appeared. Wondering at this I pushed on, bending down, for the passage was very low, and in a dozen yards came out on the other side.

"Just as I did this the sky suddenly grew lighter, the wind, I suppose, having dispersed the mists, and the moon, though not yet visible through the flying skirts of cloud, made sufficient illumination.

"I was in a circular enclosure, and above me there projected from the walls some four feet from the ground, broken stones which must have been intended to support a floor. Then simultaneously two things occurred.

"The whole of my nine months' terror came back to me, for I saw that the vision in the garden was fulfilled, and at the same moment I saw stealing towards me a little figure as of a man, but only about three foot six in height. That my eyes told me; my ears told me that he stumbled on a stone; my nostrils told me that the air I breathed was of an overpowering foulness, and my soul told me that it was sick unto death. I think I tried to scream, but could not; I know I tried to move and could not. And it crept closer.

"Then I suppose the terror which held me spellbound so spurred me that I must move, for next moment I heard a cry break from my lips, and was stumbling through the passage. I made one leap of it down the grass slope, and ran as I hope never to have to run again. What direction I took I did not pause to consider, so long as I put distance between me and that place. Luck, however, favoured me, and before long I struck the track by the river, and an hour afterwards reached the lodge.

"Next day I developed a chill, and as you know pneumonia laid me on my back for six weeks.

"Well, that is my story, and there are many explanations. You may say that I fell asleep on the lawn, and was reminded of that by finding myself, under discouraging circumstances, in an old Picts' castle, where a sheep or a goat that, like myself, had taken shelter from the storm, was moving about. Yes, there are hundreds of ways in which you may explain it. But the coincidence was an odd one, and those who believe in second sight might find an instance of their hobby in it."

"And that is all?" I asked.

"Yes, it was nearly too much for me. I think the dressing-bell has sounded."

The Gardener

E.F. Benson

TWO FRIENDS OF mine, Hugh Grainger and his wife, had taken for a month of Christmas holiday the house in which we were to witness such strange manifestations, and when I received an invitation from them to spend a fortnight there I returned them an enthusiastic affirmative. Well already did I know that pleasant heathery country-side, and most intimate was my acquaintance with the subtle hazards of its most charming golf-links. Golf, I was given to understand, was to occupy the solid day for Hugh and me, so that Margaret should never be obliged to set her hand to the implements with which the game, so detestable to her, was conducted...

I arrived there while yet the daylight lingered, and as my hosts were out, I took a ramble round the place. The house and garden stood on a plateau facing south; below it were a couple of acres of pasture that sloped down to a vagrant stream crossed by a foot-bridge, by the side of which stood a thatched cottage with a vegetable patch surrounding it. A path ran close past this across the pasture from a wicket-gate in the garden, conducted you over the foot-bridge, and, so my remembered sense of geography told me, must constitute a short cut to the links that lay not half a mile beyond. The cottage itself was clearly on the land of the little estate, and I at once supposed it to be the gardener's house. What went against so obvious and simple a theory was that it appeared to be untenanted. No wreath of smoke, though the evening was chilly, curled from its chimneys, and, coming closer, I fancied it had that air of "waiting" about it which we so often conjure into unused habitations. There it stood, with no sign of life whatever about it, though ready, as its apparently perfect state of repair seemed to warrant, for fresh tenants to put the breath of life into it again. Its little garden, too, though the palings were neat and newly painted, told the same tale; the beds were untended and unweeded, and in the flower-border by the front door was a row of chrysanthemums, which had withered on their stems. But all this was but the impression of a moment, and I did not pause as I passed it, but crossed the foot-bridge and went on up the heathery slope that lay beyond. My geography was not at fault, for presently I saw the club-house just in front of me. Hugh no doubt would be just about coming in from his afternoon round, and so we would walk back together. On reaching the club-house, however, the steward told me that not five minutes before Mrs. Grainger had called in her car for her husband, and I therefore retraced my steps by the path along which I had already come. But I made a detour, as a golfer will, to walk up the fairway of the seventeenth and eighteenth holes just for the pleasure of recognition, and looked respectfully at the yawning sandpit which so inexorably guards the eighteenth green, wondering in what circumstances I should visit it next, whether with a step complacent and superior, knowing that my ball reposed safely on the green beyond, or with the heavy footfall of one who knows that laborious delving lies before him.

The light of the winter evening had faded fast, and when I crossed the foot-bridge on my return the dusk had gathered. To my right, just beside the path, lay the cottage, the whitewashed walls of which gleamed whitely in the gloaming; and as I turned my glance back from it to the rather narrow plank which bridged the stream I thought I caught out of the tail of my eye some light from one of its windows, which thus disproved my theory that it was untenanted. But when

I looked directly at it again I saw that I was mistaken: some reflection in the glass of the red lines of sunset in the west must have deceived me, for in the inclement twilight it looked more desolate than ever. Yet I lingered by the wicket gate in its low palings, for though all exterior evidence bore witness to its emptiness, some inexplicable feeling assured me, quite irrationally, that this was not so, and that there was somebody there. Certainly there was nobody visible, but, so this absurd idea informed me, he might be at the back of the cottage concealed from me by the intervening structure, and, still oddly, still unreasonably, it became a matter of importance to my mind to ascertain whether this was so or not, so clearly had my perceptions told me that the place was empty, and so firmly had some conviction assured me that it was tenanted. To cover my inquisitiveness, in case there was someone there, I could inquire whether this path was a short cut to the house at which I was staying, and, rather rebelling at what I was doing, I went through the small garden, and rapped at the door. There was no answer, and, after waiting for a response to a second summons, and having tried the door and found it locked, I made the circuit of the house. Of course there was no one there, and I told myself that I was just like a man who looks under his bed for a burglar and would be beyond measure astonished if he found one.

My hosts were at the house when I arrived, and we spent a cheerful two hours before dinner in such desultory and eager conversation as is proper between friends who have not met for some time. Between Hugh Grainger and his wife it is always impossible to light on a subject which does not vividly interest one or other of them, and golf, politics, the needs of Russia, cooking, ghosts, the possible victory over Mount Everest, and the income tax were among the topics which we passionately discussed. With all these plates spinning, it was easy to whip up any one of them, and the subject of spooks generally was lighted upon again and again.

"Margaret is on the high road to madness," remarked Hugh on one of these occasions, "for she has begun using planchette. If you use planchette for six months, I am told, most careful doctors will conscientiously certify you as insane. She's got five months more before she goes to Bedlam."

"Does it work?" I asked.

"Yes, it says most interesting things," said Margaret. "It says things that never entered my head. We'll try it tonight."

"Oh, not tonight," said Hugh. "Let's have an evening off."

Margaret disregarded this.

"It's no use asking planchette questions," she went on, "because there is in your mind some sort of answer to them. If I ask whether it will be fine tomorrow, for instance, it is probably I – though indeed I don't mean to push – who makes the pencil say 'yes.'"

"And then it usually rains," remarked Hugh.

"Not always: don't interrupt. The interesting thing is to let the pencil write what it chooses."

"Very often it only makes loops and curves – though they may mean something – and every now and then a word comes, of the significance of which I have no idea whatever, so I clearly couldn't have suggested it. Yesterday evening, for instance, it wrote 'gardener' over and over again. Now what did that mean? The gardener here is a Methodist with a chin-beard. Could it have meant him? Oh, it's time to dress. Please don't be late, my cook is so sensitive about soup."

We rose, and some connection of ideas about "gardener" linked itself up in my mind.

"By the way, what's that cottage in the field by the foot-bridge?" I asked. "Is that the gardener's cottage?"

"It used to be," said Hugh. "But the chin-beard doesn't live there: in fact nobody lives there."

"It's empty. If I was owner here, I should put the chin-beard into it, and take the rent off his wages. Some people have no idea of economy. Why did you ask?"

I saw Margaret was looking at me rather attentively.

"Curiosity," I said. "Idle curiosity."

"I don't believe it was," said she.

"But it was," I said. "It was idle curiosity to know whether the house was inhabited. As I passed it, going down to the club-house, I felt sure it was empty, but coming back I felt so sure that there was someone there that I rapped at the door, and indeed walked round it."

Hugh had preceded us upstairs, as she lingered a little.

"And there was no one there?" she asked. "It's odd: I had just the same feeling as you about it."

"That explains planchette writing 'gardener' over and over again," said I. "You had the gardener's cottage on your mind."

"How ingenious!" said Margaret. "Hurry up and dress."

A gleam of strong moonlight between my drawn curtains when I went up to bed that night led me to look out. My room faced the garden and the fields which I had traversed that afternoon, and all was vividly illuminated by the full moon. The thatched cottage with its white walls close by the stream was very distinct, and once more, I suppose, the reflection of the light on the glass of one of its windows made it appear that the room was lit within. It struck me as odd that twice that day this illusion should have been presented to me, but now a yet odder thing happened.

Even as I looked the light was extinguished.

The morning did not at all bear out the fine promise of the clear night, for when I woke the wind was squealing, and sheets of rain from the south-west were dashed against my panes. Golf was wholly out of the question, and, though the violence of the storm abated a little in the afternoon, the rain dripped with a steady sullenness. But I wearied of indoors, and, since the two others entirely refused to set foot outside, I went forth mackintoshed to get a breath of air. By way of an object in my tramp, I took the road to the links in preference to the muddy short cut through the fields, with the intention of engaging a couple of caddies for Hugh and myself next morning, and lingered awhile over illustrated papers in the smoking-room. I must have read for longer than I knew, for a sudden beam of sunset light suddenly illuminated my page, and looking up, I saw that the rain had ceased, and that evening was fast coming on. So instead of taking the long detour by the road again, I set forth homewards by the path across the fields. That gleam of sunset was the last of the day, and once again, just as twenty-four hours ago, I crossed the foot-bridge in the gloaming. Till that moment, as far as I was aware, I had not thought at all about the cottage there, but now in a flash the light I had seen there last night, suddenly extinguished, recalled itself to my mind, and at the same moment I felt that invincible conviction that the cottage was tenanted. Simultaneously in these swift processes of thought I looked towards it, and saw standing by the door the figure of a man. In the dusk I could distinguish nothing of his face, if indeed it was turned to me, and only got the impression of a tallish fellow, thickly built. He opened the door, from which there came a dim light as of a lamp, entered, and shut it after him.

So then my conviction was right. Yet I had been distinctly told that the cottage was empty: who, then, was he that entered as if returning home? Once more, this time with a certain qualm of fear, I rapped on the door, intending to put some trivial question; and rapped again, this time more drastically, so that there could be no question that my summons was unheard. But still I got no reply, and finally I tried the handle of the door. It was locked. Then, with difficulty mastering an increasing terror, I made the circuit of the cottage, peering into each unshuttered window. All was dark within, though but two minutes ago I had seen the gleam of light escape from the opened door.

Just because some chain of conjecture was beginning to form itself in my mind, I made no allusion to this odd adventure, and after dinner Margaret, amid protests from Hugh, got out the planchette which had persisted in writing "gardener." My surmise was, of course, utterly fantastic, but I wanted to convey no suggestion of any sort to Margaret…For a long time the pencil skated over her paper making loops and curves and peaks like a temperature chart, and she had begun to yawn and weary over her experiment before any coherent word emerged. And then, in the oddest way, her head nodded forward and she seemed to have fallen asleep.

Hugh looked up from his book and spoke in a whisper to me.

"She fell asleep the other night over it," he said.

Margaret's eyes were closed, and she breathed the long, quiet breaths of slumber, and then her hand began to move with a curious firmness. Right across the big sheet of paper went a level line of writing, and at the end her hand stopped with a jerk, and she woke.

She looked at the paper.

"Hullo," she said. "Ah, one of you has been playing a trick on me!"

We assured her that this was not so, and she read what she had written.

"Gardener, gardener," it ran. "I am the gardener. I want to come in. I can't find her here."

"O Lord, that gardener again!" said Hugh.

Looking up from the paper, I saw Margaret's eyes fixed on mine, and even before she spoke I knew what her thought was.

"Did you come home by the empty cottage?" she asked.

"Yes: why?"

"Still empty?" she said in a low voice. "Or – or anything else?"

I did not want to tell her just what I had seen – or what, at any rate, I thought I had seen. If there was going to be anything odd, anything worth observation, it was far better that our respective impressions should not fortify each other.

"I tapped again, and there was no answer," I said.

Presently there was a move to bed: Margaret initiated it, and after she had gone upstairs Hugh and I went to the front door to interrogate the weather. Once more the moon shone in a clear sky, and we strolled out along the flagged path that fronted the house. Suddenly Hugh turned quickly and pointed to the angle of the house.

"Who on earth is that?" he sad. "Look! There! He has gone round the corner."

I had but the glimpse of a tallish man of heavy build.

"Didn't you see him?" asked Hugh. "I'll just go round the house, and find him; I don't want anyone prowling round us at night. Wait here, will you, and if he comes round the other corner ask him what his business is."

Hugh had left me, in our stroll, close by the front door which was open, and there I waited until he should have made his circuit. He had hardly disappeared when I heard, quite distinctly, a rather quick but heavy footfall coming along the paved walk towards me from the opposite direction. But there was absolutely no one to be seen who made this sound of rapid walking.

Closer and closer to me came the steps of the invisible one, and then with a shudder of horror I felt somebody unseen push by me as I stood on the threshold. That shudder was not merely of the spirit, for the touch of him was that of ice on my hand. I tried to seize this impalpable intruder, but he slipped from me, and next moment I heard his steps on the parquet of the floor inside. Some door within opened and shut, and I heard no more of him. Next moment Hugh came running round the corner of the house from which the sound of steps had approached.

"But where is he?" he asked. "He was not twenty yards in front of me – a big, tall fellow."

"I saw nobody," I said. "I heard his step along the walk, but there was nothing to be seen."

"And then?" asked Hugh.

"Whatever it was seemed to brush by me, and go into the house," said I.

There had certainly been no sound of steps on the bare oak stairs, and we searched room after room through the ground floor of the house. The dining-room door and that of the smoking-room were locked, that into the drawing-room was open, and the only other door which could have furnished the impression of an opening and a shutting was that into the kitchen and servants' quarters. Here again our quest was fruitless; through pantry and scullery and boot-room and servants' hall we searched, but all was empty and quiet. Finally we came to the kitchen, which too was empty. But by the fire there was set a rocking-chair, and this was oscillating to and fro as if someone, lately sitting there, had just quitted it. There it stood gently rocking, and this seemed to convey the sense of a presence, invisible now, more than even the sight of him who surely had been sitting there could have done. I remember wanting to steady it and stop it, and yet my hand refused to go forth to it.

What we had seen, and in especial what we had not seen, would have been sufficient to furnish most people with a broken night, and assuredly I was not among the strong-minded exceptions. Long I lay wide-eyed and open-eared, and when at last I dozed I was plucked from the border-land of sleep by the sound, muffled but unmistakable, of someone moving about the house. It occurred to me that the steps might be those of Hugh conducting a lonely exploration, but even while I wondered a tap came at the door of communication between our rooms, and, in answer to my response, it appeared that he had come to see whether it was I thus uneasily wandering. Even as we spoke the step passed my door, and the stairs leading to the floor above creaked to its ascent. Next moment it sounded directly above our heads in some attics in the roof.

"Those are not the servants' bedrooms," said Hugh. "No one sleeps there. Let us look once more: it must be somebody."

With lit candles we made our stealthy way upstairs, and just when we were at the top of the flight, Hugh, a step ahead of me, uttered a sharp exclamation.

"But something is passing by me!" he said, and he clutched at the empty air. Even as he spoke, I experienced the same sensation, and the moment afterwards the stairs below us creaked again, as the unseen passed down.

All night long that sound of steps moved about the passages, as if someone was searching the house, and as I lay and listened that message which had come through the pencil of the planchette to Margaret's fingers occurred to me. "I want to come in. I cannot find her here."...

Indeed someone had come in, and was sedulous in his search. He was the gardener, it would seem. But what gardener was this invisible seeker, and for whom did he seek?

Even as when some bodily pain ceases it is difficult to recall with any vividness what the pain was like, so next morning, as I dressed, I found myself vainly trying to recapture the horror of the spirit which had accompanied these nocturnal adventures. I remembered that something within me had sickened as I watched the movements of the rocking-chair the night before and as I heard the steps along the paved way outside, and by that invisible pressure against me knew that someone had entered the house. But now in the sane and tranquil morning, and all day under the serene winter sun, I could not realise what it had been. The presence, like the bodily pain, had to be there for the realisation of it, and all day it was absent. Hugh felt the same; he was even disposed to be humorous on the subject.

"Well, he's had a good look," he said, "whoever he is, and whomever he was looking for. By the way, not a word to Margaret, please. She heard nothing of these perambulations, nor of the entry of – of whatever it was. Not gardener, anyhow: who ever heard of a gardener spending his time walking about the house? If there were steps all over the potato-patch, I might have been with you."

Margaret had arranged to drive over to have tea with some friends of hers that afternoon, and in consequence Hugh and I refreshed ourselves at the club-house after our game, and it was already dusk when for the third day in succession I passed homewards by the whitewashed cottage. But tonight I had no sense of it being subtly occupied; it stood mournfully desolate, as is the way of untenanted houses, and no light nor semblance of such gleamed from its windows.

Hugh, to whom I had told the odd impressions I had received there, gave them a reception as flippant as that which he had accorded to the memories of the night, and he was still being humorous about them when we came to the door of the house.

"A psychic disturbance, old boy," he said. "Like a cold in the head. Hullo, the door's locked."

He rang and rapped, and from inside came the noise of a turned key and withdrawn bolts.

"What's the door locked for?" he asked his servant who opened it.

The man shifted from one foot to the other.

"The bell rang half an hour ago, sir," he said, "and when I came to answer it there was a man standing outside, and—"

"Well?" asked Hugh.

"I didn't like the looks of him, sir," he said, "and I asked him his business. He didn't say anything, and then he must have gone pretty smartly away, for I never saw him go."

"Where did he seem to go?" asked Hugh, glancing at me.

"I can't rightly say, sir. He didn't seem to go at all. Something seemed to brush by me."

"That'll do," said Hugh rather sharply.

Margaret had not come in from her visit, but when soon after the crunch of the motor wheels was heard Hugh reiterated his wish that nothing should be said to her about the impression which now, apparently, a third person shared with us. She came in with a flush of excitement on her face.

"Never laugh at my planchette again," she said. "I've heard the most extraordinary story from Maud Ashfield – horrible, but so frightfully interesting."

"Out with it," said Hugh.

"Well, there was a gardener here," she said. "He used to live at that little cottage by the foot-bridge, and when the family were up in London he and his wife used to be caretakers and live here."

Hugh's glance and mine met: then he turned away.

I knew, as certainly as if I was in his mind, that his thoughts were identical with my own.

"He married a wife much younger than himself," continued Margaret, "and gradually he became frightfully jealous of her. And one day in a fit of passion he strangled her with his own hands. A little while after someone came to the cottage, and found him sobbing over her, trying to restore her. They went for the police, but before they came he had cut his own throat. Isn't it all horrible? But surely it's rather curious that the planchette said 'Gardener. I am the gardener. I want to come in. I can't find her here.' You see I knew nothing about it. I shall do planchette again tonight. Oh dear me, the post goes in half an hour, and I have a whole budget to send. But respect my planchette for the future, Hughie."

We talked the situation out when she had gone, but Hugh, unwillingly convinced and yet unwilling to admit that something more than coincidence lay behind that "planchette nonsense," still insisted that Margaret should be told nothing of what we had heard and seen in the house last night, and of the strange visitor who again this evening, so we must conclude, had made his entry.

"She'll be frightened," he said, "and she'll begin imagining things. As for the planchette, as likely as not it will do nothing but scribble and make loops. What's that? Yes: come in!"

There had come from somewhere in the room one sharp, peremptory rap. I did not think it came from the door, but Hugh, when no response replied to his words of admittance, jumped up and opened it. He took a few steps into the hall outside, and returned.

"Didn't you hear it?" he asked.

"Certainly. No one there?"

"Not a soul."

Hugh came back to the fireplace and rather irritably threw a cigarette which he had just lit into the fender.

"That was rather a nasty jar," he observed; "and if you ask me whether I feel comfortable, I can tell you I never felt less comfortable in my life. I'm frightened, if you want to know, and I believe you are too."

I hadn't the smallest intention of denying this, and he went on.

"We've got to keep a hand on ourselves," he said. "There's nothing so infectious as fear, and Margaret mustn't catch it from us. But there's something more than our fear, you know."

"Something has got into the house and we're up against it. I never believed in such things before."

"Let's face it for a minute. What is it anyhow?"

"If you want to know what I think it is," said I, "I believe it to be the spirit of the man who strangled his wife and then cut his throat. But I don't see how it can hurt us. We're afraid of our own fear really."

"But we're up against it," said Hugh. "And what will it do? Good Lord, if I only knew what it would do I shouldn't mind. It's the not knowing...Well, it's time to dress."

Margaret was in her highest spirits at dinner. Knowing nothing of the manifestations of that presence which had taken place in the last twenty-four hours, she thought it absorbingly interesting that her planchette should have "guessed" (so ran her phrase) about the gardener, and from that topic she flitted to an equally interesting form of patience for three which her friend had showed her, promising to initiate us into it after dinner. This she did, and, not knowing that we both above all things wanted to keep planchette at a distance, she was delighted with the success of her game. But suddenly she observed that the evening was burning rapidly away, and swept the cards together at the conclusion of a hand.

"Now just half an hour of planchette," she said.

"Oh, mayn't we play one more hand?" asked Hugh. "It's the best game I've seen for years."

"Planchette will be dismally slow after this."

"Darling, if the gardener will only communicate again, it won't be slow," said she.

"But it is such drivel," said Hugh.

"How rude you are! Read your book, then."

Margaret had already got out her machine and a sheet of paper, when Hugh rose.

"Please don't do it tonight, Margaret," he said.

"But why? You needn't attend."

"Well, I ask you not to, anyhow," said he.

Margaret looked at him closely.

"Hughie, you've got something on your mind," she said. "Out with it. I believe you're nervous. You think there is something queer about. What is it?"

I could see Hugh hesitating as to whether to tell her or not, and I gathered that he chose the chance of her planchette inanely scribbling.

"Go on, then," he said.

Margaret hesitated: she clearly did not want to vex Hugh, but his insistence must have seemed to her most unreasonable.

"Well, just ten minutes," she said, "and I promise not to think of gardeners."

She had hardly laid her hand on the board when her head fell forward, and the machine began moving. I was sitting close to her, and as it rolled steadily along the paper the writing became visible.

"I have come in," it ran, "but still I can't find her. Are you hiding her? I will search the room where you are."

What else was written but still concealed underneath the planchette I did not know, for at that moment a current of icy air swept round the room, and at the door, this time unmistakably, came a loud, peremptory knock. Hugh sprang to his feet.

"Margaret, wake up," he said, "something is coming!"

The door opened, and there moved in the figure of a man. He stood just within the door, his head bent forward, and he turned it from side to side, peering, it would seem, with eyes staring and infinitely sad, into every corner of the room.

"Margaret, Margaret," cried Hugh again.

But Margaret's eyes were open too; they were fixed on this dreadful visitor.

"Be quiet, Hughie," she said below her breath, rising as she spoke. The ghost was now looking directly at her. Once the lips above the thick, rust-coloured beard moved, but no sound came forth, the mouth only moved and slavered. He raised his head, and, horror upon horror, I saw that one side of his neck was laid open in a red, glistening gash...

For how long that pause continued, when we all three stood stiff and frozen in some deadly inhibition to move or speak, I have no idea: I suppose that at the utmost it was a dozen seconds.

Then the spectre turned, and went out as it had come. We heard his steps pass along the parqueted floor; there was the sound of bolts withdrawn from the front door, and with a crash that shook the house it slammed to.

"It's all over," said Margaret. "God have mercy on him!"

Now the reader may put precisely what construction he pleases on this visitation from the dead.

He need not, indeed, consider it to have been a visitation from the dead at all, but say that there had been impressed on the scene, where this murder and suicide happened, some sort of emotional record, which in certain circumstances could translate itself into images visible and invisible. Waves of ether, or what not, may conceivably retain the impress of such scenes; they may be held, so to speak, in solution, ready to be precipitated. Or he may hold that the spirit of the dead man indeed made itself manifest, revisiting in some sort of spiritual penance and remorse the place where his crime was committed. Naturally, no materialist will entertain such an explanation for an instant, but then there is no one so obstinately unreasonable as the materialist. Beyond doubt a dreadful deed was done there, and Margaret's last utterance is not inapplicable.

The Horror-Horn

E.F. Benson

FOR THE PAST ten days Alhubel had basked in the radiant midwinter weather proper to its eminence of over 6,000 feet. From rising to setting the sun (so surprising to those who have hitherto associated it with a pale, tepid plate indistinctly shining through the murky air of England) had blazed its way across the sparkling blue, and every night the serene and windless frost had made the stars sparkle like illuminated diamond dust. Sufficient snow had fallen before Christmas to content the skiers, and the big rink, sprinkled every evening, had given the skaters each morning a fresh surface on which to perform their slippery antics. Bridge and dancing served to while away the greater part of the night, and to me, now for the first time tasting the joys of a winter in the Engadine, it seemed that a new heaven and a new earth had been lighted, warmed, and refrigerated for the special benefit of those who like myself had been wise enough to save up their days of holiday for the winter.

But a break came in these ideal conditions: one afternoon the sun grew vapour-veiled and up the valley from the north-west a wind frozen with miles of travel over ice-bound hill-sides began scouting through the calm halls of the heavens. Soon it grew dusted with snow, first in small flakes driven almost horizontally before its congealing breath and then in larger tufts as of swansdown. And though all day for a fortnight before the fate of nations and life and death had seemed to me of far less importance than to get certain tracings of the skate-blades on the ice of proper shape and size, it now seemed that the one paramount consideration was to hurry back to the hotel for shelter: it was wiser to leave rocking-turns alone than to be frozen in their quest.

I had come out here with my cousin, Professor Ingram, the celebrated physiologist and Alpine climber. During the serenity of the last fortnight he had made a couple of notable winter ascents, but this morning his weather-wisdom had mistrusted the signs of the heavens, and instead of attempting the ascent of the Piz Passug he had waited to see whether his misgivings justified themselves. So there he sat now in the hall of the admirable hotel with his feet on the hot-water pipes and the latest delivery of the English post in his hands. This contained a pamphlet concerning the result of the Mount Everest expedition, of which he had just finished the perusal when I entered.

"A very interesting report," he said, passing it to me, "and they certainly deserve to succeed next year. But who can tell, what that final six thousand feet may entail? Six thousand feet more when you have already accomplished twenty-three thousand does not seem much, but at present no one knows whether the human frame can stand exertion at such a height. It may affect not the lungs and heart only, but possibly the brain. Delirious hallucinations may occur. In fact, if I did not know better, I should have said that one such hallucination had occurred to the climbers already."

"And what was that?" I asked.

"You will find that they thought they came across the tracks of some naked human foot at a great altitude. That looks at first sight like an hallucination. What more natural than that a brain excited and exhilarated by the extreme height should have interpreted certain marks in the snow as the footprints of a human being? Every bodily organ at these altitudes is exerting itself to the utmost to do its work, and the brain seizes on those marks in the snow and says 'Yes, I'm all right, I'm doing my job, and I perceive marks in the snow which I affirm are human footprints.' You know, even at this altitude, how restless and eager the brain is, how vividly, as you told me, you dream at night. Multiply that stimulus and that consequent eagerness and restlessness by three, and how natural that the brain should harbour illusions! What after all is the delirium which often accompanies high fever but the effort of the brain to do its work under the pressure of feverish conditions? It is so eager to continue perceiving that it perceives things which have no existence!"

"And yet you don't think that these naked human footprints were illusions," said I. "You told me you would have thought so, if you had not known better."

He shifted in his chair and looked out of the window a moment. The air was thick now with the density of the big snow-flakes that were driven along by the squealing north-west gale.

"Quite so," he said. "In all probability the human footprints were real human footprints. I expect that they were the footprints, anyhow, of a being more nearly a man than anything else.

"My reason for saying so is that I know such beings exist. I have even seen quite near at hand – and I assure you I did not wish to be nearer in spite of my intense curiosity – the creature, shall we say, which would make such footprints. And if the snow was not so dense, I could show you the place where I saw him."

He pointed straight out of the window, where across the valley lies the huge tower of the Ungeheuerhorn with the carved pinnacle of rock at the top like some gigantic rhinoceros-horn.

On one side only, as I knew, was the mountain practicable, and that for none but the finest climbers; on the other three a succession of ledges and precipices rendered it unscalable. Two thousand feet of sheer rock form the tower; below are five hundred feet of fallen boulders, up to the edge of which grow dense woods of larch and pine.

"Upon the Ungeheuerhorn?" I asked.

"Yes. Up till twenty years ago it had never been ascended, and I, like several others, spent a lot of time in trying to find a route up it. My guide and I sometimes spent three nights together at the hut beside the Blumen glacier, prowling round it, and it was by luck really that we found the route, for the mountain looks even more impracticable from the far side than it does from this.

"But one day we found a long, transverse fissure in the side which led to a negotiable ledge; then there came a slanting ice couloir which you could not see till you got to the foot of it. However, I need not go into that."

The big room where we sat was filling up with cheerful groups driven indoors by this sudden gale and snowfall, and the cackle of merry tongues grew loud. The band, too, that invariable appanage of tea-time at Swiss resorts, had begun to tune up for the usual potpourri from the works of Puccini. Next moment the sugary, sentimental melodies began.

"Strange contrast!" said Ingram. "Here are we sitting warm and cosy, our ears pleasantly tickled with these little baby tunes and outside is the great storm growing more violent every moment, and swirling round the austere cliffs of the Ungeheuerhorn: the Horror-Horn, as indeed it was to me."

"I want to hear all about it," I said. "Every detail: make a short story long, if it's short. I want to know why it's your Horror-Horn?"

"Well, Chanton and I (he was my guide) used to spend days prowling about the cliffs, making a little progress on one side and then being stopped, and gaining perhaps five hundred feet on another side and then being confronted by some insuperable obstacle, till the day when by luck we found the route. Chanton never liked the job, for some reason that I could not fathom.

"It was not because of the difficulty or danger of the climbing, for he was the most fearless man I have ever met when dealing with rocks and ice, but he was always insistent that we should get off the mountain and back to the Blumen hut before sunset. He was scarcely easy even when we had got back to shelter and locked and barred the door, and I well remember one night when, as we ate our supper, we heard some animal, a wolf probably, howling somewhere out in the night.

"A positive panic seized him, and I don't think he closed his eyes till morning. It struck me then that there might be some grisly legend about the mountain, connected possibly with its name, and next day I asked him why the peak was called the Horror-Horn. He put the question off at first, and said that, like the Schreckhorn, its name was due to its precipices and falling stones; but when I pressed him further he acknowledged that there was a legend about it, which his father had told him. There were creatures, so it was supposed, that lived in its caves, things human in shape, and covered, except for the face and hands, with long black hair. They were dwarfs in size, four feet high or thereabouts, but of prodigious strength and agility, remnants of some wild primeval race. It seemed that they were still in an upward stage of evolution, or so I guessed, for the story ran that sometimes girls had been carried off by them, not as prey, and not for any such fate as for those captured by cannibals, but to be bred from. Young men also had been raped by them, to be mated with the females of their tribe. All this looked as if the creatures, as I said, were tending towards humanity. But naturally I did not believe a word of it, as applied to the conditions of the present day. Centuries ago, conceivably, there may have been such beings, and, with the extraordinary tenacity of tradition, the news of this had been handed down and was still current round the hearths of the peasants. As for their numbers, Chanton told me that three had been once seen together by a man who owing to his swiftness on skis had escaped to tell the tale.

"This man, he averred, was no other than his grand-father, who had been benighted one winter evening as he passed through the dense woods below the Ungeheuerhorn, and Chanton supposed that they had been driven down to these lower altitudes in search of food during severe winter weather, for otherwise the recorded sights of them had always taken place among the rocks of the peak itself. They had pursued his grandfather, then a young man, at an extraordinarily swift canter, running sometimes upright as men run, sometimes on all-fours in the manner of beasts, and their howls were just such as that we had heard that night in the Blumen hut. Such at any rate was the story Chanton told me, and, like you, I regarded it as the very moonshine of superstition.

"But the very next day I had reason to reconsider my judgment about it.

"It was on that day that after a week of exploration we hit on the only route at present known to the top of our peak. We started as soon as there was light enough to climb by, for, as you may guess, on very difficult rocks it is impossible to climb by lantern or moonlight. We hit on the long fissure I have spoken of, we explored the ledge which from below seemed to end in nothingness, and with an hour's stepcutting ascended the couloir which led upwards from it.

"From there onwards it was a rock-climb, certainly of considerable difficulty, but with no heart-breaking discoveries ahead, and it was about nine in the morning that we stood on the top. We did not wait there long, for that side of the mountain is raked by falling stones loosened, when the sun grows hot, from the ice that holds them, and we made haste to pass the ledge where the falls are most frequent. After that there was the long fissure to descend, a matter of no great difficulty, and we were at the end of our work by midday, both of us, as you may imagine, in the state of the highest elation.

"A long and tiresome scramble among the huge boulders at the foot of the cliff then lay before us. Here the hill-side is very porous and great caves extend far into the mountain. We had unroped at the base of the fissure, and were picking our way as seemed good to either of us among these fallen rocks, many of them bigger than an ordinary house, when, on coming round the corner of one of these, I saw that which made it clear that the stories Chanton had told me were no figment of traditional superstition.

"Not twenty yards in front of me lay one of the beings of which he had spoken. There it sprawled naked and basking on its back with face turned up to the sun, which its narrow eyes regarded unwinking. In form it was completely human, but the growth of hair that covered limbs and trunk alike almost completely hid the sun-tanned skin beneath. But its face, save for the down on its cheeks and chin, was hairless, and I looked on a countenance the sensual and malevolent bestiality of which froze me with horror. Had the creature been an animal, one would have felt scarcely a shudder at the gross animalism of it; the horror lay in the fact that it was a man. There lay by it a couple of gnawed bones, and, its meal finished, it was lazily licking its protuberant lips, from which came a purring murmur of content. With one hand it scratched the thick hair on its belly, in the other it held one of these bones, which presently split in half beneath the pressure of its finger and thumb. But my horror was not based on the information of what happened to those men whom these creatures caught, it was due only to my proximity to a thing so human and so infernal. The peak, of which the ascent had a moment ago filled us with such elated satisfaction, became to me an Ungeheuerhorn indeed, for it was the home of beings more awful than the delirium of nightmare could ever have conceived.

"Chanton was a dozen paces behind me, and with a backward wave of my hand I caused him to halt. Then withdrawing myself with infinite precaution, so as not to attract the gaze of that basking creature, I slipped back round the rock, whispered to him what I had seen, and with blanched faces we made a long detour, peering round every corner, and crouching low, not knowing that at any step we might not come upon another of these beings, or that from the mouth of one of these caves in the mountain-side there might not appear another of those hairless and dreadful faces, with perhaps this time the breasts and insignia of womanhood. That would have been the worst of all.

"Luck favoured us, for we made our way among the boulders and shifting stones, the rattle of which might at any moment have betrayed us, without a repetition of my experience, and once among the trees we ran as if the Furies themselves were in pursuit. Well now did I understand, though I dare say I cannot convey, the qualms of Chanton's mind when he spoke to me of these creatures. Their very humanity was what made them so terrible, the fact that they were of the same race as ourselves, but of a type so abysmally degraded that the most brutal and inhuman of men would have seemed angelic in comparison."

The music of the small band was over before he had finished the narrative, and the chattering groups round the tea-table had dispersed. He paused a moment.

"There was a horror of the spirit," he said, "which I experienced then, from which, I verily believe, I have never entirely recovered. I saw then how terrible a living thing could be, and how terrible, in consequence, was life itself. In us all I suppose lurks some inherited germ of that ineffable bestiality, and who knows whether, sterile as it has apparently become in the course of centuries, it might not fructify again. When I saw that creature sun itself, I looked into the abyss out of which we have crawled. And these creatures are trying to crawl out of it now, if they exist any longer. Certainly for the last twenty years there has been no record of their being seen, until we come to this story of the footprint seen by the climbers on Everest. If that is authentic, if the party did not mistake the footprint of some bear, or what not, for a human tread, it seems as if still this bestranded remnant of mankind is in existence."

Now, Ingram, had told his story well; but sitting in this warm and civilised room, the horror which he had clearly felt had not communicated itself to me in any very vivid manner.

Intellectually, I agreed, I could appreciate his horror, but certainly my spirit felt no shudder of interior comprehension.

"But it is odd," I said, "that your keen interest in physiology did not disperse your qualms.

"You were looking, so I take it, at some form of man more remote probably than the earliest human remains. Did not something inside you say 'This is of absorbing significance'?"

He shook his head.

"No: I only wanted to get away," said he. "It was not, as I have told you, the terror of what according to Chanton's story, might – await us if we were captured; it was sheer horror at the creature itself. I quaked at it."

The snowstorm and the gale increased in violence that night, and I slept uneasily, plucked again and again from slumber by the fierce battling of the wind that shook my windows as if with an imperious demand for admittance. It came in billowy gusts, with strange noises intermingled with it as for a moment it abated, with flutings and moanings that rose to shrieks as the fury of it returned. These noises, no doubt, mingled themselves with my drowsed and sleepy consciousness, and once I tore myself out of nightmare, imagining that the creatures of the Horror-Horn had gained footing on my balcony and were rattling at the window-bolts. But before morning the gale had died away, and I awoke to see the snow falling dense and fast in a windless air. For three days it continued, without intermission, and with its cessation there came a frost such as I have never felt before. Fifty degrees were registered one night, and more the next, and what the cold must have been on the cliffs of the Ungeheuerborn I cannot imagine. Sufficient, so I thought, to have made an end altogether of its secret inhabitants: my cousin, on that day twenty years ago, had missed an opportunity for study which would probably never fall again either to him or another.

I received one morning a letter from a friend saying that he had arrived at the neighbouring winter resort of St. Luigi, and proposing that I should come over for a morning's skating and lunch afterwards. The place was not more than a couple of miles off, if one took the path over the low, pine-clad foot-hills above which lay the steep woods below the first rocky slopes of the Ungeheuerhorn; and accordingly, with a knapsack containing skates on my back, I went on skis over the wooded slopes and down by an easy descent again on to St. Luigi. The day was overcast, clouds entirely obscured the higher peaks though the sun was visible, pale and unluminous, through the mists. But as the morning went on, it gained the upper hand, and I slid down into St. Luigi beneath a sparkling firmament. We skated and lunched, and then, since it looked as if thick weather was coming up again, I set out early about three o'clock for my return journey.

Hardly had I got into the woods when the clouds gathered thick above, and streamers and skeins of them began to descend among the pines through which my path threaded its way. In ten minutes more their opacity had so increased that I could hardly see a couple of yards in front of me. Very soon I became aware that I must have got off the path, for snow-cowled shrubs lay directly in my way, and, casting back to find it again, I got altogether confused as to direction.

But, though progress was difficult, I knew I had only to keep on the ascent, and presently I should come to the brow of these low foot-hills, and descend into the open valley where Alhubel stood. So on I went, stumbling and sliding over obstacles, and unable, owing to the thickness of the snow, to take off my skis, for I should have sunk over the knees at each step. Still the ascent continued, and looking at my watch I saw that I had already been near an hour on my way from St. Luigi, a period more than sufficient to complete my whole journey. But still I stuck to my idea that though I had certainly strayed far from my proper route a few minutes more must surely see me over the top of the upward way, and I should find the ground declining into the next valley. About now, too, I noticed that the mists were growing suffused with rose-colour, and, though the inference was that it must be close on sunset, there was consolation in the fact that they were there and might lift at any moment and disclose to me my whereabouts. But the fact that night would soon be on me made it needful to bar my mind against that despair of loneliness which so eats out the heart of a man who is lost in woods or on mountain-side, that, though still there is plenty of vigour in his limbs, his nervous force is sapped, and he can do no more than lie down and abandon himself to whatever fate may await him...And then I heard that which made the thought of loneliness seem bliss indeed, for there was a worse fate than loneliness. What I heard resembled the howl of a wolf, and it came from not far in front of me where the ridge – was it a ridge? – still rose higher in vestment of pines.

From behind me came a sudden puff of wind, which shook the frozen snow from the drooping pine-branches, and swept away the mists as a broom sweeps the dust from the floor.

Radiant above me were the unclouded skies, already charged with the red of the sunset, and in front I saw that I had come to the very edge of the wood through which I had wandered so long.

But it was no valley into which I had penetrated, for there right ahead of me rose the steep slope of boulders and rocks soaring upwards to the foot of the Ungeheuerhorn. What, then, was that cry of a wolf which had made my heart stand still? I saw.

Not twenty yards from me was a fallen tree, and leaning against the trunk of it was one of the denizens of the Horror-Horn, and it was a woman. She was enveloped in a thick growth of hair grey and tufted, and from her head it streamed down over her shoulders and her bosom, from which hung withered and pendulous breasts. And looking on her face I comprehended not with my mind alone, but with a shudder of my spirit, what Ingram had felt. Never had nightmare fashioned so terrible a countenance; the beauty of sun and stars and of the beasts of the field and the kindly race of men could not atone for so hellish an incarnation of the spirit of life. A fathomless bestiality modelled the slavering mouth and the narrow eyes; I looked into the abyss itself and knew that out of that abyss on the edge of which I leaned the generations of men had climbed. What if that ledge crumbled in front of me and pitched me headlong into its nethermost depths?...

In one hand she held by the horns a chamois that kicked and struggled. A blow from its hindleg caught her withered thigh, and with a grunt of anger she seized the leg in her other hand, and, as a man may pull from its sheath a stem of meadow-grass, she plucked it off the body, leaving the torn skin hanging round the gaping wound. Then putting the red, bleeding member to her mouth she sucked at it as a child sucks a stick of sweetmeat. Through flesh and gristle her short, brown teeth penetrated, and she licked her lips with a sound of purring. Then dropping the leg by her side, she looked again at the body of the prey now quivering in its death-convulsion, and with finger and thumb gouged out one of its eyes. She snapped her teeth on it, and it cracked like a soft-shelled nut.

It must have been but a few seconds that I stood watching her, in some indescribable catalepsy of terror, while through my brain there pealed the panic-command of my mind to my stricken limbs "Begone, begone, while there is time." Then, recovering the power of my joints and muscles, I tried to slip behind a tree and hide myself from this apparition. But the woman – shall I say? – must have caught my stir of movement, for she raised her eyes from her living feast and saw me. She craned forward her neck, she dropped her prey, and half rising began to move towards me. As she did this, she opened her mouth, and gave forth a howl such as I had heard a moment before. It was answered by another, but faintly and distantly.

Sliding and slipping, with the toes of my skis tripping in the obstacles below the snow, I plunged forward down the hill between the pine-trunks. The low sun already sinking behind some rampart of mountain in the west reddened the snow and the pines with its ultimate rays. My knapsack with the skates in it swung to and fro on my back, one ski-stick had already been twitched out of my hand by a fallen branch of pine, but not a second's pause could I allow myself to recover it. I gave no glance behind, and I knew not at what pace my pursuer was on my track, or indeed whether any pursued at all, for my whole mind and energy, now working at full power again under the stress of my panic, was devoted to getting away down the hill and out of the wood as swiftly as my limbs could bear me. For a little while I heard nothing but the hissing snow of my headlong passage, and the rustle of the covered undergrowth beneath my feet, and then, from close at hand behind me, once more the wolf-howl sounded and I heard the plunging of footsteps other than my own.

The strap of my knapsack had shifted, and as my skates swung to and fro on my back it chafed and pressed on my throat, hindering free passage of air, of which, God knew, my labouring lungs were in dire need, and without pausing I slipped it free from my neck, and held it in the hand from which my ski-stick had been jerked. I seemed to go a little more easily for this adjustment, and now, not so far distant, I could see below me the path from which I had strayed.

If only I could reach that, the smoother going would surely enable me to outdistance my pursuer, who even on the rougher ground was but slowly overhauling me, and at the sight of that riband stretching unimpeded downhill, a ray of hope pierced the black panic of my soul. With that came the desire, keen and insistent, to see who or what it was that was on my tracks, and I spared a backward glance. It was she, the hag whom I had seen at her gruesome meal; her long grey hair flew out behind her, her mouth chattered and gibbered, her fingers made grabbing movements, as if already they closed on me.

But the path was now at hand, and the nearness of it I suppose made me incautious. A hump of snow-covered bush lay in my path, and, thinking I could jump over it, I tripped and fell, smothering myself in snow. I heard a maniac noise, half scream, half laugh, from close behind, and before I could recover myself the grabbing fingers were at my neck, as if a steel vice had closed there. But my right hand in which I held my knapsack of skates was free, and with a blind back-handed movement I whirled it behind me at the full length of its strap, and knew that my desperate blow had found its billet somewhere. Even before I could look round I felt the grip on my neck relax, and something subsided into the very bush which had entangled me. I recovered my feet and turned.

There she lay, twitching and quivering. The heel of one of my skates piercing the thin alpaca of the knapsack had hit her full on the temple, from which the blood was pouring, but a hundred yards away I could see another such figure coming downwards on my tracks, leaping and bounding. At that panic rose again within me, and I sped off down the white smooth path that led to the lights of the village already beckoning. Never once did I pause in my headlong going: there was no safety until I was back among the haunts of men. I flung myself against the door of the hotel, and screamed for admittance, though I had but to turn the handle and enter; and once more as when Ingram had told his tale, there was the sound of the band, and the chatter of voices, and there, too, was he himself, who looked up and then rose swiftly to his feet as I made my clattering entrance.

"I have seen them too," I cried. "Look at my knapsack. Is there not blood on it? It is the blood of one of them, a woman, a hag, who tore off the leg of a chamois as I looked, and pursued me through the accursed wood. I—".Whether it was I who spun round, or the room which seemed to spin round me, I knew not, but I heard myself falling, collapsed on the floor, and the next time that I was conscious at all I was in bed. There was Ingram there, who told me that I was quite safe, and another man, a stranger, who pricked my arm with the nozzle of a syringe, and reassured me...

A day or two later I gave a coherent account of my adventure, and three or four men, armed with guns, went over my traces. They found the bush in which I had stumbled, with a pool of blood which had soaked into the snow, and, still following my ski-tracks, they came on the body of a chamois, from which had been torn one of its hindlegs and one eye-socket was empty. That is all the corroboration of my story that I can give the reader, and for myself I imagine that the creature which pursued me was either not killed by my blow or that her fellows removed her body...Anyhow, it is open to the incredulous to prowl about the caves of the Ungeheuerhorn, and see if anything occurs that may convince them.

The Kit-Bag

Algernon Blackwood

WHEN THE WORDS 'Not Guilty' sounded through the crowded courtroom that dark December afternoon, Arthur Wilbraham, the great criminal KC, and leader for the triumphant defence, was represented by his junior; but Johnson, his private secretary, carried the verdict across to his chambers like lightning.

'It's what we expected, I think,' said the barrister, without emotion; 'and, personally, I am glad the case is over.' There was no particular sign of pleasure that his defence of John Turk, the murderer, on a plea of insanity, had been successful, for no doubt he felt, as everybody who had watched the case felt, that no man had ever better deserved the gallows.

'I'm glad too,' said Johnson. He had sat in the court for ten days watching the face of the man who had carried out with callous detail one of the most brutal and cold-blooded murders of recent years.

Be counsel glanced up at his secretary. They were more than employer and employed; for family and other reasons, they were friends. 'Ah, I remember; yes,' he said with a kind smile, 'and you want to get away for Christmas? You're going to skate and ski in the Alps, aren't you? If I was your age I'd come with you.'

Johnson laughed shortly. He was a young man of twenty-six, with a delicate face like a girl's. 'I can catch the morning boat now,' he said; 'but that's not the reason I'm glad the trial is over. I'm glad it's over because I've seen the last of that man's dreadful face. It positively haunted me. Bat white skin, with the black hair brushed low over the forehead, is a thing I shall never forget, and the description of the way the dismembered body was crammed and packed with lime into that—'

'Don't dwell on it, my dear fellow,' interrupted the other, looking at him curiously out of his keen eyes, 'don't think about it. Such pictures have a trick of coming back when one least wants them.' He paused a moment. 'Now go,' he added presently, 'and enjoy your holiday. I shall want all your energy for my Parliamentary work when you get back. And don't break your neck skiing.'

Johnson shook hands and took his leave. At the door he turned suddenly.

'I knew there was something I wanted to ask you,' he said. 'Would you mind lendang me one of your kit-bags? It's too late to get one tonight, and I leave in the morning before the shops are open.'

'Of course; I'll send Henry over with it to your rooms. You shall have it the moment I get home.'

'I promise to take great care of it,' said Johnson gratefully, delighted to think that within thirty hours he would be nearing the brilliant sunshine of the high Alps in winter. Be thought of that criminal court was like an evil dream in his mind.

He dined at his club and went on to Bloomsbury, where he occupied the top floor in one of those old, gaunt houses in which the rooms are large and lofty. The floor below his own was vacant and unfurnished, and below that were other lodgers whom he did not know. It was cheerless, and he looked forward heartily to a change. The night was even more cheerless: it was miserable, and few people were about. A cold, sleety rain was driving down the streets before the keenest east wind he had ever felt. It howled dismally among the big, gloomy houses of the great squares, and when he reached his rooms he heard it whistling and shouting over the world of black roofs beyond his windows.

In the hall he met his landlady, shading a candle from the draughts with her thin hand. 'This come by a man from Mr Wilbr'im's, sir.'

She pointed to what was evidently the kit-bag, and Johnson thanked her and took it upstairs with him. 'I shall be going abroad in the morning for ten days, Mrs Monks,' he said. 'I'll leave an address for letters.'

'And I hope you'll 'ave a merry Christmas, sir,' she said, in a raucous, wheezy voice that suggested spirits, 'and better weather than this.'

'I hope so too,' replied her lodger, shuddering a little as the wind went roaring down the street outside.

When he got upstairs he heard the sleet volleying against the window panes. He put his kettle on to make a cup of hot coffee, and then set about putting a few things in order for his absence. 'And now I must pack – such as my packing is,' he laughed to himself, and set to work at once.

He liked the packing, for it brought the snow mountains so vividly before him, and made him forget the unpleasant scenes of the past ten days. Besides, it was not elaborate in nature. His fraend had lent him the very thing – a stout canvas kit-bag, sack-shaped, with holes round the neck for the brass bar and padlock. It was a bit shapeless, true, and not much to look at, but its capacity was unlimited, and there was no need to pack carefully. He shoved in his waterproof coat, his fur cap and gloves, his skates and climbing boots, his sweaters, snow-boots, and ear-caps; and then on the top of these he piled his woollen shirts and underwear, his thick socks, puttees, and knickerbockers. The dress suit came next, in case the hotel people dressed for dinner, and then, thinking of the best way to pack his white shirts, he paused a moment to reflect. 'Bat's the worst of these kit-bags,' he mused vaguely, standing in the centre of the sitting-room, where he had come to fetch some string.

It was after ten o'clock. A furious gust of wind rattled the windows as though to hurry him up, and he thought with pity of the poor Londoners whose Christmas would be spent in such a climate, whilst he was skimming over snowy slopes in bright sunshine, and dancing in the evening with rosy-cheeked girls – Ah! that reminded him; he must put in his dancing-pumps and evening socks. He crossed over from his sitting-room to the cupboard on the landing where he kept his linen.

And as he did so he heard someone coming softly up the stairs.

He stood still a moment on the landing to listen. It was Mrs Monks's step, he thought; she must he coming up with the last post. But then the steps ceased suddenly, and he heard no more. They were at least two flights down, and he came to the conclusion they were too heavy to be those of his bibulous landlady. No doubt they belonged to a late lodger who had mistaken his floor. He went into his bedroom and packed his pumps and dress-shirts as best he could.

Be kit-bag by this time was two-thirds full, and stood upright on its own base like a sack of flour. For the first time he noticed that it was old and dirty, the canvas faded and worn, and that it had obviously been subjected to rather rough treatment. It was not a very nice bag to have sent him – certainly not a new one, or one that his chief valued. He gave the matter a passing thought, and went on with his packing. Once or twice, however, he caught himself wondering who it could have been wandering down below, for Mrs Monks had not come up with letters, and the floor was empty and unfurnished. From time to time, moreover, he was almost certain he heard a soft tread of someone padding about over the bare boards – cautiously, stealthily, as silently as possible – and, further, that the sounds had been lately coming distinctly nearer.

For the first time in his life he began to feel a little creepy. Then, as though to emphasize this feeling, an odd thing happened: as he left the bedroom, having just packed his recalcitrant white shirts, he noticed that the top of the kit-bag lopped over towards him with an extraordinary resemblance to a human face. Be camas fell into a fold like a nose and forehead, and the brass rings for the padlock just filled the position of the eyes. A shadow – or was it a travel stain? for he could not tell exactly – looked like hair. It gave him rather a turn, for it was so absurdly, so outrageously, like the face of John Turk the murderer.

He laughed, and went into the front room, where the light was stronger.

'That horrid case has got on my mind,' he thought; 'I shall be glad of a change of scene and air.' In the sitting-room, however, he was not pleased to hear again that stealthy tread upon the stairs, and to realize that it was much closer than before, as well as unmistakably real. And this time he got up and went out to see who it could be creeping about on the upper staircase at so late an hour.

But the sound ceased; there was no one visible on the stairs. He went to the floor below, not without trepidation, and turned on the electric light to make sure that no one was hiding in the empty rooms of the unoccupied suite. There was not a stick of furniture large enough to hide a dog. Then he called over the banisters to Mrs Monks, but there was no answer, and his voice echoed down into the dark vault of the house, and was lost in the roar of the gale that howled outside. Everyone was in bed and asleep – everyone except himself and the owner of this soft and stealthy tread.

'My absurd imagination, I suppose,' he thought. 'It must have been the wind after all, although – it seemed so *very* real and close, I thought.' He went back to his packing. It was by this time getting on towards midnight. He drank his coffee up and lit another pipe – the last before turning in.

It is difficult to say exactly at what point fear begins, when the causes of that fear are not plainly before the eyes. Impressions gather on the surface of the mind, film by film, as ice gathers upon the surface of still water, but often so lightly that they claim no definite recognation from the consciousness. Then a point is reached where the accumulated impressions become a definite emotion, and the mind realizes that something has happened. With something of a start, Johnson suddenly recognized that he felt nervous – oddly nervous; also, that for some time past the causes of this feeling had been gathering slowly in has mind, but that he had only just reached the point where he was forced to acknowledge them.

It was a singular and curious malaise that had come over him, and he hardly knew what to make of it. He felt as though he were doing something that was strongly objected to by another person, another person, moreover, who had some right to object. It was a most disturbing and disagreeable feeling, not unlike the persistent promptings of conscience: almost, in fact, as if he were doing something he knew to be wrong. Yet, though he searched vigorously and honestly in his mind, he could nowhere lay his finger upon the secret of this growing uneasiness, and it perplexed him. More, it distressed and frightened him.

'Pure nerves, I suppose,' he said aloud with a forced laugh. 'Mountain air will cure all that! Ah,' he added, still speaking to himself, 'and that reminds me – my snow-glasses.'

He was standing by the door of the bedroom during this brief soliloquy, and as he passed quickly towards the sitting-room to fetch them from the cupboard he saw out of the corner of his eye the indistinct outline of a figure standing on the stairs, a few feet from the top. It was someone in a stooping position, with one hand on the banisters, and the face peering up towards the landing. And at the same moment he heard a shuffling footstep. The person who had been creeping about below all this time had at last come up to his own floor. Who in the world could it be? And what in the name of Heaven did he want?

Johnson caught his breath sharply and stood stock still. Then, after a few seconds' hesitation, he found his courage, and turned to investigate. Be stairs, he saw to his utter amazement, were empty; there was no one. He felt a series of cold shivers run over him, and something about the muscles of his legs gave a little and grew weak. For the space of several minutes he peered steadily into the shadows that congregated about the top of the staircase where he had seen the figure, and then he walked fast – almost ran, in fact – into the light of the front room; but hardly had he passed inside the doorway when he heard someone come up the stairs behind him with a quick bound and go swiftly into his bedroom. It was a heavy, but at the same time a stealthy footstep – the tread of somebody who did not wish to be seen. And it was at this precise moment that the nervousness he had hitherto experienced leaped the boundary line, and entered the state of fear, almost of acute, unreasoning fear. Before it turned into terror there was a further boundary to cross, and beyond that again lay the region of pure horror. Johnson's position was an unenviable one.

By Jove! That was someone on the stairs, then,' he muttered, his flesh crawling all over; 'and whoever it was has now gone into my bedroom.' His delicate, pale face turned absolutely white, and for some minutes he hardly knew what to think or do. Then he realized intuitively that delay only set a premium upon fear; and he crossed the landing boldly and went straight into the other room, where, a few seconds before, the steps had disappeared.

'Who's there? Is that you, Mrs Monks?' he called aloud, as he went, and heard the first half of his words echo down the empty stairs, while the second half fell dead against the curtains in a room that apparently held no other human figure than his own.

'Who's there?' he called again, in a voice unnecessarily loud and that only just held firm. 'What do you want here?'

The curtains swayed very slightly, and, as he saw it, his heart felt as if it almost missed a beat; yet he dashed forward and drew them aside with a rush. A window, streaming with rain, was all that met his gaze. He continued his search, but in vain; the cupboards held nothing but rows of clothes, hanging motionless; and under the bed there was no sign of anyone hiding. He stepped backwards into the middle of the room, and, as he did so, something all but tripped him up. Turning with a sudden spring of alarm he saw – the kit-bag.

'Odd!' he thought. 'That's not where I left it!' A few moments before it had surely been on his right, between the bed and the bath; he did not remember having moved it. It was very curious. What in the world was the matter with everything? Were all his senses gone queer? A terrific gust of wind tore at the windows, dashing the sleet against the glass with the force of small gunshot, and then fled away howling dismally over the waste of Bloomsbury roofs. A sudden vision of the Channel next day rose in his mind and recalled him sharply to realities.

There's no one here at any rate; that's quite clear!' he exclaimed aloud. Yet at the time he uttered them he knew perfectly well that his words were not true and that he did not believe them himself. He felt exactly as though someone was hiding close about him, watching all his movements, trying to hinder his packing in some way. 'And two of my senses,' he added, keeping up the pretence, 'have played me the most absurd tricks: the steps I heard and the figure I saw were both entirely imaginary.'

He went hack to the front room, poked the fire into a blaze, and sat down before it to think. What impressed him more than anythang else was the fact that the kit-bag was no longer where he had left at. It had been dragged nearer to the door.

What happened afterwards that night happened, of course, to a man already excited by fear, and was perceived by a mand that had not the full and proper control, therefore, of the senses. Outwardly, Johnson remained calm and master of himself to the end, pretending to the very last that everything he witnessed had a natural explanation, or was merely delusions of his tired nerves. But inwardly, in his very heart, he knew all along that someone had been hiding downstairs in the empty suite when he came in, that this person had watched his opportunity and then stealthily made his way up to the bedroom, and that all he saw and heard afterwards, from the moving of the kit-bag to – well, to the other things this story has to tell – were caused directly by the presence of this invisible person.

And it was here, just when he most desired to keep his mind and thoughts controlled, that the vivid pictures received day after day upon the mental plates exposed in the courtroom of the Old Bailey, came strongly to light and developed themselves in the dark room of his inner vision. Unpleasant, haunting memories have a way of coming to life again just when the mind least desires them – in the silent watches of the night, on sleepless pillows, during the lonely hours spent by sick and dying beds. And so now, in the same way, Johnson saw nothing but the dreadful face of John Turk, the murderer, lowering at him from every corner of his mental field of vision; the white skin, the evil eyes, and the fringe of black hair low over the forehead. All the pictures of those ten days in court crowded back into his mind unbidden, and very vivid.

'This is all rubbish and nerves,' he exclaimed at length, springing with sudden energy from his chair. 'I shall finish my packing and go to bed. I'm overwrought, overtired. No doubt, at this rate I shall hear steps and things all night!'

But his face was deadly white all the same. He snatched up his field-glasses and walked across to the bedroom, humming a music-hall song as he went – a trifle too loud to be natural; and the instant he crossed the threshold and stood within the room something turned cold about his heart, and he felt that every hair on his head stood up.

The kit-bag lay close in front of him, several feet nearer to the door than he had left it, and just over its crumpled top he saw a head and face slowly sinking down out of sight as though someone were crouching behind it to hide, and at the same moment a sound like a long-drawn sigh was distinctly audible in the still air about him between the gusts of the storm outside.

Johnson had more courage and will-power than the girlish indecision of his face indicated; but at first such a wave of terror came over him that for some seconds he could do nothing but stand and stare. A violent trembling ran down his back and legs, and he was conscious of a foolish, almost a hysterical, impulse to scream aloud. That sigh seemed in his very ear, and the air still quivered with it. It was unmistakably a human sigh.

'Who's there?' he said at length, findinghis voice; but thought he meant to speak with loud decision, the tones came out instead in a faint whisper, for he had partly lost the control of his tongue and lips.

He stepped forward, so that he could see all round and over the kit-bag. Of course there was nothing there, nothing but the faded carpet and the bulgang canvas sides. He put out his hands and threw open the mouth of the sack where it had fallen over, being only three parts full, and then he saw for the first time that round the inside, some six inches from the top, there ran a broad smear of dull crimson. It was an old and faded blood stain. He uttered a scream, and drew hack his hands as if they had been burnt. At the same moment the kit-bag gave a faint, but unmistakable, lurch forward towards the door.

Johnson collapsed backwards, searching with his hands for the support of something solid, and the door, being further behind him than he realized, received his weight just in time to prevent his falling, and shut to with a resounding bang. At the same moment the swinging of his left arm accidentally touched the electric switch, and the light in the room went out.

It was an awkward and disagreeable predicament, and if Johnson had not been possessed of real pluck he might have done all manner of foolish things. As it was, however, he pulled himself together, and groped furiously for the little brass knob to turn the light on again. But the rapid closing of the door had set the coats hanging on it a-swinging, and his fingers became entangled in a confusion of sleeves and pockets, so that it was some moments before he found the switch. And in those few moments of bewilderment and terror two things happened that sent him beyond recall over the boundary into the region of genuine horror – he distinctly heard the kit-bag shuffling heavily across the floor in jerks, and close in front of his face sounded once again the sigh of a human being.

In his anguished efforts to find the brass button on the wall he nearly scraped the nails from his fingers, but even then, in those frenzied moments of alarm – so swift and alert are the impressaons of a mand keyed-up by a vivid emotion – he had time to realize that he dreaded the return of the light, and that it might be better for him to stay hidden in the merciful screen of darkness. It was but the impulse of a moment, however, and before he had time to act upon it he had yielded automatically to the original desire, and the room was flooded again with light.

But the second instinct had been right. It would have been better for him to have stayed in the shelter of the kind darkness. For there, close before him, bending over the half-packed kit-bag, clear as life in the merciless glare of the electric light, stood the figure of John Turk, the murderer. Not three feet from him the man stood, the fringe of black hair marked plainly against the pallor of the forehead, the whole horrible presentment of the scoundrel, as vivid as he had seen him day after day in the Old Bailey, when he stood there in the dock, cynical and callous, under the very shadow of the gallows.

In a flash Johnson realized what it all meant: the dirty and much-used bag; the smear of crimson within the top; the dreadful stretched condition of the bulging sides. He remembered how the victim's body had been stuffed into a canvas bag for burial, the ghastly, dismembered fragments forced with lime into this very bag; and the bag itself produced as evidence – it all came back to him as clear as day...

Very softly and stealthily his hand groped behind him for the handle of the door, but before he could actually turn it the very thing that he most of all dreaded came about, and John Turk lifted his devil's face and looked at him. At the same moment that heavy sigh passed through the air of the room, formulated somehow into words: It's my bag. And I want it.'

Johnson just remembered clawing the door open, and then falling in a heap upon the floor of the landing, as he tried frantically to make his way into the front room.

He remained unconscious for a long time, and it was still dark when he opened his eyes and realized that he was lying, stiff and bruised, on the cold boards. Then the memory of what he had seen rushed back into his mind, and he promptly fainted again. When he woke the second time the wintry dawn was just beginning to peep in at the windows, painting the stairs a cheerless, dismal grey, and he managed to crawl into the front room, and cover himself with an overcoat in the armchair, where at length he fell asleep.

A great clamour woke him. He recognized Mrs Monks's voice, loud and voluble.

'What! You ain't been to bed, sir! Are you ill, or has anything 'appened? And there's an urgent gentleman to see you, though it ain't seven o'clock yet, and—'

'Who is it?' he stammered. 'I'm all right, thanks. Fell asleep in my chair, I suppose.'

'Someone from Mr Wilb'rim's, and he says he ought to see you quick before you go abroad, and I told him—'

'Show him up, please, at once,' said Johnson, whose head was whirling, and his mind was still full of dreadful visions.

Mr Wilbraham's man came in with many apologies, and explained briefly and quickly that an absurd mistake had been made, and that the wrong kit-bag had been sent over the night before.

'Henry somehow got hold of the one that came over from the courtoom, and Mr Wilbraham only discovered it when he saw his own lying in his room, and asked why it had not gone to you,' the man said.

'Oh!' said Johnson stupidly.

'And he must have brought you the one from the murder case instead, sir, I'm afraid,' the man continued, without the ghost of an expression on his face. 'The one John Turk packed the dead both in. Mr Wilbraham's awful upset about it, sir, and told me to come over first thing this morning with the right one, as you were leaving by the boat.'

He pointed to a clean-looking kit-bag on the floor, which he had just brought. 'And I was to bring the other one back, sir,' he added casually.

For some minutes Johnson could not find his voice. At last he pointed in the direction of his bedroom. 'Perhaps you would kindly unpack it for me. Just empty the things out on the floor.'

The man disappeared into the other room, and was gone for five minutes. Johnson heard the shifting to and fro of the bag, and the rattle of the skates and boots being unpacked.

'Thank you, sir,' the man said, returning with the bag folded over his arm. 'And can I do anything more to help you, sir?'

'What is it?' asked Johnson, seeing that he still had something he wished to say.

The man shuffled and looked mysterious. 'Beg pardon, sir, but knowing your interest in the Turk case, I thought you'd maybe like to know what's happened—'

'Yes.'

'John Turk killed hisself last night with poison immediately on getting his release, and he left a note for Mr Wilbraham saying as he'd be much obliged if they'd have him put away, same as the woman he murdered, in the old kit-hag.'

'What time – did he do it?' asked Johnson.

'Ten o'clock last night, sir, the warder says.'

Christmas Re-union

Sir Andrew Caldecott

I

'I CANNOT EXPLAIN what exactly it is about him; but I don't like your Mr Clarence Love, and I'm sorry that you ever asked him to stay.'

Thus Richard Dreyton to his wife Elinor on the morning of Christmas Eve.

'But one must remember the children, Richard. You know what marvellous presents he gives them.'

'Much too marvellous. He spoils them. Yet you'll have noticed that none of them likes him. Children have a wonderful intuition in regard to the character of grown-ups.'

'What on earth are you hinting about his character? He's a very nice man.'

Dreyton shuffled off his slippers in front of the study fire and began putting on his boots.

'I wonder, darling, whether you noticed his face just now at breakfast, when he opened that letter with the Australian stamps on?'

'Yes; he did seem a bit upset: but not more so than you when you get my dressmaker's bill!'

Mrs Dreyton accompanied this sally with a playful pat on her husband's back as he leant forward to do up his laces.

'Well, Elinor, all that I can say is that there's something very fishy about his antipodean history. At five-and-twenty, he left England a penniless young man and, heigh presto! he returns a stinking plutocrat at twenty-eight. And how? What he's told you doesn't altogether tally with what he's told me; but, cutting out the differences, his main story is that he duly contacted old Nelson Joy, his maternal uncle, whom he went out to join, and that they went off together, prospecting for gold. They struck it handsomely; and then the poor old uncle gets a heart-stroke or paralysis, or something, in the bush, and bids Clarence leave him there to die and get out himself before the food gives out. Arrived back in Sydney, Clarence produces a will under which he is the sole beneficiary, gets the Court to presume old Joy's death, and bunks back here with the loot.'

Mrs Dreyton frowned. 'I can see nothing wrong or suspicious about the story,' she said, 'but only in your telling of it.'

'No! No! In *his* telling of it. He never gets the details quite the same twice running, and I'm certain that he gave a different topography to their prospecting expedition this year from what he did last. It's my belief that he did the uncle in, poor old chap!'

'Don't be so absurd, Richard; and please remember that he's our guest, and that we must be hospitable: especially at Christmas. Which reminds me: on your way to office, would you mind looking in at Harridge's and making sure that they haven't forgotten our order for their Santa Claus tomorrow? He's to be here at seven; then to go on to the Simpsons at seven-thirty, and to end up at the Joneses at eight. It's lucky our getting three households to share the expenses: Harridge's charge each of us only half their catalogued fee. If they could possibly send us the same Father Christmas as last year it would be splendid. The children adored him. Don't forget to say, too, that he will find all the crackers, hats, musical toys and presents inside the big chest in the hall. Just the same as last year. What should we do nowadays without the big stores? One goes to them for everything.'

'We certainly do,' Dreyton agreed; 'and I can't see the modern child putting up with the amateur Father Christmas we used to suffer from. I shall never forget the annual exhibition Uncle Bertie used to make of himself, or the slippering I got when I stuck a darning-needle into his behind under pretence that I wanted to see if he was real! Well, so long, old girl: no, I won't forget to call in at Harridge's.'

II

By the time the festive Christmas supper had reached the dessert stage, Mrs Dreyton fully shared her husband's regret that she had ever asked Clarence Love to be of the party. The sinister change that had come over him on receipt of the letter from Australia became accentuated on the later arrival of a telegram which, he said, would necessitate his leaving towards the end of the evening to catch the eight-fifteen northbound express from King's Pancras. His valet had already gone ahead with the luggage and, as it had turned so foggy, he had announced his intention of following later by Underground, in order to avoid the possibility of being caught in a traffic-jam.

It is strange how sometimes the human mind can harbour simultaneously two entirely contradictory emotions. Mrs Dreyton was consumed with annoyance that any guest of hers should be so inconsiderate as to terminate his stay in the middle of a Christmas party; but was, at the same time, impatient to be rid of such a skeleton at the feast. One of the things that she had found attractive in Clarence Love had been an unfailing fund of small talk, which, if not brilliant, was at any rate bright and breezy. He possessed, also, a pleasant and frequent smile and, till now, had always been assiduous in his attention to her conversation. Since yesterday, however, he had turned silent, inattentive, and dour in expression. His presentation to her of a lovely emerald brooch had been unaccompanied by any greeting beyond an unflattering and perfunctory 'Happy Christmas!' He had also proved unforgivably oblivious of the mistletoe, beneath which, with a careful carelessness, she stationed herself when she heard him coming down to breakfast. It was, indeed, quite mortifying; and, when her husband described the guest as a busted balloon, she had neither the mind nor the heart to gainsay him.

Happily for the mirth and merriment of the party Dreyton seemed to derive much exhilaration from the dumb discomfiture of his wife's friend, and Elinor had never seen or heard her husband in better form. He managed, too, to infect the children with his own ebullience; and even Miss Potterby (the governess) reciprocated his fun. Even before the entry of Father Christmas it had thus become a noisy, and almost rowdy, company.

Father Christmas's salutation, on arrival, was in rhymed verse and delivered in the manner appropriate to pantomime. His lines ran thus:

To Sons of Peace
Yule brings release
From worry at this tide;
But men of crime
This holy time
Their guilty heads need hide.
So never fear,
Ye children dear,

But innocent sing 'Nowell';
For the Holy Rood
Shall save the good,
And the bad be burned in hell.
This is my carol
And Nowell my parole.

There was clapping of hands at this, for there is nothing children enjoy so much as mummery; especially if it be slightly mysterious. The only person who appeared to dislike the recitation was Love, who was seen to stop both ears with his fingers at the end of the first verse and to look ill. As soon as he had made an end of the prologue, Santa Claus went ahead with his distribution of gifts, and made many a merry quip and pun. He was quick in the uptake, too; for the children put to him many a poser, to which a witty reply was always ready. The minutes indeed slipped by all too quickly for all of them, except Love, who kept glancing uncomfortably at his wrist-watch and was plainly in a hurry to go. Hearing him mutter that it was time for him to be off, Father Christmas walked to his side and bade him pull a farewell cracker. Having done so, resentfully it seemed, he was asked to pull out the motto and read it. His hands were now visibly shaking, and his voice seemed to have caught their infection. Very falteringly, he managed to stammer out the two lines of doggerel:

Re-united heart to heart
Love and joy shall never part.

'And now,' said Father Christmas, 'I must be making for the next chimney; and, on my way, sir, I will see you into the Underground.'

So saying he took Clarence Love by the left arm and led him with mock ceremony to the door, where he turned and delivered this epilogue:

Ladies and Gentlemen, goodnight!
Let not darkness you affright.
Aught of evil here today
Santa Claus now bears away.

At this point, with sudden dramatic effect, he clicked off the electric light switch by the door; and, by the time Dreyton had groped his way to it in the darkness and turned it on again, the parlour-maid (who was awaiting Love's departure in the hall) had let both him and Father Christmas out into the street.

'Excellent!' Mrs Dreyton exclaimed, 'quite excellent! One can always depend on Harridge's. It wasn't the same man as they sent last year; but quite as good, and more original, perhaps.'

'I'm glad he's taken Mr Love away,' said young Harold.

'Yes,' Dorothy chipped in; 'he's been beastly all day, and yesterday, too: and his presents aren't nearly as expensive as last year.'

'Shut up, you spoilt children!' the father interrupted. 'I must admit, though, that the fellow was a wet blanket this evening. What was that nonsense he read out about reunion?'

Miss Potterby had developed a pedagogic habit of clearing her throat audibly, as a signal demanding her pupils' attention to some impending announcement. She did it now, and parents as well as children looked expectantly towards her.

'The motto as read by Mr Love,' she declared, 'was so palpably inconsequent that I took the liberty of appropriating it when he laid the slip of paper back on the table. Here it is, and this is how it actually reads:

Be united heart to heart,
Love and joy shall never part.

That makes sense, if it doesn't make poetry. Mr Love committed the error of reading 'be united' as 'reunited' and of not observing the comma between the two lines.'

'Thank you, Miss Potterby; that, of course, explains it. How clever of you to have spotted the mistake and tracked it down!'

Thus encouraged, Miss Potterby proceeded to further corrective edification.

'You remarked just now, Mrs Dreyton, that the gentleman impersonating Father Christmas had displayed originality. His prologue and epilogue, however, were neither of them original, but corrupted versions of passages which you will find in Professor Borleigh's *Synopsis of Nativity, Miracle and Morality Plays,* published two years ago. I happen to be familiar with the subject, as the author is a first cousin of mine, once removed.'

'How interesting!' Dreyton here broke in; 'and now, Miss Potterby, if you will most kindly preside at the piano, we will dance Sir Roger de Coverley. Come on, children, into the drawing-room.'

III

On Boxing Day there was no post and no paper. Meeting Mrs Simpson in the Park that afternoon, Mrs Dreyton was surprised to hear that Father Christmas had kept neither of his two other engagements. 'It must have been that horrid fog,' she suggested; 'but what a shame! He was even better than last year:' by which intelligence Mrs Simpson seemed little comforted.

Next morning – the second after Christmas – there were two letters on the Dreytons' breakfast-table, and both were from Harridge's.

The first conveyed that firm's deep regret that their representative should have been prevented from carrying out his engagements in Pentland Square on Christmas night owing to dislocation of traffic caused by the prevailing fog.

'But he kept ours all right,' Mrs Dreyton commented. 'I feel so sorry for the Simpsons and the Joneses.'

The second letter cancelled the first, 'which had been written in unfortunate oversight of the cancellation of the order'.

'What on earth does that mean?' Mrs Dreyton ejaculated.

'Ask me another!' returned her husband. 'Got their correspondence mixed up, I suppose.',

In contrast to the paucity of letters, the morning newspapers seemed unusually voluminous and full of pictures. Mrs Dreyton's choice of what to read in them was not that of a highbrow. The headline that attracted her first attention ran 'XMAS ON UNDERGROUND', and, among other choice items, she learned how, at Pentland Street Station (their own nearest), a man dressed as Santa Claus had been seen to guide and support an invalid, or possibly tipsy, companion down the long escalator. The red coat, mask and beard were afterwards found discarded in a passage leading to the emergency staircase, so that even Santa's sobriety might be called into question. She was just about to retail this interesting intelligence to her husband when, laying down his own paper, he stared curiously at her and muttered 'Good God!'

'What on earth's the matter, dear?'

'A very horrible thing, Elinor. Clarence Love has been killed! Listen;' here he resumed his paper and began to read aloud: "The body of the man who fell from the Pentland Street platform on Christmas night in front of an incoming train has been identified as that of Mr Clarence Love, of I I Playfair Mansions. There was a large crowd of passengers on the platform at the time, and it is conjectured that he fell backwards off it while turning to expostulate with persons exerting pressure at his back. Nobody, however, in the crush, could have seen the exact circumstances of the said fatality."'

'Hush, dear! Here come the children. They mustn't know, of course. We can talk about it afterwards.'

Dreyton, however, could not wait to talk about it afterwards. The whole of the amateur detective within him had been aroused, and, rising early from the breakfast-table, he journeyed by tube to Harridge's, where he was soon interviewing a departmental sub-manager. No: there was no possibility of one of their representatives having visited Pentland Square on Christmas evening. Our Mr Droper had got hung up in the Shenton Street traffic-block until it was too late to keep his engagements there. He had come straight back to his rooms. In any case, he would not have called at Mr Dreyton's residence in view of the cancellation of the order the previous day. Not cancelled? But he took down the telephone message himself. Yes: here was the entry in the register. Then it must have been the work of some mischief-maker; it was certainly a gentleman's, and not a lady's voice. Nobody except he and Mr Droper knew of the engagement at their end, so the practical joker must have derived his knowledge of it from somebody in Mr Dreyton's household.

This was obviously sound reasoning and, on his return home, Dreyton questioned Mrs Timmins, the cook, in the matter. She was immediately helpful and forthcoming. One of them insurance gents had called on the morning before Christmas and had been told that none of us wanted no policies or such like. He had then turned conversational and asked what sort of goings-on there would be here for Christmas. Nothing, he was told, except old Father Christmas, as usual, out of Harridge's shop. Then he asked about visitors in the house, and was told as there were none except Mr Love, who, judging by the tip what he had given Martha when he stayed last in the house, was a wealthy and openhanded gentleman. Little did she think when she spoke those words as Mr Love would forget to give any tips or boxes at Christmas, when they were most natural and proper. But perhaps he would think better on it by the New Year and send a postal order. Dreyton thought it unlikely, but deemed it unnecessary at this juncture to inform Mrs Timmins of the tragedy reported in the newspaper.

At luncheon Mrs Dreyton found her husband unusually taciturn and preoccupied; but, by the time they had come to the cheese, he announced importantly that he had made up his mind to report immediately to the police certain information that had come into his possession. Miss Potterby and the children looked suitably impressed, but knew better than to court a snub by asking questions. Mrs Dreyton took the cue admirably by replying: 'Of course, Richard, you must do your duty!'

IV

The inspector listened intently and jotted down occasional notes. At the end of the narration, he complimented the informant by asking whether he had formed any theory regarding the facts he reported. Dreyton most certainly had. That was why he had been so silent and absent-minded at lunch. His solution, put much more briefly than he expounded it to the inspector, was as follows.

Clarence Love had abandoned his uncle and partner in the Australian bush. Having returned to civilisation, got the Courts to presume the uncle's death, and taken probate of the will under which he was sole inheritor, Love returned to England a wealthy and still youngish man. The uncle, however (this was Dreyton's theory), did not die after his nephew's desertion, but was found and tended by bushmen. Having regained his power of locomotion, he trekked back to Sydney, where he discovered himself legally dead and his property appropriated by Love and removed to England. Believing his nephew to have compassed his death, he resolved to take revenge into his own hands. Having despatched a cryptic letter to Love containing dark hints of impending doom, he sailed for the Old Country and ultimately tracked Love down to the Dreytons' abode. Then, having in the guise of a travelling insurance agent ascertained the family's programme for Christmas Day, he planned his impersonation of Santa Claus. That his true identity, revealed by voice and accent, did not escape his victim was evidenced by the latter's nervous misreading of the motto in the cracker. Whether Love's death in the Underground was due to actual murder or to suicide enforced by despair and remorse, Dreyton hazarded no guess: either was possible under his theory.

The inspector's reception of Dreyton's hypothesis was less enthusiastic than his wife's.

'If you'll excuse me, Mr Dreyton,' said the former, 'you've built a mighty lot on dam' little. Still, it's ingenious and no mistake. I'll follow your ideas up and, if you'll call in a week's time, I may have something to tell you and one or two things, perhaps, to ask.'

'Why darling, how wonderful!' Mrs Dreyton applauded. 'Now that you've pieced the bits together so cleverly the thing's quite obvious, isn't it? What a horrible thing to have left poor old Mr Joy to die all alone in the jungle! I never really liked Clarence, and am quite glad now that he's dead. But of course we mustn't tell the children!'

Inquiries of the Australian Police elicited the intelligence that the presumption of Mr Joy's death had been long since confirmed by the discovery of his remains in an old prospecting pit. There were ugly rumours and suspicions against his nephew but no evidence on which to support them. On being thus informed by the inspector Dreyton amended his theory to the extent that the impersonator of Father Christmas must have been not Mr Joy himself, as he was dead, but a bosom friend determined to avenge him. This substitution deprived the cracker episode, on which Dreyton had imagined his whole story, of all relevance; and the inspector was quite frank about his disinterest in the revised version.

Mrs Dreyton also rejected it. Her husband's original theory seemed to her more obviously right and conclusive even than before. The only amendment required, and that on a mere matter of detail, was to substitute Mr Joy's ghost for Mr Joy: though of course one mustn't tell the children.

'But,' her husband remonstrated, 'you know that I don't believe in ghosts.'

'No, but your aunt Cecilia *does;* and she is such a clever woman. By the way, she called in this morning and left you a book to look at.'

'A book?'

'Yes, the collected ghost stories of M.R. James.'

'But the stupid old dear knows that I have them all in the original editions.'

'So she said: but she wants you to read the author's epilogue to the collection which, she says, is most entertaining. It's entitled "Stories I have tried to write". She said that she'd side-lined a passage that might interest you. The book's on that table by you. No, not that: the one with the black cover.'

Dreyton picked it up, found the marked passage and read it aloud.

There may be possibilities too in the Christmas cracker if the right people pull it and if the motto which they find inside has the right message on it. They will probably leave the party early, pleading indisposition; but very likely a previous engagement of long standing would be the more truthful excuse.

'There is certainly,' Dreyton commented, 'some resemblance between James's idea and our recent experience. But he could have made a perfectly good yarn out of that theme without introducing ghosts.'

His wife's mood at that moment was for compromise rather than controversy.

'Well, darling,' she temporised, 'perhaps not exactly ghosts.'

Calling Card

Ramsey Campbell

DOROTHY HARRIS stepped off the pavement and into her hall. As she stooped groaning to pick up the envelopes the front door opened, opened, a yawn that wouldn't be suppressed. She wrestled it shut – she must ask Simon to see to it, though certainly not over Christmas – then she began to open the cards.

Here was Father Christmas, and here he was again, apparently after dieting. Here was a robin like a rosy apple with a beak, and here was an envelope whose handwriting staggered: Simon's and Margery's children, perhaps?

The card showed a church on a snowy hill. The hill was bare except for a smudge of ink. Though the card was unsigned, there was writing within. A Very Happy Christmas And A Prosperous New Year, the message should have said – but now it said A Very Harried Christmas And No New Year. She turned back to the picture, her hands shaking. It wasn't just a smudge of ink; someone had drawn a smeary cross on the hill: a grave.

Though the name on the envelope was a watery blur, the address was certainly hers. Suddenly the house – the kitchen and living-room, the two bedrooms with her memories stacked neatly against the walls – seemed far too large and dim. Without moving from the front door she phoned Margery.

"Is it Grandma?" Margery had to hush the children while she said "You come as soon as you like, mummy."

Lark Lane was deserted. An unsold Christmas tree loitered in a shop doorway, a gargoyle craned out from the police station. Once Margery had moved away, the nearness of the police had been reassuring – not that Dorothy was nervous, like some of the old folk these days – but the police station was only a community centre now.

The bus already sounded like a pub. She sat outside on the ferry, though the bench looked and felt like black ice. Lights fished in the Mersey, gulls drifted down like snowflakes from the muddy sky. A whitish object grabbed the rail, but of course it was only a gull. Nevertheless she was glad that Simon was waiting with the car at Woodside.

As soon as the children had been packed off to bed so that Father Christmas could get to work, she produced the card. It felt wet, almost slimy, though it hadn't before. Simon pointed out what she'd overlooked: the age of the stamp. "We weren't even living there then," Margery said. "You wouldn't think they would bother delivering it after sixty years."

"A touch of the Christmas spirit."

"I wish they hadn't bothered," Margery said. But her mother didn't mind now; the addressee must have died years ago. She turned the conversation to old times, to Margery's father. Later she gazed from her bedroom window, at the houses of Bebington sleeping in pairs. A man was creeping about the house, but it was only Simon, laden with presents.

In the morning the house was full of cries of delight, gleaming new toys, balls of wrapping paper big as cabbages. In the afternoon the adults, bulging with turkey and pudding, lolled in chairs. When Simon drove her home that night, Dorothy noticed that the unsold Christmas tree was still there, a scrawny glistening shape at the back of the shop doorway. As soon as Simon left she found herself thinking about the unpleasant card. She tore it up, then went determinedly to bed.

Boxing Day was her busiest time, what with Christmas dinner Mark II, and making sure the house was impeccable, and hiding small presents for the children to find. She wished she could see them more often, but they and their parents had their own lives to lead.

An insect clung to a tinsel globe on the tree. When she reached out to squash the insect it wasn't there, neither on the globe nor on the floor. Could it have been the reflection of someone thin outside the window? Nobody was there now.

She liked the house best when it was full of laughter, and it would be again soon: "We'll get a sitter," Margery promised, "and first-foot you on New Year's Eve." That reminded Dorothy to offer the children a holiday treat. Everything seemed fine, even when they went to the door to leave. "Grandma, someone's left you a present," little Denise cried.

Then she cried out, and dropped the package. Perhaps the wind had snatched it from her hands. As the package, which looked wet and mouldy, struck the kerb it broke open. Did its contents scuttle out and sidle away into the dark? Surely that was the play of the wind, which tumbled carton and wrapping away down the street.

Someone must have used her doorway for a waste-bin, that was all. Dorothy lay in bed, listening to the wind which groped around the windowless side of the house, that faced onto the alley. She kept thinking she was on the ferry, backing away from the rail, forgetting that the rail was also behind her. Her nervousness annoyed her – she was acting like an old fogey – which was why, next afternoon, she walked to Otterspool promenade.

Gulls and planes sailed over the Mersey, which was deserted except for buoys. On the far bank, tiny towns and stalks of factory chimneys stood at the foot of an enormous frieze of clouds. Sunlight slipped through to Birkenhead and Wallasey, touching up the colours of microscopic streets; specks of windows glinted. She enjoyed none of this, for the slopping of water beneath the promenade seemed to be pacing her. Worse, she couldn't make herself go to the rail to prove that there was nothing.

Really, it was heartbreaking. One vicious card and she felt nervous in her own house. A blurred voice seemed to creep behind the carols on the radio, lowing out of tune. Next day she took her washing to Lark Lane, in search of distraction as much as anything.

The Westinghouse Laundromat was deserted. 000, the washing machines said emptily. There was only herself, and her dervishes of clothes, and a black plastic bag almost as tall as she was. If someone had abandoned it, whatever its lumpy contents were, she could see why, for it was leaking; she smelled stagnant water. It must be a draught that made it twitch feebly. Nevertheless, if she had been able to turn off her machine she might have fled.

She mustn't grow neurotic. She still had friends to visit. The following day she went to a friend whose flat overlooked Wavertree Park. It was all very convivial – a rainstorm outside made the mince pies more warming, the chat flowed as easily as the whisky – but she kept glancing at the thin figure who stood in the park, unmoved by the downpour. The trails of rain on the window must be lending him their colour, for his skin looked like a snail's.

Eventually the 68 bus, meandering like a drunkard's monologue, took her home to Aigburth. No, the man in the park hadn't really looked as though his clothes and his body had merged into a single greyish mass. Tomorrow she was taking the children for their treat, and that would clear her mind.

She took them to the aquarium. Piranhas sank stonily, their sides glittering like Christmas cards. Toads were bubbling lumps of tar. Finny humbugs swam, and darting fish wired with light. Had one of the tanks cracked? There seemed to be a stagnant smell.

In the museum everything was under glass: shrunken heads like sewn leathery handbags, a watchmaker's workshop, buses passing as though the windows were silent films. Here was a slum street, walled in by photographs of despair, real flagstones underfoot, overhung by streetlamps on brackets. She halted between a grid and a drinking fountain; she was trapped in the dimness between blind corners, and couldn't see either way. Why couldn't she get rid of the stagnant smell? Grey forlorn faces, pressed like specimens, peered out of the walls. "Come on, quickly," she said, pretending that only the children were nervous.

She was glad of the packed crowds in Church Street, even though the children kept letting go of her hands. But the stagnant smell was trailing her, and once, when she grabbed for little Denise's hand, she clutched someone else's, which felt soft and wet. It must have been nervousness which made her fingers seem to sink into the hand.

That night she returned to the aquarium and found she was locked in. Except for the glow of the tanks, the narrow room was oppressively dark. In the nearest tank a large dead fish floated towards her, out of weeds. Now she was in the tank, her nails scrabbling at the glass, and she saw that it wasn't a fish but a snail-coloured hand, which closed spongily on hers. When she woke, her scream made the house sound very empty.

At least it was New Year's Eve. After tonight she could stop worrying. Why had she thought that? It only made her more nervous. Even when Margery phoned to confirm they would first-foot her, that reminded her how many hours she would be on her own. As the night seeped into the house, the emptiness grew.

A knock at the front door made her start, but it was only the Harveys, inviting her next door for sherry and sandwiches. While she dodged a sudden rainstorm Mr Harvey dragged at her front door, one hand through the letter-box, until the latch clicked.

After several sherries Dorothy remembered something she'd once heard. "The lady who lived next door before me – didn't she have trouble with her son?"

"He wasn't right in the head. He got so he'd go for anyone, even if he'd never met them before. She got so scared of him she locked him out one New Year's Eve. They say he threw himself in the river, though they never found the body."

Dorothy wished she hadn't asked. She thought of the body, rotting in the depths. She must go home, in case Simon and Margery arrived. The Harveys were next door if she needed them.

The sherries had made her sleepy. Only the ticking of her clock, clipping away the seconds, kept her awake. Twenty past eleven. The splashing from the gutters sounded like wet footsteps pacing outside the window. She had never noticed she could smell the river in her house. She wished she had stayed longer with the Harveys; she would have been able to hear Simon's car.

Twenty to twelve. Surely they wouldn't wait until midnight. She switched on the radio for company. A compere was making people laugh; a man was laughing thickly, sounding waterlogged. Was he a drunk in the street? He wasn't on the radio. She mustn't brood; why, she hadn't put out the sherry glasses; that was something to do, to distract her from the intolerably measured counting of the clock, the silenced radio, the emptiness displaying her sounds –

Though the knock seemed enormously loud, she didn't start. They were here at last, though she hadn't heard the car. It was New Year's Day. She ran, and had reached the front door when the phone shrilled. That startled her so badly that she snatched the door open before lifting the receiver.

Nobody was outside – only a distant uproar of cheers and bells and horns – and Margery was on the phone. "We've been held up, mummy. There was an accident in the tunnel. We'll be over as soon as we can."

Then who had knocked? It must have been a drunk; she heard him stumbling beside the house, thumping on her window. He'd better take himself off, or she would call Mr Harvey to deal with him. But she was still inside the doorway when she saw the object on her step.

Good God, was it a rat? No, just a shoe, so ancient that it looked stuffed with mould. It wasn't mould, only a rotten old sock. There was something in the sock, something that smelled of stagnant water and worse. She stooped to peer at it, and then she was struggling to close the door, fighting to make the latch click, no breath to spare for a scream. She'd had her first foot, and now – hobbling doggedly alongside the house, its hands slithering over the wall – here came the rest of the body.

The Shallows

Donna Cuttress

DEBRA CHECKED THE rock pool before she plunged her hand into it. The water was freezing cold and as clear as glass. Seaweed fronds waved as she disturbed some pebbles. She always wished for pearlescent shells or snow white coral but this was not the caribbean. Northern coast rock pools froze fingers rather than caressing them.

The sand shuddered as she knocked a piece of driftwood, exposing a flash of metal. Debra clawed at it and inspected it in the palm of her hand. It was a small heart-shaped key. 'Probably off a desk or a wardrobe. Lost forever.' she thought. She stared at it wondering how far it had travelled.

"All that bobbing around to end up here."

She yawned, then dropped it into the pocket of her coat and wiped her hand on the leg of her jeans. She had been woken up off and on during the night by someone stomping around on one of the upper floors of the guesthouse. She blew on her mottled fingers to warm them, then thought of how *she* had washed up here? Holidaying at a guesthouse in a faded seaside resort during the Christmas holiday.

Wind blew into her face, making her eyes water. She avoided crunching the raided crab shells and burgled whelks that had been cast aside by ravenous seagulls that morning and blinked back the cold tears against the blinding winter sun. As her vision cleared, she saw someone standing in the 'The Shallows'.

The woman wore a long sage green coat. Her red hair blew around her shoulders as she balanced on the tip of one of the large rocks that protruded out of the muddy sludge around it. Debra had been warned when she had first arrived at the guesthouse.

"Don't go near *The Shallows*, love."

The manager of the guesthouse, Mr Benson, had lifted the net curtain and pointed from the window of her room.

"Right over there, those jagged rocks. Very dangerous. There's quicksand as well. The tide washes in fast. Catches you unaware. People have died there."

She had looked at where his finger had pointed, a rocky piece of land, almost out of sight.

"The rocks are lethal. Very slippery. It's cordoned off most of the year. Come winter, well, everyone knows, don't go near The Shallows."

She had heard Mr Benson giving the same speech to each guest who arrived. He'd begin as he was carrying their suitcases up the Victorian villa's winding staircase. He always used the word 'lethal'. Saying it slowly, *'Leeethal'*. Enjoying it.

Debra was transfixed by the woman. Her red hair whipped like a cyclone, obscuring her face. She gathered her coat around her, hugging herself. Debra wondered how she had climbed the rocks in the wooden-soled boots she wore.

The wind gathered in strength, but the woman stood fast. Debra thought about shouting to her, but stopped as the woman suddenly raised her arms. Her coat flapped behind her as her hair blew away from her face. She wobbled slightly on to her heels, before allowing herself to fall silently forward. Debra screamed out, but the wind snatched the sound away. Covering her mouth with her hands, she looked around her to see if anyone else had seen what she had, but there was no one. She felt pathetic as she took a few steps toward the rocks, then stopped. The wind had ceased. For a few seconds she could hear only her heart beating. The woman had disappeared.

A horrific scream echoed around her. The guttural howl sent Debra falling backwards. She stumbled, then quickly got to her feet and began running across the beach toward the promenade. The sun had disappeared behind a grey cloud. The tide had turned and rumbled ominously toward land, chasing her home.

Debra patted off the sand from her jeans, wiped her runny nose on her sleeve and dabbed at her teary eyes with her scarf. She opened the door to the guesthouse and went in, allowing the wind to close it behind her. The lock clicked. She stood before the dining room door, listening to the landlady, Mrs Benson, busying herself in the room. The door opened quickly.

"I thought I heard you come in. You look freezing, girl!"

Debra wanted to tell her she had seen, but she suddenly felt foolish. Hysterical. She unwrapped the thick scarf from around her neck and let it drop on to the chair next to the telephone table. She held out her shaking hands in front of her. Mrs Benson stopped adjusting chairs and stared at Debra.

"I've just seen a woman fall from those rocks in The Shallows! She fell about fifteen feet. I meant to help, but I couldn't. She wasn't there!!"

Mrs Benson looked at her for a few seconds, then turned abruptly and pushed her way through a set of double doors. The dining room began to fill with the scent of coffee. Debra sat at a small table set in the bay window and stared toward The Shallows. Sleet began to spatter the glass obscuring her view. Mrs Benson returned, placing a mug of steaming tea on Debra's table. She leaned against the empty chair that faced her. Her fingers twitched.

"You've obviously had a shock, but believe me when I tell you this… she's not there."

Debra went to speak, but she was silenced by Mrs Benson's raised hand. The coffee machine gurgled noisily in the kitchen.

"You know her?"

"Long red hair, green coat ? Oh yes, I know her."

"Is she on the beach frequently?"

"Yes… she died there."

Debra spilt some tea on to the white cloth. Mrs Benson began arranging cutlery and tea cups on the other tables.

"Excuse me?"

"She died there. Slipped and fell on those rocks. Cracked her skull, but that's not what killed her."

Mrs Benson smoothed a tablecloth then returned to the chair facing Debra. Her neck was flushed red.

"She drowned. The tide came in fast while she was unconscious and… there you go."

Debra nodded, surprised at the landlady's lack of emotion, obviously retelling a rehearsed story. Mrs Benson turned away.

"How can you be so normal about a *ghost*?"

Mrs Benson took an apron from a hook behind the kitchen door then returned, tying it around her waist.

"We're used to her."

She walked to the hallway and grabbed a small handbell that sat on the telephone table. She rang it. Breakfast was about to begin. There was a rumble of footsteps on the stairs. Mrs Benson replaced the bell, then returned to Debra.

"She was my sister, Clarissa."

"Your sister?"

"Yes, baby sister. Youngest is most loved they say, but she was just indulged that's all. She wasn't very well, but at least now, I know where she is."

Mrs Benson disappeared into the kitchen. The other guests greeted each other as they met on the stairs. Debra watched the tide creep along the coast line, as the sleet became snow.

"Good morning, early bird! Shame we didn't have this a couple of days ago."

Mr Lavender waved to her even though he was sitting no more than six feet away. He adjusted his knife and fork on the table, then waved to the other guests.

"A white Christmas! How lovely."

Mrs Benson placed a plate of egg and bacon in front of Debra.

"Eat up now, you've had a shock," she whispered. "Stay inside today."

She squeezed her shoulder. Debra couldn't decide whether she was being kind or threatening. She smiled at Mrs Benson, then noticed Mr Lavender staring at her as she sipped her tea.

Debra sat in the reading room, an open book on her lap, looking out of the window. The Christmas tree lights blinked softly, sending slow striations of colour across the already darkening room. She thought about the woman, Clarissa, and how her sister ignored her.

'Why would you ignore your sister's ghost?'

The thought alone sounded preposterous. A now familiar sound caught her attention. The Christmas tree lights fluttered. Slow monotonous footsteps padded around upstairs. Debra stood, letting the book drop to the floor and waited to see who descended the staircase. Nobody came down.

The dawn sky was grey. The path between the guesthouse and the beach was barely visible through the sand that had blown inland. The fallen snow had become ice. Debra kept her hands in her pockets as she stepped on to the beach. She glanced at the guesthouse. Mrs Benson was staring at her through a raised net curtain, slowly shaking her head. She dropped the curtain. The light in the room went out.

Debra kept walking. She sidestepped the rock pools that would have entranced her so much and headed toward the jagged rocks of The Shallows. She deliberately walked on the split and cracked seams of shells, enjoying the crunch beneath her feet and wondered why she was even out here at this time? What if she saw Clarissa? What would she say? Her boots began to sink and an oily ridge of sand clogged the grip underfoot. The beach felt as though it had thickened as the sands shifted, sucking each foot downwards slightly with every step. The grey light was now lilac, as snow began to fall again.

Debra walked on, pulling her coat around her. She could hear someone behind her, not footsteps but a heavy gasping breath, like they had slowed down from a sprint. There was muttering. An angry female voice, spitting bile, hissed words that she could not quite grasp, but were meant for someone. Debra sidestepped out of the way, but no one passed. She scanned around her, hearing the voice coming from every direction, echoing through and around her just like the scream the day before. There was no one else on the beach. She was a solitary figure. Debra leaned against one of the rocks, then slipped as she was aggressively pushed. Someone passed, leaving deep footprints in the wet sand. Debra watched as the form of the woman began to slowly appear, as though someone was adjusting the scene with a dimmer switch. Colours became vivid, the volume too loud and the smell of the sea became choking. Clarissa was climbing on to the rocks. Debra shouted,

"*Stop!*"

The ghost didn't move.

"*Stop! Don't!*"

The ghost raised its arms as before, and dropped forward. Debra closed her eyes. Being this close was hideous. She saw the reddened skin on Clarissa's hands, heard the scrape of her boots on the rocks, and the crack of her skull as it impacted on the rocks. Clarissa's mottled face grimaced in pain as she let out a muffled cry before closing her eyes. Debra could hear a choking sound as she began to drown. The wind became fierce, as snow hit her in the face. The shock of seeing this woman's death up close was sickening. Debra felt complicit in the nightmare of Clarissa's death but could do nothing to stop this horrific replay of the past. She gasped for air and turned into the direction of the wind letting cold air rush into her mouth.

Her boots began to sink into the quicksand. She panicked and struggled to free them, feeling herself sinking. There was a man's voice behind her. A black scarf was wrapped across his face, his pale fingers poked out of his gloves like bones. Mr Benson grabbed her shoulder.

"Come away from there! The tide's coming in!"

Sea water and sand had already passed her calf. She turned quickly, grabbing Mr Benson for leveridge. He reached under her shoulders and pulled as she fell backward. The sands released her hobbled feet as he grabbed her arm, pulling her quickly.

"Move! Move!"

She fell again, splashing water everywhere, her breath escaped, her hair covered her face, as she raked at the ground.

"Move quicker, girl!"

She followed him, gasping with each step, forcing her cold hands to reach out to him. She turned briefly. Clarissa's ghost watched from the rocks. Her face was covered in sand, blood ran from the wound on her temple – it clogged her ear and matted her hair. Their eyes locked.

"*Help me.*"

Debra heard her, though her lips didn't move. Snow blew around her, blinding Debra for a few seconds. When her vision cleared, Clarissa had gone.

"You stupid fool! Didn't I warn you? The Shallows will kill you, like it did her."

They sat on the steps that led from the beach to the promenade. The Christmas lights from the guesthouse glowed dully in the distance, the only colour around. Debra rubbed her numb hands against her coat.

"I lost track of where I was and what time it was."

Mr Benson put his face before hers. Debra flinched.

"*You needed to see her!* Vivienne told me you saw her yesterday. Don't lie to me."

She stood up quickly, forcing him to back away.

"You're right! I did come to see her!"

He glanced quickly at the guesthouse.

"That's what she does. Calls people to her. Clarissa always caused misery."

He climbed the steps and began walking toward the guesthouse. Debra followed, slowly.

The air inside was too warm. She could smell food cooking, hear chattering voices, and a radio played a Christmas hymn. She avoided the dining room, deciding to go to her room instead. Vivienne was waiting by her door, upright and tense.

"Why would you go there? I watched you leave and I thought, '*Why is she going there? I have to stop her*', but Stan wouldn't let me. 'I'll go' he said and he did, he risked his life to save you."

Debra began to apologise, but Mrs Benson continued, not listening.

"She went there to kill herself, our Clarissa *wanted* to do that. Let her be."

"She didn't look like she wanted to die."

Mrs Benson turned, her face contorted with anger.

"What would you know? I *knew* her."

"It was the look on her face. I saw it close up. She... didn't want to die. Haven't you seen her? Don't you go to The Shallows?"

"What do I need to go there for? I didn't make her kill herself."

"I didn't mean it like that, I meant that if there was a ghost of someone I loved..."

"*Who says I loved her?* Listen to me! I *saw* her on the day she died, I *found* her. Don't tell me what she looked like, because I already know."

"I know what I saw!"

Debra opened the door to her room and waited for Vivienne to finish, but Stan shouted up the stairwell, interrupting them.

"Would you like some breakfast, Vivienne? How about you, Miss Craig?"

Mrs Benson tilted her head toward Debra.

"Let Clarissa be."

She descended the staircase, retying her apron extra tightly around her waist. Before Debra closed her door, she heard the click of another on the landing. Mr Lavender across the hall looked through a narrow gap in the door to check on whose conversation he had been eavesdropping.

She had the hottest bath the old immersion heater could produce, then dried her hair and dressed. Debra sat on the bed. She felt bullied and tired. There was a low knock at her door.

She opened it to find Mr Lavender, wearing a long camel-coloured coat. A red mohair scarf was tucked into his collar to cover his withered neck, his cap was pulled low. He whispered,

"I'll be taking a slow walk to the Pier. I like to have a mid-morning coffee sometimes in the Silver Slipper cafe. I'll be there at eleven."

She didn't know what to say to him other than, "That sounds nice."

"You should join me. At eleven. We can talk."

He leaned in just a fraction too close.

"*About Clarissa.*"

The windows of The Silver Slipper cafe had steamed up with condensation, but Debra could make out the blurred lights on the small Christmas tree on the counter and the vivid red of Mr Lavender's scarf. She opened the door slowly as the paper chains pinned from corner to corner in the polystyrene ceiling tiles swayed in the draught from the door.

"Over here Debra."

He waved, despite there being no other customers. Before she had unfastened her coat, a lady placed a frothy coffee in a glass cup with a saucer on the table. Debra sat and sipped it, allowing it to warm her throat.

"Glad we didn't have to send out a St Bernard dog to find you in the snow!"

The radio volume dipped, the owner returned to her crossword puzzle in the newspaper.

"You want to know about Clarissa?"

"Yes."

He took out a pressed handkerchief from his pocket and wiped his forehead.

"She was lovely. Not at all like what Vivienne, that's Mrs Benson, will tell you. I remember Stan, Mr Benson, saying she was dangerous. Rubbish! She had a mind of her own, that's all. She wanted to go to art school. Make dresses and designs, that kind of thing. She always looked fashionable. Copied outfits from the magazines."

He stopped talking, lost in a memory. He wiped the condensation on the window with his handkerchief. The sea was roiling against the stands of the pier. Debra could feel them banging against the stanchions. Snow settled on the kiddie rides and the benches for weary pensioners.

"Vivienne wanted her to work in the guesthouse. Her and Stan bought it with the money from their dad's death. They never gave Clarissa her share. Anyway, she didn't want to stay, so they sort of made out she was no better than what she should, convinced important people she was going mad. They made her live in a bloody attic room! I kept asking after her, I always did. I would have helped her escape, you see, but… she'd gone before I could."

"Do you think she killed herself?"

"I don't know. I don't think so. Quite a few people have died in The Shallows. It's very dangerous, as you found out yourself. I've seen her ghost. I always think she'll stop when she sees me, but she never does. I gave up trying to talk to it… *her*."

"Why do you still come here?"

"To remind *them*, Viv and Stan. I knew the real Clarissa, not the bullshit they peddle about her."

They carried on sipping the coffee, watching the snow disappear into the sea.

After dinner, Debra sat in the reading room, absently staring out of the bay window at the falling snow. The other guests were in the TV room watching a comedy programme. She didn't feel like joining them and decided to go to bed, but something made her stop at the foot of the stairs. She stared upwards through the dark centre of the staircase that twisted up four floors of the villa. The crowd in the TV room laughed as one. Stan asked if anyone wanted a drink from the bar. Everyone was distracted.

She walked slowly up the stairs to her room and hesitated by her door. She looked up the centre of the staircase again. A light flickered near the attic rooms. She was drawn to carry on climbing, and did until the frayed stair carpet ended at the end of the last flight at the top of the house. She stepped tentatively on to the boards facing a door that clicked and slowly opened for her. The room invited her in.

The promenade lights cast shadows across the ceiling. There was a single bed, a chest of drawers with a lamp and some books stacked on it. In the corner was a child's wardrobe. She tried to turn on the lamp but there was no bulb in it. Sketches had been pinned to the wall, some had been ripped off and were laying on the floor. She tried to open the wardrobe but the door would not budge.

"It's locked,"

She felt inside her cardigan pocket and took out the heart-shaped key.

'Have I always been carrying this?' she thought.

The wardrobe opened without her even using it, exposing the darkness within. Inside was a sage green coat, gently swinging on a hanger. Next to it was a long brown dress, on the floor a pair of boots with wooden soles.

"This is her room…"

Her breath fogged out in front of her. Her hands shook. The coat smelled of the sea, there was still sand smeared on the arms. She touched the damp neck of the dress, then looked at her fingers in the promenade light. There was blood on them. A face slowly appeared in the wardrobe, evolving from the darkness. It was pale and bloodied and covered in strands of wet hair. It whispered slowly,

"Help me."

Debra slammed the wardrobe door. She covered her mouth, terrified, shaking, unable to breathe.

"Leave me alone!"

She ran from the attic room, taking the stairs two at a time, until she reached her room. She fumbled with her door key and let herself in.

'*Vivienne will come now. Vivienne will come and confront me!*'

Nobody came. She could only hear laughter from the TV room as she wrapped herself in the eiderdown on the bed.

Cawing seagulls swooped outside of Debra's window. She glanced at her bedside clock, but it had stopped, it had not been wound since she arrived on Boxing Day. The morning noises of the guesthouse did not begin. There was no water running in the pipes, toilets flushing or muffled chatter in cold rooms. There was only silence. She thought she must have slept through breakfast. The seagulls screamed again. She swung her legs out of the bed. Her breath fogged. The room was freezing. The small radiator was cold. She pulled the curtain back. The clouds had an orange tint, heavy with more snow to fall. The promenade lights swung gently.

The room suddenly seemed too bare. A stranger's room. Her case was still on top of the wardrobe, her wash bag on the sink and her clothes folded neatly on the wooden chair, but there was something different. The bedside clock began to tick.

A slow tapping began from inside the wardrobe. Debra moved further up the bed, leaning against the wall away from it. The bed wobbled, as the headboard banged against the wall. A voice shouted,

"Be quiet up there!"

Debra froze. She pulled the sleeves of her dress over her cold fingers and wrapped her arms around herself. The quiet tapping continued from inside the wardrobe.

'*Someone is in there. They want to get out. I have to help them.*'

She walked almost on tiptoes, trying not to make any noise with her boots on the wooden floor. The small heart-shaped key, the treasure she had found on the beach and shown to Vivienne, was already in the lock. She turned it. The tapping grew in volume, becoming a heartbeat.

Ba boom ba boom ba boom.

She turned the key over and over and thought for a moment the lock had broken. She began to panic in case the noise alerted Vivienne or Stan and they would be angry and come running up the stairs to her room and… and… what?

'*What would they do Debra?*'

The key clicked in the lock. The door swung open and the tapping ceased. Inside was the long green coat. She touched the soft mohair, tipped it off the hanger and put it on. She fastened it feeling safer at once.

The seagulls cawed again as snow began to fall. She unpinned a christmas card that was pinned to the door. It read '*Lots of lovely Christmas wishes darling, Eddy XX*'

Debra had to leave, escape this room. She ran down the stairs, not caring how noisy she was and did not stop until she came to the beach. The snow began to fall heavier, blurring her vision. Her hair blew in her face. She grabbed it and tucked it down the back of her coat, feeling its coldness on her skin. Her boots dug into the wet sand. She spoke to herself,

"How many times have I done this? How many times have I walked this beach? I must not turn around, but I have to, I always do. Vivienne will see me. Vivienne will see me and come running after me… or she will ignore me, and let the curtain fall."

Debra turned. Squinting through the wind and snow she saw a light in one of the windows. An illuminated square in the grey blizzard. Vivienne was watching her. The curtain hung like a veil around her head. Then it dropped. The light went out. Debra began to cry, yet smiled ,feeling vindicated.

"Every time."

She carried on walking as the winds blew into her from the changing tide. Snow stuck to her coat. She stopped as she approached The Shallows. Clarissa's ghost had already fallen from the rocks. Sea water foamed around her bloodied face. The green coat undulated with the wind. Her hair splayed out in thick wet points, it stuck to her face with sand and blood.

"Too late. I'm too late!"

Clarissa's eyes suddenly opened.

Debra yelled out as she fell backwards in fear. Her feet dug into the sand and began to sink beneath her. Clarissa was dead, a ghost, yet here she was, spitting out salt water and pushing herself up. Her head lolled to one side as the blood from her wound trickled down her face. Despite the wind, Debra could hear her,

"I knew you would come. I knew someone would come. Someone always does... I thought it would be her. I thought it would be our Vivienne but it never is. It's you. I knew it would be you when I saw you. I always know."

Clarissa held out a hand. Debra tried to reach for it, but found her hands had been sucked into the sands. She looked down at herself. She was not wearing the green coat or the wooden-soled boots, she was in her pyjamas and barefoot. Sand squelched between her toes as she felt the shells of sea creatures moving beneath her.

Clarissa reached forward and effortlessly pulled her to her feet. Debra felt herself drifting like the snow that fell around her. They climbed the higher rocks silently, staring down the foamy waves that had begun to rush in around them. The sky suddenly cleared and for a brief moment the sun shone through on to them.

"Do as I do," Clarissa said, and extended her arms outwards to her side. Debra did the same. They fell forward on to the rocks below. Clarissa disappeared as they dropped.

Her body was found on New Year's Day. Vivienne and Stan watched the police on the beach from the bay window in the dining room. The guests looked on from the reading room.

"How very sad," said one.

"She seemed very nice. Quiet. Solitary. But nice all the same," said another.

Mr Lavender turned away, and looked across the hall into the dining room. Stanley was picking up pieces of discarded party streamers from the carpet.

"*Vivienne?*"

The guests looked at him. It was not like Mr Lavender to raise his voice. Vivienne came to the dining room doorway.

"Yes, Eddie?"

"Another death. This has to stop!"

Stanley stood up straight.

"That's The Shallows for you. I did warn her. I warn everyone who comes here."

Mr Lavender shook his head.

"*When are you going to go to The Shallows yourself, Vivienne?*"

Vivienne went to answer, but stopped. The muffled thudding of footsteps began on the stairs. Slow step after slow step echoed like a heartbeat up to the attic rooms. Heavy dull thuds, as though someone was wearing wooden-soled boots.

The Haunted Man and the Ghost's Bargain

Charles Dickens

Chapter I
The Gift Bestowed

EVERYBODY SAID SO.

Far be it from me to assert that what everybody says must be true. Everybody is, often, as likely to be wrong as right. In the general experience, everybody has been wrong so often, and it has taken, in most instances, such a weary while to find out how wrong, that the authority is proved to be fallible. Everybody may sometimes be right; "but that's no rule," as the ghost of Giles Scroggins says in the ballad.

The dread word, Ghost, recalls me.

Everybody said he looked like a haunted man. The extent of my present claim for everybody is, that they were so far right. He did.

Who could have seen his hollow cheek; his sunken brilliant eye; his black-attired figure, indefinably grim, although well-knit and well-proportioned; his grizzled hair hanging, like tangled sea-weed, about his face, – as if he had been, through his whole life, a lonely mark for the chafing and beating of the great deep of humanity, – but might have said he looked like a haunted man?

Who could have observed his manner, taciturn, thoughtful, gloomy, shadowed by habitual reserve, retiring always and jocund never, with a distraught air of reverting to a bygone place and time, or of listening to some old echoes in his mind, but might have said it was the manner of a haunted man?

Who could have heard his voice, slow-speaking, deep, and grave, with a natural fulness and melody in it which he seemed to set himself against and stop, but might have said it was the voice of a haunted man?

Who that had seen him in his inner chamber, part library and part laboratory, – for he was, as the world knew, far and wide, a learned man in chemistry, and a teacher on whose lips and hands a crowd of aspiring ears and eyes hung daily, – who that had seen him there, upon a winter night, alone, surrounded by his drugs and instruments and books; the shadow of his shaded lamp a monstrous beetle on the wall, motionless among a crowd of spectral shapes raised there by the flickering of the fire upon the quaint objects around him; some of these phantoms (the reflection of glass vessels that held liquids), trembling at heart like things that knew his power to uncombine them, and to give back their component parts to fire and vapour; – who that had seen him then, his work done, and he pondering in his chair before the rusted grate and red flame, moving his thin mouth as if in speech, but silent as the dead, would not have said that the man seemed haunted and the chamber too?

Who might not, by a very easy flight of fancy, have believed that everything about him took this haunted tone, and that he lived on haunted ground?

His dwelling was so solitary and vault-like, – an old, retired part of an ancient endowment for students, once a brave edifice, planted in an open place, but now the obsolete whim of forgotten architects; smoke-age-and-weather-darkened, squeezed on every side by the overgrowing of the great city, and choked, like an old well, with stones and bricks; its small quadrangles, lying down in very pits formed by the streets and buildings, which, in course of time, had been constructed above its heavy chimney stacks; its old trees, insulted by the neighbouring smoke, which deigned to droop so low when it was very feeble and the weather very moody; its grass-plots, struggling with the mildewed earth to be grass, or to win any show of compromise; its silent pavements, unaccustomed to the tread of feet, and even to the observation of eyes, except when a stray face looked down from the upper world, wondering what nook it was; its sun-dial in a little bricked-up corner, where no sun had straggled for a hundred years, but where, in compensation for the sun's neglect, the snow would lie for weeks when it lay nowhere else, and the black east wind would spin like a huge humming-top, when in all other places it was silent and still.

His dwelling, at its heart and core – within doors – at his fireside – was so lowering and old, so crazy, yet so strong, with its worm-eaten beams of wood in the ceiling, and its sturdy floor shelving downward to the great oak chimney-piece; so environed and hemmed in by the pressure of the town yet so remote in fashion, age, and custom; so quiet, yet so thundering with echoes when a distant voice was raised or a door was shut, – echoes, not confined to the many low passages and empty rooms, but rumbling and grumbling till they were stifled in the heavy air of the forgotten Crypt where the Norman arches were half-buried in the earth.

You should have seen him in his dwelling about twilight, in the dead winter time.

When the wind was blowing, shrill and shrewd, with the going down of the blurred sun. When it was just so dark, as that the forms of things were indistinct and big – but not wholly lost. When sitters by the fire began to see wild faces and figures, mountains and abysses, ambuscades and armies, in the coals. When people in the streets bent down their heads and ran before the weather. When those who were obliged to meet it, were stopped at angry corners, stung by wandering snow-flakes alighting on the lashes of their eyes, – which fell too sparingly, and were blown away too quickly, to leave a trace upon the frozen ground. When windows of private houses closed up tight and warm. When lighted gas began to burst forth in the busy and the quiet streets, fast blackening otherwise. When stray pedestrians, shivering along the latter, looked down at the glowing fires in kitchens, and sharpened their sharp appetites by sniffing up the fragrance of whole miles of dinners.

When travellers by land were bitter cold, and looked wearily on gloomy landscapes, rustling and shuddering in the blast. When mariners at sea, outlying upon icy yards, were tossed and swung above the howling ocean dreadfully. When lighthouses, on rocks and headlands, showed solitary and watchful; and benighted sea-birds breasted on against their ponderous lanterns, and fell dead. When little readers of story-books, by the firelight, trembled to think of Cassim Baba cut into quarters, hanging in the Robbers' Cave, or had some small misgivings that the fierce little old woman, with the crutch, who used to start out of the box in the merchant Abudah's bedroom, might, one of these nights, be found upon the stairs, in the long, cold, dusky journey up to bed.

When, in rustic places, the last glimmering of daylight died away from the ends of avenues; and the trees, arching overhead, were sullen and black. When, in parks and woods, the high wet fern and sodden moss, and beds of fallen leaves, and trunks of trees, were lost to view, in masses of impenetrable shade. When mists arose from dyke, and fen, and river. When lights in old halls and in cottage windows, were a cheerful sight. When the mill stopped, the wheelwright and the blacksmith shut their workshops, the turnpike-gate closed, the plough and harrow were left lonely in the fields, the labourer and team went home, and the striking of the church clock had a deeper sound than at noon, and the churchyard wicket would be swung no more that night.

When twilight everywhere released the shadows, prisoned up all day, that now closed in and gathered like mustering swarms of ghosts. When they stood lowering, in corners of rooms, and frowned out from behind half-opened doors. When they had full possession of unoccupied apartments. When they danced upon the floors, and walls, and ceilings of inhabited chambers, while the fire was low, and withdrew like ebbing waters when it sprang into a blaze. When they fantastically mocked the shapes of household objects, making the nurse an ogress, the rocking-horse a monster, the wondering child, half-scared and half-amused, a stranger to itself, – the very tongs upon the hearth, a straddling giant with his arms a-kimbo, evidently smelling the blood of Englishmen, and wanting to grind people's bones to make his bread.

When these shadows brought into the minds of older people, other thoughts, and showed them different images. When they stole from their retreats, in the likenesses of forms and faces from the past, from the grave, from the deep, deep gulf, where the things that might have been, and never were, are always wandering.

When he sat, as already mentioned, gazing at the fire. When, as it rose and fell, the shadows went and came. When he took no heed of them, with his bodily eyes; but, let them come or let them go, looked fixedly at the fire. You should have seen him, then.

When the sounds that had arisen with the shadows, and come out of their lurking-places at the twilight summons, seemed to make a deeper stillness all about him. When the wind was rumbling in the chimney, and sometimes crooning, sometimes howling, in the house. When the old trees outside were so shaken and beaten, that one querulous old rook, unable to sleep, protested now and then, in a feeble, dozy, high-up "Caw!" When, at intervals, the window trembled, the rusty vane upon the turret-top complained, the clock beneath it recorded that another quarter of an hour was gone, or the fire collapsed and fell in with a rattle.

When a knock came at his door, in short, as he was sitting so, and roused him.

"Who's that?" said he. "Come in!"

Surely there had been no figure leaning on the back of his chair; no face looking over it. It is certain that no gliding footstep touched the floor, as he lifted up his head, with a start, and spoke. And yet there was no mirror in the room on whose surface his own form could have cast its shadow for a moment; and, Something had passed darkly and gone!

"I'm humbly fearful, sir," said a fresh-coloured busy man, holding the door open with his foot for the admission of himself and a wooden tray he carried, and letting it go again by very gentle and careful degrees, when he and the tray had got in, lest it should close noisily, "that it's a good bit past the time tonight. But Mrs. William has been taken off her legs so often—"

"By the wind? Ay! I have heard it rising."

"—By the wind, sir – that it's a mercy she got home at all. Oh dear, yes. Yes. It was by the wind, Mr. Redlaw. By the wind."

He had, by this time, put down the tray for dinner, and was employed in lighting the lamp, and spreading a cloth on the table. From this employment he desisted in a hurry, to stir and feed the fire, and then resumed it; the lamp he had lighted, and the blaze that rose under his hand, so quickly changing the appearance of the room, that it seemed as if the mere coming in of his fresh red face and active manner had made the pleasant alteration.

"Mrs. William is of course subject at any time, sir, to be taken off her balance by the elements. She is not formed superior to that."

"No," returned Mr. Redlaw good-naturedly, though abruptly.

"No, sir. Mrs. William may be taken off her balance by Earth; as for example, last Sunday week, when sloppy and greasy, and she going out to tea with her newest sister-in-law, and having a pride in herself, and wishing to appear perfectly spotless though pedestrian. Mrs. William may be taken off her balance by Air; as being once over-persuaded by a friend to try a swing at Peckham Fair, which acted on her constitution instantly like a steam-boat. Mrs. William may be taken off her balance by Fire; as on a false alarm of engines at her mother's, when she went two miles in her nightcap. Mrs. William may be taken off her balance by Water; as at Battersea, when rowed into the piers by her young nephew, Charley Swidger junior, aged twelve, which had no idea of boats whatever. But these are elements. Mrs. William must be taken out of elements for the strength of her character to come into play."

As he stopped for a reply, the reply was "Yes," in the same tone as before.

"Yes, sir. Oh dear, yes!" said Mr. Swidger, still proceeding with his preparations, and checking them off as he made them. "That's where it is, sir. That's what I always say myself, sir. Such a many of us Swidgers! – Pepper. Why there's my father, sir, superannuated keeper and custodian of this Institution, eighty-seven year old. He's a Swidger! – Spoon."

"True, William," was the patient and abstracted answer, when he stopped again.

"Yes, sir," said Mr. Swidger. "That's what I always say, sir. You may call him the trunk of the tree! – Bread. Then you come to his successor, my unworthy self – Salt – and Mrs. William, Swidgers both. – Knife and fork. Then you come to all my brothers and their families, Swidgers, man and woman, boy and girl. Why, what with cousins, uncles, aunts, and relationships of this, that, and t'other degree, and whatnot degree, and marriages, and lyings-in, the Swidgers – Tumbler – might take hold of hands, and make a ring round England!"

Receiving no reply at all here, from the thoughtful man whom he addressed, Mr. William approached, him nearer, and made a feint of accidentally knocking the table with a decanter, to rouse him. The moment he succeeded, he went on, as if in great alacrity of acquiescence.

"Yes, sir! That's just what I say myself, sir. Mrs. William and me have often said so. 'There's Swidgers enough,' we say, 'without our voluntary contributions,' – Butter. In fact, sir, my father is a family in himself – Castors – to take care of; and it happens all for the best that we have no child of our own, though it's made Mrs. William rather quiet-like, too. Quite ready for the fowl and mashed potatoes, sir? Mrs. William said she'd dish in ten minutes when I left the Lodge."

"I am quite ready," said the other, waking as from a dream, and walking slowly to and fro.

"Mrs. William has been at it again, sir!" said the keeper, as he stood warming a plate at the fire, and pleasantly shading his face with it. Mr. Redlaw stopped in his walking, and an expression of interest appeared in him.

"What I always say myself, sir. She will do it! There's a motherly feeling in Mrs. William's breast that must and will have went."

"What has she done?"

"Why, sir, not satisfied with being a sort of mother to all the young gentlemen that come up from a variety of parts, to attend your courses of lectures at this ancient foundation – its surprising how stone-chaney catches the heat this frosty weather, to be sure!" Here he turned the plate, and cooled his fingers.

"Well?" said Mr. Redlaw.

"That's just what I say myself, sir," returned Mr. William, speaking over his shoulder, as if in ready and delighted assent. "That's exactly where it is, sir! There ain't one of our students but appears to regard Mrs. William in that light. Every day, right through the course, they puts their heads into the Lodge, one after another, and have all got something to tell her, or something to ask her. 'Swidge' is the appellation by which they speak of Mrs. William in general, among themselves, I'm told; but that's what I say, sir. Better be called ever so far out of your name, if it's done in real liking, than have it made ever so much of, and not cared about! What's a name for? To know a person by. If Mrs. William is known by something better than her name – I allude to Mrs. William's qualities and disposition – never mind her name, though it is Swidger, by rights. Let 'em call her Swidge, Widge, Bridge – Lord! London Bridge, Blackfriars, Chelsea, Putney, Waterloo, or Hammersmith Suspension – if they like."

The close of this triumphant oration brought him and the plate to the table, upon which he half laid and half dropped it, with a lively sense of its being thoroughly heated, just as the subject of his praises entered the room, bearing another tray and a lantern, and followed by a venerable old man with long grey hair.

Mrs. William, like Mr. William, was a simple, innocent-looking person, in whose smooth cheeks the cheerful red of her husband's official waistcoat was very pleasantly repeated. But whereas Mr. William's light hair stood on end all over his head, and seemed to draw his eyes up with it in an excess of bustling readiness for anything, the dark brown hair of Mrs. William was carefully smoothed down, and waved away under a trim tidy cap, in the most exact and quiet manner imaginable. Whereas Mr. William's very trousers hitched themselves up at the ankles, as if it were not in their iron-grey nature to rest without looking about them, Mrs. William's neatly-flowered skirts – red and white, like her own pretty face – were as composed and orderly, as if the very wind that blew so hard out of doors could not disturb one of their folds. Whereas his coat had something of a fly-away and half-off appearance about the collar and breast, her little bodice was so placid and neat, that there should have been protection for her, in it, had she needed any, with the roughest people. Who could have had the heart to make so calm a bosom swell with grief, or throb with fear, or flutter with a thought of shame! To whom would its repose and peace have not appealed against disturbance, like the innocent slumber of a child!

"Punctual, of course, Milly," said her husband, relieving her of the tray, "or it wouldn't be you. Here's Mrs. William, sir! – He looks lonelier than ever tonight," whispering to his wife, as he was taking the tray, "and ghostlier altogether."

Without any show of hurry or noise, or any show of herself even, she was so calm and quiet, Milly set the dishes she had brought upon the table, – Mr. William, after much clattering and running about, having only gained possession of a butter-boat of gravy, which he stood ready to serve.

"What is that the old man has in his arms?" asked Mr. Redlaw, as he sat down to his solitary meal.

"Holly, sir," replied the quiet voice of Milly.

"That's what I say myself, sir," interposed Mr. William, striking in with the butter-boat. "Berries is so seasonable to the time of year! – Brown gravy!"

"Another Christmas come, another year gone!" murmured the Chemist, with a gloomy sigh. "More figures in the lengthening sum of recollection that we work and work at to our torment, till Death idly jumbles all together, and rubs all out. So, Philip!" breaking off, and raising his voice as he addressed the old man, standing apart, with his glistening burden in his arms, from which the quiet Mrs. William took small branches, which she noiselessly trimmed with her scissors, and decorated the room with, while her aged father-in-law looked on much interested in the ceremony.

"My duty to you, sir," returned the old man. "Should have spoke before, sir, but know your ways, Mr. Redlaw – proud to say – and wait till spoke to! Merry Christmas, sir, and Happy New Year, and many of 'em. Have had a pretty many of 'em myself – ha, ha! – and may take the liberty of wishing 'em. I'm eighty-seven!"

"Have you had so many that were merry and happy?" asked the other.

"Ay, sir, ever so many," returned the old man.

"Is his memory impaired with age? It is to be expected now," said Mr. Redlaw, turning to the son, and speaking lower.

"Not a morsel of it, sir," replied Mr. William. "That's exactly what I say myself, sir. There never was such a memory as my father's. He's the most wonderful man in the world. He don't know what forgetting means. It's the very observation I'm always making to Mrs. William, sir, if you'll believe me!"

Mr. Swidger, in his polite desire to seem to acquiesce at all events, delivered this as if there were no iota of contradiction in it, and it were all said in unbounded and unqualified assent.

The Chemist pushed his plate away, and, rising from the table, walked across the room to where the old man stood looking at a little sprig of holly in his hand.

"It recalls the time when many of those years were old and new, then?" he said, observing him attentively, and touching him on the shoulder. "Does it?"

"Oh many, many!" said Philip, half awaking from his reverie. "I'm eighty-seven!"

"Merry and happy, was it?" asked the Chemist in a low voice. "Merry and happy, old man?"

"Maybe as high as that, no higher," said the old man, holding out his hand a little way above the level of his knee, and looking retrospectively at his questioner, "when I first remember 'em! Cold, sunshiny day it was, out a-walking, when someone – it was my mother as sure as you stand there, though I don't know what her blessed face was like, for she took ill and died that Christmas-time – told me they were food for birds. The pretty little fellow thought – that's me, you understand – that birds' eyes were so bright, perhaps, because the berries that they lived on in the winter were so bright. I recollect that. And I'm eighty-seven!"

"Merry and happy!" mused the other, bending his dark eyes upon the stooping figure, with a smile of compassion. "Merry and happy – and remember well?"

"Ay, ay, ay!" resumed the old man, catching the last words. "I remember 'em well in my school time, year after year, and all the merry-making that used to come along with them. I was a strong chap then, Mr. Redlaw; and, if you'll believe me, hadn't my match at football within ten mile. Where's my son William? Hadn't my match at football, William, within ten mile!"

"That's what I always say, father!" returned the son promptly, and with great respect. "You ARE a Swidger, if ever there was one of the family!"

"Dear!" said the old man, shaking his head as he again looked at the holly. "His mother – my son William's my youngest son – and I, have sat among 'em all, boys and girls, little children and babies, many a year, when the berries like these were not shining half so bright all round us, as their bright faces. Many of 'em are gone; she's gone; and my son George (our eldest, who was her pride more than all the rest!) is fallen very low: but I can see them, when I look here, alive and healthy, as they used to be in those days; and I can see him, thank God, in his innocence. It's a blessed thing to me, at eighty-seven."

The keen look that had been fixed upon him with so much earnestness, had gradually sought the ground.

"When my circumstances got to be not so good as formerly, through not being honestly dealt by, and I first come here to be custodian," said the old man, " – which was upwards of fifty years ago – where's my son William? More than half a century ago, William!"

"That's what I say, father," replied the son, as promptly and dutifully as before, "that's exactly where it is. Two times ought's an ought, and twice five ten, and there's a hundred of 'em."

"It was quite a pleasure to know that one of our founders – or more correctly speaking," said the old man, with a great glory in his subject and his knowledge of it, "one of the learned gentlemen that helped endow us in Queen Elizabeth's time, for we were founded afore her day – left in his will, among the other bequests he made us, so much to buy holly, for garnishing the walls and windows, come Christmas. There was something homely and friendly in it. Being but strange here, then, and coming at Christmas time, we took a liking for his very picter that hangs in what used to be, anciently, afore our ten poor gentlemen commuted for an annual stipend in money, our great Dinner Hall. – A sedate gentleman in a peaked beard, with a ruff round his neck, and a scroll below him, in old English letters, 'Lord! keep my memory green!' You know all about him, Mr. Redlaw?"

"I know the portrait hangs there, Philip."

"Yes, sure, it's the second on the right, above the panelling. I was going to say – he has helped to keep my memory green, I thank him; for going round the building every year, as I'm a doing now, and freshening up the bare rooms with these branches and berries, freshens up my bare old brain. One year brings back another, and that year another, and those others numbers! At last, it seems to me as if the birth-time of our Lord was the birth-time of all I have ever had affection for, or mourned for, or delighted in, – and they're a pretty many, for I'm eighty-seven!"

"Merry and happy," murmured Redlaw to himself.

The room began to darken strangely.

"So you see, sir," pursued old Philip, whose hale wintry cheek had warmed into a ruddier glow, and whose blue eyes had brightened while he spoke, "I have plenty to keep, when I keep this present season. Now, where's my quiet Mouse? Chattering's the sin of my time of life, and there's half the building to do yet, if the cold don't freeze us first, or the wind don't blow us away, or the darkness don't swallow us up."

The quiet Mouse had brought her calm face to his side, and silently taken his arm, before he finished speaking.

"Come away, my dear," said the old man. "Mr. Redlaw won't settle to his dinner, otherwise, till it's cold as the winter. I hope you'll excuse me rambling on, sir, and I wish you good night, and, once again, a merry—"

"Stay!" said Mr. Redlaw, resuming his place at the table, more, it would have seemed from his manner, to reassure the old keeper, than in any remembrance of his own appetite. "Spare me another moment, Philip. William, you were going to tell me something to your excellent wife's honour. It will not be disagreeable to her to hear you praise her. What was it?"

"Why, that's where it is, you see, sir," returned Mr. William Swidger, looking toward his wife in considerable embarrassment. "Mrs. William's got her eye upon me."

"But you're not afraid of Mrs. William's eye?"

"Why, no, sir," returned Mr. Swidger, "that's what I say myself. It wasn't made to be afraid of. It wouldn't have been made so mild, if that was the intention. But I wouldn't like to – Milly! – him, you know. Down in the Buildings."

Mr. William, standing behind the table, and rummaging disconcertedly among the objects upon it, directed persuasive glances at Mrs. William, and secret jerks of his head and thumb at Mr. Redlaw, as alluring her toward him.

"Him, you know, my love," said Mr. William. "Down in the Buildings. Tell, my dear! You're the works of Shakespeare in comparison with myself. Down in the Buildings, you know, my love. – Student."

"Student?" repeated Mr. Redlaw, raising his head.

"That's what I say, sir!" cried Mr. William, in the utmost animation of assent. "If it wasn't the poor student down in the Buildings, why should you wish to hear it from Mrs. William's lips? Mrs. William, my dear – Buildings."

"I didn't know," said Milly, with a quiet frankness, free from any haste or confusion, "that William had said anything about it, or I wouldn't have come. I asked him not to. It's a sick young gentleman, sir – and very poor, I am afraid – who is too ill to go home this holiday-time, and lives, unknown to any one, in but a common kind of lodging for a gentleman, down in Jerusalem Buildings. That's all, sir."

"Why have I never heard of him?" said the Chemist, rising hurriedly. "Why has he not made his situation known to me? Sick! – give me my hat and cloak. Poor! – what house? – what number?"

"Oh, you mustn't go there, sir," said Milly, leaving her father-in-law, and calmly confronting him with her collected little face and folded hands.

"Not go there?"

"Oh dear, no!" said Milly, shaking her head as at a most manifest and self-evident impossibility. "It couldn't be thought of!"

"What do you mean? Why not?"

"Why, you see, sir," said Mr. William Swidger, persuasively and confidentially, "that's what I say. Depend upon it, the young gentleman would never have made his situation known to one of his own sex. Mrs. Williams has got into his confidence, but that's quite different. They all confide in Mrs. William; they all trust her. A man, sir, couldn't have got a whisper out of him; but woman, sir, and Mrs. William combined—!"

"There is good sense and delicacy in what you say, William," returned Mr. Redlaw, observant of the gentle and composed face at his shoulder. And laying his finger on his lip, he secretly put his purse into her hand.

"Oh dear no, sir!" cried Milly, giving it back again. "Worse and worse! Couldn't be dreamed of!"

Such a staid matter-of-fact housewife she was, and so unruffled by the momentary haste of this rejection, that, an instant afterwards, she was tidily picking up a few leaves which had strayed from between her scissors and her apron, when she had arranged the holly.

Finding, when she rose from her stooping posture, that Mr. Redlaw was still regarding her with doubt and astonishment, she quietly repeated – looking about, the while, for any other fragments that might have escaped her observation:

"Oh dear no, sir! He said that of all the world he would not be known to you, or receive help from you – though he is a student in your class. I have made no terms of secrecy with you, but I trust to your honour completely."

"Why did he say so?"

"Indeed I can't tell, sir," said Milly, after thinking a little, "because I am not at all clever, you know; and I wanted to be useful to him in making things neat and comfortable about him, and employed myself that way. But I know he is poor, and lonely, and I think he is somehow neglected too. – How dark it is!"

The room had darkened more and more. There was a very heavy gloom and shadow gathering behind the Chemist's chair.

"What more about him?" he asked.

"He is engaged to be married when he can afford it," said Milly, "and is studying, I think, to qualify himself to earn a living. I have seen, a long time, that he has studied hard and denied himself much. – How very dark it is!"

"It's turned colder, too," said the old man, rubbing his hands. "There's a chill and dismal feeling in the room. Where's my son William? William, my boy, turn the lamp, and rouse the fire!"

Milly's voice resumed, like quiet music very softly played:

"He muttered in his broken sleep yesterday afternoon, after talking to me" (this was to herself) "about someone dead, and some great wrong done that could never be forgotten; but whether to him or to another person, I don't know. Not by him, I am sure."

"And, in short, Mrs. William, you see – which she wouldn't say herself, Mr. Redlaw, if she was to stop here till the new year after this next one—" said Mr. William, coming up to him to speak in his ear, "has done him worlds of good! Bless you, worlds of good! All at home just the same as ever – my father made as snug and comfortable – not a crumb of litter to be found in the house, if you were to offer fifty pound ready money for it – Mrs. William apparently never out of the way – yet Mrs. William backwards and forwards, backwards and forwards, up and down, up and down, a mother to him!"

The room turned darker and colder, and the gloom and shadow gathering behind the chair was heavier.

"Not content with this, sir, Mrs. William goes and finds, this very night, when she was coming home (why it's not above a couple of hours ago), a creature more like a young wild beast than a young child, shivering upon a door-step. What does Mrs. William do, but brings it home to dry it, and feed it, and keep it till our old Bounty of food and flannel is given away, on Christmas morning! If it ever felt a fire before, it's as much as ever it did; for it's sitting in the old Lodge chimney, staring at ours as if its ravenous eyes would never shut again. It's sitting there, at least," said Mr. William, correcting himself, on reflection, "unless it's bolted!"

"Heaven keep her happy!" said the Chemist aloud, "and you too, Philip! and you, William! I must consider what to do in this. I may desire to see this student, I'll not detain you any longer now. Good-night!"

"I thank'ee, sir, I thank'ee!" said the old man, "for Mouse, and for my son William, and for myself. Where's my son William? William, you take the lantern and go on first, through them long dark passages, as you did last year and the year afore. Ha ha! I remember – though I'm eighty-seven! 'Lord, keep my memory green!' It's a very good prayer, Mr. Redlaw, that of the learned gentleman in the peaked beard, with a ruff round his neck – hangs up, second on the right above the panelling, in what used to be, afore our ten poor gentlemen commuted, our great Dinner Hall. 'Lord, keep my memory green!' It's very good and pious, sir. Amen! Amen!"

As they passed out and shut the heavy door, which, however carefully withheld, fired a long train of thundering reverberations when it shut at last, the room turned darker.

As he fell a musing in his chair alone, the healthy holly withered on the wall, and dropped – dead branches.

As the gloom and shadow thickened behind him, in that place where it had been gathering so darkly, it took, by slow degrees, – or out of it there came, by some unreal, unsubstantial process – not to be traced by any human sense, – an awful likeness of himself!

Ghastly and cold, colourless in its leaden face and hands, but with his features, and his bright eyes, and his grizzled hair, and dressed in the gloomy shadow of his dress, it came into his terrible appearance of existence, motionless, without a sound. As he leaned his arm upon the elbow of his chair, ruminating before the fire, it leaned upon the chair-back, close above him, with its appalling copy of his face looking where his face looked, and bearing the expression his face bore.

This, then, was the Something that had passed and gone already. This was the dread companion of the haunted man!

It took, for some moments, no more apparent heed of him, than he of it. The Christmas Waits were playing somewhere in the distance, and, through his thoughtfulness, he seemed to listen to the music. It seemed to listen too.

At length he spoke; without moving or lifting up his face.

"Here again!" he said.

"Here again," replied the Phantom.

"I see you in the fire," said the haunted man; "I hear you in music, in the wind, in the dead stillness of the night."

The Phantom moved its head, assenting.

"Why do you come, to haunt me thus?"

"I come as I am called," replied the Ghost.

"No. Unbidden," exclaimed the Chemist.

"Unbidden be it," said the Spectre. "It is enough. I am here."

Hitherto the light of the fire had shone on the two faces – if the dread lineaments behind the chair might be called a face – both addressed toward it, as at first, and neither looking at the other. But, now, the haunted man turned, suddenly, and stared upon the Ghost. The Ghost, as sudden in its motion, passed to before the chair, and stared on him.

The living man, and the animated image of himself dead, might so have looked, the one upon the other. An awful survey, in a lonely and remote part of an empty old pile of building, on a winter night, with the loud wind going by upon its journey of mystery – whence or whither, no man knowing since the world began – and the stars, in unimaginable millions, glittering through it, from eternal space, where the world's bulk is as a grain, and its hoary age is infancy.

"Look upon me!" said the Spectre. "I am he, neglected in my youth, and miserably poor, who strove and suffered, and still strove and suffered, until I hewed out knowledge from the mine where it was buried, and made rugged steps thereof, for my worn feet to rest and rise on."

"I am that man," returned the Chemist.

"No mother's self-denying love," pursued the Phantom, "no father's counsel, aided me. A stranger came into my father's place when I was but a child, and I was easily an alien from my mother's heart. My parents, at the best, were of that sort whose care soon ends, and whose duty is soon done; who cast their offspring loose, early, as birds do theirs; and, if they do well, claim the merit; and, if ill, the pity."

It paused, and seemed to tempt and goad him with its look, and with the manner of its speech, and with its smile.

"I am he," pursued the Phantom, "who, in this struggle upward, found a friend. I made him – won him – bound him to me! We worked together, side by side. All the love and confidence that in my earlier youth had had no outlet, and found no expression, I bestowed on him."

"Not all," said Redlaw, hoarsely.

"No, not all," returned the Phantom. "I had a sister."

The haunted man, with his head resting on his hands, replied "I had!" The Phantom, with an evil smile, drew closer to the chair, and resting its chin upon its folded hands, its folded hands upon the back, and looking down into his face with searching eyes, that seemed instinct with fire, went on:

"Such glimpses of the light of home as I had ever known, had streamed from her. How young she was, how fair, how loving! I took her to the first poor roof that I was master of, and made it rich. She came into the darkness of my life, and made it bright. – She is before me!"

"I saw her, in the fire, but now. I hear her in music, in the wind, in the dead stillness of the night," returned the haunted man.

"Did he love her?" said the Phantom, echoing his contemplative tone. "I think he did, once. I am sure he did. Better had she loved him less – less secretly, less dearly, from the shallower depths of a more divided heart!"

"Let me forget it!" said the Chemist, with an angry motion of his hand. "Let me blot it from my memory!"

The Spectre, without stirring, and with its unwinking, cruel eyes still fixed upon his face, went on:

"A dream, like hers, stole upon my own life."

"It did," said Redlaw.

"A love, as like hers," pursued the Phantom, "as my inferior nature might cherish, arose in my own heart. I was too poor to bind its object to my fortune then, by any thread of promise or entreaty. I loved her far too well, to seek to do it. But, more than ever I had striven in my life, I strove to climb! Only an inch gained, brought me something nearer to the height. I toiled up! In the late pauses of my labour at that time, – my sister (sweet companion!) still sharing with me the expiring embers and the cooling hearth, – when day was breaking, what pictures of the future did I see!"

"I saw them, in the fire, but now," he murmured. "They come back to me in music, in the wind, in the dead stillness of the night, in the revolving years."

"—Pictures of my own domestic life, in aftertime, with her who was the inspiration of my toil. Pictures of my sister, made the wife of my dear friend, on equal terms – for he had some inheritance, we none – pictures of our sobered age and mellowed happiness, and of the golden links, extending back so far, that should bind us, and our children, in a radiant garland," said the Phantom.

"Pictures," said the haunted man, "that were delusions. Why is it my doom to remember them too well!"

"Delusions," echoed the Phantom in its changeless voice, and glaring on him with its changeless eyes. "For my friend (in whose breast my confidence was locked as in my own), passing between me and the centre of the system of my hopes and struggles, won her to himself, and shattered my frail universe. My sister, doubly dear, doubly devoted, doubly cheerful in my home, lived on to see me famous, and my old ambition so rewarded when its spring was broken, and then—"

"Then died," he interposed. "Died, gentle as ever; happy; and with no concern but for her brother. Peace!"

The Phantom watched him silently.

"Remembered!" said the haunted man, after a pause. "Yes. So well remembered, that even now, when years have passed, and nothing is more idle or more visionary to me than the boyish love so long outlived, I think of it with sympathy, as if it were a younger brother's or a son's. Sometimes I even wonder when her heart first inclined to him, and how it had been affected towards me. – Not lightly, once, I think. – But that is nothing. Early unhappiness, a wound from a hand I loved and trusted, and a loss that nothing can replace, outlive such fancies."

"Thus," said the Phantom, "I bear within me a Sorrow and a Wrong. Thus I prey upon myself. Thus, memory is my curse; and, if I could forget my sorrow and my wrong, I would!"

"Mocker!" said the Chemist, leaping up, and making, with a wrathful hand, at the throat of his other self. "Why have I always that taunt in my ears?"

"Forbear!" exclaimed the Spectre in an awful voice. "Lay a hand on Me, and die!"

He stopped midway, as if its words had paralysed him, and stood looking on it. It had glided from him; it had its arm raised high in warning; and a smile passed over its unearthly features, as it reared its dark figure in triumph.

"If I could forget my sorrow and wrong, I would," the Ghost repeated. "If I could forget my sorrow and my wrong, I would!"

"Evil spirit of myself," returned the haunted man, in a low, trembling tone, "my life is darkened by that incessant whisper."

"It is an echo," said the Phantom.

"If it be an echo of my thoughts – as now, indeed, I know it is," rejoined the haunted man, "why should I, therefore, be tormented? It is not a selfish thought. I suffer it to range beyond myself. All men and women have their sorrows, – most of them their wrongs; ingratitude, and sordid jealousy, and interest, besetting all degrees of life. Who would not forget their sorrows and their wrongs?"

"Who would not, truly, and be happier and better for it?" said the Phantom.

"These revolutions of years, which we commemorate," proceeded Redlaw, "what do they recall! Are there any minds in which they do not re-awaken some sorrow, or some trouble? What is the remembrance of the old man who was here tonight? A tissue of sorrow and trouble."

"But common natures," said the Phantom, with its evil smile upon its glassy face, "unenlightened minds and ordinary spirits, do not feel or reason on these things like men of higher cultivation and profounder thought."

"Tempter," answered Redlaw, "whose hollow look and voice I dread more than words can express, and from whom some dim foreshadowing of greater fear is stealing over me while I speak, I hear again an echo of my own mind."

"Receive it as a proof that I am powerful," returned the Ghost. "Hear what I offer! Forget the sorrow, wrong, and trouble you have known!"

"Forget them!" he repeated.

"I have the power to cancel their remembrance – to leave but very faint, confused traces of them, that will die out soon," returned the Spectre. "Say! Is it done?"

"Stay!" cried the haunted man, arresting by a terrified gesture the uplifted hand. "I tremble with distrust and doubt of you; and the dim fear you cast upon me deepens into a nameless horror I can hardly bear. – I would not deprive myself of any kindly recollection, or any sympathy that is good for me, or others. What shall I lose, if I assent to this? What else will pass from my remembrance?"

"No knowledge; no result of study; nothing but the intertwisted chain of feelings and associations, each in its turn dependent on, and nourished by, the banished recollections. Those will go."

"Are they so many?" said the haunted man, reflecting in alarm.

"They have been wont to show themselves in the fire, in music, in the wind, in the dead stillness of the night, in the revolving years," returned the Phantom scornfully.

"In nothing else?"

The Phantom held its peace.

But having stood before him, silent, for a little while, it moved towards the fire; then stopped.

"Decide!" it said, "before the opportunity is lost!"

"A moment! I call Heaven to witness," said the agitated man, "that I have never been a hater of any kind, – never morose, indifferent, or hard, to anything around me. If, living here alone, I have made too much of all that was and might have been, and too little of what is, the evil, I believe, has fallen on me, and not on others. But, if there were poison in my body, should I not, possessed of antidotes and knowledge how to use them, use them? If there be poison in my mind, and through this fearful shadow I can cast it out, shall I not cast it out?"

"Say," said the Spectre, "is it done?"

"A moment longer!" he answered hurriedly. "I would forget it if I could! Have I thought that, alone, or has it been the thought of thousands upon thousands, generation after generation? All human memory is fraught with sorrow and trouble. My memory is as the memory of other men, but other men have not this choice. Yes, I close the bargain. Yes! I WILL forget my sorrow, wrong, and trouble!"

"Say," said the Spectre, "is it done?"

"It is!"

"It is. And take this with you, man whom I here renounce! The gift that I have given, you shall give again, go where you will. Without recovering yourself the power that you have yielded up, you shall henceforth destroy its like in all whom you approach. Your wisdom has discovered that the memory of sorrow, wrong, and trouble is the lot of all mankind, and that mankind would be the happier, in its other memories, without it. Go! Be its benefactor! Freed from such remembrance, from this hour, carry involuntarily the blessing of such freedom with you. Its diffusion is inseparable and inalienable from you. Go! Be happy in the good you have won, and in the good you do!"

The Phantom, which had held its bloodless hand above him while it spoke, as if in some unholy invocation, or some ban; and which had gradually advanced its eyes so close to his, that he could see how they did not participate in the terrible smile upon its face, but were a fixed, unalterable, steady horror melted before him and was gone.

As he stood rooted to the spot, possessed by fear and wonder, and imagining he heard repeated in melancholy echoes, dying away fainter and fainter, the words, "Destroy its like in all whom you approach!" a shrill cry reached his ears. It came, not from the passages beyond the door, but from another part of the old building, and sounded like the cry of some one in the dark who had lost the way.

He looked confusedly upon his hands and limbs, as if to be assured of his identity, and then shouted in reply, loudly and wildly; for there was a strangeness and terror upon him, as if he too were lost.

The cry responding, and being nearer, he caught up the lamp, and raised a heavy curtain in the wall, by which he was accustomed to pass into and out of the theatre where he lectured, – which adjoined his room. Associated with youth and animation, and a high amphitheatre of faces which his entrance charmed to interest in a moment, it was a ghostly place when all this life was faded out of it, and stared upon him like an emblem of Death.

"Halloa!" he cried. "Halloa! This way! Come to the light!" When, as he held the curtain with one hand, and with the other raised the lamp and tried to pierce the gloom that filled the place, something rushed past him into the room like a wild-cat, and crouched down in a corner.

"What is it?" he said, hastily.

He might have asked "What is it?" even had he seen it well, as presently he did when he stood looking at it gathered up in its corner.

A bundle of tatters, held together by a hand, in size and form almost an infant's, but in its greedy, desperate little clutch, a bad old man's. A face rounded and smoothed by some half-dozen years, but pinched and twisted by the experiences of a life. Bright eyes, but not youthful. Naked feet, beautiful in their childish delicacy, – ugly in the blood and dirt that cracked upon them. A baby savage, a young monster, a child who had never been a child, a creature who might live to take the outward form of man, but who, within, would live and perish a mere beast.

Used, already, to be worried and hunted like a beast, the boy crouched down as he was looked at, and looked back again, and interposed his arm to ward off the expected blow.

"I'll bite," he said, "if you hit me!"

The time had been, and not many minutes since, when such a sight as this would have wrung the Chemist's heart. He looked upon it now, coldly; but with a heavy effort to remember something – he did not know what – he asked the boy what he did there, and whence he came.

"Where's the woman?" he replied. "I want to find the woman."

"Who?"

"The woman. Her that brought me here, and set me by the large fire. She was so long gone, that I went to look for her, and lost myself. I don't want you. I want the woman."

He made a spring, so suddenly, to get away, that the dull sound of his naked feet upon the floor was near the curtain, when Redlaw caught him by his rags.

"Come! you let me go!" muttered the boy, struggling, and clenching his teeth. "I've done nothing to you. Let me go, will you, to the woman!"

"That is not the way. There is a nearer one," said Redlaw, detaining him, in the same blank effort to remember some association that ought, of right, to bear upon this monstrous object. "What is your name?"

"Got none."

"Where do you live?

"Live! What's that?"

The boy shook his hair from his eyes to look at him for a moment, and then, twisting round his legs and wrestling with him, broke again into his repetition of "You let me go, will you? I want to find the woman."

The Chemist led him to the door. "This way," he said, looking at him still confusedly, but with repugnance and avoidance, growing out of his coldness. "I'll take you to her."

The sharp eyes in the child's head, wandering round the room, lighted on the table where the remnants of the dinner were.

"Give me some of that!" he said, covetously.

"Has she not fed you?"

"I shall be hungry again tomorrow, sha'n't I? Ain't I hungry every day?"

Finding himself released, he bounded at the table like some small animal of prey, and hugging to his breast bread and meat, and his own rags, all together, said:

"There! Now take me to the woman!"

As the Chemist, with a new-born dislike to touch him, sternly motioned him to follow, and was going out of the door, he trembled and stopped.

"The gift that I have given, you shall give again, go where you will!"

The Phantom's words were blowing in the wind, and the wind blew chill upon him.

"I'll not go there, tonight," he murmured faintly. "I'll go nowhere tonight. Boy! straight down this long-arched passage, and past the great dark door into the yard, – you see the fire shining on the window there."

"The woman's fire?" inquired the boy.

He nodded, and the naked feet had sprung away. He came back with his lamp, locked his door hastily, and sat down in his chair, covering his face like one who was frightened at himself.

For now he was, indeed, alone. Alone, alone.

Chapter II
The Gift Diffused

A small man sat in a small parlour, partitioned off from a small shop by a small screen, pasted all over with small scraps of newspapers. In company with the small man, was almost any amount of small children you may please to name – at least it seemed so; they made, in that very limited sphere of action, such an imposing effect, in point of numbers.

Of these small fry, two had, by some strong machinery, been got into bed in a corner, where they might have reposed snugly enough in the sleep of innocence, but for a constitutional propensity to keep awake, and also to scuffle in and out of bed. The immediate occasion of these predatory dashes at the waking world, was the construction of an oyster-shell wall in a corner, by two other youths of tender age; on which fortification the two in bed made harassing descents (like those accursed Picts and Scots who beleaguer the early historical studies of most young Britons), and then withdrew to their own territory.

In addition to the stir attendant on these inroads, and the retorts of the invaded, who pursued hotly, and made lunges at the bed-clothes under which the marauders took refuge, another little boy, in another little bed, contributed his mite of confusion to the family stock, by casting his boots upon the waters; in other words, by launching these and several small objects, inoffensive in themselves, though of a hard substance considered as missiles, at the disturbers of his repose, – who were not slow to return these compliments.

Besides which, another little boy – the biggest there, but still little – was tottering to and fro, bent on one side, and considerably affected in his knees by the weight of a large baby, which he was supposed by a fiction that obtains sometimes in sanguine families, to be hushing to sleep. But oh! the inexhaustible regions of contemplation and watchfulness into which this baby's eyes were then only beginning to compose themselves to stare, over his unconscious shoulder!

It was a very Moloch of a baby, on whose insatiate altar the whole existence of this particular young brother was offered up a daily sacrifice. Its personality may be said to have consisted in its never being quiet, in any one place, for five consecutive minutes, and never going to sleep when required. "Tetterby's baby" was as well known in the neighbourhood as the postman or the pot-boy. It roved from door-step to door-step, in the arms of little Johnny Tetterby, and lagged heavily at the rear of troops of juveniles who followed the Tumblers or the Monkey, and came up, all on one side, a little too late for everything that was attractive, from Monday morning until Saturday night. Wherever childhood congregated to play, there was little Moloch making Johnny fag and toil. Wherever Johnny desired to stay, little Moloch became fractious, and would not remain. Whenever Johnny wanted to go out, Moloch was asleep, and must be watched. Whenever Johnny wanted to stay at home, Moloch was awake, and must be taken out. Yet Johnny was verily persuaded that it was a faultless baby, without its peer in the realm of England, and was quite content to catch meek glimpses of things in general from behind its skirts, or over its limp flapping bonnet, and to go staggering about with it like a very little porter with a very large parcel, which was not directed to anybody, and could never be delivered anywhere.

The small man who sat in the small parlour, making fruitless attempts to read his newspaper peaceably in the midst of this disturbance, was the father of the family, and the chief of the firm described in the inscription over the little shop front, by the name and title of A. Tetterby and Co., Newsmen. Indeed, strictly speaking, he was the only personage answering to that designation, as Co. was a mere poetical abstraction, altogether baseless and impersonal.

Tetterby's was the corner shop in Jerusalem Buildings. There was a good show of literature in the window, chiefly consisting of picture-newspapers out of date, and serial pirates, and footpads. Walking-sticks, likewise, and marbles, were included in the stock in trade. It had once extended into the light confectionery line; but it would seem that those elegancies of life were not in demand about Jerusalem Buildings, for nothing connected with that branch of commerce remained in the window, except a sort of small glass lantern containing a languishing mass of bull's-eyes, which had melted in the summer and congealed in the winter until all hope of ever getting them out, or of eating them without eating the lantern too, was gone for ever. Tetterby's had tried its hand at several things. It had once made a feeble little dart at the toy business; for, in another lantern, there was a heap of minute wax dolls, all sticking together upside down, in the direst confusion, with their feet on one another's heads, and a precipitate of broken arms and legs at the bottom. It had made a move in the millinery direction, which a few dry, wiry bonnet-shapes remained in a corner of the window to attest. It had fancied that a living might lie hidden in the tobacco trade, and had stuck up a representation of a native of each of the three integral portions of the British Empire, in the act of consuming that fragrant weed; with a poetic legend attached, importing that united in one cause they sat and joked, one chewed tobacco, one took snuff, one smoked: but nothing seemed to have come of it – except flies. Time had been when it had put a forlorn trust in imitative jewellery, for in one pane of glass there was a card of cheap seals, and another of pencil-cases, and a mysterious black amulet of inscrutable intention, labelled ninepence. But, to that hour, Jerusalem Buildings had bought none of them. In short, Tetterby's had tried so hard to get a livelihood out of Jerusalem Buildings in one way or other, and appeared to have done so indifferently in all, that the best position in the firm was too evidently Co.'s; Co., as a bodiless creation, being untroubled with the vulgar inconveniences of hunger and thirst, being chargeable neither to the poor's-rates nor the assessed taxes, and having no young family to provide for.

Tetterby himself, however, in his little parlour, as already mentioned, having the presence of a young family impressed upon his mind in a manner too clamorous to be disregarded, or to comport with the quiet perusal of a newspaper, laid down his paper, wheeled, in his distraction, a few times round the parlour, like an undecided carrier-pigeon, made an ineffectual rush at one or two flying little figures in bed-gowns that skimmed past him, and then, bearing suddenly down upon the only unoffending member of the family, boxed the ears of little Moloch's nurse.

"You bad boy!" said Mr. Tetterby, "haven't you any feeling for your poor father after the fatigues and anxieties of a hard winter's day, since five o'clock in the morning, but must you wither his rest, and corrode his latest intelligence, with *your* wicious tricks? Isn't it enough, sir, that your brother 'Dolphus is toiling and moiling in the fog and cold, and you rolling in the lap of luxury with a – with a baby, and everything you can wish for," said Mr. Tetterby, heaping this up as a great climax of blessings, "but must you make a wilderness of home, and maniacs of your parents? Must you, Johnny? Hey?" At each interrogation, Mr. Tetterby made a feint of boxing his ears again, but thought better of it, and held his hand.

"Oh, father!" whimpered Johnny, "when I wasn't doing anything, I'm sure, but taking such care of Sally, and getting her to sleep. Oh, father!"

"I wish my little woman would come home!" said Mr. Tetterby, relenting and repenting, "I only wish my little woman would come home! I ain't fit to deal with 'em. They make my head go round, and get the better of me. Oh, Johnny! Isn't it enough that your dear mother has provided you with that sweet sister?" indicating Moloch; "isn't it enough that you were seven boys before without a ray of gal, and that your dear mother went through what she *did* go through, on purpose that you might all of you have a little sister, but must you so behave yourself as to make my head swim?"

Softening more and more, as his own tender feelings and those of his injured son were worked on, Mr. Tetterby concluded by embracing him, and immediately breaking away to catch one of the real delinquents. A reasonably good start occurring, he succeeded, after a short but smart run, and some rather severe cross-country work under and over the bedsteads, and in and out among the intricacies of the chairs, in capturing this infant, whom he condignly punished, and bore to bed. This example had a powerful, and apparently, mesmeric influence on him of the boots, who instantly fell into a deep sleep, though he had been, but a moment before, broad awake, and in the highest possible feather. Nor was it lost upon the two young architects, who retired to bed, in an adjoining closet, with great privacy and speed. The comrade of the Intercepted One also shrinking into his nest with similar discretion, Mr. Tetterby, when he paused for breath, found himself unexpectedly in a scene of peace.

"My little woman herself," said Mr. Tetterby, wiping his flushed face, "could hardly have done it better! I only wish my little woman had had it to do, I do indeed!"

Mr. Tetterby sought upon his screen for a passage appropriate to be impressed upon his children's minds on the occasion, and read the following.

"'It is an undoubted fact that all remarkable men have had remarkable mothers, and have respected them in after life as their best friends.' Think of your own remarkable mother, my boys," said Mr. Tetterby, "and know her value while she is still among you!"

He sat down again in his chair by the fire, and composed himself, cross-legged, over his newspaper.

"Let anybody, I don't care who it is, get out of bed again," said Tetterby, as a general proclamation, delivered in a very soft-hearted manner, "and astonishment will be the portion of that respected contemporary!" – which expression Mr. Tetterby selected from his screen. "Johnny, my child, take care of your only sister, Sally; for she's the brightest gem that ever sparkled on your early brow."

Johnny sat down on a little stool, and devotedly crushed himself beneath the weight of Moloch.

"Ah, what a gift that baby is to you, Johnny!" said his father, "and how thankful you ought to be! 'It is not generally known, Johnny,'" he was now referring to the screen again, "'but it is a fact ascertained, by accurate calculations, that the following immense percentage of babies never attain to two years old; that is to say—'"

"Oh, don't, father, please!" cried Johnny. "I can't bear it, when I think of Sally."

Mr. Tetterby desisting, Johnny, with a profound sense of his trust, wiped his eyes, and hushed his sister.

"Your brother 'Dolphus," said his father, poking the fire, "is late tonight, Johnny, and will come home like a lump of ice. What's got your precious mother?"

"Here's mother, and 'Dolphus too, father!" exclaimed Johnny, "I think."

"You're right!" returned his father, listening. "Yes, that's the footstep of my little woman."

The process of induction, by which Mr. Tetterby had come to the conclusion that his wife was a little woman, was his own secret. She would have made two editions of himself, very easily. Considered as an individual, she was rather remarkable for being robust and portly; but considered with reference to her husband, her dimensions became magnificent. Nor did they assume a less imposing proportion, when studied with reference to the size of her seven sons, who were but diminutive. In the case of Sally, however, Mrs. Tetterby had asserted herself, at last; as nobody knew better than the victim Johnny, who weighed and measured that exacting idol every hour in the day.

Mrs. Tetterby, who had been marketing, and carried a basket, threw back her bonnet and shawl, and sitting down, fatigued, commanded Johnny to bring his sweet charge to her straightway, for a kiss. Johnny having complied, and gone back to his stool, and again crushed himself, Master Adolphus Tetterby, who had by this time unwound his torso out of a prismatic comforter, apparently interminable, requested the same favour. Johnny having again complied, and again gone back to his stool, and again crushed himself, Mr. Tetterby, struck by a sudden thought, preferred the same claim on his own parental part. The satisfaction of this third desire completely exhausted the sacrifice, who had hardly breath enough left to get back to his stool, crush himself again, and pant at his relations.

"Whatever you do, Johnny," said Mrs. Tetterby, shaking her head, "take care of her, or never look your mother in the face again."

"Nor your brother," said Adolphus.

"Nor your father, Johnny," added Mr. Tetterby.

Johnny, much affected by this conditional renunciation of him, looked down at Moloch's eyes to see that they were all right, so far, and skilfully patted her back (which was uppermost), and rocked her with his foot.

"Are you wet, 'Dolphus, my boy?" said his father. "Come and take my chair, and dry yourself."

"No, father, thank'ee," said Adolphus, smoothing himself down with his hands. "I an't very wet, I don't think. Does my face shine much, father?"

"Well, it *does* look waxy, my boy," returned Mr. Tetterby.

"It's the weather, father," said Adolphus, polishing his cheeks on the worn sleeve of his jacket. "What with rain, and sleet, and wind, and snow, and fog, my face gets quite brought out into a rash sometimes. And shines, it does – oh, don't it, though!"

Master Adolphus was also in the newspaper line of life, being employed, by a more thriving firm than his father and Co., to vend newspapers at a railway station, where his chubby little person, like a shabbily-disguised Cupid, and his shrill little voice (he was not much more than ten years old), were as well known as the hoarse panting of the locomotives, running in and out. His juvenility might have been at some loss for a harmless outlet, in this early application to traffic, but for a fortunate discovery he made of a means of entertaining himself, and of dividing the long day into stages of interest, without neglecting business. This ingenious invention, remarkable, like many great discoveries, for its simplicity, consisted in varying the first vowel in the word "paper," and substituting, in its stead, at different periods of the day, all the other vowels in grammatical succession. Thus, before daylight in the winter-time, he went to and fro, in his little oilskin cap and cape, and his big comforter, piercing the heavy air with his cry of "Morn-ing Pa-per!" which, about an hour before noon, changed to "Morn-ing Pepper!" which, at about two, changed to "Morn-ing Pip-per!" which in a couple of hours changed to "Morn-ing Pop-per!" and so declined with the sun into "Eve-ning Pup-per!" to the great relief and comfort of this young gentleman's spirits.

Mrs. Tetterby, his lady-mother, who had been sitting with her bonnet and shawl thrown back, as aforesaid, thoughtfully turning her wedding-ring round and round upon her finger, now rose, and divesting herself of her out-of-door attire, began to lay the cloth for supper.

"Ah, dear me, dear me, dear me!" said Mrs. Tetterby. "That's the way the world goes!"

"Which is the way the world goes, my dear?" asked Mr. Tetterby, looking round.

"Oh, nothing," said Mrs. Tetterby.

Mr. Tetterby elevated his eyebrows, folded his newspaper afresh, and carried his eyes up it, and down it, and across it, but was wandering in his attention, and not reading it.

Mrs. Tetterby, at the same time, laid the cloth, but rather as if she were punishing the table than preparing the family supper; hitting it unnecessarily hard with the knives and forks, slapping it with the plates, dinting it with the salt-cellar, and coming heavily down upon it with the loaf.

"Ah, dear me, dear me, dear me!" said Mrs. Tetterby. "That's the way the world goes!"

"My duck," returned her husband, looking round again, "you said that before. Which is the way the world goes?"

"Oh, nothing!" said Mrs. Tetterby.

"Sophia!" remonstrated her husband, "you said *that* before, too."

"Well, I'll say it again if you like," returned Mrs. Tetterby. "Oh nothing – there! And again if you like, oh nothing – there! And again if you like, oh nothing – now then!"

Mr. Tetterby brought his eye to bear upon the partner of his bosom, and said, in mild astonishment:

"My little woman, what has put you out?"

"I'm sure *I* don't know," she retorted. "Don't ask me. Who said I was put out at all? *I* never did."

Mr. Tetterby gave up the perusal of his newspaper as a bad job, and, taking a slow walk across the room, with his hands behind him, and his shoulders raised – his gait according perfectly with the resignation of his manner – addressed himself to his two eldest offspring.

"Your supper will be ready in a minute, 'Dolphus," said Mr. Tetterby. "Your mother has been out in the wet, to the cook's shop, to buy it. It was very good of your mother so to do. *You* shall get some supper too, very soon, Johnny. Your mother's pleased with you, my man, for being so attentive to your precious sister."

Mrs. Tetterby, without any remark, but with a decided subsidence of her animosity towards the table, finished her preparations, and took, from her ample basket, a substantial slab of hot pease pudding wrapped in paper, and a basin covered with a saucer, which, on being uncovered, sent forth an odour so agreeable, that the three pair of eyes in the two beds opened wide and fixed themselves upon the banquet. Mr. Tetterby, without regarding this tacit invitation to be seated, stood repeating slowly, "Yes, yes, your supper will be ready in a minute, 'Dolphus – your mother went out in the wet, to the cook's shop, to buy it. It was very good of your mother so to do" – until Mrs. Tetterby, who had been exhibiting sundry tokens of contrition behind him, caught him round the neck, and wept.

"Oh, Dolphus!" said Mrs. Tetterby, "how could I go and behave so?"

This reconciliation affected Adolphus the younger and Johnny to that degree, that they both, as with one accord, raised a dismal cry, which had the effect of immediately shutting up the round eyes in the beds, and utterly routing the two remaining little Tetterbys, just then stealing in from the adjoining closet to see what was going on in the eating way.

"I am sure, 'Dolphus," sobbed Mrs. Tetterby, "coming home, I had no more idea than a child unborn—"

Mr. Tetterby seemed to dislike this figure of speech, and observed, "Say than the baby, my dear."

"—Had no more idea than the baby," said Mrs. Tetterby. – "Johnny, don't look at me, but look at her, or she'll fall out of your lap and be killed, and then you'll die in agonies of a broken heart, and serve you right. – No more idea I hadn't than that darling, of being cross when I came home; but somehow, 'Dolphus—" Mrs. Tetterby paused, and again turned her wedding-ring round and round upon her finger.

"I see!" said Mr. Tetterby. "I understand! My little woman was put out. Hard times, and hard weather, and hard work, make it trying now and then. I see, bless your soul! No wonder! Dolf, my man," continued Mr. Tetterby, exploring the basin with a fork, "here's your mother been and bought, at the cook's shop, besides pease pudding, a whole knuckle of a lovely roast leg of pork, with lots of crackling left upon it, and with seasoning gravy and mustard quite unlimited. Hand in your plate, my boy, and begin while it's simmering."

Master Adolphus, needing no second summons, received his portion with eyes rendered moist by appetite, and withdrawing to his particular stool, fell upon his supper tooth and nail. Johnny was not forgotten, but received his rations on bread, lest he should, in a flush of gravy, trickle any on the baby. He was required, for similar reasons, to keep his pudding, when not on active service, in his pocket.

There might have been more pork on the knucklebone, – which knucklebone the carver at the cook's shop had assuredly not forgotten in carving for previous customers – but there was no stint of seasoning, and that is an accessory dreamily suggesting pork, and pleasantly cheating the sense of taste. The pease pudding, too, the gravy and mustard, like the Eastern rose in respect of the nightingale, if they were not absolutely pork, had lived near it; so, upon the whole, there was the flavour of a middle-sized pig. It was irresistible to the Tetterbys in bed, who, though professing to slumber peacefully, crawled out when unseen by their parents, and silently appealed to their brothers for any gastronomic token of fraternal affection. They, not hard of heart, presenting scraps in return, it resulted that a party of light skirmishers in nightgowns were careering about the parlour all through supper, which harassed Mr. Tetterby exceedingly, and once or twice imposed upon him the necessity of a charge, before which these guerilla troops retired in all directions and in great confusion.

Mrs. Tetterby did not enjoy her supper. There seemed to be something on Mrs. Tetterby's mind. At one time she laughed without reason, and at another time she cried without reason, and at last she laughed and cried together in a manner so very unreasonable that her husband was confounded.

"My little woman," said Mr. Tetterby, "if the world goes that way, it appears to go the wrong way, and to choke you."

"Give me a drop of water," said Mrs. Tetterby, struggling with herself, "and don't speak to me for the present, or take any notice of me. Don't do it!"

Mr. Tetterby having administered the water, turned suddenly on the unlucky Johnny (who was full of sympathy), and demanded why he was wallowing there, in gluttony and idleness, instead of coming forward with the baby, that the sight of her might revive his mother. Johnny immediately approached, borne down by its weight; but Mrs. Tetterby holding out her hand to signify that she was not in a condition to bear that trying appeal to her feelings, he was interdicted from advancing another inch, on pain of perpetual hatred from all his dearest connections; and accordingly retired to his stool again, and crushed himself as before.

After a pause, Mrs. Tetterby said she was better now, and began to laugh.

"My little woman," said her husband, dubiously, "are you quite sure you're better? Or are you, Sophia, about to break out in a fresh direction?"

"No, 'Dolphus, no," replied his wife. "I'm quite myself." With that, settling her hair, and pressing the palms of her hands upon her eyes, she laughed again.

"What a wicked fool I was, to think so for a moment!" said Mrs. Tetterby. "Come nearer, 'Dolphus, and let me ease my mind, and tell you what I mean. Let me tell you all about it."

Mr. Tetterby bringing his chair closer, Mrs. Tetterby laughed again, gave him a hug, and wiped her eyes.

"You know, Dolphus, my dear," said Mrs. Tetterby, "that when I was single, I might have given myself away in several directions. At one time, four after me at once; two of them were sons of Mars."

"We're all sons of Ma's, my dear," said Mr. Tetterby, "jointly with Pa's."

"I don't mean that," replied his wife, "I mean soldiers – serjeants."

"Oh!" said Mr. Tetterby.

"Well, 'Dolphus, I'm sure I never think of such things now, to regret them; and I'm sure I've got as good a husband, and would do as much to prove that I was fond of him, as—"

"As any little woman in the world," said Mr. Tetterby. "Very good. *Very* good."

If Mr. Tetterby had been ten feet high, he could not have expressed a gentler consideration for Mrs. Tetterby's fairy-like stature; and if Mrs. Tetterby had been two feet high, she could not have felt it more appropriately her due.

"But you see, 'Dolphus," said Mrs. Tetterby, "this being Christmas-time, when all people who can, make holiday, and when all people who have got money, like to spend some, I did, somehow, get a little out of sorts when I was in the streets just now. There were so many things to be sold – such delicious things to eat, such fine things to look at, such delightful things to have – and there was so much calculating and calculating necessary, before I durst lay out a sixpence for the commonest thing; and the basket was so large, and wanted so much in it; and my stock of money was so small, and would go such a little way; – you hate me, don't you, 'Dolphus?"

"Not quite," said Mr. Tetterby, "as yet."

"Well! I'll tell you the whole truth," pursued his wife, penitently, "and then perhaps you will. I felt all this, so much, when I was trudging about in the cold, and when I saw a lot of other calculating faces and large baskets trudging about, too, that I began to think whether I mightn't have done better, and been happier, if—I—hadn't—" the wedding-ring went round again, and Mrs. Tetterby shook her downcast head as she turned it.

"I see," said her husband quietly; "if you hadn't married at all, or if you had married somebody else?"

"Yes," sobbed Mrs. Tetterby. "That's really what I thought. Do you hate me now, 'Dolphus?"

"Why no," said Mr. Tetterby. "I don't find that I do, as yet."

Mrs. Tetterby gave him a thankful kiss, and went on.

"I begin to hope you won't, now, 'Dolphus, though I'm afraid I haven't told you the worst. I can't think what came over me. I don't know whether I was ill, or mad, or what I was, but I couldn't call up anything that seemed to bind us to each other, or to reconcile me to my fortune. All the pleasures and enjoyments we had ever had – they seemed so poor and insignificant, I hated them. I could have trodden on them. And I could think of nothing else, except our being poor, and the number of mouths there were at home."

"Well, well, my dear," said Mr. Tetterby, shaking her hand encouragingly, "that's truth, after all. We are poor, and there are a number of mouths at home here."

"Ah! but, Dolf, Dolf!" cried his wife, laying her hands upon his neck, "my good, kind, patient fellow, when I had been at home a very little while – how different! Oh, Dolf, dear, how different it was! I felt as if there was a rush of recollection on me, all at once, that softened my hard heart, and filled it up till it was bursting. All our struggles for a livelihood, all our cares and wants since we have been married, all the times of sickness, all the hours of watching, we have ever had, by one another, or by the children, seemed to speak to me, and say that they had made us one, and that I never might have been, or could have been, or would have been, any other than the wife and mother I am. Then, the cheap enjoyments that I could have trodden on so cruelly, got to be so precious to me – Oh so priceless, and dear! – that I couldn't bear to think how much I had wronged them; and I said, and say again a hundred times, how could I ever behave so, 'Dolphus, how could I ever have the heart to do it!"

The good woman, quite carried away by her honest tenderness and remorse, was weeping with all her heart, when she started up with a scream, and ran behind her husband. Her cry was so terrified, that the children started from their sleep and from their beds, and clung about her. Nor did her gaze belie her voice, as she pointed to a pale man in a black cloak who had come into the room.

"Look at that man! Look there! What does he want?"

"My dear," returned her husband, "I'll ask him if you'll let me go. What's the matter! How you shake!"

"I saw him in the street, when I was out just now. He looked at me, and stood near me. I am afraid of him."

"Afraid of him! Why?"

"I don't know why—I—stop! husband!" for he was going towards the stranger.

She had one hand pressed upon her forehead, and one upon her breast; and there was a peculiar fluttering all over her, and a hurried unsteady motion of her eyes, as if she had lost something.

"Are you ill, my dear?"

"What is it that is going from me again?" she muttered, in a low voice. "What *is* this that is going away?"

Then she abruptly answered: "Ill? No, I am quite well," and stood looking vacantly at the floor.

Her husband, who had not been altogether free from the infection of her fear at first, and whom the present strangeness of her manner did not tend to reassure, addressed himself to the pale visitor in the black cloak, who stood still, and whose eyes were bent upon the ground.

"What may be your pleasure, sir," he asked, "with us?"

"I fear that my coming in unperceived," returned the visitor, "has alarmed you; but you were talking and did not hear me."

"My little woman says – perhaps you heard her say it," returned Mr. Tetterby, "that it's not the first time you have alarmed her tonight."

"I am sorry for it. I remember to have observed her, for a few moments only, in the street. I had no intention of frightening her."

As he raised his eyes in speaking, she raised hers. It was extraordinary to see what dread she had of him, and with what dread he observed it – and yet how narrowly and closely.

"My name," he said, "is Redlaw. I come from the old college hard by. A young gentleman who is a student there, lodges in your house, does he not?"

"Mr. Denham?" said Tetterby.

"Yes."

It was a natural action, and so slight as to be hardly noticeable; but the little man, before speaking again, passed his hand across his forehead, and looked quickly round the room, as though he were sensible of some change in its atmosphere. The Chemist, instantly transferring to him the look of dread he had directed towards the wife, stepped back, and his face turned paler.

"The gentleman's room," said Tetterby, "is upstairs, sir. There's a more convenient private entrance; but as you have come in here, it will save your going out into the cold, if you'll take this little staircase," showing one communicating directly with the parlour, "and go up to him that way, if you wish to see him."

"Yes, I wish to see him," said the Chemist. "Can you spare a light?"

The watchfulness of his haggard look, and the inexplicable distrust that darkened it, seemed to trouble Mr. Tetterby. He paused; and looking fixedly at him in return, stood for a minute or so, like a man stupefied, or fascinated.

At length he said, "I'll light you, sir, if you'll follow me."

"No," replied the Chemist, "I don't wish to be attended, or announced to him. He does not expect me. I would rather go alone. Please to give me the light, if you can spare it, and I'll find the way."

In the quickness of his expression of this desire, and in taking the candle from the newsman, he touched him on the breast. Withdrawing his hand hastily, almost as though he had wounded him by accident (for he did not know in what part of himself his new power resided, or how it was communicated, or how the manner of its reception varied in different persons), he turned and ascended the stair.

But when he reached the top, he stopped and looked down. The wife was standing in the same place, twisting her ring round and round upon her finger. The husband, with his head bent forward on his breast, was musing heavily and sullenly. The children, still clustering about the mother, gazed timidly after the visitor, and nestled together when they saw him looking down.

"Come!" said the father, roughly. "There's enough of this. Get to bed here!"

"The place is inconvenient and small enough," the mother added, "without you. Get to bed!"

The whole brood, scared and sad, crept away; little Johnny and the baby lagging last. The mother, glancing contemptuously round the sordid room, and tossing from her the fragments of their meal, stopped on the threshold of her task of clearing the table, and sat down, pondering idly and dejectedly. The father betook himself to the chimney-corner, and impatiently raking the small fire together, bent over it as if he would monopolise it all. They did not interchange a word.

The Chemist, paler than before, stole upward like a thief; looking back upon the change below, and dreading equally to go on or return.

"What have I done!" he said, confusedly. "What am I going to do!"

"To be the benefactor of mankind," he thought he heard a voice reply.

He looked round, but there was nothing there; and a passage now shutting out the little parlour from his view, he went on, directing his eyes before him at the way he went.

"It is only since last night," he muttered gloomily, "that I have remained shut up, and yet all things are strange to me. I am strange to myself. I am here, as in a dream. What interest have I in this place, or in any place that I can bring to my remembrance? My mind is going blind!"

There was a door before him, and he knocked at it. Being invited, by a voice within, to enter, he complied.

"Is that my kind nurse?" said the voice. "But I need not ask her. There is no one else to come here."

It spoke cheerfully, though in a languid tone, and attracted his attention to a young man lying on a couch, drawn before the chimney-piece, with the back towards the door. A meagre scanty stove, pinched and hollowed like a sick man's cheeks, and bricked into the centre of a hearth that it could scarcely warm, contained the fire, to which his face was turned. Being so near the windy house-top, it wasted quickly, and with a busy sound, and the burning ashes dropped down fast.

"They chink when they shoot out here," said the student, smiling, "so, according to the gossips, they are not coffins, but purses. I shall be well and rich yet, some day, if it please God, and shall live perhaps to love a daughter Milly, in remembrance of the kindest nature and the gentlest heart in the world."

He put up his hand as if expecting her to take it, but, being weakened, he lay still, with his face resting on his other hand, and did not turn round.

The Chemist glanced about the room; – at the student's books and papers, piled upon a table in a corner, where they, and his extinguished reading-lamp, now prohibited and put away, told of the attentive hours that had gone before this illness, and perhaps caused it; – at such signs of his old health and freedom, as the out-of-door attire that hung idle on the wall;—at those remembrances of other and less solitary scenes, the little miniatures upon the chimney-piece, and the drawing of home; – at that token of his emulation, perhaps, in some sort, of his personal attachment too, the framed engraving of himself, the looker-on. The time had been, only yesterday, when not one of these objects, in its remotest association of interest with the living figure before him, would have been lost on Redlaw. Now, they were but objects; or, if any gleam of such connexion shot upon him, it perplexed, and not enlightened him, as he stood looking round with a dull wonder.

The student, recalling the thin hand which had remained so long untouched, raised himself on the couch, and turned his head.

"Mr. Redlaw!" he exclaimed, and started up.

Redlaw put out his arm.

"Don't come nearer to me. I will sit here. Remain you, where you are!"

He sat down on a chair near the door, and having glanced at the young man standing leaning with his hand upon the couch, spoke with his eyes averted towards the ground.

"I heard, by an accident, by what accident is no matter, that one of my class was ill and solitary. I received no other description of him, than that he lived in this street. Beginning my inquiries at the first house in it, I have found him."

"I have been ill, sir," returned the student, not merely with a modest hesitation, but with a kind of awe of him, "but am greatly better. An attack of fever – of the brain, I believe—has weakened me, but I am much better. I cannot say I have been solitary, in my illness, or I should forget the ministering hand that has been near me."

"You are speaking of the keeper's wife," said Redlaw.

"Yes." The student bent his head, as if he rendered her some silent homage.

The Chemist, in whom there was a cold, monotonous apathy, which rendered him more like a marble image on the tomb of the man who had started from his dinner yesterday at the first mention of this student's case, than the breathing man himself, glanced again at the student leaning with his hand upon the couch, and looked upon the ground, and in the air, as if for light for his blinded mind.

"I remembered your name," he said, "when it was mentioned to me down stairs, just now; and I recollect your face. We have held but very little personal communication together?"

"Very little."

"You have retired and withdrawn from me, more than any of the rest, I think?"

The student signified assent.

"And why?" said the Chemist; not with the least expression of interest, but with a moody, wayward kind of curiosity. "Why? How comes it that you have sought to keep especially from me, the knowledge of your remaining here, at this season, when all the rest have dispersed, and of your being ill? I want to know why this is?"

The young man, who had heard him with increasing agitation, raised his downcast eyes to his face, and clasping his hands together, cried with sudden earnestness and with trembling lips:

"Mr. Redlaw! You have discovered me. You know my secret!"

"Secret?" said the Chemist, harshly. "I know?"

"Yes! Your manner, so different from the interest and sympathy which endear you to so many hearts, your altered voice, the constraint there is in everything you say, and in your looks," replied the student, "warn me that you know me. That you would conceal it, even now, is but a proof to me (God knows I need none!) of your natural kindness and of the bar there is between us."

A vacant and contemptuous laugh, was all his answer.

"But, Mr. Redlaw," said the student, "as a just man, and a good man, think how innocent I am, except in name and descent, of participation in any wrong inflicted on you or in any sorrow you have borne."

"Sorrow!" said Redlaw, laughing. "Wrong! What are those to me?"

"For Heaven's sake," entreated the shrinking student, "do not let the mere interchange of a few words with me change you like this, sir! Let me pass again from your knowledge and notice. Let me occupy my old reserved and distant place among those whom you instruct. Know me only by the name I have assumed, and not by that of Longford—"

"Longford!" exclaimed the other.

He clasped his head with both his hands, and for a moment turned upon the young man his own intelligent and thoughtful face. But the light passed from it, like the sun-beam of an instant, and it clouded as before.

"The name my mother bears, sir," faltered the young man, "the name she took, when she might, perhaps, have taken one more honoured. Mr. Redlaw," hesitating, "I believe I know that history. Where my information halts, my guesses at what is wanting may supply something not remote from the truth. I am the child of a marriage that has not proved itself a well-assorted or a happy one. From infancy, I have heard you spoken of with honour and respect – with something that was almost reverence. I have heard of such devotion, of such fortitude and tenderness, of such rising up against the obstacles which press men down, that my fancy, since I learnt my little lesson from my mother, has shed a lustre on your name. At last, a poor student myself, from whom could I learn but you?"

Redlaw, unmoved, unchanged, and looking at him with a staring frown, answered by no word or sign.

"I cannot say," pursued the other, "I should try in vain to say, how much it has impressed me, and affected me, to find the gracious traces of the past, in that certain power of winning gratitude and confidence which is associated among us students (among the humblest of us, most) with Mr. Redlaw's generous name. Our ages and positions are so different, sir, and I am so accustomed to regard you from a distance, that I wonder at my own presumption when I touch, however lightly, on that theme. But to one who – I may say, who felt no common interest in my mother once – it may be something to hear, now that all is past, with what indescribable feelings of affection I have, in my obscurity, regarded him; with what pain and reluctance I have kept aloof from his encouragement, when a word of it would have made me rich; yet how I have felt it fit that I should hold my course, content to know him, and to be unknown. Mr. Redlaw," said the student, faintly, "what I would have said, I have said ill, for my strength is strange to me as yet; but for anything unworthy in this fraud of mine, forgive me, and for all the rest forget me!"

The staring frown remained on Redlaw's face, and yielded to no other expression until the student, with these words, advanced towards him, as if to touch his hand, when he drew back and cried to him:

"Don't come nearer to me!"

The young man stopped, shocked by the eagerness of his recoil, and by the sternness of his repulsion; and he passed his hand, thoughtfully, across his forehead.

"The past is past," said the Chemist. "It dies like the brutes. Who talks to me of its traces in my life? He raves or lies! What have I to do with your distempered dreams? If you want money, here it is. I came to offer it; and that is all I came for. There can be nothing else that brings me here," he muttered, holding his head again, with both his hands. "There *can* be nothing else, and yet—"

He had tossed his purse upon the table. As he fell into this dim cogitation with himself, the student took it up, and held it out to him.

"Take it back, sir," he said proudly, though not angrily. "I wish you could take from me, with it, the remembrance of your words and offer."

"You do?" he retorted, with a wild light in his eyes. "You do?"

"I do!"

The Chemist went close to him, for the first time, and took the purse, and turned him by the arm, and looked him in the face.

"There is sorrow and trouble in sickness, is there not?" he demanded, with a laugh.

The wondering student answered, "Yes."

"In its unrest, in its anxiety, in its suspense, in all its train of physical and mental miseries?" said the Chemist, with a wild unearthly exultation. "All best forgotten, are they not?"

The student did not answer, but again passed his hand, confusedly, across his forehead. Redlaw still held him by the sleeve, when Milly's voice was heard outside.

"I can see very well now," she said, "thank you, Dolf. Don't cry, dear. Father and mother will be comfortable again, tomorrow, and home will be comfortable too. A gentleman with him, is there!"

Redlaw released his hold, as he listened.

"I have feared, from the first moment," he murmured to himself, "to meet her. There is a steady quality of goodness in her, that I dread to influence. I may be the murderer of what is tenderest and best within her bosom."

She was knocking at the door.

"Shall I dismiss it as an idle foreboding, or still avoid her?" he muttered, looking uneasily around.

She was knocking at the door again.

"Of all the visitors who could come here," he said, in a hoarse alarmed voice, turning to his companion, "this is the one I should desire most to avoid. Hide me!"

The student opened a frail door in the wall, communicating where the garret-roof began to slope towards the floor, with a small inner room. Redlaw passed in hastily, and shut it after him.

The student then resumed his place upon the couch, and called to her to enter.

"Dear Mr. Edmund," said Milly, looking round, "they told me there was a gentleman here."

"There is no one here but I."

"There has been someone?"

"Yes, yes, there has been someone."

She put her little basket on the table, and went up to the back of the couch, as if to take the extended hand – but it was not there. A little surprised, in her quiet way, she leaned over to look at his face, and gently touched him on the brow.

"Are you quite as well tonight? Your head is not so cool as in the afternoon."

"Tut!" said the student, petulantly, "very little ails me."

A little more surprise, but no reproach, was expressed in her face, as she withdrew to the other side of the table, and took a small packet of needlework from her basket. But she laid it down again, on second thoughts, and going noiselessly about the room, set everything exactly in its place, and in the neatest order; even to the cushions on the couch, which she touched with so light a hand, that he hardly seemed to know it, as he lay looking at the fire. When all this was done, and she had swept the hearth, she sat down, in her modest little bonnet, to her work, and was quietly busy on it directly.

"It's the new muslin curtain for the window, Mr. Edmund," said Milly, stitching away as she talked. "It will look very clean and nice, though it costs very little, and will save your eyes, too, from the light. My William says the room should not be too light just now, when you are recovering so well, or the glare might make you giddy."

He said nothing; but there was something so fretful and impatient in his change of position, that her quick fingers stopped, and she looked at him anxiously.

"The pillows are not comfortable," she said, laying down her work and rising. "I will soon put them right."

"They are very well," he answered. "Leave them alone, pray. You make so much of everything."

He raised his head to say this, and looked at her so thanklessly, that, after he had thrown himself down again, she stood timidly pausing. However, she resumed her seat, and her needle, without having directed even a murmuring look towards him, and was soon as busy as before.

"I have been thinking, Mr. Edmund, that *you* have been often thinking of late, when I have been sitting by, how true the saying is, that adversity is a good teacher. Health will be more precious to you, after this illness, than it has ever been. And years hence, when this time of year comes round, and you remember the days when you lay here sick, alone, that the knowledge of your illness might not afflict those who are dearest to you, your home will be doubly dear and doubly blest. Now, isn't that a good, true thing?"

She was too intent upon her work, and too earnest in what she said, and too composed and quiet altogether, to be on the watch for any look he might direct towards her in reply; so the shaft of his ungrateful glance fell harmless, and did not wound her.

"Ah!" said Milly, with her pretty head inclining thoughtfully on one side, as she looked down, following her busy fingers with her eyes. "Even on me – and I am very different from you, Mr. Edmund, for I have no learning, and don't know how to think properly – this view of such things has made a great impression, since you have been lying ill. When I have seen you so touched by the kindness and attention of the poor people downstairs, I have felt that you thought even that experience some repayment for the loss of health, and I have read in your face, as plain as if it was a book, that but for some trouble and sorrow we should never know half the good there is about us."

His getting up from the couch, interrupted her, or she was going on to say more.

"We needn't magnify the merit, Mrs. William," he rejoined slightingly. "The people downstairs will be paid in good time I dare say, for any little extra service they may have rendered me; and perhaps they anticipate no less. I am much obliged to you, too."

Her fingers stopped, and she looked at him.

"I can't be made to feel the more obliged by your exaggerating the case," he said. "I am sensible that you have been interested in me, and I say I am much obliged to you. What more would you have?"

Her work fell on her lap, as she still looked at him walking to and fro with an intolerant air, and stopping now and then.

"I say again, I am much obliged to you. Why weaken my sense of what is your due in obligation, by preferring enormous claims upon me? Trouble, sorrow, affliction, adversity! One might suppose I had been dying a score of deaths here!"

"Do you believe, Mr. Edmund," she asked, rising and going nearer to him, "that I spoke of the poor people of the house, with any reference to myself? To me?" laying her hand upon her bosom with a simple and innocent smile of astonishment.

"Oh! I think nothing about it, my good creature," he returned. "I have had an indisposition, which your solicitude – observe! I say solicitude – makes a great deal more of, than it merits; and it's over, and we can't perpetuate it."

He coldly took a book, and sat down at the table.

She watched him for a little while, until her smile was quite gone, and then, returning to where her basket was, said gently:

"Mr. Edmund, would you rather be alone?"

"There is no reason why I should detain you here," he replied.

"Except—" said Milly, hesitating, and showing her work.

"Oh! the curtain," he answered, with a supercilious laugh. "That's not worth staying for."

She made up the little packet again, and put it in her basket. Then, standing before him with such an air of patient entreaty that he could not choose but look at her, she said:

"If you should want me, I will come back willingly. When you did want me, I was quite happy to come; there was no merit in it. I think you must be afraid, that, now you are getting well, I may be troublesome to you; but I should not have been, indeed. I should have come no longer than your weakness and confinement lasted. You owe me nothing; but it is right that you should deal as justly by me as if I was a lady – even the very lady that you love; and if you suspect me of meanly making much of the little I have tried to do to comfort your sick room, you do yourself more wrong than ever you can do me. That is why I am sorry. That is why I am very sorry."

If she had been as passionate as she was quiet, as indignant as she was calm, as angry in her look as she was gentle, as loud of tone as she was low and clear, she might have left no sense of her departure in the room, compared with that which fell upon the lonely student when she went away.

He was gazing drearily upon the place where she had been, when Redlaw came out of his concealment, and came to the door.

"When sickness lays its hand on you again," he said, looking fiercely back at him, "—may it be soon! – Die here! Rot here!"

"What have you done?" returned the other, catching at his cloak. "What change have you wrought in me? What curse have you brought upon me? Give me back *myself*!"

"Give me back myself!" exclaimed Redlaw like a madman. "I am infected! I am infectious! I am charged with poison for my own mind, and the minds of all mankind. Where I felt interest, compassion, sympathy, I am turning into stone. Selfishness and ingratitude spring up in my blighting footsteps. I am only so much less base than the wretches whom I make so, that in the moment of their transformation I can hate them."

As he spoke – the young man still holding to his cloak – he cast him off, and struck him: then, wildly hurried out into the night air where the wind was blowing, the snow falling, the cloud-drift sweeping on, the moon dimly shining; and where, blowing in the wind, falling with the snow, drifting with the clouds, shining in the moonlight, and heavily looming in the darkness, were the Phantom's words, "The gift that I have given, you shall give again, go where you will!"

Whither he went, he neither knew nor cared, so that he avoided company. The change he felt within him made the busy streets a desert, and himself a desert, and the multitude around him, in their manifold endurances and ways of life, a mighty waste of sand, which the winds tossed into unintelligible heaps and made a ruinous confusion of. Those traces in his breast which the Phantom had told him would "die out soon," were not, as yet, so far upon their way to death, but that he understood enough of what he was, and what he made of others, to desire to be alone.

This put it in his mind – he suddenly bethought himself, as he was going along, of the boy who had rushed into his room. And then he recollected, that of those with whom he had communicated since the Phantom's disappearance, that boy alone had shown no sign of being changed.

Monstrous and odious as the wild thing was to him, he determined to seek it out, and prove if this were really so; and also to seek it with another intention, which came into his thoughts at the same time.

So, resolving with some difficulty where he was, he directed his steps back to the old college, and to that part of it where the general porch was, and where, alone, the pavement was worn by the tread of the students' feet.

The keeper's house stood just within the iron gates, forming a part of the chief quadrangle. There was a little cloister outside, and from that sheltered place he knew he could look in at the window of their ordinary room, and see who was within. The iron gates were shut, but his hand was familiar with the fastening, and drawing it back by thrusting in his wrist between the bars, he passed through softly, shut it again, and crept up to the window, crumbling the thin crust of snow with his feet.

The fire, to which he had directed the boy last night, shining brightly through the glass, made an illuminated place upon the ground. Instinctively avoiding this, and going round it, he looked in at the window. At first, he thought that there was no one there, and that the blaze was reddening only the old beams in the ceiling and the dark walls; but peering in more narrowly, he saw the object of his search coiled asleep before it on the floor. He passed quickly to the door, opened it, and went in.

The creature lay in such a fiery heat, that, as the Chemist stooped to rouse him, it scorched his head. So soon as he was touched, the boy, not half awake, clutching his rags together with the instinct of flight upon him, half rolled and half ran into a distant corner of the room, where, heaped upon the ground, he struck his foot out to defend himself.

"Get up!" said the Chemist. "You have not forgotten me?"

"You let me alone!" returned the boy. "This is the woman's house – not yours."

The Chemist's steady eye controlled him somewhat, or inspired him with enough submission to be raised upon his feet, and looked at.

"Who washed them, and put those bandages where they were bruised and cracked?" asked the Chemist, pointing to their altered state.

"The woman did."

"And is it she who has made you cleaner in the face, too?"

"Yes, the woman."

Redlaw asked these questions to attract his eyes towards himself, and with the same intent now held him by the chin, and threw his wild hair back, though he loathed to touch him. The boy watched his eyes keenly, as if he thought it needful to his own defence, not knowing what he might do next; and Redlaw could see well that no change came over him.

"Where are they?" he inquired.

"The woman's out."

"I know she is. Where is the old man with the white hair, and his son?"

"The woman's husband, d'ye mean?" inquired the boy.

"Ay. Where are those two?"

"Out. Something's the matter, somewhere. They were fetched out in a hurry, and told me to stop here."

"Come with me," said the Chemist, "and I'll give you money."

"Come where? and how much will you give?"

"I'll give you more shillings than you ever saw, and bring you back soon. Do you know your way to where you came from?"

"You let me go," returned the boy, suddenly twisting out of his grasp. "I'm not a going to take you there. Let me be, or I'll heave some fire at you!"

He was down before it, and ready, with his savage little hand, to pluck the burning coals out.

What the Chemist had felt, in observing the effect of his charmed influence stealing over those with whom he came in contact, was not nearly equal to the cold vague terror with which he saw this baby-monster put it at defiance. It chilled his blood to look on the immovable impenetrable thing, in the likeness of a child, with its sharp malignant face turned up to his, and its almost infant hand, ready at the bars.

"Listen, boy!" he said. "You shall take me where you please, so that you take me where the people are very miserable or very wicked. I want to do them good, and not to harm them. You shall have money, as I have told you, and I will bring you back. Get up! Come quickly!" He made a hasty step towards the door, afraid of her returning.

"Will you let me walk by myself, and never hold me, nor yet touch me?" said the boy, slowly withdrawing the hand with which he threatened, and beginning to get up.

"I will!"

"And let me go, before, behind, or anyways I like?"

"I will!"

"Give me some money first, then, and go."

The Chemist laid a few shillings, one by one, in his extended hand. To count them was beyond the boy's knowledge, but he said "one," every time, and avariciously looked at each as it was given, and at the donor. He had nowhere to put them, out of his hand, but in his mouth; and he put them there.

Redlaw then wrote with his pencil on a leaf of his pocket-book, that the boy was with him; and laying it on the table, signed to him to follow. Keeping his rags together, as usual, the boy complied, and went out with his bare head and naked feet into the winter night.

Preferring not to depart by the iron gate by which he had entered, where they were in danger of meeting her whom he so anxiously avoided, the Chemist led the way, through some of those passages among which the boy had lost himself, and by that portion of the building where he lived, to a small door of which he had the key. When they got into the street, he stopped to ask his guide – who instantly retreated from him – if he knew where they were.

The savage thing looked here and there, and at length, nodding his head, pointed in the direction he designed to take. Redlaw going on at once, he followed, something less suspiciously; shifting his money from his mouth into his hand, and back again into his mouth, and stealthily rubbing it bright upon his shreds of dress, as he went along.

Three times, in their progress, they were side by side. Three times they stopped, being side by side. Three times the Chemist glanced down at his face, and shuddered as it forced upon him one reflection.

The first occasion was when they were crossing an old churchyard, and Redlaw stopped among the graves, utterly at a loss how to connect them with any tender, softening, or consolatory thought.

The second was, when the breaking forth of the moon induced him to look up at the Heavens, where he saw her in her glory, surrounded by a host of stars he still knew by the names and histories which human science has appended to them; but where he saw nothing else he had been wont to see, felt nothing he had been wont to feel, in looking up there, on a bright night.

The third was when he stopped to listen to a plaintive strain of music, but could only hear a tune, made manifest to him by the dry mechanism of the instruments and his own ears, with no address to any mystery within him, without a whisper in it of the past, or of the future, powerless upon him as the sound of last year's running water, or the rushing of last year's wind.

At each of these three times, he saw with horror that, in spite of the vast intellectual distance between them, and their being unlike each other in all physical respects, the expression on the boy's face was the expression on his own.

They journeyed on for some time – now through such crowded places, that he often looked over his shoulder thinking he had lost his guide, but generally finding him within his shadow on his other side; now by ways so quiet, that he could have counted his short, quick, naked footsteps coming on behind – until they arrived at a ruinous collection of houses, and the boy touched him and stopped.

"In there!" he said, pointing out one house where there were scattered lights in the windows, and a dim lantern in the doorway, with "Lodgings for Travellers" painted on it.

Redlaw looked about him; from the houses to the waste piece of ground on which the houses stood, or rather did not altogether tumble down, unfenced, undrained, unlighted, and bordered by a sluggish ditch; from that, to the sloping line of arches, part of some neighbouring viaduct or bridge with which it was surrounded, and which lessened gradually towards them, until the last but one was a mere kennel for a dog, the last a plundered little heap of bricks; from that, to the child, close to him, cowering and trembling with the cold, and limping on one little foot, while he coiled the other round his leg to warm it, yet staring at all these things with that frightful likeness of expression so apparent in his face, that Redlaw started from him.

"In there!" said the boy, pointing out the house again. "I'll wait."

"Will they let me in?" asked Redlaw.

"Say you're a doctor," he answered with a nod. "There's plenty ill here."

Looking back on his way to the house-door, Redlaw saw him trail himself upon the dust and crawl within the shelter of the smallest arch, as if he were a rat. He had no pity for the thing, but he was afraid of it; and when it looked out of its den at him, he hurried to the house as a retreat.

"Sorrow, wrong, and trouble," said the Chemist, with a painful effort at some more distinct remembrance, "at least haunt this place darkly. He can do no harm, who brings forgetfulness of such things here!"

With these words, he pushed the yielding door, and went in.

There was a woman sitting on the stairs, either asleep or forlorn, whose head was bent down on her hands and knees. As it was not easy to pass without treading on her, and as she was perfectly regardless of his near approach, he stopped, and touched her on the shoulder. Looking up, she showed him quite a young face, but one whose bloom and promise were all swept away, as if the haggard winter should unnaturally kill the spring.

With little or no show of concern on his account, she moved nearer to the wall to leave him a wider passage.

"What are you?" said Redlaw, pausing, with his hand upon the broken stair-rail.

"What do you think I am?" she answered, showing him her face again.

He looked upon the ruined Temple of God, so lately made, so soon disfigured; and something, which was not compassion – for the springs in which a true compassion for such miseries has its rise, were dried up in his breast – but which was nearer to it, for the moment, than any feeling that had lately struggled into the darkening, but not yet wholly darkened, night of his mind – mingled a touch of softness with his next words.

"I am come here to give relief, if I can," he said. "Are you thinking of any wrong?"

She frowned at him, and then laughed; and then her laugh prolonged itself into a shivering sigh, as she dropped her head again, and hid her fingers in her hair.

"Are you thinking of a wrong?" he asked once more.

"I am thinking of my life," she said, with a momentary look at him.

He had a perception that she was one of many, and that he saw the type of thousands, when he saw her, drooping at his feet.

"What are your parents?" he demanded.

"I had a good home once. My father was a gardener, far away, in the country."

"Is he dead?"

"He's dead to me. All such things are dead to me. You a gentleman, and not know that!" She raised her eyes again, and laughed at him.

"Girl!" said Redlaw, sternly, "before this death, of all such things, was brought about, was there no wrong done to you? In spite of all that you can do, does no remembrance of wrong cleave to you? Are there not times upon times when it is misery to you?"

So little of what was womanly was left in her appearance, that now, when she burst into tears, he stood amazed. But he was more amazed, and much disquieted, to note that in her awakened recollection of this wrong, the first trace of her old humanity and frozen tenderness appeared to show itself.

He drew a little off, and in doing so, observed that her arms were black, her face cut, and her bosom bruised.

"What brutal hand has hurt you so?" he asked.

"My own. I did it myself!" she answered quickly.

"It is impossible."

"I'll swear I did! He didn't touch me. I did it to myself in a passion, and threw myself down here. He wasn't near me. He never laid a hand upon me!"

In the white determination of her face, confronting him with this untruth, he saw enough of the last perversion and distortion of good surviving in that miserable breast, to be stricken with remorse that he had ever come near her.

"Sorrow, wrong, and trouble!" he muttered, turning his fearful gaze away. "All that connects her with the state from which she has fallen, has those roots! In the name of God, let me go by!"

Afraid to look at her again, afraid to touch her, afraid to think of having sundered the last thread by which she held upon the mercy of Heaven, he gathered his cloak about him, and glided swiftly up the stairs.

Opposite to him, on the landing, was a door, which stood partly open, and which, as he ascended, a man with a candle in his hand, came forward from within to shut. But this man, on seeing him, drew back, with much emotion in his manner, and, as if by a sudden impulse, mentioned his name aloud.

In the surprise of such a recognition there, he stopped, endeavouring to recollect the wan and startled face. He had no time to consider it, for, to his yet greater amazement, old Philip came out of the room, and took him by the hand.

"Mr. Redlaw," said the old man, "this is like you, this is like you, sir! you have heard of it, and have come after us to render any help you can. Ah, too late, too late!"

Redlaw, with a bewildered look, submitted to be led into the room. A man lay there, on a truckle-bed, and William Swidger stood at the bedside.

"Too late!" murmured the old man, looking wistfully into the Chemist's face; and the tears stole down his cheeks.

"That's what I say, father," interposed his son in a low voice. "That's where it is, exactly. To keep as quiet as ever we can while he's a dozing, is the only thing to do. You're right, father!"

Redlaw paused at the bedside, and looked down on the figure that was stretched upon the mattress. It was that of a man, who should have been in the vigour of his life, but on whom it was not likely the sun would ever shine again. The vices of his forty or fifty years' career had so branded him, that, in comparison with their effects upon his face, the heavy hand of Time upon the old man's face who watched him had been merciful and beautifying.

"Who is this?" asked the Chemist, looking round.

"My son George, Mr. Redlaw," said the old man, wringing his hands. "My eldest son, George, who was more his mother's pride than all the rest!"

Redlaw's eyes wandered from the old man's grey head, as he laid it down upon the bed, to the person who had recognised him, and who had kept aloof, in the remotest corner of the room. He seemed to be about his own age; and although he knew no such hopeless decay and broken man as he appeared to be, there was something in the turn of his figure, as he stood with his back towards him, and now went out at the door, that made him pass his hand uneasily across his brow.

"William," he said in a gloomy whisper, "who is that man?"

"Why you see, sir," returned Mr. William, "that's what I say, myself. Why should a man ever go and gamble, and the like of that, and let himself down inch by inch till he can't let himself down any lower!"

"Has *he* done so?" asked Redlaw, glancing after him with the same uneasy action as before.

"Just exactly that, sir," returned William Swidger, "as I'm told. He knows a little about medicine, sir, it seems; and having been wayfaring towards London with my unhappy brother that you see here," Mr. William passed his coat-sleeve across his eyes, "and being lodging up stairs for the night

– what I say, you see, is that strange companions come together here sometimes – he looked in to attend upon him, and came for us at his request. What a mournful spectacle, sir! But that's where it is. It's enough to kill my father!"

Redlaw looked up, at these words, and, recalling where he was and with whom, and the spell he carried with him – which his surprise had obscured – retired a little, hurriedly, debating with himself whether to shun the house that moment, or remain.

Yielding to a certain sullen doggedness, which it seemed to be a part of his condition to struggle with, he argued for remaining.

"Was it only yesterday," he said, "when I observed the memory of this old man to be a tissue of sorrow and trouble, and shall I be afraid, tonight, to shake it? Are such remembrances as I can drive away, so precious to this dying man that I need fear for *him*? No! I'll stay here."

But he stayed in fear and trembling none the less for these words; and, shrouded in his black cloak with his face turned from them, stood away from the bedside, listening to what they said, as if he felt himself a demon in the place.

"Father!" murmured the sick man, rallying a little from stupor.

"My boy! My son George!" said old Philip.

"You spoke, just now, of my being mother's favourite, long ago. It's a dreadful thing to think now, of long ago!"

"No, no, no;" returned the old man. "Think of it. Don't say it's dreadful. It's not dreadful to me, my son."

"It cuts you to the heart, father." For the old man's tears were falling on him.

"Yes, yes," said Philip, "so it does; but it does me good. It's a heavy sorrow to think of that time, but it does me good, George. Oh, think of it too, think of it too, and your heart will be softened more and more! Where's my son William? William, my boy, your mother loved him dearly to the last, and with her latest breath said, 'Tell him I forgave him, blessed him, and prayed for him.' Those were her words to me. I have never forgotten them, and I'm eighty-seven!"

"Father!" said the man upon the bed, "I am dying, I know. I am so far gone, that I can hardly speak, even of what my mind most runs on. Is there any hope for me beyond this bed?"

"There is hope," returned the old man, "for all who are softened and penitent. There is hope for all such. Oh!" he exclaimed, clasping his hands and looking up, "I was thankful, only yesterday, that I could remember this unhappy son when he was an innocent child. But what a comfort it is, now, to think that even God himself has that remembrance of him!"

Redlaw spread his hands upon his face, and shrank, like a murderer.

"Ah!" feebly moaned the man upon the bed. "The waste since then, the waste of life since then!"

"But he was a child once," said the old man. "He played with children. Before he lay down on his bed at night, and fell into his guiltless rest, he said his prayers at his poor mother's knee. I have seen him do it, many a time; and seen her lay his head upon her breast, and kiss him. Sorrowful as it was to her and me, to think of this, when he went so wrong, and when our hopes and plans for him were all broken, this gave him still a hold upon us, that nothing else could have given. Oh, Father, so much better than the fathers upon earth! Oh, Father, so much more afflicted by the errors of Thy children! take this wanderer back! Not as he is, but as he was then, let him cry to Thee, as he has so often seemed to cry to us!"

As the old man lifted up his trembling hands, the son, for whom he made the supplication, laid his sinking head against him for support and comfort, as if he were indeed the child of whom he spoke.

When did man ever tremble, as Redlaw trembled, in the silence that ensued! He knew it must come upon them, knew that it was coming fast.

"My time is very short, my breath is shorter," said the sick man, supporting himself on one arm, and with the other groping in the air, "and I remember there is something on my mind concerning the man who was here just now, Father and William – wait! – is there really anything in black, out there?"

"Yes, yes, it is real," said his aged father.

"Is it a man?"

"What I say myself, George," interposed his brother, bending kindly over him. "It's Mr. Redlaw."

"I thought I had dreamed of him. Ask him to come here."

The Chemist, whiter than the dying man, appeared before him. Obedient to the motion of his hand, he sat upon the bed.

"It has been so ripped up, tonight, sir," said the sick man, laying his hand upon his heart, with a look in which the mute, imploring agony of his condition was concentrated, "by the sight of my poor old father, and the thought of all the trouble I have been the cause of, and all the wrong and sorrow lying at my door, that—"

Was it the extremity to which he had come, or was it the dawning of another change, that made him stop?

"—that what I *can* do right, with my mind running on so much, so fast, I'll try to do. There was another man here. Did you see him?"

Redlaw could not reply by any word; for when he saw that fatal sign he knew so well now, of the wandering hand upon the forehead, his voice died at his lips. But he made some indication of assent.

"He is penniless, hungry, and destitute. He is completely beaten down, and has no resource at all. Look after him! Lose no time! I know he has it in his mind to kill himself."

It was working. It was on his face. His face was changing, hardening, deepening in all its shades, and losing all its sorrow.

"Don't you remember? Don't you know him?" he pursued.

He shut his face out for a moment, with the hand that again wandered over his forehead, and then it lowered on Redlaw, reckless, ruffianly, and callous.

"Why, d-n you!" he said, scowling round, "what have you been doing to me here! I have lived bold, and I mean to die bold. To the Devil with you!"

And so lay down upon his bed, and put his arms up, over his head and ears, as resolute from that time to keep out all access, and to die in his indifference.

If Redlaw had been struck by lightning, it could not have struck him from the bedside with a more tremendous shock. But the old man, who had left the bed while his son was speaking to him, now returning, avoided it quickly likewise, and with abhorrence.

"Where's my boy William?" said the old man hurriedly. "William, come away from here. We'll go home."

"Home, father!" returned William. "Are you going to leave your own son?"

"Where's my own son?" replied the old man.

"Where? why, there!"

"That's no son of mine," said Philip, trembling with resentment. "No such wretch as that, has any claim on me. My children are pleasant to look at, and they wait upon me, and get my meat and drink ready, and are useful to me. I've a right to it! I'm eighty-seven!"

"You're old enough to be no older," muttered William, looking at him grudgingly, with his hands in his pockets. "I don't know what good you are, myself. We could have a deal more pleasure without you."

"*My* son, Mr. Redlaw!" said the old man. "*My* son, too! The boy talking to me of *my* son! Why, what has he ever done to give me any pleasure, I should like to know?"

"I don't know what you have ever done to give *me* any pleasure," said William, sulkily.

"Let me think," said the old man. "For how many Christmas times running, have I sat in my warm place, and never had to come out in the cold night air; and have made good cheer, without being disturbed by any such uncomfortable, wretched sight as him there? Is it twenty, William?"

"Nigher forty, it seems," he muttered. "Why, when I look at my father, sir, and come to think of it," addressing Redlaw, with an impatience and irritation that were quite new, "I'm whipped if I can see anything in him but a calendar of ever so many years of eating and drinking, and making himself comfortable, over and over again."

"I—I'm eighty-seven," said the old man, rambling on, childishly and weakly, "and I don't know as I ever was much put out by anything. I'm not going to begin now, because of what he calls my son. He's not my son. I've had a power of pleasant times. I recollect once – no I don't – no, it's broken off. It was something about a game of cricket and a friend of mine, but it's somehow broken off. I wonder who he was – I suppose I liked him? And I wonder what became of him – I suppose he died? But I don't know. And I don't care, neither; I don't care a bit."

In his drowsy chuckling, and the shaking of his head, he put his hands into his waistcoat pockets. In one of them he found a bit of holly (left there, probably last night), which he now took out, and looked at.

"Berries, eh?" said the old man. "Ah! It's a pity they're not good to eat. I recollect, when I was a little chap about as high as that, and out a walking with – let me see – who was I out a walking with? – no, I don't remember how that was. I don't remember as I ever walked with any one particular, or cared for any one, or any one for me. Berries, eh? There's good cheer when there's berries. Well; I ought to have my share of it, and to be waited on, and kept warm and comfortable; for I'm eighty-seven, and a poor old man. I'm eigh-ty-seven. Eigh-ty-seven!"

The drivelling, pitiable manner in which, as he repeated this, he nibbled at the leaves, and spat the morsels out; the cold, uninterested eye with which his youngest son (so changed) regarded him; the determined apathy with which his eldest son lay hardened in his sin; impressed themselves no more on Redlaw's observation, – for he broke his way from the spot to which his feet seemed to have been fixed, and ran out of the house.

His guide came crawling forth from his place of refuge, and was ready for him before he reached the arches.

"Back to the woman's?" he inquired.

"Back, quickly!" answered Redlaw. "Stop nowhere on the way!"

For a short distance the boy went on before; but their return was more like a flight than a walk, and it was as much as his bare feet could do, to keep pace with the Chemist's rapid strides. Shrinking from all who passed, shrouded in his cloak, and keeping it drawn closely about him, as though there were mortal contagion in any fluttering touch of his garments, he made no pause until they reached the door by which they had come out. He unlocked it with his key, went in, accompanied by the boy, and hastened through the dark passages to his own chamber.

The boy watched him as he made the door fast, and withdrew behind the table, when he looked round.

"Come!" he said. "Don't you touch me! You've not brought me here to take my money away."

Redlaw threw some more upon the ground. He flung his body on it immediately, as if to hide it from him, lest the sight of it should tempt him to reclaim it; and not until he saw him seated by his lamp, with his face hidden in his hands, began furtively to pick it up. When he had done so, he crept near the fire, and, sitting down in a great chair before it, took from his breast some broken scraps of food, and fell to munching, and to staring at the blaze, and now and then to glancing at his shillings, which he kept clenched up in a bunch, in one hand.

"And this," said Redlaw, gazing on him with increased repugnance and fear, "is the only one companion I have left on earth!"

How long it was before he was aroused from his contemplation of this creature, whom he dreaded so – whether half-an-hour, or half the night – he knew not. But the stillness of the room was broken by the boy (whom he had seen listening) starting up, and running towards the door.

"Here's the woman coming!" he exclaimed.

The Chemist stopped him on his way, at the moment when she knocked.

"Let me go to her, will you?" said the boy.

"Not now," returned the Chemist. "Stay here. Nobody must pass in or out of the room now. Who's that?"

"It's I, sir," cried Milly. "Pray, sir, let me in!"

"No! not for the world!" he said.

"Mr. Redlaw, Mr. Redlaw, pray, sir, let me in."

"What is the matter?" he said, holding the boy.

"The miserable man you saw, is worse, and nothing I can say will wake him from his terrible infatuation. William's father has turned childish in a moment, William himself is changed. The shock has been too sudden for him; I cannot understand him; he is not like himself. Oh, Mr. Redlaw, pray advise me, help me!"

"No! No! No!" he answered.

"Mr. Redlaw! Dear sir! George has been muttering, in his doze, about the man you saw there, who, he fears, will kill himself."

"Better he should do it, than come near me!"

"He says, in his wandering, that you know him; that he was your friend once, long ago; that he is the ruined father of a student here – my mind misgives me, of the young gentleman who has been ill. What is to be done? How is he to be followed? How is he to be saved? Mr. Redlaw, pray, oh, pray, advise me! Help me!"

All this time he held the boy, who was half-mad to pass him, and let her in.

"Phantoms! Punishers of impious thoughts!" cried Redlaw, gazing round in anguish, "look upon me! From the darkness of my mind, let the glimmering of contrition that I know is there, shine up and show my misery! In the material world as I have long taught, nothing can be spared; no step or atom in the wondrous structure could be lost, without a blank being made in the great universe. I know, now, that it is the same with good and evil, happiness and sorrow, in the memories of men. Pity me! Relieve me!"

There was no response, but her "Help me, help me, let me in!" and the boy's struggling to get to her.

"Shadow of myself! Spirit of my darker hours!" cried Redlaw, in distraction, "come back, and haunt me day and night, but take this gift away! Or, if it must still rest with me, deprive me of the dreadful power of giving it to others. Undo what I have done. Leave me benighted, but restore the day to those whom I have cursed. As I have spared this woman from the first, and as I never will go forth again, but will die here, with no hand to tend me, save this creature's who is proof against me, – hear me!"

The only reply still was, the boy struggling to get to her, while he held him back; and the cry, increasing in its energy, "Help! let me in. He was your friend once, how shall he be followed, how shall he be saved? They are all changed, there is no one else to help me, pray, pray, let me in!"

Chapter III
The Gift Reversed

Night was still heavy in the sky. On open plains, from hill-tops, and from the decks of solitary ships at sea, a distant low-lying line, that promised by-and-by to change to light, was visible in the dim horizon; but its promise was remote and doubtful, and the moon was striving with the night-clouds busily.

The shadows upon Redlaw's mind succeeded thick and fast to one another, and obscured its light as the night-clouds hovered between the moon and earth, and kept the latter veiled in darkness. Fitful and uncertain as the shadows which the night-clouds cast, were their concealments from him, and imperfect revelations to him; and, like the night-clouds still, if the clear light broke forth for a moment, it was only that they might sweep over it, and make the darkness deeper than before.

Without, there was a profound and solemn hush upon the ancient pile of building, and its buttresses and angles made dark shapes of mystery upon the ground, which now seemed to retire into the smooth white snow and now seemed to come out of it, as the moon's path was more or less beset. Within, the Chemist's room was indistinct and murky, by the light of the expiring lamp; a ghostly silence had succeeded to the knocking and the voice outside; nothing was audible but, now and then, a low sound among the whitened ashes of the fire, as of its yielding up its last breath. Before it on the ground the boy lay fast asleep. In his chair, the Chemist sat, as he had sat there since the calling at his door had ceased – like a man turned to stone.

At such a time, the Christmas music he had heard before, began to play. He listened to it at first, as he had listened in the church-yard; but presently – it playing still, and being borne towards him on the night air, in a low, sweet, melancholy strain – he rose, and stood stretching his hands about him, as if there were some friend approaching within his reach, on whom his desolate touch might rest, yet do no harm. As he did this, his face became less fixed and wondering; a gentle trembling came upon him; and at last his eyes filled with tears, and he put his hands before them, and bowed down his head.

His memory of sorrow, wrong, and trouble, had not come back to him; he knew that it was not restored; he had no passing belief or hope that it was. But some dumb stir within him made him capable, again, of being moved by what was hidden, afar off, in the music. If it were only that it told him sorrowfully the value of what he had lost, he thanked Heaven for it with a fervent gratitude.

As the last chord died upon his ear, he raised his head to listen to its lingering vibration. Beyond the boy, so that his sleeping figure lay at its feet, the Phantom stood, immovable and silent, with its eyes upon him.

Ghastly it was, as it had ever been, but not so cruel and relentless in its aspect – or he thought or hoped so, as he looked upon it trembling. It was not alone, but in its shadowy hand it held another hand.

And whose was that? Was the form that stood beside it indeed Milly's, or but her shade and picture? The quiet head was bent a little, as her manner was, and her eyes were looking down, as if in pity, on the sleeping child. A radiant light fell on her face, but did not touch the Phantom; for, though close beside her, it was dark and colourless as ever.

"Spectre!" said the Chemist, newly troubled as he looked, "I have not been stubborn or presumptuous in respect of her. Oh, do not bring her here. Spare me that!"

"This is but a shadow," said the Phantom; "when the morning shines seek out the reality whose image I present before you."

"Is it my inexorable doom to do so?" cried the Chemist.

"It is," replied the Phantom.

"To destroy her peace, her goodness; to make her what I am myself, and what I have made of others!"

"I have said seek her out," returned the Phantom. "I have said no more."

"Oh, tell me," exclaimed Redlaw, catching at the hope which he fancied might lie hidden in the words. "Can I undo what I have done?"

"No," returned the Phantom.

"I do not ask for restoration to myself," said Redlaw. "What I abandoned, I abandoned of my own free will, and have justly lost. But for those to whom I have transferred the fatal gift; who never sought it; who unknowingly received a curse of which they had no warning, and which they had no power to shun; can I do nothing?"

"Nothing," said the Phantom.

"If I cannot, can any one?"

The Phantom, standing like a statue, kept its gaze upon him for a while; then turned its head suddenly, and looked upon the shadow at its side.

"Ah! Can she?" cried Redlaw, still looking upon the shade.

The Phantom released the hand it had retained till now, and softly raised its own with a gesture of dismissal. Upon that, her shadow, still preserving the same attitude, began to move or melt away.

"Stay," cried Redlaw with an earnestness to which he could not give enough expression. "For a moment! As an act of mercy! I know that some change fell upon me, when those sounds were in the air just now. Tell me, have I lost the power of harming her? May I go near her without dread? Oh, let her give me any sign of hope!"

The Phantom looked upon the shade as he did – not at him – and gave no answer.

"At least, say this – has she, henceforth, the consciousness of any power to set right what I have done?"

"She has not," the Phantom answered.

"Has she the power bestowed on her without the consciousness?"

The phantom answered: "Seek her out."

And her shadow slowly vanished.

They were face to face again, and looking on each other, as intently and awfully as at the time of the bestowal of the gift, across the boy who still lay on the ground between them, at the Phantom's feet.

"Terrible instructor," said the Chemist, sinking on his knee before it, in an attitude of supplication, "by whom I was renounced, but by whom I am revisited (in which, and in whose milder aspect, I would fain believe I have a gleam of hope), I will obey without inquiry, praying that the cry I have sent up in the anguish of my soul has been, or will be, heard, in behalf of those whom I have injured beyond human reparation. But there is one thing—"

"You speak to me of what is lying here," the Phantom interposed, and pointed with its finger to the boy.

"I do," returned the Chemist. "You know what I would ask. Why has this child alone been proof against my influence, and why, why, have I detected in its thoughts a terrible companionship with mine?"

"This," said the Phantom, pointing to the boy, "is the last, completest illustration of a human creature, utterly bereft of such remembrances as you have yielded up. No softening memory of sorrow, wrong, or trouble enters here, because this wretched mortal from his birth has been abandoned to a worse condition than the beasts, and has, within his knowledge, no one contrast, no humanising touch, to make a grain of such a memory spring up in his hardened breast. All within this desolate creature is barren wilderness. All within the man bereft of what you have resigned, is the same barren wilderness. Woe to such a man! Woe, tenfold, to the nation that shall count its monsters such as this, lying here, by hundreds and by thousands!"

Redlaw shrank, appalled, from what he heard.

"There is not," said the Phantom, "one of these – not one – but sows a harvest that mankind MUST reap. From every seed of evil in this boy, a field of ruin is grown that shall be gathered in, and garnered up, and sown again in many places in the world, until regions are overspread with wickedness enough to raise the waters of another Deluge. Open and unpunished murder in a city's streets would be less guilty in its daily toleration, than one such spectacle as this."

It seemed to look down upon the boy in his sleep. Redlaw, too, looked down upon him with a new emotion.

"There is not a father," said the Phantom, "by whose side in his daily or his nightly walk, these creatures pass; there is not a mother among all the ranks of loving mothers in this land; there is no one risen from the state of childhood, but shall be responsible in his or her degree for this enormity. There is not a country throughout the earth on which it would not bring a curse. There is no religion upon earth that it would not deny; there is no people upon earth it would not put to shame."

The Chemist clasped his hands, and looked, with trembling fear and pity, from the sleeping boy to the Phantom, standing above him with his finger pointing down.

"Behold, I say," pursued the Spectre, "the perfect type of what it was your choice to be. Your influence is powerless here, because from this child's bosom you can banish nothing. His thoughts have been in 'terrible companionship' with yours, because you have gone down to his unnatural level. He is the growth of man's indifference; you are the growth of man's presumption. The beneficent design of Heaven is, in each case, overthrown, and from the two poles of the immaterial world you come together."

The Chemist stooped upon the ground beside the boy, and, with the same kind of compassion for him that he now felt for himself, covered him as he slept, and no longer shrank from him with abhorrence or indifference.

Soon, now, the distant line on the horizon brightened, the darkness faded, the sun rose red and glorious, and the chimney stacks and gables of the ancient building gleamed in the clear air, which turned the smoke and vapour of the city into a cloud of gold. The very sun-dial in his shady corner, where the wind was used to spin with such unwindy constancy, shook off the finer particles of snow that had accumulated on his dull old face in the night, and looked out at the little white wreaths eddying round and round him. Doubtless some blind groping of the morning made its way down into the forgotten crypt so cold and earthy, where the Norman arches were half buried in the ground, and stirred the dull sap in the lazy vegetation hanging to the walls, and quickened the slow principle of life within the little world of wonderful and delicate creation which existed there, with some faint knowledge that the sun was up.

The Tetterbys were up, and doing. Mr. Tetterby took down the shutters of the shop, and, strip by strip, revealed the treasures of the window to the eyes, so proof against their seductions, of Jerusalem Buildings. Adolphus had been out so long already, that he was halfway on to "Morning Pepper." Five small Tetterbys, whose ten round eyes were much inflamed by soap and friction, were in the tortures of a cool wash in the back kitchen; Mrs. Tetterby presiding. Johnny, who was pushed and hustled through his toilet with great rapidity when Moloch chanced to be in an exacting frame of mind (which was always the case), staggered up and down with his charge before the shop door, under greater difficulties than usual; the weight of Moloch being much increased by a complication of defences against the cold, composed of knitted worsted-work, and forming a complete suit of chain-armour, with a head-piece and blue gaiters.

It was a peculiarity of this baby to be always cutting teeth. Whether they never came, or whether they came and went away again, is not in evidence; but it had certainly cut enough, on the showing of Mrs. Tetterby, to make a handsome dental provision for the sign of the Bull and Mouth. All sorts of objects were impressed for the rubbing of its gums, notwithstanding that it always carried, dangling at its waist (which was immediately under its chin), a bone ring, large enough to have represented the rosary of a young nun. Knife-handles, umbrella-tops, the heads of walking-sticks selected from the stock, the fingers of the family in general, but especially of Johnny, nutmeg-graters, crusts, the handles of doors, and the cool knobs on the tops of pokers, were among the commonest instruments indiscriminately applied for this baby's relief. The amount of electricity that must have been rubbed out of it in a week, is not to be calculated. Still Mrs. Tetterby always said "it was coming through, and then the child would be herself;" and still it never did come through, and the child continued to be somebody else.

The tempers of the little Tetterbys had sadly changed with a few hours. Mr. and Mrs. Tetterby themselves were not more altered than their offspring. Usually they were an unselfish, good-natured, yielding little race, sharing short commons when it happened (which was pretty often) contentedly and even generously, and taking a great deal of enjoyment out of a very little meat. But they were fighting now, not only for the soap and water, but even for the breakfast which was yet in perspective. The hand of every little Tetterby was against the other little Tetterbys; and even Johnny's hand – the patient, much-enduring, and devoted Johnny – rose against the baby! Yes, Mrs. Tetterby, going to the door by mere accident, saw him viciously pick out a weak place in the suit of armour where a slap would tell, and slap that blessed child.

Mrs. Tetterby had him into the parlour by the collar, in that same flash of time, and repaid him the assault with usury thereto.

"You brute, you murdering little boy," said Mrs. Tetterby. "Had you the heart to do it?"

"Why don't her teeth come through, then," retorted Johnny, in a loud rebellious voice, "instead of bothering me? How would you like it yourself?"

"Like it, sir!" said Mrs. Tetterby, relieving him of his dishonoured load.

"Yes, like it," said Johnny. "How would you? Not at all. If you was me, you'd go for a soldier. I will, too. There an't no babies in the Army."

Mr. Tetterby, who had arrived upon the scene of action, rubbed his chin thoughtfully, instead of correcting the rebel, and seemed rather struck by this view of a military life.

"I wish I was in the Army myself, if the child's in the right," said Mrs. Tetterby, looking at her husband, "for I have no peace of my life here. I'm a slave – a Virginia slave:" some indistinct association with their weak descent on the tobacco trade perhaps suggested this aggravated expression to Mrs. Tetterby. "I never have a holiday, or any pleasure at all, from year's end to year's end! Why, Lord bless and save the child," said Mrs. Tetterby, shaking the baby with an irritability hardly suited to so pious an aspiration, "what's the matter with her now?"

Not being able to discover, and not rendering the subject much clearer by shaking it, Mrs. Tetterby put the baby away in a cradle, and, folding her arms, sat rocking it angrily with her foot.

"How you stand there, 'Dolphus," said Mrs. Tetterby to her husband. "Why don't you do something?"

"Because I don't care about doing anything," Mr. Tetterby replied.

"I am sure *I* don't," said Mrs. Tetterby.

"I'll take my oath *I* don't," said Mr. Tetterby.

A diversion arose here among Johnny and his five younger brothers, who, in preparing the family breakfast table, had fallen to skirmishing for the temporary possession of the loaf, and were buffeting one another with great heartiness; the smallest boy of all, with precocious discretion, hovering outside the knot of combatants, and harassing their legs. Into the midst of this fray, Mr. and Mrs. Tetterby both precipitated themselves with great ardour, as if such ground were the only ground on which they could now agree; and having, with no visible remains of their late soft-heartedness, laid about them without any lenity, and done much execution, resumed their former relative positions.

"You had better read your paper than do nothing at all," said Mrs. Tetterby.

"What's there to read in a paper?" returned Mr. Tetterby, with excessive discontent.

"What?" said Mrs. Tetterby. "Police."

"It's nothing to me," said Tetterby. "What do I care what people do, or are done to?"

"Suicides," suggested Mrs. Tetterby.

"No business of mine," replied her husband.

"Births, deaths, and marriages, are those nothing to you?" said Mrs. Tetterby.

"If the births were all over for good, and all today; and the deaths were all to begin to come off tomorrow; I don't see why it should interest me, till I thought it was a coming to my turn," grumbled Tetterby. "As to marriages, I've done it myself. I know quite enough about *them*."

To judge from the dissatisfied expression of her face and manner, Mrs. Tetterby appeared to entertain the same opinions as her husband; but she opposed him, nevertheless, for the gratification of quarrelling with him.

"Oh, you're a consistent man," said Mrs. Tetterby, "an't you? You, with the screen of your own making there, made of nothing else but bits of newspapers, which you sit and read to the children by the half-hour together!"

"Say used to, if you please," returned her husband. "You won't find me doing so any more. I'm wiser now."

"Bah! wiser, indeed!" said Mrs. Tetterby. "Are you better?"

The question sounded some discordant note in Mr. Tetterby's breast. He ruminated dejectedly, and passed his hand across and across his forehead.

"Better!" murmured Mr. Tetterby. "I don't know as any of us are better, or happier either. Better, is it?"

He turned to the screen, and traced about it with his finger, until he found a certain paragraph of which he was in quest.

"This used to be one of the family favourites, I recollect," said Tetterby, in a forlorn and stupid way, "and used to draw tears from the children, and make 'em good, if there was any little bickering or discontent among 'em, next to the story of the robin redbreasts in the wood. 'Melancholy case of destitution. Yesterday a small man, with a baby in his arms, and surrounded by half-a-dozen ragged little ones, of various ages between ten and two, the whole of whom were evidently in a famishing condition, appeared before the worthy magistrate, and made the following recital:' – Ha! I don't understand it, I'm sure," said Tetterby; "I don't see what it has got to do with us."

"How old and shabby he looks," said Mrs. Tetterby, watching him. "I never saw such a change in a man. Ah! dear me, dear me, dear me, it was a sacrifice!"

"What was a sacrifice?" her husband sourly inquired.

Mrs. Tetterby shook her head; and without replying in words, raised a complete sea-storm about the baby, by her violent agitation of the cradle.

"If you mean your marriage was a sacrifice, my good woman—" said her husband.

"I *do* mean it," said his wife.

"Why, then I mean to say," pursued Mr. Tetterby, as sulkily and surlily as she, "that there are two sides to that affair; and that I was the sacrifice; and that I wish the sacrifice hadn't been accepted."

"I wish it hadn't, Tetterby, with all my heart and soul I do assure you," said his wife. "You can't wish it more than I do, Tetterby."

"I don't know what I saw in her," muttered the newsman, "I'm sure; – certainly, if I saw anything, it's not there now. I was thinking so, last night, after supper, by the fire. She's fat, she's ageing, she won't bear comparison with most other women."

"He's common-looking, he has no air with him, he's small, he's beginning to stoop and he's getting bald," muttered Mrs. Tetterby.

"I must have been half out of my mind when I did it," muttered Mr. Tetterby.

"My senses must have forsook me. That's the only way in which I can explain it to myself," said Mrs. Tetterby with elaboration.

In this mood they sat down to breakfast. The little Tetterbys were not habituated to regard that meal in the light of a sedentary occupation, but discussed it as a dance or trot; rather resembling a savage ceremony, in the occasionally shrill whoops, and brandishings of bread and butter, with which it was accompanied, as well as in the intricate filings off into the street and back again, and the hoppings up and down the door-steps, which were incidental to the performance. In the present instance, the contentions between these Tetterby children for the milk-and-water jug, common to all, which stood upon the table, presented so lamentable an instance of angry passions risen very high indeed, that it was an outrage on the memory of Dr. Watts. It was not until Mr. Tetterby had driven the whole herd out at the front door, that a moment's peace was secured; and even that was broken by the discovery that Johnny had surreptitiously come back, and was at that instant choking in the jug like a ventriloquist, in his indecent and rapacious haste.

"These children will be the death of me at last!" said Mrs. Tetterby, after banishing the culprit. "And the sooner the better, I think."

"Poor people," said Mr. Tetterby, "ought not to have children at all. They give *us* no pleasure."

He was at that moment taking up the cup which Mrs. Tetterby had rudely pushed towards him, and Mrs. Tetterby was lifting her own cup to her lips, when they both stopped, as if they were transfixed.

"Here! Mother! Father!" cried Johnny, running into the room. "Here's Mrs. William coming down the street!"

And if ever, since the world began, a young boy took a baby from a cradle with the care of an old nurse, and hushed and soothed it tenderly, and tottered away with it cheerfully, Johnny was that boy, and Moloch was that baby, as they went out together!

Mr. Tetterby put down his cup; Mrs. Tetterby put down her cup. Mr. Tetterby rubbed his forehead; Mrs. Tetterby rubbed hers. Mr. Tetterby's face began to smooth and brighten; Mrs. Tetterby's began to smooth and brighten.

"Why, Lord forgive me," said Mr. Tetterby to himself, "what evil tempers have I been giving way to? What has been the matter here!"

"How could I ever treat him ill again, after all I said and felt last night!" sobbed Mrs. Tetterby, with her apron to her eyes.

"Am I a brute," said Mr. Tetterby, "or is there any good in me at all? Sophia! My little woman!"

"'Dolphus dear," returned his wife.

"I—I've been in a state of mind," said Mr. Tetterby, "that I can't abear to think of, Sophy."

"Oh! It's nothing to what I've been in, Dolf," cried his wife in a great burst of grief.

"My Sophia," said Mr. Tetterby, "don't take on. I never shall forgive myself. I must have nearly broke your heart, I know."

"No, Dolf, no. It was me! Me!" cried Mrs. Tetterby.

"My little woman," said her husband, "don't. You make me reproach myself dreadful, when you show such a noble spirit. Sophia, my dear, you don't know what I thought. I showed it bad enough, no doubt; but what I thought, my little woman!—"

"Oh, dear Dolf, don't! Don't!" cried his wife.

"Sophia," said Mr. Tetterby, "I must reveal it. I couldn't rest in my conscience unless I mentioned it. My little woman—"

"Mrs. William's very nearly here!" screamed Johnny at the door.

"My little woman, I wondered how," gasped Mr. Tetterby, supporting himself by his chair, "I wondered how I had ever admired you – I forgot the precious children you have brought about me, and thought you didn't look as slim as I could wish. I—I never gave a recollection," said Mr. Tetterby, with severe self-accusation, "to the cares you've had as my wife, and along of me and mine, when you might have had hardly any with another man, who got on better and was luckier than me (anybody might have found such a man easily I am sure); and I quarrelled with you for having aged a little in the rough years you have lightened for me. Can you believe it, my little woman? I hardly can myself."

Mrs. Tetterby, in a whirlwind of laughing and crying, caught his face within her hands, and held it there.

"Oh, Dolf!" she cried. "I am so happy that you thought so; I am so grateful that you thought so! For I thought that you were common-looking, Dolf; and so you are, my dear, and may you be the commonest of all sights in my eyes, till you close them with your own good hands. I thought that you were small; and so you are, and I'll make much of you because you are, and more of you because I love my husband. I thought that you began to stoop; and so you do, and you shall lean on me, and I'll do all I can to keep you up. I thought there was no air about you; but there is, and it's the air of home, and that's the purest and the best there is, and God bless home once more, and all belonging to it, Dolf!"

"Hurrah! Here's Mrs. William!" cried Johnny.

So she was, and all the children with her; and so she came in, they kissed her, and kissed one another, and kissed the baby, and kissed their father and mother, and then ran back and flocked and danced about her, trooping on with her in triumph.

Mr. and Mrs. Tetterby were not a bit behind-hand in the warmth of their reception. They were as much attracted to her as the children were; they ran towards her, kissed her hands, pressed round her, could not receive her ardently or enthusiastically enough. She came among them like the spirit of all goodness, affection, gentle consideration, love, and domesticity.

"What! are *you* all so glad to see me, too, this bright Christmas morning?" said Milly, clapping her hands in a pleasant wonder. "Oh dear, how delightful this is!"

More shouting from the children, more kissing, more trooping round her, more happiness, more love, more joy, more honour, on all sides, than she could bear.

"Oh dear!" said Milly, "what delicious tears you make me shed. How can I ever have deserved this! What have I done to be so loved?"

"Who can help it!" cried Mr. Tetterby.

"Who can help it!" cried Mrs. Tetterby.

"Who can help it!" echoed the children, in a joyful chorus. And they danced and trooped about her again, and clung to her, and laid their rosy faces against her dress, and kissed and fondled it, and could not fondle it, or her, enough.

"I never was so moved," said Milly, drying her eyes, "as I have been this morning. I must tell you, as soon as I can speak. – Mr. Redlaw came to me at sunrise, and with a tenderness in his manner, more as if I had been his darling daughter than myself, implored me to go with him to where William's brother George is lying ill. We went together, and all the way along he was so kind, and so subdued, and seemed to put such trust and hope in me, that I could not help crying with pleasure. When we got to the house, we met a woman at the door (somebody had bruised and hurt her, I am afraid), who caught me by the hand, and blessed me as I passed."

"She was right!" said Mr. Tetterby. Mrs. Tetterby said she was right. All the children cried out that she was right.

"Ah, but there's more than that," said Milly. "When we got up stairs, into the room, the sick man who had lain for hours in a state from which no effort could rouse him, rose up in his bed, and, bursting into tears, stretched out his arms to me, and said that he had led a mis-spent life, but that he was truly repentant now, in his sorrow for the past, which was all as plain to him as a great prospect, from which a dense black cloud had cleared away, and that he entreated me to ask his poor old father for his pardon and his blessing, and to say a prayer beside his bed. And when I did so, Mr. Redlaw joined in it so fervently, and then so thanked and thanked me, and thanked Heaven, that my heart quite overflowed, and I could have done nothing but sob and cry, if the sick man had not begged me to sit down by him, – which made me quiet of course. As I sat there, he held my hand in his until he sank in a doze; and even then, when I withdrew my hand to leave him to come here (which Mr. Redlaw was very earnest indeed in wishing me to do), his hand felt for mine, so that some one else was obliged to take my place and make believe to give him my hand back. Oh dear, oh dear," said Milly, sobbing. "How thankful and how happy I should feel, and do feel, for all this!"

While she was speaking, Redlaw had come in, and, after pausing for a moment to observe the group of which she was the centre, had silently ascended the stairs. Upon those stairs he now appeared again; remaining there, while the young student passed him, and came running down.

"Kind nurse, gentlest, best of creatures," he said, falling on his knee to her, and catching at her hand, "forgive my cruel ingratitude!"

"Oh dear, oh dear!" cried Milly innocently, "here's another of them! Oh dear, here's somebody else who likes me. What shall I ever do!"

The guileless, simple way in which she said it, and in which she put her hands before her eyes and wept for very happiness, was as touching as it was delightful.

"I was not myself," he said. "I don't know what it was – it was some consequence of my disorder perhaps – I was mad. But I am so no longer. Almost as I speak, I am restored. I heard the children crying out your name, and the shade passed from me at the very sound of it. Oh, don't weep! Dear Milly, if you could read my heart, and only knew with what affection and what grateful homage it is glowing, you would not let me see you weep. It is such deep reproach."

"No, no," said Milly, "it's not that. It's not indeed. It's joy. It's wonder that you should think it necessary to ask me to forgive so little, and yet it's pleasure that you do."

"And will you come again? and will you finish the little curtain?"

"No," said Milly, drying her eyes, and shaking her head. "You won't care for my needlework now."

"Is it forgiving me, to say that?"

She beckoned him aside, and whispered in his ear.

"There is news from your home, Mr. Edmund."

"News? How?"

"Either your not writing when you were very ill, or the change in your handwriting when you began to be better, created some suspicion of the truth; however that is – but you're sure you'll not be the worse for any news, if it's not bad news?"

"Sure."

"Then there's someone come!" said Milly.

"My mother?" asked the student, glancing round involuntarily towards Redlaw, who had come down from the stairs.

"Hush! No," said Milly.

"It can be no one else."

"Indeed?" said Milly, "are you sure?"

"It is not—" Before he could say more, she put her hand upon his mouth.

"Yes it is!" said Milly. "The young lady (she is very like the miniature, Mr. Edmund, but she is prettier) was too unhappy to rest without satisfying her doubts, and came up, last night, with a little servant-maid. As you always dated your letters from the college, she came there; and before I saw Mr. Redlaw this morning, I saw her. *She* likes me too!" said Milly. "Oh dear, that's another!"

"This morning! Where is she now?"

"Why, she is now," said Milly, advancing her lips to his ear, "in my little parlour in the Lodge, and waiting to see you."

He pressed her hand, and was darting off, but she detained him.

"Mr. Redlaw is much altered, and has told me this morning that his memory is impaired. Be very considerate to him, Mr. Edmund; he needs that from us all."

The young man assured her, by a look, that her caution was not ill-bestowed; and as he passed the Chemist on his way out, bent respectfully and with an obvious interest before him.

Redlaw returned the salutation courteously and even humbly, and looked after him as he passed on. He drooped his head upon his hand too, as trying to reawaken something he had lost. But it was gone.

The abiding change that had come upon him since the influence of the music, and the Phantom's reappearance, was, that now he truly felt how much he had lost, and could compassionate his own condition, and contrast it, clearly, with the natural state of those who were around him. In this, an interest in those who were around him was revived, and a meek, submissive sense of his calamity was bred, resembling that which sometimes obtains in age, when its mental powers are weakened, without insensibility or sullenness being added to the list of its infirmities.

He was conscious that, as he redeemed, through Milly, more and more of the evil he had done, and as he was more and more with her, this change ripened itself within him. Therefore, and because of the attachment she inspired him with (but without other hope), he felt that he was quite dependent on her, and that she was his staff in his affliction.

So, when she asked him whether they should go home now, to where the old man and her husband were, and he readily replied "yes" – being anxious in that regard – he put his arm through hers, and walked beside her; not as if he were the wise and learned man to whom the wonders of Nature were an open book, and hers were the uninstructed mind, but as if their two positions were reversed, and he knew nothing, and she all.

He saw the children throng about her, and caress her, as he and she went away together thus, out of the house; he heard the ringing of their laughter, and their merry voices; he saw their bright faces, clustering around him like flowers; he witnessed the renewed contentment and affection of their parents; he breathed the simple air of their poor home, restored to its tranquillity; he thought of the unwholesome blight he had shed upon it, and might, but for her, have been diffusing then; and perhaps it is no wonder that he walked submissively beside her, and drew her gentle bosom nearer to his own.

When they arrived at the Lodge, the old man was sitting in his chair in the chimney-corner, with his eyes fixed on the ground, and his son was leaning against the opposite side of the fire-place, looking at him. As she came in at the door, both started, and turned round towards her, and a radiant change came upon their faces.

"Oh dear, dear, dear, they are all pleased to see me like the rest!" cried Milly, clapping her hands in an ecstasy, and stopping short. "Here are two more!"

Pleased to see her! Pleasure was no word for it. She ran into her husband's arms, thrown wide open to receive her, and he would have been glad to have her there, with her head lying on his shoulder, through the short winter's day. But the old man couldn't spare her. He had arms for her too, and he locked her in them.

"Why, where has my quiet Mouse been all this time?" said the old man. "She has been a long while away. I find that it's impossible for me to get on without Mouse. I – where's my son William? – I fancy I have been dreaming, William."

"That's what I say myself, father," returned his son. "I have been in an ugly sort of dream, I think. – How are you, father? Are you pretty well?"

"Strong and brave, my boy," returned the old man.

It was quite a sight to see Mr. William shaking hands with his father, and patting him on the back, and rubbing him gently down with his hand, as if he could not possibly do enough to show an interest in him.

"What a wonderful man you are, father! – How are you, father? Are you really pretty hearty, though?" said William, shaking hands with him again, and patting him again, and rubbing him gently down again.

"I never was fresher or stouter in my life, my boy."

"What a wonderful man you are, father! But that's exactly where it is," said Mr. William, with enthusiasm. "When I think of all that my father's gone through, and all the chances and changes, and sorrows and troubles, that have happened to him in the course of his long life, and under which his head has grown grey, and years upon years have gathered on it, I feel as if we couldn't do enough to honour the old gentleman, and make his old age easy. – How are you, father? Are you really pretty well, though?"

Mr. William might never have left off repeating this inquiry, and shaking hands with him again, and patting him again, and rubbing him down again, if the old man had not espied the Chemist, whom until now he had not seen.

"I ask your pardon, Mr. Redlaw," said Philip, "but didn't know you were here, sir, or should have made less free. It reminds me, Mr. Redlaw, seeing you here on a Christmas morning, of the time when you was a student yourself, and worked so hard that you were backwards and forwards in our Library even at Christmas time. Ha! ha! I'm old enough to remember that; and I remember it right well, I do, though I am eighty-seven. It was after you left here that my poor wife died. You remember my poor wife, Mr. Redlaw?"

The Chemist answered yes.

"Yes," said the old man. "She was a dear creetur. – I recollect you come here one Christmas morning with a young lady – I ask your pardon, Mr. Redlaw, but I think it was a sister you was very much attached to?"

The Chemist looked at him, and shook his head. "I had a sister," he said vacantly. He knew no more.

"One Christmas morning," pursued the old man, "that you come here with her – and it began to snow, and my wife invited the lady to walk in, and sit by the fire that is always a burning on Christmas Day in what used to be, before our ten poor gentlemen commuted, our great Dinner Hall. I was there; and I recollect, as I was stirring up the blaze for the young lady to warm her pretty feet by, she read the scroll out loud, that is underneath that pictur, 'Lord, keep my memory green!' She and my poor wife fell a talking about it; and it's a strange thing to think of, now, that they both said (both being so unlike to die) that it was a good prayer, and that it was one they would put up very earnestly, if they were called away young, with reference to those who were dearest to them. 'My brother,' says the young lady – 'My husband,' says my poor wife. – 'Lord, keep his memory of me, green, and do not let me be forgotten!'"

Tears more painful, and more bitter than he had ever shed in all his life, coursed down Redlaw's face. Philip, fully occupied in recalling his story, had not observed him until now, nor Milly's anxiety that he should not proceed.

"Philip!" said Redlaw, laying his hand upon his arm, "I am a stricken man, on whom the hand of Providence has fallen heavily, although deservedly. You speak to me, my friend, of what I cannot follow; my memory is gone."

"Merciful power!" cried the old man.

"I have lost my memory of sorrow, wrong, and trouble," said the Chemist, "and with that I have lost all man would remember!"

To see old Philip's pity for him, to see him wheel his own great chair for him to rest in, and look down upon him with a solemn sense of his bereavement, was to know, in some degree, how precious to old age such recollections are.

The boy came running in, and ran to Milly.

"Here's the man," he said, "in the other room. I don't want *him*."

"What man does he mean?" asked Mr. William.

"Hush!" said Milly.

Obedient to a sign from her, he and his old father softly withdrew. As they went out, unnoticed, Redlaw beckoned to the boy to come to him.

"I like the woman best," he answered, holding to her skirts.

"You are right," said Redlaw, with a faint smile. "But you needn't fear to come to me. I am gentler than I was. Of all the world, to you, poor child!"

The boy still held back at first, but yielding little by little to her urging, he consented to approach, and even to sit down at his feet. As Redlaw laid his hand upon the shoulder of the child, looking on him with compassion and a fellow-feeling, he put out his other hand to Milly. She stooped down on that side of him, so that she could look into his face, and after silence, said:

"Mr. Redlaw, may I speak to you?"

"Yes," he answered, fixing his eyes upon her. "Your voice and music are the same to me."

"May I ask you something?"

"What you will."

"Do you remember what I said, when I knocked at your door last night? About one who was your friend once, and who stood on the verge of destruction?"

"Yes. I remember," he said, with some hesitation.

"Do you understand it?"

He smoothed the boy's hair – looking at her fixedly the while, and shook his head.

"This person," said Milly, in her clear, soft voice, which her mild eyes, looking at him, made clearer and softer, "I found soon afterwards. I went back to the house, and, with Heaven's help, traced him. I was not too soon. A very little and I should have been too late."

He took his hand from the boy, and laying it on the back of that hand of hers, whose timid and yet earnest touch addressed him no less appealingly than her voice and eyes, looked more intently on her.

"He *is* the father of Mr. Edmund, the young gentleman we saw just now. His real name is Longford. – You recollect the name?"

"I recollect the name."

"And the man?"

"No, not the man. Did he ever wrong me?"

"Yes!"

"Ah! Then it's hopeless – hopeless."

He shook his head, and softly beat upon the hand he held, as though mutely asking her commiseration.

"I did not go to Mr. Edmund last night," said Milly, – "You will listen to me just the same as if you did remember all?"

"To every syllable you say."

"Both, because I did not know, then, that this really was his father, and because I was fearful of the effect of such intelligence upon him, after his illness, if it should be. Since I have known who this person is, I have not gone either; but that is for another reason. He has long been separated from his wife and son – has been a stranger to his home almost from this son's infancy, I learn from him – and has abandoned and deserted what he should have held most dear. In all that time he has been falling from the state of a gentleman, more and more, until—" she rose up, hastily, and going out for a moment, returned, accompanied by the wreck that Redlaw had beheld last night.

"Do you know me?" asked the Chemist.

"I should be glad," returned the other, "and that is an unwonted word for me to use, if I could answer no."

The Chemist looked at the man, standing in self-abasement and degradation before him, and would have looked longer, in an ineffectual struggle for enlightenment, but that Milly resumed her late position by his side, and attracted his attentive gaze to her own face.

"See how low he is sunk, how lost he is!" she whispered, stretching out her arm towards him, without looking from the Chemist's face. "If you could remember all that is connected with him, do you not think it would move your pity to reflect that one you ever loved (do not let us mind how long ago, or in what belief that he has forfeited), should come to this?"

"I hope it would," he answered. "I believe it would."

His eyes wandered to the figure standing near the door, but came back speedily to her, on whom he gazed intently, as if he strove to learn some lesson from every tone of her voice, and every beam of her eyes.

"I have no learning, and you have much," said Milly; "I am not used to think, and you are always thinking. May I tell you why it seems to me a good thing for us, to remember wrong that has been done us?"

"Yes."

"That we may forgive it."

"Pardon me, great Heaven!" said Redlaw, lifting up his eyes, "for having thrown away thine own high attribute!"

"And if," said Milly, "if your memory should one day be restored, as we will hope and pray it may be, would it not be a blessing to you to recall at once a wrong and its forgiveness?"

He looked at the figure by the door, and fastened his attentive eyes on her again; a ray of clearer light appeared to him to shine into his mind, from her bright face.

"He cannot go to his abandoned home. He does not seek to go there. He knows that he could only carry shame and trouble to those he has so cruelly neglected; and that the best reparation he can make them now, is to avoid them. A very little money carefully bestowed, would remove him to some distant place, where he might live and do no wrong, and make such atonement as is left within his power for the wrong he has done. To the unfortunate lady who is his wife, and to his son, this would be the best and kindest boon that their best friend could give them – one too that they need never know of; and to him, shattered in reputation, mind, and body, it might be salvation."

He took her head between her hands, and kissed it, and said: "It shall be done. I trust to you to do it for me, now and secretly; and to tell him that I would forgive him, if I were so happy as to know for what."

As she rose, and turned her beaming face towards the fallen man, implying that her mediation had been successful, he advanced a step, and without raising his eyes, addressed himself to Redlaw.

"You are so generous," he said, "– you ever were – that you will try to banish your rising sense of retribution in the spectacle that is before you. I do not try to banish it from myself, Redlaw. If you can, believe me."

The Chemist entreated Milly, by a gesture, to come nearer to him; and, as he listened looked in her face, as if to find in it the clue to what he heard.

"I am too decayed a wretch to make professions; I recollect my own career too well, to array any such before you. But from the day on which I made my first step downward, in dealing falsely by you, I have gone down with a certain, steady, doomed progression. That, I say."

Redlaw, keeping her close at his side, turned his face towards the speaker, and there was sorrow in it. Something like mournful recognition too.

"I might have been another man, my life might have been another life, if I had avoided that first fatal step. I don't know that it would have been. I claim nothing for the possibility. Your sister is at rest, and better than she could have been with me, if I had continued even what you thought me; even what I once supposed myself to be."

Redlaw made a hasty motion with his hand, as if he would have put that subject on one side.

"I speak," the other went on, "like a man taken from the grave. I should have made my own grave, last night, had it not been for this blessed hand."

"Oh dear, he likes me too!" sobbed Milly, under her breath. "That's another!"

"I could not have put myself in your way, last night, even for bread. But, today, my recollection of what has been is so strongly stirred, and is presented to me, I don't know how, so vividly, that I have dared to come at her suggestion, and to take your bounty, and to thank you for it, and to beg you, Redlaw, in your dying hour, to be as merciful to me in your thoughts, as you are in your deeds."

He turned towards the door, and stopped a moment on his way forth.

"I hope my son may interest you, for his mother's sake. I hope he may deserve to do so. Unless my life should be preserved a long time, and I should know that I have not misused your aid, I shall never look upon him more."

Going out, he raised his eyes to Redlaw for the first time. Redlaw, whose steadfast gaze was fixed upon him, dreamily held out his hand. He returned and touched it – little more – with both his own; and bending down his head, went slowly out.

In the few moments that elapsed, while Milly silently took him to the gate, the Chemist dropped into his chair, and covered his face with his hands. Seeing him thus, when she came back, accompanied by her husband and his father (who were both greatly concerned for him), she avoided disturbing him, or permitting him to be disturbed; and kneeled down near the chair to put some warm clothing on the boy.

"That's exactly where it is. That's what I always say, father!" exclaimed her admiring husband. "There's a motherly feeling in Mrs. William's breast that must and will have went!"

"Ay, ay," said the old man; "you're right. My son William's right!"

THE HAUNTED MAN AND THE GHOST'S BARGAIN

"It happens all for the best, Milly dear, no doubt," said Mr. William, tenderly, "that we have no children of our own; and yet I sometimes wish you had one to love and cherish. Our little dead child that you built such hopes upon, and that never breathed the breath of life – it has made you quiet-like, Milly."

"I am very happy in the recollection of it, William dear," she answered. "I think of it every day."

"I was afraid you thought of it a good deal."

"Don't say, afraid; it is a comfort to me; it speaks to me in so many ways. The innocent thing that never lived on earth, is like an angel to me, William."

"You are like an angel to father and me," said Mr. William, softly. "I know that."

"When I think of all those hopes I built upon it, and the many times I sat and pictured to myself the little smiling face upon my bosom that never lay there, and the sweet eyes turned up to mine that never opened to the light," said Milly, "I can feel a greater tenderness, I think, for all the disappointed hopes in which there is no harm. When I see a beautiful child in its fond mother's arms, I love it all the better, thinking that my child might have been like that, and might have made my heart as proud and happy."

Redlaw raised his head, and looked towards her.

"All through life, it seems by me," she continued, "to tell me something. For poor neglected children, my little child pleads as if it were alive, and had a voice I knew, with which to speak to me. When I hear of youth in suffering or shame, I think that my child might have come to that, perhaps, and that God took it from me in His mercy. Even in age and grey hair, such as father's, it is present: saying that it too might have lived to be old, long and long after you and I were gone, and to have needed the respect and love of younger people."

Her quiet voice was quieter than ever, as she took her husband's arm, and laid her head against it.

"Children love me so, that sometimes I half fancy – it's a silly fancy, William – they have some way I don't know of, of feeling for my little child, and me, and understanding why their love is precious to me. If I have been quiet since, I have been more happy, William, in a hundred ways. Not least happy, dear, in this – that even when my little child was born and dead but a few days, and I was weak and sorrowful, and could not help grieving a little, the thought arose, that if I tried to lead a good life, I should meet in Heaven a bright creature, who would call me, Mother!"

Redlaw fell upon his knees, with a loud cry.

"O Thou," he said, "who through the teaching of pure love, hast graciously restored me to the memory which was the memory of Christ upon the Cross, and of all the good who perished in His cause, receive my thanks, and bless her!"

Then, he folded her to his heart; and Milly, sobbing more than ever, cried, as she laughed, "He is come back to himself! He likes me very much indeed, too! Oh, dear, dear, dear me, here's another!"

Then, the student entered, leading by the hand a lovely girl, who was afraid to come. And Redlaw so changed towards him, seeing in him and his youthful choice, the softened shadow of that chastening passage in his own life, to which, as to a shady tree, the dove so long imprisoned in his solitary ark might fly for rest and company, fell upon his neck, entreating them to be his children.

Then, as Christmas is a time in which, of all times in the year, the memory of every remediable sorrow, wrong, and trouble in the world around us, should be active with us, not less than our own experiences, for all good, he laid his hand upon the boy, and, silently calling Him to witness who laid His hand on children in old time, rebuking, in the majesty of His prophetic knowledge, those who kept them from Him, vowed to protect him, teach him, and reclaim him.

Then, he gave his right hand cheerily to Philip, and said that they would that day hold a Christmas dinner in what used to be, before the ten poor gentlemen commuted, their great Dinner Hall; and that they would bid to it as many of that Swidger family, who, his son had told him, were so numerous that they might join hands and make a ring round England, as could be brought together on so short a notice.

And it was that day done. There were so many Swidgers there, grown up and children, that an attempt to state them in round numbers might engender doubts, in the distrustful, of the veracity of this history. Therefore the attempt shall not be made. But there they were, by dozens and scores – and there was good news and good hope there, ready for them, of George, who had been visited again by his father and brother, and by Milly, and again left in a quiet sleep. There, present at the dinner, too, were the Tetterbys, including young Adolphus, who arrived in his prismatic comforter, in good time for the beef. Johnny and the baby were too late, of course, and came in all on one side, the one exhausted, the other in a supposed state of double-tooth; but that was customary, and not alarming.

It was sad to see the child who had no name or lineage, watching the other children as they played, not knowing how to talk with them, or sport with them, and more strange to the ways of childhood than a rough dog. It was sad, though in a different way, to see what an instinctive knowledge the youngest children there had of his being different from all the rest, and how they made timid approaches to him with soft words and touches, and with little presents, that he might not be unhappy. But he kept by Milly, and began to love her – that was another, as she said! – and, as they all liked her dearly, they were glad of that, and when they saw him peeping at them from behind her chair, they were pleased that he was so close to it.

All this, the Chemist, sitting with the student and his bride that was to be, Philip, and the rest, saw.

Some people have said since, that he only thought what has been herein set down; others that he read it in the fire, one winter night about the twilight time; others, that the Ghost was but the representation of his gloomy thoughts, and Milly the embodiment of his better wisdom. *I* say nothing.

—Except this. That as they were assembled in the old Hall, by no other light than that of a great fire (having dined early), the shadows once more stole out of their hiding-places, and danced about the room, showing the children marvellous shapes and faces on the walls, and gradually changing what was real and familiar there, to what was wild and magical. But that there was one thing in the Hall, to which the eyes of Redlaw, and of Milly and her husband, and of the old man and of the student, and his bride that was to be, were often turned, which the shadows did not obscure or change. Deepened in its gravity by the fire-light, and gazing from the darkness of the panelled wall like life, the sedate face in the portrait, with the beard and ruff, looked down at them from under its verdant wreath of holly, as they looked up at it; and, clear and plain below, as if a voice had uttered them, were the words.

Lord keep my Memory green.

*

The Story of the Goblins Who Stole a Sexton

Charles Dickens

"**IN AN OLD** abbey town, down in this part of the country, a long, long while ago – so long, that the story must be a true one, because our great grandfathers implicitly believed it – there officiated as sexton and grave-digger in the church-yard, one Gabriel Grub. It by no means follows that because a man is a sexton, and constantly surrounded by emblems of mortality, therefore he should be a morose and melancholy man; your undertakers are the merriest fellows in the world, and I once had the honour of being on intimate terms with a mute, who in private life, and off duty, was as comical and jocose a little fellow as ever chirped out a devil-may-care song, without a hitch in his memory, or drained off a good stiff glass of grog without stopping for breath. But notwithstanding these precedents to the contrary, Gabriel Grub was an ill-conditioned, cross-grained, surly fellow – a morose and lonely man, who consorted with nobody but himself, and an old wicker bottle which fitted into his large deep waistcoat pocket; and who eyed each merry face as it passed him by, with such a deep scowl of malice and ill-humour, as it was difficult to meet without feeling something the worse for.

"A little before twilight one Christmas Eve, Gabriel shouldered his spade, lighted his lantern, and betook himself towards the old church-yard, for he had got a grave to finish by next morning, and feeling very low he thought it might raise his spirits perhaps, if he went on with his work at once. As he wended his way up the ancient street, he saw the cheerful light of the blazing fires gleam through the old casements, and heard the loud laugh and the cheerful shouts of those who were assembled around them; he marked the bustling preparations for next day's good cheer, and smelt the numerous savoury odours consequent thereupon, as they steamed up from the kitchen windows in clouds. All this was gall and wormwood to the heart of Gabriel Grub; and as groups of children bounded out of the houses, tripped across the road, and were met, before they could knock at the opposite door, by half a dozen curly-headed little rascals who crowded round them as they flocked up stairs to spend the evening in their Christmas games, Gabriel smiled grimly, and clutched the handle of his spade with a firmer grasp, as he thought of measles, scarlet-fever, thrush, hooping-cough, and a good many other sources of consolation beside.

"In this happy frame of mind, Gabriel strode along, returning a short, sullen growl to the good-humoured greetings of such of his neighbours as now and then passed him, until he turned into the dark lane which led to the church-yard. Now Gabriel had been looking forward to reaching the dark lane, because it was, generally speaking, a nice gloomy mournful place, into which the towns-people did not much care to go, except in broad daylight, and when the sun was shining; consequently he was not a little indignant to hear a young urchin roaring out some jolly song about a merry Christmas, in this very sanctuary, which had been called Coffin Lane ever since the days of the old abbey, and the time of the shaven-headed monks. As Gabriel walked on, and the voice drew nearer, he found it proceeded from a small boy, who was hurrying along, to join one of the little parties in the old street, and who, partly to keep himself company, and partly to prepare himself for the occasion, was shouting out the song at the highest pitch of his lungs. So Gabriel waited till the boy came up, and then dodged him into a corner, and rapped him over the head with his lantern five or six times, just to teach him to modulate his voice. And as the boy hurried away with his hand to his head, singing quite a different sort of tune, Gabriel Grub chuckled very heartily to himself, and entered the church-yard, locking the gate behind him.

"He took off his coat, set down his lantern, and getting into the unfinished grave, worked at it for an hour or so, with right good-will. But the earth was hardened with the frost, and it was no very easy matter to break it up, and shovel it out; and although there was a moon, it was a very young one, and shed little light upon the grave, which was in the shadow of the church. At any other time, these obstacles would have made Gabriel Grub very moody and miserable, but he was so well pleased with having stopped the small boy's singing, that he took little heed of the scanty progress he had made, and looked down into the grave when he had finished work for the night, with grim satisfaction, murmuring as he gathered up his things –

Brave lodgings for one, brave lodgings for one,
A few feet of cold earth, when life is done;
A stone at the head, a stone at the feet,
A rich, juicy meal for the worms to eat;
Rank grass over head, and damp clay around,
Brave lodgings for one, these, in holy ground!

"'Ho! ho!' laughed Gabriel Grub, as he sat himself down on a flat tombstone which was a favourite resting place of his and drew forth his wicker bottle. 'A coffin at Christmas – a Christmas Box. Ho! ho! ho!'

"'Ho! ho! ho!' repeated a voice which sounded close behind him.

"Gabriel paused in some alarm, in the act of raising the wicker bottle to his lips, and looked round. The bottom of the oldest grave about him, was not more still and quiet, than the church-yard in the pale moonlight. The cold hoar frost glistened on the tombstones, and sparkled like rows of gems among the stone carvings of the old church. The snow lay hard and crisp upon the ground, and spread over the thickly-strewn mounds of earth, so white and smooth a cover, that it seemed as if corpses lay there, hidden only by their winding sheets. Not the faintest rustle broke the profound tranquillity of the solemn scene. Sound itself appeared to be frozen up, all was so cold and still.

"'It was the echoes,' said Gabriel Grub, raising the bottle to his lips again.

"'It was *not*,' said a deep voice.

"Gabriel started up, and stood rooted to the spot with astonishment and terror; for his eyes rested on a form which made his blood run cold.

"Seated on an upright tombstone, close to him, was a strange unearthly figure, whom Gabriel felt at once, was no being of this world. His long fantastic legs which might have reached the ground, were cocked up, and crossed after a quaint, fantastic fashion; his sinewy arms were bare, and his hands rested on his knees. On his short round body he wore a close covering, ornamented with small slashes; and a short cloak dangled at his back; the collar was cut into curious peaks, which served the goblin in lieu of ruff or neckerchief; and his shoes curled up at the toes into long points. On his head he wore a broad-brimmed sugar loaf hat, garnished with a single feather. The hat was covered with the white frost, and the goblin looked as if he had sat on the same tombstone very comfortably, for two or three hundred years. He was sitting perfectly still; his tongue was put out, as if in derision; and he was grinning at Gabriel Grub with such a grin as only a goblin could call up.

"'It was *not* the echoes,' said the goblin.

"Gabriel Grub was paralysed, and could make no reply.

"'What do you do here on Christmas eve?' said the goblin, sternly.

"'I came to dig a grave Sir,' stammered Gabriel Grub.

"'What man wanders among graves and church-yards on such a night as this?' said the goblin.

"'Gabriel Grub! Gabriel Grub!' screamed a wild chorus of voices that seemed to fill the church-yard. Gabriel looked fearfully round – nothing was to be seen.

"'What have you got in that bottle?' said the goblin.

"'Hollands, Sir,' replied the sexton, trembling more than ever; for he had bought it of the smugglers, and he thought that perhaps his questioner might be in the excise department of the goblins.

"'Who drinks Hollands alone, and in a church-yard, on such a night as this?' said the goblin.

"'Gabriel Grub! Gabriel Grub!' exclaimed the wild voices again.

"The goblin leered maliciously at the terrified sexton, and then raising his voice, exclaimed –

"'And who, then, is our fair and lawful prize?'

"To this inquiry the invisible chorus replied, in a strain that sounded like the voices of many choristers singing to the mighty swell of the old church organ – a strain that seemed borne to the sexton's ears upon a gentle wind, and to die away as its soft breath passed onward – but the burden of the reply was still the same, 'Gabriel Grub! Gabriel Grub!'

"The goblin grinned a broader grin than before, as he said, 'Well, Gabriel, what do you say to this?'

"The sexton gasped for breath.

"'What do you think of this, Gabriel?' said the goblin, kicking up his feet in the air on either side the tombstone, and looking at the turned-up points with as much complacency as if he had been contemplating the most fashionable pair of Wellingtons in all Bond Street.

"'It's—it's—very curious, Sir,' replied the sexton, half dead with fright, 'very curious, and very pretty, but I think I'll go back and finish my work, Sir, if you please.'

"'Work!' said the goblin, 'what work?'

"'The grave, Sir, making the grave,' stammered the sexton.

"'Oh, the grave, eh?' said the goblin, 'who makes graves at a time when all other men are merry, and takes a pleasure in it?'

"Again the mysterious voices replied, 'Gabriel Grub! Gabriel Grub!'

"'I'm afraid my friends want you, Gabriel,' said the goblin, thrusting his tongue further into his cheek than ever – and a most astonishing tongue it was – 'I'm afraid my friends want you, Gabriel,' said the goblin.

"'Under favour, Sir,' replied the horror-struck sexton, 'I don't think they can, Sir; they don't know me, Sir, I don't think the gentlemen have ever seen me, Sir.'

"'Oh yes they have,' replied the goblin; 'we know the man with the sulky face and the grim scowl, that came down the street tonight, throwing his evil looks at the children, and grasping his burying spade the tighter. We know the man that struck the boy in the envious malice of his heart, because the boy could be merry, and he could not. We know him, we know him.'

"Here the goblin gave a loud shrill laugh, that the echoes returned twenty-fold, and throwing his legs up in the air, stood upon his head, or rather upon the very point of his sugar-loaf hat, on the narrow edge of the tombstone, from whence he threw a summerset with extraordinary agility, right to the sexton's feet, at which he planted himself in the attitude in which tailors generally sit upon the shop-board.

"'I—I—am afraid I must leave you, Sir,' said the sexton, making an effort to move.

"'Leave us!' said the goblin, 'Gabriel Grub going to leave us. Ho! ho! ho!'

"As the goblin laughed, the sexton observed for one instant a brilliant illumination within the windows of the church, as if the whole building were lighted up; it disappeared, the organ pealed forth a lively air, and whole troops of goblins, the very counterpart of the first one, poured into the church-yard, and began playing at leap-frog with the tombstones, never stopping for an instant to take breath, but overing the highest among them, one after the other, with the most marvellous dexterity. The first goblin was a most astonishing leaper, and none of the others could come near him; even in the extremity of his terror the sexton could not help observing, that while his friends were content to leap over the common-sized gravestones, the first one took the family vaults, iron railings and all, with as much ease as if they had been so many street posts.

"At last the game reached to a most exciting pitch; the organ played quicker and quicker, and the goblins leaped faster and faster, coiling themselves up, rolling head over heels upon the ground, and bounding over the tombstones like foot-balls. The sexton's brain whirled round with the rapidity of the motion he beheld, and his legs reeled beneath him, as the spirits flew before his eyes, when the goblin king suddenly darting towards him, laid his hand upon his collar, and sank with him through the earth.

"When Gabriel Grub had had time to fetch his breath, which the rapidity of his descent had for the moment taken away, he found himself in what appeared to be a large cavern, surrounded on all sides by crowds of goblins, ugly and grim; in the centre of the room, on an elevated seat, was stationed his friend of the church-yard; and close beside him stood Gabriel Grub himself, without the power of motion.

"'Cold tonight,' said the king of the goblins, 'very cold. A glass of something warm, here.'

"At this command, half a dozen officious goblins, with a perpetual smile upon their faces, whom Gabriel Grub imagined to be courtiers, on that account, hastily disappeared, and presently returned with a goblet of liquid fire, which they presented to the king.

"'Ah!' said the goblin, whose cheeks and throat were quite transparent, as he tossed down the flame, 'This warms one, indeed: bring a bumper of the same, for Mr. Grub.'

"It was in vain for the unfortunate sexton to protest that he was not in the habit of taking anything warm at night; for one of the goblins held him while another poured the blazing liquid down his throat, and the whole assembly screeched with laughter as he coughed and choked, and wiped away the tears which gushed plentifully from his eyes, after swallowing the burning draught.

"'And now,' said the king, fantastically poking the taper corner of his sugar-loaf hat into the sexton's eye, and thereby occasioning him the most exquisite pain – 'And now, show the man of misery and gloom a few of the pictures from our own great storehouse.'

"As the goblin said this, a thick cloud which obscured the further end of the cavern, rolled gradually away, and disclosed, apparently at a great distance, a small and scantily furnished, but neat and clean apartment. A crowd of little children were gathered round a bright fire, clinging to their mother's gown, and gambolling round her chair. The mother occasionally rose, and drew aside the window-curtain as if to look for some expected object; a frugal meal was ready spread upon the table, and an elbow chair was placed near the fire. A knock was heard at the door: the mother opened it, and the children crowded round her, and clapped their hands for joy, as their father entered. He was wet and weary, and shook the snow from his garments, as the children crowded round him, and seizing his cloak, hat, stick, and gloves, with busy zeal, ran with them from the room. Then as he sat down to his meal before the fire, the children climbed about his knee, and the mother sat by his side, and all seemed happiness and comfort.

"But a change came upon the view, almost imperceptibly. The scene was altered to a small bedroom, where the fairest and youngest child lay dying; the roses had fled from his cheek, and the light from his eye; and even as the sexton looked upon him with an interest he had never felt or known before, he died. His young brothers and sisters crowded round his little bed, and seized his tiny hand, so cold and heavy; but they shrunk back from its touch, and looked with awe on his infant face; for calm and tranquil as it was, and sleeping in rest and peace as the beautiful child seemed to be, they saw that he was dead, and they knew that he was an angel looking down upon, and blessing them, from a bright and happy Heaven."

Again the light cloud passed across the picture, and again the subject changed. The father and mother were old and helpless now, and the number of those about them was diminished more than half; but content and cheerfulness sat on every face, and beamed in every eye, as they crowded round the fireside, and told and listened to old stories of earlier and bygone days. Slowly and peacefully the father sank into the grave, and, soon after, the sharer of all his cares and troubles followed him to a place of rest and peace. The few, who yet survived them, knelt by their tomb, and watered the green turf which covered it with their tears; then rose and turned away, sadly and mournfully, but not with bitter cries, or despairing lamentations, for they knew that they should one day meet again; and once more they mixed with the busy world, and their content and cheerfulness were restored. The cloud settled upon the picture, and concealed it from the sexton's view.

"'What do you think of *that*?' said the goblin, turning his large face towards Gabriel Grub.

"Gabriel murmured out something about its being very pretty, and looked somewhat ashamed, as the goblin bent his fiery eyes upon him.

"'*You* a miserable man!' said the goblin, in a tone of excessive contempt. 'You!' He appeared disposed to add more, but indignation choked his utterance, so he lifted up one of his very pliable legs, and flourishing it above his head a little, to insure his aid, administered a good sound kick to Gabriel Grub; immediately after which, all the goblins in waiting crowded round the wretched sexton, and kicked him without mercy, according to the established and invariable custom of courtiers upon earth, who kick whom royalty kicks, and hug whom royalty hugs.

"'Show him some more,' said the king of the goblins.

"At these words the cloud was again dispelled, and a rich and beautiful landscape was disclosed to view – there is just such another to this day, within half a mile of the old abbey town. The sun shone from out the clear blue sky, the water sparkled beneath his rays, and the trees looked greener, and the flowers more gay, beneath his cheering influence. The water rippled on, with a pleasant sound, the trees rustled in the light wind that murmured among their leaves, the birds sang upon the boughs, and the lark carolled on high, her welcome to the morning. Yes, it was morning, the bright, balmy morning of summer; the minutest leaf, the smallest blade of grass, was instinct with life. The ant crept forth to her daily toil, the butterfly fluttered and basked in the warm rays of the sun; myriads of insects spread their transparent wings, and revelled in their brief but happy existence. Man walked forth, elated with the scene; and all was brightness and splendour.

"'*You* a miserable man!' said the king of the goblins, in a more contemptuous tone than before. And again the king of the goblins gave his leg a flourish; again it descended on the shoulders of the sexton; and again the attendant goblins imitated the example of their chief.

"Many a time the cloud went and came, and many a lesson it taught to Gabriel Grub, who although his shoulders smarted with pain from the frequent applications of the goblin's feet thereunto, looked on with an interest which nothing could diminish. He saw that men who worked hard, and earned their scanty bread with lives of labour, were cheerful and happy; and that to the most ignorant, the sweet face of nature was a never-failing source of cheerfulness and joy. He saw those who had been delicately nurtured, and tenderly brought up, cheerful under privations, and superior to suffering, that would have crushed many of a rougher grain, because they bore within their own bosoms the materials of happiness, contentment, and peace. He saw that women, the tenderest and most fragile of all God's creatures, were the oftenest superior to sorrow, adversity, and distress; and he saw that it was because they bore in their own hearts an inexhaustible wellspring of affection and devotedness. Above all, he saw that men like himself, who snarled at the mirth and cheerfulness of others, were the foulest weeds on the fair surface of the earth; and setting all the good of the world against the evil, he came to the conclusion that it was a very decent and respectable sort of world after all. No sooner had he formed it, than the cloud which had closed over the last picture, seemed to settle on his senses, and lull him to repose. One by one, the goblins faded from his sight, and as the last one disappeared, he sunk to sleep."

The day had broken when Gabriel Grub awoke, and found himself lying at full length on the flat gravestone in the church-yard, with the wicker bottle lying empty by his side, and his coat, spade, and lantern, all well whitened by the last night's frost, scattered on the ground. The stone on which he had first seen the goblin seated, stood bolt upright before him, and the grave at which he had worked, the night before, was not far off. At first he began to doubt the reality of his adventures, but the acute pain in his shoulders when he attempted to rise, assured him that the kicking of the goblins was certainly not ideal. He was staggered again, by observing no traces of footsteps in the snow on which the goblins had played at leap-frog with the gravestones, but he speedily accounted for this circumstance when he remembered that being spirits, they would leave no visible impression behind them. So Gabriel Grub got on his feet as well as he could, for the pain in his back; and brushing the frost off his coat, put it on, and turned his face towards the town.

But he was an altered man, and he could not bear the thought of returning to a place where his repentance would be scoffed at, and his reformation disbelieved. He hesitated for a few moments; and then turned away to wander where he might, and seek his bread elsewhere.

The lantern, the spade, and the wicker bottle, were found that day in the church-yard. There were a great many speculations about the sexton's fate at first, but it was speedily determined that he had been carried away by the goblins; and there were not wanting some very credible witnesses who had distinctly seen him whisked through the air on the back of a chestnut horse blind of one eye, with the hind quarters of a lion, and the tail of a bear. At length all this was devoutly believed; and the new sexton used to exhibit to the curious for a trifling emolument, a good-sized piece of the church weathercock which had been accidentally kicked off by the aforesaid horse in his aërial flight, and picked up by himself in the church-yard, a year or two afterwards.

"Unfortunately these stories were somewhat disturbed by the unlooked-for reappearance of Gabriel Grub himself, some ten years afterwards, a ragged, contented, rheumatic old man. He told his story to the clergyman, and also to the mayor; and in course of time it began to be received as a matter of history, in which form it has continued down to this very day. The believers in the weathercock tale, having misplaced their confidence once, were not easily prevailed upon to part with it again, so they looked as wise as they could, shrugged their shoulders, touched their foreheads, and murmured something about Gabriel Grub's having drunk all the Hollands, and then fallen asleep on the flat tombstone; and they affected to explain what he supposed he had witnessed in the goblin's cavern, by saying that he had seen the world, and grown wiser. But this opinion, which was by no means a popular one at any time, gradually died off; and be the matter how it may, as Gabriel Grub was afflicted with rheumatism to the end of his days, this story has at least one moral, if it teach no better one – and that is, that if a man turns sulky and drinks by himself at Christmas time, he may make up his mind to be not a bit the better for it, let the spirits be ever so good, or let them be even as many degrees beyond proof, as those which Gabriel Grub saw, in the goblin's cavern."

Elvis Saves Christmas

James Dodds

IT WAS THE night before Christmas and Elvis was nowhere to be found. Madison combed through the house twice, sweeping basement to attic. During the second search she called and whistled for him. "Elvis? Hound dog? Here, boy! C'mon Elvis!" Madison stepped out into the back yard, hugging herself against the bitter cold. "Elvis!" she shouted into the howling wind. "Elll… *vis*!" No bark answered her call, no dog loped through the snow to his best friend's side. Madison began trembling; not from the frosty air, but from the chill settling on her heart.

Madison's parents, David and Sandra, huddled together in their living room as they listened to her fruitless journey. Their Christmas tree, with its warm lights and bright decorations, tried bravely to be a lighthouse against the dark clouds gathering inside their home.

"Oh David," said Sandra, "I so hoped he would last a few more days. If she loses him tonight or tomorrow, Christmas will never be the same for her." David embraced Sandra, pulling her close. His heart ached that Madison's future Christmases might be tinged with sadness.

"It's the night of our Savior's birth, darling," he said. "It's a night for miracles. Keep a candle lit in your heart."

Madison's footsteps approached. Voice shaking, she called for her dog once more. As she walked into the room, her lower lip quivering, David knew a sadness that only fathers with daughters know. Here, too soon, was her first heartbreak.

"Mom? Dad? I can't find Elvis," she said. Her face crumpled as she looked at each parent. "He's never not come when I called."

* * *

This was true. David and Sandra eagerly welcomed the black Labrador puppy right after their honeymoon, twelve years before. They wanted a family dog. One year later, Madison arrived. Two years after that, Elvis's unwavering devotion to their toddler made it clear that while there was a dog in the family, he was not a family dog.

He liked David and Sandra well enough. Especially at feeding time. Elvis would wolf down his food, reward his server with a hearty tail wag, then bound off in search of Madison. While both grownups performed useful functions in Elvis's world, that world revolved around Madison.

The two became inseparable, day and night. Madison had friends, but life on a hay farm in eastern Washington state can be isolated. Elvis filled the gap. He was playmate, horsey, fellow explorer, guardian, confidante of little girl secrets and extra blanket on the bed.

Shortly after she turned five, Madison discovered there had been a human Elvis. When she asked David about him, he showed her an internet video of young Elvis Presley dancing and singing "Blue Suede Shoes." Fascinated, she watched it over and over.

For the next few days, Madison hummed and sang the song. She even danced like Elvis. "Her first earworm," Sandra smiled. They didn't know the half of it until a week later, when Madison called to them from her room.

"Mommy? Daddy? Come watch us!"

Both girl and dog were wriggling with excitement. "You ready?" said Madison. "Okay, watch!" She turned to her dog. "Elvis! Blue Suede Shoes!" He sat up, paws out; eyes focused on his little human. As she sang, "Well it's one for the money," he reached his right paw forward and up. She clasped it with her left hand.

"And two for the show." He reached his left paw out to her right hand.

"Three to get ready." She paused.

Elvis barked, "Rarf, rarf, rarf!"

"Now go, dog, go!" she shouted. She did her best Elvis hip swivel and he stood up on his hind legs to wiggle along as she joggled his upper body. After a few seconds she wrapped with, "Don't you step on my blue suede shoes." She let go and Elvis pounced for her feet, batting at them with his paws as she danced away, giggling madly.

"Didja like it? Didja?" she squealed as she pranced around the room, Elvis chasing her.

David stared at Elvis; eyes wide in disbelief. Sandra stared at Madison, mouth agape and momentarily speechless. After a long moment, both parents stared at each other. "Um," said David, "Could we see that again?"

Two repeat performances later, her parents were over their shock and singing along with "Now go, dog, go!"

David grabbed Madison up and both he and Sandra hugged her. "Baby girl, that is amazing!" David yelled. "You are absolutely amazing!"

"Honey?" Sandra raised her eyebrows and looked down at Elvis. The dog stared up at the three of them, the tip of his tail wagging expectantly.

"Oh, right!" said David. He put his daughter down and pulled Elvis into a four-way family hug. After a warm moment, he leaned back and smiled at his daughter and her dog. "You two are pretty special," he said.

* * *

Girl and dog stayed special to each other through the years. Time brought the slow changes that always seem to arrive so quickly. Now eleven, Madison teetered toward her teens. At twelve, Elvis was a senior citizen who had acquired a grizzled muzzle and distinct limp. Plus, at some point in the last year, cancer.

David's first grim suspicion hit him at Thanksgiving. As family and guests stretched out after the feast, David made Elvis his traditional 'one spoonful of everything' dinner. "Here you go, Big Pig. Remember to say grace and don't inhale it this time." Instead of diving in like a starving vacuum cleaner, Elvis snuffled at the bowl, finally taking a tentative bite.

David knelt to inspect the food offering. "Getting picky in your old age, pal?" He started to get up and join his family, but something made him linger. Under David's gaze, Elvis grazed for a minute then turned away, his bowl still full. He looked up at David and gave him a slow tail wag.

Heart sinking, David took Elvis's head in his hands. "No boy," he said, "You're not in trouble. And you're right, that gravy was too salty." David put his head against Elvis's and gently tugged on his ears. "Dear God," he murmured, "Please let me be wrong." He heard Madison approaching and quickly dashed the remains of Elvis's dinner into the garbage bin. "Too early to be sure and way too early for questions, right boy?" Elvis wagged his tail enthusiastically.

Two weeks later, David knew. "Are you sure, dear?" Sandra said when he confided his fears to her. They were washing dishes in the kitchen. She gripped the windowsill as she watched Madison skipping around the yard, Elvis struggling to keep up.

"I'm sorry, darling, but there's no doubt." A farm boy, David had known many dogs. The low energy and the lumps underneath Elvis's skin flashed unmistakable signs. Signs that called up canine angels from David's past. He winced as Elvis stumbled, rose back up, shook it off and continued on after Madison. In the last few days Elvis's appetite and weight had dropped dramatically. "His time is very near."

* * *

Now, the family had come to it. Madison studied her parents' faces, searching for the reassurance they could make everything okay. She didn't find it. David saw her shoulders slump. Was this something they couldn't fix? Unthinkable.

Madison saw David's gaze on her and moved toward him. He pulled her on to his lap and stroked her hair. "Daddy?" she said. She hadn't called him that for three years. "Daddy, can you help me find Elvis?"

"Yes, pumpkin. I'm pretty sure I know where he is. Let's all go find him and rarffle his tail off!" This family game involved pushing Elvis down and tickle-scratching him all over. He growled fiercely and bit their arms with a gentleness that wouldn't break an egg. When they stopped, he snuffled indignantly and nosed at their hands until they continued.

"We'll check the barn first. Everybody get a coat," said David. To Sandra he added, "Better bring some blankets too."

David picked the barn because there were already other dogs there – a mother and her pups. This particular wandering dog appeared in mid-summer and took up residence in the barn. This occurred frequently. Sometimes the wanderer stayed for a few days, other times longer. As long as they didn't bother the livestock, David enjoyed their presence. Dogs provided a natural deterrent to undesirable animals like rodents, rabbits and coyotes. He fed them occasionally – enough to keep them from starving, but not so much that they felt at home.

This dog was female and, as best as he could tell, part Golden Lab, part Border Collie and part Who Knows. She barked at all the right varmints and tagged along with Madison and Elvis as they rambled about the place.

A few weeks after her arrival, it was clear that she was pregnant. "Looks like we're going to have puppies in about two months," David said to Sandra as the dog lumbered past them at an ungainly trot. "They'll be ready for adoption right before Christmas."

"Was she pregnant when she got here?" Sandra said. "Or… you don't suppose that Elvis…." She smiled in disbelieving admiration.

David laughed. "Not likely at his age, honey!"

But when the puppies arrived, it was clear Elvis had been involved. Some resembled the mother and some were a mix, but one little black puppy was a carbon copy of Elvis. He stood over the wriggling mass of whimpering puppies, wagging his tail proudly.

"I can't believe it!" said Sandra, as she watched the mother lick each puppy, cleaning it up to meet the big world. "Talk about an old dog still up to his old tricks!"

"Hey!" said David, "They didn't call him The King for nothing, you know."

* * *

The three approached the barn. Brightly lit by a yard light glowing high overhead, the ancient structure seemed like a manger from the past. They hurried through the door and Madison immediately saw Elvis. He lay stretched out full length, ten feet from the mother dog. She braced herself against a pile of hay while her puppies, minus one, dozed, played, nursed and dozed some more.

The little black one lay nose-to-nose with Elvis. Elvis's chest rose and fell slowly, his breathing labored. Small sounds escaped his mouth, as if he was talking to the puppy. Occasionally the black puppy yipped in reply.

Elvis saw his humans. He "hrrffd" a few more times at the puppy, then gently nosed him away.

Madison knelt down and took Elvis's head in her hands. His tail thump sounded like someone beating on the door. The family settled themselves around him. David leaned back and inhaled the rich, earthy barn smells. For him, it was all here. The fragrant, familiar scents spoke of birth, death and the sweat and toil of everything in between.

Sandra sighed and spread a blanket over Elvis's spare frame. Madison scooted forward and lifted his head into her lap. Her lips quivered. "Oh, Elvis," she whispered. Tears started down her cheeks.

Elvis gazed up at her and stretched his paw forward to rest on her foot. All her life, when he sensed his charge was upset, he'd comforted her this way. Madison gently stroked his head and looked up at her father. "Dad, what do we do?" Her voice cracked with pain and uncertainty.

David cast his memory back over all the dogs he'd loved and lost. He put his arm around her. "We celebrate his time in our world. The best thing about a dog is they adore you with a perfect love. The worst thing about a dog is they're only yours for a short time. When you take one into your life, you're making a bargain. You get years of love, but the price is a broken heart.

"But it's a good bargain. The love and the memories stay with you. This pain won't. Don't fight the pain. It's part of how we let our loved ones go."

He reached down to stroke Elvis's snout and got a low "hrrrr" in response.

David laughed. "I remember the first time he made that noise. Binging him home from the breeder, I held the puppy curled up in my lap. Who knew he had motion sickness! I pulled into the driveway, rubbed his tummy and said, "Well boy, you're home." He raised his head and promptly barfed in my lap. Yuck! I almost barfed myself."

"We never did get the stain out of the car seat," added Sandra.

"Or my pants."

All three chuckled, awkwardly. Elvis thumped his tail on the floorboards, encouraging another story.

Sandra began. "I remember when Elvis discovered chipmunks. He was two and had anointed himself Lord and Protector of the house, against all comers. That spring, when the 'munks started zipping around the garden, Elvis tried to chase them out. They thought he was hilarious. After one led him into a rose bush, he decided they were no longer worth noticing."

The laughter sounded a bit more genuine.

Madison cleared her throat. "I remember Elvis and I walking out on the old wagon trail. It was hot and dusty and I scuffed along in the new cowboy boots I'd got for my birthday. I was so taken with them, I wasn't watching the trail. Suddenly I heard the rattle of that big fat snake who lived up there."

Her parents looked at each other, eyebrows raised. They hadn't heard this story before.

"I never told you cuz I thought you'd be mad at me. 'Stay away from the trail up there, it's snake territory,'" she added in her 'naggy grownup voice.' "Elvis jumped in front of me and started barking like I'd never heard before. He roared like a lion at that snake. It hissed and slithered off."

They went on, sharing warm memories in the chilly barn while they petted and held their dog. He occasionally wagged his tail and looked up at each one. The little black puppy sat motionless in the circle beside them.

Eventually, the stories flagged. So did Elvis. His breathing became more ragged and then, after a harsh coughing spell, it smoothed out for the last time. He raised his head, gazed for a long moment at Madison and then, after a sharp look at the black puppy, he laid his head back down. It was over.

Madison started to sob. The puppy crept over to her and rested his paw on her foot. Her parents leaned in and wrapped their arms around her.

When she finished crying, she hugged her parents and stood up. Wiping her eyes and nose on her sleeve, she declared, "I never want another dog again. And I don't want Christmas breakfast or presents or anything tomorrow! I can't care about The Birth when all I can think of is death." Back stiff, she stomped toward the door.

The black puppy scampered in front of her. He stopped, sat up and gave three short barks.

"Shoo, puppy!" she said, brushing past him. "No more dogs!"

He dashed past her again, stopped and sat up. This time he raised his right paw, teetered a bit and then raised his left paw. Madison stopped and stared. The puppy barked again, three high puppy yips, the third so insistent that he fell over and wriggled on the floor.

"Impossible," Madison whispered. The little dog stood back up, looking at her expectantly. "Mom? Dad? What is this?" David and Sandra joined her and they all stared down at the dog. He jumped toward Madison and barked up at her.

Madison knelt down; her breath caught in her throat. "Okay puppy. Blue Suede Shoes!" The dog sat up straight, again teetering on the brink of falling over.

In a low voice, Madison said, "Well it's one for the money." The puppy considered both its front legs, then stretched his right paw forward. She gasped, then grabbed it as his balance crumbled.

"Two for the show." Steadied, he had no trouble extending the other paw. She took it.

Louder now, "Three to get ready!" On cue, the pup barked, "Rarf, rarf, rarf!"

"Now go, dog, go!" she yelled. The puppy wriggled madly and then fell right down.

Madison sang, "Don't you step on my blue suede shoes, you hound!" He raced forward and grabbed one of her shoestrings in his mouth. Growling furiously, he backed away until it was taut and shook his head as hard as he could. Madison picked him up, pulled his face to hers and stared hard into his eyes. She got a big wet puppy lick.

"This can't be happening, can it Dad?" Wonder tinged her voice as she looked up at David.

"Sweetie," he replied, "It's Christmas. Today we celebrate the biggest miracle ever. I don't see any reason to doubt a little miracle like this one."

All three gathered around the wriggling mass of warm puppy. He looked up at them and gave a low "wuff."

"Call me crazy," said Sandra, "But that sure sounded like 'Hey – I know you!'"

"Looks like I need to rethink my 'no more dogs' policy," said Madison. "Frankie here is going to need a home." She hugged him close, a smile beginning to appear through the tear-streak smudges.

"Frankie?" said David. "Where did that come from?"

"Short for Frankincense."

Her father looked puzzled. Madison sighed. At the lofty age of eleven, she was starting to notice just how dense grownups could be at times. "Um, it's *Christmas*, we're in a *manger* and we just got a *gift*, right? Jeesh, Dad, who ever heard of calling a dog Myrrh? Duh."

Having clarified the point with her hapless father, Madison put the puppy down and returned to Elvis. She kneeled and gently grasped both his ears with her special Elvis ear scrunch. Madison nestled her head to his and began whispering. David watched her lips move, but couldn't make out the words. After a minute, she stood. New tears were coursing down her face, but behind them glimmered a look of peace.

Madison scooped Frankie up. Holding him eye to eye she said, "I knew you wouldn't leave me, hound dog." She started off to the house, carrying Frankie. As the two moved away, her parents heard her cooing to him.

David and Sandra knelt down beside Elvis. They took each other's hand, humbly accepting this sign of Christmas spirit. All was silent. Every other puppy was asleep.

Finally, Sandra inhaled deeply. "Best Christmas gift ever, Elvis. Thank you."

"Good dog," said David, patting his head, "Good dog."

Yule Cat

JG Faherty

Excitement hovered over the town of Fox Run in much the same way the snow-filled clouds had done all week. The day seemed ordinary enough, but children and adults alike knew differently.

Tonight would be special.

All day long, women bustled about in kitchens, grandmothers and mothers and daughters, cooking and baking the feasts for that night. The savory, grease-laden scents of fried ham, roast lamb, and *hamborgarhyryggur* – smoked pork rack – competed with the heavenly aromas of fresh-baked breads and desserts. For those with a sweet tooth, plates stacked high with jelly-covered pancakes and twisted fried dough – *lummer* and *kleinur* – sat on tables and counters, wherever there was room.

It was the traditional Yule feast, part of the celebration of the winter solstice.

The longest night of the year.

The night when ghosts ride the winds and the Yule Cat roams in search of lazy humans to eat.

* * *

"Aw, Grandpa, that's just a silly old tale to scare little kids," Jacob Anders said, as his grandfather finished his annual telling of the Yule story.

"Don't talk to your Farfar like that," Grandma Anders said, her thin face pulled tight in one of her mock-serious scowls. She worked hard to keep up her brusque appearance to the rest of the family, only occasionally letting her old-country veneer slip, as she'd done earlier when she let Jacob and his older sister Erika lick the spoons after she iced the traditional Yule cake.

Like most of Fox Run's residents, the Anders had emigrated from Scandinavia, eventually settling in Western Pennsylvania, where the Appalachians provided the same backdrop as the *Kölen* of their homeland.

Although they'd celebrated Yule at their grandparents' since before they could remember, this year was the first year Jacob and Erika's parents weren't with them. They'd dropped the children off the day before, with kisses and hugs and promises to return in four days loaded with gifts from their cruise.

For Jacob and Erika, the four days loomed over them in much the same way as the mountains loomed over Fox Run. Their grandparents' house wasn't exactly child friendly. They had no cable TV, no video games, and cell phone service was spotty on the best of days.

His temper frayed by boredom, Jacob, who'd always been overly energetic, even for a nine-year-old, made a face. "It's the same old boring story every year. Why can't we go into town and do something? Maybe see a movie?"

"Because Yule is for being with family." Grandma Anders shook a bony finger at him. "Children today have forgotten the old ways. They think only of themselves."

"Ja." Grandpa Anders sucked on his empty pipe. He'd given up tobacco years before, but never the habit of clenching the pipe between his teeth while sitting by the fire. "And those are the ones who get no presents from *Jule-nissen* later tonight."

"Grandpa, we don't believe in Santa or the Easter Bunny. What makes you think we're gonna believe in an elf who rides a talking goat and leaves gifts for children?" Jacob laughed, but his grandparents didn't smile.

"Ah. No talking to children today." Grandpa Anders got up and shook his head. "Goodnight, then. If you think the tales of your ancestors are such...foof..." he said, waving his hand at them, "perhaps you should stay up and watch for the *Jule-nissen* yourself."

"Maybe I will."

"Jacob, hush." Erika gave her brother a poke. Normally she wouldn't care, but with her parents gone she felt responsible for her brother, and she didn't want him being rude.

"I think perhaps bed is a good idea for all of us," Grandma Anders said, taking her tea cup into the kitchen.

"No way! It's not even nine o'clock yet. We never go to bed this early at home."

"You're not at home, young man." Grandma Anders glared at him, giving him what the children secretly called her 'stink eye.' It meant she'd reached the point where she'd put up with no more nonsense. "So off to bed. Now!" She clapped her hands twice, the sudden sound like branches snapping under the weight of too much ice.

"But—"

"C'mon, Jacob. I think you had too much sugar tonight." Erika grabbed him by the arm.

"Lemme go!" He yanked himself from her grasp and stormed down the hall to the guest bedroom they were sharing.

"I'm sorry, Grandma," Erika said.

Grandma Anders patted her shoulder and planted a soft, whiskery kiss on her cheek. "Don't fret, child. Someday he will learn the truth."

* * *

Jacob and Erika lay awake in their room. Upstairs, the grumbling, wheezing sounds emanating from their grandparents' bedroom told them Mormor and Farfar Anders were fast asleep.

"I'm hungry," Jakob whispered.

"No, you're not. You had two plates for dinner, and at least three desserts, plus the one I saw you sneak while everyone was sitting by the fire."

"Fine. Then I'm thirsty."

Erika sighed. "What you are is bored and a brat. Go to sleep." She wished she could do the same. She'd been trying to doze off for over an hour. But too much sugar and a day of doing nothing but helping in the kitchen had her wide awake.

"Did you hear that?" Jakob asked.

"All I hear is you talking."

"Sssh!"

She started to scold him for being such a pain, and then stopped.

Because she did hear it.

A low, distant moaning, winter-cold and ethereal as the wind. A dozen voices; a hundred. A thousand, perhaps, all sighing at once, all lamenting a sadness older than time but not forgotten.

Jacob climbed out of bed and went to the window. His body was a gray shadow among all the others in the room. When he pulled the white lace curtain aside, he revealed a scene that was almost alien, as the snow, so white it almost glowed, hid the ordinary beneath weird mounds and featureless plains.

"Don't!" Erika couldn't explain it, but she felt something deep in her bones.

Danger waited outside.

As usual, Jacob didn't listen. He pressed his face to the glass and peered out.

"I don't see anything," he whispered.

Against her better judgment, Erika joined him at the window, barely noticing the chill of the floor against her bare feet.

Jacob's breath left twin ovals of fog on the frigid glass as he pushed closer to look up and down the street.

Shaped like a heart, Erika thought, and that scared her just as much as the distant susserations of grief.

Outside, nothing seemed different than any other night. The houses were dark. Like the hard-working towns around it, Fox Run rose early and went to bed early.

Just when Erika thought her chattering teeth might wake her grandparents, new sounds joined the mourning dirge. A triumphant cry, accompanied by the bellow of a horn and the baying of hounds.

"Something's happening!" Before Erika could stop him, Jacob dashed from room. For a moment she stood frozen by indecision. Then she heard the slam of the back door and the spell holding her in place broke like an ice dagger snapping from the gutter.

Pausing just long enough to put on boots and grab her coat from the hook by the door, she hurried outside and spotted Jacob already running down the road.

"Jacob, stop! Come back!" He didn't, so despite the glacial air that threatened to freeze her blood and stop her heart, Erika ran after him.

It took three blocks to catch up with Jacob, and by the time she did, her face burned and tiny icicles of snot crusted her nose and upper lip.

"I'm gonna kill you when we get back," she said, grabbing a fistful of his coat.

"Quiet!" He put a finger to his lips. "It's almost here."

Since the sounds were no louder, Erika wanted to ask him how he knew, but then she understood. He felt it, and she could, too.

A heartbeat later, the source of the supernatural noise appeared. Swirling towers of mist, so many she couldn't count them, appeared out of nowhere and sailed down the road as fast as racing cars. As they swept past, she glimpsed faces, twisted and horrible. The moaning of the apparitions vibrated her teeth like a dentist's drill. Next to her, Jacob pressed his hands over his ears.

The line of spirits – for she knew that's what they were – seemed to go on forever, but it was only seconds before they were past, and the reason for their wailing became apparent.

Behind them came more ghosts, mounted on ephemeral horses and surrounded by massive hounds with glowing red eyes. Leading the pack was a giant of a man wearing the antlered skull of a colossal deer as a helmet. It was his exultant war cries that had the other spirits fleeing, as he led his phantom troop in pursuit.

Ten heartbeats later, the streets lay empty again.

"Did you see that?" Jacob asked. "What were they?"

"I don't know." Erika pulled at him. "Let's go home before we freeze to death."

"'Tis not the cold you should be worrying about."

Erika screamed and Jacob gasped at the unknown voice behind them. Turning, they found themselves face to face with a goat wearing a green jacket. On its back perched a tiny man with a long, pointed beard. Like the goat, the man's yellow eyes had horizontal pupils, and he wore green clothes as well.

"Jule-nissen." Jacob's eyes were wide. "You're real!"

The elf shook his head. "Yes, but you'll be nothing but a memory if the Cat gets you."

"The cat? What cat?"

"The Yule Cat, sonny-boy. He's been stalking you since you left your house."

"I didn't see any—"

"There!" The elf pointed down the street.

Between two houses, a shadow, darker than the sky and impossibly huge, slid across the snow. Before Erika could think of anything to say, a giant tabby cat, taller than a lion and twice as broad, stalked into view, yellowish-green eyes glowing and a hungry smile on its face.

Jacob moaned, and the Cat, even from a hundred yards away, heard. Its ears twitched and it crouched down in the middle of the street, tail whipping back and forth behind it.

"Run," Erika said.

Jacob stood still, frozen in fear.

"Run!" This time she shouted it. At the same time, the cat sprang forward.

"This way," the elf called to them, as the goat carried him down a side street.

Jacob and Erika followed. Each step took them further from their grandparents' house, but they didn't care. All that mattered was eluding the impossible feline sprinting down the road after them.

The goat led them around a corner and Erika felt a rush of relief as the Cat skidded on the slippery road and missed the turn. Then her relief turned to horror as the Cat sprang out from behind a house and swung a massive paw that sent the goat and its elvin rider tumbling across the icy blacktop. It swung again and Jacob cried out as a white cloud exploded from his chest. Erika screamed, sure the cat had disemboweled her brother and she was watching the air from his lungs freeze as it escaped. Then she saw it was just the front of his down jacket torn open and gushing feathers into the night.

"Get up!" Erika grabbed Jacob and pulled as he kicked his legs in a frantic attempt to get his feet under himself.

The Yule cat took a half-swing at them and hot liquid ran down her legs. She remembered how Mittens, the cat they'd had when she was younger, used to play with field mice and birds the same way, toying with them until it was ready to bite their heads off.

Now she knew how they felt.

"Ho, Yule Cat! Train your eyes this way!"

Erika jumped at the *Jule-nissen's* shout. In her worry for Jacob, she'd forgotten about the elf and his goat. She watched in amazement as the diminutive man waved his arms while the goat jumped and danced on its hind legs.

"What are you doing?"

"Saving your lazy hides," the elf said. "This is your chance. Return to your house. We'll be fine."

Erika didn't argue. Hand in hand, she and Jacob ran as fast as they could, the December air burning their lungs, hearts pounding in time with their feet. They ran without looking back, deathly afraid the Cat might be only a whisker's length away.

Suddenly Jacob cut sharply to the right. Erika started to shout at him and then realized they'd reached their grandparents' house. They pounded up the front steps and flung open the door so hard it hit the wall and sent knick-knacks clattering to the floor.

"Who's there? What's going on?" Josef Anders appeared at the top of the stairs, his wife close behind him.

"Grandma! Grandpa! It's after us! The Yule Cat!"

Erika slammed the door shut and twisted the lock. Grandma Anders said something, but Erika couldn't hear over the sounds of her and Jacob gasping for air.

"Into the living room! Hurry!" Grandpa Anders hurried down the stairs and tugged at their sleeves.

"But we're safe now. The goat—" The rest of Jacob's words disappeared in a crash of breaking glass as a pumpkin-sized paw came through the window next to the door.

"There's no hiding from the Cat," Grandma Anders shouted. "Only one thing can save you. Come!"

Erika and Jacob followed their grandparents into the living room, where the sweet scent of pine still decorated the air from the Yule log smoldering in the fireplace. Behind them, the Cat let out a fierce yowl at being denied its prey yet again.

Grandma Anders grabbed two small boxes from beneath the Christmas tree. "Here, open these. Quickly now."

"What?" Erika took the box but could only stare at it. With everything that had happened, the merry green and red wrapping paper seemed unreal.

"Do as your Mormor says." Grandpa Anders threw an angry scowl at them as he pulled the drapes shut. With his head turned away, he never saw the movement outside the window, never knew the Yule Cat was there until it burst through the glass and knocked him sideways into a bookcase. Shaking shards from its fur, the Cat let out a roar.

"Grandpa!" Jacob cried.

Erika turned to run but her grandmother stopped her by slapping her across the face. "Open the fordømt box!"

Hoping box contained some kind of magic weapon, Erika tore at the paper and cardboard. When she saw what was inside, her hands went limp and the box fell to the floor.

"A shirt?" She sank to her knees, knowing there was no hope left. Hot, fetid breath blew past her face, carrying the stench of rotten meat. Tears ran down Erika's face as she closed her eyes and waited for the end.

The carrion stink grew stronger and a whimper escaped her throat as something cold and wet bumped ever so lightly against her neck. Then it was gone.

"That's right, one for the girl and one for the boy, too. Now be gone."

Erika heard her grandmother's voice but the words didn't make sense. She opened her eyes and risked turning her head, just in time to see the Yule Cat climb out through the shattered picture window. Grandpa Anders was leaning against the bookcase, a cut on his forehead dripping blood. Jacob stood near him, his open box in his hands.

Eyes still on the departing feline, Erika asked, "What happened?"

"I can answer that, young miss."

Erika turned and saw the *Jule-nissen* atop his goat, right next to Grandma Anders, who didn't seem at all surprised by their presence.

"'Twas the gifts. A shirt for each of you."

"On Yule Eve, the Jule-nissen leaves a gift of clothing for all the children," Jacob said in a soft voice, "except for the lazy ones."

"And for them?" the elf asked.

"The Yule Cat eats them."

"So, you did listen to my stories." Grandpa Anders put a hand on the boy's shoulder.

"You really brought us gifts?" Jacob asked.

The goat snorted and the *Jule-nissen* shook his head. "Not me. You haven't done anything to deserve them, in my eyes. But lucky for you, someone thought different, and to the Cat, a gift's a gift." The elf snapped his fingers and he and his goat disappeared in a burst of golden sparkles.

"Then who...?" Jacob looked confused, but Erika knew exactly where the gifts had come from.

"You knew the tales were true," she said to her grandmother. "You did it to protect us."

Grandma Anders gave them the briefest of smiles. "We follow tradition, even if you do not. All families make sure to keep gifts handy in case the Yule Cat appears."

"You have to be careful on Yule," Grandpa Anders said.

Jacob nodded. "'Cause of the Yule Cat."

"Yes, but not just the Cat. 'Tis also the night of the Hunt, when the spirits of the Oak King arise to drive away the spirits of the Holly King, and put an end to nights growing longer. Get in their way and you'll become like them, doomed to Hunt forever."

"The Hunt," Erika whispered. She shivered, remembering the wailings of the Holly King's spirits as the Oak King banished them until June.

Grandma Anders noticed her reaction. "Go put on dry clothes. I'll make hot cocoa."

After the children left the room, Grandma Anders went into the kitchen, where her husband was already filling a pot with milk.

"Well?" he asked.

"I think from now on they'll listen when you tell your stories."

So distant they wouldn't have heard it if not for the broken window, a child's voice screamed in pain.

Josef Anders nodded. "Ja. Let us hope so. For their sakes."

Mr. Anders Meets a Stranger

Marina Favila

*The snake in the garden may know
it's in a garden, but not necessarily
know it is a snake*
Poppies and other Dangerous Beauties
M.V. Helsinger

MR. ANDERS REMEMBERS very little of his life before he met the stranger. He was a toymaker in Chelsea, that he was sure, sometime after the Second World War. And successful too, he thought, though that was mostly due to his wife's clever marketing. Mrs. Anders changed the name of their shop to Hans Christian Anders' Toys and Trains, and often let drop to customers and friends that her husband might well be related to that famous Danish storyteller. She even hired a local artist to paint a little mermaid on the shop window. Mr. Anders remembers strange colors for the mermaid's hair: twisted strands of salmon pink and pine green. Mrs. Anders added glitter to the tail, a source of fascination for the children in the town, at least in the early days, before wind and rain had scrubbed the window clean of all its sparkle.

Mr. Anders also remembers, or thinks he remembers, that he specialized in Christmas toys: stuffed animals from the North Pole (reindeer, penguins, white fur foxes) and overstuffed Santas, each with their own red leather sleigh. Some had silver bells, some gold, and some had mistletoe woven into the reins – a Mrs. Anders touch, her husband liked to say. There was a polar bear that popped out of a barrel when sufficiently wound, a Christmas elf with a bobble head filled with chocolates, and a crimson-red sailboat with Happy Holidays printed on its bow.

But what Mr. Anders was known for was trains, electric trains that ran through little towns with miniature trees and miniature bridges all lit up in bright white lights. A mirror lake with tiny skaters sold separately, along with an array of buildings of various shapes and sizes, lit from within.

These were Mr. Anders' pride and joy, in high demand from customers in the holiday season, especially those who wanted to surprise and delight their children, regardless of the cost. Mr. Anders worked very hard on these trains – sometimes all night, often falling into bed right before sunrise, exhausted but content, thinking of the boys and girls who would skip with joy when they saw his trains on Christmas morning.

It was, in fact, this bad habit of working through the night that led to his present dilemma, for a stranger saw his light on in the middle of the night, and knocked on his door one week before Christmas.

"I'm afraid we are closed…" But before Mr. Anders could shut the shop door, a tall, angular man begged entrance with such a piteous cry that it startled the toymaker.

"Par-*don*, par-*don*, sir!" The stranger had a slight, but familiar accent. Middle-aged, perhaps the same age as Mr. Anders himself. His coat was worn, but still an expensive cut from one of the finer shops in the city. Mr. Anders remembers shivering as the stranger stepped closer, the cold night air seeming to emanate from his very being.

"What do you desire... *Monsieur?*" Mr. Anders was not French, nor did he speak French, but the man on his stoop was so distinguished-looking that he felt sure he was European, and 'monsieur' was the only European word he knew.

"Forgive me," the man responded. "But yours was the only light on, and I suffer a terrible plight. I have been traveling on the continent for months, and have just returned – so close, is it not, to Christmas? I cannot go home to my family without some marvellous gift for my little boy. What welcome could I expect?"

Mr. Anders was kind-hearted, though a bit naïve. He immediately brought the stranger into his shop, and ushered him into a wingback chair, covered in berry-red corduroy. His wife had ordered the chair from London to dress up the shop for the holidays and to give her husband a comfortable place to rest. "Well, sit down then," Mr. Anders said. "Perhaps a cup of tea? For you look..." and the toymaker paused. The man was very pale, and for all his European charm seemed a bit the worse for wear.

When the stranger hesitated, Mr. Anders said in a low voice, "Or something stronger. A glass of sherry?

"Wine, if you have it." The man relaxed into the pillowed folds of his seat. "Red – anything deep red, perhaps a Cabernet."

The two men smiled, and Mr. Anders briefly touched the tip of his nose, as if suddenly aware of its own rosy flush. He too loved wine. "Give me a moment."

When both men were seated with Mrs. Anders' anniversary goblets filled to the brim with wine, Mr. Anders began to rattle off his huge catalogue of toys: rocking horses, pogo sticks, dangling mobiles of stars and planets, baby dolls with baby blankets and matching baby bottles, a plastic hippo that spat water when you squeezed it, a lion with a mane and a comb to comb it... When he came to the trains, the stranger's eyes glowed. "A train! My son would love a train. They are such romantic objects. They carry you away from the present and into some fabulous adventure."

"I have always thought so," Mr. Anders nodded. "When I was a little boy, I dreamed of being a conductor on the Orient Express! My mother bought me a dark blue cap that looked like a conductor's hat, and I would wear it everywhere, even to school. I remember getting into trouble for not removing it at the school assembly, but it was worth it."

The stranger chuckled. "Do you have children?"

"No. Mrs. Anders and I were not so lucky in that respect," and the toymaker blushed, for reasons he did not explain.

"Tell me about the train you are working on."

"Well!" Mr. Anders popped out of his chair and motioned to his visitor to join him at Train Central. That's what he called his workplace, a large table with a showcase display of all his newest additions. "This is the Day Racer. See the racing stripe on both sides of the train? It goes very fast and the headlights can be turned on and off. And this is the Red Rider, which can both speed up and slow down with the touch of a switch. And this – *this* is the Christmas Express."

The stranger moved slowly to the toymaker's side, entranced by the train before him. It was much larger than the other trains, and split down the middle, for it was not a train for a track or a train that could move, but a doll house-train, three cars long and decorated for the holidays. There was a diner car, with a bar and two booths, the tables set with tiny plates and tiny silverware, and little red and green porcelain cups. A silver pot was on the counter (for hot chocolate, Mr. Anders said) and a little cake server with a mound of Christmas cookies. The floor was black and white check and made of shiny plastic tiles, and a banner pronouncing Merry Christmas was strung up behind the bar.

The second car was a sleeper, with two fold-down beds. Imagine: real sheets, like a sleeping bag, just loose enough for a little doll to be tucked in tight for a good long rest. The blankets were remnants of Scottish plaid; and a tiny box wrapped in gold foil was placed nearby on a comfy seat, a miniature of the berry-red corduroy chair picked out by his loving wife.

The last car was the locomotive, with a little shovel and a little pail of coal to heap into the burner. Red tinsel fluttered in the furnace.

The stranger seemed entranced by it all, but he was particularly interested in the sleeper car. He pulled down the window shade, a jaunty candy cane stripe, and his hand shook as he did. Mr. Anders beamed with pleasure that his visitor had noticed this tiny detail. "Yes, it's a train for Christmas Eve. The sleeper car must have a heavy shade to allow its passengers to sleep in on Christmas morning. Otherwise the sun might wake them at dawn!"

"A train that could keep out the day even as it carried you into it. What a novel idea. Why did I never think of that?"

Mr. Anders smiled enthusiastically, though he did not understand the stranger's comment. "Have you never travelled on a red-eye, Monsieur?"

"No. I cannot travel in the day. I have a skin condition that makes it impossible for me to be out in the sun. That wasn't always true. As a child I loved playing outside, as soon as my morning chores were done and until the lights of the sunset faded, when my mother called me home. My eyes and skin would drink up the sunshine like a glass of life itself." His voice trailed off, then he added huskily, "Now I live and work only at night."

"Another drink perhaps?" Mr. Anders suggested, seeing his visitor turn melancholy at this happy childhood memory.

"No, I must be going soon. But tell me, sir, would it be possible to build this train, say, on a larger scale?"

"How large?"

"I was thinking what a wonderful playhouse it would be for... for my little boy," he said in a rush. "It wouldn't have to be the whole train, just two compartments. The diner car and the sleeper car – yes! A bed he could sleep in, like the ones on your train, with a large window and a heavy window shade that would allow him to sleep as late as he wished on Christmas morning."

"A playroom of that size, Monsieur, would be terribly expensive and take some time. This is my busiest month, as I'm sure you understand." Mr. Anders stood awkwardly, afraid of embarrassing his guest with this rejection.

"Yes," the stranger said slowly, "of course." But instead of getting up to leave – as Mr. Anders had hoped, for it was now quite late, and the warmth of the wine was rouging his nose and fluttering his eyes – the visitor sat back down in the berry-red chair, as if he intended to stay. "But, but... you see, Mr. Anders, I am rich – *very* rich. I could easily pay what you would make on other sales in the coming weeks, even into the winter months."

The stranger looked around. "And... and... and you have a cellar, yes? I thought I saw one from the outside. You could build it there. And I and my little boy could spend Christmas Eve and Christmas Day here in your shop! I know this must be a terrible imposition, but I have never spent Christmas Day with my son."

Mr. Anders was dumbfounded. "But, sir, what would your wife think?"

"My wife died in childbirth, Mr. Anders, and my work is such that I rarely see my child. Our London flat is cold and spare. I'll have no time to decorate it. But a Christmas train ride, even a pretend one, what a wonderful holiday that would be for us both. And... I would pay you very well, more than you can imagine. Anything you wish."

Mr. Anders paused, and then, to his own surprise, he said yes – not to the money, or, at least, not just to the money. The toymaker worked hard all year and made enough for his livelihood and more. He said yes to the challenge: building a life-size train, or close to it. Could he do it, and in such a short time? He thought he could. Perhaps he would put parts of it in the shop window next Christmas to decorate for the holidays. Mrs. Anders would approve, he was sure – if she were here, that is. And here, too, was another reason Mr. Anders said yes, for his wife had also died in childbirth, along with his infant son ten years ago. Since then he had thrown himself into his work and only his work, filling up his time making toys and toys for no child of his own. But now – now he was filled with sudden joy, for he was charged with making, not just any toy, not just any train you could play with, but a train you could play in, live in, a train to change your reality. Mr. Anders worked hard at his desk, mapping his plans, till the first touch of dawn light-lit the shop window.

* * *

For the next two weeks, Mr. Anders barely slept. Breakfast: black coffee, a half sandwich late in the day for lunch. He usually forgot dinner alltogether, so taken he was with some minor detail or measurement. Night, as always, was his special time, when the world stopped turning, and Mr. Anders could hammer and saw, needle and thread to his heart's content. This time, though, was different. He felt driven by some demon to get the job done, and not just done: it must be perfect – *perfect.* By the time Mr. Anders got into bed it was time to get up.

And what fun he was having! The two train cars fitted perfectly in the cellar, and the high ceiling afforded some space for a little platform. Mr. Anders created a short two-step hop: his holiday passengers would literally have to climb on board. (The toymaker was especially proud of that.) He used walnut planks for the train car panelling, and set the dining booth tables with Christmas plates he'd found in the attic. An antique mirror was set to the side to be hung at the back of the bar, and two lengths of Irish wool from Mrs. Anders' old fragment bin would be used for the blankets. The soft green plush had a goldish tint and would warm up the beds nicely.

Three times the stranger returned at night to check on the toymaker's progress. He applauded the silver tea set that would be used for hot chocolate, and the Christmas tree lights strung up on the bar. Tickets? The stranger would create them himself. Would Mr. Anders be willing to act, just for the early part of the evening, mind you, as conductor, accepting their passes and inviting them on to the train? "Of course!"

The stranger's only real concern was the sleeper car window. Built so close to the outside wall meant the train window was pushed up next to the cellar window. "I don't want my little boy awakened too early," he said. "Please black out the edges with paint or paper, to prohibit any light while the shade is in place. I want to be the one to welcome my son to Christmas Day. I want us to do it together." This seemed a strange request to Mr. Anders, but the generosity of his new patron was beyond belief. "All of us are a little strange", he breathed to himself.

On Christmas Eve, Mr. Anders was ready. Hot chocolate steamed on the counter, next to an impressive mound of goodies from the local bakery. A porcelain Christmas tree decorated the dining club table, and tinsel and garlands hung in the doorways. Mr. Anders even wore a blue cap, though not the same blue cap he had championed as a child, but one with a silver braid. He had a silver whistle too, which he would toot at the appropriate time. So much joy filled his heart that Mr. Anders wanted to give something back to his guests, leave some personal mark on this, his toy masterpiece. So he wrapped up Mrs. Anders' favorite book of fairy tales in winking gold foil, and placed it on his own berry-red corduroy chair, now part of the sleeper car set.

* * *

"Welcome aboard!" Mr. Anders cried.

Father and son stood at the bottom of the stairs, waiting for permission to enter. Both were in shadow. The boy looked young, huddled against his father: seven, maybe eight years old, and slight of build. In silhouette, he could have been some bashful elfin child. Mr. Anders extended his arm to greet his small guest and was surprised when the little boy placed two large passes into his hand. *Ticket to Christmas* it said on the front, in a delicate scrolled print and on bright gold cardboard paper. Tiny fir trees were carefully drawn on the corners.

Mr. Anders' mouth made a joyful O at this last addition to the Christmas journey he'd worked so hard to create, but his pleasure was marred with a second look at the small hands holding those elaborate tickets. They were white, incredibly white, the bones and the blue veins swimming in skeletal skim-milk skin, like a Ming vase, pearlescent and fragile. Mr. Anders looked up and into a face just as pale, the skin pulled tight around bird-like features that could have snapped with half a breath. The boy's eyes were sunk deep into his skull, ringed in lavender-gray, the irises bright pink. Was the child sick? He must be. Perhaps he'd been starved, near-starved to death? An accusatory glance at the stranger lasted no more than a second. Only love and pride shone in the father's eyes.

"Sir, this is my son, Nicolai. A finer or more well-behaved boy you will not meet." The two stepped on to the train in unison. The boy's eyes were radiant, filled with wonder. He smiled shyly at Mr. Anders, who responded in kind by reaching to shake the boy's hand. It was cold as ice.

"We are pleased to have you both aboard, Monsieur. Would you like to wait in our club car before retiring?"

"Yes!" The stranger and his son sat at the booth, while Mr. Anders quickly took the role as server. "Hot chocolate? You both must be…" and he looked, again, at his newest guest, and shivered.

"Cookies?" Mr. Anders passed a serving plate to the little boy, whose eyes grew large, but who seemed unable to accept the offer. The stranger picked out a cutout star sprinkled with colored sugar. He dipped it into the hot chocolate and offered it to his son. The boy's smile widened as he gobbled up the shortbread, his teeth very white.

Once the two were settled in, Mr. Anders offered to play a little Christmas music. From behind the counter, he brought out a small turntable. But as he shuffled through a stack of holiday records he'd found in the attic, he noted something strange in the mirror. Some trick of light had made the boy and his father disappear from view. He looked back to the booth – there they were, laughing, talking, sipping their cocoa, the boy holding his mug with two hands, as if he held the Lord's chalice itself. But when the toymaker looked again to the mirror, no reflection of his guests was apparent. Again, he looked to his passengers, again, to the mirror, then round the dark cellar to find some source of the mirror's error. There was none.

At last, he turned to the stranger. Their two eyes locked over the little boy's head. Mr. Anders read horror in that ashen glance, then danger – an anger, barely controlled, white hot, rising to the surface of his white-white face. And something else too… was it sorrow? The toymaker thought he felt a pull, a certain pleading in the vampire's glistening eyes, something trying to pierce his mind, something he recognized but did not fully comprehend. Mr. Anders turned on the music, motioned to the sleeping car, and quickly made his exit. At the top of the cellar stairs, he said "Good night," and then, softly, "Merry Christmas."

Nicolai's high sweet voice called out, "And to you, too, sir. Merry Christmas!"

* * *

Mr. Anders did not sleep that night. He merely cowered in his bed, behind a locked door, with the sheets and the blankets and the eiderdown quilt and the eiderdown pillows over his head, trying to decide what to do. If he left, might not the vampires swoop down upon him and devour him immediately? But why had they not done so already? The boy seemed genuinely thrilled to be playing at Christmas on the life-size toy train; and the father too, for his eyes were warm when he climbed aboard, and filled with gratitude. *But they are demons*, Mr. Anders shivered, *the undead!*

By the time the sun rose, the toymaker still had no plan, no thought of what to do; and so he returned to the cellar, for even adults do stupid things when they are afraid. Standing at the top of the stairs, he listened. Silence. One step down, two. Silence. With a Bible in his hand and his wife's silver crucifix strung round his neck, Mr. Anders cautiously descended.

Shimmering in the dark below, the toymaker saw a shaft of light, rectangular in shape, floating in the air. It was very bright in that dark cellar, like an alien ship hovering in the night, or some slanted intersecting plane from another dimension, revealing our own as absent of color or life. Two steps more, and Mr. Anders could see that someone had rolled up the sleeper-car window shade a good six inches, and all the glory of Christmas Day had come sweeping into the dark cellar. That square beam of gold anointed the soft-green plaid and berry-red chair, making them shine like jewels in a cave.

Yet another two steps and Mr. Anders thought, why, they are gone! And I am safe once more in my little shop. But then he heard a muffled laugh, pitched high, almost a giggle. There in the shadow of the cellar he made out two forms, standing within reach of the bright bar of sun floating in the dark.

Mr. Anders stood transfixed by what he saw: father and son facing the light, one behind the other, the father's hands wrapped round his little boy's shoulders, holding him with a firm grasp; for the boy repeatedly reached to touch the sunbeam, and laughed as his father repeatedly pulled him back. Some game, the child thought, the two were playing; but even in the dark Mr. Anders could see the vampire crying, his cheeks a translucent wash, the color of dark pearls.

"This is Christmas Day," the vampire said softly to his son. The two took one step closer to the blinding shaft of light.

Mr. Anders audibly gasped, seeing the boy's delight as he reached once more to touch the sun. Surely a father would not do such a thing to his own child, and on Christmas Day! But at this faintest rasp of horror, the vampire's eyes flew to the toymaker's perch above. And whether it was the horror he read in the toymaker's face, or some other horror in his heart, the vampire let out an anguished cry and thrust the child back into the recess of the dark cellar. He alone rushed into the light.

What Mr. Anders saw and heard cannot be easily described: screaming, terrible screams, flashes of darkness and dark grey smoke pervading that sunlit shaft. Millions of tiny black flecks of dust, like a swarm of bees, rose up and spread out, taking on various forms: a man with a swollen head, then a great gaping mouth; the mouth twisting then turning into the jaws of a wolf, open wide and howling; and then some winged creature with demon eyes, its face and body blurred by its own fast-flapping wings. And through it all, a screeching cacophony of great clanking sounds.

Somewhere from within the mass of smoke and shadow and flying black bits, the toymaker thought he heard a voice calling – something. And though he could not make out the words, he saw the boy leap up and run towards the mottled light. Without thought, Mr. Anders swooped down the stairs and clamped a hold on the little boy's shoulders. He's only a child, he thought. He doesn't deserve to die.

But the boy would not be deterred. And in the struggle, he bit the toymaker's arm, two sharp-toothed punctures, sinking fast and deep into the flesh of his forearm, like anchors falling in a calm sea. The fangs of an asp or tiger cub could not have proved more fatal. Mr. Anders felt ice sweep through his body. He let the boy go.

Within seconds Nicolai, too, had disintegrated in the light, joining the mass of dust and darkness and shadow-laced sun, now swirling together amid thunderous claps and moans. Mr. Anders shrunk back in the corner, covering his ears. He thought he might faint at the scene before him: millions of dust particles trapped in the light, crashing against one another in a violent frenzy to be free.

And then...

Everything slowed, and the light and the dark and the dust moved as one, like a languorous wave far from the shore. Those bits of dust that had blackened the sun began to twirl, in and of themselves, catching the light like crystals. Mr. Anders watched them for hours, rotating in the air, and fancied he sometimes heard a peal of laughter, though the sound could have been church bells in the distance, ringing Christmas mass.

As the day faded into cellar-night, the rectangular beam became smaller and smaller. Those floating diamond chips finally lost their buoyancy and sank into two small piles of glitter on the berry-red chair. Mr. Anders promptly swept them up in a dustpan and returned to his shop.

* * *

Mr. Anders has not been seen from that day forward. He hired a girl from the local college, who opened and closed the shop, but reportedly claimed never to have met her employer. He paid well, she said, and always left clear instructions on the workstation table.

As winter turned to spring, the shop's business, always healthy before, became exceedingly prosperous – famous even; for Mr. Anders no longer made everyday toys, not even trains, but fantastic flying objects, both to play with and to admire: shiny silver jets and brass-plated rockets that shot up in the sky fifty to sixty feet, giant ufos with rotating lights and helium balloon-type ships that could hover in the air for hours. Mechanical birds of unusual colors could sing high-pitched notes only dogs could hear, and dragon-kites with huge wingspans shot red tinsel fire out of their mouths as they flew high in the wind. The only cuddly toy in the shop was a soft furry bat, which seemed to hang in the air when you threw it, then folded up like an umbrella to be hung in your closet when done.

Mr. Anders became so famous that the Queen Mother once visited his shop to buy a gift for her secretary's child (so said the local paper), and it was rumored H.G. Wells himself tried to interview the toymaker, but to no avail. Mr. Anders would see no one.

On January 6th of the following year, Mr. Anders' shop girl returned from her Christmas vacation to find her last set of instructions.

> *Dear Miss P.,*
>
> *First, let me thank you for your faithful work this past year. No employer could be more pleased at your attention to detail. So pleased, I have decided to leave you my shop. The deed is in the lockbox, under the cellar steps. The keys you already have.*
>
> *I ask one thing: downstairs in the cellar, you should find a pile of glitter on or around the berry-red chair. Sweep it up, every drop. A broom and dustpan are close by. Then take the glitter and spread it with some glue on the painted mermaid's tail on the*

shop-front window. I know it doesn't need it. The glitter I used last Christmas still looks brand new. But this is my request.

Be a good girl, Miss P., and say a prayer for me. I am taking the early train home – to see my family, I hope. I'm unsure of my arrival. I will not return.

Bone Chill

Kevin M. Folliard

ON CHRISTMAS EVE, Doctor Gunther Holloway settled into a wingback chair in his study and pored over his latest scientific journal. Outside his window, snow blanketed the grounds and silver moonlight filtered through twisted branches. Logs crackled in his fireplace. Embers escaped up the chimney like swirling fireflies.

Dr. Holloway was entrenched in a fascinating study on the reaction times of caffeinated mice when a frantic rapping sounded at the door.

He huffed, slapped his article on the side table, and hurried to the front hall. The rapping continued.

"One moment!"

Dr. Holloway unlatched the gilded locks, opened the door, and gaped in bewilderment.

Standing on his front stoop, offering a doughnut-shaped green and red speckled fruitcake, stood a lanky skeleton with bones as white as the piling snow. The skeleton's jaw grinned. Its shadowy eye sockets stared. Bony fingers clutched the cake platter.

"Good evening. Merry Christmas," the skeleton said. "I have come to give you this." Its jaw flexed as it spoke.

Dr. Holloway shook his head in frustration. He searched behind the skeleton, in the bushes nearby, and scoured the grounds for any sign of pranksters, wires, or robotic parts.

"What is the matter?" the skeleton enquired. "Are you frightened?"

"Certainly not!" Dr. Holloway peered between the skeleton's ribs and under its skull. But it appeared perfectly real, standing by some invisible power. The doctor furrowed his brow. "I just need to wrap my head around this."

"I am a skeleton."

"Obviously!" Dr. Holloway scoffed.

"I have come to provide a gift." The skeleton's spidery white fingertips gestured to the cake. "But I understand your fear."

"Why on Earth should I be frightened of a skeleton? You have no muscle. You shouldn't be able to move, let alone speak without a tongue and lips."

"May I come inside?" Powdery snowflakes dusted its ribs and sternum.

"Why should I let a skeleton into my home?"

"You are a smart man," the skeleton said. "I saw nice things through your windows: maps, paintings, sculptures. Shelves full of books."

"How could you see *anything*?" Dr. Holloway demanded. "You have no eyes."

"You like to learn."

"I am a professor of anatomy," the doctor boasted.

"Would you like to learn more about skeletons?"

"I know *everything* there is to know about skeletons. I can recite all 206 bones in my sleep."

"Does that help you to understand how I walk, talk, see, and offer cake?" The skeleton's wrists inched the cake closer to the doctor's face.

The doctor scrutinized the cake, and then glared into the contours of the skeleton's dark, hollow eye sockets. The skeleton's existence contradicted everything he knew to be true about the human body.

And yet, if he could determine and record the rational explanation for its means of locomotion and communication – perhaps even persuade the skeleton to become his specimen and test subject – the study would revolutionize medical science and transform his career.

Dr. Holloway smiled. "All right." He beckoned the skeleton inside. "Come in. Come in."

The skeleton stepped inside and wiped its snowy tarsals on the carpet.

"I'll take that." Dr. Holloway brought the fruitcake into the study. He set it on the table near the fireplace and gestured toward an armchair. "Have a seat. I'll fetch utensils."

The skeleton settled as Dr. Holloway headed toward the kitchen. "It's quite cold out there. You must be chilled to the–" He caught himself and laughed. "I imagine that expression could bother you? Chilled to the bone!" he called out.

"It does not bother me."

"Do skeletons have a sense of humor?" Dr. Holloway reappeared and set the table.

"Some do. I only mean I cannot be chilled. I am only bone."

"You have no nerves then? No sense of touch?"

"All I know is that I find it quite merry outside."

"You prefer the cold?" Dr. Holloway gestured to the fireplace. "Is this too hot for you?"

"I am made of bone, not ice. I just like to be outside. Most skeletons do."

"Interesting." Dr. Holloway sliced a piece of fruitcake and offered it to the skeleton.

His guest waved the cake away. "No, thank you. I have no digestive tract, you see."

Dr. Holloway dropped the plate on the table. Silverware rattled. "Why ever does a skeleton bring cake to someone's door if it doesn't eat?"

The skeleton tilted its skull. "For Christmas. Why else?"

Dr. Holloway sighed. "What is the purpose of this visitation?"

"You seem frustrated," the skeleton observed.

"Well, I suppose I am." Dr. Holloway shrugged. "I was enjoying reading in my cozy study, when – if you'll excuse my bluntness – a rather inappropriately grim guest interrupted an otherwise pleasant holiday."

"Why read alone on Christmas Eve?" the skeleton inquired. "Have you no friends?"

Dr. Holloway rolled his eyes. "This encounter would have been downright charming on Halloween. I am quite content on my own, if you must know."

"People are never alone," the skeleton said. "Is that what you wish? To be alone on a holiday?"

"I'm not trying to hurry you back out. At least stay and explain yourself for a bit before you go. What is your name?"

"My name?" The skeleton scratched its mandible. "I have no name. I am a skeleton."

"We've covered that part, haven't we?" The doctor groaned. "Surely you *had* a name when you were alive, covered in flesh and filled with blood."

The skeleton pointed to its skull. "A brain was in here, and it had a name. But that was not my name. I do not recall much about that person."

"Where did you come from? The cemetery? The morgue? Why are you wandering about?"

"I sense a kindred spirit in you. I only wished to deliver a Christmas gift."

The doctor sneered. "What does a skeleton know about Christmas?"

The fireplace sputtered. The skeleton's spine curled toward Dr. Holloway. "*You* were alone, reading. *I* came bearing a gift for a new friend. It seems that I know more about this holiday than you." The skeleton folded its fingers. Its jaw grinned with satisfaction.

Dr. Holloway sighed. "Fair enough." He lifted the fork and took a bite. Spongy fruitcake melted into sugary sweetness on his tongue. "That's rather good, actually!" He reached for another bite. "Did you make this?"

The skeleton grinned and nodded. "You ought to come outside."

"It's freezing!" Dr. Holloway took another bite. "Those with nerves prefer a warm fire."

"Why be trapped inside?" the skeleton asked. "The outside is liberating."

"I'm not a total curmudgeon," Dr. Holloway said between bites. "I'll take a walk tomorrow morning, when the sun is shining."

"Not tomorrow," the skeleton insisted. "Come outside now."

Dr. Holloway stopped chewing. He set his plate on the table with a clank. "This is better than fruitcake has any right to be. What's in it?"

The skeleton smiled. "Fruit. And cake. I would like you to come outs–"

"Outside, yes." Dr. Holloway stared into dark sockets. "Why do you keep saying outside?"

"Why are you still inside?" his guest inquired.

Dr. Holloway glared. "You're quite the aberration, you know. Until you arrived, I had understood absolutely everything just fine."

"Is that a problem?" the skeleton asked.

"You're not going to tell me where you come from?"

"Is it necessary for you to know?"

The doctor stood and pointed to the door. "I am afraid you've overstayed your welcome, skeleton. You promised a fascinating learning experience, and so far you have answered my every question with *another* question. Either start educating me about magic Christmas skeletons or go back to your precious outside."

The skeleton stood. "Join me." It reached toward Dr. Holloway.

A terrible aching sensation crept into Dr. Holloway's bones. Pain bolted through his limbs. Muscles twitched. Joints cracked, popped and twisted. Chills shuddered along his spine. A throbbing headache exploded in the doctor's skull. Screams snagged in his throat. Teeth clattered. Jaws pried open. His eyes turned up in their sockets as skin peeled from his face and rolled down his neck.

The doctor's hands, arms and shoulders folded into useless flaps as bones slipped away from connecting tissue. Arm bones wriggled and worked their way back into Dr. Holloway's chest. Fingertips poked through his skin and clawed his chest open. Dr. Holloway's skeleton ripped him apart from the inside.

The doctor's heart, lungs and organs slipped from his ribcage and splattered inside a pile of skin and innards on the floor. His eyes tilted back into loose, inside-out sockets and blurred into focus for just a moment. He watched in horror as his own skeleton strode out of his legs on to the carpet. The doctor's skeleton wiped blood and bits of tissue from its wet bones.

"Much better outside, isn't it?" came the voice of the skeleton guest.

"Indeed," Dr. Holloway's skeleton replied. "What a terrible bore that man was."

Where the Christmas-Tree Grew

Mary E. Wilkins Freeman

IT WAS AFTERNOON recess at No. 4 District School, in Warner. There was a heavy snow-storm; so every one was in the warm school-room, except a few adventurous spirits who were tumbling about in the snow-drifts out in the yard, getting their clothes wet and preparing themselves for chidings at home. Their shrill cries and shouts of laughter floated into the school-room, but the small group near the stove did not heed them at all. There were five or six little girls and one boy. The girls, with the exception of Jenny Brown, were trim and sweet in their winter dresses and neat school-aprons; they perched on the desks and the arms of the settee with careless grace, like birds. Some of them had their arms linked. The one boy lounged against the blackboard. His dark, straight-profiled face was all aglow as he talked. His big brown eyes gazed now soberly and impressively at Jenny, then gave a gay dance in the direction of the other girls.

"Yes, it does – *honest!*" said he.

The other girls nudged one another softly; but Jenny Brown stood with her innocent, solemn eyes fixed upon Earl Munroe's face, drinking in every word.

"You ask anybody who knows," continued Earl; "ask Judge Barker, ask – the minister—"

"Oh!" cried the little girls; but the boy shook his head impatiently at them.

"Yes," said he; "you just go and ask Mr. Fisher tomorrow, and you'll see what he'll tell you. Why, look here" – Earl straightened himself and stretched out an arm like an orator – "it's nothing more than *reasonable* that Christmas-trees grow wild with the presents all on 'em! What sense would there be in 'em if they didn't, I'd like to know? They grow in different places, of course; but these around here grow mostly on the mountain over there. They come up every spring, and they all blossom out about Christmas-time, and folks go hunting for them to give to the children. Father and Ben are over on the mountain today—"

"Oh, oh!" cried the little girls.

"I mean, I guess they are," amended Earl, trying to put his feet on the boundary – line of truth. "I hope they'll find a full one."

Jenny Brown had a little, round, simple face; her thin brown hair was combed back and braided tightly in one tiny braid tied with a bit of shoe-string. She wore a nondescript gown, which nearly trailed behind, and showed in front her little, coarsely-shod feet, which toed-in helplessly. The gown was of a faded green color; it was scalloped and bound around the bottom, and had some green ribbon-bows down the front. It was, in fact, the discarded polonaise of a benevolent woman, who aided the poor substantially but not tastefully.

Jenny Brown was eight, and small for her age – a strange, gentle, ignorant little creature, never doubting the truth of what she was told, which sorely tempted the other children to impose upon her. Standing there in the school-room that stormy recess, in the midst of that group of wiser, richer, mostly older girls, and that one handsome, mischievous boy, she believed every word she heard.

This was her first term at school, and she had never before seen much of other children. She had lived her eight years all alone at home with her mother, and she had never been told about

Christmas. Her mother had other things to think about. She was a dull, spiritless, reticent woman, who had lived through much trouble. She worked, doing washings and cleanings, like a poor feeble machine that still moves but has no interest in its motion. Sometimes the Browns had almost enough to eat, at other times they half starved. It was half-starving time just then; Jenny had not had enough to eat that day.

There was a pinched look on the little face up-turned toward Earl Munroe's.

Earl's words gained authority by coming from himself. Jenny had always regarded him with awe and admiration. It was much that he should speak at all to her.

Earl Munroe was quite the king of this little district school. He was the son of the wealthiest man in town. No other boy was so well dressed, so gently bred, so luxuriously lodged and fed. Earl himself realized his importance, and had at times the loftiness of a young prince in his manner. Occasionally, some independent urchin would bristle with democratic spirit, and tell him to his face that he was "stuck up," and that he hadn't so much more to be proud of than other folks; that his grandfather wasn't anything but an old ragman!

Then Earl would wilt. Arrogance in a free country is likely to have an unstable foundation. Earl tottered at the mention of his paternal grandfather, who had given the first impetus to the family fortune by driving a tin-cart about the country. Moreover, the boy was really pleasant and generous hearted, and had no mind, in the long run, for lonely state and disagreeable haughtiness. He enjoyed being lordly once in a while, that was all.

He did now, with Jenny – he eyed her with a gay condescension, which would have greatly amused his tin-peddler grandfather.

Soon the bell rung, and they all filed to their seats, and the lessons were begun.

After school was done that night, Earl stood in the door when Jenny passed out.

"Say, Jenny," he called, "when are you going over on the mountain to find the Christmas-tree? You'd better go pretty soon, or they'll be gone."

"That's so!" chimed in one of the girls. "You'd better go right off, Jenny."

She passed along, her face shyly dimpling with her little innocent smile, and said nothing. She would never talk much.

She had quite a long walk to her home. Presently, as she was pushing weakly through the new snow, Earl went flying past her in his father's sleigh, with the black horses and the fur-capped coachman. He never thought of asking her to ride. If he had, he would not have hesitated a second before doing so.

Jenny, as she waded along, could see the mountain always before her. This road led straight to it, then turned and wound around its base. It had stopped snowing, and the sun was setting clear. The great white mountain was all rosy. It stood opposite the red western sky. Jenny kept her eyes fixed upon the mountain. Down in the valley shadows her little simple face, pale and colorless, gathered another kind of radiance.

There was no school the next day, which was the one before Christmas. It was pleasant, and not very cold. Everybody was out; the little village stores were crowded; sleds trailing Christmas-greens went flying; people were hastening with parcels under their arms, their hands full.

Jenny Brown also was out. She was climbing Franklin Mountain. The snowy pine boughs bent so low that they brushed her head. She stepped deeply into the untrodden snow; the train of her green polonaise dipped into it, and swept it along. And all the time she was peering through those white fairy columns and arches for – a Christmas-tree.

That night, the mountain had turned rosy, and faded, and the stars were coming out, when a frantic woman, panting, crying out now and then in her distress, went running down the road to the Munroe house. It was the only one between her own and the mountain. The woman rained some clattering knocks on the door – she could not stop for the bell. Then she burst into the house, and threw open the dining-room door, crying out in gasps:

"Hev you seen her? Oh, hev you? My Jenny's lost! She's lost! Oh, oh, oh! They said they saw her comin' up this way, this mornin'. *Hev* you seen her, *hev* you?"

Earl and his father and mother were having tea there in the handsome oak-panelled dining-room. Mr. Munroe rose at once, and went forward, Mrs. Munroe looked with a pale face around her silver tea-urn, and Earl sat as if frozen. He heard his father's soothing questions, and the mother's answers. She had been out at work all day; when she returned, Jenny was gone. Some one had seen her going up the road to the Munroes' that morning about ten o'clock. That was her only clew.

Earl sat there, and saw his mother draw the poor woman into the room and try to comfort her; he heard, with a vague understanding, his father order the horses to be harnessed immediately; he watched him putting on his coat and hat out in the hall.

When he heard the horses trot up the drive, he sprang to his feet. When Mr. Munroe opened the door, Earl, with his coat and cap on, was at his heels.

"Why, you can't go, Earl!" said his father, when he saw him. "Go back at once."

Earl was white and trembling. He half sobbed: "Oh, father, I must go!" said he.

"Earl, be reasonable. You want to help, don't you, and not hinder?" his mother called out of the dining-room.

Earl caught hold of his father's coat. "Father – look here – I—*I believe I know where she is*!"

Then his father faced sharply around, his mother and Jenny's stood listening in bewilderment, and Earl told his ridiculous, childish, and cruel little story. "I—didn't dream—she'd really be— such a little—goose as to—go," he choked out; "but she must have, for" – with brave candor – "I know she believed every word I told her."

It seemed a fantastic theory, yet a likely one. It would give method to the search, yet more alarm to the searchers. The mountain was a wide region in which to find one little child.

Jenny's mother screamed out, "Oh, if she's lost on the mountain, they'll never find her! They never will, they never will! Oh, Jenny, Jenny, Jenny!"

Earl gave a despairing glance at her, and bolted up-stairs to his own room. His mother called pityingly after him; but he only sobbed back, "Don't, mother – please!" and kept on.

The boy, lying face downward on his bed, crying as if his heart would break, heard presently the church-bell clang out fast and furious. Then he heard loud voices down in the road, and the flurry of sleigh-bells. His father had raised the alarm, and the search was organized.

After a while Earl arose, and crept over to the window. It looked toward the mountain, which towered up, cold and white and relentless, like one of the ice-hearted giants of the old Indian tales. Earl shuddered as he looked at it. Presently he crawled down-stairs and into the parlor. In the bay-window stood, like a gay mockery, the Christmas-tree. It was a quite small one that year, only for the family – some expected guests had failed to come – but it was well laden. After tea the presents were to have been distributed. There were some for his father and mother, and some for the servants, but the bulk of them were for Earl.

By-and-by his mother, who had heard him come down-stairs, peeped into the room, and saw him busily taking his presents from the tree. Her heart sank with sad displeasure and amazement. She would not have believed that her boy could be so utterly selfish as to think of Christmas-presents *then*.

But she said nothing. She stole away, and returned to poor Mrs. Brown, whom she was keeping with her; still she continued to think of it all that long, terrible night, when they sat there waiting, listening to the signal-horns over on the mountain.

Morning came at last and Mr. Munroe with it. No success so far. He drank some coffee and was off again. That was quite early. An hour or two later the breakfast-bell rang. Earl did not respond to it, so his mother went to the foot of the stairs and called him. There was a stern ring in her soft voice. All the time she had in mind his heartlessness and greediness over the presents. When Earl did not answer she went up-stairs, and found that he was not in his room. Then she looked in the parlor, and stood staring in bewilderment. Earl was not there, but neither were the Christmas-tree and his presents – they had vanished bodily!

Just at that moment Earl Munroe was hurrying down the road, and he was dragging his big sled, on which were loaded his Christmas-presents and the Christmas-tree. The top of the tree trailed in the snow, its branches spread over the sled on either side, and rustled. It was a heavy load, but Earl tugged manfully in an enthusiasm of remorse and atonement – a fantastic, extravagant atonement, planned by that same fertile fancy which had invented that story for poor little Jenny, but instigated by all the good, repentant impulses in the boy's nature.

On every one of those neat parcels, above his own name, was written in his big crooked, childish hand, "Jenny Brown, from—" Earl Munroe had not saved one Christmas-present for himself.

Pulling along, his eyes brilliant, his cheeks glowing, he met Maud Barker. She was Judge Barker's daughter, and the girl who had joined him in advising Jenny to hunt on the mountain for the Christmas-tree.

Maud stepped along, placing her trim little feet with dainty precision; she wore some new high-buttoned overshoes. She also carried a new beaver muff, but in one hand only. The other dangled mittenless at her side; it was pink with cold, but on its third finger sparkled a new gold ring with a blue stone in it.

"Oh, Earl!" she called out, "have they found Jenny Brown? I was going up to your house to – Why, Earl Munroe, what have you got there?"

"I'm carrying up my Christmas-presents and the tree up to Jenny's – so she'll find 'em when she comes back," said the boy, flushing red. There was a little defiant choke in his voice.

"Why, what for?"

"I rather think they belong to her more'n they do to me, after what's happened."

"Does your mother know?"

"No; she wouldn't care. She'd think I was only doing what I ought."

"All of 'em?" queried Maud, feebly.

"You don't s'pose I'd keep any back?"

Maud stood staring. It was beyond her little philosophy.

Earl was passing on when a thought struck him.

"Say, Maud," he cried, eagerly, "haven't you something you can put in? Girls' things might please her better, you know. Some of mine are – rather queer, I'm afraid."

"What have you got?" demanded Maud.

"Well, some of the things are well enough. There's a lot of candy and oranges and figs and books; there's one by Jules Verne I guess she'll like; but there's a great big jack-knife, and – a brown velvet bicycle suit?"

"Why, Earl Munroe! what could she do with a bicycle suit?"

"I thought, maybe, she could rip the seams to 'em, an' sew 'em some way, an' get a basque cut, or something. Don't you s'pose she could?" Earl asked, anxiously.

"I don't know; her mother could tell," said Maud.

"Well, I'll hang it on, anyhow. Maud, haven't you anything to give her?"

"I—don't know."

Earl eyed her sharply. "Isn't that muff new?"

"Yes."

"And that ring?"

Maud nodded. "She'd be delighted with 'em. Oh, Maud, put 'em in!"

Maud looked at him. Her pretty mouth quivered a little; some tears twinkled in her blue eyes. "I don't believe my mother would let me," faltered she. "You – come with me, and I'll ask her."

"All right," said Earl, with a tug at his sled-rope.

He waited with his load in front of Maud's house until she came forth radiant, lugging a big basket. She had her last winter's red cashmere dress, a hood, some mittens, cake and biscuit, and nice slices of cold meat.

"Mother said these would be much more *suitable* for her," said Maud, with a funny little imitation of her mother's manner.

Over across the street another girl stood at the gate, waiting for news.

"Have they found her?" she cried. "Where are you going with all those things?"

Somehow, Earl's generous, romantic impulse spread like an epidemic. This little girl soon came flying out with her contribution; then there were more – quite a little procession filed finally down the road to Jenny Brown's house.

The terrible possibilities of the case never occurred to them. The idea never entered their heads that little, innocent, trustful Jenny might never come home to see that Christmas-tree which they set up in her poor home.

It was with no surprise whatever that they saw, about noon, Mr. Munroe's sleigh, containing Jenny and her mother and Mrs. Munroe, drive up to the door.

Afterwards they heard how a wood-cutter had found Jenny crying, over on the east side of the mountain, at sunset, and had taken her home with him. He lived five miles from the village, and was an old man, not able to walk so far that night to tell them of her safety. His wife had been very good to the child. About eleven o'clock some of the searchers had met the old man plodding along the mountain-road with the news.

They did not stop for this now. They shouted to Jenny to "come in, quick!" They pulled her with soft violence into the room where they had been at work. Then the child stood with her hands clasped, staring at the Christmas-tree. All too far away had she been searching for it. The Christmas-tree grew not on the wild mountainside, in the lonely woods, but at home, close to warm, loving hearts; and that was where she found it.

The Old Nurse's Story

Elizabeth Gaskell

YOU KNOW, my dears, that your mother was an orphan, and an only child; and I daresay you have heard that your grandfather was a clergyman up in Westmoreland, where I come from. I was just a girl in the village school, when, one day, your grandmother came in to ask the mistress if there was any scholar there who would do for a nurse-maid; and mighty proud I was, I can tell ye, when the mistress called me up, and spoke of me being a good girl at my needle, and a steady, honest girl, and one whose parents were very respectable, though they might be poor. I thought I should like nothing better than to serve the pretty young lady, who was blushing as deep as I was, as she spoke of the coming baby, and what I should have to do with it. However, I see you don't care so much for this part of my story, as for what you think is to come, so I'll tell you at once. I was engaged and settled at the parsonage before Miss Rosamond (that was the baby, who is now your mother) was born. To be sure, I had little enough to do with her when she came, for she was never out of her mother's arms, and slept by her all night long; and proud enough was I sometimes when missis trusted her to me. There never was such a baby before or since, though you've all of you been fine enough in your turns; but for sweet, winning ways, you've none of you come up to your mother. She took after her mother, who was a real lady born; a Miss Furnivall, a grand-daughter of Lord Furnivall's, in Northumberland. I believe she had neither brother nor sister, and had been brought up in my lord's family till she had married your grandfather, who was just a curate, son to a shopkeeper in Carlisle – but a clever, fine gentleman as ever was – and one who was a right-down hard worker in his parish, which was very wide, and scattered all abroad over the Westmoreland Fells. When your mother, little Miss Rosamond, was about four or five years old, both her parents died in a fortnight – one after the other. Ah! that was a sad time. My pretty young mistress and me was looking for another baby, when my master came home from one of his long rides, wet and tired, and took the fever he died of; and then she never held up her head again, but just lived to see her dead baby, and have it laid on her breast, before she sighed away her life. My mistress had asked me, on her death-bed, never to leave Miss Rosamond; but if she had never spoken a word, I would have gone with the little child to the end of the world.

The next thing, and before we had well stilled our sobs, the executors and guardians came to settle the affairs. They were my poor young mistress's own cousin, Lord Furnivall, and Mr. Esthwaite, my master's brother, a shopkeeper in Manchester; not so well to do then as he was afterwards, and with a large family rising about him. Well! I don't know if it were their settling, or because of a letter my mistress wrote on her death-bed to her cousin, my lord; but somehow it was settled that Miss Rosamond and me were to go to Furnivall Manor House, in Northumberland, and my lord spoke as if it had been her mother's wish that she should live with his family, and as if he had no objections, for that one or two more or less could make no difference in so grand a household. So, though that was not the way in which I should have wished the coming of my bright and pretty pet to have been looked at – who was like a sunbeam in any family, be it never so grand – I was well pleased that all the folks in the Dale should stare and admire, when they heard I was going to be young lady's maid at my Lord Furnivall's at Furnivall Manor.

But I made a mistake in thinking we were to go and live where my lord did. It turned out that the family had left Furnivall Manor House fifty years or more. I could not hear that my poor young mistress had never been there, though she had been brought up in the family; and I was sorry for that, for I should have liked Miss Rosamond's youth to have passed where her mother's had been.

My lord's gentleman, from whom I asked as many questions as I durst, said that the Manor House was at the foot of the Cumberland Fells, and a very grand place; that an old Miss Furnivall, a great-aunt of my lord's, lived there, with only a few servants; but that it was a very healthy place, and my lord had thought that it would suit Miss Rosamond very well for a few years, and that her being there might perhaps amuse his old aunt.

I was bidden by my lord to have Miss Rosamond's things ready by a certain day. He was a stern, proud man, as they say all the Lords Furnivall were; and he never spoke a word more than was necessary. Folk did say he had loved my young mistress; but that, because she knew that his father would object, she would never listen to him, and married Mr. Esthwaite; but I don't know. He never married, at any rate. But he never took much notice of Miss Rosamond; which I thought he might have done if he had cared for her dead mother. He sent his gentleman with us to the Manor House, telling him to join him at Newcastle that same evening; so there was no great length of time for him to make us known to all the strangers before he, too, shook us off; and we were left, two lonely young things (I was not eighteen) in the great old Manor House. It seems like yesterday that we drove there. We had left our own dear parsonage very early, and we had both cried as if our hearts would break, though we were travelling in my lord's carriage, which I thought so much of once. And now it was long past noon on a September day, and we stopped to change horses for the last time at a little smoky town, all full of colliers and miners. Miss Rosamond had fallen asleep, but Mr. Henry told me to waken her, that she might see the park and the Manor House as we drove up. I thought it rather a pity; but I did what he bade me, for fear he should complain of me to my lord. We had left all signs of a town, or even a village, and were then inside the gates of a large wild park – not like the parks here in the south, but with rocks, and the noise of running water, and gnarled thorn-trees, and old oaks, all white and peeled with age.

The road went up about two miles, and then we saw a great and stately house, with many trees close around it, so close that in some places their branches dragged against the walls when the wind blew; and some hung broken down; for no one seemed to take much charge of the place; – to lop the wood, or to keep the moss-covered carriage-way in order. Only in front of the house all was clear. The great oval drive was without a weed; and neither tree nor creeper was allowed to grow over the long, many-windowed front; at both sides of which a wing protected, which were each the ends of other side fronts; for the house, although it was so desolate, was even grander than I expected. Behind it rose the Fells; which seemed unenclosed and bare enough; and on the left hand of the house, as you stood facing it, was a little, old-fashioned flower-garden, as I found out afterwards. A door opened out upon it from the west front; it had been scooped out of the thick, dark wood for some old Lady Furnivall; but the branches of the great forest-trees had grown and overshadowed it again, and there were very few flowers that would live there at that time.

When we drove up to the great front entrance, and went into the hall, I thought we would be lost – it was so large, and vast and grand. There was a chandelier all of bronze, hung down from the middle of the ceiling; and I had never seen one before, and looked at it all in amaze. Then, at one end of the hall, was a great fire-place, as large as the sides of the houses in my country, with massy andirons and dogs to hold the wood; and by it were heavy, old-fashioned sofas. At the opposite end of the hall, to the left as you went in – on the western side – was an organ built into the wall, and so large that it filled up the best part of that end. Beyond it, on the same side, was a door; and opposite, on each side of the fire-place, were also doors leading to the east front; but those I never went through as long as I stayed in the house, so I can't tell you what lay beyond.

The afternoon was closing in, and the hall, which had no fire lighted in it, looked dark and gloomy, but we did not stay there a moment. The old servant, who had opened the door for us, bowed to Mr. Henry, and took us in through the door at the further side of the great organ, and led us through several smaller halls and passages into the west drawing-room, where he said that Miss Furnivall was sitting. Poor little Miss Rosamond held very tight to me, as if she were scared and lost in that great place; and as for myself, I was not much better. The west drawing-room was very cheerful-looking, with a warm fire in it, and plenty of good, comfortable furniture about. Miss Furnivall was an old lady not far from eighty, I should think, but I do not know. She was thin and tall, and had a face as full of fine wrinkles as if they had been drawn all over it with a needle's point. Her eyes were very watchful, to make up, I suppose, for her being so deaf as to be obliged to use a trumpet. Sitting with her, working at the same great piece of tapestry, was Mrs. Stark, her maid and companion, and almost as old as she was. She had lived with Miss Furnivall ever since they both were young, and now she seemed more like a friend than a servant; she looked so cold, and grey, and stony, as if she had never loved or cared for any one; and I don't suppose she did care for any one, except her mistress; and, owing to the great deafness of the latter, Mrs. Stark treated her very much as if she were a child. Mr. Henry gave some message from my lord, and then he bowed good-by to us all, – taking no notice of my sweet little Miss Rosamond's outstretched hand – and left us standing there, being looked at by the two old ladies through their spectacles.

I was right glad when they rung for the old footman who had shown us in at first, and told him to take us to our rooms. So we went out of that great drawing-room and into another sitting-room, and out of that, and then up a great flight of stairs, and along a broad gallery – which was something like a library, having books all down one side, and windows and writing-tables all down the other – till we came to our rooms, which I was not sorry to hear were just over the kitchens; for I began to think I should be lost in that wilderness of a house. There was an old nursery, that had been used for all the little lords and ladies long ago, with a pleasant fire burning in the grate, and the kettle boiling on the hob, and tea-things spread out on the table; and out of that room was the night-nursery, with a little crib for Miss Rosamond close to my bed. And old James called up Dorothy, his wife, to bid us welcome; and both he and she were so hospitable and kind, that by-and-by Miss Rosamond and me felt quite at home; and by the time tea was over, she was sitting on Dorothy's knee, and chattering away as fast as her little tongue could go. I soon found out that Dorothy was from Westmoreland, and that bound her and me together, as it were; and I would never wish to meet with kinder people than were old James and his wife. James had lived pretty nearly all his life in my lord's family, and thought there was no one so grand as they. He even looked down a little on his wife; because, till he had married her, she had never lived in any but a farmer's household. But he was very fond of her, as well he might be. They had one servant under them, to do all the rough work. Agnes they called her; and she and me, and James and Dorothy, with Miss Furnivall and Mrs. Stark, made up the family; always remembering my sweet little Miss Rosamond! I used to wonder what they had done before she came, they thought so much of her now. Kitchen and drawing-room, it was all the same. The hard, sad Miss Furnivall, and the cold Mrs. Stark, looked pleased when she came fluttering in like a bird, playing and pranking hither and thither, with a continual murmur, and pretty prattle of gladness. I am sure, they were sorry many a time when she flitted away into the kitchen, though they were too proud to ask her to stay with them, and were a little surprised at her taste; though to be sure, as Mrs. Stark said, it was not to be wondered at, remembering what stock her father had come of. The great, old rambling house was a famous place for little Miss Rosamond. She made expeditions all over it, with me at her heels; all, except the east wing, which was never opened, and whither we never thought of going. But in the western and northern part was many a pleasant room; full of things that were curiosities to us, though they might not have been to people who had seen more. The windows were darkened by the sweeping boughs of the trees, and the ivy which had overgrown them; but, in the green gloom, we could manage to see old china jars and carved ivory boxes, and great heavy books, and, above all, the old pictures!

Once, I remember, my darling would have Dorothy go with us to tell us who they all were; for they were all portraits of some of my lord's family, though Dorothy could not tell us the names of every one. We had gone through most of the rooms, when we came to the old state drawing-room over the hall, and there was a picture of Miss Furnivall; or, as she was called in those days, Miss Grace, for she was the younger sister. Such a beauty she must have been! but with such a set, proud look, and such scorn looking out of her handsome eyes, with her eyebrows just a little raised, as if she wondered how anyone could have the impertinence to look at her, and her lip curled at us, as we stood there gazing. She had a dress on, the like of which I had never seen before, but it was all the fashion when she was young; a hat of some soft white stuff like beaver, pulled a little over her brows, and a beautiful plume of feathers sweeping round it on one side; and her gown of blue satin was open in front to a quilted white stomacher.

'Well, to be sure!' said I, when I had gazed my fill. 'Flesh is grass, they do say; but who would have thought that Miss Furnivall had been such an out-and-out beauty, to see her now.'

'Yes,' said Dorothy. 'Folks change sadly. But if what my master's father used to say was true, Miss Furnivall, the elder sister, was handsomer than Miss Grace. Her picture is here somewhere; but, if I show it you, you must never let on, even to James, that you have seen it. Can the little lady hold her tongue, think you?' asked she.

I was not so sure, for she was such a little sweet, bold, open-spoken child, so I set her to hide herself; and then I helped Dorothy to turn a great picture, that leaned with its face toward the wall, and was not hung up as the others were. To be sure, it beat Miss Grace for beauty; and, I think, for scornful pride, too, though in that matter it might be hard to choose. I could have looked at it an hour, but Dorothy seemed half frightened at having shown it to me, and hurried it back again, and bade me run and find Miss Rosamond, for that there were some ugly places about the house, where she should like ill for the child to go. I was a brave, high-spirited girl, and thought little of what the old woman said, for I liked hide-and-seek as well as any child in the parish; so off I ran to find my little one.

As winter drew on, and the days grew shorter, I was sometimes almost certain that I heard a noise as if someone was playing on the great organ in the hall. I did not hear it every evening; but, certainly, I did very often, usually when I was sitting with Miss Rosamond, after I had put her to bed, and keeping quite still and silent in the bedroom. Then I used to hear it booming and swelling away in the distance. The first night, when I went down to my supper, I asked Dorothy who had been playing music, and James said very shortly that I was a gowk to take the wind soughing among the trees for music; but I saw Dorothy look at him very fearfully, and Bessy, the kitchen-maid, said something beneath her breath, and went quite white. I saw they did not like my question, so I held my peace till I was with Dorothy alone, when I knew I could get a good deal out of her. So, the next day, I watched my time, and I coaxed and asked her who it was that played the organ; for I knew that it was the organ and not the wind well enough, for all I had kept silence before James. But Dorothy had had her lesson, I'll warrant, and never a word could I get from her. So then I tried Bessy, though I had always held my head rather above her, as I was evened to James and Dorothy, and she was little better than their servant. So she said I must never, never tell; and if ever I told, I was never to say *she* had told me; but it was a very strange noise, and she had heard it many a time, but most of all on winter nights, and before storms; and folks did say it was the old lord playing on the great organ in the hall, just as he used to do when he was alive; but who the old lord was, or why he played, and why he played on stormy winter evenings in particular, she either could not or would not tell me. Well! I told you I had a brave heart; and I thought it was rather pleasant to have that grand music rolling about the house, let who would be the player; for now it rose above the great gusts of wind, and wailed and triumphed just like a living creature, and then it fell to a softness most complete, only it was always music, and tunes, so it was nonsense to call it the wind. I thought at first, that it might be Miss Furnivall who played, unknown to Bessy; but one day, when I was in the hall by myself, I opened the organ and peeped all about it and around it, as I had done to the organ in Crosthwaite church once before, and I saw it was all broken and destroyed inside, though it looked so brave and fine; and then, though it was noon-day, my flesh began to creep a little, and I shut it up, and run away pretty quickly to my own bright nursery; and I did not like hearing the music for some time after that, any more than James and Dorothy did. All this time Miss Rosamond was making herself more and more beloved. The old ladies liked her to dine with them at their early dinner. James stood behind Miss Furnivall's chair, and I behind Miss Rosamond's all in state; and after dinner, she would play about in a corner of the great drawing-room as still as any mouse, while Miss Furnivall slept, and I had my dinner in the kitchen. But she was glad enough to come to me in the nursery afterwards; for, as she said, Miss Furnivall was so sad, and Mrs. Stark so dull; but she and I were merry enough; and by-and-by, I got not to care for that weird rolling music, which did one no harm, if we did not know where it came from.

That winter was very cold. In the middle of October the frosts began, and lasted many, many weeks. I remember one day, at dinner, Miss Furnivall lifted up her sad, heavy eyes, and said to Mrs. Stark, 'I am afraid we shall have a terrible winter,' in a strange kind of meaning way. But Mrs. Stark pretended not to hear, and talked very loud of something else. My little lady and I did not care for the frost; not we! As long as it was dry, we climbed up the steep brows behind the house, and went up on the Fells, which were bleak and bare enough, and there we ran races in the fresh, sharp air; and once we came down by a new path, that took us past the two old gnarled holly-trees, which grew about half-way down by the east side of the house. But the days grew shorter and shorter, and the old lord, if it was he, played away, more and more stormily and sadly, on the great organ. One Sunday afternoon – it must have been towards the end of November – I asked Dorothy to take charge of little missy when she came out of the drawing-room, after Miss Furnivall had had her nap; for it was too cold to take her with me to church, and yet I wanted to go. And Dorothy was glad enough to promise, and was so fond of the child, that all seemed well; and Bessy and I set off very briskly, though the sky hung heavy and black over the white earth, as if the night had never fully gone away, and the air, though still, was very biting and keen.

'We shall have a fall of snow,' said Bessy to me. And sure enough, even while we were in church, it came down thick, in great large flakes, – so thick, it almost darkened the windows. It had stopped snowing before we came out, but it lay soft, thick and deep beneath our feet, as we tramped home. Before we got to the hall, the moon rose, and I think it was lighter then – what with the moon, and what with the white dazzling snow – than it had been when we went to church, between two and three o'clock. I have not told you that Miss Furnivall and Mrs. Stark never went to church; they used to read the prayers together, in their quiet, gloomy way; they seemed to feel the Sunday very long without their tapestry-work to be busy at. So when I went to Dorothy in the kitchen, to fetch Miss Rosamond and take her upstairs with me, I did not much wonder when the old woman told me that the ladies had kept the child with them, and that she had never come to the kitchen, as I had bidden her, when she was tired of behaving pretty in the drawing-room. So I took off my things and went to find her, and bring her to her supper in the

THE OLD NURSE'S STORY

nursery. But when I went into the best drawing-room, there sat the two old ladies, very still and quiet, dropping out a word now and then, but looking as if nothing so bright and merry as Miss Rosamond had ever been near them. Still I thought she might be hiding from me; it was one of her pretty ways, – and that she had persuaded them to look as if they knew nothing about her; so I went softly peeping under this sofa, and behind that chair, making believe I was sadly frightened at not finding her.

'What's the matter, Hester?' said Mrs. Stark, sharply. I don't know if Miss Furnivall had seen me, for, as I told you, she was very deaf, and she sat quite still, idly staring into the fire, with her hopeless face. 'I'm only looking for my little Rosy Posy,' replied I, still thinking that the child was there, and near me, though I could not see her.

'Miss Rosamond is not here,' said Mrs. Stark. 'She went away, more than an hour ago, to find Dorothy.' And she, too, turned and went on looking into the fire.

My heart sank at this, and I began to wish I had never left my darling. I went back to Dorothy and told her. James was gone out for the day, but she, and me, and Bessy took lights, and went up into the nursery first; and then we roamed over the great, large house, calling and entreating Miss Rosamond to come out of her hiding-place, and not frighten us to death in that way. But there was no answer; no sound.

'Oh!' said I, at last, 'can she have got into the east wing and hidden there?'

But Dorothy said it was not possible, for that she herself had never been in there; that the doors were always locked, and my lord's steward had the keys, she believed; at any rate, neither she nor James had ever seen them: so I said I would go back, and see if, after all, she was not hidden in the drawing-room, unknown to the old ladies; and if I found her there, I said, I would whip her well for the fright she had given me; but I never meant to do it. Well, I went back to the west drawing-room, and I told Mrs. Stark we could not find her anywhere, and asked for leave to look all about the furniture there, for I thought now that she might have fallen asleep in some warm, hidden corner; but no! we looked – Miss Furnivall got up and looked, trembling all over – and she was nowhere there; then we set off again, every one in the house, and looked in all the places we had searched before, but we could not find her. Miss Furnivall shivered and shook so much, that Mrs. Stark took her back into the warm drawing-room; but not before they had made me promise to bring her to them when she was found. Well-a-day! I began to think she never would be found, when I bethought me to look into the great front court, all covered with snow. I was upstairs when I looked out; but, it was such clear moonlight, I could see, quite plain, two little footprints, which might be traced from the hall-door and round the corner of the east wing. I don't know how I got down, but I tugged open the great stiff hall-door, and, throwing the skirt of my gown over my head for a cloak, I ran out. I turned the east corner, and there a black shadow fell on the snow; but when I came again into the moonlight, there were the little foot-marks going up – up to the Fells. It was bitter cold; so cold, that the air almost took the skin off my face as I ran; but I ran on crying to think how my poor little darling must be perished and frightened. I was within sight of the holly-trees, when I saw a shepherd coming down the hill, bearing something in his arms wrapped in his maud. He shouted to me, and asked me if I had lost a bairn; and, when I could not speak for crying, he bore towards me, and I saw my wee bairnie, lying still, and white, and stiff in his arms, as if she had been dead. He told me he had been up the Fells to gather in his sheep, before the deep cold of night came on, and that under the holly-trees (black marks on the hill-side, where no other bush was for miles around) he had found my little lady – my lamb – my queen – my darling – stiff and cold in the terrible sleep which is frost-begotten. Oh! the joy and the tears of having her in my arms once again! for I would not let him carry her; but took her, maud and all, into my own arms, and held her near my own warm neck and heart, and felt the life stealing slowly back again into

205

her little gentle limbs. But she was still insensible when we reached the hall, and I had no breath for speech. We went in by the kitchen-door.

'Bring me the warming-pan,' said I; and I carried her upstairs and began undressing her by the nursery fire, which Bessy had kept up. I called my little lammie all the sweet and playful names I could think of, – even while my eyes were blinded by my tears; and at last, oh! at length she opened her large blue eyes. Then I put her into her warm bed, and sent Dorothy down to tell Miss Furnivall that all was well; and I made up my mind to sit by my darling's bedside the live-long night. She fell away into a soft sleep as soon as her pretty head had touched the pillow, and I watched by her till morning light; when she wakened up bright and clear – or so I thought at first – and, my dears, so I think now.

She said, that she had fancied that she should like to go to Dorothy, for that both the old ladies were asleep, and it was very dull in the drawing-room; and that, as she was going through the west lobby, she saw the snow through the high window falling – falling – soft and steady; but she wanted to see it lying pretty and white on the ground; so she made her way into the great hall; and then, going to the window, she saw it bright and soft upon the drive; but while she stood there, she saw a little girl, not so old as she was, 'but so pretty,' said my darling, 'and this little girl beckoned to me to come out; and oh, she was so pretty and so sweet, I could not choose but go.' And then this other little girl had taken her by the hand, and side by side the two had gone round the east corner.

'Now you are a naughty little girl, and telling stories,' said I. 'What would your good mamma, that is in heaven, and never told a story in her life, say to her little Rosamond, if she heard her – and I daresay she does – telling stories!'

'Indeed, Hester,' sobbed out my child, 'I'm telling you true. Indeed I am.'

'Don't tell me!' said I, very stern. 'I tracked you by your foot-marks through the snow; there were only yours to be seen: and if you had had a little girl to go hand-in-hand with you up the hill, don't you think the footprints would have gone along with yours?'

'I can't help it, dear, dear Hester,' said she, crying, 'if they did not; I never looked at her feet, but she held my hand fast and tight in her little one, and it was very, very cold. She took me up the Fell-path, up to the holly-trees; and there I saw a lady weeping and crying; but when she saw me, she hushed her weeping, and smiled very proud and grand, and took me on her knee, and began to lull me to sleep; and that's all, Hester – but that is true; and my dear mamma knows it is,' said she, crying. So I thought the child was in a fever, and pretended to believe her, as she went over her story – over and over again, and always the same. At last Dorothy knocked at the door with Miss Rosamond's breakfast; and she told me the old ladies were down in the eating parlour, and that they wanted to speak to me. They had both been into the night-nursery the evening before, but it was after Miss Rosamond was asleep; so they had only looked at her – not asked me any questions.

'I shall catch it,' thought I to myself, as I went along the north gallery. 'And yet,' I thought, taking courage, 'it was in their charge I left her; and it's they that's to blame for letting her steal away unknown and unwatched.' So I went in boldly, and told my story. I told it all to Miss Furnivall, shouting it close to her ear; but when I came to the mention of the other little girl out in the snow, coaxing and tempting her out, and willing her up to the grand and beautiful lady by the holly-tree, she threw her arms up – her old and withered arms – and cried aloud, 'Oh! Heaven forgive! Have mercy!'

Mrs. Stark took hold of her; roughly enough, I thought; but she was past Mrs. Stark's management, and spoke to me, in a kind of wild warning and authority.

'Hester! keep her from that child! It will lure her to her death! That evil child! Tell her it is a wicked, naughty child.' Then, Mrs. Stark hurried me out of the room; where, indeed, I was glad enough to go; but Miss Furnivall kept shrieking out, 'Oh, have mercy! Wilt Thou never forgive! It is many a long year ago—'

I was very uneasy in my mind after that. I durst never leave Miss Rosamond, night or day, for fear lest she might slip off again, after some fancy or other; and all the more, because I thought I could make out that Miss Furnivall was crazy, from their odd ways about her; and I was afraid lest something of the same kind (which might be in the family, you know) hung over my darling. And the great frost never ceased all this time; and, whenever it was a more stormy night than usual, between the gusts, and through the wind, we heard the old lord playing on the great organ. But, old lord, or not, wherever Miss Rosamond went, there I followed; for my love for her, pretty, helpless orphan, was stronger than my fear for the grand and terrible sound. Besides, it rested with me to keep her cheerful and merry, as beseemed her age. So we played together, and wandered together, here and there, and everywhere; for I never dared to lose sight of her again in that large and rambling house. And so it happened, that one afternoon, not long before Christmas-day, we were playing together on the billiard-table in the great hall (not that we knew the right way of playing, but she liked to roll the smooth ivory balls with her pretty hands, and I liked to do whatever she did); and, by-and-by, without our noticing it, it grew dusk indoors, though it was still light in the open air, and I was thinking of taking her back into the nursery, when, all of a sudden, she cried out,

'Look, Hester! look! there is my poor little girl out in the snow!'

I turned towards the long narrow windows, and there, sure enough, I saw a little girl, less than my Miss Rosamond – dressed all unfit to be out-of-doors such a bitter night – crying, and beating against the window-panes, as if she wanted to be let in. She seemed to sob and wail, till Miss Rosamond could bear it no longer, and was flying to the door to open it, when, all of a sudden, and close upon us, the great organ pealed out so loud and thundering, it fairly made me tremble; and all the more, when I remembered me that, even in the stillness of that dead-cold weather, I had heard no sound of little battering hands upon the windowglass, although the phantom child had seemed to put forth all its force; and, although I had seen it wail and cry, no faintest touch of sound had fallen upon my ears. Whether I remembered all this at the very moment, I do not know; the great organ sound had so stunned me into terror; but this I know, I caught up Miss Rosamond before she got the hall-door opened, and clutched her, and carried her away, kicking and screaming, into the large, bright kitchen, where Dorothy and Agnes were busy with their mince-pies.

'What is the matter with my sweet one?' cried Dorothy, as I bore in Miss Rosamond, who was sobbing as if her heart would break.

'She won't let me open the door for my little girl to come in; and she'll die if she is out on the Fells all night. Cruel, naughty Hester,' she said, slapping me; but she might have struck harder, for I had seen a look of ghastly terror on Dorothy's face, which made my very blood run cold.

'Shut the back-kitchen door fast, and bolt it well,' said she to Agnes. She said no more; she gave me raisins and almonds to quiet Miss Rosamond; but she sobbed about the little girl in the snow, and would not touch any of the good things. I was thankful when she cried herself to sleep in bed. Then I stole down to the kitchen, and told Dorothy I had made up my mind. I would carry my darling back to my father's house in Applethwaite; where, if we lived humbly, we lived at peace. I said I had been frightened enough with the old lord's organ-playing; but now that I had seen for myself this little moaning child, all decked out as no child in the neighbourhood could be, beating and battering to get in, yet always without any sound or noise – with the dark wound on its right shoulder; and that Miss Rosamond had known it again for the phantom that had nearly lured her to her death (which Dorothy knew was true); I would stand it no longer.

I saw Dorothy change colour once or twice. When I had done, she told me she did not think I could take Miss Rosamond with me, for that she was my lord's ward, and I had no right over her; and she asked me would I leave the child that I was so fond of just for sounds and sights that could do me no harm; and that they had all had to get used to in their turns? I was all in a hot, trembling passion; and I said it was very well for her to talk; that knew what these sights and noises betokened, and that had, perhaps, had something to do with the spectre child while it was alive. And I taunted her so, that she told me all she knew at last; and then I wished I had never been told, for it only made me more afraid than ever.

She said she had heard the tale from old neighbours that were alive when she was first married; when folks used to come to the hall sometimes, before it had got such a bad name on the country side: it might not be true, or it might, what she had been told.

The old lord was Miss Furnivall's father – Miss Grace, as Dorothy called her, for Miss Maude was the elder, and Miss Furnivall by rights. The old lord was eaten up with pride. Such a proud man was never seen or heard of; and his daughters were like him. No one was good enough to wed them, although they had choice enough; for they were the great beauties of their day, as I had seen by their portraits, where they hung in the state drawing-room. But, as the old saying is, 'Pride will have a fall;' and these two haughty beauties fell in love with the same man, and he no better than a foreign musician, whom their father had down from London to play music with him at the Manor House. For, above all things, next to his pride, the old lord loved music. He could play on nearly every instrument that ever was heard of, and it was a strange thing it did not soften him; but he was a fierce dour old man, and had broken his poor wife's heart with his cruelty, they said. He was mad after music, and would pay any money for it. So he got this foreigner to come; who made such beautiful music, that they said the very birds on the trees stopped their singing to listen. And, by degrees, this foreign gentleman got such a hold over the old lord, that nothing would serve him but that he must come every year; and it was he that had the great organ brought from Holland, and built up in the hall, where it stood now. He taught the old lord to play on it; but many and many a time, when Lord Furnivall was thinking of nothing but his fine organ, and his finer music, the dark foreigner was walking abroad in the woods with one of the young ladies; now Miss Maude, and then Miss Grace.

Miss Maude won the day and carried off the prize, such as it was; and he and she were married, all unknown to any one; and before he made his next yearly visit, she had been confined of a little girl at a farm-house on the Moors, while her father and Miss Grace thought she was away at Doncaster Races. But though she was a wife and a mother, she was not a bit softened, but as haughty and as passionate as ever; and perhaps more so, for she was jealous of Miss Grace, to whom her foreign husband paid a deal of court – by way of blinding her – as he told his wife. But Miss Grace triumphed over Miss Maude, and Miss Maude grew fiercer and fiercer, both with her husband and with her sister; and the former – who could easily shake off what was disagreeable, and hide himself in foreign countries – went away a month before his usual time that summer, and half-threatened that he would never come back again. Meanwhile, the little girl was left at the farm-house, and her mother used to have her horse saddled and gallop wildly over the hills to see her once every week, at the very least; for where she loved she loved, and where she hated she hated. And the old lord went on playing – playing on his organ; and the servants thought the sweet music he made had soothed down his awful temper, of which (Dorothy said) some terrible tales could be told. He grew infirm too, and had to walk with a crutch; and his son – that was the present Lord Furnivall's father – was with the army in America, and the other son at sea; so Miss Maude had it pretty much her own way, and she and Miss Grace grew colder and bitterer to each other every day; till at last they hardly ever spoke, except when the old lord was by. The foreign musician came again the next summer, but it was for the last time; for they led him such a life with their jealousy and their passions, that he grew weary, and went away, and never was heard of again. And Miss Maude, who had always meant to have her marriage acknowledged when her father should be dead, was left now a deserted wife, whom nobody knew to have been married, with a child that she dared not own, although she loved it to distraction; living with a father whom she feared, and a sister whom she hated. When the next summer passed over, and the dark foreigner never came, both Miss Maude and Miss Grace grew gloomy and sad; they had a haggard look about them, though they looked handsome as ever. But, by-and-by, Maude brightened; for her father grew more and more infirm, and more than ever carried away by his music; and she and Miss Grace lived almost entirely apart, having separate rooms, the one on the west side, Miss Maude on the east – those very rooms which were now shut up. So she thought she might have her little girl with her, and no one need ever know except those who dared not speak about it, and were bound to believe that it was, as she said, a cottager's child she had taken a fancy to. All this, Dorothy said, was pretty well known; but what came afterwards no one knew, except Miss Grace and Mrs. Stark, who was even then her maid, and much more of a friend to her than ever her sister had been. But the servants supposed, from words that were dropped, that Miss Maude had triumphed over Miss Grace, and told her that all the time the dark foreigner had been mocking her with pretended love – he was her own husband. The colour left Miss Grace's cheek and lips that very day for ever, and she was heard to say many a time that sooner or later she would have her revenge; and Mrs. Stark was for ever spying about the east rooms.

One fearful night, just after the New Year had come in, when the snow was lying thick and deep; and the flakes were still falling – fast enough to blind any one who might be out and abroad – there was a great and violent noise heard, and the old lord's voice above all, cursing and swearing awfully, and the cries of a little child, and the proud defiance of a fierce woman, and the sound of a blow, and a dead stillness, and moans and wailings dying away on the hill-side! Then the old lord summoned all his servants, and told them, with terrible oaths, and words more terrible, that his daughter had disgraced herself, and that he had turned her out of doors – her, and her child – and that if ever they gave her help, or food, or shelter, he prayed that they might never enter heaven. And, all the while, Miss Grace stood by him, white and still as any stone; and, when he had ended, she heaved a great sigh, as much as to say her work was done, and her end was accomplished. But the old lord never touched his organ again, and died within the year; and no wonder! for, on the morrow of that wild and fearful night, the shepherds, coming down the Fell side, found Miss Maude sitting, all crazy and smiling, under the holly-trees, nursing a dead child, with a terrible mark on its right shoulder. 'But that was not what killed it,' said Dorothy: 'it was the frost and the cold. Every wild creature was in its hole, and every beast in its fold, while the child and its mother were turned out to wander on the Fells! And now you know all! and I wonder if you are less frightened now?'

I was more frightened than ever; but I said I was not. I wished Miss Rosamond and myself well out of that dreadful house for ever; but I would not leave her, and I dared not take her away. But oh, how I watched her, and guarded her! We bolted the doors, and shut the window-shutters fast, an hour or more before dark, rather than leave them open five minutes too late. But my little lady still heard the weird child crying and mourning; and not all we could do or say could keep her from wanting to go to her, and let her in from the cruel wind and the snow. All this time I kept away from Miss Furnivall and Mrs. Stark, as much as ever I could; for I feared them – I knew no good could be about them, with their grey, hard faces, and their dreamy eyes, looking back into the ghastly years that were gone. But, even in my fear, I had a kind of pity for Miss Furnivall, at least. Those gone down to the pit can hardly have a more hopeless look than that which was ever on her face. At last I even got so sorry for her – who never said a word but what was quite forced from her – that I prayed for her; and I taught Miss Rosamond to pray for one who had done a deadly sin; but often when she came to those words, she would listen, and start up from her knees and say, 'I hear my little girl plaining and crying very sad – oh, let her in, or she will die!'

One night – just after New Year's Day had come at last, and the long winter had taken a turn, as I hoped – I heard the west drawing-room bell ring three times, which was the signal for me. I would not leave Miss Rosamond alone, for all she was asleep – for the old lord had been playing wilder than ever – and I feared lest my darling should waken to hear the spectre child; see her, I knew she could not. I had fastened the windows too well for that. So I took her out of her bed, and wrapped her up in such outer clothes as were most handy, and carried her down to the drawing-room, where the old ladies sat at their tapestry-work as usual. They looked up when I came in, and Mrs. Stark asked, quite astounded, 'Why did I bring Miss Rosamond there, out of her warm bed? I had begun to whisper, 'Because I was afraid of her being tempted out while I was away, by the wild child in the snow,' when she stopped me short (with a glance at Miss Furnivall), and said Miss Furnivall wanted me to undo some work she had done wrong, and which neither of them could see to unpick. So I laid my pretty dear on the sofa, and sat down on a stool by them, and hardened my heart against them, as I heard the wind rising and howling.

Miss Rosamond slept on sound, for all the wind blew so Miss Furnivall said never a word, nor looked round when the gusts shook the windows. All at once she started up to her full height, and put up one hand, as if to bid us to listen.

'I hear voices!' said she. 'I hear terrible screams – I hear my father's voice!'

Just at that moment my darling wakened with a sudden start: 'My little girl is crying, oh, how she is crying!' and she tried to get up and go to her, but she got her feet entangled in the blanket, and I caught her up; for my flesh had begun to creep at these noises, which they heard while we could catch no sound. In a minute or two the noises came, and gathered fast, and filled our ears; we, too, heard voices and screams, and no longer heard the winter's wind that raged abroad. Mrs. Stark looked at me, and I at her, but we dared not speak. Suddenly Miss Furnivall went towards the door, out into the ante-room, through the west lobby, and opened the door into the great hall. Mrs. Stark followed, and I durst not be left, though my heart almost stopped beating for fear. I wrapped my darling tight in my arms, and went out with them. In the hall the screams were louder than ever; they seemed to come from the east wing – nearer and nearer – close on the other side of the locked-up doors – close behind them. Then I noticed that the great bronze chandelier seemed all alight, though the hall was dim, and that a fire was blazing in the vast hearth-place, though it gave no heat; and I shuddered up with terror, and folded my darling closer to me. But as I did so the east door shook, and she, suddenly struggling to get free from me, cried, 'Hester! I must go. My little girl is there! I hear her; she is coming! Hester, I must go!'

I held her tight with all my strength; with a set will, I held her. If I had died, my hands would have grasped her still, I was so resolved in my mind. Miss Furnivall stood listening, and paid no regard to my darling, who had got down to the ground, and whom I, upon my knees now, was holding with both my arms clasped round her neck; she still striving and crying to get free.

All at once, the east door gave way with a thundering crash, as if torn open in a violent passion, and there came into that broad and mysterious light, the figure of a tall old man, with grey hair and gleaming eyes. He drove before him, with many a relentless gesture of abhorrence, a stern and beautiful woman, with a little child clinging to her dress.

'Oh, Hester! Hester!' cried Miss Rosamond; 'it's the lady! the lady below the holly-trees; and my little girl is with her. Hester! Hester! let me go to her; they are drawing me to them. I feel them – I feel them. I must go!'

Again she was almost convulsed by her efforts to get away; but I held her tighter and tighter, till I feared I should do her a hurt; but rather that than let her go towards those terrible phantoms. They passed along towards the great hall-door, where the winds howled and ravened for their prey; but before they reached that, the lady turned; and I could see that she defied the old man with a fierce and proud defiance; but then she quailed – and then she threw up her arms wildly and piteously to save her child – her little child – from a blow from his uplifted crutch.

And Miss Rosamond was torn as by a power stronger than mine and writhed in my arms, and sobbed (for by this time the poor darling was growing faint).

'They want me to go with them on to the Fells – they are drawing me to them. Oh, my little girl! I would come, but cruel, wicked Hester holds me very tight.' But when she saw the uplifted crutch, she swooned away, and I thanked God for it. Just at this moment – when the tall old man, his hair streaming as in the blast of a furnace, was going to strike the little shrinking child – Miss Furnivall, the old woman by my side, cried out, 'Oh father! father! spare the little innocent child!' But just then I saw – we all saw – another phantom shape itself, and grow clear out of the blue and misty light that filled the hall; we had not seen her till now, for it was another lady who stood by the old man, with a look of relentless hate and triumphant scorn. That figure was very beautiful to look upon, with a soft, white hat drawn down over the proud brows, and a red and curling lip. It was dressed in an open robe of blue satin. I had seen that figure before. It was the likeness of Miss Furnivall in her youth; and the terrible phantoms moved on, regardless of old Miss Furnivall's wild entreaty, – and the uplifted crutch fell on the right shoulder of the little child, and the younger sister looked on, stony, and deadly serene. But at that moment, the dim lights, and the fire that gave no heat, went out of themselves, and Miss Furnivall lay at our feet stricken down by the palsy – death-stricken.

Yes! she was carried to her bed that night never to rise again. She lay with her face to the wall, muttering low, but muttering always: 'Alas! alas! what is done in youth can never be undone in age! What is done in youth can never be undone in age!'

Aunt Hetty

John Linwood Grant

I DID NOT recognise the old woman seated in the corner of our hall.

Whilst other guests clustered around the great hearth, mindful of winter's grip on the estate, she remained quiet, silent, her chair placed almost in the corridor to the kitchen. A shadow lay across half her face, placing her even further from the murmurs and laughter of the gathered revellers.

"Who's that over there, by the passage?" I asked my wife, tipping my head slightly in the direction of the stranger.

Muriel turned from one of our neighbours – a Mrs Buckley or Bentley – and frowned.

"Some dowager from your side of the family, I assumed."

"Not that I know of."

"Then go ask her, Philip." And she swivelled on sharp heels to continue her former conversation.

I thought of employing one of the children to enquire if the old woman needed anything, and hopefully discover her name – but Muriel approved only of the most practical and direct route to any solution. So I went over myself.

Stepping closer, I could make out drooping eyelids and a broad face; her skin was weather-lined, painted only with such blemishes as come to us all with age, her hair a tight grey coif. Her clothes were... I had no eye for fashion, but decades must have passed since such a show of black bombazine was in vogue.

"Quite a gathering!" I said with feigned cheer. "Would you like me to draw your chair closer to the fire? There's frost on the lawn already."

Her gaze lifted slowly, like a sleeper roused.

"Thank you, but the cold does not bother me."

Hardly an opening for conversation. I tried again.

"Good to have the family under one roof – yet so many I barely know. Forgive me, madam. I'm Philip Carlen, your host – and you'd be...?"

"A Brulier. Henrietta Brulier."

I stopped myself from remarking that I thought that line extinct. My grandfather's cousins, as best I could recall – French émigrés from long ago.

"And yes, I am the last."

"I did not–"

"People always ask." That was softened by a dry smile. "Call me Hetty, if you will."

More curious than before, I took two glasses of sherry from one of the circulating maids.

"You've not visited Thwale House before? I fear I don't remember you from previous Christmas gatherings, not even when Father was alive."

She looked upwards, and I instinctively copied her. I had grown up with those blackened timbers high above, and my mother's talk of their age had instilled in me a vague fear that one day they would crash down on me – something which my surveyor, Trevis, denied with vigour. 'They've seen more than ever we will, Mr Cullen, and will stand as long again.'

"Can you see the particular darkness up there, in places?" Henrietta Brulier pointed one gloved finger. "The scorching of the wood?"

I could not, and answered so, but I don't think she was listening.

"It is more than sixty years since I last stood inside Thwale. Odd to be back, to say farewell."

"You are ill, Aunt Hetty?" It seemed only polite to call her so.

"No, no, I was built strong, and stay as much. Still, as we grow old, we shed much of the clutter we have gathered over the years – knick-knacks to favourites; ugly and solid furniture to the salesrooms, and so forth. My memories of Thwale are clutter, and no comfort to me. Nor were they ever."

I glanced to where my wife and my sister-in-law were amusing neighbours, nephews and nieces by the roaring open fire; my brother was 'deep in' with Bob Carstairs, lately recovered after his time in the Flanders trenches.

"I'm sorry to hear that. You had some difficult times here? The family and so forth?"

Cullens, Fullers, Blakes, a handful of Bruliers – the clan had been larger in Grandfather's day. I hardly knew their names except through lists at the back of bibles and a bookplate or two.

"I was here, when it happened. That Christmas when flames ran through the house."

I knew that parts of the manor house had been rebuilt after a fire in Grandfather's day, in the middle of last century, but I had never enquired as to the details. Nor had I thought to ask Trevis, who would probably be able to say which sections were original.

"That would be…"

"Just after another war. The Crimean, which is so rarely remembered. In those days, we had the cholera; now we have the influenza. War and disease, Mr Cullen, war and disease."

"Philip, please," I said. "Was it… I mean, were you hurt in the fire? I imagine it was quite frightening."

Bombazine rustled as she shifted in her seat; the logs in the massive hearth crackled, and it was if she was trying to press her chair further back into the wall and the shadows. The glass of sherry was untouched.

"Frightening? I can tell you, if you wish?"

A quandary. I could smell cooking from the passage, but it lacked an hour yet before dinner, and I was less than eager to throw myself into the fray by the hearth. My brother and I were currently at odds over politics, and my wife's sister was far too friendly for my liking after more than one sip from the decanter.

I dragged a straight-backed chair over, and sat down; Henrietta Brulier regarded me with a solemn expression, and began to speak…

* * *

Henry Cullen, your grandfather, was a good man, and when we were all asked to join him for Christmas – the winter of 1857, this was, and I would be fifteen years old – we understood that he was trying to hold up some sense of family, at a time when the world was changing. So my parents brought me with them from Suffolk, along with another relative, my cousin Michael Brulier, whose own father was away on business.

Michael had been in some trouble at his school – the school pavilion burned down, cause unknown, and Michael had been near, nothing proven, of course. He was known as a ruffler of feathers, full of his own plans and purposes. I believe my father was trying to steer him into the Cullen business, hoping your grandfather might employ him in industry, and thus tame him.

So there we were, almost two dozen of us. Your Great-Uncle Beresford Cullen – the Colonel – who lost three fingers to frostbite in the Crimean campaign; your grandmother, great-aunts and various of their dependents, and a large clutch of cousins.

Thwale was grander then, and darker – no electric lights nor gas here, this far out into the countryside, but only candles, lanterns and rush-lights. The nearest gas lighting was in Selby; the nearest fine society in York. There was riding here, and shooting, a little fishing, but nothing else. This left Michael and I, and a girl of barely fourteen, Maria, with little to do but circle each other.

To be of such an age is to hover, always watched, between the safe retreat of childhood and the cunning maze of adult life. I was not cunning, but Michael was. I soon say how he toyed with Maria, and threw sly glances in my direction at the same time; he teased me on my height – an inch more than his – but made as if he liked it really when Maria was near. I saw his game; she was taken in, and grew possessive of his time.

On our second evening at Thwale, the twentieth of December, entertainments played out in this very hall – harmless card tricks from the Colonel, and other diversions, a song from a young lady, a recitation from one of the men. The hearth was burning bright, an equally prodigious Yule log laid ready nearby to be lit on Christmas Eve. As one of the aunts finished a tedious song, Michael came forward into the centre of the hall, dark eyes intent.

"Fire from Prometheus," he announced to the family as they turned, curious.

He had not my height, but he had presence, I grant him that, when he wanted it so. His brown hair was tossed idly back, his youthful jacket was too tight, his trousers a little too short. A man erupting from a boy.

"A trick?" asked Uncle Beresford, coarse grey whiskers around a face still scarred by Inkerman and Balaclava. "Be at it then, lad."

Michael requested that a path be cleared to the great fire. With mock theatrics, he strode to the hearth, and stretched one hand almost into the flames.

"Careful now, dear!" my mother called.

"It is quite safe, Mrs Brulier," he reassured her. "For those in the know."

He passed his left hand swiftly over the bulk of fire, and ran back to the centre of the room; some of the women present gasped, for at his fingertips bloomed orange-yellow flames. I remember clearly that your grandfather reached for the soda syphon, a proud new possession of his, but Michael waved him back – and as we looked on, unsure, these sizeable flames ran up his sleeve, across the collar, and down the other sleeve, to be extinguished as mysteriously as they came.

There was an awkward hush.

"Chemicals, I wager!" declared Uncle Beresford. "Reminds me of the Turkish artillerymen, and their confounded powders."

Michael bowed; the family applauded with various degrees of enthusiasm. I held back, watching his lean, proud face. Was his 'entertainment' so simple as chemicals and powders?

Something about his expression told me that it was not.

* * *

She sipped her sherry, lapsing into silence.

"What else could it have been?" I asked at last, drawn into her vision of over sixty years before. "A machination with lens or mirrors? Mesmerism?"

"All of those are possible," she agreed. "For a young man with too much time to brood."

"Why 'brood'? You mentioned his father. Had something happened to his mother?"

"She died of a fever, not long after his birth. Another reason why he had been so easily permitted to come up to Yorkshire – his father was not over-fond of him. If he had received more love, perhaps... we shall never know."

The clock stood only at twenty-one past six. Dinner not until seven...

"Please, Aunt Hetty – continue your tale."

* * *

On the morning of the twenty-second, after a service of carols, Thwale bustled with preparations which excluded us. I strolled the gardens, and as I walked by the rear of the house, between yew hedges and a tired rose garden, I heard a soft laugh.

Forswearing the crunch of the gravel path for the quieter grass border, I crept forward, and beneath a twisted yew, saw Michael with Maria in his grasp. Her struggles were more music-hall than alarm, her smile unsoured. I could not hear what they were saying, but when he turned his head for a second and looked in my direction, I had no doubt he knew I was there. His tryst with Maria was once more a manoeuvre for effect.

I left swiftly, considering how best to deal with him.

Of more immediate concern was that Maria took a fever after dinner the same day. There being no resident doctor nearby, Uncle Beresford – with considerable experience of sickness overseas – examined her, and declared that her temperature was high, but she showed no signs of failure of the organs, only a certain hysterical distress when awake. A powder and rest, he prescribed – and observation.

I asked if I might sit and read to her, to which her mother readily agreed. Reading was pointless; she turned and fretted, eyes closed, beneath the counterpane, so much so that I pulled it down. When my fingers touched her bare arm, there was an unnatural heat in her, and I wished I had ice to hand. Which I did, I realised! I rushed down to the kitchen and begged a bowl, taking this into the courtyard and filling it with snow.

Back in her room, I smoothed her arms, upper chest and face with the snow, mopping it with a towel as it melted. A half hour, and she was more calm, opening her eyes.

"You have caught a chill, Maria dear. It will soon pass."

"No... it was him. Your cousin from Suffolk – he pressed himself to me, and he burned. 'Let proud Henrietta learn a lesson,' he said to me..."

I frowned. "Burned?"

"Oh, he was so hot! I liked it at first – they say in books that love burns, do they not? But it became uncomfortable, and I pulled from him, at which he scowled and walked back with me, unspeaking."

I mopped her brow, read a few passages from my facile romance, and when she was asleep, I left to find Michael.

He was outside, by the woodsheds.

"It will pass by morning," he said, before I opened my mouth. "It always does. The silly girl. What I could do for you, though..."

Raising his left hand as he had in the house, he clicked his fingers, and a flame greater than most candles flickered into existence above his thumb. "These stacked logs would burn nicely, a signal to be seen for miles. A token for you, if you like?"

I put scorn into my laugh, and turned on my heel.

His tone had been light, but his expression was one I had seen before. It was one not of affection, but of desire.

Michael wanted me.

* * *

Her sudden directness surprised me; I spluttered my mouthful of sherry, turning it into a cough.

"Smoky in here," I said, but the old woman knew better. As we looked at each other, I could see it now – large blue eyes beneath those lids, a hint of raven in the grey hair, and those broad cheekbones… she must have been quite striking. Perhaps she still was. She wore black silk gloves, but her hands seemed straight, not clawed or wizened, and I realised that she must have been tall once.

It should not have been a surprise that someone had wanted Henrietta Brulier.

"That flame could have been a trick with a lucifer," I offered, rather weakly.

"It could." Her reply left neither of us in doubt that more than a simple match had been in play. "What did you do?"

"I sought counsel…"

* * *

Maria recovered fully by the next morning, leaving the family puzzled. Michael professed concern when adults were present; acted heedless when they left. When he suggested that he and I explore the attics to alleviate our boredom, I snapped out my refusal.

It seemed to me that I must share my concerns, but with who?

Uncle Beresford was at ease in your grandfather's study, a cheroot to his lips. When I knocked and entered, he smiled.

"Edwin's daughter. I remember you. I showed you and your friends a dried snake once – they squealed and fled; you asked if I had taken it myself, and how was it despatched."

"I have a problem, Colonel."

He tugged at his whiskers, and closed the study door.

"Licence to speak freely," he said, as if with one of his officers.

I told him, without preamble, every doubt I had about Michael, keeping my head high. He listened and paced, without speaking. I still remember the sound of his heavy boots on the floorboards, the musty tobacco smell of him. A veteran of more than one war, listening to a girl with a fantastical tale.

When I finished, he stopped his pacing.

"So, you bring me your suspicion that we have an unpredictable incendiary among us – or a worry that stranger concerns might threaten Thwale."

"Stranger concerns, sir?"

"The gifts of Allah and those of a *shaitan* can be hard to separate." He smiled again. "But we are not Mussulmans, are we?"

I did not entirely understand, but agreed we were not.

"My brother is not a fanciful man; I, on the other hand, have seen many odd things in the lands of the Turks, and amongst the fellahin. Will you take a duty directly from me, Hetty, as if you were one of my troops?"

"Yes, sir. But… does this mean you believe me?"

"I believe that you are worried, that you have made a concise report of your observations so far. It is what I expect of my people. Keep your eyes on that young man, Hetty, and tell me if aught else amiss comes to your attention."

If he was humouring me, there was no sign of it. Glad that I had unburdened myself, I agreed I would do his bidding.

I managed to keep clear of a sullen Michael the next day, but there was a grand civic ball in York the night before Christmas Eve. Your grandfather was unenthusiastic, but your grandmother insisted that they should take carriages and attend; with a dearth of males, even Uncle Beresford was pressed to accompany them.

Untutored in higher society, Maria, Michael and I were left in the care of the servants, and instructed to do as we were told, to amuse ourselves in harmless pursuits and then take ourselves to our bedrooms until the party returned. Should the two or three youngest members of the family become troublesome, we were to settle them, and be obedient to the housekeeper, Mrs Fentley.

Maria volunteered – with haste – to play with the little ones until their bedtime, and insisted she needed no assistance. Thus Michael and I were left to our own devices.

I could not avoid him this time – nor ignore what I now saw as his wider influence. After the carriages departed, it seemed that the hearths blazed high, needing more than usual replenishment, and the candles throughout Thwale seemed brighter, more urgent than they should be. One of the maids had a sweat upon her brow and remarked that it felt unseasonal, yet outside lay ice, and the drive was freezing mud. I was sure this was his doing.

"Have you fully recognised what I possess? And what I can offer?" Michael asked as we sat apart in the drawing room.

I put down my book, a harmless romance with clueless girls and unscrupulous uncles.

"Your arrogance? Your tricks? Yes, I recognise those, Michael Brulier."

His lips curled unpleasantly. He was a man in waiting, but the man to come did not appeal. An achiever, possibly, but one who would do so at others' expense, preening in his own abilities.

He leaped from the settee, cheeks red. "Tricks, eh? Must I still prove myself to you?"

One hand swept behind him, and the smouldering fire in the drawing room hearth began to stir, sudden flickers in the coals; he lifted his other arm high, and the candles in the antique chandelier blazed in swift response, small suns against a plaster firmament. Worse, those on the sideboard flared, catching the frayed edge of a tapestry. Old and dry, it caught in seconds.

Michael laughed.

I have never shrieked, never fainted, in my life. I rose and struck him, hard, on the cheekbone; staggering, he fell back against the curtains, which erupted into flame at his touch. Smoke wreathed the room, and a cry of alarm came from not far away – one of the servants.

"End it!" I yelled at him. "Quench or quieten what you have started."

"Some men are not meant to be quenched! But as you ask…"

His initial gestures were confident; his expression, when the fire showed no signs of abating, less so.

"It's a matter of will," he muttered, but his look grew wilder.

Full half of the room was burning.

"Come away, you idiot!" I cried. "You cannot control this!"

I grabbed at him, burning my hand, but he stood there still, trapped in anger and determination, as if that would bring the fires around him back under his control. Choking on fumes, I staggered for the French doors which led on to the carriageway.

He remained.

Half-collapsed on the gravel drive, I saw your grandfather's valet, trying to enter the drawing room from the hall, driven back by heat and smoke, and two gardeners ran past outside, not noticing me.

"Is there anyone inside?" cried Mrs Fentley.

"Michael was there..."

I had seen him clearly enough at the end, a pillar of fire within the flames; seen the way he seemed to bathe in the conflagration, even when the joists above gave way and part of the first floor fell, finally obscuring my view.

The carriages returned not long after. Your grandfather organised the chain of buckets and foot-pumps which saved the bulk of the house; Uncle Beresford alone came to me. He placed a blanket around me, and sat me by the carriage-house.

"Michael?"

I nodded.

"Where is he?"

I pointed to the collapsing west face of the house. "In there, sir."

His face grew grim. "I suppose we must dig, when the wreckage is cooler."

"You will find nothing but ashes."

He squinted at me. "That was the way of it, eh? And you saw all?"

I nodded. He wrapped the blanket tighter around me, squeezing my shoulder.

"Did you know, Henrietta, that your family name was once not Brulier, but de Brûlure. It changed with the centuries. You know the word?"

I had reasonable French from my lessons. "A scorch or burn."

"The de Brûlures were long associated with the *oriflamme*, the pennon of the French kings. The golden flame. When it flew in battle, no quarter was to be given. No survivors."

And together we turned to stare at the still-burning wreckage...

* * *

A child shrieked at a joke; my sister-in-law's alcohol-fuelled laughter cut across the hall. My thoughts remained between two Thwales, six decades apart.

"There will be no more Bruliers," Aunt Hetty said softly. "And so whether the line truly held any abnormal gift... it does not matter. What Michael was does not matter. But you have begun to wonder – is this tale why I keep my distance from open fires, and Thwale's hearths in particular."

"Because you fear them? After your... experience here?"

From a face that had survived some seventy-five years, the clear blue eyes of a fifteen-year-old girl regarded me, steady.

"Since that night," she said, "I have never felt the cold. If I were naked in the fields outside, I would not suffer the slightest chill."

I had not a single reason to believe her fantastical tale – nor any cause to doubt it. Not once had she pressured me to accept her word, and throughout, her tone had been as blunt as someone reciting a list of groceries.

The old woman peeled off one glove, and reached over to me with a fingers which were scarred, as if they had been in a conflagration. As she touched the back of my own hand, for a heartbeat only, I felt the heat of her flesh.

"I keep away from fires, Philip," she said, "because I might be tempted. I might reach forward, idly, to caress the flames – and find it good..."

* * *

Henrietta Brulier died on the second of January, 1926. Seven years had passed since she spoke to me at Thwale. She left no will, and it turned out – following months of enquiry by solicitors – that I was her nearest living relative. After many sleepless nights, I instructed that she be buried, not cremated.

Let her lie in the cool earth, and be at peace.

Horror: A True Tale

John Berwick Harwood

I WAS BUT nineteen years of age when the incident occurred which has thrown a shadow over my life; and, ah me! how many and many a weary year has dragged by since then! Young, happy, and beloved I was in those long-departed days. They said that I was beautiful. The mirror now reflects a haggard old woman, with ashen lips and face of deadly pallor. But do not fancy that you are listening to a mere puling lament. It is not the flight of years that has brought me to be this wreck of my former self: had it been so I could have borne the loss cheerfully, patiently, as the common lot of all; but it was no natural progress of decay which has robbed me of bloom, of youth, of the hopes and joys that belong to youth, snapped the link that bound my heart to another's, and doomed me to a lone old age. I try to be patient, but my cross has been heavy, and my heart is empty and weary, and I long for the death that comes so slowly to those who pray to die.

I will try and relate, exactly as it happened, the event which blighted my life. Though it occurred many years ago, there is no fear that I should have forgotten any of the minutest circumstances: they were stamped on my brain too clearly and burningly, like the brand of a red-hot iron. I see them written in the wrinkles of my brow, in the dead whiteness of my hair, which was a glossy brown once, and has known no gradual change from dark to gray, from gray to white, as with those happy ones who were the companions of my girlhood, and whose honored age is soothed by the love of children and grandchildren. But I must not envy them. I only meant to say that the difficulty of my task has no connection with want of memory – I remember but too well. But as I take my pen my hand trembles, my head swims, the old rushing faintness and Horror comes over me again, and the well-remembered fear is upon me. Yet I will go on.

This, briefly, is my story: I was a great heiress, I believe, though I cared little for the fact; but so it was. My father had great possessions, and no son to inherit after him. His three daughters, of whom I was the youngest, were to share the broad acres among them. I have said, and truly, that I cared little for the circumstance; and, indeed, I was so rich then in health and youth and love that I felt myself quite indifferent to all else. The possession of all the treasures of earth could never have made up for what I then had – and lost, as I am about to relate. Of course, we girls knew that we were heiresses, but I do not think Lucy and Minnie were any the prouder or the happier on that account. I know I was not. Reginald did not court me for my money. Of THAT I felt assured. He proved it, Heaven be praised! when he shrank from my side after the change. Yes, in all my lonely age, I can still be thankful that he did not keep his word, as some would have done – did not clasp at the altar a hand he had learned to loathe and shudder at, because it was full of gold – much gold! At least he spared me that. And I know that I was loved, and the knowledge has kept me from going mad through many a weary day and restless night, when my hot eyeballs had not a tear to shed, and even to weep was a luxury denied me.

Our house was an old Tudor mansion. My father was very particular in keeping the smallest peculiarities of his home unaltered. Thus the many peaks and gables, the numerous turrets, and the mullioned windows with their quaint lozenge panes set in lead, remained very nearly as they had been three centuries back. Over and above the quaint melancholy of our dwelling, with the deep woods of its park and the sullen waters of the mere, our neighborhood was thinly peopled and primitive, and the people round us were ignorant, and tenacious of ancient ideas and traditions. Thus it was a superstitious atmosphere that we children were reared in, and we heard, from our infancy, countless tales of horror, some mere fables doubtless, others legends of dark deeds of the olden time, exaggerated by credulity and the love of the marvelous. Our mother had died when we were young, and our other parent being, though a kind father, much absorbed in affairs of various kinds, as an active magistrate and landlord, there was no one to check the unwholesome stream of tradition with which our plastic minds were inundated in the company of nurses and servants. As years went on, however, the old ghostly tales partially lost their effects, and our undisciplined minds were turned more towards balls, dress, and partners, and other matters airy and trivial, more welcome to our riper age. It was at a county assembly that Reginald and I first met – met and loved. Yes, I am sure that he loved me with all his heart. It was not as deep a heart as some, I have thought in my grief and anger; but I never doubted its truth and honesty. Reginald's father and mine approved of our growing attachment; and as for myself, I know I was so happy then, that I look back upon those fleeting moments as on some delicious dream. I now come to the change. I have lingered on my childish reminiscences, my bright and happy youth, and now I must tell the rest – the blight and the sorrow.

It was Christmas, always a joyful and a hospitable time in the country, especially in such an old hall as our home, where quaint customs and frolics were much clung to, as part and parcel of the very dwelling itself. The hall was full of guests – so full, indeed, that there was great difficulty in providing sleeping accommodation for all. Several narrow and dark chambers in the turrets – mere pigeon-holes, as we irreverently called what had been thought good enough for the stately gentlemen of Elizabeth's reign – were now allotted to bachelor visitors, after having been empty for a century. All the spare rooms in the body and wings of the hall were occupied, of course; and the servants who had been brought down were lodged at the farm and at the keeper's, so great was the demand for space. At last the unexpected arrival of an elderly relative, who had been asked months before, but scarcely expected, caused great commotion. My aunts went about wringing their hands distractedly. Lady Speldhurst was a personage of some consequence; she was a distant cousin, and had been for years on cool terms with us all, on account of some fancied affront or slight when she had paid her LAST visit, about the time of my christening. She was seventy years old; she was infirm, rich, and testy; moreover, she was my godmother, though I had forgotten the fact; but it seems that though I had formed no expectations of a legacy in my favor, my aunts had done so for me. Aunt Margaret was especially eloquent on the subject. "There isn't a room left," she said; "was ever anything so unfortunate! We cannot put Lady Speldhurst into the turrets, and yet where IS she to sleep? And Rosa's godmother, too! Poor, dear child, how dreadful! After all these years of estrangement, and with a hundred thousand in the funds, and no comfortable, warm room at her own unlimited disposal – and Christmas, of all times in the year!" What WAS to be done? My aunts could not resign their own chambers to Lady Speldhurst, because they had already given them up to some of the married guests. My father was the most hospitable of men, but he was rheumatic, gouty, and methodical. His sisters-in-law dared not propose to shift his quarters; and, indeed, he would have far sooner dined on prison fare than have been translated to a strange bed. The matter ended in my giving up my room. I had a strange reluctance to making the offer, which surprised myself. Was it a boding of evil to come? I cannot say. We are strangely and wonderfully made. It MAY have been. At any rate, I do not think it was any selfish unwillingness to make an old and infirm lady comfortable by a trifling sacrifice. I was perfectly healthy and strong. The weather was not cold for the time of the year. It was a dark, moist

Yule – not a snowy one, though snow brooded overhead in the darkling clouds. I DID make the offer, which became me, I said with a laugh, as the youngest. My sisters laughed too, and made a jest of my evident wish to propitiate my godmother. "She is a fairy godmother, Rosa," said Minnie, "and you know she was affronted at your christening, and went away muttering vengeance. Here she is coming back to see you; I hope she brings golden gifts with her."

I thought little of Lady Speldhurst and her possible golden gifts. I cared nothing for the wonderful fortune in the funds that my aunts whispered and nodded about so mysteriously. But since then I have wondered whether, had I then showed myself peevish or obstinate – had I refused to give up my room for the expected kinswoman – it would not have altered the whole of my life? But then Lucy or Minnie would have offered in my stead, and been sacrificed – what do I say? – better that the blow should have fallen as it did than on those dear ones.

The chamber to which I removed was a dim little triangular room in the western wing, and was only to be reached by traversing the picture-gallery, or by mounting a little flight of stone stairs which led directly upward from the low-browed arch of a door that opened into the garden. There was one more room on the same landing-place, and this was a mere receptacle for broken furniture, shattered toys, and all the lumber that WILL accumulate in a country-house. The room I was to inhabit for a few nights was a tapestry-hung apartment, with faded green curtains of some costly stuff, contrasting oddly with a new carpet and the bright, fresh hangings of the bed, which had been hurriedly erected. The furniture was half old, half new; and on the dressing-table stood a very quaint oval mirror, in a frame of black wood – unpolished ebony, I think. I can remember the very pattern of the carpet, the number of chairs, the situation of the bed, the figures on the tapestry. Nay, I can recollect not only the color of the dress I wore on that fated evening, but the arrangement of every scrap of lace and ribbon, of every flower, every jewel, with a memory but too perfect.

Scarcely had my maid finished spreading out my various articles of attire for the evening (when there was to be a great dinner-party) when the rumble of a carriage announced that Lady Speldhurst had arrived. The short winter's day drew to a close, and a large number of guests were gathered together in the ample drawing-room, around the blaze of the wood-fire, after dinner. My father, I recollect, was not with us at first. There were some squires of the old, hard-riding, hard-drinking stamp still lingering over their port in the dining-room, and the host, of course, could not leave them. But the ladies and all the younger gentlemen – both those who slept under our roof and those who would have a dozen miles of fog and mire to encounter on their road home – were all together. Need I say that Reginald was there? He sat near me – my accepted lover, my plighted future husband. We were to be married in the spring. My sisters were not far off; they, too, had found eyes that sparkled and softened in meeting theirs, had found hearts that beat responsive to their own. And, in their cases, no rude frost nipped the blossom ere it became the fruit; there was no canker in their flowerets of young hope, no cloud in their sky. Innocent and loving, they were beloved by men worthy of their esteem.

The room – a large and lofty one, with an arched roof – had somewhat of a somber character from being wainscoted and ceiled with polished black oak of a great age. There were mirrors and there were pictures on the walls, and handsome furniture, and marble chimney-pieces, and a gay Tournay carpet; but these merely appeared as bright spots on the dark background of the Elizabethan woodwork. Many lights were burning, but the blackness of the walls and roof seemed absolutely to swallow up their rays, like the mouth of a cavern. A hundred candles could not have given that apartment the cheerful lightness of a modern drawing room. But the gloomy richness of the panels matched well with the ruddy gleam from the enormous wood-fire, in which crackling and glowing, now lay the mighty Yule log. Quite a blood-red luster poured forth from the fire, and quivered on the walls and the groined roof. We had gathered round the vast antique hearth in a wide circle. The quivering light of the fire and candles fell upon us all, but not equally, for some were in shadow. I remember still how tall and manly and handsome Reginald looked that night, taller by the head than any there, and full of high spirits and gayety. I, too, was in the highest spirits; never had my bosom felt lighter, and I believe it was my mirth that gradually gained the rest, for I recollect what a blithe, joyous company we seemed. All save one. Lady Speldhurst, dressed in gray silk and wearing a quaint head- dress, sat in her armchair, facing the fire, very silent, with her hands and her sharp chin propped on a sort of ivory-handled crutch that she walked with (for she was lame), peering at me with half- shut eyes. She was a little, spare old woman, with very keen, delicate features of the French type. Her gray silk dress, her spotless lace, old-fashioned jewels, and prim neatness of array, were well suited to the intelligence of her face, with its thin lips, and eyes of a piercing black, undimmed by age. Those eyes made me uncomfortable, in spite of my gayety, as they followed my every movement with curious scrutiny. Still I was very merry and gay; my sisters even wondered at my ever-ready mirth, which was almost wild in its excess. I have heard since then of the Scottish belief that those doomed to some great calamity become fey, and are never so disposed for merriment and laughter as just before the blow falls. If ever mortal was fey, then I was so on that evening. Still, though I strove to shake it off, the pertinacious observation of old Lady Speldhurst's eyes DID make an impression on me of a vaguely disagreeable nature. Others, too, noticed her scrutiny of me, but set it down as a mere eccentricity of a person always reputed whimsical, to say the least of it.

However, this disagreeable sensation lasted but a few moments. After a short pause my aunt took her part in the conversation, and we found ourselves listening to a weird legend, which the old lady told exceedingly well. One tale led to another. Everyone was called on in turn to contribute to the public entertainment, and story after story, always relating to demonology and witchcraft, succeeded. It was Christmas, the season for such tales; and the old room, with its dusky walls and pictures, and vaulted roof, drinking up the light so greedily, seemed just fitted to give effect to such legendary lore. The huge logs crackled and burned with glowing warmth; the blood-red glare of the Yule log flashed on the faces of the listeners and narrator, on the portraits, and the holly wreathed about their frames, and the upright old dame, in her antiquated dress and trinkets, like one of the originals of the pictures, stepped from the canvas to join our circle. It threw a shimmering luster of an ominously ruddy hue upon the oaken panels. No wonder that the ghost and goblin stories had a new zest. No wonder that the blood of the more timid grew chill and curdled, that their flesh crept, that their hearts beat irregularly, and the girls peeped fearfully over their shoulders, and huddled close together like frightened sheep, and half fancied they beheld some impish and malignant face gibbering at them from the darkling corners of the old room. By degrees my high spirits died out, and I felt the childish tremors, long latent, long forgotten, coming over me. I followed each story with painful interest; I did not ask myself if I believed the dismal tales. I listened, and fear grew upon me – the blind, irrational fear of our nursery days. I am sure most of the other ladies present, young or middle-aged, were affected by the circumstances under which these traditions were heard, no less than by the wild and fantastic character of them. But with them the impression would die out next morning, when the bright sun should shine on the frosted boughs, and the rime on the grass, and the scarlet berries and green spikelets of the holly; and with me – but, ah! what was to happen ere another day dawn? Before we had made an end of this talk my father and the other squires came in, and we ceased our ghost stories, ashamed to speak of such matters before these new-comers – hard-headed, unimaginative men, who had no sympathy with idle legends. There was now a stir and bustle.

Servants were handing round tea and coffee, and other refreshments. Then there was a little music and singing. I sang a duet with Reginald, who had a fine voice and good musical skill. I remember that my singing was much praised, and indeed I was surprised at the power and pathos of my own voice, doubtless due to my excited nerves and mind. Then I heard someone say to another that I was by far the cleverest of the Squire's daughters, as well as the prettiest. It did not make me vain. I had no rivalry with Lucy and Minnie. But Reginald whispered some soft, fond words in my ear a little before he mounted his horse to set off homeward, which DID make me happy and proud. And to think that the next time we met – but I forgave him long ago. Poor Reginald! And now shawls and cloaks were in request, and carriages rolled up to the porch, and the guests gradually departed. At last no one was left but those visitors staying in the house. Then my father, who had been called out to speak with the bailiff of the estate, came back with a look of annoyance on his face.

"A strange story I have just been told," said he; "here has been my bailiff to inform me of the loss of four of the choicest ewes out of that little flock of Southdowns I set such store by, and which arrived in the north but two months since. And the poor creatures have been destroyed in so strange a manner, for their carcasses are horribly mangled."

Most of us uttered some expression of pity or surprise, and some suggested that a vicious dog was probably the culprit.

"It would seem so," said my father; "it certainly seems the work of a dog; and yet all the men agree that no dog of such habits exists near us, where, indeed, dogs are scarce, excepting the shepherds' collies and the sporting dogs secured in yards. Yet the sheep are gnawed and bitten, for they show the marks of teeth. Something has done this, and has torn their bodies wolfishly; but apparently it has been only to suck the blood, for little or no flesh is gone."

"How strange!" cried several voices. Then some of the gentlemen remembered to have heard of cases when dogs addicted to sheep- killing had destroyed whole flocks, as if in sheer wantonness, scarcely deigning to taste a morsel of each slain wether.

My father shook his head. "I have heard of such cases, too," he said; "but in this instance I am tempted to think the malice of some unknown enemy has been at work. The teeth of a dog have been busy, no doubt, but the poor sheep have been mutilated in a fantastic manner, as strange as horrible; their hearts, in especial, have been torn out, and left at some paces off, half- gnawed. Also, the men persist that they found the print of a naked human foot in the soft mud of the ditch, and near it – this." And he held up what seemed a broken link of a rusted iron chain.

Many were the ejaculations of wonder and alarm, and many and shrewd the conjectures, but none seemed exactly to suit the bearings of the case. And when my father went on to say that two lambs of the same valuable breed had perished in the same singular manner three days previously, and that they also were found mangled and gore- stained, the amazement reached a higher pitch. Old Lady Speldhurst listened with calm, intelligent attention, but joined in none of our exclamations. At length she said to my father, "Try and recollect – have you no enemy among your neighbors?" My father started, and knit his brows. "Not one that I know of," he replied; and indeed he was a popular man and a kind landlord. "The more lucky you," said the old dame, with one of her grim smiles. It was now late, and we retired to rest before long. One by one the guests dropped off. I was the member of the family selected to escort old Lady Speldhurst to her room – the room I had vacated in her favor. I did not much like the office. I felt a remarkable repugnance to my godmother, but my worthy aunts insisted so much that I should ingratiate myself with one who had so much to leave that I could not but comply. The visitor hobbled up the broad oaken stairs actively enough, propped on my arm and her ivory crutch. The room never had looked more genial and pretty, with its brisk fire, modern furniture, and the gay French paper on the walls

"A nice room, my dear, and I ought to be much obliged to you for it, since my maid tells me it is yours," said her ladyship; "but I am pretty sure you repent your generosity to me, after all those ghost stories, and tremble to think of a strange bed and chamber, eh?" I made some commonplace reply. The old lady arched her eyebrows. "Where have they put you, child?" she asked; "in some cock-loft of the turrets, eh? or in a lumber-room – a regular ghost-trap? I can hear your heart beating with fear this moment. You are not fit to be alone." I tried to call up my pride, and laugh off the accusation against my courage, all the more, perhaps, because I felt its truth. "Do you want anything more that I can get you, Lady Speldhurst?" I asked, trying to feign a yawn of sleepiness. The old dame's keen eyes were upon me. "I rather like you, my dear," she said, "and I liked your mamma well enough before she treated me so shamefully about the christening dinner. Now, I know you are frightened and fearful, and if an owl should but flap your window tonight, it might drive you into fits. There is a nice little sofa-bed in this dressing closet – call your maid to arrange it for you, and you can sleep there snugly, under the old witch's protection, and then no goblin dare harm you, and nobody will be a bit the wiser, or quiz you for being afraid." How little I knew what hung in the balance of my refusal or acceptance of that trivial proffer! Had the veil of the future been lifted for one instant! but that veil is impenetrable to our gaze.

I left her door. As I crossed the landing a bright gleam came from another room, whose door was left ajar; it (the light) fell like a bar of golden sheen across my path. As I approached the door opened and my sister Lucy, who had been watching for me, came out. She was already in a white cashmere wrapper, over which her loosened hair hung darkly and heavily, like tangles of silk. "Rosa, love," she whispered, "Minnie and I can't bear the idea of your sleeping out there, all alone, in that solitary room – the very room too Nurse Sherrard used to talk about! So, as you know Minnie has given up her room, and come to sleep in mine, still we should so wish you to stop with us tonight at any rate, and I could make up a bed on the sofa for myself or you – and—" I stopped Lucy's mouth with a kiss. I declined her offer. I would not listen to it. In fact, my pride was up in arms, and I felt I would rather pass the night in the churchyard itself than accept a proposal dictated, I felt sure, by the notion that my nerves were shaken by the ghostly lore we had been raking up, that I was a weak, superstitious creature, unable to pass a night in a strange chamber. So I would not listen to Lucy, but kissed her, bade her good-night, and went on my way laughing, to show my light heart. Yet, as I looked back in the dark corridor, and saw the friendly door still ajar, the yellow bar of light still crossing from wall to wall, the sweet, kind face still peering after me from amidst its clustering curls, I felt a thrill of sympathy, a wish to return, a yearning after human love and companionship. False shame was strongest, and conquered. I waved a gay adieu. I turned the corner, and peeping over my shoulder, I saw the door close; the bar of yellow light was there no longer in the darkness of the passage. I thought at that instant that I heard a heavy sigh. I looked sharply round. No one was there. No door was open, yet I fancied, and fancied with a wonderful vividness, that I did hear an actual sigh breathed not far off, and plainly distinguishable from the groan of the sycamore branches as the wind tossed them to and fro in the outer blackness. If ever a mortal's good angel had cause to sigh for sorrow, not sin, mine had cause to mourn that night. But imagination plays us strange tricks and my nervous system was not over-composed or very fitted for judicial analysis. I had to go through the picture-gallery. I had never entered this apartment by candle-light before and I was struck by the gloomy array of the tall portraits, gazing moodily from the canvas on the lozenge-paned or painted windows, which rattled to the blast as it swept howling by. Many of the faces looked stern, and very different from their daylight expression. In others a furtive, flickering smile seemed to mock me as my candle illumined them; and in all, the eyes, as usual with artistic portraits, seemed to follow my motions with a scrutiny and an interest the more marked for the apathetic immovability of the other features. I felt ill at ease under this stony gaze, though conscious how absurd were my apprehensions; and I called up a smile and an air of mirth, more as if acting a part under the eyes of human beings than of their mere shadows on the wall. I even laughed as I confronted them. No echo had my short- lived laughter but from the hollow armor and arching roof, and I continued on my way in silence.

By a sudden and not uncommon revulsion of feeling I shook off my aimless terrors, blushed at my weakness, and sought my chamber only too glad that I had been the only witness of my late tremors. As I entered my chamber I thought I heard something stir in the neglected lumber room, which was the only neighboring apartment. But I was determined to have no more panics, and resolutely shut my eyes to this slight and transient noise, which had nothing unnatural in it; for surely, between rats and wind, an old manor- house on a stormy night needs no sprites to disturb it. So I entered my room, and rang for my maid. As I did so I looked around me, and a most unaccountable repugnance to my temporary abode came over me, in spite of my efforts. It was no more to be shaken off than a chill is to be shaken off when we enter some damp cave. And, rely upon it, the feeling of dislike and apprehension with which we regard, at first sight, certain places and people, was not implanted in us without some wholesome purpose. I grant it is irrational – mere animal instinct – but is not instinct God's gift, and is it for us to despise it? It is by instinct that children know their friends from their enemies – that they distinguish with such unerring accuracy between those who like them and those who only flatter and hate them. Dogs do the same; they will fawn on one person, they slink snarling from another. Show me a man whom children and dogs shrink from, and I will show you a false, bad man – lies on his lips, and murder at his heart. No; let none despise the heaven-sent gift of innate antipathy, which makes the horse quail when the lion crouches in the thicket – which makes the cattle scent the shambles from afar, and low in terror and disgust as their nostrils snuff the blood-polluted air. I felt this antipathy strongly as I looked around me in my new sleeping-room, and yet I could find no reasonable pretext for my dislike. A very good room it was, after all, now that the green damask curtains were drawn, the fire burning bright and clear, candles burning on the mantel-piece, and the various familiar articles of toilet arranged as usual. The bed, too, looked peaceful and inviting – a pretty little white bed, not at all the gaunt funereal sort of couch which haunted apartments generally contain.

My maid entered, and assisted me to lay aside the dress and ornaments I had worn, and arranged my hair, as usual, prattling the while, in Abigail fashion. I seldom cared to converse with servants; but on that night a sort of dread of being left alone – a longing to keep some human being near me possessed me – and I encouraged the girl to gossip, so that her duties took her half an hour longer to get through than usual. At last, however, she had done all that could be done, and all my questions were answered, and my orders for the morrow reiterated and vowed obedience to, and the clock on the turret struck one. Then Mary, yawning a little, asked if I wanted anything more, and I was obliged to answer no, for very shame's sake; and she went. The shutting of the door, gently as it was closed, affected me unpleasantly. I took a dislike to the curtains, the tapestry, the dingy pictures – everything. I hated the room. I felt a temptation to put on a cloak, run, half-dressed, to my sisters' chamber, and say I had changed my mind and come for shelter. But they must be asleep, I thought, and I could not be so unkind as to wake them. I said my prayers with unusual earnestness and a heavy heart. I extinguished the candles, and was just about to lay my head on my pillow, when the idea seized me that I would fasten the door. The candles were extinguished, but the firelight was amply sufficient to guide me. I gained the door. There was a lock, but it was rusty or hampered; my utmost strength could not turn the key. The bolt was broken and worthless. Balked of my intention, I consoled myself by remembering that I had never had need of fastenings yet, and returned to my bed. I lay awake for a good while, watching the red glow of the burning coals in the grate. I was quiet now, and more composed. Even the light gossip of the maid, full of petty human cares and joys, had done me good – diverted my thoughts from brooding. I was on the point of dropping asleep, when I was twice disturbed. Once, by an owl, hooting in the ivy outside – no unaccustomed sound, but harsh and melancholy; once, by a long and mournful howling set up by the mastiff, chained in the yard beyond the wing I occupied. A long-drawn, lugubrious howling was this latter, and much such a note as the vulgar declare to herald a death in the family. This was a fancy I had never shared; but yet I could not help feeling that the dog's mournful moans were sad, and expressive of terror, not at all like his fierce, honest bark of anger, but rather as if something evil and unwonted were abroad. But soon I fell asleep.

How long I slept I never knew. I awoke at once with that abrupt start which we all know well, and which carries us in a second from utter unconsciousness to the full use of our faculties. The fire was still burning, but was very low, and half the room or more was in deep shadow. I knew, I felt, that some person or thing was in the room, although nothing unusual was to be seen by the feeble light. Yet it was a sense of danger that had aroused me from slumber. I experienced, while yet asleep, the chill and shock of sudden alarm, and I knew, even in the act of throwing off sleep like a mantle, WHY I awoke, and that some intruder was present. Yet, though I listened intently, no sound was audible, except the faint murmur of the fire – the dropping of a cinder from the bars – the loud, irregular beatings of my own heart. Notwithstanding this silence, by some intuition I knew that I had not been deceived by a dream, and felt certain that I was not alone. I waited. My heart beat on; quicker, more sudden grew its pulsations, as a bird in a cage might flutter in presence of the hawk. And then I heard a sound, faint, but quite distinct, the clank of iron, the rattling of a chain! I ventured to lift my head from the pillow. Dim and uncertain as the light was, I saw the curtains of my bed shake, and caught a glimpse of something beyond, a darker spot in the darkness. This confirmation of my fears did not surprise me so much as it shocked me. I strove to cry aloud, but could not utter a word. The chain rattled again, and this time the noise was louder and clearer. But though I strained my eyes, they could not penetrate the obscurity that shrouded the other end of the chamber whence came the sullen clanking. In a moment several distinct trains of thought, like many-colored strands of thread twining into one, became palpable to my mental vision. Was it a robber? Could it be a supernatural visitant? Or was I the victim of a cruel trick, such as I had heard of, and which some thoughtless persons love to practice on the timid, reckless of its dangerous results? And then a new idea, with some ray of comfort in it, suggested itself. There was a fine young dog of the Newfoundland breed, a favorite of my father's, which was usually chained by night in an outhouse. Neptune might have broken loose, found his way to my room, and, finding the door imperfectly closed, have pushed it open and entered. I breathed more freely as this harmless interpretation of the noise forced itself upon me. It was – it must be – the dog, and I was distressing myself uselessly. I resolved to call to him; I strove to utter his name – "Neptune, Neptune," but a secret apprehension restrained me, and I was mute.

Then the chain clanked nearer and nearer to the bed, and presently I saw a dusky, shapeless mass appear between the curtains on the opposite side to where I was lying. How I longed to hear the whine of the poor animal that I hoped might be the cause of my alarm. But no; I heard no sound save the rustle of the curtains and the clash of the iron chains. Just then the dying flame of the fire leaped up, and with one sweeping, hurried glance I saw that the door was shut, and, horror! it is not the dog! it is the semblance of a human form that now throws itself heavily on the bed, outside the clothes, and lies there, huge and swart, in the red gleam that treacherously died away after showing so much to affright, and sinks into dull darkness. There was now no light left, though the red cinders yet glowed with a ruddy gleam like the eyes of wild beasts. The chain rattled no more. I tried to speak, to scream wildly for help; my mouth was parched, my tongue refused to obey. I could not utter a cry, and, indeed, who could have heard me, alone as I was in that solitary chamber, with no living neighbor, and the picture-gallery between me and any aid that even the loudest, most piercing shriek could summon. And the storm that howled without would have drowned my voice, even if help had been at hand. To call aloud – to demand who was there – alas! how useless, how perilous! If the intruder were a robber, my outcries would but goad him to fury; but what robber would act thus? As for a trick, that seemed impossible. And yet, WHAT lay by my side, now wholly unseen? I strove to pray aloud as there rushed on my memory a flood of weird legends – the dreaded yet fascinating lore of my childhood. I had heard and read of the spirits of the wicked men forced to revisit the scenes of their earthly crimes – of demons that lurked in certain accursed spots – of the ghoul and vampire of the east, stealing amidst the graves they rifled for their ghostly banquets; and then I shuddered as I gazed on the blank darkness where I knew it lay. It stirred – it moaned hoarsely; and again I heard the chain clank close beside me – so close that it must almost have touched me. I drew myself from it, shrinking away in loathing and terror of the evil thing – what, I knew not, but felt that something malignant was near.

And yet, in the extremity of my fear, I dared not speak; I was strangely cautious to be silent, even in moving farther off; for I had a wild hope that it – the phantom, the creature, whichever it was – had not discovered my presence in the room. And then I remembered all the events of the night – Lady Speldhurst's ill-omened vaticinations, her half-warnings, her singular look as we parted, my sister's persuasions, my terror in the gallery, the remark that "this was the room nurse Sherrard used to talk of." And then memory, stimulated by fear, recalled the long-forgotten past, the ill-repute of this disused chamber, the sins it had witnessed, the blood spilled, the poison administered by unnatural hate within its walls, and the tradition which called it haunted. The green room – I remembered now how fearfully the servants avoided it – how it was mentioned rarely, and in whispers, when we were children, and how we had regarded it as a mysterious region, unfit for mortal habitation. Was It – the dark form with the chain – a creature of this world, or a specter? And again – more dreadful still – could it be that the corpses of wicked men were forced to rise and haunt in the body the places where they had wrought their evil deeds? And was such as these my grisly neighbor? The chain faintly rattled. My hair bristled; my eyeballs seemed starting from their sockets; the damps of a great anguish were on my brow. My heart labored as if I were crushed beneath some vast weight. Sometimes it appeared to stop its frenzied beatings, sometimes its pulsations were fierce and hurried; my breath came short and with extreme difficulty, and I shivered as if with cold; yet I feared to stir. IT moved, it moaned, its fetters clanked dismally, the couch creaked and shook. This was no phantom, then – no air-drawn specter. But its very solidity, its palpable presence, were a thousand times more terrible. I felt that I was in the very grasp of what could not only affright but harm; of something whose contact sickened the soul with deathly fear. I made a desperate resolve: I glided from the bed, I seized a warm wrapper, threw it around me, and tried to grope, with extended hands, my way to the door. My heart beat high at the hope of escape. But I had scarcely taken one step before the moaning was renewed – it changed into a threatening growl that would have suited a wolf's throat, and a hand clutched at my sleeve. I stood motionless. The muttering growl sank to a moan again, the chain sounded no more, but still the hand held its gripe of my garment, and I feared to move. It knew of my presence, then. My brain reeled, the blood boiled in my ears, and my knees lost all strength, while my heart panted like that of a deer in the wolf's jaws. I sank back, and the benumbing influence of excessive terror reduced me to a state of stupor.

When my full consciousness returned I was sitting on the edge of the bed, shivering with cold, and barefooted. All was silent, but I felt that my sleeve was still clutched by my unearthly visitant.

The silence lasted a long time. Then followed a chuckling laugh that froze my very marrow, and the gnashing of teeth as in demoniac frenzy; and then a wailing moan, and this was succeeded by silence. Hours may have passed – nay, though the tumult of my own heart prevented my hearing the clock strike, must have passed – but they seemed ages to me. And how were they passed? Hideous visions passed before the aching eyes that I dared not close, but which gazed ever into the dumb darkness where It lay – my dread companion through the watches of the night. I pictured It in every abhorrent form which an excited fancy could summon up: now as a skeleton; with hollow eye-holes and grinning, fleshless jaws; now as a vampire, with livid face and bloated form, and dripping mouth wet with blood. Would it never be light! And yet, when day should dawn I should be forced to see It face to face. I had heard that specter and fiend were compelled to fade as morning brightened, but this creature was too real, too foul a thing of earth, to vanish at cock-crow. No! I should see it – the Horror – face to face! And then the cold prevailed, and my teeth chattered, and shiverings ran through me, and yet there was the damp of agony on my bursting brow. Some instinct made me snatch at a shawl or cloak that lay on a chair within reach, and wrap it round me. The moan was renewed, and the chain just stirred. Then I sank into apathy, like an Indian at the stake, in the intervals of torture. Hours fled by, and I remained like a statue of ice, rigid and mute. I even slept, for I remember that I started to find the cold gray light of an early winter's day was on my face, and stealing around the room from between the heavy curtains of the window.

Shuddering, but urged by the impulse that rivets the gaze of the bird upon the snake, I turned to see the Horror of the night. Yes, it was no fevered dream, no hallucination of sickness, no airy phantom unable to face the dawn. In the sickly light I saw it lying on the bed, with its grim head on the pillow. A man? Or a corpse arisen from its unhallowed grave, and awaiting the demon that animated it? There it lay – a gaunt, gigantic form, wasted to a skeleton, half-clad, foul with dust and clotted gore, its huge limbs flung upon the couch as if at random, its shaggy hair streaming over the pillows like a lion's mane. His face was toward me. Oh, the wild hideousness of that face, even in sleep! In features it was human, even through its horrid mask of mud and half-dried bloody gouts, but the expression was brutish and savagely fierce; the white teeth were visible between the parted lips, in a malignant grin; the tangled hair and beard were mixed in leonine confusion, and there were scars disfiguring the brow. Round the creature's waist was a ring of iron, to which was attached a heavy but broken chain – the chain I had heard clanking. With a second glance I noted that part of the chain was wrapped in straw to prevent its galling the wearer. The creature – I cannot call it a man – had the marks of fetters on its wrists, the bony arm that protruded through one tattered sleeve was scarred and bruised; the feet were bare, and lacerated by pebbles and briers, and one of them was wounded, and wrapped in a morsel of rag. And the lean hands, one of which held my sleeve, were armed with talons like an eagle's. In an instant the horrid truth flashed upon me – I was in the grasp of a madman. Better the phantom that scares the sight than the wild beast that rends and tears the quivering flesh – the pitiless human brute that has no heart to be softened, no reason at whose bar to plead, no compassion, naught of man save the form and the cunning. I gasped in terror. Ah! the mystery of those ensanguined fingers, those gory, wolfish jaws! that face, all besmeared with blackening blood, is revealed!

The slain sheep, so mangled and rent – the fantastic butchery – the print of the naked foot – all, all were explained; and the chain, the broken link of which was found near the slaughtered animals – it came from his broken chain – the chain he had snapped, doubtless, in his escape from the asylum where his raging frenzy had been fettered and bound, in vain! in vain! Ah me! how had this grisly Samson broken manacles and prison bars – how had he eluded guardian and keeper and a hostile world, and come hither on his wild way, hunted like a beast of prey, and snatching his hideous banquet like a beast of prey, too! Yes, through the tatters of his mean and ragged garb I could see the marks of the seventies, cruel and foolish, with which men in that time tried to tame the might of madness. The scourge – its marks were there; and the scars of the hard iron fetters, and many a cicatrice and welt, that told a dismal tale of hard usage. But now he was loose, free to play the brute – the baited, tortured brute that they had made him – now without the cage, and ready to gloat over the victims his strength should overpower. Horror! horror! I was the prey – the victim – already in the tiger's clutch; and a deadly sickness came over me, and the iron entered into my soul, and I longed to scream, and was dumb! I died a thousand deaths as that morning wore on. I DARED NOT faint. But words cannot paint what I suffered as I waited – waited till the moment when he should open his eyes and be aware of my presence; for I was assured he knew it not. He had entered the chamber as a lair, when weary and gorged with his horrid orgy; and he had flung himself down to sleep without a suspicion that he was not alone. Even his grasping my sleeve was doubtless an act done betwixt sleeping and waking, like his unconscious moans and laughter, in some frightful dream.

Hours went on; then I trembled as I thought that soon the house would be astir, that my maid would come to call me as usual, and awake that ghastly sleeper. And might he not have time to tear me, as he tore the sheep, before any aid could arrive? At last what I dreaded came to pass – a light footstep on the landing – there is a tap at the door. A pause succeeds, and then the tapping is renewed, and this time more loudly. Then the madman stretched his limbs, and uttered his moaning cry, and his eyes slowly opened – very slowly opened and met mine. The girl waited a while ere she knocked for the third time. I trembled lest she should open the door unbidden – see that grim thing, and bring about the worst.

I saw the wondering surprise in his haggard, bloodshot eyes; I saw him stare at me half vacantly, then with a crafty yet wondering look; and then I saw the devil of murder begin to peep forth from those hideous eyes, and the lips to part as in a sneer, and the wolfish teeth to bare themselves. But I was not what I had been. Fear gave me a new and a desperate composure – a courage foreign to my nature. I had heard of the best method of managing the insane; I could but try; I DID try. Calmly, wondering at my own feigned calm, I fronted the glare of those terrible eyes. Steady and undaunted was my gaze – motionless my attitude. I marveled at myself, but in that agony of sickening terror I was OUTWARDLY firm. They sink, they quail, abashed, those dreadful eyes, before the gaze of a helpless girl; and the shame that is never absent from insanity bears down the pride of strength, the bloody cravings of the wild beast. The lunatic moaned and drooped his shaggy head between his gaunt, squalid hands.

I lost not an instant. I rose, and with one spring reached the door, tore it open, and, with a shriek, rushed through, caught the wondering girl by the arm, and crying to her to run for her life, rushed like the wind along the gallery, down the corridor, down the stairs. Mary's screams filled the house as she fled beside me. I heard a long-drawn, raging cry, the roar of a wild animal mocked of its prey, and I knew what was behind me. I never turned my head – I flew rather than ran. I was in the hall already; there was a rush of many feet, an outcry of many voices, a sound of scuffling feet, and brutal yells, and oaths, and heavy blows, and I fell to the ground crying, "Save me!" and lay in a swoon. I awoke from a delirious trance. Kind faces were around my bed, loving looks were bent on me by all, by my dear father and dear sisters; but I scarcely saw them before I swooned again.

When I recovered from that long illness, through which I had been nursed so tenderly, the pitying looks I met made me tremble. I asked for a looking-glass. It was long denied me, but my importunity prevailed at last – a mirror was brought. My youth was gone at one fell swoop. The glass showed me a livid and haggard face, blanched and bloodless as of one who sees a specter;

and in the ashen lips, and wrinkled brow, and dim eyes, I could trace nothing of my old self. The hair, too, jetty and rich before, was now as white as snow; and in one night the ravages of half a century had passed over my face. Nor have my nerves ever recovered their tone after that dire shock. Can you wonder that my life was blighted, that my lover shrank from me, so sad a wreck was I?

I am old now – old and alone. My sisters would have had me to live with them, but I chose not to sadden their genial homes with my phantom face and dead eyes. Reginald married another. He has been dead many years. I never ceased to pray for him, though he left me when I was bereft of all. The sad weird is nearly over now. I am old, and near the end, and wishful for it. I have not been bitter or hard, but I cannot bear to see many people, and am best alone. I try to do what good I can with the worthless wealth Lady Speldhurst left me, for, at my wish, my portion was shared between my sisters. What need had I of inheritance? – I, the shattered wreck made by that one night of horror!

The Christmas Banquet

Nathaniel Hawthorne

"I HAVE HERE attempted," said Roderick, unfolding a few sheets of manuscript, as he sat with Rosina and the sculptor in the summer-house, – "I have attempted to seize hold of a personage who glides past me, occasionally, in my walk through life. My former sad experience, as you know, has gifted me with some degree of insight into the gloomy mysteries of the human heart, through which I have wandered like one astray in a dark cavern, with his torch fast flickering to extinction. But this man, this class of men, is a hopeless puzzle."

"Well, but propound him," said the sculptor. "Let us have an idea of hint, to begin with."

"Why, indeed," replied Roderick, "he is such a being as I could conceive you to carve out of marble, and some yet unrealized perfection of human science to endow with an exquisite mockery of intellect; but still there lacks the last inestimable touch of a divine Creator. He looks like a man; and, perchance, like a better specimen of man than you ordinarily meet. You might esteem him wise; he is capable of cultivation and refinement, and has at least an external conscience; but the demands that spirit makes upon spirit are precisely those to which he cannot respond. When at last you come close to him you find him chill and unsubstantial, – a mere vapor."

"I believe," said Rosina, "I have a glimmering idea of what you mean."

"Then be thankful," answered her husband, smiling; "but do not anticipate any further illumination from what I am about to read. I have here imagined such a man to be – what, probably, he never is – conscious of the deficiency in his spiritual organization. Methinks the result would be a sense of cold unreality wherewith he would go shivering through the world, longing to exchange his load of ice for any burden of real grief that fate could fling upon a human being."

Contenting himself with this preface, Roderick began to read.

In a certain old gentleman's last will and testament there appeared a bequest, which, as his final thought and deed, was singularly in keeping with a long life of melancholy eccentricity. He devised a considerable sum for establishing a fund, the interest of which was to be expended, annually forever, in preparing a Christmas Banquet for ten of the most miserable persons that could be found. It seemed not to be the testator's purpose to make these half a score of sad hearts merry, but to provide that the stern or fierce expression of human discontent should not be drowned, even for that one holy and joyful day, amid the acclamations of festal gratitude which all Christendom sends up. And he desired, likewise, to perpetuate his own remonstrance against the earthly course of Providence, and his sad and sour dissent from those systems of religion or philosophy which either find sunshine in the world or draw it down from heaven.

The task of inviting the guests, or of selecting among such as might advance their claims to partake of this dismal hospitality, was confided to the two trustees or stewards of the fund. These gentlemen, like their deceased friend, were sombre humorists, who made it their principal occupation to number the sable threads in the web of human life, and drop all the golden ones out of the reckoning. They performed their present office with integrity and judgment. The aspect of the assembled company, on the day of the first festival, might not, it is true, have satisfied every beholder that these were especially the individuals, chosen forth from all the world, whose griefs were worthy to stand as indicators of the mass of human suffering. Yet, after due consideration, it could not be disputed that here was a variety of hopeless discomfort, which, if it sometimes arose from causes apparently inadequate, was thereby only the shrewder imputation against the nature and mechanism of life.

The arrangements and decorations of the banquet were probably intended to signify that death in life which had been the testator's definition of existence. The hall, illuminated by torches, was hung round with curtains of deep and dusky purple, and adorned with branches of cypress and wreaths of artificial flowers, imitative of such as used to be strewn over the dead. A sprig of parsley was laid by every plate. The main reservoir of wine, was a sepulchral urn of silver, whence the liquor was distributed around the table in small vases, accurately copied from those that held the tears of ancient mourners. Neither had the stewards – if it were their taste that arranged these details – forgotten the fantasy of the old Egyptians, who seated a skeleton at every festive board, and mocked their own merriment with the imperturbable grin of a death's-head. Such a fearful guest, shrouded in a black mantle, sat now at the head of the table. It was whispered, I know not with what truth, that the testator himself had once walked the visible world with the machinery of that sane skeleton, and that it was one of the stipulations of his will, that he should thus be permitted to sit, from year to year, at the banquet which he had instituted. If so, it was perhaps covertly implied that he had cherished no hopes of bliss beyond the grave to compensate for the evils which he felt or imagined here. And if, in their bewildered conjectures as to the purpose of earthly existence, the banqueters should throw aside the veil, and cast an inquiring glance at this figure of death, as seeking thence the solution otherwise unattainable, the only reply would be a stare of the vacant eye-caverns and a grin of the skeleton jaws. Such was the response that the dead man had fancied himself to receive when he asked of Death to solve the riddle of his life; and it was his desire to repeat it when the guests of his dismal hospitality should find themselves perplexed with the same question.

"What means that wreath?" asked several of the company, while viewing the decorations of the table.

They alluded to a wreath of cypress, which was held on high by a skeleton arm, protruding from within the black mantle.

"It is a crown," said one of the stewards, "not for the worthiest, but for the wofulest, when he shall prove his claim to it."

The guest earliest bidden to the festival was a man of soft and gentle character, who had not energy to struggle against the heavy despondency to which his temperament rendered him liable; and therefore with nothing outwardly to excuse him from happiness, he had spent a life of quiet misery that made his blood torpid, and weighed upon his breath, and sat like a ponderous night-fiend upon every throb of his unresisting heart. His wretchedness seemed as deep as his original nature, if not identical with it. It was the misfortune of a second guest to cherish within his bosom a diseased heart, which had become so wretchedly sore that the continual and unavoidable rubs of the world, the blow of an enemy, the careless jostle of a stranger, and even the faithful and loving touch of a friend, alike made ulcers in it. As is the habit of people thus afflicted, he found his chief employment in exhibiting these miserable sores to any who would give themselves the pain of viewing them. A third guest was a hypochondriac, whose imagination wrought necromancy in his outward and inward world, and caused him to see monstrous faces in the household fire, and dragons in the clouds of sunset, and fiends in the guise of beautiful women, and something ugly or wicked beneath all the pleasant surfaces of nature. His neighbor at table was one who, in his early youth, had trusted mankind too much, and hoped too highly in their behalf, and, in meeting with many disappointments, had become desperately soured. For several years back this misanthrope had employed himself in accumulating motives for hating and despising his race, – such as murder, lust, treachery, ingratitude, faithlessness of trusted friends, instinctive vices of children, impurity of women, hidden guilt in men of saint-like aspect, – and, in short, all manner of black realities that sought to decorate themselves with outward grace or glory. But at every atrocious fact that was added to his catalogue, at every increase of the sad knowledge which he spent his life to collect, the native impulses of the poor man's loving and confiding heart made him groan with anguish. Next, with his heavy brow bent downward, there stole into the hall a man naturally earnest and impassioned, who, from his immemorial infancy, had felt the consciousness of a high message to the world; but, essaying to deliver it, had found either no voice or form of speech, or else no ears to listen. Therefore his whole life was a bitter questioning of himself: "Why have not men acknowledged my mission? Am I not a self-deluding fool? What business have I on earth? Where is my grave?" Throughout the festival, he quaffed frequent draughts from the sepulchral urn of wine, hoping thus to quench the celestial fire that tortured his own breast and could not benefit his race.

Then there entered, having flung away a ticket for a ball, a gay gallant of yesterday, who had found four or five wrinkles in his brow, and more gray hairs than he could well number on his head. Endowed with sense and feeling, he had nevertheless spent his youth in folly, but had reached at last that dreary point in life where Folly quits us of her own accord, leaving us to make friends with Wisdom if we can. Thus, cold and desolate, he had come to seek Wisdom at the banquet, and wondered if the skeleton were she. To eke out the company, the stewards had invited a distressed poet from his home in the almshouse, and a melancholy idiot from the street-corner. The latter had just the glimmering of sense that was sufficient to make him conscious of a vacancy, which the poor fellow, all his life long, had mistily sought to fill up with intelligence, wandering up and down the streets, and groaning miserably because his attempts were ineffectual. The only lady in the hall was one who had fallen short of absolute and perfect beauty, merely by the trifling defect of a slight cast in her left eye. But this blemish, minute as it was, so shocked the pure ideal of her soul, rather than her vanity, that she passed her life in solitude, and veiled her countenance even from her own gaze. So the skeleton sat shrouded at one end of the table, and this poor lady at the other.

One other guest remains to be described. He was a young man of smooth brow, fair cheek, and fashionable mien. So far as his exterior developed him, he might much more suitably have found a place at some merry Christmas table, than have been numbered among the blighted, fate-stricken, fancy-tortured set of ill-starred banqueters. Murmurs arose among the guests as they noted, the glance of general scrutiny which the intruder threw over his companions. What had he to do among them? Why did not the skeleton of the dead founder of the feast unbend its rattling joints, arise, and motion the unwelcome stranger from the board?

"Shameful!" said the morbid man, while a new ulcer broke out in his heart. "He comes to mock us! we shall be the jest of his tavern friends I—he will make a farce of our miseries, and bring it out upon the stage!"

"O, never mind him!" said the hypochondriac, smiling sourly. "He shall feast from yonder tureen of viper-soup; and if there is a fricassee of scorpions on the table, pray let him have his share of it. For the dessert, he shall taste the apples of Sodom, then, if he like our Christmas fare, let him return again next year!"

"Trouble him not," murmured the melancholy man, with gentleness. "What matters it whether the consciousness of misery come a few years sooner or later? If this youth deem himself happy now, yet let him sit with us for the sake of the wretchedness to come."

The poor idiot approached the young man with that mournful aspect of vacant inquiry which his face continually wore, and which caused people to say that he was always in search of his missing wits. After no little examination he touched the stranger's hand, but immediately drew back his own, shaking his head and shivering.

"Cold, cold, cold!" muttered the idiot.

The young man shivered too, and smiled.

"Gentlemen, and you, madam," said one of the stewards of the festival, "do not conceive so ill either of our caution or judgment, as to imagine that we have admitted this young stranger – Gervayse Hastings by name – without a full investigation and thoughtful balance of his claims. Trust me, not a guest at the table is better entitled to his seat."

The steward's guaranty was perforce satisfactory. The company, therefore, took their places, and addressed themselves to the serious business of the feast, but were soon disturbed by the hypochondriac, who thrust back his chair, complaining that a dish of stewed toads and vipers was set before him, and that there was green ditchwater in his cup of wine. This mistake being amended, he quietly resumed his seat. The wine, as it flowed freely from the sepulchral urn, seemed to come imbued with all gloomy inspirations; so that its influence was not to cheer, but either to sink the revellers into a deeper melancholy, or elevate their spirits to an enthusiasm of wretchedness. The conversation was various. They told sad stories about people who might have been Worthy guests at such a festival as the present. They talked of grisly incidents in human history; of strange crimes, which, if truly considered, were but convulsions of agony; of some lives that had been altogether wretched, and of others, which, wearing a general semblance of happiness, had yet been deformed, sooner or later, by misfortune, as by the intrusion of a grim face at a banquet; of death-bed scenes, and what dark intimations might be gathered from the words of dying men; of suicide, and whether the more eligible mode were by halter, knife, poison, drowning, gradual starvation, or the fumes of charcoal. The majority of the guests, as is the custom with people thoroughly and profoundly sick at heart, were anxious to make their own woes the theme of discussion, and prove themselves most excellent in anguish. The misanthropist went deep into the philosophy of evil, and wandered about in the darkness, with now and then a gleam of discolored light hovering on ghastly shapes and horrid scenery. Many a miserable thought, such as men have stumbled upon from age to age, did he now rake up again, and gloat over it as an inestimable gem, a diamond, a treasure far preferable to those bright, spiritual revelations of a better world, which are like precious stones from heaven's pavement. And then, amid his lore of wretchedness he hid his face and wept.

It was a festival at which the woful man of Uz might suitably have been a guest, together with all, in each succeeding age, who have tasted deepest of the bitterness of life. And be it said, too, that every son or daughter of woman, however favored with happy fortune, might, at one sad moment or another, have claimed the privilege of a stricken heart, to sit down at this table. But, throughout the feast, it was remarked that the young stranger, Gervayse Hastings, was unsuccessful in his attempts to catch its pervading spirit. At any deep, strong thought that found utterance, and which was torn out, as it were, from the saddest recesses of human consciousness, he looked mystified and bewildered; even more than the poor idiot, who seemed to grasp at such things with his earnest heart, and thus occasionally to comprehend them. The young man's conversation was of a colder and lighter kind, often brilliant, but lacking the powerful characteristics of a nature that had been developed by suffering.

"Sir," said the misanthropist, bluntly, in reply to some observation by Gervayse Hastings, "pray do not address me again. We have no right to talk together. Our minds have nothing in common. By what claim you appear at this banquet I cannot guess; but methinks, to a man who could say what you have just now said, my companions and myself must seem no more than shadows flickering on the wall. And precisely such a shadow are you to us."

The young man smiled and bowed, but, drawing himself back in his chair, he buttoned his coat over his breast, as if the banqueting-hall were growing chill. Again the idiot fixed his melancholy stare upon the youth, and murmured, "Cold! cold! cold!"

The banquet drew to its conclusion, and the guests departed. Scarcely had they stepped across the threshold of the hall, when the scene that had there passed seemed like the vision of a sick fancy, or an exhalation from a stagnant heart. Now and then, however, during the year that ensued, these melancholy people caught glimpses of one another, transient, indeed, but enough to prove that they walked the earth with the ordinary allotment of reality. Sometimes a pair of them came face to face, while stealing through the evening twilight, enveloped in their sable cloaks. Sometimes they casually met in churchyards. Once, also, it happened that two of the dismal banqueters mutually started at recognizing each other in the noonday sunshine of a crowded street, stalking there like ghosts astray. Doubtless they wondered why the skeleton did not come abroad at noonday too.

But whenever the necessity of their affairs compelled these Christmas guests into the bustling world, they were sure to encounter the young man who had so unaccountably been admitted to the festival. They saw him among the gay and fortunate; they caught the sunny sparkle of his eye; they heard the light and careless tones of his voice, and muttered to themselves with such indignation as only the aristocracy of wretchedness could kindle, "The traitor! The vile impostor! Providence, in its own good time, may give him a right to feast among us!" But the young man's unabashed eye dwelt upon their gloomy figures as they passed him, seeming to say, perchance with somewhat of a sneer, "First, know my secret then, measure your claims with mine!"

The step of Time stole onward, and soon brought merry Christmas round again, with glad and solemn worship in the churches, and sports, games, festivals, and everywhere the bright face of Joy beside the household fire. Again likewise the hall, with its curtains of dusky purple, was illuminated by the death-torches gleaming on the sepulchral decorations of the banquet. The veiled, skeleton sat in state, lifting the cypress-wreath above its head, as the guerdon of some guest illustrious in the qualifications which there claimed precedence. As the stewards deemed the world inexhaustible in misery, and were desirous of recognizing it in all its forms, they had not seen fit to reassemble the company of the former year. New faces now threw their gloom across the table.

There was a man of nice conscience, who bore a blood-stain in his heart – the death of a fellow-creature – which, for his more exquisite torture, had chanced with such a peculiarity of circumstances, that he could not absolutely determine whether his will had entered into the deed or not. Therefore, his whole life was spent in the agony of an inward trial for murder, with a continual sifting of the details of his terrible calamity, until his mind had no longer any thought, nor his soul any emotion, disconnected with it, There was a mother, too, – a mother once, but a desolation now, – who, many years before, had gone out on a pleasure-party, and, returning, found her infant smothered in its little bed. And ever since she has been tortured with the fantasy that her buried baby lay smothering in its coffin. Then there was an aged lady, who had lived from time immemorial with a constant tremor quivering through her frame. It was terrible to discern her dark shadow tremulous upon the wall; her lips, likewise, were tremulous; and the expression of her eye seemed to indicate that her soul was trembling too. Owing to the bewilderment and confusion which made almost a chaos of her intellect, it was impossible to discover what dire misfortune had thus shaken her nature to its depths; so that the stewards had admitted her to the table, not from any acquaintance with her history, but on the safe testimony of her miserable aspect. Some surprise was expressed at the presence of a bluff, red-faced gentleman, a certain Mr. Smith, who had evidently the fat of many a rich feast within him, and the habitual twinkle of whose eye betrayed a disposition to break forth into uproarious laughter for little cause or none. It turned out, however, that, with the best possible flow of spirits, our poor friend was afflicted with a physical disease of the heart, which threatened instant death on the slightest cachinnatory indulgence, or even that titillation of the bodily frame produced by merry thoughts. In this dilemma he had sought admittance to the banquet, on the ostensible plea of his irksome and miserable state, but, in reality, with the hope of imbibing a life-preserving melancholy.

A married couple had been invited from a motive of bitter humor, it being well understood that they rendered each other unutterably miserable whenever they chanced to meet, and therefore must necessarily be fit associates at the festival. In contrast with these was another couple still unmarried, who had interchanged their hearts in early life, but had been divided by circumstances as impalpable as morning mist, and kept apart so long that their spirits now found it impossible to meet, Therefore, yearning for communion, yet shrinking from one another and choosing none beside, they felt themselves companionless in life, and looked upon eternity as a boundless desert. Next to the skeleton sat a mere son of earth, – a hunter of the Exchange, – a gatherer of shining dust, – a man whose life's record was in his ledger, and whose soul's prison-house the vaults of the bank where he kept his deposits. This person had been greatly perplexed at his invitation, deeming himself one of the most fortunate men in the city; but the stewards persisted in demanding his presence, assuring him that he had no conception how miserable he was.

And now appeared a figure which we must acknowledge as our acquaintance of the former festival. It was Gervayse Hastings, whose presence had then caused so much question and criticism, and who now took his place with the composure of one whose claims were satisfactory to himself and must needs be allowed by others. Yet his easy and unruffled face betrayed no sorrow.

The well-skilled beholders gazed a moment into his eyes and shook their heads, to miss the unuttered sympathy – the countersign never to be falsified – of those whose hearts are cavern-mouths through which they descend into a region of illimitable woe and recognize other wanderers there.

"Who is this youth?" asked the man with a bloodstain on his conscience. "Surely he has never gone down into the depths! I know all the aspects of those who have passed through the dark valley. By what right is he among us?"

"Ah, it is a sinful thing to come hither without a sorrow," murmured the aged lady, in accents that partook of the eternal tremor which pervaded her whole being "Depart, young man! Your soul has never been shaken, and, therefore, I tremble so much the more to look at you."

"His soul shaken! No; I'll answer for it," said bluff Mr. Smith, pressing his hand upon his heart and making himself as melancholy as he could, for fear of a fatal explosion of laughter. "I know the lad well; he has as fair prospects as any young man about town, and has no more right among us miserable creatures than the child unborn. He never was miserable and probably never will be!"

"Our honored guests," interposed the stewards, "pray have patience with us, and believe, at least, that our deep veneration for the sacredness of this solemnity would preclude any wilful violation of it. Receive this young man to your table. It may not be too much to say, that no guest here would exchange his own heart for the one that beats within that youthful bosom!"

"I'd call it a bargain, and gladly, too," muttered Mr. Smith, with a perplexing mixture of sadness and mirthful conceit. "A plague upon their nonsense! My own heart is the only really miserable one in the company; it will certainly be the death of me at last!"

Nevertheless, as on the former occasion, the judgment of the stewards being without appeal, the company sat down. The obnoxious guest made no more attempt to obtrude his conversation on those about him, but appeared to listen to the table-talk with peculiar assiduity, as if some inestimable secret, otherwise beyond his reach, might be conveyed in a casual word. And in truth, to those who could understand and value it, there was rich matter in the upgushings and outpourings of these initiated souls to whom sorrow had been a talisman, admitting them into spiritual depths which no other spell can open. Sometimes out of the midst of densest gloom there flashed a momentary radiance, pure as crystal, bright as the flame of stars, and shedding such a glow upon the mysteries of life, that the guests were ready to exclaim, "Surel the riddle is on the point of being solved!" At such illuminated intervals the saddest mourner felt it to be revealed that mortal griefs are but shadowy and external; no more than the sable robes voluminously shrouding a certain divine reality, and thus indicating what migh otherwise be altogether invisible to mortal eye.

"Just now," remarked the trembling old woman, "I seemed to see beyond the outside. And then my everlasting tremor passed away!"

"Would that I could dwell always in these momentary gleams of light!" said the man o stricken conscience. "Then the blood-stain in my heart would be washed clean away."

This strain of conversation appeared so unintelligibly absurd to good Mr. Smith, that h burst into precisely the fit of laughter which his physicians had warned him against, as likely to prove instantaneously fatal. In effect, he fell back in his chair a corpse, with a broad grin upor his face, while his ghost, perchance, remained beside it bewildered at its unpremeditated exit This catastrophe of course broke up the festival.

"How is this? You do not tremble!" observed the tremulous old woman to Gervayse Hastings, who was gazing at the dead man with singular intentness. "Is it not awful to see hir so suddenly vanish out of the midst of life, – this man of flesh and blood, whose earthly natur was so warm and strong? There is a never-ending tremor in my soul, but it trembles afresh a this! And you are calm!"

"Would that he could teach me somewhat!" said Gervayse Hastings, drawing a long breath "Men pass before me like shadows on the wall; their actions, passions, feelings, are flickering of the light, and then they vanish! Neither the corpse, nor yonder skeleton, nor this ol woman's everlasting tremor, can give me what I seek."

And then the company departed.

We cannot linger to narrate, in such detail, more circumstances of these singular festival: which, in accordance with the founder's will, continued to be kept with the regularity of a established institution. In process of time the stewards adopted the custom of inviting, from fa and near, those individuals whose misfortunes were prominent above other men's, and whos mental and moral development might, therefore, be supposed to possess a correspondin interest. The exiled noble of the French Revolution, and the broken soldier of the Empire were alike represented at the table. Fallen monarchs, wandering about the earth, have foun places at that forlorn and miserable feast. The statesman, when his party flung him off, migh if he chose it, be once more a great man for the space of a single banquet. Aaron Burr's nam appears on the record at a period when his ruin – the profoundest and most striking, with more of moral circumstance in it than that of almost any other man – was complete in hi lonely age. Stephen Guard, when his wealth weighed upon him like a mountain, once sougr admittance of his own accord. It is not probable, however, that these men had any lesson t teach in the lore of discontent and misery which might not equally well have been studie in the common walks of life. Illustrious unfortunates attract a wider sympathy, not becaus their griefs are more intense, but because, being set on lofty pedestals, they the better serv mankind as instances and bywords of calamity.

It concerns our present purpose to say that, at each successive festival, Gervayse Hasting showed his face, gradually changing from the smooth beauty of his youth to the thoughtfu comeliness of manhood, and thence to the bald, impressive dignity of age. He was the only individual invariably present. Yet on every occasion there were murmurs, both from those who knew his character and position, and from them whose hearts shrank back as denying his companionship in their mystic fraternity.

"Who is this impassive man?" had been asked a hundred times. "Has he suffered? Has he sinned? There are no traces of either. Then wherefore is he here?"

"You must inquire of the stewards or of himself," was the constant reply. "We seem to know him well here in our city, and know nothing of him but what is creditable and fortunate. Yet hither he comes, year after year, to this gloomy banquet, and sits among the guests like a marble statue. Ask yonder skeleton, perhaps that may solve the riddle!"

It was in truth a wonder. The life of Gervayse Hastings was not merely a prosperous, but a brilliant one. Everything had gone well with him. He was wealthy, far beyond the expenditure that was required by habits of magnificence, a taste of rare purity and cultivation, a love of travel, a scholar's instinct to collect a splendid library, and, moreover, what seemed a magnificent liberality to the distressed. He had sought happiness, and not vainly, if a lovely and tender wife, and children of fair promise, could insure it. He had, besides, ascended above the limit which separates the obscure from the distinguished, and had won a stainless reputation in affairs of the widest public importance. Not that he was a popular character, or had within him the mysterious attributes which are essential to that species of success. To the public he was a cold abstraction, wholly destitute of those rich lines of personality, that living warmth, and the peculiar faculty of stamping his own heart's impression on a multitude of hearts, by which the people recognize their favorites. And it must be owned that, after his most intimate associates had done their best to know him thoroughly, and love him warmly, they were startled to find how little hold he had upon their affections. They approved, they admired, but still in those moments when the human spirit most craves reality, they shrank back from Gervayse Hastings, as powerless to give them what they sought. It was the feeling of distrustful regret with which we should draw back the hand after extending it, in an illusive twilight, to grasp the hand of a shadow upon the wall.

As the superficial fervency of youth decayed, this peculiar effect of Gervayse Hastings's character grew more perceptible. His children, when he extended his arms, came coldly to his knees, but never climbed them of their own accord. His wife wept secretly, and almost adjudged herself a criminal because she shivered in the chill of his bosom. He, too, occasionally appeared not unconscious of the chillness of his moral atmosphere, and willing, if it might be so, to warm himself at a kindly fire. But age stole onward and benumbed him snore and more. As the hoar-frost began to gather on him his wife went to her grave, and was doubtless warmer there; his children either died or were scattered to different homes of their own; and old Gervayse Hastings, unscathed by grief, – alone, but needing no companionship, – continued his steady walk through life, and still one very Christmas day attended at the dismal banquet. His privilege as a guest had become prescriptive now. Had he claimed the head of the table, even the skeleton would have been ejected from its seat.

Finally, at the merry Christmas-tide, when he had numbered fourscore years complete, this pale, highbrowed, marble-featured old man once more entered the long-frequented hall, with the same impassive aspect that had called forth so much dissatisfied remark at his first attendance. Time, except in matters merely external, had done nothing for him, either of good or evil. As he took his place he threw a calm, inquiring glance around the table, as if to ascertain whether any guest had yet appeared, after so many unsuccessful banquets, who might impart to him the mystery – the deep, warm secret – the life within the life – which, whether manifested in joy or sorrow, is what gives substance to a world of shadows.

"My friends," said Gervayse Hastings, assuming a position which his long conversance with the festival caused to appear natural, "you are welcome! I drink to you all in this cup of sepulchral wine."

The guests replied courteously, but still in a manner that proved them unable to receive the old man as a member of their sad fraternity. It may be well to give the reader an idea of the present company at the banquet.

One was formerly a clergyman, enthusiastic in his profession, and apparently of the genuine dynasty of those old Puritan divines whose faith in their calling, and stern exercise of it, had placed them among the mighty of the earth. But yielding to the speculative tendency of the age, he had gone astray from the firm foundation of an ancient faith, and wandered into a cloud-region, where everything was misty and deceptive, ever mocking him with a semblance of reality, but still dissolving when he flung himself upon it for support and rest. His instinct and early training demanded something steadfast; but, looking forward, he beheld vapors piled on vapors, and behind him an impassable gulf between the man of yesterday and today on the borders of which he paced to and fro, sometimes wringing his hands in agony, and often making his own woe a theme of scornful merriment. This surely was a miserable man. Next, there was a theorist, – one of a numerous tribe, although he deemed himself unique since the creation, – a theorist, who had conceived a plan by which all the wretchedness of earth, moral and physical, might be done away, and the bliss of the millennium at once accomplished. But, the incredulity of mankind debarring him from action, he was smitten with as much grief as if the whole mass of woe which he was denied the opportunity to remedy were crowded into his own bosom. A plain old man in black attracted much of the company's notice, on the supposition that he was no other than Father Miller, who, it seemed had given himself up to despair at the tedious delay of the final conflagration. Then there was a man distinguished for native pride and obstinacy, who, a little while before, had possessed immense wealth, and held the control of a vast moneyed interest which he had wielded in the same spirit as a despotic monarch would wield the power of his empire, carrying on a tremendous moral warfare, the roar and tremor of which was felt at every fireside in the land. At length came a crushing ruin, – a total overthrow of fortune, power, and character, – the effect of which on his imperious and, in many respects, noble and lofty nature might have entitled him to a place, not merely at our festival, but among the peers of Pandemonium.

There was a modern philanthropist, who had become so deeply sensible of the calamities of thousands and millions of his fellow-creatures, and of the impracticableness of any general measures for their relief, that he had no heart to do what little good lay immediately within his power, but contented himself with being miserable for sympathy. Near him sat a gentleman in a predicament hitherto unprecedented, but of which the present epoch probably affords numerous examples. Ever since he was of capacity to read a newspaper, this person had prided himself on his consistent adherence to one political party, but, in the confusion of these latter days, had got bewildered and knew not whereabouts his party was. This wretched condition, so morally desolate and disheartening to a man who has long accustomed himself to merge his individuality in the mass of a great body, can only be conceived by such as have experienced it. His next companion was a popular orator who had lost his voice, and – as it was pretty much all that he had to lose – had fallen into a state of hopeless melancholy. The table was likewise graced by two of the gentler sex, – one, a half-starved, consumptive seamstress, the representative of thousands just as wretched; the other, a woman of unemployed energy who found herself in the world with nothing to achieve, nothing to enjoy, and nothing even to suffer. She had, therefore, driven herself to the verge of madness by dark broodings over the wrongs of her sex, and its exclusion from a proper field of action. The roll of guests being thus complete, a side-table had been set for three or four disappointed office-seekers, with hearts as sick as death, whom the stewards had admitted partly because their calamities really entitled them to entrance here, and partly that they were in especial need of a good dinner. There was likewise a homeless dog, with his tail between his legs, licking up the crumbs and gnawing the fragments of the feast, – such a melancholy cur as one sometimes sees about the streets without a master, and willing to follow the first that will accept his service.

In their own way, these were as wretched a set of people as ever had assembled at the festival. There they sat, with the veiled skeleton of the founder holding aloft the cypress-wreath, at one end of the table, and at the other, wrapped in furs, the withered figure of Gervayse Hastings, stately, calm, and cold, impressing the company with awe, yet so little interesting their sympathy that he might have vanished into thin air without their once exclaiming, "Whither is he gone?"

"Sir," said the philanthropist, addressing the old man, "you have been so long a guest at this annual festival, and have thus been conversant with so many varieties of human affliction, that, not improbably, you have thence derived some great and important lessons. How blessed were your lot could you reveal a secret by which all this mass of woe might be removed!"

"I know of but one misfortune," answered Gervayse Hastings, quietly, "and that is my own."

"Your own!" rejoined the philanthropist. "And looking back on your serene and prosperous life, how can you claim to be the sole unfortunate of the human race?"

"You will not understand it," replied Gervayse Hastings, feebly, and with a singular inefficiency of pronunciation, and sometimes putting one word for another. "None have understood it, not even those who experience the like. It is a chillness, a want of earnestness, a feeling as if what should be my heart were a thing of vapor, a haunting perception of unreality! Thus seeming to possess all that other men have, all that men aim at, I have really possessed nothing, neither joy nor griefs. All things, all persons, – as was truly said to me at this table long and long ago, – have been like shadows flickering on the wall. It was so with my wife and children, with those who seemed my friends: it is so with yourselves, whom I see now before one. Neither have I myself any real existence, but am a shadow like the rest."

"And how is it with your views of a future life?" inquired the speculative clergyman.

"Worse than with you," said the old man, in a hollow and feeble tone; "for I cannot conceive it earnestly enough to feel either hope or fear. Mine,—mine is the wretchedness! This cold heart, – this unreal life! Ah! it grows colder still."

It so chanced that at this juncture the decayed ligaments of the skeleton gave way, and the dry bones fell together in a heap, thus causing the dusty wreath of cypress to drop upon the table. The attention of the company being thus diverted for a single instant from Gervayse Hastings, they perceived, on turning again towards him, that the old man had undergone a change. His shadow had ceased to flicker on the wall.

"Well, Rosina, what is your criticism?" asked Roderick, as he rolled up the manuscript.

"Frankly, your success is by no means complete," replied she. "It is true, I have an idea of the character you endeavor to describe; but it is rather by dint of my own thought than your expression."

"That is unavoidable," observed the sculptor, "because the characteristics are all negative. If Gervayse Hastings could have imbibed one human grief at the gloomy banquet, the task of describing him would have been infinitely easier. Of such persons – and we do meet with these moral monsters now and then – it is difficult to conceive how they came to exist here, or what there is in them capable of existence hereafter. They seem to be on the outside of everything; and nothing wearies the soul more than an attempt to comprehend them within its grasp."

The Unforgiven

K. M. Hazel

A little over twenty years ago, I managed a community arts initiative which, for three weeks prior to the Christmas holiday, occupied a vacant retail unit in the Queen's Square shopping centre in West Bromwich. The project's remit was to record garrulous local folk while they reminisced about bygone Christmas celebrations. The audio recordings formed the basis of both a travelling exhibition and a lavishly illustrated book, *The Stockings on the Mantelpiece Were Filled with Coal: Recollections of Christmas in the Black Country*, which I'm proud to say won the Six Towns Medal for best factual publication.

It was on the last day of the acquisition phase of the project, on a Christmas Eve which had seen Queen's Square bustling with record numbers of frenzied, last-minute shoppers, that an elderly gentleman hobbled into our makeshift recording studio on the arm of his daughter. My colleagues had already decamped to the pub by this time, leaving me to hold the fort for the hour or so remaining to us before we handed back the keys of the shop to the centre manager. Experience had taught me that there is always one more story to capture if one only has the patience to await its arrival, but had I known beforehand what would come of my diligence, then I would surely have abandoned my post in favour of a celebratory drink.

The project archive identifies the man who was to be our final contributor by nothing more illuminating than his initials. I, however, remember his name well. I saw it again last night – quite by chance – when it happened to catch my eye amongst the fresh crop of obituaries in the evening paper. Alfred Beale, as I shall refer to him in this document, 'passed peacefully in the night at the age of ninety-six', according to his notice of remembrance; if true, his was a happier end by far than the one which befell the man at the heart of the tale Alfred told me.

Unsurprisingly, the project's funding body felt at the time that Alfred's contribution was too disturbing for general publication, and so it has languished in obscurity until now.

Alfred was in his seventies back then. Tall but stooped, he maintained an air of quiet dignity in the face of growing physical infirmity. Pain flickered over his spare features as he settled into a seat at my desk. Time had etched deep lines around his piercing blue eyes, which remained the most vital part of him. His pleading gaze spoke of the need to share a painful memory with a non-judgmental stranger; I had seen the same look countless times before.

Alfred's daughter left us alone to chat. After locking the door of the shop, I offered Alfred a homemade mince pie and a glass of mulled wine, but these humble offerings sat untouched while the softly spoken pensioner gathered his thoughts. At the end of a companionable silence, Alfred signalled with a nod of his head that he was ready to begin.

I pressed the appropriate buttons on the cassette recorder, then leaned back to listen to a story that has troubled me ever since.

* * *

Christmas lost all its charm for me in 1935, the year I turned ten. We lived at the time in Clayton

Road in Wednesbury, a family of nine with another one on the way, all packed like sardines into a corporation house designed for half that number. I shared a bedroom with three brothers: we slept two to a bed, huddled together like mismatched spoons under blankets as scratchy as my old man's chin on a Sunday morning. Fewer people in authority looking to poke their nose into your business in those days, so the working class had no other choice than to make the best of a challenging situation.

My father had become friendly with an old man who drank in his favourite boozer. Edgar Drayton had worked the railways out Kidderminster way before his retirement. He lived alone on the edge of our brand-new housing development in a quaint little house which he had inherited from his older sister.

My mother felt sorry for those poor souls who found themselves isolated during the festive period. Even though money was tight, and we barely had the means to feed ourselves most days of the year, she considered it the Christian thing to do to invite Mr Drayton to join us for Christmas dinner. 'No man deserves to lose a wife and child at so young an age,' I overheard her say, referring to the shocking admission made to my father in the pub on Christmas Eve when Mr Drayton was the worse for drink. 'And to lose them both at this time of year, in the way that he did, can only add to his endless sorrow.'

Being the most sensible member of an unruly brood ensured that I was the bearer of the note inviting Mr Drayton to lunch. Mother had written the invitation in a handmade Christmas card, which my sister had illustrated with the chalks she'd found in her Christmas stocking.

Snow had fallen that morning and the entire world seemed freshly minted in white as I traipsed the half-mile to Mr Drayton's house, shivering inside my hand-me-down clothes.

Rose Cottage was situated beside a brook on a surviving scrap of heathland. The countryside around the cottage had shrunk massively since Mr Drayton had entered the world seventy years before. The once picturesque spot was now fighting a losing battle against the forces of modernisation: Elwell's factory, black with soot, sprawled like a cathedral for the damned on the far side of the polluted brook, its machines eerily silent for once; while behind the cottage, barely a quarter-mile distant, the noisy goods yard at Bescot junction never rested and had plans for further expansion.

As I unlatched the cottage's rickety gate, I heard the mournful whistle of a freight train as it left the yard on the next leg of its journey. I felt a momentary sense of unease at the sound, even though I must have heard the same note of warning a thousand times before, but I attributed my nervousness to the fact that I was about to make the acquaintance of a stranger.

Mr Drayton had not long returned from the morning service at St Paul's, I discovered after applying the lion's head door knocker to its sounding plate. He was still in his Sunday best as he stood on his doorstep peering down at me over the spectacles perched on his red nose. He was a short, stocky man who seemed to draw himself up with the thumbs hooked under his black braces. He still had a full complement of curling grey hair that topped an owlish face with apples in its cheeks from the trudge back from church.

Nailed to the lintel above his head was a brown plaque emblazoned with the name of the cottage along with clusters of crudely daubed roses. I found it easier to gawp at the sign rather than meet the bemused gaze of this initially intimidating man. But after a bit of gentle cajoling on his part, I was able to state my business and hand over my sister's gaily coloured card.

As Mr Drayton read Mother's heartfelt message, his eyes welled up with tears, forcing him to turn away momentarily so that he could dry them with a handkerchief. After recovering his composure, he smiled kindly down at me and said, 'Please tell your mum and dad that I'd be honoured to come to dinner.'

I had never seen a grown man cry before, and when I told Mother about Mr Drayton's reaction, she felt amply rewarded for her simple act of kindness.

Mr Drayton arrived a little after one o'clock. Mother lined her nippers up like regimental soldiers before formally introducing Father's friend. Mr Drayton had an easy way with children, and I could tell he had taken a real shine to me. He insisted on helping Mother with the final preparations for lunch. Mother's pregnancy had two months to run, but even without this additional strain, the demands of a large family meant that she rarely had a moment to herself and always looked worn out. Mr Drayton seemed genuinely concerned for her welfare, and I liked him all the more for that. When he carried in the goose from the kitchen like a toff's butler, we famished kids banged our cutlery on the table in appreciation.

The strange thing is, I still remember that Christmas Day – the first part of it, at any rate – with a great deal of affection; to my mind, there was a sense of the festive spirit at work in all our hearts. Though our circumstances meant we could hardly set a feast before our guest, I can honestly say that no one left Mother's table wanting more.

After the plum pudding, Mr Drayton lifted a glass with my Father in honour of King George, after which, they played dominoes while my mother and sisters washed the dishes and began to prepare the evening meal. You might well smirk at that, young man, but in those days, menfolk barely lifted a finger around the house. Society allotted rigid roles to the sexes, which is why, I suppose, Mr Drayton's sentimental display at the cottage had so intrigued me. Nonetheless, I'm sure he would have lent a hand in the kitchen had there not been another chap present to help maintain the status quo.

It was dark by the time Mr Drayton left for home. After shaking hands with my father, he loitered at the gate to watch my brothers and I chucking snowballs in the street. Our excited shrieks filled the frigid air as we tried to knock each other's heads off with our well-aimed missiles. After a minute or two of indulgent silence, Mr Drayton called out to me, and reluctantly, I withdrew from the fray. He wanted me to walk back to Rose Cottage with him.

The shimmering snow held the darkness at bay; it was as if the sun had forgotten to set, and I remember remarking that I had never seen the dirty streets look so clean. During our journey, Mr Drayton regaled me with stories of his time as an engine driver, but when I happened to mention that a classmate of mine had fallen under the wheels of a train while trespassing on the railway, he abruptly changed the subject.

I waited on the doorstep until Mr Drayton beckoned me into the parlour of Rose Cottage. An ancient coal-fired range, dull and black, occupied the fireplace, its coal basket filled with last night's ashes. The lack of cheering warmth made the barely furnished room seem like a dismal place for a man to take his ease.

After lighting a spirit lamp, Mr Drayton carried it from the mantelpiece to the bookcase tucked beneath the angle of the stairs. As the lamplight played over the contents of the shelves, I realised that I had never seen so many books outside of a classroom. Before long, Mr Drayton found the volume he wanted and withdrew it from the bottom shelf. He rose on creaking knees, blowing away a film of dust from the top of the book as he turned towards me.

'My sister gave me this when I was about your age,' he said, handing me a well-thumbed copy of A Christmas Carol by Charles Dickens. 'Now I'd like to pass it on to you. Mirrored in that book is all the kindness your family showed me today. I hope it brings you the same pleasure that I once found within its pages.'

On the flyleaf, his sister had written, 'May the joys of Christmas keep you rich in spirit your whole life long' – a sentiment, I would come to realise, that summarised all that Scrooge would grow to love about the season of goodwill. I still have the book, but unlike Mr Drayton, I would never willingly part with it.

At the end of his speech, Mr Drayton offered me his hand, his sad eyes twinkling in the golden glow of the lamp. I slipped his gift into the pocket of my jacket, then shook his hand with all the youthful vigour at my disposal.

The house seemed to come to life as our fingers parted company.

A sound, as horrible as it was unexpected, floated down from the ceiling, as in the room above, a baby in distress began to cry.

Mr Drayton stiffened as his eyes grew wide with fear. The lamp trembled so violently in his hand that I felt certain he would drop it. We stood there for upwards of half a minute, shivering in the chilly gloom of the Spartan room, listening to that unearthly wailing.

When the crying stopped, Mr Drayton released the breath he had been holding into an uneasy silence.

'Who's up there?' I inquired in a terrified whisper.

Mr Drayton spoke without considering the effect his words might have on an impressionable child.

'Little Archie', he muttered. 'God rest his soul.'

Without warning, the flame of the lamp flared with a hiss that elicited a whimper from Mr Drayton; in the next moment, its glow dwindled until it was little more than a guttering spark.

I smelled the smoke before I saw it; the air in the room turned foul in an instant, and then the smoke began to wrap itself around us, swirling up through gaps in the floorboards like a rancid fog. A yellowish tinge gave the smoke a strangely luminescent quality which allowed me to see that in the corner, by the front door, a denser portion of the filthy cloud had assumed a human shape. The rudimentary arms of the manifestation spread in a widening circle that quickly encompassed the room and the hapless spectators within it.

Beside me, Mr Drayton had begun to pant like a dog, his mouth hanging open in slack-jawed terror.

Impulsively, I grabbed his hand and dragged him towards a door which I assumed led to the scullery. He followed me without resistance, his panicked gaze never leaving the thing whose very essence we were inhaling.

As I broke through the wavering circle of phantom arms, my mind's eye thrust before me a vision of a smoke-filled tunnel, lit at the far end by moonlight. As the smoke thinned in the dreary passage, I glimpsed the starkly outlined figure of a woman standing beneath the distant archway in an attitude that conveyed a sense of infinite menace to my onlooking mind. I seemed to spend far longer in the tunnel than the second or two in which I must have lingered at the door; long enough, certainly, to see the fearsome woman begin to move crookedly in my direction. Thankfully, this unwanted impression faded as I burst into the scullery and made a dash for the back door.

As we stumbled into the fresh air, Mr Drayton dropped the lamp in the snow, then turned away to be sick.

The stiff breeze blowing into the scullery had stopped the advance of the mysterious smoke, which I saw withdraw into the parlour like a disagreeable host who had just ejected a couple of uninvited guests.

This experience left Mr Drayton in a terrible state. Not knowing what else to do, I decided to take him home with me. Mother always said that I was 'old headed' for my age and so I coped with this reversal of the natural order with surprising calmness.

Shocked by Mr Drayton's appearance and manner, my parents took the pair of us upstairs so that we could talk in private. I gave an account of what had happened at the cottage while Mr

Drayton – ashen-faced and still trembling – merely nodded to confirm that I was telling the truth. When I had said my piece, Mother crossed herself and then wrapped me tightly in her arms while telling me that I had been a brave boy. Once she had finished fussing, Father sent me downstairs with the instruction to keep what I'd seen to myself.

That night, I couldn't sleep for thinking about the visitation at the cottage: every time I closed my eyes, I saw a face of pale smoke leering at me from the darkness.

At about three o'clock, Muriel, our youngest, began to howl. Ordinarily, I would have slept through the din just like my softly snoring brothers, but on that occasion, her cries could not help but remind me of what I had heard in Rose Cottage. Mother clambered noisily out of bed to soothe my sister, and soon, all was peaceful again.

When my brother, Ron, turned over, taking my share of the blankets with him, I stopped chasing sleep and went downstairs to see if Mr Drayton was still awake.

He was spending the night in an armchair by the fire. Helping to keep him warm was Father's bottle of whisky, which was almost empty, I saw, after quietly opening the living room door.

A look of fearful expectation fell from his haggard face on seeing that it was only me who had come to visit.

I noticed, too, that he had opened the curtains to allow the snow's radiance to brighten the room. He could have turned on the electric light – which we had in the new house – but I daresay he didn't want anyone to know how badly the dark frightened him. Peering in at us through the uncovered window was the jolly looking snowman my brothers had built with his back to the street. I was glad to see that it was snowing again because fresh snow guaranteed our frosty friend a stay of execution.

I sat down on the hearth rug beside the remains of the fire.

Mr Drayton gazed uneasily at me. He took another drink of whisky, then placed the empty glass beside the chair.

'What's on your mind, lad?'

'Is Rose Cottage haunted?' I asked with the honest frankness of a child.

He let the question hang in the air before answering.

'I don't know that it's the cottage so much as the old bones that rattle around inside it. But what you saw was my wife, Elsie, and what you heard was the son she bore me. They've been in spirit these forty years.'

I took a moment to absorb this information, because as young as I was, I knew that it begged a more troubling question.

'How did they die?'

Mr Drayton flinched at my bluntness and then seemed to look through me to the distant past. 'Badly,' he murmured at last. 'They died badly.'

He slumped forward and buried his head in his hands.

After a few moments of sobbing reflection, he looked at me once more, his eyes glistening with tears.

'I thought on Christmas Day I'd be free of Elsie and the little one, otherwise I never would have let you into the cottage. It was seeing me happy for once,' he concluded bitterly; 'that's what brought that she-devil back on such a holy day.'

Before he could say another word, an agonised shriek from above had us leaping to our feet.

I raced upstairs ahead of Mr Drayton and was the first to see the distress Mother was in. Father was already half-dressed. 'Baby's coming,' he said, buttoning his shirt while Mother lay groaning in bed, her sallow face drenched with sweat. 'I'm going to fetch the midwife.'

As Mr Drayton and I looked on from the doorway, Mother suddenly sat bolt upright, her eyes rolling back in her head as a second harrowing scream erupted from her lips. The scream seemed to catch in her throat with a horrible rattling sound before giving way to a final venting of breath. Mother fell back on the mattress, leaving us to watch in helpless horror as smoke began to seep from beneath the blankets to which her lifeless hands still clung.

Father dropped the boot he had been about to put on and staggered back, goggle-eyed, until he collided with the wardrobe. In a collective daze, we watched the smoke rise and gather beneath the ceiling, where the vapour seemed to boil in the air, as if seething with emotion, before shaping itself into the rudiments of a baleful face and then fading away.

In the meantime, the passage behind us had become a bedlam of confused and frightened children. Father, in the grip of shock, lurched towards the bed, but one look at Mother's face was enough to convince him that she was beyond mortal help. He dropped to his knees and began to weep like one of his own pitiful offspring.

My older siblings pushed past Mr Drayton to join Father in his tearful mourning. As they bustled into the room, Mr Drayton's fingers dug painfully into my shoulders as he reacted to the unnatural quiet which then fell over both of us. I could no longer hear the despairing cries of my family and somehow knew that Mr Drayton was experiencing the same auditory phenomenon. The sense of deafness would have been absolute had the sound of a crying baby not then infiltrated the void. Though this was merely a repetition of the intolerable keening we had heard at the cottage, the sobbing seemed infinitely more chilling when set against the backdrop of induced silence. The infant wailing rose to its shrillest pitch of distress, then all at once transformed into the drawn-out shriek of a train whistle.

I pressed my hands to my ears to escape the maddening sound and then, before I was entirely sensible of my actions, I shook off Mr Drayton's grasping hands and ran downstairs to the living room.

Once there, a disturbing intuition made me halt in front of the bay window. As I turned to face the icy glass, I unstopped my ears and heard the hammering of my frantic heart in a continuation of the hush that had wiped every other natural sound from the world.

To begin with, I saw nothing notable out of the window other than the snowman in the front garden, his friendly face greeting me with a crooked smile made of coal. But then, by degrees, what lurked behind this towering figure made its presence known. The woman who slithered into view had the solid appearance of a real human being to my eyes but clinging to her like tattered rags were wispy traces of the smoke in which she had manifested at the cottage. Her old-fashioned clothes were badly torn and uniformly black. She seemed to glide towards me, even though, beneath her skirt, her feet continued to take dainty steps that left no trace upon the garden's unblemished carpet of snow. There was almost nothing left of her face. Her fleshless jaw opened with a distinct click, and I heard the most hateful laughter ring from her rotted throat.

The next thing I remember with any clarity is waking up in bed after collapsing from a seizure that had left me with a dangerously elevated temperature. 'A fever without apparent cause' was how the doctor described my affliction, but then his science could not admit of the horror I had seen through the window. At one point in my delirium, I began to cry out for my mother, forgetting that she would never again be there to comfort me. Elsie came in her place and continued to do so every night until my fever broke three weeks later.

Mr Drayton followed Mother into the ground within a year. The guilt at what he had done to our family wore him down, though none of us held him responsible. He bequeathed us Rose Cottage in his will, but Father was unable to sell it at any price. To me, he left the sum of one hundred pounds – held in trust until I was twenty-one – along with a letter which completed the picture I had already formed of the Drayton family's tragic history.

Elsie Drayton had become troubled in her mind after giving birth to her son, spending time in an institution as a result. However, her doctor had deemed her well enough to return home in time for Archie's first birthday in the December of 1895.

Never an easy person to live with, Elsie had seemed like a different woman on her return: kind and pleasant and above all, a good mother to Archie. But this charade had merely concealed the true depths of her disorder.

On Christmas Eve, with the baby in her arms, Elsie jumped from a railway bridge near Old Hill into the path of a train driven by her husband. Mr Drayton witnessed the act from the footplate without realising who was involved and brought the train to a rapid halt inside the tunnel.

There was no wind that night. Smoke from the boiler lingered beneath the tunnel's dripping bricks, mingling with the evening mist to hamper the search for the woman whose reckless act had seen her broken body flung into the dark passage.

Shining a lantern on the victim's face, Mr Drayton had at first failed to recognise his wife because of the injuries she had sustained. Miraculously, a thread of life had still connected the wretched woman to this world. As he bent over her in a horrible moment of recognition, Elsie reached up and drew his head down so that she could whisper in his ear with her dying breath.

'Your turn to suffer, my sweet.'

The light had left her eyes, then, and a sound that would haunt Mr Drayton for the rest of his life began to resound through the hazy interior of the cavernous tunnel...

I often hear the same thing myself, but with an additional turn of the screw, so to speak. For what comes in the night to disturb my peace of mind is the tormented wailing of *two* pitiful infants.

You see, little Archie has company in that black tunnel far from the everlasting light. The child who perished with Mother cries with him still. The sister I never knew; Isobel...

* * *

At this point in his narrative, Alfred's daughter returned from her shopping expedition to collect him. As she waited for me to unlock the door, Alfred added a footnote to his story, even though I had already turned off the tape recorder.

'I can think of no worse fate,' he said, 'than to have the most demented part of one's being pass into the hereafter. That being said, I reckon Mr Drayton's suffering was the equal of Elsie's in the end.'

Before we said our goodbyes, I asked Alfred if crying children were now the extent of the haunting.

The dreadful look of fear that flitted across his face answered for him.

Christmas Interrupted

Larry Hodges

In recent years, Santa Claus had found it more difficult to keep up the cheery facade as he and the elves loaded up the sleigh. He knew something was wrong but couldn't quite remember what. He didn't feel lively and quick any more and hadn't looked in a mirror in a millennium, not since that last time when an old, emaciated man in a shabby and faded red coat stared back at him. The belly full of jelly was long gone, as was his hair, other than a few long strands still bravely clinging to his chin. His cheeks were as sunken as that sleigh he vaguely remembered crashing over the Pacific – how long ago was that? He couldn't remember. But it was Christmas Eve, and he knew what that meant.

"Load up the sleigh!" he cried. He'd barely slept the night before, alternating between excitement as he thought about all the joy he had brought to children in so many thousands of past Christmases, and perplexity when he tried to remember them. It was like grabbing smoke with your eyes closed.

"Still loaded up from last year," said Head-Elf Bernie. "Remember?"

"Remember what?" When had the elves switched from green outfits to torn blue jeans and rock band t-shirts? And when did Bernie get so old?

"See, I told you," said Head-Elf-in-Training Charlie, not attempting to hide his yawn and no doubt assuming Santa wouldn't notice – but Santa did, behind his forced smile. "He doesn't remember."

"We didn't give out any of the presents last year, or the year before, and for many years before that," said Bernie. "There are no more humans in the world, no more children, and so nobody to give them to. Remember? So we never unloaded the sleigh last year. Again. And the worker elves got another year off."

"We just gave the toys on top a good dusting," added Charlie. "Kind of pointless, though."

"That's not possible," Santa said. But as he said it, vague memories of disappointment came to him. No children? How was that possible? No, it was Christmas Eve, and he had a job to do. A billion kids were counting on him. His elves were testing him, that was it. Well, by God, he'd pass the test!

"I know you two are joking, so let's get on with it," Santa said. "Load up the sleigh!"

"We already did," said Bernie. "We just told you that."

"Um, right. Then fuel 'em up!"

"Already fed the reindeer," said Charlie. "All seven of them."

"Huh? There should be eight."

"Blitzen died ten years ago, remember?" said Bernie.

"Really?" Santa struggled to remember, but smoke just wafted through his fingers and mind. Yet he felt a deep sadness when he thought of poor Blitzen even if he couldn't remember why.

But Santa knew that he and sadness didn't go together, so he thought of sugarplums and chocolate eggnog, and the sadness evaporated into smoke that he waved away with a smile. He walked over and gave each of the reindeer a pat on the head. They grunted and nodded back.

"Did you give them the special candy canes I made?"

"Sure did," said Charlie. "But they're on a modern scientific diet that has all the vitamins, minerals, electrolytes, roughage and calories they need, and chocolate candy sticks really isn't a part of it. But I gave them each a lick."

"A lick! Why, you whippersnappel—"

"You're all set to go," interrupted Bernie in a monotone.

"Oh, right," he said. "But—" There was something he was angry about – something about the reindeer? But he couldn't remember what. Probably not important. But he did notice the elves' obvious lack of enthusiasm. Did they really think he didn't notice? He remembered his own boyhood, and sometimes treating elders with respect, but other times as if they weren't there, just as they were doing here. Strange how he could remember so much from so long ago but couldn't remember what he'd done last Christmas or even yesterday. But it was time to go to work.

"Okay, fuel 'em up!" he cried. The two elves exchanged glances. "I already said that, didn't I? Never mind, let's get going!" He climbed into the sleigh and gave the huge 4-D bag of toys a pat. He'd once tried to understand how the elves jammed a billion toys into a bag the size of a corpulent polar bear, but when the explanation got into relativistic quantum mechanics, he'd told them to never mind. He'd had the elves paint a nice snowy night mural on the bag.

"Do we really have to go through this charade again?" asked Head-Elf-in-Training-But-Not-Much-Longer Charlie. "How many more years will we be doing this?" He shook his head as he walked away.

"Have a good one," said Bernie. "Don't go too fast – you don't want to crash again."

Santa grabbed the reins in his gloved hands. But there was a lump under his left glove. He removed the glove – he was wearing a gold ring. His wedding ring. It brought back joyful memories though he couldn't quite make them out.

"Tell Mrs. Claus I'll be back!" he cried out.

Bernie had a pained expression. Then he remembered… Mrs. Claus… the long illness… how could he have forgotten?

"Never mind, I remember now." Sadness flooded over him. Think sugarplums, chocolate eggnog. He put the glove back on and grabbed the reins again, perhaps too tightly, and muscle memory took over. "Now Dasher! Now, Dancer! Now Prancer and Vixen! On, Comet! On Cupid! On Donner and Blitzen!" Then he frowned. Where the blazes was Blitzen? Somehow, she'd gotten left behind. No problem, he'd make do with seven reindeer.

The reindeer began prancing and the sleigh picked up speed. Within seconds they were in the air and off into the night. He directed them south – the only direction you could go from the North Pole – and they zoomed out over the Arctic Ocean.

"Strange, didn't that used to be covered with ice?" he pondered. He didn't remember the waters being so close to their North Pole home. Wait, wasn't there that time when… some big construction project where they put the North Pole on flotation devices? He vaguely remembered the big hassle, but the elves said it was either that or they'd fall into the sea. Why had all the ice melted? Shrugging, he looked ahead. Soon they would be flying over the city lights of Norilsk in Siberia, the northernmost city.

"Dang it, they should be coming up now," he muttered. But there were no lights in sight. The reindeer flew on.

After a while he directed them to fly west. Soon they would see the lights of Scandinavia. But again, no lights. The reindeer flew on.

"Something's wrong," Santa said.

When he saw Atlantic Ocean beneath them, he directed the reindeer to go south until they reached England. There were still no lights, but the full moon had come out. He had the reindeer fly lower and searched about until he found what he was sure was London.

They flew over it, just a few hundred feet up. By the light of the moon and stars he stared at it, refusing to believe, his mind a whir.

Nothing but rubble.

"Ready to go home now, boss?" Santa almost fell out of his seat and into the rubble below. He twisted around to see who it was. "There's nothing left," said Definitely-No-Longer-Head-Elf-in-Training Charlie, leaning against the big bag of toys and tapping a toy magic wand against the floor. "They killed themselves off long ago with their stupid wars and hunger when the climate got hot. We go through this charade every year, but Head-Elf says we should humor you."

"How'd you get on my sleigh? And give me that toy wand you stole from the bag, it's meant for—"... but he couldn't remember who it was for. Strange. He snatched it away anyway.

"The Head-Elf asked me to keep an eye on you. So I hid behind the big bag."

"Look after me? Why, you whoopersnopple—"

"boss, it's time to stop looking. There are no more children. They're all dead. Like the planet itself."

Santa felt his cheeks turning red like roses. The children – dead? It was too overwhelming to be true. And yet... he had vague memories, something about wars and famine. No, that was just a dream, it wasn't true. "You're lying! They're out there!" He gestured into the distance with the toy wand. But... where?

"Stop crying, boss, you do this every year." He handed Santa a red handkerchief with a big 'S' embroidered on it.

Crying? He wiped his face on a fading pink sleeve that had once been red. Santa and crying didn't go together. Sugarplums, chocolate eggnog.

He noticed a lump under his left glove. He removed it and stared at the gold ring underneath. "Why am I wearing a gold ring?"

"It's your wedding band, remember? You were married to Mrs. Claus. Before she died."

"Oh," Santa said as a thousand sleighs in his head came crashing together. How long had they been married? When had she died?

He couldn't remember what she looked like.

"Can we go home now?" Charlie asked.

"No!" Santa cried. "We'll keep looking! There must be children left!" What had he been thinking about a moment ago? It was something sad...

"Here we go again," said Charlie, sighing. "Suit yourself." He leaned back against the big bag, stretched out his legs, and stuck his long, skinny nose into a worn-out copy of "Little Elves."

They circled London a few times, looking for something, *anything*. But there was nothing, just more rubble of the once great city.

And then Santa saw it. "Look!" he cried, pointing with the toy wand. "Downward, Dasher, and the rest of you! Land, I say, land!"

"What's going on?" shouted Charlie, tossing his book aside as the sleigh hit the ground, skidded, and came to a stop.

"There are five children standing right over there! You were wrong, they're alive!" Santa exclaimed. He leaped from his sleigh, as lively and quick as he'd ever been. He rushed over "*Merry Christmas, Merry Christmas!*"

But the five children, three girls and two boys, just stood and sat there, holding bags. Two were looking at him, the others looking away. They wore dark, brown clothing that matched their dark skin. One of the girls sat on a suitcase holding a teddy bear. They seemed frozen at the sight of Santa Claus in their midst – he often had that effect on children.

"boss, stop it," said Charlie.

"Oh, give it up!" Santa cried. "There are five children here, and no doubt many more! It's going to be a great Christmas!"

"That's the Kindertransport Commemorative Statue. It commemorates the thousands of Jewish children from Germany and Austria sent to England before World War II to escape persecution. We're standing in the remains of the Liverpool Street Station in London. I guess bronze doesn't crumble as easily as concrete."

"What do you mean?" But now Santa stood next to them. He tapped one of the children on the arm and heard a metallic *thunk*.

Charlie was right. How had he mistaken bronze statues for real children? He was supposed to be an expert on the latter!

Something moved among the rubble. In the darkness it was hard to see, even under the light of the moon. "What's that?" he exclaimed, pointing down.

Charlie moved closer, then quickly stepped back. "Rats."

Santa stepped back even more quickly as shivers exploded down his spine. At least something had survived. But did it have to be rats? He shuddered.

Then he looked up at the faces of the bronze children. In his mind he saw the happy faces of billions and billions of children from the many millennia, smiling on many a Christmas morning as they unwrapped their gifts. Now just ashes and dust.

All dead.

The wand dropped from his shivering hand.

"Now can we go home?" Charlie pleaded.

* * *

Many years had gone by since the statue fiasco, though he wasn't really sure how long. Sometimes he remembered the past and was determined to prove it was just a bad memory; other years he did not. Sometimes Bernie accompanied him, and sometimes Charlie. Then Bernie stopped showing up. When Santa visited the toy factory, the elves looked incredibly old, playing video games on aging game devices as they withered away with no purpose. After years of abstinence, he'd made the mistake of glancing at his reflection in the mirror. Was that really him? It would have given Edgar Allan Poe nightmares.

And now it was Christmas Eve. Again. But Santa didn't want to get up. He'd spent the day in bed, as he always did the day before Christmas, getting as much sleep as possible before the long night. But what was the point?

He'd once written down what the elves had told him about humankind and their terrible fate, and often read it over. Eventually he was able to remember it on his own, usually. Now he wished he had not. If there were no humans, what was the point of delivering toys to non-existent children?

What was the point of getting up?

What was the point of existing without a purpose, with the constant sadness of reality? Even he was mortal, if he took the appropriate steps. A sharpened stick to the heart. Poison. Or a convenient fall from a flying sleigh. These thoughts now invaded his mind all too often.

To quote a famous human, to be or not to be?

Then he sat up suddenly. "*No!*" he cried out. "*I will not give up!* The children live on, whether in body, spirit or just in my mind." He hesitated. "No, not just in my mind. They are out there. They *must* be! *And I will find them!*"

253

"You okay in there?" called out an elf from outside the door.

"I'm fine," Santa said as he rose from his bed.

It was time to go. Nothing would keep him from his rounds. He dressed quickly and ate a quick dinner... or was it breakfast? Soon he was beside the sleigh.

"Go get 'em, Tiger," said Head-Elf Charlie. He yawned.

"Load up the sleigh!" Santa cried, putting memory of that sight out of his mind. But his body felt like his body looked. His muscles and bones ached no matter how much chocolate eggnog he drank.

"You already said that," said Charlie. "Still loaded from last year. We had to replace some of the wooden components – they don't last as long as metal, and of course plastic lasts forever. Re inflated the balls as well."

"Then fuel up the reindeer!"

"Already done, remember?"

"Don't get twickety with me, you whopperdiddle—"

"You're all set to go. Again."

Santa stood next to the small escalator the elves had made for him. Climbing up used to be so easy! Then he looked at his reindeer.

"Where are the rest?" he demanded.

"That's all that's left, boss," said Charlie. "Just Prancer and Vixen. The rest died off over the years, one by one. You don't remember." He didn't say it as a question.

"Of course I remember!" Santa cried, but he did not. Fighting back tears, he gave the two remaining reindeer each a pat on the head, and then, when Charlie wasn't looking, sneaked each a chocolate candy cane. They grunted and snorted their delight. Then he took the escalator up into the sleigh and grabbed the reins.

There was a lump under his left glove. He removed the glove and stared.

"Why am I wearing a gold ring?" he asked.

"You don't remember?" Charlie asked.

"If I remembered, I wouldn't be asking!"

Charlie nodded and looked off into the distance for a moment, then smiled. "It's an award they gave you a long time ago for your distinguished service to children all over the world."

"Really?" Santa felt warm all over. "They recognized me? Then I better live up to their award! Time to make deliveries! The children are waiting, all snug in their beds!"

"Let me drive," said Charlie. "You crashed again last year, remember?"

"I did not!" Santa declared, some of warmth receding. But perhaps he had.

"We had to fix up the sleigh. We put in some safety devices – it's practically crash-proof now. You couldn't crash it if you tried, all sorts of alarms would go off and it would take preventative action. It pretty much flies itself now, you don't even need reindeer. But we also trained Prancer and Vixen to change course if anything goes wrong. Wasn't easy, but it turns out they really like those unhealthy candy canes you feed them, and so we used those as training incentive."

"If it's crash-proof, then why do you need to come?"

"Because—"

"Look, we both know you only do this because you think you have to. You elves are incredibly loyal. But you don't have any Christmas spirit left, and I don't blame you – yeah, my memory is foggy these last few millennia—"

"A lot longer than that!"

"—but I remember much of it. No more people, right? All dead from wars and hunger?"

"Exactly."

"Then, with my new crash-proof sleigh, let me go on my own this year. You don't have to come."

"Are you sure, boss? You are kind of old."

"And how old are you?" He felt a twinkle in his eye.

"Touché, boss, almost as old as you, percentage-wise! Tell you what, you drive, and I'll just take a nap in the back." Charlie clambered aboard – he was amazingly spry for an elf of his age – and curled up behind the huge bag of toys.

Santa gave a light tug of the reins. The two reindeer looked back at him over their shoulders. *Just two?* He bit his lip – hadn't Charlie just said something about that? Sighing, he said, "Now Prancer and Vixen... oh, just go."

Soon Santa was out over the night, ignoring Charlie's snores, once again doing the rounds, looking for children in all the rubble to give presents to, as he had done for... how long? The years all blended together. How had so much time gone by so quickly? And where were Blitzen and the other reindeer?

He looked over the side of the sleigh. They were a long way up. It could be over in seconds. No, don't think that, he thought, making it impossible *not* to think about it. One more time, he thought, one more attempt to find the children. And if not...

Soon he was over London under a full moon, site of his last child-sighting – sort of. For many years he'd visited the rat-infested bronze statues each year, the closest thing to real children left. They were so calm and peaceful. But they were a constant reminder that the human race was dead, as were all the children that had ever been born. It always sent him into convulsions of sobs that sugarplums and chocolate eggnog couldn't repel. So he'd stopped seeing them, directing the reindeer to give the place a wide clearance. How many years had it been since he'd last seen his fake metal friends? He wasn't sure – but he decided to see them this year. He had the reindeer land. But – there were only two reindeer? Where were the others?

Then the aging statues came into view and a deep depression hit him. Their surfaces were blotchy and had lost their shininess, and the children looked like sick caricatures. But – there was something different. The rubble around the statues' feet had been removed, leaving a clear area. Who had done that? Could a storm have blown all that rubble away? Perhaps a tornado? Sadness overwhelmed him as he moved closer to this final memorial to a dead race. All those children... sugarplums and chocolate eggnog, he thought furiously, as tears flowed. He should have jumped.

Then he saw movement and flickering light. Two dark figures scurried about the clearing at the statue's feet. He took a quick step back – rats! Then he gasped – both rats were walking on their hind legs, kicking a round stone back and forth with their bare, pink feet. It looked painful.

Around the rubble were larger rats, squirrel-sized, also standing on their hind feet, pointing at him and making squeaky sounds. Their faces were hairless and whiskerless. They had only vestigial tails. One wore a sprig of leaves in its hair. Several stood over a fire at the foot of the girl statue holding the teddy bear, roasting something whose scent brought back memories of backyard barbecues from long ago.

"*Oh my God,*" whispered a now-awake Charlie.

Very slowly, Santa reached into his bag. He found a box of ping-pong balls – plastic lasts for ever. He pulled one out and held it in his hand for the rats to see. They wiggled their noses and stomped their paws on the ground as they stared at him. Slowly, so as not to scare them, he rolled the ping-pong ball towards the children with the stone ball.

The parents squeaked even louder, and several disappeared into the surrounding rubble. But one of the two child rats grabbed the new ball in its front legs – its hands. Soon the two child rats were kicking the ping-pong ball back and forth with glee.

"*Merry Christmas!*" Santa exclaimed.

"*Melly Kithmas!*" one of the child rats squeaked back with wide, shining eyes and an almost human smile.

"Santa," said Charlie. "We're back in business."

Bring Me a Light!
A Ghost Story
Jane Margaret Hooper

MY NAME IS Thomas Whinmore, and when I was a young man I went to spend a college vacation with a gentleman in Westmoreland. He had known my father's family, and had been appointed the trustee of a small estate left me by my great aunt, Lady Jane Whinmore. At the time I speak of I was one-and-twenty, and he was anxious to give up the property into my hands. I accepted his invitation to "come down to the old place and look about me." When I arrived at the nearest point to the said "old place," to which the Carlisle coach would carry me, I and my portmanteau were put into a little cart, which was the only wheeled thing I could get at the little way-side inn.

"How far is it to Whinmore?" I asked of a tall grave-looking lad, who had already informed me I could have "t'horse and cairt" for a shilling a mile.

"Twal mile to t'ould Hall gaet – a mile ayont that to Squire Erle's farm."

As I looked at the shaggy wild horse, just caught from the moor for the purpose of drawing t'cairt," I felt doubtful as to which of us would be the master on the road. I had ascertained that the said road lay over moor and mountain – just the sort of ground on which such a steed would gambol away at his own sweet will. I had no desire to be run away with.

"Is there any one here who can drive me to Mr. Erle's?" I asked of the tall grave lad.

"Nobbut fayther."

I was puzzled; and was about to ask for an explanation, when a tall, strong old man, as like the young one as might be, came out from the door of the house with his hat on, and a whip in his hand. He got up into the cart, and looking at me, said,

"Ye munna stan here, sir. We shan't pass Whinmore Hall afore t'deevil brings a light."

"But I want something to eat before we start," I remonstrated. "I've had no dinner."

"Then ye maun keep your appetite till supper time," replied the old man. "I canna gae past Whinmore lights for na man – nor t'horse neither. Get up wi' ye! Joe, lend t'gentleman a hand."

Joe did as he was desired, and then said—

"Will ye be home the night, fayther?"

"May be yees, may be na, lad; take care of t'place."

In a moment the horse started, and we were rattling over the moor at the rate of eight miles an hour. Surprise, indignation, and hunger possessed me. Was it possible I had been whirled off dinnerless into this wilderness against my own desire?

"I say, my good man," I began.

"My name is Ralph Thirlston."

"Well! Mr. Thirlston, I want something to eat. Is there any inn between this desert and Mr. Erle's house!"

"Nobbut Whinmore Hall," said the old man, with a grin.

"I suppose I can get something to eat there, without being obliged to anybody. It is my own property."

Mr. Thirlston glanced at me sharply.

"Be ye t'maister, lad?"

"I am, Mr. Thirlston," said I. "My name is Whinmore."

"Maister Tom!"

"The same. Do you know anything about me and my old house?"

" 'Deed do I. You're the heir of t'ould leddy. Mr. Erle is your guardian, and farms your lands."

"I know so much, myself," I replied. "I want you to tell me who lives in Whinmore Hall now, and whether I can get a dinner there, for I'm *clem*, as you say here."

"Weel, weel. It is a sore trial to a young stomach! You must e'en bear it till we get to Mr. Erle's."

"But surely there is somebody, some old woman or other, who lives in the old house and airs the rooms!"

" 'Deed is there. But it's nobbut ghosts and deevil's spawn of that sort."

"I am surprised, Mr. Thirlston, to hear a man like you talk such nonsense."

"What like man do ye happen know that I am, Maister Whinmore? Tho' if I talk nonsense (and I'm no gainsaying what a learned colleger like you can tell about nonsense), yet it's just the thing I have heard and seen mysell I am speaking of."

"What have you heard and seen at Whinmore Hall?"

"What a' body hears and sees to Whinmore, 'twixt sunset and moonlight; – and what I used to see times and oft, when I lived there farming-man to t'ould Leddy Jane, – what I'm not curious to see again, now. So get on, Timothy," he added to the horse, "or we may chance to come in for a fright."

I did not trouble myself about the delay, as he did, but watched him.

This man is no fool, I thought. I wonder what strange delusion has got possession of the people about this old house of mine. I remembered that Mr. Erle had told me in one of the very few letters I ever received from him, that it was difficult to find a tenant for Whinmore Hall. Curiosity took precedence of hunger, and I began to think how I could best soothe my irritated companion, and get him to tell me what he believed.

We were back on the road again, and going across the shoulder of a great fell; – the sun had just disappeared behind a distant range of similar fells; it left no rosy clouds, no orange streaks in the sky – black rain-clouds spread all over the great concave, and in a very few minutes they burst upon us. There was a cold, piercing wind in our teeth. I felt my spirits rise. The vast monotonous moor, the threatening sky, and the fierce rushing blast had something for me sublime and invigorating. I looked round at the new range of moorland which we were gradually commanding as we rounded the hill.

"I like this wild place, Mr. Thirlston," I said.

"Wild enough!" he grumbled in reply. " 'Tis college learning is a deal better than such house and land. Beggars won't live in th' house, and th' land is the poorest in all England."

"Is that the house, yonder, on the right?"

"There's na ither house, good or bad, to be seen from this," he replied: but I observed that he did not turn his head in the direction I had indicated. He kept a look-out straight between the horse's ears; I, on the contrary, never took my eyes off the grey building which we were approaching. Nearer and nearer we came, and I saw that there was a sort of large garden or pleasure-ground enclosed round the house, and that the road ran past a part of this enclosure, and also past a large open-worked iron gate, which was the chief entrance. Very desolate, cold, and inhospitable looked this old house of mine; wild and tangled looked the garden. The tall smokeless chimneys were numerous, and stood up white against the blackness of the sky; the windows, more numerous still, looked black, in contrast with the whitish-grey stone of the wall.

Just as we entered the shadow cast by the trees of the shrubbery, our horse snorted, and sprang several yards from the enclosure.

"Now for it! It is your own fault for running away, and bringing us late," muttered Ralph Thirlston, grasping the reins and standing up to get a better hold of the horse. Timothy now stood still; and to my surprise he was trembling in every limb, and shaking with terror.

"Something has frightened the beast," said I. "I shall just go and see what it was," and was about to jump down, when I felt Ralph Thirlston's great hand on my arm: it was a powerful grip.

"For the love of God, lad, stay where ye are!" he said, in a frightened whisper. "It's just here that my brother met his death, for doing what you want to do now."

"What! For walking up to that fence and seeing what trifle frightened a skittish horse?" And I looked at the fence intently. There was nothing to be seen but a straggling bough of an elder bush which had forced its way through a chink in the rotten wood and was waving in the wind.

Finding that the man was really frightened as well as the horse, I humoured him. He still held my arm.

"There is no need for any one to go closer to see the cause of poor Timothy's fear," I said, laughing. "If you will look, Mr. Thirlston, you will see what it was."

"Na! lad, na! I'm not going to turn my face towards the deevil and his works. 'Lord have mercy upon us! Christ have mercy upon us! Our Father which art in heaven—'" and he repeated the whole prayer with emphasis, slowness, and with his eyes closed. I sat still, an amazed witness of his state of mind. When he had said "Amen," he opened his eyes, and looking down at the horse, who seemed to have recovered, as I judged by his putting his head down to graze, he gave a low whistle, and tightening the reins once more, Timothy allowed himself to be driven forward. Thirlston kept his face away from the enclosure on his right hand, and looked steadily at Timothy. I gave another glance towards the innocent elder bough, – but what was my astonishment to see where it had been, or seemed to be, the figure of a man with a drawn sword in his hand.

"Stop, Thirlston! stop!" I cried. "There is somebody there. I see a man with a sword. Look! Turn back, and I'll soon see what he is doing there."

"Na! na! Never turn back to meet the deevil, when ye have once got past him!" And Thirlston drove on rapidly.

"But he may overtake you," I cried, laughing. But as I looked back I saw that a pursuit was not intended, for the figure I had seen was gone. "I'll pay a visit to that devil tomorrow," I added. "I shall not harbour such game in my preserves."

"Lord's sake, don't talk like that, Maister Whinmore!" whispered Thirlston. "We're just coming to the gaet! May be they may strike Timothy dead!"

"They? – who? Not the ghosts, surely?" I looked through the great gate as we passed, and saw the whole front of the house. "Why, Mr. Thirlston, you said no one lived in the old Hall! Look! there are lights in the windows."

"Ay! ay! I thought you would see them," he said, in a terrified whisper, without turning his head.

"Why, look at them yourself," cried I, pointing to the house.

"God forbid!" he exclaimed; and he gave Timothy a stroke with the whip, that sent him flying past the rest of the garden of the Hall. Our ground rose again, and in a few minutes a good view of the place was obtained. I looked back at it with vivid interest. No lights were to be seen now; no moving thing; the black windows contrasted with the grey walls, and the grey chimneys with the black clouds, as when the place first appeared to me. The moon now rose above a dark hill on our left. Thirlston allowed Timothy to slacken his speed, and, turning round his head, he also looked back at Whinmore Hall.

"We are safe enough now," he said. "The only dangerous time is betwixt sunset and moonrise when people are passing close to the accursed ould place."

About a mile further, the barking of a housedog indicated that we were approaching Mr. Erle's. The driver stopped at a small wicket-gate leading into a shrubbery, got down, and invited me to do the same. He then fastened Timothy to the gatepost. The garden and the house have nothing to do with my present tale, and are far too dear to me to be flung in as an episodical adornment. They form the scenery of the romantic part of my own life; for Miss Erle became my wife a few years after this first visit to Whinmore. I saw her that evening, and forgot Ralph Thirlston, the old Hall, its ghosts and mysterious lights. However, the next morning I was forced back to this work-a-day world in her father's study. There I heard Mr. Erle's account of my property. All the land was farmed by himself, except the few acres round the Hall, which no one would take because it was not worth tillage, and because of the evil name of the house itself.

"I suppose you know why no tenant can be found for the Hall, since Ralph Thirlston drove you over?"

"Yes," I said, smiling. "But I could get no rational account from him. What is this nonsense about ghosts and lights? Who lives in the Hall?"

"No one, my good fellow. Why, you would not get the stoutest man in the parish, and that's Thirlston, to go into the house after sunset, much less live in it."

"But I have seen lights in some of the windows myself."

"So have I," he replied.

"Do you mean to say that no human beings make use of the house, in virtue of the superstition about it? Tricks of this kind are not uncommon."

"At the risk of seeming foolish in your eyes, I must reply, that I believe no human beings now living have any hand in the operations which go on in Whinmore Hall." Mr. Erle looked perfectly grave as he said this.

"I saw a man with a sword in his hand start from a part of the fence. I think he frightened our horse."

"I, too, have seen the figure you speak of. But I do not think it is a living man."

"What do you suppose it to be?" I asked, in amazement; for Mr. Erle was no ignorant or weak-minded person. He had already impressed me with real respect for his character and intellect.

He smiled at my impetuous tone.

"I live apart from what is called the world," said he. "Grace and I are not polite enough to think everything which we cannot account for either impossible or ridiculous. Ten years ago, I myself was a new resident in this county, and wishing to improve your property, I determined to occupy the old Hall myself. I had it prepared for my family. No mechanic would work about the place after sunset. However, I brought all my servants from a distance; and took care that they should have no intercourse with any neighbour for the first three days. On the third evening they all came to me, and said that they must leave the next morning – all but Grace's nurse, who had been her mother's attendant, and was attached to the family. She told me that she did not think it safe for the child to remain another night, and that I must give her permission to take her away."

"What did you do?" said I.

"I asked for some account of the things that had frightened them. Of course, I heard some wild and exaggerated tales; but the main phenomena related were what I myself had seen and heard, and which I was as fully determined as they were not to see and hear again, or to let my child have a chance of encountering. I told them so, candidly; and at the same time declared that it was my belief God's Providence or punishment was at work in that old house, as everywhere else in creation, and not the devil's mischievous hand. Once more I made a rigorous search for secret devices and means for producing the sights and sounds which so many had heard and seen; but without any discovery: and before sunset that afternoon the Hall was cleared of all human occupants. And so it has remained until this day."

"Will you tell me the things you saw and heard?"

"Nay, you had better see and hear them for yourself. We have plenty of time before sunset. I can show you over the whole house, and if your courage holds good, I will leave you there to pass an hour or so between sunset and moonrise. You can come back here when you like; and if you are in a condition to hear, and care to hear, the story which peoples your old Hall with horrors, I will tell it you."

"Thank you," said I. "Will you lend me a gun and pistols to assist me in my investigations?"

"Surely." And taking down the weapons I had pointed out, he began to examine them.

"You want them loaded?"

"Certainly, and with bullets. I am not going to play."

Mr. Erle loaded both gun and pistols. I put the latter into my pocket, and we left the room by the window. Grace Erle met us on the moor, riding a shaggy pony.

"Where are you going, so near dinner time?" she asked.

"Mr. Whinmore is going to look at the old Hall."

"And his gun?" she asked, smiling.

"I want to shoot vermin there."

She looked as if she were about to say something eagerly, but checked herself, and rode slowly away. I looked after her, and wondered what she was going to say. Perhaps she wished to prevent me from going.

Presently we stood before the great iron gate of Whinmore. Mr. Erle took two keys from his pocket. With one he unlocked the gate, with the other the chief door. There were no other fastenings. These were very rusty, and were moved with difficulty.

"People don't get in this way," said I. "That is clear."

The garden was a sad wilderness, and grass grew on the broad steps which led up to the door. As soon as we had crossed the threshold, I felt the influence of that desolate dwelling creep over my spirits. There was a cold stagnation in the air – a deathly stillness – a murky light in the old rooms that was indescribably depressing. All the lower windows had their pierced shutters fastened, and cobwebs and dust adorned them plentifully.

Yet I could have sworn I saw lights in two, at least, of these lower windows. I said so to my companion. He replied –

"Yes. It was in this very room you saw a light, I dare say. This is one in which I have seen lights myself. But I do not wish to spoil my dinner by seeing anything supernatural now. We will leave it, and I will hasten to the lady's bed-chamber and dressing-room, where the apparitions and noises are most numerous."

I followed him, but cast a glance round the room before I shut the door carefully. It was partly furnished like a library, but on one side was a bed, and beside it an easy-chair. "What name is given to this room? It looks ominous of some evil deed," I said.

"It is called 't'ould Squire's Murder Room,' by the people who know the story connected with it."

"Ah!" I said; "then I may look for a ghost there?"

"You will perhaps see one, or more, if you stay long enough," said Mr. Erle, with the utmost composure. "This way."

I followed him along a gallery on the first floor to the door of a room. He opened it, and we entered what had been apparently one of the principal bedrooms. It was a regular lady's chamber, of the seventeenth century, with dark plumes waving on the top of the bed-pillars of black oak.

The massy toilette, with its oval looking-glass, set in silver and shrouded in old lace – the carved chairs and lofty mantelpiece – gave an air of quaint elegance to the dignity of the apartment. I had but little time to examine the objects here, for Mr. Erle had passed on to an inner room, which was reached by ascending a short flight of steps.

"Come up here," cried a voice which did not sound like Mr. Erle's. I ran up the stairs and found him alone in a small room which contained little else than an escritoire, a cabinet, and two great chairs. On one side, a large Parisian looking-glass, *à la Régence*, was fixed on the wall. The branches for lights still held some yellow bits of wax-candle covered with dust. I joined Mr. Erle, who was looking through the window over a vast expanse of mountainous moorland. "What a grand prospect!" I exclaimed. "I like these two rooms very much. I shall certainly come and live here."

"You shall tell me your opinion about that tomorrow," said Mr. Erle. "I must go now."

Concealing as much as possible the contempt I felt for his absurd superstition, I accompanied him down-stairs again. "Are these the only rooms worth looking at?" I asked.

"No; most of the rooms are good enough for a gentleman's household. The rooms I have shown you, and the passages and staircase which lead from one to the other, are the only portions of the house in which you are subjected to annoyance. I have slept in both the rooms, and advise no one else to do so."

"You had bad dreams?" I asked, with an involuntary smile, as I took my gun from the hall-table, where I had left it.

"As you please," said Mr. Erle, smiling also.

I stretched out my hand to him when we stood at the gate together.

"Good night!" said I. "I think I shall sleep in one of those rooms, and return to you in the morning."

Mr. Erle shook his head. "You will be back at my house within three hours, Tom Whinmore; so, *au revoir!*"

He strode away over the moor. His fine figure appeared almost gigantic as it moved between me and the setting sun.

"That does not look like a man who should be a prey to weak superstition, any more than good Ralph Thirlston, who drove home alone willingly enough past this same gate and fence at nine o'clock last night! The witching hour, it seems, is just after sunset. Well, it wants a quarter of an hour of that now," I continued, thinking silently. "There will be time enough for me to explore the garden a little, before I return to the house and wait for my evening's entertainment."

As I walked through the shrubbery, I recollected the figure I had seen outside the fence on the previous evening. I must find out how *that* trick is managed, thought I, and if I get a chance I will certainly wing that ghost, *pour encourager les autres.*

Ascertaining, as well as I was able, the part of the shrubbery near which I saw the man, I began to search for footsteps or marks of human ingenuity. I soon discovered the elder bush that had sent some of its branches through a hole in the fence. I crept round it, and examined the fence. No plank was loose, though some boughs had grown through the hole. I could see no footstep except my own on the moist, dank leafy mould. I got over the fence and saw no marks outside. Baffled, and yet suspicious, I went back and continued my walk, in the course of which I came upon sundry broken and decayed summer-houses and seats. In the tangled flower-garden, on the south-west side, were a few rich blossoms, growing amicably with the vilest weeds. I tore up a great root of hemlock to get at a branch of Provence rose, and then seeing that the sun had disappeared below the opposite fell, I pursued my course and arrived again at the broad gravel path leading from the gate to the hall-door.

Both stood open, as I had left them. I lingered on the grass-grown steps to look at the last rays of the sun, reddening the heather on the distant fell. As I leaned on my gun enjoying the profound stillness of this place, far from all sounds of village, or wood, or sea – a stillness that seemed to deepen and deepen into unearthly intensity – the charm was broken by a human voice speaking near me – the tone was hollow and full of agony – "*Bring me a light! Bring me a light!*" it cried. It was like a sick or dying man. The voice came, I thought, from the room next to me on the right hand of the Hall. I rushed into the house and to the door of that room; it was the first which Mr. Irle had shown me. I remembered shutting the door – it now stood wide open; and there was a sound of hurrying footsteps within.

"Who is there?" I shouted. No answer came. But there passed by me, as it were, in the very doorway, the figure of a young and, as I could see at a glance, very beautiful woman.

When she moved onwards I could not choose but follow, trembling with an indefinable fear, yet borne on by a mystic attraction. At the foot of the stairs she turned on me again, and smiled, and beckoned me with an upraised arm, whereon great jewels flashed in the gloom. I followed her quickly, but could not overtake her. My limbs – I am not ashamed to say it – shook with strange fear; yet I could not turn back from following that fair form. Onward she led me – up the stairs and through the gallery to the door of the lady's chamber. There she paused a moment, and again turned her bewitching face, radiant with smiles, upon me before she disappeared within the dark doorway. I followed into the room, and saw her stand before the antique toilette and arrange in her bosom a spray of roses – the very spray that I had so lately pulled in the garden, it seemed – then she kissed her hand to me and glided to the narrow stairs that led to the little room above. Then came a loud haughty voice – the voice of a woman accustomed to command. It sounded from the little room above, and it could not be the voice of that fair girl, I felt sure. It said:

"*Bring me a light! Bring me a light!*"

I shuddered at the sound; I knew not why, but I stood there still. I then saw the figure of an old female servant, rise from a chair by one of the windows. She approached the toilette, and there I saw her light two tapers, with her breath, it seemed.

"*Bring me a light!*" was repeated in an angry tone from the upper room.

The old woman passed rapidly to the stairs. Thither I followed in obedience to a sign from her; and, mounting to the top, saw into the room.

That beautiful girl stood in the centre, with her costly lace gown sweeping the floor, and her bright curls drooping to the waist. Her back was towards me, but I could see her innocent, sweet face in the great glass. What a lovely, happy face it was!

Behind her stood another lady, taller, and more majestic. She pretended to caress her, but her proud eyes, unseen by the young lady, brightened with triumphant malice. They danced gladly in the light of the taper which she took from the maid. "God of heaven! can a woman look so wicked?" I thought.

"*Watch her!*" whispered a voice in my ear – a voice that stirred my hair.

I did watch her. Would to God I could forget that vision! She – the woman, the fiend – bent carefully to the floor, as though to set right something amiss in the border of the fair bride's robe. I saw her lower the flame of the candle, and set fire to the dress of the smiling, trusting girl. Ere I could move she was enveloped in flames, and I heard her wild shrieks mingling with the low demoniac laughter of her murderess.

I remember suddenly raising the gun in my hand and firing at the horrid apparition. But still she laughed and pointed with mocking gestures to the flames and the writhing figure they enveloped. I ran forward to extinguish them; – my arms struck against the wall, and I fell down insensible.

* * *

When I recovered my senses I found myself lying on the floor of that little room, with the bright cold moon looking in on me. I waited without moving, listening for some more of those demon sounds. All was still. I rose – went to the window – the moon was high in heaven, and all the great moor seemed light as day. The air of that room was stifling. I turned and fled. Hastily I ran down those few steps – quicker yet through the great chamber and out into the gallery. As I began to go down the stairs, I saw a figure coming up.

I was now a very coward. Grasping the banister with one hand, and feeling for the unused pistol with the other, I called out –

"Who are you?" and with stupid terror I fired at the thing, without pausing.

There was a slight cry; a very human one. Then a little laugh.

"Don't fire any more pistols at me, Mr. Whinmore. I'm not a ghost."

Something in the voice sent the blood once more coursing through my veins.

"Is it ——?" I could not utter another word.

"It is I, Grace Erle."

"What brought you here?" I said, at length, after I had descended the stairs, and had seized her hand that I might feel sure it was of flesh and blood.

"My pony. We began to get uneasy about you. It is nearly midnight. So papa and I set off to see what you were doing."

"What the devil are you firing at, Whinmore?" asked Mr. Erle, coming hurriedly from a search in the lower rooms.

"Only at *me*, papa!" answered his daughter, archly, glancing up at my face. "But he is a bad shot, for he didn't hit me."

"Thank God!" I ejaculated – "Miss Erle, I was mad."

"No, only very frightened. Look at him, papa!"

Mr. Erle looked at me. He took my arm.

"Why! Whinmore, you don't look the better for seeing the spirits of your ancestors. However, I see it is no longer a joking matter with you. You do not wish to take up your abode here immediately."

I rallied under their kindly *badinage*.

"Let me get out of this horrible place," said I.

Mr. Erle led me beyond the gate. I leaned against it, in a state of exhaustion.

"Here. Try your hand at my other pocket-pistol!" said Mr. Erle, as he put a precious flask of that kind to my lips. After a second application of the remedy I was decidedly better.

Miss Erle mounted her pony, and we set off across the moor. I was very silent, and my companions talked a little with each other. My mind was too confused to recollect just then all that I had experienced during my stay in the house, and I wished to arrange my thoughts and compose my nerves before I conversed with Mr. Erle on the strange visions of that night.

I excused myself to my host and his daughter, in the best way I could, and after taking a slice of bread and a glass of water, I went to bed.

The next day I rose late; but in my right mind. I was much shocked to think of the cowardly fear which had led me to fire a pistol at Miss Erle. I began my interview with my host, by uttering some expressions of this feeling. But it was an awkward thing to declare myself a fool and a coward.

"The less we say about that the better," said her father, gravely. "Fear is the strongest human passion, my boy; and will lead us to commit the vilest acts, if we let it get the mastery."

"I acknowledge that I was beside myself with terror at the sights and sounds of that accursed house. I was not sane, at the moment, I saw your daughter! I shall never—"

"Whinmore, she hopes you will never mention it again! We certainly shall not. Now, if you are disposed to hear the story of your ancestor's evil deeds, I am ready to fulfil the promise I made you last night. I see you know too much, now, to think me a fool for believing my own senses, and keeping clear of disagreeable creatures that will not trouble themselves about me. I don't raise the question of *what* they are, or *how* they exist – nor even whether they exist at all. It is sufficient that they appear; and that by their appearance they put a stop to normal human life. You may be a philosopher; and may find some means of banishing these supernatural horrors. I shall like you none the less, if you can do what I cannot."

"I will try. Will you tell the story?"

"Yes, if you will take a cigar with me first."

After we had composed ourselves comfortably before the fire in his study, Mr. Erle began.

"How long ago, I can't exactly find out, but some time between the Reformation and the Great Rebellion, the Whinmores settled in this part of the county, and owned a large tract of land. They were of gentle blood, and most ungentle manners; for they quarrelled with every one, and carried themselves in an insolent fashion, to the simple below them, and to the noble above. The Whinmores were iron-handed and iron-hearted, staunch Catholics and staunch Jacobites, during the religious and political dissensions of the end of the seventeenth and beginning of the eighteenth centuries. After the establishment of Protestantism in the reigns of William III. and Anne, the position of the proud house of Whinmore was materially altered. The cadets went early into foreign service as soldiers and priests, and the first-born remained at home to keep up a blighted dignity. After the establishment of the Hanoverian dynasty, the Whinmores of Whinmore Hall ceased to take any part in public affairs. They were too proud to farm their own land; and putting trust in a nefarious steward, the Whinmore who reigned at the Hall when King George the Second reigned over England was compelled to keep up appearances by selling half the family estate.

"The Whinmore in question, 't'ould squire,' as the people call him, was a melancholy man, not much blest in the matrimonial lottery. His wife, Lady Henrietta Whinmore, was the daughter of a poor Catholic Earl. Tradition says she was equally beautiful and proud; and I believe it.

"To return. This couple had only one child, a son. When Lady Henrietta found that her husband was a gentleman of a moping and unenterprising turn of mind, that she could not persuade him to compromise his principles, and so find favour with the new government, she devoted herself to the education of her son, Graham. As he was a clever boy, with strong health and good looks, she determined that he should retrieve the fortunes of the family. She kept him under her own superintendence till he was ten years of age. She then sent him to Eton, with his cousin the little Earl of ——. He was brought up a Protestant, and thus the civil disabilities of the family would be removed. He was early accustomed to the society of all ranks, to be found in a first-class English public school; and his personal gifts as well as his mental excellence helped to win him the good opinion of others. Graham came home from Oxford in his twenty-third year, a first-class man."

"Indeed!" I exclaimed. "I hope I am descended from him, and that his good luck will be a part of my inheritance. Is there any portrait of this fine young English gentleman of the olden time?"

"A very good one. It is in my daughter's sitting-room. We are both struck by your likeness to your grandfather, Graham Whinmore."

"I shall never take a first-class," I sighed; "but go on."

"When Graham returned home after his success at college, he found his father a hopeless valetudinarian, who had had his bed brought down to his library, because he thought himself too feeble to go up and down stairs. He showed little emotion at sight of his son, and seemed to be fast sinking to idiotcy. His mother, on the contrary, was radiant with joy; and had made the old ruined house look its best to welcome the heir. For, at that time, the place was much dilapidated, and only a small portion was habitable, that is the part you saw yesterday, the south front.

"And Graham stayed at home for a month or two in repose, after the fatigues of study. One afternoon as he rode home from a distant town, he paused on the top of Whinmore Hill, which commands a good view of the Hall. The simple bareness of the great hills around, the antique beauty and retirement of the Hall – above all, the sweet impressive stillness of the place, had often charmed Graham, as a boy. Now he gazed with far stronger feeling at it all.

" 'It shall *not* be lost to me and my children,' he vowed, inwardly. 'I will redeem the mortgage on the house, I will win back every acre of the old Whinmore land. Yes, I will work for wealth; but I must lose no time, or my opportunity will be gone.'

"He looked at the ruined part of the house, and began to calculate the cost of rebuilding as he hastened forward. As soon as he entered the house he went to see his father, whom he had not seen that day. He found him in his bed, with the nurse asleep in the easy chair beside it. His father did not recognise him, and to Graham's mind, looked very much changed since the previous day. He left the room in search of his mother; thinking, in spite of his love for her, that she neglected her duty as a wife. 'She should be beside him now,' he thought. Still, he framed the best excuse he could for her then, for he loved and reverenced her. She was so strong-minded, so beautiful. Above all, she loved him with such passionate devotion. He dreaded to tell her the resolution he had formed. She was an aristocrat and a woman. She did not understand the mutation of things in that day; she would not believe that the best way to wealth and power was not through the Court influence, but by commercial enterprise. He went to her bed-room, the Lady's Chamber, in which you were last night. She was not there, and he was about to retreat, when he heard her voice in anger speaking to some one, in the dressing-room or oratory above. Graham went towards the stairs, and was met by an old female servant who was in his mother's confidence, and acted as her maid and head-nurse to his father. She came down in tears, murmuring, 'I cannot bear it. It was you gave me the draught for him. I will send for a doctor.'

" 'A doctor, indeed! He wants no doctor,' cried the angry mistress. 'And don't talk any more nonsense, my good woman, if you value your place.'

"In her agitation the woman did not see her young master, and hastily left the room.

"Astonished at the woman's words, he slowly ascended the steps to the dressing-room. He found his mother standing before the long looking-glass arrayed in a rich dress of old point lace, over a brocaded petticoat, with necklace, bracelets, and tiara of diamonds. She looked very handsome as her great eyes still flashed and her cheek was yet crimson with anger. She turned hastily as her son's foot was heard on the topmost stair. When she saw who it was her face softened with a smile.

" 'You here, Graham! I have been wanting you. Read that.'

"He could scarcely take his admiring eyes from the brilliant figure before him as he received the letter.

"It was addressed to his mother, and came from his cousin, the Earl, informing her that he had obtained a certain post under government for Graham.

"She kissed him as he sat down after reading the letter.

" 'There is your first step on fortune's ladder, my son. You are sure to rise.'

" 'I hope so, mother. But where are you going decked out in the family diamonds and lace?'

" 'Have you forgotten? – To the ball at the Lord-Lieutenant's. You must dress quickly, or we shall be late. Your cousin will be there, and we must thank him for that letter.'

" 'Yes, mother,' he replied, 'but we must refuse the place – I have other views.'

"Lady Henrietta's brow darkened.

" 'Mother! I have vowed to recover the estate of my ancestors. It will require a large fortune to do this. I cannot get a large fortune by dangling about the Court – I am going to turn merchant.'

"Lady Henrietta stared at him in amazement.

" 'You? – My son become a merchant?'

" 'Why not, mother? Sons of nobler houses have done so; and I have advantages that few have ever had. Listen, dear mother. I saved the life of a college friend, who was drowning. His father is one of the wealthiest merchants in London – in all England. He wrote to tell me that if it suited my views and those of my family, he was ready to receive me, at once, as a junior partner in his firm. He had learned from his son that I wished to become rich that I might buy back my ancestral estate. His offer puts it in my power to become rich in a comparatively short space of time. – I intend to accept his munificent offer.'

"Lady Henrietta's proud bosom swelled; but there was something in her son's tone which made her feel that anger and persuasion were alike vain. After some minutes' silence, she said bitterly:

" 'The world is changed indeed, Graham, if men of gentle blood can become traders and not lose their gentility.'

" 'They can, mother. And I do not think the world can be much changed in that particular. A man of gentle blood, who is, in very truth, a gentleman, cannot lose that distinction in any occupation. Come, good mother, give me a smile! I am about to go forth to win an inheritance. I shall fight with modern weapons – the pen and the ledger – instead of sword and shield.'

"At that moment hasty steps were heard in the chamber below, and a voice called:

" 'My lady! my lady! come quick! The Squire is dying!'

"Mother and son went fast to Mr. Whinmore's room. They arrived in time to see the old man die. He pointed to her, and cried with his last breath,

She did it! She did it!'

"Lady Henrietta sat beside his bed and listened to these incoherent words without any outward emotion. She watched the breath leave the body, and then closed the eyes herself. But though she kept up so bravely then, she was dangerously ill for several months after her husband's death, and was lovingly tended by her son and the old servant.

* * *

"I must now pass over ten years. Before the end of that time Graham Whinmore had become rich enough to buy back every acre of the land and to build a bran new house, twenty times finer than the old one, if he were so minded. But he was by no means so minded. He restored the old house – made it what it now is. He would not have accepted Chatsworth or Stowe in exchange.

"The Lady Henrietta lived there still; and superintended all the improvements. She had become reconciled to her son's occupation for the sake of the result in wealth. She entered eagerly into all his plans for the improvement of his property, and she had some of her own to propose.

"It was the autumn of the tenth year since her husband's death, and she was expecting Graham shortly for his yearly visit to the Hall. She sat looking over papers of importance in her dressing-room; the old servant (who seems to have grown no older) sat sewing in the bedroom below, when a housemaid brought in a letter which the old servant took immediately to her mistress.

"Lady Henrietta opened the letter quickly, for she saw that the handwriting was her son's. 'Perhaps he is coming this week,' she thought with a thrill of delight. 'Yes, he will come to take me to the Lord-Lieutenant's ball. He is proud of his mother yet, and I must look my best.' But she had not read a dozen words before the expression of her face changed. Surprise darkened into contempt and anger – anger deepened into rage and hatred. She uttered a sharp cry of pain. The old servant ran to her in alarm; but her mistress had composed herself, though her cheek was livid.

"'Did your ladyship call me?'

"'Yes. Bring me a light!'

"In this letter Graham announced his return home the following week – with a wife; – a beautiful girl – penniless and without connections of gentility. No words can describe the bitter rage and disappointment of this proud woman. He had a second time thwarted her plans for his welfare, and each time he had outraged her strongest feelings. He had turned merchant, and by his plebeian peddling had bought the land which his ancestors had won at the point of the sword. She had borne that, and had submitted to help him in his schemes. But receive a beggarly, low-born wench for her daughter-in-law? – No! She would never do that. She paced the room with soft, firm steps, like a panther. After a time thought became clearer, and she saw that there was no question of her willingness to receive her daughter-in-law, but of that daughter-in-law's willingness to allow her to remain in the house. Ah! but it was an awful thing to see the proud woman when she looked that fact fully in the face. She hated her unseen daughter with a keen cold hate – a remorseless hate born of that terrible sin, Pride. But she was not a woman to hate passively. She paced to and fro, turning and returning with savage, stealthy quickness. The day waned, and night began. Her servant came to see if she were wanted, and was sent away with a haughty negative. 'She is busy with some wicked thought,' murmured the old woman.

* * *

"Graham Whinmore's bride was, as he had said, 'so good and so lovely, that no one ever thought of asking who were her parents.' She was also accomplished and elegant in manner. She was in all respects but birth superior to the Duke's daughter whom Lady Henrietta had selected for her son's wife. The beautiful Lilian's father was a music master, and she had given lessons in singing herself. Lady Henrietta learned this and everything else concerning her young daughter-in-law that could be considered disgraceful in her present station. But she put restraint on her contempt, and received her with an outward show of courtesy and stately kindness. Graham believed that for his sake his mother was determined to forget his wife's low origin, and he became easy about the result of their connection after he had seen his mother caress his wife once or twice. He felt sure that no one could know Lilian and not love her. He was proud and happy to think that two such beautiful women belonged to him.

"The Lord-Lieutenant's ball was expected to be unusually brilliant that year, and Graham was anxious that his wife should be the queen of the assembly.

"'I should like her to wear the old lace and the jewels, mother,' said Graham.

"The Lady Henrietta's eyebrows were contracted for a moment, and she shot forth a furtive glance at Lilian, who sat near, playing with a greyhound.

"If Graham had seen that glance! But her words he believed.

"'Certainly, my son. It is quite proper that your wife should wear such magnificent heirlooms. There is no woman of quality in this county that can match them. I am proud to abdicate my right in her favour.'

"'There, Lilian! Do you hear, you are to eclipse the Duchess herself!'

"I will do so, if you wish it,' said Lilian. 'But I do not think that will amuse me so much as dancing.'

* * *

"Balls, in those times, began at a reasonable hour. Ladies who went to a ball early in November, began to dress by daylight.

"Lilian had been dressed by her maid. Owing to a certain sentimental secret between her and her husband, she wore her wedding-dress of white Indian muslin, instead of a rich brocaded silk petticoat, underneath the grand lace robe. The diamonds glittered gaily round her head and her softly-rounded throat and arms. She went to the old library, where Graham sat awaiting the ladies. She wanted his opinion concerning her appearance. The legend does not tell how he behaved on this occasion, but leaves it to young husbands to imagine.

"'You must go to my mother, and let her see how lovely you look. Walk first, that I may see how you look behind.' So she took from his hand a spray of roses he had gathered, and preceded him from the room, and up the staircase to his mother's chamber. She was in the dressing-room above.

"'Go up by yourself,' said Graham; 'I will remain on the stairs, and watch you both. I should like to hear what she says, when she does not think I hear; for she never praises you much to me, for fear of increasing my blind adoration, I suppose.'

"Lilian smiled at him, and disappeared up the stairs. It was now becoming dark, and as he approached the stairs, a few minutes afterwards, to hear what was said, his mother's voice, in a strange, eager tone, called from above,

"*Bring me a light! Bring me a light!*'

"Then Graham saw his mother's old servant run quickly from her seat by the window, and light a tall taper on the toilette. She carried this up to her mistress, and found Graham on the stair on her return. She grasped his arm, and whispered fearfully,

"'Watch her! Watch her!'

"He did watch, and saw—"

"For God's sake, Mr. Erle," I interrupted, "don't tell me what he saw – for I saw the same dreadful sight!"

"I have no doubt you did, since you say so; and because I have seen it myself."

We were silent for some moments, and then I asked if he knew anything more of these people.

"Yes – the rest is well known to every one who lives within twenty miles. Graham Whinmore vowed not to remain under the same roof with his mother, after he had seen his wife's blackened corpse. His grief and resentment were quiet and enduring. He would not leave the corpse in the house; but before midnight had it carried to a summer-house in the shrubbery, where he watched beside it, and allowed no one to approach, except the old servant who figures in this story. She brought him food, and carried his commands to the household. From the day of Lilian's death till the day of her burial in the family vault at Whinmore Church, Graham guarded the summer-house where his wife lay, with his drawn sword as he walked by night round about. It was known that he would not allow the family jewels to be taken from the body, and that they were to be buried with it. Some say that he finally took them from the body himself, and buried them in the shrubbery, lest the undertakers, tempted by the sight of the jewels on the corpse, might desecrate her tomb afterwards for the sake of stealing

CHRISTMAS GOTHIC SHORT STORIES

them. This opinion is supported by the fact that a portion of the shrubbery is haunted by the apparition of Graham Whinmore, in mourning garments, and with a drawn sword in his hand.

"Would you advise me to institute a search for those old jewels?" I asked smiling.

"I would," said he. "But take no one into your confidence, Tom Whinmore. You may raise a laugh against you, if you are unsuccessful. And if you find them, and take them away—"

"Which I certainly should do," I interrupted.

"You will raise a popular outcry against you. The superstitious people will believe that you have outraged the ghost of your great-grandfather, who will become mischievous, in consequence."

I saw the prudence of this remark; and it was agreed between us, that we should do all the digging ourselves, unknown to any one. I then asked how it was that I was descended from this unfortunate gentleman.

Mr. Erle's story continued thus: –

"After his wife's funeral, Graham Whinmore did not return to the Hall, but went away to the south, and never came here again, not even to visit his mother on her death-bed, a year after. In a few years he married again, and had sons and daughters. To an unmarried daughter, Jane Whinmore, – always called 'Leddy Jane' by our neighbours, – he left the house and lands. He did not care to keep it in the family, and she might leave it to a stranger, or sell it, if she pleased. It was but a small portion of Graham Whinmore's property, as you must know. She, however – this 'Leddy Jane' – took a great fancy to the old place. She is said to have lived on terms of familiarity with the ghost of her grandmother, and still more affectionately with her father's first wife. She heard nothing of the buried jewels, and saw nothing of her own father's ghost during his lifetime. That part of the story did not come to light until after the death of Graham Whinmore; when the 'Leddy Jane' herself was startled one evening in the shrubbery, by meeting the apparition of her father. It is said that she left her property to her youngest nephew's youngest son, in obedience to his injunctions during that interview."

"So that though unborn at the time, I may consider myself lord of Whinmore Hall, by the will of my great-grandfather!" I said.

"Precisely so. I think it an indication that the ghostly power is to die out in your time. The last year of the wicked Lady Henrietta's life was very wretched, as you may suppose. Her besetting and cherished sins brought their own reward – and her crowning crime was avenged without the terror of the law. For it is said that every evening at sunset the apparition of her murdered daughter-in-law came before her, wearing the rich dress which was so dear to the proud woman; and that she was compelled to repeat the cruel act, and to hear her screams and the farewell curses of her adored son. The servants all left the Hall in affright; and no one lived with the wicked Lady except the faithful old servant, Margaret Thirlston, who stayed with her to the last, followed her to the grave, and died soon after.

"Her son and his wife were sought for by Jane Whinmore on her arrival here. She gave them a home and everything they wanted as housekeeper and farm-manager at the Hall. And at the death of Giles Thirlston, his son Ralph became farm-manager in his place. He continued there till 't' Leddy's' death, when he settled at the little wayside inn which you have seen, and which he calls 'Leddy Jane's Gift.'"

* * *

I have but little more to say. Mr. Erle and I sought long for the hidden treasure. We found it, after reading a letter secreted in the escritoire, addressed to 'My youngest nephew's youngest son.' In that letter directions were given for recovering the hidden jewels of the family. They were buried outside the garden fence, on the open moor, on the very spot where I can swear I saw the figure of a man with a sword – my great-grandfather, Graham Whinmore.

After I married, we came to live in the south; and I took every means to let my little estate of Whinmore. To my regret the Hall has never found a tenant, and it is still without a tenant after these twenty-five years.

Will any reader of ONCE A WEEK make me an offer? They shall have it cheap.

"Oh, Whistle, and I'll Come to You, My Lad"

M.R. James

"I SUPPOSE YOU will be getting away pretty soon, now Full Term is over, Professor," said a person not in the story to the Professor of Ontography, soon after they had sat down next to each other at a feast in the hospitable hall of St James's College.

The Professor was young, neat, and precise in speech.

"Yes," he said; "my friends have been making me take up golf this term, and I mean to go to the East Coast – in point of fact to Burnstow – (I dare say you know it) for a week or ten days, to improve my game. I hope to get off tomorrow."

"Oh, Parkins," said his neighbour on the other side, "if you are going to Burnstow, I wish you would look at the site of the Templars' preceptory, and let me know if you think it would be any good to have a dig there in the summer."

It was, as you might suppose, a person of antiquarian pursuits who said this, but, since he merely appears in this prologue, there is no need to give his entitlements.

"Certainly," said Parkins, the Professor: "if you will describe to me whereabouts the site is, I will do my best to give you an idea of the lie of the land when I get back; or I could write to you about it, if you would tell me where you are likely to be."

"Don't trouble to do that, thanks. It's only that I'm thinking of taking my family in that direction in the Long, and it occurred to me that, as very few of the English preceptories have ever been properly planned, I might have an opportunity of doing something useful on off-days."

The Professor rather sniffed at the idea that planning out a preceptory could be described as useful. His neighbour continued:

"The site – I doubt if there is anything showing above ground – must be down quite close to the beach now. The sea has encroached tremendously, as you know, all along that bit of coast. I should think, from the map, that it must be about three-quarters of a mile from the Globe Inn, at the north end of the town. Where are you going to stay?"

"Well, *at* the Globe Inn, as a matter of fact," said Parkins; "I have engaged a room there. I couldn't get in anywhere else; most of the lodging-houses are shut up in winter, it seems; and, as it is, they tell me that the only room of any size I can have is really a double-bedded one, and that they haven't a corner in which to store the other bed, and so on. But I must have a fairly large room, for I am taking some books down, and mean to do a bit of work; and though I don't quite fancy having an empty bed – not to speak of two – in what I may call for the time being my study, I suppose I can manage to rough it for the short time I shall be there."

"Do you call having an extra bed in your room roughing it, Parkins?" said a bluff person opposite. "Look here, I shall come down and occupy it for a bit; it'll be company for you."

The Professor quivered, but managed to laugh in a courteous manner.

"By all means, Rogers; there's nothing I should like better. But I'm afraid you would find it rather dull; you don't play golf, do you?"

"No, thank Heaven!" said rude Mr Rogers.

"Well, you see, when I'm not writing I shall most likely be out on the links, and that, as I say, would be rather dull for you, I'm afraid."

"Oh, I don't know! There's certain to be somebody I know in the place; but, of course, if you don't want me, speak the word, Parkins; I shan't be offended. Truth, as you always tell us, is never offensive."

Parkins was, indeed, scrupulously polite and strictly truthful. It is to be feared that Mr Rogers sometimes practised upon his knowledge of these characteristics. In Parkins's breast there was a conflict now raging, which for a moment or two did not allow him to answer. That interval being over, he said:

"Well, if you want the exact truth, Rogers, I was considering whether the room I speak of would really be large enough to accommodate us both comfortably; and also whether (mind, I shouldn't have said this if you hadn't pressed me) you would not constitute something in the nature of a hindrance to my work."

Rogers laughed loudly.

"Well done, Parkins!" he said. "It's all right. I promise not to interrupt your work; don't you disturb yourself about that. No, I won't come if you don't want me; but I thought I should do so nicely to keep the ghosts off." Here he might have been seen to wink and to nudge his next neighbour. Parkins might also have been seen to become pink. "I beg pardon, Parkins," Rogers continued; "I oughtn't to have said that. I forgot you didn't like levity on these topics."

"Well," Parkins said, "as you have mentioned the matter, I freely own that I do *not* like careless talk about what you call ghosts. A man in my position," he went on, raising his voice a little, "cannot, I find, be too careful about appearing to sanction the current beliefs on such subjects. As you know, Rogers, or as you ought to know; for I think I have never concealed my views—"

"No, you certainly have not, old man," put in Rogers *sotto voce.*

"—I hold that any semblance, any appearance of concession to the view that such things might exist is equivalent to a renunciation of all that I hold most sacred. But I'm afraid I have not succeeded in securing your attention."

"Your *undivided* attention, was what Dr Blimber actually *said,*" Rogers interrupted, with every appearance of an earnest desire for accuracy. "But I beg your pardon, Parkins: I'm stopping you."

"No, not at all," said Parkins. "I don't remember Blimber; perhaps he was before my time. But I needn't go on. I'm sure you know what I mean."

"Yes, yes," said Rogers, rather hastily – "just so. We'll go into it fully at Burnstow, or somewhere."

In repeating the above dialogue I have tried to give the impression which it made on me, that Parkins was something of an old woman – rather henlike, perhaps, in his little ways; totally destitute, alas! of the sense of humour, but at the same time dauntless and sincere in his convictions, and a man deserving of the greatest respect. Whether or not the reader has gathered so much, that was the character which Parkins had.

On the following day Parkins did, as he had hoped, succeed in getting away from his college, and in arriving at Burnstow. He was made welcome at the Globe Inn, was safely installed in the large double-bedded room of which we have heard, and was able before retiring to rest to arrange his materials for work in apple-pie order upon a commodious table which occupied the outer end of the room, and was surrounded on three sides by windows looking out seaward; that is to say, the central window looked straight out to sea, and those on the left and right commanded prospects along the shore to the north and south respectively. On the south you saw the village of Burnstow. On the north no houses were to be seen, but only the beach and the low cliff backing it. Immediately in front was a strip – not considerable – of rough grass, dotted with old anchors, capstans, and so forth; then a broad path; then the beach. Whatever may have been the original distance between the Globe Inn and the sea, not more than sixty yards now separated them.

The rest of the population of the inn was, of course, a golfing one, and included few elements that call for a special description. The most conspicuous figure was, perhaps, that of an *ancien militaire*, secretary of a London club, and possessed of a voice of incredible strength, and of views of a pronouncedly Protestant type. These were apt to find utterance after his attendance upon the ministrations of the Vicar, an estimable man with inclinations towards a picturesque ritual, which he gallantly kept down as far as he could out of deference to East Anglian tradition.

Professor Parkins, one of whose principal characteristics was pluck, spent the greater part of the day following his arrival at Burnstow in what he had called improving his game, in company with this Colonel Wilson: and during the afternoon – whether the process of improvement were to blame or not, I am not sure – the Colonel's demeanour assumed a colouring so lurid that even Parkins jibbed at the thought of walking home with him from the links. He determined, after a short and furtive look at that bristling moustache and those incarnadined features, that it would be wiser to allow the influences of tea and tobacco to do what they could with the Colonel before the dinner-hour should render a meeting inevitable.

"I might walk home tonight along the beach," he reflected – "yes, and take a look – there will be light enough for that – at the ruins of which Disney was talking. I don't exactly know where they are, by the way; but I expect I can hardly help stumbling on them."

This he accomplished, I may say, in the most literal sense, for in picking his way from the links to the shingle beach his foot caught, partly in a gorse-root and partly in a biggish stone and over he went. When he got up and surveyed his surroundings, he found himself in a patch of somewhat broken ground covered with small depressions and mounds. These latter, when he came to examine them, proved to be simply masses of flints embedded in mortar and grown over with turf. He must, he quite rightly concluded, be on the site of the preceptory he had promised to look at. It seemed not unlikely to reward the spade of the explorer; enough of the foundations was probably left at no great depth to throw a good deal of light on the general plan. He remembered vaguely that the Templars, to whom this site had belonged, were in the habit of building round churches, and he thought a particular series of the humps or mounds near him did appear to be arranged in something of a circular form. Few people can resist the temptation to try a little amateur research in a department quite outside their own, if only for the satisfaction of showing how successful they would have been had they only taken it up seriously. Our Professor, however if he felt something of this mean desire, was also truly anxious to oblige Mr Disney. So he paced with care the circular area he had noticed, and wrote down its rough dimensions in his pocket book. Then he proceeded to examine an oblong eminence which lay east of the centre of the circle, and seemed to his thinking likely to be the base of a platform or altar. At one end of it, the northern, a patch of the turf was gone – removed by some boy or other creature *feræ naturæ* It might, he thought, be as well to probe the soil here for evidences of masonry, and he took out his knife and began scraping away the earth. And now followed another little discovery: a portion of soil fell inward as he scraped, and disclosed a small cavity. He lighted one match after another to help him to see of what nature the hole was, but the wind was too strong for them all By tapping and scratching the sides with his knife, however, he was able to make out that it must be an artificial hole in masonry. It was rectangular, and the sides, top, and bottom, if not actually plastered, were smooth and regular. Of course it was empty. No! As he withdrew the knife he heard a metallic clink, and when he introduced his hand it met with a cylindrical object lying on the floor of the hole. Naturally enough, he picked it up, and when he brought it into the light, now fast fading, he could see that it, too, was of man's making – a metal tube about four inches long, and evidently of some considerable age.

By the time Parkins had made sure that there was nothing else in this odd receptacle, it was too late and too dark for him to think of undertaking any further search. What he had done had proved so unexpectedly interesting that he determined to sacrifice a little more of the daylight on the morrow to archaeology. The object which he now had safe in his pocket was bound to be of some slight value at least, he felt sure.

Bleak and solemn was the view on which he took a last look before starting homeward. A faint yellow light in the west showed the links, on which a few figures moving towards the club-house were still visible, the squat martello tower, the lights of Aldsey village, the pale ribbon of sands intersected at intervals by black wooden groynings, the dim and murmuring sea. The wind was bitter from the north, but was at his back when he set out for the Globe. He quickly rattled and clashed through the shingle and gained the sand, upon which, but for the groynings which had to be got over every few yards, the going was both good and quiet. One last look behind, to measure the distance he had made since leaving the ruined Templars' church, showed him a prospect of company on his walk, in the shape of a rather indistinct personage, who seemed to be making great efforts to catch up with him, but made little, if any, progress. I mean that there was an appearance of running about his movements, but that the distance between him and Parkins did not seem materially to lessen. So, at least, Parkins thought, and decided that he almost certainly did not know him, and that it would be absurd to wait until he came up. For all that, company, he began to think, would really be very welcome on that lonely shore, if only you could choose your companion. In his unenlightened days he had read of meetings in such places which even now would hardly bear thinking of. He went on thinking of them, however, until he reached home, and particularly of one which catches most people's fancy at some time of their childhood. "Now I saw in my dream that Christian had gone but a very little way when he saw a foul fiend coming over the field to meet him." "What should I do now," he thought, "if I looked back and caught sight of a black figure sharply defined against the yellow sky, and saw that it had horns and wings? I wonder whether I should stand or run for it. Luckily, the gentleman behind is not of that kind, and he seems to be about as far off now as when I saw him first. Well, at this rate, he won't get his dinner as soon as I shall; and, dear me! it's within a quarter of an hour of the time now. I must run!"

Parkins had, in fact, very little time for dressing. When he met the Colonel at dinner, Peace – or as much of her as that gentleman could manage – reigned once more in the military bosom; nor was she put to flight in the hours of bridge that followed dinner, for Parkins was a more than respectable player. When, therefore, he retired towards twelve o'clock, he felt that he had spent his evening in quite a satisfactory way, and that, even for so long as a fortnight or three weeks, life at the Globe would be supportable under similar conditions – "especially," thought he, "if I go on improving my game."

As he went along the passages he met the boots of the Globe, who stopped and said:

"Beg your pardon, sir, but as I was a-brushing your coat just now there was somethink fell out of the pocket. I put it on your chest of drawers, sir, in your room, sir – a piece of a pipe or somethink of that, sir. Thank you, sir. You'll find it on your chest of drawers, sir – yes, sir. Good night, sir."

The speech served to remind Parkins of his little discovery of that afternoon. It was with some considerable curiosity that he turned it over by the light of his candles. It was of bronze, he now saw, and was shaped very much after the manner of the modern dog-whistle; in fact it was – yes, certainly it was – actually no more nor less than a whistle. He put it to his lips, but it was quite full of a fine, caked-up sand or earth, which would not yield to knocking, but must be loosened with a knife. Tidy as ever in his habits, Parkins cleared out the earth on to a piece of paper, and took the latter to the window to empty it out. The night was clear and bright, as he saw when he had opened the casement, and he stopped for an instant to look at the sea and note a belated wanderer stationed on the shore in front of the inn. Then he shut the window, a little surprised at the late hours people kept at Burnstow, and took his whistle to the light again. Why, surely there were marks on it, and not merely marks, but letters! A very little rubbing rendered the deeply-cut inscription quite legible, but the Professor had to confess, after some earnest thought, that the meaning of it was as obscure to him as the writing on the wall to Belshazzar. There were legends both on the front and on the back of the whistle. The one read thus:

FLA FUR BIS FLE

The other:

QUIS EST ISTE QUI VENIT

"I ought to be able to make it out," he thought; "but I suppose I am a little rusty in my Latin. When I come to think of it, I don't believe I even know the word for a whistle. The long one does seem simple enough. It ought to mean, 'Who is this who is coming?' Well, the best way to find out is evidently to whistle for him."

He blew tentatively and stopped suddenly, startled and yet pleased at the note he had elicited. It had a quality of infinite distance in it, and, soft as it was, he somehow felt it must be audible for miles round. It was a sound, too, that seemed to have the power (which many scents possess) of forming pictures in the brain. He saw quite clearly for a moment a vision of a wide, dark expanse at night, with a fresh wind blowing, and in the midst a lonely figure – how employed, he could not tell. Perhaps he would have seen more had not the picture been broken by the sudden surge of a gust of wind against his casement, so sudden that it made him look up, just in time to see the white glint of a seabird's wing somewhere outside the dark panes.

The sound of the whistle had so fascinated him that he could not help trying it once more, this time more boldly. The note was little, if at all, louder than before, and repetition broke the illusion – no picture followed, as he had half hoped it might. 'But what is this? Goodness! what force the wind can get up in a few minutes! What a tremendous gust! There! I knew that window-fastening was no use! Ah! I thought so – both candles out. It is enough to tear the room to pieces.'

The first thing was to get the window shut. While you might count twenty Parkins was struggling with the small casement, and felt almost as if he were pushing back a sturdy burglar, so strong was the pressure. It slackened all at once, and the window banged to and latched itself. Now to relight the candles and see what damage, if any, had been done. No, nothing seemed amiss; no glass even was broken in the casement. But the noise had evidently roused at least one member of the household: the Colonel was to be heard stumping in his stockinged feet on the floor above and growling.

Quickly as it had risen, the wind did not fall at once. On it went, moaning and rushing past the house, at times rising to a cry so desolate that, as Parkins disinterestedly said, it might have made fanciful people feel quite uncomfortable; even the unimaginative, he thought after a quarter of an hour, might be happier without it.

Whether it was the wind, or the excitement of golf, or of the researches in the preceptory that kept Parkins awake, he was not sure. Awake he remained, in any case, long enough to fancy (as I am afraid I often do myself under such conditions) that he was the victim of all manner of fatal disorders: he would lie counting the beats of his heart, convinced that it was going to stop work every moment, and would entertain grave suspicions of his lungs, brain, liver, etc. – suspicions which he was sure would be dispelled by the return of daylight, but which until then refused to be put aside. He found a little vicarious comfort in the idea that someone else was in the same boat

A near neighbour (in the darkness it was not easy to tell his direction) was tossing and rustling in his bed, too.

The next stage was that Parkins shut his eyes and determined to give sleep every chance. Here again over-excitement asserted itself in another form – that of making pictures. *Experto crede*, pictures do come to the closed eyes of one trying to sleep, and are often so little to his taste that he must open his eyes and disperse them.

Parkins's experience on this occasion was a very distressing one. He found that the picture which presented itself to him was continuous. When he opened his eyes, of course, it went; but when he shut them once more it framed itself afresh, and acted itself out again, neither quicker nor slower than before. What he saw was this:

A long stretch of shore – shingle edged by sand, and intersected at short intervals with black groynes running down to the water – a scene, in fact, so like that of his afternoon's walk that, in the absence of any landmark, it could not be distinguished therefrom. The light was obscure, conveying an impression of gathering storm, late winter evening, and slight cold rain. On this bleak stage at first no actor was visible. Then, in the distance, a bobbing black object appeared; a moment more, and it was a man running, jumping, clambering over the groynes, and every few seconds looking eagerly back. The nearer he came the more obvious it was that he was not only anxious, but even terribly frightened, though his face was not to be distinguished. He was, moreover, almost at the end of his strength. On he came; each successive obstacle seemed to cause him more difficulty than the last. "Will he get over this next one?" thought Parkins; "it seems a little higher than the others." Yes; half climbing, half throwing himself, he did get over, and fell all in a heap on the other side (the side nearest to the spectator). There, as if really unable to get up again, he remained crouching under the groyne, looking up in an attitude of painful anxiety.

So far no cause whatever for the fear of the runner had been shown; but now there began to be seen, far up the shore, a little flicker of something light-coloured moving to and fro with great swiftness and irregularity. Rapidly growing larger, it, too, declared itself as a figure in pale, fluttering draperies, ill-defined. There was something about its motion which made Parkins very unwilling to see it at close quarters. It would stop, raise arms, bow itself towards the sand, then run stooping across the beach to the water-edge and back again; and then, rising upright, once more continue its course forward at a speed that was startling and terrifying. The moment came when the pursuer was hovering about from left to right only a few yards beyond the groyne where the runner lay in hiding. After two or three ineffectual castings hither and thither it came to a stop, stood upright, with arms raised high, and then darted straight forward towards the groyne.

It was at this point that Parkins always failed in his resolution to keep his eyes shut. With many misgivings as to incipient failure of eyesight, overworked brain, excessive smoking, and so on, he finally resigned himself to light his candle, get out a book, and pass the night waking, rather than be tormented by this persistent panorama, which he saw clearly enough could only be a morbid reflection of his walk and his thoughts on that very day.

The scraping of match on box and the glare of light must have startled some creatures of the night – rats or what not – which he heard scurry across the floor from the side of his bed with much rustling. Dear, dear! the match is out! Fool that it is! But the second one burnt better, and a candle and book were duly procured, over which Parkins pored till sleep of a wholesome kind came upon him, and that in no long space. For about the first time in his orderly and prudent life he forgot to blow out the candle, and when he was called next morning at eight there was still a flicker in the socket and a sad mess of guttered grease on the top of the little table.

After breakfast he was in his room, putting the finishing touches to his golfing costume – fortune had again allotted the Colonel to him for a partner – when one of the maids came in.

"Oh, if you please," she said, "would you like any extra blankets on your bed, sir?"

"Ah! thank you," said Parkins. "Yes, I think I should like one. It seems likely to turn rather colder." In a very short time the maid was back with the blanket.

"Which bed should I put it on, sir?" she asked.

"What? Why, that one – the one I slept in last night," he said, pointing to it.

"Oh yes! I beg your pardon, sir, but you seemed to have tried both of 'em; leastways, we had to make 'em both up this morning."

"Really? How very absurd!" said Parkins. "I certainly never touched the other, except to lay some things on it. Did it actually seem to have been slept in?"

"Oh yes, sir!" said the maid. "Why, all the things was crumpled and throwed about all ways, if you'll excuse me, sir – quite as if anyone 'adn't passed but a very poor night, sir."

"Dear me," said Parkins. "Well, I may have disordered it more than I thought when I unpacked my things. I'm very sorry to have given you the extra trouble, I'm sure. I expect a friend of mine soon, by the way – a gentleman from Cambridge – to come and occupy it for a night or two. That will be all right, I suppose, won't it?"

"Oh yes, to be sure, sir. Thank you, sir. It's no trouble, I'm sure," said the maid, and departed to giggle with her colleagues.

Parkins set forth, with a stern determination to improve his game.

I am glad to be able to report that he succeeded so far in this enterprise that the Colonel, who had been rather repining at the prospect of a second day's play in his company, became quite chatty as the morning advanced; and his voice boomed out over the flats, as certain also of our own minor poets have said, "like some great bourdon in a minster tower".

"Extraordinary wind, that, we had last night," he said. "In my old home we should have said someone had been whistling for it."

"Should you, indeed!" said Parkins. "Is there a superstition of that kind still current in your part of the country?"

"I don't know about superstition," said the Colonel. "They believe in it all over Denmark and Norway, as well as on the Yorkshire coast; and my experience is, mind you, that there's generally something at the bottom of what these country-folk hold to, and have held to for generations. But it's your drive" (or whatever it might have been: the golfing reader will have to imagine appropriate digressions at the proper intervals).

When conversation was resumed, Parkins said, with a slight hesitancy:

"A propos of what you were saying just now, Colonel, I think I ought to tell you that my own views on such subjects are very strong. I am, in fact, a convinced disbeliever in what is called the 'supernatural'."

"What!" said the Colonel, "do you mean to tell me you don't believe in second-sight, or ghosts, or anything of that kind?"

"In nothing whatever of that kind," returned Parkins firmly.

"Well," said the Colonel, "but it appears to me at that rate, sir, that you must be little better than a Sadducee."

Parkins was on the point of answering that, in his opinion, the Sadducees were the most sensible persons he had ever read of in the Old Testament; but, feeling some doubt as to whether much mention of them was to be found in that work, he preferred to laugh the accusation off.

"Perhaps I am," he said; "but – Here, give me my cleek, boy! – Excuse me one moment, Colonel." A short interval. "Now, as to whistling for the wind, let me give you my theory about it. The laws which govern winds are really not at all perfectly known – to fisherfolk and such, of course, not known at all. A man or woman of eccentric habits, perhaps, or a stranger, is seen repeatedly on the beach at some unusual hour, and is heard whistling. Soon afterwards a violent wind rises; a man who could read the sky perfectly or who possessed a barometer could have foretold that it would. The simple people of a fishing-village have no barometers, and only a few rough rules for prophesying weather. What more natural than that the eccentric personage I postulated should be regarded as having raised the wind, or that he or she should clutch eagerly at the reputation of being able to do so? Now, take last night's wind: as it happens, I myself was whistling. I blew a whistle twice, and the wind seemed to come absolutely in answer to my call. If anyone had seen me—"

The audience had been a little restive under this harangue, and Parkins had, I fear, fallen somewhat into the tone of a lecturer; but at the last sentence the Colonel stopped.

"Whistling, were you?" he said. "And what sort of whistle did you use? Play this stroke first." Interval.

"About that whistle you were asking, Colonel. It's rather a curious one. I have it in my – No; I see I've left it in my room. As a matter of fact, I found it yesterday."

And then Parkins narrated the manner of his discovery of the whistle, upon hearing which the Colonel grunted, and opined that, in Parkins's place, he should himself be careful about using a thing that had belonged to a set of Papists, of whom, speaking generally, it might be affirmed that you never knew what they might not have been up to. From this topic he diverged to the enormities of the Vicar, who had given notice on the previous Sunday that Friday would be the Feast of St Thomas the Apostle, and that there would be service at eleven o'clock in the church. This and other similar proceedings constituted in the Colonel's view a strong presumption that the Vicar was a concealed Papist, if not a Jesuit; and Parkins, who could not very readily follow the Colonel in this region, did not disagree with him. In fact, they got on so well together in the morning that there was no talk on either side of their separating after lunch.

Both continued to play well during the afternoon, or, at least, well enough to make them forget everything else until the light began to fail them. Not until then did Parkins remember that he had meant to do some more investigating at the preceptory; but it was of no great importance, he reflected. One day was as good as another; he might as well go home with the Colonel.

As they turned the corner of the house, the Colonel was almost knocked down by a boy who rushed into him at the very top of his speed, and then, instead of running away, remained hanging on to him and panting. The first words of the warrior were naturally those of reproof and objurgation, but he very quickly discerned that the boy was almost speechless with fright. Inquiries were useless at first. When the boy got his breath he began to howl, and still clung to the Colonel's legs. He was at last detached, but continued to howl.

"What in the world *is* the matter with you? What have you been up to? What have you seen?" said the two men.

"Ow, I seen it wive at me out of the winder," wailed the boy, "and I don't like it."

"What window?" said the irritated Colonel. "Come, pull yourself together, my boy."

"The front winder it was, at the 'otel," said the boy.

At this point Parkins was in favour of sending the boy home, but the Colonel refused; he wanted to get to the bottom of it, he said; it was most dangerous to give a boy such a fright as this one had had, and if it turned out that people had been playing jokes, they should suffer for it in some way. And by a series of questions he made out this story: The boy had been playing about on the grass in front of the Globe with some others; then they had gone home to their teas, and he was just going, when he happened to look up at the front winder and see it a-wiving at him. *It* seemed to be a figure of some sort, in white as far as he knew – couldn't see its face; but it wived at him, and it warn't a right thing – not to say not a right person. Was there a light in the room? No, he didn't think to look if there was a light. Which was the window? Was it the top one or the second one? The seckind one it was – the big winder what got two little uns at the sides.

"Very well, my boy," said the Colonel, after a few more questions. "You run away home now. I expect it was some person trying to give you a start. Another time, like a brave English boy, you just throw a stone – well, no, not that exactly, but you go and speak to the waiter, or to Mr Simpson, the landlord, and – yes – and say that I advised you to do so."

The boy's face expressed some of the doubt he felt as to the likelihood of Mr Simpson's lending a favourable ear to his complaint, but the Colonel did not appear to perceive this, and went on:

"And here's a sixpence – no, I see it's a shilling – and you be off home, and don't think any more about it."

The youth hurried off with agitated thanks, and the Colonel and Parkins went round to the front of the Globe and reconnoitred. There was only one window answering to the description they had been hearing.

"Well, that's curious," said Parkins; "it's evidently my window the lad was talking about. Will you come up for a moment, Colonel Wilson? We ought to be able to see if anyone has been taking liberties in my room."

They were soon in the passage, and Parkins made as if to open the door. Then he stopped and felt in his pockets.

"This is more serious than I thought," was his next remark. "I remember now that before I started this morning I locked the door. It is locked now, and, what is more, here is the key." And he held it up. "Now," he went on, "if the servants are in the habit of going into one's room during the day when one is away, I can only say that – well, that I don't approve of it at all." Conscious of a somewhat weak climax, he busied himself in opening the door (which was indeed locked) and in lighting candles. "No," he said, "nothing seems disturbed."

"Except your bed," put in the Colonel.

"Excuse me, that isn't my bed," said Parkins. "I don't use that one. But it does look as if someone had been playing tricks with it."

It certainly did: the clothes were bundled up and twisted together in a most tortuous confusion. Parkins pondered.

"That must be it," he said at last: "I disordered the clothes last night in unpacking, and they haven't made it since. Perhaps they came in to make it, and that boy saw them through the window; and then they were called away and locked the door after them. Yes, I think that must be it."

"Well, ring and ask," said the Colonel, and this appealed to Parkins as practical.

The maid appeared, and, to make a long story short, deposed that she had made the bed in the morning when the gentleman was in the room, and hadn't been there since. No, she hadn't no other key. Mr Simpson he kep' the keys; he'd be able to tell the gentleman if anyone had been up.

This was a puzzle. Investigation showed that nothing of value had been taken, and Parkins remembered the disposition of the small objects on tables and so forth well enough to be pretty sure that no pranks had been played with them. Mr and Mrs Simpson furthermore agreed that neither of them had given the duplicate key of the room to any person whatever during the day. Nor could Parkins, fair-minded man as he was, detect anything in the demeanour of master, mistress, or maid that indicated guilt. He was much more inclined to think that the boy had been imposing on the Colonel.

The latter was unwontedly silent and pensive at dinner and throughout the evening. When he bade goodnight to Parkins, he murmured in a gruff undertone:

"You know where I am if you want me during the night."

"Why, yes, thank you, Colonel Wilson, I think I do; but there isn't much prospect of my disturbing you, I hope. By the way," he added, "did I show you that old whistle I spoke of? I think not. Well, here it is."

The Colonel turned it over gingerly in the light of the candle.

"Can you make anything of the inscription?" asked Parkins, as he took it back.

"No, not in this light. What do you mean to do with it?"

"Oh, well, when I get back to Cambridge I shall submit it to some of the archaeologists there, and see what they think of it; and very likely, if they consider it worth having, I may present it to one of the museums."

"'M!" said the Colonel. "Well, you may be right. All I know is that, if it were mine, I should chuck it straight into the sea. It's no use talking, I'm well aware, but I expect that with you it's a case of live and learn. I hope so, I'm sure, and I wish you a good night."

He turned away, leaving Parkins in act to speak at the bottom of the stair, and soon each was in his own bedroom.

By some unfortunate accident, there were neither blinds nor curtains to the windows of the Professor's room. The previous night he had thought little of this, but tonight there seemed every prospect of a bright moon rising to shine directly on his bed, and probably wake him later on. When he noticed this he was a good deal annoyed, but, with an ingenuity which I can only envy, he succeeded in rigging up, with the help of a railway-rug, some safety-pins, and a stick and umbrella, a screen which, if it only held together, would completely keep the moonlight off his bed. And shortly afterwards he was comfortably in that bed. When he had read a somewhat solid work long enough to produce a decided wish for sleep, he cast a drowsy glance round the room, blew out the candle, and fell back upon the pillow.

He must have slept soundly for an hour or more, when a sudden clatter shook him up in a most unwelcome manner. In a moment he realized what had happened: his carefully-constructed screen had given way, and a very bright frosty moon was shining directly on his face. This was highly annoying. Could he possibly get up and reconstruct the screen? or could he manage to sleep if he did not?

For some minutes he lay and pondered over the possibilities; then he turned over sharply, and with his eyes open lay breathlessly listening. There had been a movement, he was sure, in the empty bed on the opposite side of the room. Tomorrow he would have it moved, for there must be rats or something playing about in it. It was quiet now. No! the commotion began again. There was a rustling and shaking: surely more than any rat could cause.

I can figure to myself something of the Professor's bewilderment and horror, for I have in a dream thirty years back seen the same thing happen; but the reader will hardly, perhaps, imagine how dreadful it was to him to see a figure suddenly sit up in what he had known was an empty bed. He was out of his own bed in one bound, and made a dash towards the window, where lay his only weapon, the stick with which he had propped his screen. This was, as it turned out, the worst thing he could have done, because the personage in the empty bed, with a sudden smooth motion, slipped from the bed and took up a position, with outspread arms, between the two beds, and in front of the door. Parkins watched it in a horrid perplexity. Somehow, the idea of getting past it and escaping through the door was intolerable to him; he could not have borne – he didn't know why – to touch it; and as for its touching him, he would sooner dash himself through the window than have that happen. It stood for the moment in a band of dark shadow, and he had not seen what its face was like. Now it began to move, in a stooping posture, and all at once the spectator realized, with some horror and some relief, that it must be blind, for it seemed to feel about it with its muffled arms in a groping and random fashion. Turning half away from him, it became suddenly conscious of the bed he had just left, and darted towards it, and bent and felt over the pillows in a way which made Parkins shudder as he had never in his life thought it possible. In a very few moments it seemed to know that the bed was empty, and then, moving forward into the area of light and facing the window, it showed for the first time what manner of thing it was.

Parkins, who very much dislikes being questioned about it, did once describe something of it in my hearing, and I gathered that what he chiefly remembers about it is a horrible, an intensely horrible, face *of crumpled linen*. What expression he read upon it he could not or would not tell, but that the fear of it went nigh to maddening him is certain.

But he was not at leisure to watch it for long. With formidable quickness it moved into the middle of the room, and, as it groped and waved, one corner of its draperies swept across Parkins's face. He could not, though he knew how perilous a sound was – he could not keep back a cry of disgust, and this gave the searcher an instant clue. It leapt towards him upon the instant, and the next moment he was half-way through the window backwards, uttering cry upon cry at the utmost pitch of his voice, and the linen face was thrust close into his own. At this, almost the last possible second, deliverance came, as you will have guessed: the Colonel burst the door open, and was just in time to see the dreadful group at the window. When he reached the figures only one was left. Parkins sank forward into the room in a faint, and before him on the floor lay a tumbled heap of bed-clothes.

Colonel Wilson asked no questions, but busied himself in keeping everyone else out of the room and in getting Parkins back to his bed; and himself, wrapped in a rug, occupied the other bed, for the rest of the night. Early on the next day Rogers arrived, more welcome than he would have been a day before, and the three of them held a very long consultation in the Professor's room. At the end of it the Colonel left the hotel door carrying a small object between his finger and thumb, which he cast as far into the sea as a very brawny arm could send it. Later on the smoke of a burning ascended from the back premises of the Globe.

Exactly what explanation was patched up for the staff and visitors at the hotel I must confess I do not recollect. The Professor was somehow cleared of the ready suspicion of delirium tremens, and the hotel of the reputation of a troubled house.

There is not much question as to what would have happened to Parkins if the Colonel had not intervened when he did. He would either have fallen out of the window or else lost his wits. But it is not so evident what more the creature that came in answer to the whistle could have done than frighten. There seemed to be absolutely nothing material about it save the bedclothes of which it had made itself a body. The Colonel, who remembered a not very dissimilar occurrence in India, was of the opinion that if Parkins had closed with it it could really have done very little, and that its one power was that of frightening. The whole thing, he said, served to confirm his opinion of the Church of Rome.

There is really nothing more to tell, but, as you may imagine, the Professor's views on certain points are less clear cut than they used to be. His nerves, too, have suffered: he cannot even now see a surplice hanging on a door quite unmoved, and the spectacle of a scarecrow in a field late on a winter afternoon has cost him more than one sleepless night.

The Story of a Disappearance and an Appearance

M.R. James

THE LETTERS which I now publish were sent to me recently by a person who knows me to be interested in ghost stories. There is no doubt about their authenticity. The paper on which they are written, the ink, and the whole external aspect put their date beyond the reach of question.

The only point which they do not make clear is the identity of the writer. He signs with initials only, and as none of the envelopes of the letters are preserved, the surname of his correspondent – obviously a married brother – is as obscure as his own. No further preliminary explanation is needed, I think. Luckily the first letter supplies all that could be expected.

Letter I

Great Chrishall, Dec. 22, 1837.

My Dear Robert, – It is with great regret for the enjoyment I am losing, and for a reason which you will deplore equally with myself, that I write to inform you that I am unable to join your circle for this Christmas: but you will agree with me that it is unavoidable when I say that I have within these few hours received a letter from Mrs. Hunt at B——, to the effect that our Uncle Henry has suddenly and mysteriously disappeared, and begging me to go down there immediately and join the search that is being made for him. Little as I, or you either, I think, have ever seen of Uncle, I naturally feel that this is not a request that can be regarded lightly, and accordingly I propose to go to B—— by this afternoon's mail, reaching it late in the evening. I shall not go to the Rectory, but put up at the King's Head, and to which you may address letters. I enclose a small draft, which you will please make use of for the benefit of the young people. I shall write you daily (supposing me to be detained more than a single day) what goes on, and you may be sure, should the business be cleared up in time to permit of my coming to the Manor after all, I shall present myself. I have but a few minutes at disposal. With cordial greetings to you all, and many regrets, believe me, your affectionate Bro.,

W. R.

Letter II

King's Head, Dec. 23, '37.

My Dear Robert, – In the first place, there is as yet no news of Uncle H., and I think you may finally dismiss any idea – I won't say hope – that I might after all "turn up" for Xmas. However, my thoughts will be with you, and you have my best wishes for a really festive day. Mind that none of my nephews or nieces expend any fraction of their guineas on presents for me.

Since I got here I have been blaming myself for taking this affair of Uncle H. too easily. From what people here say, I gather that there is very little hope that he can still be alive; but whether it is accident or design that carried him off I cannot judge. The facts are these. On Friday the 19th, he went as usual shortly before five o'clock to read evening prayers at the Church; and when they were over the clerk brought him a message, in response to which he set off to pay a visit to a sick person at an outlying cottage the better part of two miles away. He paid the visit, and started on his return journey at about half-past six. This is the last that is known of him. The people here are very much grieved at his loss; he had been here many years, as you know, and though, as you also know, he was not the most genial of men, and had more than a little of the *martinet* in his composition, he seems to have been active in good works, and unsparing of trouble to himself.

Poor Mrs. Hunt, who has been his housekeeper ever since she left Woodley, is quite overcome: it seems like the end of the world to her. I am glad that I did not entertain the idea of taking quarters at the Rectory; and I have declined several kindly offers of hospitality from people in the place, preferring as I do to be independent, and finding myself very comfortable here.

You will, of course, wish to know what has been done in the way of inquiry and search. First, nothing was to be expected from investigation at the Rectory; and to be brief, nothing has transpired. I asked Mrs. Hunt – as others had done before – whether there was either any unfavourable symptom in her master such as might portend a sudden stroke, or attack of illness, or whether he had ever had reason to apprehend any such thing: but both she, and also his medical man, were clear that this was not the case. He was quite in his usual health. In the second place, naturally, ponds and streams have been dragged, and fields in the neighbourhood which he is known to have visited last, have been searched – without result. I have myself talked to the parish clerk and – more important – have been to the house where he paid his visit.

There can be no question of any foul play on these people's part. The one man in the house is ill in bed and very weak: the wife and the children of course could do nothing themselves, nor is there the shadow of a probability that they or any of them should have agreed to decoy poor Uncle H. out in order that he might be attacked on the way back. They had told what they knew to several other inquirers already, but the woman repeated it to me. The Rector was looking just as usual: he wasn't very long with the sick man – "He ain't," she said, "like some what has a gift in prayer; but there, if we was all that way, 'owever would the chapel people get their living?" He left some money when he went away, and one of the children saw him cross the stile into the next field. He was dressed as he always was: wore his bands – I gather he is nearly the last man remaining who does so – at any rate in this district.

You see I am putting down everything. The fact is that I have nothing else to do, having brought no business papers with me; and, moreover, it serves to clear my own mind, and may suggest points which have been overlooked. So I shall continue to write all that passes, even to conversations if need be – you may read or not as you please, but pray keep the letters. I have another reason for writing so fully, but it is not a very tangible one.

You may ask if I have myself made any search in the fields near the cottage. Something – a good deal – has been done by others, as I mentioned; but I hope to go over the ground tomorrow. Bow Street has now been informed, and will send down by tonight's coach, but I do not think they will make much of the job. There is no snow, which might have helped us. The fields are all grass. Of course I was on the *qui vive* for any indication today both going and returning; but there was a thick mist on the way back, and I was not in trim for wandering about unknown pastures, especially on an evening when bushes looked like men, and a cow lowing in the distance might have been the last trump. I assure you, if Uncle Henry had stepped out from among the trees in a little copse which borders the path at one place, carrying his head under his arm, I should have been very little more uncomfortable than I was. To tell you the truth, I was rather expecting something of the kind. But I must drop my pen for the moment: Mr. Lucas, the curate, is announced.

Later. Mr. Lucas has been, and gone, and there is not much beyond the decencies of ordinary sentiment to be got from him. I can see that he has given up any idea that the Rector can be alive, and that, so far as he can be, he is truly sorry. I can also discern that even in a more emotional person than Mr. Lucas, Uncle Henry was not likely to inspire strong attachment.

Besides Mr. Lucas, I have had another visitor in the shape of my Boniface – mine host of the "King's Head" – who came to see whether I had everything I wished, and who really requires the pen of a Boz to do him justice. He was very solemn and weighty at first. "Well, sir," he said, "I suppose we must bow our 'ead beneath the blow, as my poor wife had used to say. So far as I can gather there's been neither hide nor yet hair of our late respected incumbent scented out as yet; not that he was what the Scripture terms a hairy man in any sense of the word."

I said – as well as I could – that I supposed not, but could not help adding that I had heard he was sometimes a little difficult to deal with. Mr. Bowman looked at me sharply for a moment, and then passed in a flash from solemn sympathy to impassioned declamation. "When I think," he said, "of the language that man see fit to employ to me in this here parlour over no more a matter than a cask of beer – such a thing as I told him might happen any day of the week to a man with a family – though as it turned out he was quite under a mistake, and that I knew at the time, only I was that shocked to hear him I couldn't lay my tongue to the right expression."

He stopped abruptly and eyed me with some embarrassment. I only said, "Dear me, I'm sorry to hear you had any little differences; I suppose my uncle will be a good deal missed in the parish?" Mr. Bowman drew a long breath. "Ah, yes!" he said; "your uncle! You'll understand me when I say that for the moment it had slipped my remembrance that he was a relative; and natural enough, I must say, as it should, for as to you bearing any resemblance to – to him, the notion of any such a thing is clean ridiculous. All the same, 'ad I 'ave bore it in my mind, you'll be among the first to feel, I'm sure, as I should have abstained my lips, or rather I should *not* have abstained my lips with no such reflections."

I assured him that I quite understood, and was going to have asked him some further questions, but he was called away to see after some business. By the way, you need not take it into your head that he has anything to fear from the inquiry into poor Uncle Henry's disappearance – though, no doubt, in the watches of the night it will occur to him that *I* think he has, and I may expect explanations tomorrow.

I must close this letter: it has to go by the late coach.

Letter III

Dec. 25, '37.

My Dear Robert, – This is a curious letter to be writing on Christmas Day, and yet after all there is nothing much in it. Or there may be – you shall be the judge. At least, nothing decisive. The Bow Street men practically say that they have no clue. The length of time and the weather conditions have made all tracks so faint as to be quite useless: nothing that belonged to the dead man – I'm afraid no other word will do – has been picked up.

As I expected, Mr. Bowman was uneasy in his mind this morning; quite early I heard him holding forth in a very distinct voice – purposely so, I thought – to the Bow Street officers in the bar, as to the loss that the town had sustained in their Rector, and as to the necessity of leaving no stone unturned (he was very great on this phrase) in order to come at the truth. I suspect him of being an orator of repute at convivial meetings.

When I was at breakfast he came to wait on me, and took an opportunity when handing a muffin to say in a low tone, "I 'ope, sir, you reconize as my feelings towards your relative is not actuated by any taint of what you may call melignity – you can leave the room, Eliza, I will see the gentleman 'as all he requires with my own hands – I ask your pardon, sir, but you must be well aware a man is not always master of himself: and when that man has been 'urt in his mind by the application of expressions which I will go so far as to say 'ad not ought to have been made use of (his voice was rising all this time and his face growing redder); no, sir; and 'ere, if you will permit of it, I should like to explain to you in a very few words the exact state of the bone of contention. This cask – I might more truly call it a firkin – of beer—"

I felt it was time to interpose, and said that I did not see that it would help us very much to go into that matter in detail. Mr. Bowman acquiesced, and resumed more calmly:

"Well, sir, I bow to your ruling, and as you say, be that here or be it there, it don't contribute a great deal, perhaps, to the present question. All I wish you to understand is that I am prepared as you are yourself to lend every hand to the business we have afore us, and – as I took the opportunity to say as much to the Orficers not three-quarters of an hour ago – to leave no stone unturned as may throw even a spark of light on this painful matter."

In fact, Mr. Bowman did accompany us on our exploration, but though I am sure his genuine wish was to be helpful, I am afraid he did not contribute to the serious side of it. He appeared to be under the impression that we were likely to meet either Uncle Henry or the person responsible for his disappearance, walking about the fields – and did a great deal of shading his eyes with his hand and calling our attention, by pointing with his stick, to distant cattle and labourers. He held several long conversations with old women whom we met, and was very strict and severe in his manner – but on each occasion returned to our party saying, "Well, I find she don't seem to 'ave no connexion with this sad affair. I think you may take it from me, sir, as there's little or no light to be looked for from that quarter; not without she's keeping somethink back intentional."

We gained no appreciable result, as I told you at starting; the Bow Street men have left the town, whether for London or not, I am not sure.

This evening I had company in the shape of a bagman, a smartish fellow. He knew what was going forward, but though he has been on the roads for some days about here, he had nothing to tell of suspicious characters – tramps, wandering sailors or gipsies. He was very full of a capital Punch and Judy Show he had seen this same day at W——, and asked if it had been here yet, and advised me by no means to miss it if it does come. The best Punch and the best Toby dog, he said, he had ever come across. Toby dogs, you know, are the last new thing in the shows. I have only seen one myself, but before long all the men will have them.

Now why, you will want to know, do I trouble to write all this to you? I am obliged to do it, because it has something to do with another absurd trifle (as you will inevitably say), which in my present state of rather unquiet fancy – nothing more, perhaps – I have to put down. It is a dream, sir, which I am going to record, and I must say it is one of the oddest I have had. Is there anything in it beyond what the bagman's talk and Uncle Henry's disappearance could have suggested? You, I repeat, shall judge: I am not in a sufficiently cool and judicial frame to do so.

It began with what I can only describe as a pulling aside of curtains: and I found myself seated in a place – I don't know whether in doors or out. There were people – only a few – on either side of me, but I did not recognize them, or indeed think much about them. They never spoke, but, so far as I remember were all grave and pale-faced and looked fixedly before them. Facing me there was a Punch and Judy Show, perhaps rather larger than the ordinary ones, painted with black figures on a reddish-yellow ground. Behind it and on each side was only darkness, but in front there was a sufficiency of light. I was "strung up" to a high degree of expectation and listened every moment to hear the panpipes and the Roo-too-too-it. Instead of that there came suddenly an enormous – I can use no other word – an enormous single toll of a bell, I don't know from how far off – somewhere behind. The little curtain flew up and the drama began.

I believe someone once tried to re-write Punch as a serious tragedy; but whoever he may have been, this performance would have suited him exactly. There was something Satanic about the hero. He varied his methods of attack: for some of his victims he lay in wait, and to see his horrible face – it was yellowish white, I may remark – peering round the wings made me think of the Vampyre in Fuseli's foul sketch. To others he was polite and carneying – particularly to the unfortunate alien who can only say *Shallabalah* – though what Punch said I never could catch. But with all of them I came to dread the moment of death. The crack of the stick on their skulls, which in the ordinary way delights me, had here a crushing sound as if the bone was giving way, and the victims quivered and kicked as they lay. The baby – it sounds more ridiculous as I go on – the baby, I am sure, was alive. Punch wrung its neck, and if the choke or squeak which it gave were not real, I know nothing of reality.

The stage got perceptibly darker as each crime was consummated, and at last there was one murder which was done quite in the dark, so that I could see nothing of the victim, and took some time to effect. It was accompanied by hard breathing and horrid muffled sounds, and after it Punch came and sat on the foot-board and fanned himself and looked at his shoes, which were bloody, and hung his head on one side, and sniggered in so deadly a fashion that I saw some of those beside me cover their faces, and I would gladly have done the same. But in the meantime the scene behind Punch was clearing, and showed, not the usual house front, but something more ambitious – a grove of trees and the gentle slope of a hill, with a very natural – in fact, I should say a real – moon shining on it. Over this there rose slowly an object which I soon perceived to be a human figure with something peculiar about the head – what, I was unable at first to see. It did not stand on its feet, but began creeping or dragging itself across the middle distance towards Punch, who still sat back to it; and by this time, I may remark (though it did not occur to me at the moment) that all pretence of this being a puppet show had vanished. Punch was still Punch, it is true, but, like the others, was in some sense a live creature, and both moved themselves at their own will.

When I next glanced at him he was sitting in malignant reflection; but in another instant something seemed to attract his attention, and he first sat up sharply and then turned round, and evidently caught sight of the person that was approaching him and was in fact now very near. Then, indeed, did he show unmistakable signs of terror: catching up his stick, he rushed towards the wood, only just eluding the arm of his pursuer, which was suddenly flung out to intercept him. It was with a revulsion which I cannot easily express that I now saw more or less clearly what this pursuer was like. He was a sturdy figure clad in black, and, as I thought, wearing bands: his head was covered with a whitish bag.

The chase which now began lasted I do not know how long, now among the trees, now along the slope of the field, sometimes both figures disappearing wholly for a few seconds, and only some uncertain sounds letting one know that they were still afoot. At length there came a moment when Punch, evidently exhausted, staggered in from the left and threw himself down among the trees. His pursuer was not long after him, and came looking uncertainly from side to side. Then, catching sight of the figure on the ground, he too threw himself down – his back was turned to the audience – with a swift motion twitched the covering from his head, and thrust his face into that of Punch. Everything on the instant grew dark.

There was one long, loud, shuddering scream, and I awoke to find myself looking straight into the face of – what in all the world do you think? – but a large owl, which was seated on my window-sill immediately opposite my bed-foot, holding up its wings like two shrouded arms. I caught the fierce glance of its yellow eyes, and then it was gone. I heard the single enormous bell again – very likely, as you are saying to yourself, the church clock; but I do not think so – and then I was broad awake.

All this, I may say, happened within the last half-hour. There was no probability of my getting to sleep again, so I got up, put on clothes enough to keep me warm, and am writing this rigmarole in the first hours of Christmas Day. Have I left out anything? Yes, there was no Toby dog, and the names over the front of the Punch and Judy booth were Kidman and Gallop, which were certainly not what the bagman told me to look out for.

By this time, I feel a little more as if I could sleep, so this shall be sealed and wafered.

Letter IV

Dec. 26, '37.

My Dear Robert, – All is over. The body has been found. I do not make excuses for not having sent off my news by last night's mail, for the simple reason that I was incapable of putting pen to paper. The events that attended the discovery bewildered me so completely that I needed what I could get of a night's rest to enable me to face the situation at all. Now I can give you my journal of the day, certainly the strangest Christmas Day that ever I spent or am likely to spend.

The first incident was not very serious. Mr. Bowman had, I think, been keeping Christmas Eve, and was a little inclined to be captious: at least, he was not on foot very early, and to judge from what I could hear, neither men or maids could do anything to please him. The latter were certainly reduced to tears; nor am I sure that Mr. Bowman succeeded in preserving a manly composure. At any rate, when I came downstairs, it was in a broken voice that he wished me the compliments of the season, and a little later on, when he paid his visit of ceremony at breakfast, he was far from cheerful: even Byronic, I might almost say, in his outlook on life.

"I don't know," he said, "if you think with me, sir; but every Christmas as comes round the world seems a hollerer thing to me. Why, take an example now from what lays under my own eye. There's my servant Eliza – been with me now for going on fifteen years. I thought I could have placed my confidence in Elizar, and yet this very morning – Christmas morning too, of all the blessed days in the year – with the bells a ringing and – and – all like that – I say, this very morning, had it not have been for Providence watching over us all, that girl would have put – indeed I may go so far as to say, 'ad put the cheese on your breakfast table—" He saw I was about to speak, and waved his hand at me. "It's all very well for you to say, 'Yes, Mr. Bowman, but you took away the cheese and locked it up in the cupboard,' which I did, and have the key here, or if not the actual key one very much about the same size. That's true enough, sir, but what do you think is the effect of that action on me? Why it's no exaggeration for me to say that the ground is cut from under my feet. And yet when I said as much to Eliza, not nasty, mind you, but just firm like, what was my return? 'Oh,' she says: 'Well,' she says, 'there wasn't no bones broke, I suppose.' Well, sir, it 'urt me, that's all I can say: it 'urt me, and I don't like to think of it now."

There was an ominous pause here, in which I ventured to say something like, "Yes, very trying," and then asked at what hour the church service was to be. "Eleven o'clock," Mr. Bowman said with a heavy sigh. "Ah, you won't have no such discourse from poor Mr. Lucas as what you would have done from our late Rector. Him and me may have had our little differences, and did do, more's the pity."

I could see that a powerful effort was needed to keep him off the vexed question of the cask of beer, but he made it. "But I will say this, that a better preacher, nor yet one to stand faster by his rights, or what he considered to be his rights – however, that's not the question now – I for one, never set under. Some might say, 'Was he a eloquent man?' and to that my answer would be: 'Well, there you've a better right per'aps to speak of your own uncle than what I have.' Others might ask, 'Did he keep a hold of his congregation?' and there again I should reply, 'That depends.' But as I say – Yes, Eliza, my girl, I'm coming – eleven o'clock, sir, and you inquire for the King's Head pew."

I believe Eliza had been very near the door, and shall consider it in my vail.

The next episode was church: I felt Mr. Lucas had a difficult task in doing justice to Christmas sentiments, and also to the feeling of disquiet and regret which, whatever Mr. Bowman might say, was clearly prevalent. I do not think he rose to the occasion. I was uncomfortable. The organ evolved – you know what I mean: the wind died – twice in the Christmas Hymn, and the tenor bell, I suppose owing to some negligence on the part of the ringers, kept sounding faintly about once in a minute during the sermon. The clerk sent up a man to see to it, but he seemed unable to do much. I was glad when it was over. There was an odd incident, too, before the service. I went in rather early, and came upon two men carrying the parish bier back to its place under the tower. From what I overheard them saying, it appeared that it had been put out by mistake, by some one who was not there. I also saw the clerk busy folding up a moth-eaten velvet pall – not a sight for Christmas Day.

I dined soon after this, and then, feeling disinclined to go out, took my seat by the fire in the parlour, with the last number of *Pickwick*, which I had been saving up for some days. I thought I could be sure of keeping awake over this, but I turned out as bad as our friend Smith. I suppose it was half-past two when I was roused by a piercing whistle and laughing and talking voices outside in the market-place. It was a Punch and Judy – I had no doubt the one that my bagman had seen at W——. I was half delighted, half not – the latter because my unpleasant dream came back to me so vividly; but, anyhow, I determined to see it through, and I sent Eliza out with a crown-piece to the performers and a request that they would face my window if they could manage it.

The show was a very smart new one; the names of the proprietors, I need hardly tell you, were Italian, Foresta and Calpigi. The Toby dog was there, as I had been led to expect. All B—— turned out, but did not obstruct my view, for I was at the large first-floor window and not ten yards away.

The play began on the stroke of a quarter to three by the church clock. Certainly it was very good; and I was soon relieved to find that the disgust my dream had given me for Punch's onslaughts on his ill-starred visitors was only transient. I laughed at the demise of the Turncock, the Foreigner, the Beadle, and even the baby. The only drawback was the Toby dog's developing a tendency to howl in the wrong place. Something had occurred, I suppose, to upset him, and something considerable: for, I forget exactly at what point, he gave a most lamentable cry, leapt off the foot board, and shot away across the market-place and down a side street. There was a stage-wait, but only a brief one. I suppose the men decided that it was no good going after him, and that he was likely to turn up again at night.

We went on. Punch dealt faithfully with Judy, and in fact with all comers; and then came the moment when the gallows was erected, and the great scene with Mr. Ketch was to be enacted. It was now that something happened of which I can certainly not yet see the import fully. You have witnessed an execution, and know what the criminal's head looks like with the cap on. If you are like me, you never wish to think of it again, and I do not willingly remind you of it. It was just such a head as that, that I, from my somewhat higher post, saw in the inside of the show-box; but at first the audience did not see it. I expected it to emerge into their view, but instead of that there slowly rose for a few seconds an uncovered face, with an expression of terror upon it, of which I have never imagined the like. It seemed as if the man, whoever he was, was being forcibly lifted, with his arms somehow pinioned or held back, towards the little gibbet on the stage. I could just see the nightcapped head behind him. Then there was a cry and a crash. The whole show-box fell over backwards; kicking legs were seen among the ruins, and then two figures – as some said; can only answer for one – were visible running at top speed across the square and disappearing in a lane which leads to the fields.

Of course everybody gave chase. I followed; but the pace was killing, and very few were in literally, at the death. It happened in a chalk pit: the man went over the edge quite blindly and broke his neck. They searched everywhere for the other, until it occurred to me to ask whether he had ever left the market-place. At first everyone was sure that he had; but when we came to look he was there, under the show-box, dead too.

But in the chalk pit it was that poor Uncle Henry's body was found, with a sack over the head, the throat horribly mangled. It was a peaked corner of the sack sticking out of the soil that attracted attention. I cannot bring myself to write in greater detail.

I forgot to say the men's real names were Kidman and Gallop. I feel sure I have heard them, but no one here seems to know anything about them.

I am coming to you as soon as I can after the funeral. I must tell you when we meet what think of it all.

Told After Supper

Jerome K. Jerome

Introductory

IT WAS CHRISTMAS EVE.

I begin this way because it is the proper, orthodox, respectable way to begin, and I have been brought up in a proper, orthodox, respectable way, and taught to always do the proper, orthodox, respectable thing; and the habit clings to me.

Of course, as a mere matter of information it is quite unnecessary to mention the date at all. The experienced reader knows it was Christmas Eve, without my telling him. It always is Christmas Eve, in a ghost story,

Christmas Eve is the ghosts' great gala night. On Christmas Eve they hold their annual fete. On Christmas Eve everybody in Ghostland who IS anybody – or rather, speaking of ghosts, one should say, I suppose, every nobody who IS any nobody – comes out to show himself or herself, to see and to be seen, to promenade about and display their winding-sheets and grave-clothes to each other, to criticise one another's style, and sneer at one another's complexion.

"Christmas Eve parade," as I expect they themselves term it, is a function, doubtless, eagerly prepared for and looked forward to throughout Ghostland, especially the swagger set, such as the murdered Barons, the crime-stained Countesses, and the Earls who came over with the Conqueror, and assassinated their relatives, and died raving mad.

Hollow moans and fiendish grins are, one may be sure, energetically practised up. Blood-curdling shrieks and marrow-freezing gestures are probably rehearsed for weeks beforehand. Rusty chains and gory daggers are over-hauled, and put into good working order; and sheets and shrouds, laid carefully by from the previous year's show, are taken down and shaken out, and mended, and aired.

Oh, it is a stirring night in Ghostland, the night of December the twenty-fourth!

Ghosts never come out on Christmas night itself, you may have noticed. Christmas Eve, we suspect, has been too much for them; they are not used to excitement. For about a week after Christmas Eve, the gentlemen ghosts, no doubt, feel as if they were all head, and go about making solemn resolutions to themselves that they will stop in next Christmas Eve; while lady spectres are contradictory and snappish, and liable to burst into tears and leave the room hurriedly on being spoken to, for no perceptible cause whatever.

Ghosts with no position to maintain – mere middle-class ghosts – occasionally, I believe, do a little haunting on off-nights: on All-hallows Eve, and at Midsummer; and some will even run up for a mere local event – to celebrate, for instance, the anniversary of the hanging of somebody's grandfather, or to prophesy a misfortune.

He does love prophesying a misfortune, does the average British ghost. Send him out to prognosticate trouble to somebody, and he is happy. Let him force his way into a peaceful home, and turn the whole house upside down by foretelling a funeral, or predicting a bankruptcy, or hinting at a coming disgrace, or some other terrible disaster, about which nobody in their senses would want to know sooner than they could possibly help, and the prior knowledge of which can serve no useful purpose whatsoever, and he feels that he is combining duty with pleasure. He would never forgive himself if anybody in his family had a trouble and he had not been there for a couple of months beforehand, doing silly tricks on the lawn, or balancing himself on somebody's bed-rail.

Then there are, besides, the very young, or very conscientious ghosts with a lost will or an undiscovered number weighing heavy on their minds, who will haunt steadily all the year round; and also the fussy ghost, who is indignant at having been buried in the dust-bin or in the village pond, and who never gives the parish a single night's quiet until somebody has paid for a first-class funeral for him.

But these are the exceptions. As I have said, the average orthodox ghost does his one turn a year, on Christmas Eve, and is satisfied.

Why on Christmas Eve, of all nights in the year, I never could myself understand. It is invariably one of the most dismal of nights to be out in – cold, muddy, and wet. And besides, at Christmas time, everybody has quite enough to put up with in the way of a houseful of living relations, without wanting the ghosts of any dead ones mooning about the place, I am sure.

There must be something ghostly in the air of Christmas – something about the close, muggy atmosphere that draws up the ghosts, like the dampness of the summer rains brings out the frogs and snails.

And not only do the ghosts themselves always walk on Christmas Eve, but live people always sit and talk about them on Christmas Eve. Whenever five or six English-speaking people meet round a fire on Christmas Eve, they start telling each other ghost stories. Nothing satisfies us on Christmas Eve but to hear each other tell authentic anecdotes about spectres. It is a genial, festive season, and we love to muse upon graves, and dead bodies, and murders, and blood.

There is a good deal of similarity about our ghostly experiences; but this of course is not our fault but the fault of ghosts, who never will try any new performances, but always will keep steadily to old, safe business. The consequence is that, when you have been at one Christmas Eve party, and heard six people relate their adventures with spirits, you do not require to hear any more ghost stories. To listen to any further ghost stories after that would be like sitting out two farcical comedies, or taking in two comic journals; the repetition would become wearisome.

There is always the young man who was, one year, spending the Christmas at a country house, and, on Christmas Eve, they put him to sleep in the west wing. Then in the middle of the night, the room door quietly opens and somebody – generally a lady in her night-dress – walks slowly in, and comes and sits on the bed. The young man thinks it must be one of the visitors, or some relative of the family, though he does not remember having previously seen her, who, unable to go to sleep, and feeling lonesome, all by herself, has come into his room for a chat. He has no idea it is a ghost: he is so unsuspicious. She does not speak, however; and, when he looks again, she is gone!

The young man relates the circumstance at the breakfast-table next morning, and asks each of the ladies present if it were she who was his visitor. But they all assure him that it was not, and the host, who has grown deadly pale, begs him to say no more about the matter, which strikes the young man as a singularly strange request.

After breakfast the host takes the young man into a corner, and explains to him that what he saw was the ghost of a lady who had been murdered in that very bed, or who had murdered somebody else there – it does not really matter which: you can be a ghost by murdering somebody else or by being murdered yourself, whichever you prefer. The murdered ghost is, perhaps, the more popular; but, on the other hand, you can frighten people better if you are the murdered one, because then you can show your wounds and do groans.

Then there is the sceptical guest – it is always 'the guest' who gets let in for this sort of thing, by-the-bye. A ghost never thinks much of his own family: it is 'the guest' he likes to haunt who after listening to the host's ghost story, on Christmas Eve, laughs at it, and says that he does not believe there are such things as ghosts at all; and that he will sleep in the haunted chamber that very night, if they will let him.

Everybody urges him not to be reckless, but he persists in his foolhardiness, and goes up to the Yellow Chamber (or whatever colour the haunted room may be) with a light heart and a candle, and wishes them all good-night, and shuts the door.

Next morning he has got snow-white hair.

He does not tell anybody what he has seen: it is too awful.

There is also the plucky guest, who sees a ghost, and knows it is a ghost, and watches it, as it comes into the room and disappears through the wainscot, after which, as the ghost does not seem to be coming back, and there is nothing, consequently, to be gained by stopping awake, he goes to sleep.

He does not mention having seen the ghost to anybody, for fear of frightening them – some people are so nervous about ghosts, – but determines to wait for the next night, and see if the apparition appears again.

It does appear again, and, this time, he gets out of bed, dresses himself and does his hair, and follows it; and then discovers a secret passage leading from the bedroom down into the beer-cellar,- -a passage which, no doubt, was not unfrequently made use of in the bad old days of yore.

After him comes the young man who woke up with a strange sensation in the middle of the night, and found his rich bachelor uncle standing by his bedside. The rich uncle smiled a weird sort of smile and vanished. The young man immediately got up and looked at his watch. It had stopped at half-past four, he having forgotten to wind it.

He made inquiries the next day, and found that, strangely enough, his rich uncle, whose only nephew he was, had married a widow with eleven children at exactly a quarter to twelve, only two days ago,

The young man does not attempt to explain the circumstance. All he does is to vouch for the truth of his narrative.

And, to mention another case, there is the gentleman who is returning home late at night, from a Freemasons' dinner, and who, noticing a light issuing from a ruined abbey, creeps up, and looks through the keyhole. He sees the ghost of a 'grey sister' kissing the ghost of a brown monk, and is so inexpressibly shocked and frightened that he faints on the spot, and is discovered there the next morning, lying in a heap against the door, still speechless, and with his faithful latch-key clasped tightly in his hand.

All these things happen on Christmas Eve, they are all told of on Christmas Eve. For ghost stories to be told on any other evening than the evening of the twenty-fourth of December would be impossible in English society as at present regulated. Therefore, in introducing the sad but authentic ghost stories that follow hereafter, I feel that it is unnecessary to inform the student of Anglo-Saxon literature that the date on which they were told and on which the incidents took place was – Christmas Eve.

Nevertheless, I do so.

Now The Stories Came To Be Told

It was Christmas Eve! Christmas Eve at my Uncle John's; Christmas Eve (There is too much 'Christmas Eve' about this book. I can see that myself. It is beginning to get monotonous even to me. But I don't see how to avoid it now.) at No. 47 Laburnham Grove, Tooting! Christmas Eve in the dimly-lighted (there was a gas-strike on) front parlour, where the flickering fire-light threw strange shadows on the highly coloured wall-paper, while without, in the wild street, the storm raged pitilessly, and the wind, like some unquiet spirit, flew, moaning, across the square, and passed, wailing with a troubled cry, round by the milk-shop.

We had had supper, and were sitting round, talking and smoking.

We had had a very good supper – a very good supper, indeed. Unpleasantness has occurred since, in our family, in connection with this party. Rumours have been put about in our family, concerning the matter generally, but more particularly concerning my own share in it, and remarks have been passed which have not so much surprised me, because I know what our family are, but which have pained me very much. As for my Aunt Maria, I do not know when I shall care to see her again. I should have thought Aunt Maria might have known me better.

But although injustice – gross injustice, as I shall explain later on – has been done to myself, that shall not deter me from doing justice to others; even to those who have made unfeeling insinuations. I will do justice to Aunt Maria's hot veal pasties, and toasted lobsters, followed by her own special make of cheesecakes, warm (there is no sense, to my thinking, in cold cheesecakes; you lose half the flavour), and washed down by Uncle John's own particular old ale, and acknowledge that they were most tasty. I did justice to them then; Aunt Maria herself could not but admit that.

After supper, Uncle brewed some whisky-punch. I did justice to that also; Uncle John himself said so. He said he was glad to notice that I liked it.

Aunt went to bed soon after supper, leaving the local curate, old Dr. Scrubbles, Mr. Samuel Coombes, our member of the County Council, Teddy Biffles, and myself to keep Uncle company. We agreed that it was too early to give in for some time yet, so Uncle brewed another bowl of punch; and I think we all did justice to that – at least I know I did. It is a passion with me, is the desire to do justice.

We sat up for a long while, and the Doctor brewed some gin-punch later on, for a change, though I could not taste much difference myself. But it was all good, and we were very happy – everybody was so kind.

Uncle John told us a very funny story in the course of the evening. Oh, it WAS a funny story! I forget what it was about now, but I know it amused me very much at the time; I do not think I ever laughed so much in all my life. It is strange that I cannot recollect that story too, because he told it us four times. And it was entirely our own fault that he did not tell it us a fifth. After that, the Doctor sang a very clever song, in the course of which he imitated all the different animals in a farmyard. He did mix them a bit. He brayed for the bantam cock, and crowed for the pig; but we knew what he meant all right.

I started relating a most interesting anecdote, but was somewhat surprised to observe, as I went on, that nobody was paying the slightest attention to me whatever. I thought this rather rude of them at first, until it dawned upon me that I was talking to myself all the time, instead of out aloud, so that, of course, they did not know that I was telling them a tale at all, and were probably puzzled to understand the meaning of my animated expression and eloquent gestures. It was a most curious mistake for any one to make. I never knew such a thing happen to me before.

Later on, our curate did tricks with cards. He asked us if we had ever seen a game called the "Three Card Trick." He said it was an artifice by means of which low, unscrupulous men, frequenters of race-meetings and such like haunts, swindled foolish young fellows out of their money. He said it was a very simple trick to do: it all depended on the quickness of the hand. It was the quickness of the hand deceived the eye.

He said he would show us the imposture so that we might be warned against it, and not be taken in by it; and he fetched Uncle's pack of cards from the tea-caddy, and, selecting three cards from the pack, two plain cards and one picture card, sat down on the hearthrug, and explained to us what he was going to do.

He said: "Now I shall take these three cards in my hand – so – and let you all see them. And then I shall quietly lay them down on the rug, with the backs uppermost, and ask you to pick out the picture card. And you'll think you know which one it is." And he did it.

Old Mr. Coombes, who is also one of our churchwardens, said it was the middle card.

"You fancy you saw it," said our curate, smiling.

"I don't 'fancy' anything at all about it," replied Mr. Coombes, "I tell you it's the middle card. I'll bet you half a dollar it's the middle card."

"There you are, that's just what I was explaining to you," said our curate, turning to the rest of us; "that's the way these foolish young fellows that I was speaking of are lured on to lose their money. They make sure they know the card, they fancy they saw it. They don't grasp the idea that it is the quickness of the hand that has deceived their eye."

He said he had known young men go off to a boat race, or a cricket match, with pounds in their pocket, and come home, early in the afternoon, stone broke; having lost all their money at this demoralising game.

He said he should take Mr. Coombes's half-crown, because it would teach Mr. Coombes a very useful lesson, and probably be the means of saving Mr. Coombes's money in the future; and he should give the two-and-sixpence to the blanket fund.

"Don't you worry about that," retorted old Mr. Coombes. "Don't you take the half-crown OUT of the blanket fund: that's all."

And he put his money on the middle card, and turned it up.

Sure enough, it really was the queen!

We were all very much surprised, especially the curate.

He said that it did sometimes happen that way, though – that a man did sometimes lay on the right card, by accident.

Our curate said it was, however, the most unfortunate thing a man could do for himself, if he only knew it, because, when a man tried and won, it gave him a taste for the so-called sport, and it lured him on into risking again and again; until he had to retire from the contest, a broken and ruined man.

Then he did the trick again. Mr. Coombes said it was the card next the coal-scuttle this time, and wanted to put five shillings on it.

We laughed at him, and tried to persuade him against it. He would listen to no advice, however, but insisted on plunging.

Our curate said very well then: he had warned him, and that was all that he could do. If he (Mr. Coombes) was determined to make a fool of himself, he (Mr. Coombes) must do so.

Our curate said he should take the five shillings and that would put things right again with the blanket fund.

So Mr. Coombes put two half-crowns on the card next the coal-scuttle and turned it up.

Sure enough, it was the queen again!

After that, Uncle John had a florin on, and HE won.

And then we all played at it; and we all won. All except the curate, that is. He had a very bad quarter of an hour. I never knew a man have such hard luck at cards. He lost every time.

We had some more punch after that; and Uncle made such a funny mistake in brewing it: he left out the whisky. Oh, we did laugh at him, and we made him put in double quantity afterwards, as a forfeit.

Oh, we did have such fun that evening!

And then, somehow or other, we must have got on to ghosts; because the next recollection I have is that we were telling ghost stories to each other.

Teddy Biffles' Story

Teddy Biffles told the first story, I will let him repeat it here in his own words.

(Do not ask me how it is that I recollect his own exact words – whether I took them down in shorthand at the time, or whether he had the story written out, and handed me the MS. afterwards for publication in this book, because I should not tell you if you did. It is a trade secret.)

Biffles called his story –

Johnson And Emily, or The Faithful Ghost
(Teddy Biffles' Story)

I was little more than a lad when I first met with Johnson. I was home for the Christmas holidays, and, it being Christmas Eve, I had been allowed to sit up very late. On opening the door of my little bedroom, to go in, I found myself face to face with Johnson, who was coming out. It passed through me, and uttering a long low wail of misery, disappeared out of the staircase window.

I was startled for the moment – I was only a schoolboy at the time, and had never seen a ghost before, – and felt a little nervous about going to bed. But, on reflection, I remembered that it was only sinful people that spirits could do any harm to, and so tucked myself up, and went to sleep.

In the morning I told the Pater what I had seen.

"Oh yes, that was old Johnson," he answered. "Don't you be frightened of that; he lives here." And then he told me the poor thing's history.

It seemed that Johnson, when it was alive, had loved, in early life, the daughter of a former lessee of our house, a very beautiful girl, whose Christian name had been Emily. Father did not know her other name.

Johnson was too poor to marry the girl, so he kissed her good-bye, told her he would soon be back, and went off to Australia to make his fortune.

But Australia was not then what it became later on. Travellers through the bush were few and far between in those early days; and, even when one was caught, the portable property found upon the body was often of hardly sufficiently negotiable value to pay the simple funeral expenses rendered necessary. So that it took Johnson nearly twenty years to make his fortune.

The self-imposed task was accomplished at last, however, and then, having successfully eluded the police, and got clear out of the Colony, he returned to England, full of hope and joy, to claim his bride.

He reached the house to find it silent and deserted. All that the neighbours could tell him was that, soon after his own departure, the family had, on one foggy night, unostentatiously disappeared, and that nobody had ever seen or heard anything of them since, although the landlord and most of the local tradesmen had made searching inquiries.

Poor Johnson, frenzied with grief, sought his lost love all over the world. But he never found her, and, after years of fruitless effort, he returned to end his lonely life in the very house where, in the happy bygone days, he and his beloved Emily had passed so many blissful hours.

He had lived there quite alone, wandering about the empty rooms, weeping and calling to his Emily to come back to him; and when the poor old fellow died, his ghost still kept the business on.

It was there, the Pater said, when he took the house, and the agent had knocked ten pounds a year off the rent in consequence.

After that, I was continually meeting Johnson about the place at all times of the night, and so, indeed, were we all. We used to walk round it and stand aside to let it pass, at first; but, when we grew at home with it, and there seemed no necessity for so much ceremony, we used to walk straight through it. You could not say it was ever much in the way.

It was a gentle, harmless, old ghost, too, and we all felt very sorry for it, and pitied it. The women folk, indeed, made quite a pet of it, for a while. Its faithfulness touched them so.

But as time went on, it grew to be a bit of a bore. You see it was full of sadness. There was nothing cheerful or genial about it. You felt sorry for it, but it irritated you. It would sit on the stairs and cry for hours at a stretch; and, whenever we woke up in the night, one was sure to hear it pottering about the passages and in and out of the different rooms, moaning and sighing, so that we could not get to sleep again very easily. And when we had a party on, it would come and sit outside the drawing-room door, and sob all the time. It did not do anybody any harm exactly, but it cast a gloom over the whole affair.

"Oh, I'm getting sick of this old fool," said the Pater, one evening (the Dad can be very blunt, when he is put out, as you know), after Johnson had been more of a nuisance than usual, and had spoiled a good game of whist, by sitting up the chimney and groaning, till nobody knew what were trumps or what suit had been led, even. "We shall have to get rid of him, somehow or other. I wish I knew how to do it."

"Well," said the Mater, "depend upon it, you'll never see the last of him until he's found Emily's grave. That's what he is after. You find Emily's grave, and put him on to that, and he'll stop there. That's the only thing to do. You mark my words."

The idea seemed reasonable, but the difficulty in the way was that we none of us knew where Emily's grave was any more than the ghost of Johnson himself did. The Governor suggested palming off some other Emily's grave upon the poor thing, but, as luck would have it, there did not seem to have been an Emily of any sort buried anywhere for miles round. I never came across a neighbourhood so utterly destitute of dead Emilies.

I thought for a bit, and then I hazarded a suggestion myself.

"Couldn't we fake up something for the old chap?" I queried. "He seems a simple-minded old sort. He might take it in. Anyhow, we could but try."

"By Jove, so we will," exclaimed my father; and the very next morning we had the workmen in, and fixed up a little mound at the bottom of the orchard with a tombstone over it, bearing the following inscription:-

SACRED TO THE MEMORY OF EMILY HER LAST WORDS
WERE – "TELL JOHNSON I LOVE HIM"

"That ought to fetch him," mused the Dad as he surveyed the work when finished. "I am sure I hope it does."

It did!

We lured him down there that very night; and – well, there, it was one of the most pathetic things I have ever seen, the way Johnson sprang upon that tombstone and wept. Dad and old Squibbins, the gardener, cried like children when they saw it.

Johnson has never troubled us any more in the house since then. It spends every night now, sobbing on the grave, and seems quite happy.

"There still?" Oh yes. I'll take you fellows down and show you it, next time you come to our place: 10 p.m. to 4 a.m. are its general hours, 10 to 2 on Saturdays.

Interlude – The Doctor's Story

It made me cry very much, that story, young Biffles told it with so much feeling. We were all a little thoughtful after it, and I noticed even the old Doctor covertly wipe away a tear. Uncle John brewed another bowl of punch, however, and we gradually grew more resigned.

The Doctor, indeed, after a while became almost cheerful, and told us about the ghost of one of his patients.

I cannot give you his story. I wish I could. They all said afterwards that it was the best of the lot – the most ghastly and terrible – but I could not make any sense of it myself. It seemed so incomplete.

He began all right and then something seemed to happen, and then he was finishing it. I cannot make out what he did with the middle of the story.

It ended up, I know, however, with somebody finding something; and that put Mr. Coombes in mind of a very curious affair that took place at an old Mill, once kept by his brother-in-law.

Mr. Coombes said he would tell us his story, and before anybody could stop him, he had begun.

Mr Coombes said the story was called –

The Haunted Mill, or The Ruined Home
(Mr. Coombes's Story)

Well, you all know my brother-in-law, Mr. Parkins (began Mr. Coombes, taking the long clay pipe from his mouth, and putting it behind his ear: we did not know his brother-in-law, but we said we did, so as to save time), and you know of course that he once took a lease of an old Mill in Surrey, and went to live there.

Now you must know that, years ago, this very mill had been occupied by a wicked old miser, who died there, leaving – so it was rumoured- -all his money hidden somewhere about the place. Naturally enough, every one who had since come to live at the mill had tried to find the treasure; but none had ever succeeded, and the local wiseacres said that nobody ever would, unless the ghost of the miserly miller should, one day, take a fancy to one of the tenants, and disclose to him the secret of the hiding-place.

My brother-in-law did not attach much importance to the story, regarding it as an old woman's tale, and, unlike his predecessors, made no attempt whatever to discover the hidden gold.

"Unless business was very different then from what it is now," said my brother-in-law, "I don't see how a miller could very well have saved anything, however much of a miser he might have been: at all events, not enough to make it worth the trouble of looking for it."

Still, he could not altogether get rid of the idea of that treasure.

One night he went to bed. There was nothing very extraordinary about that, I admit. He often did go to bed of a night. What WAS remarkable, however, was that exactly as the clock of the village church chimed the last stroke of twelve, my brother-in-law woke up with a start, and felt himself quite unable to go to sleep again.

Joe (his Christian name was Joe) sat up in bed, and looked around.

At the foot of the bed something stood very still, wrapped in shadow.

It moved into the moonlight, and then my brother-in-law saw that it was the figure of a wizened little old man, in knee-breeches and a pig-tail.

In an instant the story of the hidden treasure and the old miser flashed across his mind.

"He's come to show me where it's hid," thought my brother-in-law; and he resolved that he would not spend all this money on himself, but would devote a small percentage of it towards doing good to others.

The apparition moved towards the door: my brother-in-law put on his trousers and followed it. The ghost went downstairs into the kitchen, glided over and stood in front of the hearth, sighed and disappeared.

Next morning, Joe had a couple of bricklayers in, and made them haul out the stove and pull down the chimney, while he stood behind with a potato-sack in which to put the gold.

They knocked down half the wall, and never found so much as a four- penny bit. My brother-in-law did not know what to think.

The next night the old man appeared again, and again led the way into the kitchen. This time, however, instead of going to the fireplace, it stood more in the middle of the room, and sighed there.

"Oh, I see what he means now," said my brother-in-law to himself; "it's under the floor. Why did the old idiot go and stand up against the stove, so as to make me think it was up the chimney?"

They spent the next day in taking up the kitchen floor; but the only thing they found was a three-pronged fork, and the handle of that was broken.

On the third night, the ghost reappeared, quite unabashed, and for a third time made for the kitchen. Arrived there, it looked up at the ceiling and vanished.

"Umph! he don't seem to have learned much sense where he's been to," muttered Joe, as he trotted back to bed; "I should have thought he might have done that at first."

Still, there seemed no doubt now where the treasure lay, and the first thing after breakfast they started pulling down the ceiling. They got every inch of the ceiling down, and they took up the boards of the room above.

They discovered about as much treasure as you would expect to find in an empty quart-pot.

On the fourth night, when the ghost appeared, as usual, my brother- in-law was so wild that he threw his boots at it; and the boots passed through the body, and broke a looking-glass.

On the fifth night, when Joe awoke, as he always did now at twelve, the ghost was standing in a dejected attitude, looking very miserable. There was an appealing look in its large sad eyes that quite touched my brother-in-law.

"After all," he thought, "perhaps the silly chap's doing his best. Maybe he has forgotten where he really did put it, and is trying to remember. I'll give him another chance."

The ghost appeared grateful and delighted at seeing Joe prepare to follow him, and led the way into the attic, pointed to the ceiling, and vanished.

"Well, he's hit it this time, I do hope," said my brother-in-law; and next day they set to work to take the roof off the place.

It took them three days to get the roof thoroughly off, and all they found was a bird's nest; after securing which they covered up the house with tarpaulins, to keep it dry.

You might have thought that would have cured the poor fellow of looking for treasure. But it didn't.

He said there must be something in it all, or the ghost would never keep on coming as it did; and that, having gone so far, he would go on to the end, and solve the mystery, cost what it might.

Night after night, he would get out of his bed and follow that spectral old fraud about the house. Each night, the old man would indicate a different place; and, on each following day, my brother- in-law would proceed to break up the mill at the point indicated, and look for the treasure. At the end of three weeks, there was not a room in the mill fit to live in. Every wall had been pulled down, every floor had been taken up, every ceiling had had a hole knocked in it. And then, as suddenly as they had begun, the ghost's visits ceased; and my brother-in-law was left in peace, to rebuild the place at his leisure.

"What induced the old image to play such a silly trick upon a family man and a ratepayer?" Ah! that's just what I cannot tell you.

Some said that the ghost of the wicked old man had done it to punish my brother-in-law for not believing in him at first; while others held that the apparition was probably that of some deceased local plumber and glazier, who would naturally take an interest in seeing a house knocked about and spoilt. But nobody knew anything for certain.

Interlude

We had some more punch, and then the curate told us a story.

I could not make head or tail of the curate's story, so I cannot retail it to you. We none of us could make head or tail of that story. It was a good story enough, so far as material went. There seemed to be an enormous amount of plot, and enough incident to have made a dozen novels. I never before heard a story containing so much incident, nor one dealing with so many varied characters.

I should say that every human being our curate had ever known or met, or heard of, was brought into that story. There were simply hundreds of them. Every five seconds he would introduce into the tale a completely fresh collection of characters accompanied by a brand new set of incidents.

This was the sort of story it was:-

"Well, then, my uncle went into the garden, and got his gun, but, of course, it wasn't there, and Scroggins said he didn't believe it."

"Didn't believe what? Who's Scroggins?"

"Scroggins! Oh, why he was the other man, you know – it was his wife."

"WHAT was his wife – what's SHE got to do with it?"

"Why, that's what I'm telling you. It was she that found the hat. She'd come up with her cousin to London – her cousin was my sister- in-law, and the other niece had married a man named Evans, and Evans, after it was all over, had taken the box round to Mr. Jacobs', because Jacobs' father had seen the man, when he was alive, and when he was dead, Joseph—"

"Now look here, never you mind Evans and the box; what's become of your uncle and the gun?"

"The gun! What gun?"

"Why, the gun that your uncle used to keep in the garden, and that wasn't there. What did he do with it? Did he kill any of these people with it – these Jacobses and Evanses and Scrogginses and Josephses? Because, if so, it was a good and useful work, and we should enjoy hearing about it."

"No – oh no – how could he? – he had been built up alive in the wall, you know, and when Edward IV spoke to the abbot about it, my sister said that in her then state of health she could not and would not, as it was endangering the child's life. So they christened it Horatio, after her own son, who had been killed at Waterloo before he was born, and Lord Napier himself said—"

"Look here, do you know what you are talking about?" we asked him at this point.

He said "No," but he knew it was every word of it true, because his aunt had seen it herself. Whereupon we covered him over with the tablecloth, and he went to sleep.

And then Uncle told us a story.

Uncle said his was a real story.

The Ghost Of The Blue Chamber
(My Uncle's Story)

"I don't want to make you fellows nervous," began my uncle in a peculiarly impressive, not to say blood-curdling, tone of voice, "and if you would rather that I did not mention it, I won't; but, as a matter of fact, this very house, in which we are now sitting, is haunted."

"You don't say that!" exclaimed Mr. Coombes.

"What's the use of your saying I don't say it when I have just said it?" retorted my uncle somewhat pettishly. "You do talk so foolishly. I tell you the house is haunted. Regularly on Christmas Eve the Blue Chamber [they called the room next to the nursery the 'blue chamber,' at my uncle's, most of the toilet service being of that shade] is haunted by the ghost of a sinful man – a man who once killed a Christmas wait with a lump of coal."

"How did he do it?" asked Mr. Coombes, with eager anxiousness. "Was it difficult?"

"I do not know how he did it," replied my uncle; "he did not explain the process. The wait had taken up a position just inside the front gate, and was singing a ballad. It is presumed that, when he opened his mouth for B flat, the lump of coal was thrown by the sinful man from one of the windows, and that it went down the wait's throat and choked him."

"You want to be a good shot, but it is certainly worth trying," murmured Mr. Coombes thoughtfully.

"But that was not his only crime, alas!" added my uncle. "Prior to that he had killed a solo cornet-player."

"No! Is that really a fact?" exclaimed Mr. Coombes.

"Of course it's a fact," answered my uncle testily; "at all events, as much a fact as you can expect to get in a case of this sort.

"How very captious you are this evening. The circumstantial evidence was overwhelming. The poor fellow, the cornet-player, had been in the neighbourhood barely a month. Old Mr. Bishop, who kept the 'Jolly Sand Boys' at the time, and from whom I had the story, said he had never known a more hard-working and energetic solo cornet-player. He, the cornet-player, only knew two tunes, but Mr. Bishop said that the man could not have played with more vigour, or for more hours in a day, if he had known forty. The two tunes he did play were "Annie Laurie" and "Home, Sweet Home"; and as regarded his performance of the former melody, Mr. Bishop said that a mere child could have told what it was meant for.

"This musician – this poor, friendless artist used to come regularly and play in this street just opposite for two hours every evening. One evening he was seen, evidently in response to an invitation, going into this very house, BUT WAS NEVER SEEN COMING OUT OF IT!"

"Did the townsfolk try offering any reward for his recovery?" asked Mr. Coombes.

"Not a ha'penny," replied my uncle.

"Another summer," continued my uncle, "a German band visited here, intending – so they announced on their arrival – to stay till the autumn.

"On the second day from their arrival, the whole company, as fine and healthy a body of men as one could wish to see, were invited to dinner by this sinful man, and, after spending the whole of the next twenty-four hours in bed, left the town a broken and dyspeptic crew; the parish doctor, who had attended them, giving it as his opinion that it was doubtful if they would, any of them, be fit to play an air again."

"You – you don't know the recipe, do you?" asked Mr. Coombes.

"Unfortunately I do not," replied my uncle; "but the chief ingredient was said to have been railway refreshment-room pork-pie.

"I forget the man's other crimes," my uncle went on; "I used to know them all at one time, but my memory is not what it was. I do not, however, believe I am doing his memory an injustice in believing that he was not entirely unconnected with the death, and subsequent burial, of a gentleman who used to play the harp with his toes; and that neither was he altogether unresponsible for the lonely grave of an unknown stranger who had once visited the neighbourhood, an Italian peasant lad, a performer upon the barrel-organ.

"Every Christmas Eve," said my uncle, cleaving with low impressive tones the strange awed silence that, like a shadow, seemed to have slowly stolen into and settled down upon the room, "the ghost of this sinful man haunts the Blue Chamber, in this very house. There, from midnight until cock-crow, amid wild muffled shrieks and groans and mocking laughter and the ghostly sound of horrid blows, it does fierce phantom fight with the spirits of the solo cornet- player and the murdered wait, assisted at intervals, by the shades of the German band; while the ghost of the strangled harpist plays mad ghostly melodies with ghostly toes on the ghost of a broken harp.

Uncle said the Blue Chamber was comparatively useless as a sleeping-apartment on Christmas Eve.

"Hark!" said uncle, raising a warning hand towards the ceiling, while we held our breath, and listened; "Hark! I believe they are at it now – in the BLUE CHAMBER!"

THE BLUE CHAMBER

I rose up, and said that I would sleep in the Blue Chamber.

Before I tell you my own story, however – the story of what happened in the Blue Chamber – I would wish to preface it with –

A Personal Explanation

I feel a good deal of hesitation about telling you this story of my own. You see it is not a story like the other stories that I have been telling you, or rather that Teddy Biffles, Mr. Coombes, and my uncle have been telling you: it is a true story. It is not a story told by a person sitting round a fire on Christmas Eve, drinking whisky punch: it is a record of events that actually happened.

Indeed, it is not a 'story' at all, in the commonly accepted meaning of the word: it is a report. It is, I feel, almost out of place in a book of this kind. It is more suitable to a biography, or an English history.

There is another thing that makes it difficult for me to tell you this story, and that is, that it is all about myself. In telling you this story, I shall have to keep on talking about myself; and talking about ourselves is what we modern-day authors have a strong objection to doing. If we literary men of the new school have one praiseworthy yearning more ever present to our minds than another it is the yearning never to appear in the slightest degree egotistical.

I myself, so I am told, carry this coyness – this shrinking reticence concerning anything connected with my own personality, almost too far; and people grumble at me because of it. People come to me and say -

"Well, now, why don't you talk about yourself a bit? That's what we want to read about. Tell us something about yourself."

But I have always replied, "No." It is not that I do not think the subject an interesting one. I cannot myself conceive of any topic more likely to prove fascinating to the world as a whole, or at all events to the cultured portion of it. But I will not do it, on principle. It is inartistic, and it sets a bad example to the younger men. Other writers (a few of them) do it, I know; but I will not – not as a rule.

Under ordinary circumstances, therefore, I should not tell you this story at all. I should say to myself, "No! It is a good story, it is a moral story, it is a strange, weird, enthralling sort of a story; and the public, I know, would like to hear it; and I should like to tell it to them; but it is all about myself – about what I said, and what I saw, and what I did, and I cannot do it. My retiring, anti-egotistical nature will not permit me to talk in this way about myself."

But the circumstances surrounding this story are not ordinary, and there are reasons prompting me, in spite of my modesty, to rather welcome the opportunity of relating it.

As I stated at the beginning, there has been unpleasantness in our family over this party of ours, and, as regards myself in particular, and my share in the events I am now about to set forth, gross injustice has been done me.

As a means of replacing my character in its proper light – of dispelling the clouds of calumny and misconception with which it has been darkened, I feel that my best course is to give a simple, dignified narration of the plain facts, and allow the unprejudiced to judge for themselves. My chief object, I candidly confess, is to clear myself from unjust aspersion. Spurred by this motive – and I think it is an honourable and a right motive – I find I am enabled to overcome my usual repugnance to talking about myself, and can thus tell –

My Own Story

As soon as my uncle had finished his story, I, as I have already told you, rose up and said that *I* would sleep in the Blue Chamber that very night.

"Never!" cried my uncle, springing up. "You shall not put yourself in this deadly peril. Besides, the bed is not made."

"Never mind the bed," I replied. "I have lived in furnished apartments for gentlemen, and have been accustomed to sleep on beds that have never been made from one year's end to the other. Do not thwart me in my resolve. I am young, and have had a clear conscience now for over a month. The spirits will not harm me. I may even do them some little good, and induce them to be quiet and go away. Besides, I should like to see the show."

Saying which, I sat down again. (How Mr. Coombes came to be in my chair, instead of at the other side of the room, where he had been all the evening; and why he never offered to apologise when I sat right down on top of him; and why young Biffles should have tried to palm himself off upon me as my Uncle John, and induced me, under that erroneous impression, to shake him by the hand for nearly three minutes, and tell him that I had always regarded him as father, – are matters that, to this day, I have never been able to fully understand.)

They tried to dissuade me from what they termed my foolhardy enterprise, but I remained firm, and claimed my privilege. I was 'the guest.' 'The guest' always sleeps in the haunted chamber on Christmas Eve; it is his perquisite.

They said that if I put it on that footing, they had, of course, no answer; and they lighted a candle for me, and accompanied me upstairs in a body.

Whether elevated by the feeling that I was doing a noble action, or animated by a mere general consciousness of rectitude, is not for me to say, but I went upstairs that night with remarkable buoyancy. It was as much as I could do to stop at the landing when I came to it; I felt I wanted to go on up to the roof. But, with the help of the banisters, I restrained my ambition, wished them all good- night, and went in and shut the door.

Things began to go wrong with me from the very first. The candle tumbled out of the candlestick before my hand was off the lock. It kept on tumbling out of the candlestick, and every time I picked put it up and put it in, it tumbled out again: I never saw such a slippery candle. I gave up attempting to use the candlestick at last, and carried the candle about in my hand; and, even then, it would not keep upright. So I got wild and threw it out of window, and undressed and went to bed in the dark.

I did not go to sleep, – I did not feel sleepy at all, – I lay on my back, looking up at the ceiling, and thinking of things. I wish I could remember some of the ideas that came to me as I lay there, because they were so amusing. I laughed at them myself till the bed shook.

I had been lying like this for half an hour or so, and had forgotten all about the ghost, when, on casually casting my eyes round the room, I noticed for the first time a singularly contented-looking phantom, sitting in the easy-chair by the fire, smoking the ghost of a long clay pipe.

I fancied for the moment, as most people would under similar circumstances, that I must be dreaming. I sat up, and rubbed my eyes.

No! It was a ghost, clear enough. I could see the back of the chair through his body. He looked over towards me, took the shadowy pipe from his lips, and nodded.

The most surprising part of the whole thing to me was that I did not feel in the least alarmed. If anything, I was rather pleased to see him. It was company.

I said, "Good evening. It's been a cold day!"

He said he had not noticed it himself, but dared say I was right.

We remained silent for a few seconds, and then, wishing to put it pleasantly, I said, "I believe I have the honour of addressing the ghost of the gentleman who had the accident with the wait?"

He smiled, and said it was very good of me to remember it. One wait was not much to boast of, but still, every little helped.

I was somewhat staggered at his answer. I had expected a groan of remorse. The ghost appeared, on the contrary, to be rather conceited over the business. I thought that, as he had taken my reference to the wait so quietly, perhaps he would not be offended if I questioned him about the organ-grinder. I felt curious about that poor boy.

"Is it true," I asked, "that you had a hand in the death of that Italian peasant lad who came to the town once with a barrel-organ that played nothing but Scotch airs?"

He quite fired up. "Had a hand in it!" he exclaimed indignantly. "Who has dared to pretend that he assisted me? I murdered the youth myself. Nobody helped me. Alone I did it. Show me the man who says I didn't."

I calmed him. I assured him that I had never, in my own mind, doubted that he was the real and only assassin, and I went on and asked him what he had done with the body of the cornet-player he had killed.

He said, "To which one may you be alluding?"

"Oh, were there any more then?" I inquired.

He smiled, and gave a little cough. He said he did not like to appear to be boasting, but that, counting trombones, there were seven.

"Dear me!" I replied, "you must have had quite a busy time of it, one way and another."

He said that perhaps he ought not to be the one to say so, but that really, speaking of ordinary middle-society, he thought there were few ghosts who could look back upon a life of more sustained usefulness.

He puffed away in silence for a few seconds, while I sat watching him. I had never seen a ghost smoking a pipe before, that I could remember, and it interested me.

I asked him what tobacco he used, and he replied, "The ghost of cut cavendish, as a rule."

He explained that the ghost of all the tobacco that a man smoked in life belonged to him when he became dead. He said he himself had smoked a good deal of cut cavendish when he was alive, so that he was well supplied with the ghost of it now.

I observed that it was a useful thing to know that, and I made up my mind to smoke as much tobacco as ever I could before I died.

I thought I might as well start at once, so I said I would join him in a pipe, and he said, "Do, old man"; and I reached over and got out the necessary paraphernalia from my coat pocket and lit up.

We grew quite chummy after that, and he told me all his crimes. He said he had lived next door once to a young lady who was learning to play the guitar, while a gentleman who practised on the bass- viol lived opposite. And he, with fiendish cunning, had introduced these two unsuspecting young people to one another, and had persuaded them to elope with each other against their parents' wishes, and take their musical instruments with them; and they had done so, and, before the honeymoon was over, SHE had broken his head with the bass-viol, and HE had tried to cram the guitar down her throat, and had injured her for life.

My friend said he used to lure muffin-men into the passage and then stuff them with their own wares till they burst and died. He said he had quieted eighteen that way.

Young men and women who recited long and dreary poems at evening parties, and callow youths who walked about the streets late at night, playing concertinas, he used to get together and poison in batches of ten, so as to save expense; and park orators and temperance lecturers he used to shut up six in a small room with a glass of water and a collection-box apiece, and let them talk each other to death.

It did one good to listen to him.

I asked him when he expected the other ghosts – the ghosts of the wait and the cornet-player, and the German band that Uncle John had mentioned. He smiled, and said they would never come again, any of them.

I said, "Why; isn't it true, then, that they meet you here every Christmas Eve for a row?"

He replied that it WAS true. Every Christmas Eve, for twenty-five years, had he and they fought in that room; but they would never trouble him nor anybody else again. One by one, had he laid them out, spoilt, and utterly useless for all haunting purposes. He had finished off the last German-band ghost that very evening, just before I came upstairs, and had thrown what was left of it out through the slit between the window-sashes. He said it would never be worth calling a ghost again.

"I suppose you will still come yourself, as usual?" I said. "They would be sorry to miss you, I know."

"Oh, I don't know," he replied; "there's nothing much to come for now. Unless," he added kindly, "YOU are going to be here. I'll come if you will sleep here next Christmas Eve."

"I have taken a liking to you," he continued; "you don't fly off, screeching, when you see a party, and your hair doesn't stand on end. You've no idea," he said, "how sick I am of seeing people's hair standing on end."

He said it irritated him.

Just then a slight noise reached us from the yard below, and he started and turned deathly black.

"You are ill," I cried, springing towards him; "tell me the best thing to do for you. Shall I drink some brandy, and give you the ghost of it?"

He remained silent, listening intently for a moment, and then he gave a sigh of relief, and the shade came back to his cheek.

"It's all right," he murmured; "I was afraid it was the cock."

"Oh, it's too early for that," I said. "Why, it's only the middle of the night."

"Oh, that doesn't make any difference to those cursed chickens," he replied bitterly. "They would just as soon crow in the middle of the night as at any other time – sooner, if they thought it would spoil a chap's evening out. I believe they do it on purpose."

He said a friend of his, the ghost of a man who had killed a water- rate collector, used to haunt a house in Long Acre, where they kept fowls in the cellar, and every time a policeman went by and flashed his bull's-eye down the grating, the old cock there would fancy it was the sun, and start crowing like mad; when, of course, the poor ghost had to dissolve, and it would, in consequence, get back home sometimes as early as one o'clock in the morning, swearing fearfully because it had only been out for an hour.

I agreed that it seemed very unfair.

"Oh, it's an absurd arrangement altogether," he continued, quite angrily. "I can't imagine what our old man could have been thinking of when he made it. As I have said to him, over and over again, 'Have a fixed time, and let everybody stick to it – say four o'clock in summer, and six in winter. Then one would know what one was about.'"

"How do you manage when there isn't any cock handy?" I inquired.

He was on the point of replying, when again he started and listened. This time I distinctly heard Mr. Bowles's cock, next door, crow twice.

"There you are," he said, rising and reaching for his hat; "that's the sort of thing we have to put up with. What IS the time?"

I looked at my watch, and found it was half-past three.

"I thought as much," he muttered. "I'll wring that blessed bird's neck if I get hold of it." And he prepared to go.

"If you can wait half a minute," I said, getting out of bed, "I'll go a bit of the way with you."

"It's very good of you," he rejoined, pausing, "but it seems unkind to drag you out."

"Not at all," I replied; "I shall like a walk." And I partially dressed myself, and took my umbrella; and he put his arm through mine, and we went out together.

Just by the gate we met Jones, one of the local constables.

"Good-night, Jones," I said (I always feel affable at Christmas- time).

"Good-night, sir," answered the man a little gruffly, I thought. "May I ask what you're a-doing of?"

"Oh, it's all right," I responded, with a wave of my umbrella; "I'm just seeing my friend part of the way home."

He said, "What friend?"

"Oh, ah, of course," I laughed; "I forgot. He's invisible to you. He is the ghost of the gentleman that killed the wait. I'm just going to the corner with him."

"Ah, I don't think I would, if I was you, sir," said Jones severely. "If you take my advice, you'll say good-bye to your friend here, and go back indoors. Perhaps you are not aware that you are walking about with nothing on but a night-shirt and a pair of boots and an opera-hat. Where's your trousers?"

I did not like the man's manner at all. I said, "Jones! I don't wish to have to report you, but it seems to me you've been drinking. My trousers are where a man's trousers ought to be – on his legs. I distinctly remember putting them on."

"Well, you haven't got them on now," he retorted.

"I beg your pardon," I replied. "I tell you I have; I think I ought to know."

"I think so, too," he answered, "but you evidently don't. Now you come along indoors with me, and don't let's have any more of it."

Uncle John came to the door at this point, having been awaked, I suppose, by the altercation; and, at the same moment, Aunt Maria appeared at the window in her nightcap.

I explained the constable's mistake to them, treating the matter as lightly as I could, so as not to get the man into trouble, and I turned for confirmation to the ghost.

He was gone! He had left me without a word – without even saying good-bye!

It struck me as so unkind, his having gone off in that way, that I burst into tears; and Uncle John came out, and led me back into the house.

On reaching my room, I discovered that Jones was right. I had not put on my trousers, after all. They were still hanging over the bed-rail. I suppose, in my anxiety not to keep the ghost waiting, I must have forgotten them.

Such are the plain facts of the case, out of which it must, doubtless, to the healthy, charitable mind appear impossible that calumny could spring.

But it has.

Persons – I say 'persons' – have professed themselves unable to understand the simple circumstances herein narrated, except in the light of explanations at once misleading and insulting. Slurs have been cast and aspersions made on me by those of my own flesh and blood.

But I bear no ill-feeling. I merely, as I have said, set forth this statement for the purpose of clearing my character from injurious suspicion.

The Dead

James Joyce

LILY, THE CARETAKER'S daughter, was literally run off her feet. Hardly had she brought one gentleman into the little pantry behind the office on the ground floor and helped him off with his overcoat than the wheezy hall-door bell clanged again and she had to scamper along the bare hallway to let in another guest. It was well for her she had not to attend to the ladies also. But Miss Kate and Miss Julia had thought of that and had converted the bathroom upstairs into a ladies' dressing-room. Miss Kate and Miss Julia were there, gossiping and laughing and fussing, walking after each other to the head of the stairs, peering down over the banisters and calling down to Lily to ask her who had come.

It was always a great affair, the Misses Morkan's annual dance. Everybody who knew them came to it, members of the family, old friends of the family, the members of Julia's choir, any of Kate's pupils that were grown up enough, and even some of Mary Jane's pupils too. Never once had it fallen flat. For years and years it had gone off in splendid style as long as anyone could remember; ever since Kate and Julia, after the death of their brother Pat, had left the house in Stoney Batter and taken Mary Jane, their only niece, to live with them in the dark gaunt house on Usher's Island, the upper part of which they had rented from Mr Fulham, the corn-factor on the ground floor. That was a good thirty years ago if it was a day. Mary Jane, who was then a little girl in short clothes, was now the main prop of the household, for she had the organ in Haddington Road. She had been through the Academy and gave a pupils' concert every year in the upper room of the Antient Concert Rooms. Many of her pupils belonged to the better-class families on the Kingstown and Dalkey line. Old as they were, her aunts also did their share. Julia, though she was quite grey, was still the leading soprano in Adam and Eve's, and Kate, being too feeble to go about much, gave music lessons to beginners on the old square piano in the back room. Lily, the caretaker's daughter, did housemaid's work for them. Though their life was modest they believed in eating well; the best of everything: diamond-bone sirloins, three-shilling tea and the best bottled stout. But Lily seldom made a mistake in the orders so that she got on well with her three mistresses. They were fussy, that was all. But the only thing they would not stand was back answers.

Of course they had good reason to be fussy on such a night. And then it was long after ten o'clock and yet there was no sign of Gabriel and his wife. Besides they were dreadfully afraid that Freddy Malins might turn up screwed. They would not wish for worlds that any of Mary Jane's pupils should see him under the influence; and when he was like that it was sometimes very hard to manage him. Freddy Malins always came late but they wondered what could be keeping Gabriel: and that was what brought them every two minutes to the banisters to ask Lily had Gabriel or Freddy come.

"O, Mr Conroy," said Lily to Gabriel when she opened the door for him, "Miss Kate and Miss Julia thought you were never coming. Good-night, Mrs Conroy."

"I'll engage they did," said Gabriel, "but they forget that my wife here takes three mortal hours to dress herself."

He stood on the mat, scraping the snow from his goloshes, while Lily led his wife to the foot of the stairs and called out:

"Miss Kate, here's Mrs Conroy."

Kate and Julia came toddling down the dark stairs at once. Both of them kissed Gabriel's wife, said she must be perished alive and asked was Gabriel with her.

"Here I am as right as the mail, Aunt Kate! Go on up. I'll follow," called out Gabriel from the dark.

He continued scraping his feet vigorously while the three women went upstairs, laughing, to the ladies' dressing-room. A light fringe of snow lay like a cape on the shoulders of his overcoat and like toecaps on the toes of his goloshes; and, as the buttons of his overcoat slipped with a squeaking noise through the snow-stiffened frieze, a cold, fragrant air from out-of-doors escaped from crevices and folds.

"Is it snowing again, Mr Conroy?" asked Lily.

She had preceded him into the pantry to help him off with his overcoat. Gabriel smiled at the three syllables she had given his surname and glanced at her. She was a slim, growing girl, pale in complexion and with hay-coloured hair. The gas in the pantry made her look still paler. Gabriel had known her when she was a child and used to sit on the lowest step nursing a rag doll.

"Yes, Lily," he answered, "and I think we're in for a night of it."

He looked up at the pantry ceiling, which was shaking with the stamping and shuffling of feet on the floor above, listened for a moment to the piano and then glanced at the girl, who was folding his overcoat carefully at the end of a shelf.

"Tell me, Lily," he said in a friendly tone, "do you still go to school?"

"O no, sir," she answered. "I'm done schooling this year and more."

"O, then," said Gabriel gaily, "I suppose we'll be going to your wedding one of these fine days with your young man, eh?"

The girl glanced back at him over her shoulder and said with great bitterness:

"The men that is now is only all palaver and what they can get out of you."

Gabriel coloured as if he felt he had made a mistake and, without looking at her, kicked off his goloshes and flicked actively with his muffler at his patent-leather shoes.

He was a stout tallish young man. The high colour of his cheeks pushed upwards even to his forehead where it scattered itself in a few formless patches of pale red; and on his hairless face there scintillated restlessly the polished lenses and the bright gilt rims of the glasses which screened his delicate and restless eyes. His glossy black hair was parted in the middle and brushed in a long curve behind his ears where it curled slightly beneath the groove left by his hat.

When he had flicked lustre into his shoes he stood up and pulled his waistcoat down more tightly on his plump body. Then he took a coin rapidly from his pocket.

"O Lily," he said, thrusting it into her hands, "it's Christmas-time, isn't it? Just... here's a little...."

He walked rapidly towards the door.

"O no, sir!" cried the girl, following him. "Really, sir, I wouldn't take it."

"Christmas-time! Christmas-time!" said Gabriel, almost trotting to the stairs and waving his hand to her in deprecation.

The girl, seeing that he had gained the stairs, called out after him:

"Well, thank you, sir."

He waited outside the drawing-room door until the waltz should finish, listening to the skirts that swept against it and to the shuffling of feet. He was still discomposed by the girl's bitter and sudden retort. It had cast a gloom over him which he tried to dispel by arranging his cuffs and the bows of his tie. He then took from his waistcoat pocket a little paper and glanced at the headings he had made for his speech. He was undecided about the lines from Robert Browning for he feared they would be above the heads of his hearers. Some quotation that they would recognise from Shakespeare or from the Melodies would be better. The indelicate clacking of the men's heels and the shuffling of their soles reminded him that their grade of culture differed from his. He would only make himself ridiculous by quoting poetry to them which they could not understand. They would think that he was airing his superior education. He would fail with them just as he had failed with the girl in the pantry. He had taken up a wrong tone. His whole speech was a mistake from first to last, an utter failure.

Just then his aunts and his wife came out of the ladies' dressing-room. His aunts were two small plainly dressed old women. Aunt Julia was an inch or so the taller. Her hair, drawn low over the tops of her ears, was grey; and grey also, with darker shadows, was her large flaccid face. Though she was stout in build and stood erect her slow eyes and parted lips gave her the appearance of a woman who did not know where she was or where she was going. Aunt Kate was more vivacious. Her face, healthier than her sister's, was all puckers and creases, like a shrivelled red apple, and her hair, braided in the same old-fashioned way, had not lost its ripe nut colour.

They both kissed Gabriel frankly. He was their favourite nephew, the son of their dead elder sister, Ellen, who had married T. J. Conroy of the Port and Docks.

"Gretta tells me you're not going to take a cab back to Monkstown tonight, Gabriel," said Aunt Kate.

"No," said Gabriel, turning to his wife, "we had quite enough of that last year, hadn't we? Don't you remember, Aunt Kate, what a cold Gretta got out of it? Cab windows rattling all the way, and the east wind blowing in after we passed Merrion. Very jolly it was. Gretta caught a dreadful cold."

Aunt Kate frowned severely and nodded her head at every word.

"Quite right, Gabriel, quite right," she said. "You can't be too careful."

"But as for Gretta there," said Gabriel, "she'd walk home in the snow if she were let."

Mrs Conroy laughed.

"Don't mind him, Aunt Kate," she said. "He's really an awful bother, what with green shades for Tom's eyes at night and making him do the dumb-bells, and forcing Eva to eat the stirabout. The poor child! And she simply hates the sight of it!... O, but you'll never guess what he makes me wear now!"

She broke out into a peal of laughter and glanced at her husband, whose admiring and happy eyes had been wandering from her dress to her face and hair. The two aunts laughed heartily too, for Gabriel's solicitude was a standing joke with them.

"Goloshes!" said Mrs Conroy. "That's the latest. Whenever it's wet underfoot I must put on my goloshes. Tonight even he wanted me to put them on, but I wouldn't. The next thing he'll buy me will be a diving suit."

Gabriel laughed nervously and patted his tie reassuringly while Aunt Kate nearly doubled herself, so heartily did she enjoy the joke. The smile soon faded from Aunt Julia's face and her mirthless eyes were directed towards her nephew's face. After a pause she asked:

"And what are goloshes, Gabriel?"

"Goloshes, Julia!" exclaimed her sister. "Goodness me, don't you know what goloshes are? You wear them over your... over your boots, Gretta, isn't it?"

"Yes," said Mrs Conroy. "Guttapercha things. We both have a pair now. Gabriel says everyone wears them on the continent."

"O, on the continent," murmured Aunt Julia, nodding her head slowly.

Gabriel knitted his brows and said, as if he were slightly angered:

"It's nothing very wonderful but Gretta thinks it very funny because she says the word reminds her of Christy Minstrels."

"But tell me, Gabriel," said Aunt Kate, with brisk tact. "Of course, you've seen about the room. Gretta was saying…."

"O, the room is all right," replied Gabriel. "I've taken one in the Gresham."

"To be sure," said Aunt Kate, "by far the best thing to do. And the children, Gretta, you're not anxious about them?"

"O, for one night," said Mrs Conroy. "Besides, Bessie will look after them."

"To be sure," said Aunt Kate again. "What a comfort it is to have a girl like that, one you can depend on! There's that Lily, I'm sure I don't know what has come over her lately. She's not the girl she was at all."

Gabriel was about to ask his aunt some questions on this point but she broke off suddenly to gaze after her sister who had wandered down the stairs and was craning her neck over the banisters.

"Now, I ask you," she said almost testily, "where is Julia going? Julia! Julia! Where are you going?"

Julia, who had gone half way down one flight, came back and announced blandly:

"Here's Freddy."

At the same moment a clapping of hands and a final flourish of the pianist told that the waltz had ended. The drawing-room door was opened from within and some couples came out. Aunt Kate drew Gabriel aside hurriedly and whispered into his ear:

"Slip down, Gabriel, like a good fellow and see if he's all right, and don't let him up if he's screwed. I'm sure he's screwed. I'm sure he is."

Gabriel went to the stairs and listened over the banisters. He could hear two persons talking in the pantry. Then he recognised Freddy Malins' laugh. He went down the stairs noisily.

"It's such a relief," said Aunt Kate to Mrs Conroy, "that Gabriel is here. I always feel easier in my mind when he's here…. Julia, there's Miss Daly and Miss Power will take some refreshment. Thanks for your beautiful waltz, Miss Daly. It made lovely time."

A tall wizen-faced man, with a stiff grizzled moustache and swarthy skin, who was passing out with his partner said:

"And may we have some refreshment, too, Miss Morkan?"

"Julia," said Aunt Kate summarily, "and here's Mr Browne and Miss Furlong. Take them in, Julia, with Miss Daly and Miss Power."

"I'm the man for the ladies," said Mr Browne, pursing his lips until his moustache bristled and smiling in all his wrinkles. "You know, Miss Morkan, the reason they are so fond of me is—"

He did not finish his sentence, but, seeing that Aunt Kate was out of earshot, at once led the three young ladies into the back room. The middle of the room was occupied by two square tables placed end to end, and on these Aunt Julia and the caretaker were straightening and smoothing a large cloth. On the sideboard were arrayed dishes and plates, and glasses and bundles of knives and forks and spoons. The top of the closed square piano served also as a sideboard for viands and sweets. At a smaller sideboard in one corner two young men were standing, drinking hop-bitters.

Mr Browne led his charges thither and invited them all, in jest, to some ladies' punch, hot, strong and sweet. As they said they never took anything strong he opened three bottles of lemonade for them. Then he asked one of the young men to move aside, and, taking hold of the decanter, filled out for himself a goodly measure of whisky. The young men eyed him respectfully while he took a trial sip.

"God help me," he said, smiling, "it's the doctor's orders."

His wizened face broke into a broader smile, and the three young ladies laughed in musical echo to his pleasantry, swaying their bodies to and fro, with nervous jerks of their shoulders. The boldest said:

"O, now, Mr Browne, I'm sure the doctor never ordered anything of the kind."

Mr Browne took another sip of his whisky and said, with sidling mimicry:

"Well, you see, I'm like the famous Mrs Cassidy, who is reported to have said: 'Now, Mary Grimes, if I don't take it, make me take it, for I feel I want it.'"

His hot face had leaned forward a little too confidentially and he had assumed a very low Dublin accent so that the young ladies, with one instinct, received his speech in silence. Miss Furlong, who was one of Mary Jane's pupils, asked Miss Daly what was the name of the pretty waltz she had played; and Mr Browne, seeing that he was ignored, turned promptly to the two young men who were more appreciative.

A red-faced young woman, dressed in pansy, came into the room, excitedly clapping her hands and crying:

"Quadrilles! Quadrilles!"

Close on her heels came Aunt Kate, crying:

"Two gentlemen and three ladies, Mary Jane!"

"O, here's Mr Bergin and Mr Kerrigan," said Mary Jane. "Mr Kerrigan, will you take Miss Power? Miss Furlong, may I get you a partner, Mr Bergin. O, that'll just do now."

"Three ladies, Mary Jane," said Aunt Kate.

The two young gentlemen asked the ladies if they might have the pleasure, and Mary Jane turned to Miss Daly.

"O, Miss Daly, you're really awfully good, after playing for the last two dances, but really we're so short of ladies tonight."

"I don't mind in the least, Miss Morkan."

"But I've a nice partner for you, Mr Bartell D'Arcy, the tenor. I'll get him to sing later on. All Dublin is raving about him."

"Lovely voice, lovely voice!" said Aunt Kate.

As the piano had twice begun the prelude to the first figure Mary Jane led her recruits quickly from the room. They had hardly gone when Aunt Julia wandered slowly into the room, looking behind her at something.

"What is the matter, Julia?" asked Aunt Kate anxiously. "Who is it?"

Julia, who was carrying in a column of table-napkins, turned to her sister and said, simply, as if the question had surprised her:

"It's only Freddy, Kate, and Gabriel with him."

In fact right behind her Gabriel could be seen piloting Freddy Malins across the landing. The latter, a young man of about forty, was of Gabriel's size and build, with very round shoulders. His face was fleshy and pallid, touched with colour only at the thick hanging lobes of his ears and at the wide wings of his nose. He had coarse features, a blunt nose, a convex and receding brow, tumid and protruded lips. His heavy-lidded eyes and the disorder of his scanty hair made him look sleepy. He was laughing heartily in a high key at a story which he had been telling Gabriel on the stairs and at the same time rubbing the knuckles of his left fist backwards and forwards into his left eye.

"Good-evening, Freddy," said Aunt Julia.

Freddy Malins bade the Misses Morkan good-evening in what seemed an offhand fashion by reason of the habitual catch in his voice and then, seeing that Mr Browne was grinning at him from the sideboard, crossed the room on rather shaky legs and began to repeat in an undertone the story he had just told to Gabriel.

"He's not so bad, is he?" said Aunt Kate to Gabriel.

Gabriel's brows were dark but he raised them quickly and answered:

"O, no, hardly noticeable."

"Now, isn't he a terrible fellow!" she said. "And his poor mother made him take the pledge on New Year's Eve. But come on, Gabriel, into the drawing-room."

Before leaving the room with Gabriel she signalled to Mr Browne by frowning and shaking her forefinger in warning to and fro. Mr Browne nodded in answer and, when she had gone, said to Freddy Malins:

"Now, then, Teddy, I'm going to fill you out a good glass of lemonade just to buck you up."

Freddy Malins, who was nearing the climax of his story, waved the offer aside impatiently but Mr Browne, having first called Freddy Malins' attention to a disarray in his dress, filled out and handed him a full glass of lemonade. Freddy Malins' left hand accepted the glass mechanically, his right hand being engaged in the mechanical readjustment of his dress. Mr Browne, whose face was once more wrinkling with mirth, poured out for himself a glass of whisky while Freddy Malins exploded, before he had well reached the climax of his story, in a kink of high-pitched bronchitic laughter and, setting down his untasted and overflowing glass, began to rub the knuckles of his left fist backwards and forwards into his left eye, repeating words of his last phrase as well as his fit of laughter would allow him.

* * *

Gabriel could not listen while Mary Jane was playing her Academy piece, full of runs and difficult passages, to the hushed drawing-room. He liked music but the piece she was playing had no melody for him and he doubted whether it had any melody for the other listeners, though they had begged Mary Jane to play something. Four young men, who had come from the refreshment-room to stand in the doorway at the sound of the piano, had gone away quietly in couples after a few minutes. The only persons who seemed to follow the music were Mary Jane herself, her hands racing along the keyboard or lifted from it at the pauses like those of a priestess in momentary imprecation, and Aunt Kate standing at her elbow to turn the page.

Gabriel's eyes, irritated by the floor, which glittered with beeswax under the heavy chandelier, wandered to the wall above the piano. A picture of the balcony scene in *Romeo and Juliet* hung there and beside it was a picture of the two murdered princes in the Tower which Aunt Julia had worked in red, blue and brown wools when she was a girl. Probably in the school they had gone to as girls that kind of work had been taught for one year. His mother had worked for him as a birthday present a waistcoat of purple tabinet, with little foxes' heads upon it, lined with brown satin and having round mulberry buttons. It was strange that his mother had had no musical talent though Aunt Kate used to call her the brains carrier of the Morkan family. Both she and Julia had always seemed a little proud of their serious and matronly sister. Her photograph stood before the pierglass. She held an open book on her knees and was pointing out something in it to Constantine who, dressed in a man-o'-war suit, lay at her feet. It was she who had chosen the name of her sons for she was very sensible of the dignity of family life. Thanks to her, Constantine was now senior curate in Balbrigan and, thanks to her, Gabriel himself had taken his degree in the Royal University. A shadow passed over his face as he remembered her sullen opposition to his marriage. Some slighting phrases she had used still rankled in his memory; she had once spoken of Gretta as being country cute and that was not true of Gretta at all. It was Gretta who had nursed her during all her last long illness in their house at Monkstown.

He knew that Mary Jane must be near the end of her piece for she was playing again the opening melody with runs of scales after every bar and while he waited for the end the resentment died down in his heart. The piece ended with a trill of octaves in the treble and a final deep octave in the bass. Great applause greeted Mary Jane as, blushing and rolling up her music nervously, she escaped from the room. The most vigorous clapping came from the four young men in the doorway who had gone away to the refreshment-room at the beginning of the piece but had come back when the piano had stopped.

Lancers were arranged. Gabriel found himself partnered with Miss Ivors. She was a frank-mannered talkative young lady, with a freckled face and prominent brown eyes. She did not wear a low-cut bodice and the large brooch which was fixed in the front of her collar bore on it an Irish device and motto.

When they had taken their places she said abruptly:

"I have a crow to pluck with you."

"With me?" said Gabriel.

She nodded her head gravely.

"What is it?" asked Gabriel, smiling at her solemn manner.

"Who is G. C.?" answered Miss Ivors, turning her eyes upon him.

Gabriel coloured and was about to knit his brows, as if he did not understand, when she said bluntly:

"O, innocent Amy! I have found out that you write for *The Daily Express*. Now, aren't you ashamed of yourself?"

"Why should I be ashamed of myself?" asked Gabriel, blinking his eyes and trying to smile.

"Well, I'm ashamed of you," said Miss Ivors frankly. "To say you'd write for a paper like that. I didn't think you were a West Briton."

A look of perplexity appeared on Gabriel's face. It was true that he wrote a literary column every Wednesday in *The Daily Express*, for which he was paid fifteen shillings. But that did not make him a West Briton surely. The books he received for review were almost more welcome than the paltry cheque. He loved to feel the covers and turn over the pages of newly printed books. Nearly every day when his teaching in the college was ended he used to wander down the quays to the second-hand booksellers, to Hickey's on Bachelor's Walk, to Webb's or Massey's on Aston's Quay, or to O'Clohissey's in the by-street. He did not know how to meet her charge. He wanted to say that literature was above politics. But they were friends of many years' standing and their careers had been parallel, first at the university and then as teachers: he could not risk a grandiose phrase with her. He continued blinking his eyes and trying to smile and murmured lamely that he saw nothing political in writing reviews of books.

When their turn to cross had come he was still perplexed and inattentive. Miss Ivors promptly took his hand in a warm grasp and said in a soft friendly tone:

"Of course, I was only joking. Come, we cross now."

When they were together again she spoke of the University question and Gabriel felt more at ease. A friend of hers had shown her his review of Browning's poems. That was how she had found out the secret: but she liked the review immensely. Then she said suddenly:

"O, Mr Conroy, will you come for an excursion to the Aran Isles this summer? We're going to stay there a whole month. It will be splendid out in the Atlantic. You ought to come. Mr Clancy is coming, and Mr Kilkelly and Kathleen Kearney. It would be splendid for Gretta too if she'd come. She's from Connacht, isn't she?"

"Her people are," said Gabriel shortly.

"But you will come, won't you?" said Miss Ivors, laying her warm hand eagerly on his arm.

"The fact is," said Gabriel, "I have just arranged to go"

"Go where?" asked Miss Ivors.

"Well, you know, every year I go for a cycling tour with some fellows and so—"

"But where?" asked Miss Ivors.

"Well, we usually go to France or Belgium or perhaps Germany," said Gabriel awkwardly.

"And why do you go to France and Belgium," said Miss Ivors, "instead of visiting your own land?"

"Well," said Gabriel, "it's partly to keep in touch with the languages and partly for a change."

"And haven't you your own language to keep in touch with – Irish?" asked Miss Ivors.

"Well," said Gabriel, "if it comes to that, you know, Irish is not my language."

Their neighbours had turned to listen to the cross-examination. Gabriel glanced right and left nervously and tried to keep his good humour under the ordeal which was making a blush invade his forehead.

"And haven't you your own land to visit," continued Miss Ivors, "that you know nothing of, your own people, and your own country?"

"O, to tell you the truth," retorted Gabriel suddenly, "I'm sick of my own country, sick of it!"

"Why?" asked Miss Ivors.

Gabriel did not answer for his retort had heated him.

"Why?" repeated Miss Ivors.

They had to go visiting together and, as he had not answered her, Miss Ivors said warmly:

"Of course, you've no answer."

Gabriel tried to cover his agitation by taking part in the dance with great energy. He avoided her eyes for he had seen a sour expression on her face. But when they met in the long chain he was surprised to feel his hand firmly pressed. She looked at him from under her brows for a moment quizzically until he smiled. Then, just as the chain was about to start again, she stood on tiptoe and whispered into his ear:

"West Briton!"

When the lancers were over Gabriel went away to a remote corner of the room where Freddy Malins' mother was sitting. She was a stout feeble old woman with white hair. Her voice had a catch in it like her son's and she stuttered slightly. She had been told that Freddy had come and that he was nearly all right. Gabriel asked her whether she had had a good crossing. She lived with her married daughter in Glasgow and came to Dublin on a visit once a year. She answered placidly that she had had a beautiful crossing and that the captain had been most attentive to her. She spoke also of the beautiful house her daughter kept in Glasgow, and of all the friends they had there. While her tongue rambled on Gabriel tried to banish from his mind all memory of the unpleasant incident with Miss Ivors. Of course the girl or woman, or whatever she was, was an enthusiast but there was a time for all things. Perhaps he ought not to have answered her like that. But she had no right to call him a West Briton before people, even in joke. She had tried to make him ridiculous before people, heckling him and staring at him with her rabbit's eyes.

He saw his wife making her way towards him through the waltzing couples. When she reached him she said into his ear:

"Gabriel, Aunt Kate wants to know won't you carve the goose as usual. Miss Daly will carve the ham and I'll do the pudding."

"All right," said Gabriel.

"She's sending in the younger ones first as soon as this waltz is over so that we'll have the table to ourselves."

"Were you dancing?" asked Gabriel.

"Of course I was. Didn't you see me? What row had you with Molly Ivors?"

"No row. Why? Did she say so?"

"Something like that. I'm trying to get that Mr D'Arcy to sing. He's full of conceit, I think."

"There was no row," said Gabriel moodily, "only she wanted me to go for a trip to the west of Ireland and I said I wouldn't."

His wife clasped her hands excitedly and gave a little jump.

"O, do go, Gabriel," she cried. "I'd love to see Galway again."

"You can go if you like," said Gabriel coldly.

She looked at him for a moment, then turned to Mrs Malins and said:

"There's a nice husband for you, Mrs Malins."

While she was threading her way back across the room Mrs Malins, without adverting to the interruption, went on to tell Gabriel what beautiful places there were in Scotland and beautiful scenery. Her son-in-law brought them every year to the lakes and they used to go fishing. Her son-in-law was a splendid fisher. One day he caught a beautiful big fish and the man in the hotel cooked it for their dinner.

Gabriel hardly heard what she said. Now that supper was coming near he began to think again about his speech and about the quotation. When he saw Freddy Malins coming across the room to visit his mother Gabriel left the chair free for him and retired into the embrasure of the window. The room had already cleared and from the back room came the clatter of plates and knives. Those who still remained in the drawing-room seemed tired of dancing and were conversing quietly in little groups. Gabriel's warm trembling fingers tapped the cold pane of the window. How cool it must be outside! How pleasant it would be to walk out alone, first along by the river and then through the park! The snow would be lying on the branches of the trees and forming a bright cap on the top of the Wellington Monument. How much more pleasant it would be there than at the supper-table!

He ran over the headings of his speech: Irish hospitality, sad memories, the Three Graces, Paris, the quotation from Browning. He repeated to himself a phrase he had written in his review: "One feels that one is listening to a thought-tormented music." Miss Ivors had praised the review. Was she sincere? Had she really any life of her own behind all her propagandism? There had never been any ill-feeling between them until that night. It unnerved him to think that she would be at the supper-table, looking up at him while he spoke with her critical quizzing eyes. Perhaps she would not be sorry to see him fail in his speech. An idea came into his mind and gave him courage. He would say, alluding to Aunt Kate and Aunt Julia: "Ladies and Gentlemen, the generation which is now on the wane among us may have had its faults but for my part I think it had certain qualities of hospitality, of humour, of humanity, which the new and very serious and hypereducated generation that is growing up around us seems to me to lack." Very good: that was one for Miss Ivors. What did he care that his aunts were only two ignorant old women?

A murmur in the room attracted his attention. Mr Browne was advancing from the door, gallantly escorting Aunt Julia, who leaned upon his arm, smiling and hanging her head. An irregular musketry of applause escorted her also as far as the piano and then, as Mary Jane seated herself on the stool, and Aunt Julia, no longer smiling, half turned so as to pitch her voice fairly into the room, gradually ceased. Gabriel recognised the prelude. It was that of an old song of Aunt Julia's – *Arrayed for the Bridal*. Her voice, strong and clear in tone, attacked with great spirit the runs which embellish the air and though she sang very rapidly she did not miss even the smallest of the grace notes. To follow the voice, without looking at the singer's face, was to feel and share the excitement of swift and secure flight. Gabriel applauded loudly with all the others at the close of the song and loud applause was borne in from the invisible supper-table. It sounded so genuine that a little colour struggled into Aunt Julia's face as she bent to replace in the music-stand the old leather-bound songbook that had her initials on the cover. Freddy Malins, who had listened with his head perched sideways to hear her better, was still applauding when everyone else had ceased and talking animatedly to his mother who nodded her head gravely and slowly in acquiescence. At last, when he could clap no more, he stood up suddenly and hurried across the room to Aunt Julia whose hand he seized and held in both his hands, shaking it when words failed him or the catch in his voice proved too much for him.

"I was just telling my mother," he said, "I never heard you sing so well, never. No, I never heard your voice so good as it is tonight. Now! Would you believe that now? That's the truth. Upon my word and honour that's the truth. I never heard your voice sound so fresh and so... so clear and fresh, never."

Aunt Julia smiled broadly and murmured something about compliments as she released her hand from his grasp. Mr Browne extended his open hand towards her and said to those who were near him in the manner of a showman introducing a prodigy to an audience:

"Miss Julia Morkan, my latest discovery!"

He was laughing very heartily at this himself when Freddy Malins turned to him and said:

"Well, Browne, if you're serious you might make a worse discovery. All I can say is I never heard her sing half so well as long as I am coming here. And that's the honest truth."

"Neither did I," said Mr Browne. "I think her voice has greatly improved."

Aunt Julia shrugged her shoulders and said with meek pride:

"Thirty years ago I hadn't a bad voice as voices go."

"I often told Julia," said Aunt Kate emphatically, "that she was simply thrown away in that choir. But she never would be said by me."

She turned as if to appeal to the good sense of the others against a refractory child while Aunt Julia gazed in front of her, a vague smile of reminiscence playing on her face.

"No," continued Aunt Kate, "she wouldn't be said or led by anyone, slaving there in that choir night and day, night and day. Six o'clock on Christmas morning! And all for what?"

"Well, isn't it for the honour of God, Aunt Kate?" asked Mary Jane, twisting round on the piano-stool and smiling.

Aunt Kate turned fiercely on her niece and said:

"I know all about the honour of God, Mary Jane, but I think it's not at all honourable for the pope to turn out the women out of the choirs that have slaved there all their lives and put little whipper-snappers of boys over their heads. I suppose it is for the good of the Church if the pope does it. But it's not just, Mary Jane, and it's not right."

She had worked herself into a passion and would have continued in defence of her sister for it was a sore subject with her but Mary Jane, seeing that all the dancers had come back, intervened pacifically:

"Now, Aunt Kate, you're giving scandal to Mr Browne who is of the other persuasion."

Aunt Kate turned to Mr Browne, who was grinning at this allusion to his religion, and said hastily:

"O, I don't question the pope's being right. I'm only a stupid old woman and I wouldn't presume to do such a thing. But there's such a thing as common everyday politeness and gratitude. And if I were in Julia's place I'd tell that Father Healey straight up to his face...."

"And besides, Aunt Kate," said Mary Jane, "we really are all hungry and when we are hungry we are all very quarrelsome."

"And when we are thirsty we are also quarrelsome," added Mr Browne.

"So that we had better go to supper," said Mary Jane, "and finish the discussion afterwards."

On the landing outside the drawing-room Gabriel found his wife and Mary Jane trying to persuade Miss Ivors to stay for supper. But Miss Ivors, who had put on her hat and was buttoning her cloak, would not stay. She did not feel in the least hungry and she had already overstayed her time.

"But only for ten minutes, Molly," said Mrs Conroy. "That won't delay you."

"To take a pick itself," said Mary Jane, "after all your dancing."

"I really couldn't," said Miss Ivors.

"I am afraid you didn't enjoy yourself at all," said Mary Jane hopelessly.

"Ever so much, I assure you," said Miss Ivors, "but you really must let me run off now."

"But how can you get home?" asked Mrs Conroy.

"O, it's only two steps up the quay."

Gabriel hesitated a moment and said:

"If you will allow me, Miss Ivors, I'll see you home if you are really obliged to go."

But Miss Ivors broke away from them.

"I won't hear of it," she cried. "For goodness' sake go in to your suppers and don't mind me. I'm quite well able to take care of myself."

"Well, you're the comical girl, Molly," said Mrs Conroy frankly.

"*Beannacht libh*," cried Miss Ivors, with a laugh, as she ran down the staircase.

Mary Jane gazed after her, a moody puzzled expression on her face, while Mrs Conroy leaned over the banisters to listen for the hall-door. Gabriel asked himself was he the cause of her abrupt departure. But she did not seem to be in ill humour: she had gone away laughing. He stared blankly down the staircase.

At the moment Aunt Kate came toddling out of the supper-room, almost wringing her hands in despair.

"Where is Gabriel?" she cried. "Where on earth is Gabriel? There's everyone waiting in there, stage to let, and nobody to carve the goose!"

"Here I am, Aunt Kate!" cried Gabriel, with sudden animation, "ready to carve a flock of geese if necessary."

A fat brown goose lay at one end of the table and at the other end, on a bed of creased paper strewn with sprigs of parsley, lay a great ham, stripped of its outer skin and peppered over with crust crumbs, a neat paper frill round its shin and beside this was a round of spiced beef. Between these rival ends ran parallel lines of side-dishes: two little minsters of jelly, red and yellow; a shallow dish full of blocks of blancmange and red jam, a large green leaf-shaped dish with a stalk shaped handle, on which lay bunches of purple raisins and peeled almonds, a companion dish on which lay a solid rectangle of Smyrna figs, a dish of custard topped with grated nutmeg, a small bowl full of chocolates and sweets wrapped in gold and silver papers and a glass vase in which stood some tall celery stalks. In the centre of the table there stood, as sentries to a fruit-stand which upheld a pyramid of oranges and American apples, two squat old-fashioned decanters of cut glass, one containing port and the other dark sherry. On the closed square piano a pudding in a huge yellow dish lay in waiting and behind it were three squads of bottles of stout and ale and minerals, drawn up according to the colours of their uniforms, the first two black, with brown and red labels, the third and smallest squad white, with transverse green sashes.

Gabriel took his seat boldly at the head of the table and, having looked to the edge of the carver, plunged his fork firmly into the goose. He felt quite at ease now for he was an expert carver and liked nothing better than to find himself at the head of a well-laden table.

"Miss Furlong, what shall I send you?" he asked. "A wing or a slice of the breast?"

"Just a small slice of the breast."

"Miss Higgins, what for you?"

"O, anything at all, Mr Conroy."

While Gabriel and Miss Daly exchanged plates of goose and plates of ham and spiced beef Lily went from guest to guest with a dish of hot floury potatoes wrapped in a white napkin. This was Mary Jane's idea and she had also suggested apple sauce for the goose but Aunt Kate had said that plain roast goose without any apple sauce had always been good enough for her and she hoped she might never eat worse. Mary Jane waited on her pupils and saw that they got the best slices and Aunt Kate and Aunt Julia opened and carried across from the piano bottles of stout and ale for the gentlemen and bottles of minerals for the ladies. There was a great deal of confusion and laughter and noise, the noise of orders and counter-orders, of knives and forks, of corks and glass-stoppers. Gabriel began to carve second helpings as soon as he had finished the first round without serving himself. Everyone protested loudly so that he compromised by taking a long draught of stout for he had found the carving hot work. Mary Jane settled down quietly to her supper but Aunt Kate and Aunt Julia were still toddling round the table, walking on each other's heels, getting in each other's way and giving each other unheeded orders. Mr Browne begged of them to sit down and eat their suppers and so did Gabriel but they said they were time enough so that, at last, Freddy Malins stood up and, capturing Aunt Kate, plumped her down on her chair amid general laughter.

When everyone had been well served Gabriel said, smiling:

"Now, if anyone wants a little more of what vulgar people call stuffing let him or her speak."

A chorus of voices invited him to begin his own supper and Lily came forward with three potatoes which she had reserved for him.

"Very well," said Gabriel amiably, as he took another preparatory draught, "kindly forget my existence, ladies and gentlemen, for a few minutes."

He set to his supper and took no part in the conversation with which the table covered Lily's removal of the plates. The subject of talk was the opera company which was then at the Theatre Royal. Mr Bartell D'Arcy, the tenor, a dark-complexioned young man with a smart moustache, praised very highly the leading contralto of the company but Miss Furlong thought she had a rather vulgar style of production. Freddy Malins said there was a negro chieftain singing in the second part of the Gaiety pantomime who had one of the finest tenor voices he had ever heard.

"Have you heard him?" he asked Mr Bartell D'Arcy across the table.

"No," answered Mr Bartell D'Arcy carelessly.

"Because," Freddy Malins explained, "now I'd be curious to hear your opinion of him. I think he has a grand voice."

"It takes Teddy to find out the really good things," said Mr Browne familiarly to the table.

"And why couldn't he have a voice too?" asked Freddy Malins sharply. "Is it because he's only a black?"

Nobody answered this question and Mary Jane led the table back to the legitimate opera. One of her pupils had given her a pass for *Mignon*. Of course it was very fine, she said, but it made her think of poor Georgina Burns. Mr Browne could go back farther still, to the old Italian companies that used to come to Dublin – Tietjens, Ilma de Murzka, Campanini, the great Trebelli, Giuglini, Ravelli, Aramburo. Those were the days, he said, when there was something like singing to be heard in Dublin. He told too of how the top gallery of the old Royal used to be packed night after night, of how one night an Italian tenor had sung five encores to *Let me like a Soldier fall*, introducing a high C every time, and of how the gallery boys would sometimes in their enthusiasm unyoke the horses from the carriage of some great *prima donna* and pull her themselves through the streets to her hotel. Why did they never play the grand old operas now, he asked, *Dinorah*, *Lucrezia Borgia?* Because they could not get the voices to sing them: that was why.

"Oh, well," said Mr Bartell D'Arcy, "I presume there are as good singers today as there were then."

"Where are they?" asked Mr Browne defiantly.

"In London, Paris, Milan," said Mr Bartell D'Arcy warmly. "I suppose Caruso, for example, is quite as good, if not better than any of the men you have mentioned."

"Maybe so," said Mr Browne. "But I may tell you I doubt it strongly."

"O, I'd give anything to hear Caruso sing," said Mary Jane.

"For me," said Aunt Kate, who had been picking a bone, "there was only one tenor. To please me, I mean. But I suppose none of you ever heard of him."

"Who was he, Miss Morkan?" asked Mr Bartell D'Arcy politely.

"His name," said Aunt Kate, "was Parkinson. I heard him when he was in his prime and I think he had then the purest tenor voice that was ever put into a man's throat."

"Strange," said Mr Bartell D'Arcy. "I never even heard of him."

"Yes, yes, Miss Morkan is right," said Mr Browne. "I remember hearing of old Parkinson but he's too far back for me."

"A beautiful pure sweet mellow English tenor," said Aunt Kate with enthusiasm.

Gabriel having finished, the huge pudding was transferred to the table. The clatter of forks and spoons began again. Gabriel's wife served out spoonfuls of the pudding and passed the plates down the table. Midway down they were held up by Mary Jane, who replenished them with raspberry or orange jelly or with blancmange and jam. The pudding was of Aunt Julia's making and she received praises for it from all quarters. She herself said that it was not quite brown enough.

"Well, I hope, Miss Morkan," said Mr Browne, "that I'm brown enough for you because, you know, I'm all brown."

All the gentlemen, except Gabriel, ate some of the pudding out of compliment to Aunt Julia. As Gabriel never ate sweets the celery had been left for him. Freddy Malins also took a stalk of celery and ate it with his pudding. He had been told that celery was a capital thing for the blood and he was just then under doctor's care. Mrs Malins, who had been silent all through the supper, said that her son was going down to Mount Melleray in a week or so. The table then spoke of Mount Melleray, how bracing the air was down there, how hospitable the monks were and how they never asked for a penny-piece from their guests.

"And do you mean to say," asked Mr Browne incredulously, "that a chap can go down there and put up there as if it were a hotel and live on the fat of the land and then come away without paying anything?"

"O, most people give some donation to the monastery when they leave." said Mary Jane.

"I wish we had an institution like that in our Church," said Mr Browne candidly.

He was astonished to hear that the monks never spoke, got up at two in the morning and slept in their coffins. He asked what they did it for.

"That's the rule of the order," said Aunt Kate firmly.

"Yes, but why?" asked Mr Browne.

Aunt Kate repeated that it was the rule, that was all. Mr Browne still seemed not to understand. Freddy Malins explained to him, as best he could, that the monks were trying to make up for the sins committed by all the sinners in the outside world. The explanation was not very clear for Mr Browne grinned and said:

"I like that idea very much but wouldn't a comfortable spring bed do them as well as a coffin?"

"The coffin," said Mary Jane, "is to remind them of their last end."

As the subject had grown lugubrious it was buried in a silence of the table during which Mrs Malins could be heard saying to her neighbour in an indistinct undertone:

"They are very good men, the monks, very pious men."

The raisins and almonds and figs and apples and oranges and chocolates and sweets were now passed about the table and Aunt Julia invited all the guests to have either port or sherry. At first

Mr Bartell D'Arcy refused to take either but one of his neighbours nudged him and whispered something to him upon which he allowed his glass to be filled. Gradually as the last glasses were being filled the conversation ceased. A pause followed, broken only by the noise of the wine and by unsettlings of chairs. The Misses Morkan, all three, looked down at the tablecloth. Someone coughed once or twice and then a few gentlemen patted the table gently as a signal for silence. The silence came and Gabriel pushed back his chair.

The patting at once grew louder in encouragement and then ceased altogether. Gabriel leaned his ten trembling fingers on the tablecloth and smiled nervously at the company. Meeting a row of upturned faces he raised his eyes to the chandelier. The piano was playing a waltz tune and he could hear the skirts sweeping against the drawing-room door. People, perhaps, were standing in the snow on the quay outside, gazing up at the lighted windows and listening to the waltz music. The air was pure there. In the distance lay the park where the trees were weighted with snow. The Wellington Monument wore a gleaming cap of snow that flashed westward over the white field of Fifteen Acres.

He began:

"Ladies and Gentlemen,

"It has fallen to my lot this evening, as in years past, to perform a very pleasing task but a task for which I am afraid my poor powers as a speaker are all too inadequate."

"No, no!" said Mr Browne.

"But, however that may be, I can only ask you tonight to take the will for the deed and to lend me your attention for a few moments while I endeavour to express to you in words what my feelings are on this occasion.

"Ladies and Gentlemen, it is not the first time that we have gathered together under this hospitable roof, around this hospitable board. It is not the first time that we have been the recipients – or perhaps, I had better say, the victims – of the hospitality of certain good ladies."

He made a circle in the air with his arm and paused. Everyone laughed or smiled at Aunt Kate and Aunt Julia and Mary Jane who all turned crimson with pleasure. Gabriel went on more boldly:

"I feel more strongly with every recurring year that our country has no tradition which does it so much honour and which it should guard so jealously as that of its hospitality. It is a tradition that is unique as far as my experience goes (and I have visited not a few places abroad) among the modern nations. Some would say, perhaps, that with us it is rather a failing than anything to be boasted of. But granted even that, it is, to my mind, a princely failing, and one that I trust will long be cultivated among us. Of one thing, at least, I am sure. As long as this one roof shelters the good ladies aforesaid – and I wish from my heart it may do so for many and many a long year to come – the tradition of genuine warm-hearted courteous Irish hospitality, which our forefathers have handed down to us and which we in turn must hand down to our descendants, is still alive among us."

A hearty murmur of assent ran round the table. It shot through Gabriel's mind that Miss Ivors was not there and that she had gone away discourteously: and he said with confidence in himself:

"Ladies and Gentlemen,

"A new generation is growing up in our midst, a generation actuated by new ideas and new principles. It is serious and enthusiastic for these new ideas and its enthusiasm, even when it is misdirected, is, I believe, in the main sincere. But we are living in a sceptical and, if I may use the phrase, a thought-tormented age: and sometimes I fear that this new generation, educated or hypereducated as it is, will lack those qualities of humanity, of hospitality, of kindly humour which belonged to an older day. Listening tonight to the names of all those great singers of the past it seemed to me, I must confess, that we were living in a less spacious age. Those days might, without exaggeration, be called spacious days: and if they are gone beyond recall let us hope, at least, that in gatherings such as this we shall still speak of them with pride and affection, still cherish in our hearts the memory of those dead and gone great ones whose fame the world will not willingly let die."

"Hear, hear!" said Mr Browne loudly.

"But yet," continued Gabriel, his voice falling into a softer inflection, "there are always in gatherings such as this sadder thoughts that will recur to our minds: thoughts of the past, of youth, of changes, of absent faces that we miss here tonight. Our path through life is strewn with many such sad memories: and were we to brood upon them always we could not find the heart to go on bravely with our work among the living. We have all of us living duties and living affections which claim, and rightly claim, our strenuous endeavours.

"Therefore, I will not linger on the past. I will not let any gloomy moralising intrude upon us here tonight. Here we are gathered together for a brief moment from the bustle and rush of our everyday routine. We are met here as friends, in the spirit of good-fellowship, as colleagues, also to a certain extent, in the true spirit of *camaraderie*, and as the guests of – what shall I call them? – the Three Graces of the Dublin musical world."

The table burst into applause and laughter at this allusion. Aunt Julia vainly asked each of her neighbours in turn to tell her what Gabriel had said.

"He says we are the Three Graces, Aunt Julia," said Mary Jane.

Aunt Julia did not understand but she looked up, smiling, at Gabriel, who continued in the same vein:

"Ladies and Gentlemen,

"I will not attempt to play tonight the part that Paris played on another occasion. I will not attempt to choose between them. The task would be an invidious one and one beyond my poor powers. For when I view them in turn, whether it be our chief hostess herself, whose good heart, whose too good heart, has become a byword with all who know her, or her sister, who seems to be gifted with perennial youth and whose singing must have been a surprise and a revelation to us all tonight, or, last but not least, when I consider our youngest hostess, talented, cheerful, hard-working and the best of nieces, I confess, Ladies and Gentlemen, that I do not know to which of them I should award the prize."

Gabriel glanced down at his aunts and, seeing the large smile on Aunt Julia's face and the tears which had risen to Aunt Kate's eyes, hastened to his close. He raised his glass of port gallantly while every member of the company fingered a glass expectantly, and said loudly:

"Let us toast them all three together. Let us drink to their health, wealth, long life, happiness and prosperity and may they long continue to hold the proud and self-won position which they hold in their profession and the position of honour and affection which they hold in our hearts."

All the guests stood up, glass in hand, and turning towards the three seated ladies, sang in unison, with Mr Browne as leader:

For they are jolly gay fellows,
For they are jolly gay fellows,
For they are jolly gay fellows,
Which nobody can deny.

Aunt Kate was making frank use of her handkerchief and even Aunt Julia seemed moved. Freddy Malins beat time with his pudding-fork and the singers turned towards one another, as if in melodious conference, while they sang with emphasis:

Unless he tells a lie,
Unless he tells a lie.

Then, turning once more towards their hostesses, they sang:

For they are jolly gay fellows,
For they are jolly gay fellows,
For they are jolly gay fellows,
Which nobody can deny.

The acclamation which followed was taken up beyond the door of the supper-room by many of the other guests and renewed time after time, Freddy Malins acting as officer with his fork on high.

* * *

The piercing morning air came into the hall where they were standing so that Aunt Kate said:

"Close the door, somebody. Mrs Malins will get her death of cold."

"Browne is out there, Aunt Kate," said Mary Jane.

"Browne is everywhere," said Aunt Kate, lowering her voice.

Mary Jane laughed at her tone.

"Really," she said archly, "he is very attentive."

"He has been laid on here like the gas," said Aunt Kate in the same tone, "all during the Christmas."

She laughed herself this time good-humouredly and then added quickly:

"But tell him to come in, Mary Jane, and close the door. I hope to goodness he didn't hear me."

At that moment the hall-door was opened and Mr Browne came in from the doorstep, laughing as if his heart would break. He was dressed in a long green overcoat with mock astrakhan cuffs and collar and wore on his head an oval fur cap. He pointed down the snow-covered quay from where the sound of shrill prolonged whistling was borne in.

"Teddy will have all the cabs in Dublin out," he said.

Gabriel advanced from the little pantry behind the office, struggling into his overcoat and, looking round the hall, said:

"Gretta not down yet?"

"She's getting on her things, Gabriel," said Aunt Kate.

"Who's playing up there?" asked Gabriel.

"Nobody. They're all gone."

"O no, Aunt Kate," said Mary Jane. "Bartell D'Arcy and Miss O'Callaghan aren't gone yet."

"Someone is fooling at the piano anyhow," said Gabriel.

Mary Jane glanced at Gabriel and Mr Browne and said with a shiver:

"It makes me feel cold to look at you two gentlemen muffled up like that. I wouldn't like to face your journey home at this hour."

"I'd like nothing better this minute," said Mr Browne stoutly, "than a rattling fine walk in the country or a fast drive with a good spanking goer between the shafts."

"We used to have a very good horse and trap at home," said Aunt Julia sadly.

"The never-to-be-forgotten Johnny," said Mary Jane, laughing.

Aunt Kate and Gabriel laughed too.

"Why, what was wonderful about Johnny?" asked Mr Browne.

"The late lamented Patrick Morkan, our grandfather, that is," explained Gabriel, "commonly known in his later years as the old gentleman, was a glue-boiler."

"O now, Gabriel," said Aunt Kate, laughing, "he had a starch mill."

"Well, glue or starch," said Gabriel, "the old gentleman had a horse by the name of Johnny. And Johnny used to work in the old gentleman's mill, walking round and round in order to drive the mill. That was all very well; but now comes the tragic part about Johnny. One fine day the old gentleman thought he'd like to drive out with the quality to a military review in the park."

"The Lord have mercy on his soul," said Aunt Kate compassionately.

"Amen," said Gabriel. "So the old gentleman, as I said, harnessed Johnny and put on his very best tall hat and his very best stock collar and drove out in grand style from his ancestral mansion somewhere near Back Lane, I think."

Everyone laughed, even Mrs Malins, at Gabriel's manner and Aunt Kate said:

"O now, Gabriel, he didn't live in Back Lane, really. Only the mill was there."

"Out from the mansion of his forefathers," continued Gabriel, "he drove with Johnny. And everything went on beautifully until Johnny came in sight of King Billy's statue: and whether he fell in love with the horse King Billy sits on or whether he thought he was back again in the mill, anyhow he began to walk round the statue."

Gabriel paced in a circle round the hall in his goloshes amid the laughter of the others.

"Round and round he went," said Gabriel, "and the old gentleman, who was a very pompous old gentleman, was highly indignant. 'Go on, sir! What do you mean, sir? Johnny! Johnny! Most extraordinary conduct! Can't understand the horse!'"

The peal of laughter which followed Gabriel's imitation of the incident was interrupted by a resounding knock at the hall door. Mary Jane ran to open it and let in Freddy Malins. Freddy Malins, with his hat well back on his head and his shoulders humped with cold, was puffing and steaming after his exertions.

"I could only get one cab," he said.

"O, we'll find another along the quay," said Gabriel.

"Yes," said Aunt Kate. "Better not keep Mrs Malins standing in the draught."

Mrs Malins was helped down the front steps by her son and Mr Browne and, after many manœuvres, hoisted into the cab. Freddy Malins clambered in after her and spent a long time settling her on the seat, Mr Browne helping him with advice. At last she was settled comfortably and Freddy Malins invited Mr Browne into the cab. There was a good deal of confused talk, and then Mr Browne got into the cab. The cabman settled his rug over his knees, and bent down for the address. The confusion grew greater and the cabman was directed differently by Freddy Malins and Mr Browne, each of whom had his head out through a window of the cab. The difficulty was to know where to drop Mr Browne along the route, and Aunt Kate, Aunt Julia and Mary Jane helped the discussion from the doorstep with cross-directions and contradictions and abundance of laughter. As for Freddy Malins he was speechless with laughter. He popped his head in and out of the window every moment to the great danger of his hat, and told his mother how the discussion was progressing, till at last Mr Browne shouted to the bewildered cabman above the din of everybody's laughter:

"Do you know Trinity College?"

"Yes, sir," said the cabman.

"Well, drive bang up against Trinity College gates," said Mr Browne, "and then we'll tell you where to go. You understand now?"

"Yes, sir," said the cabman.

"Make like a bird for Trinity College."

"Right, sir," said the cabman.

The horse was whipped up and the cab rattled off along the quay amid a chorus of laughter and adieus.

Gabriel had not gone to the door with the others. He was in a dark part of the hall gazing up the staircase. A woman was standing near the top of the first flight, in the shadow also. He could not see her face but he could see the terracotta and salmon-pink panels of her skirt which the shadow made appear black and white. It was his wife. She was leaning on the banisters, listening to something. Gabriel was surprised at her stillness and strained his ear to listen also. But he could hear little save the noise of laughter and dispute on the front steps, a few chords struck on the piano and a few notes of a man's voice singing.

He stood still in the gloom of the hall, trying to catch the air that the voice was singing and gazing up at his wife. There was grace and mystery in her attitude as if she were a symbol of something. He asked himself what is a woman standing on the stairs in the shadow, listening to distant music, a symbol of. If he were a painter he would paint her in that attitude. Her blue felt hat would show off the bronze of her hair against the darkness and the dark panels of her skirt would show off the light ones. *Distant Music* he would call the picture if he were a painter.

The hall-door was closed; and Aunt Kate, Aunt Julia and Mary Jane came down the hall, still laughing.

"Well, isn't Freddy terrible?" said Mary Jane. "He's really terrible."

Gabriel said nothing but pointed up the stairs towards where his wife was standing. Now that the hall-door was closed the voice and the piano could be heard more clearly. Gabriel held up his hand for them to be silent. The song seemed to be in the old Irish tonality and the singer seemed uncertain both of his words and of his voice. The voice, made plaintive by distance and by the singer's hoarseness, faintly illuminated the cadence of the air with words expressing grief:

> *O, the rain falls on my heavy locks*
> *And the dew wets my skin,*
> *My babe lies cold....*

"O," exclaimed Mary Jane. "It's Bartell D'Arcy singing and he wouldn't sing all the night. O, I'll get him to sing a song before he goes."

"O do, Mary Jane," said Aunt Kate.

Mary Jane brushed past the others and ran to the staircase, but before she reached it the singing stopped and the piano was closed abruptly.

"O, what a pity!" she cried. "Is he coming down, Gretta?"

Gabriel heard his wife answer yes and saw her come down towards them. A few steps behind her were Mr Bartell D'Arcy and Miss O'Callaghan.

"O, Mr D'Arcy," cried Mary Jane, "it's downright mean of you to break off like that when we were all in raptures listening to you."

"I have been at him all the evening," said Miss O'Callaghan, "and Mrs Conroy too and he told us he had a dreadful cold and couldn't sing."

"O, Mr D'Arcy," said Aunt Kate, "now that was a great fib to tell."

"Can't you see that I'm as hoarse as a crow?" said Mr D'Arcy roughly.

He went into the pantry hastily and put on his overcoat. The others, taken aback by his rude speech, could find nothing to say. Aunt Kate wrinkled her brows and made signs to the others to drop the subject. Mr D'Arcy stood swathing his neck carefully and frowning.

"It's the weather," said Aunt Julia, after a pause.

"Yes, everybody has colds," said Aunt Kate readily, "everybody."

"They say," said Mary Jane, "we haven't had snow like it for thirty years; and I read this morning in the newspapers that the snow is general all over Ireland."

"I love the look of snow," said Aunt Julia sadly.

"So do I," said Miss O'Callaghan. "I think Christmas is never really Christmas unless we have the snow on the ground."

"But poor Mr D'Arcy doesn't like the snow," said Aunt Kate, smiling.

Mr D'Arcy came from the pantry, fully swathed and buttoned, and in a repentant tone told them the history of his cold. Everyone gave him advice and said it was a great pity and urged him to be very careful of his throat in the night air. Gabriel watched his wife, who did not join in the conversation. She was standing right under the dusty fanlight and the flame of the gas lit up the rich bronze of her hair, which he had seen her drying at the fire a few days before. She was in the same attitude and seemed unaware of the talk about her. At last she turned towards them and Gabriel saw that there was colour on her cheeks and that her eyes were shining. A sudden tide of joy went leaping out of his heart.

"Mr D'Arcy," she said, "what is the name of that song you were singing?"

"It's called *The Lass of Aughrim*," said Mr D'Arcy, "but I couldn't remember it properly. Why? Do you know it?"

"*The Lass of Aughrim*," she repeated. "I couldn't think of the name."

"It's a very nice air," said Mary Jane. "I'm sorry you were not in voice tonight."

"Now, Mary Jane," said Aunt Kate, "don't annoy Mr D'Arcy. I won't have him annoyed."

Seeing that all were ready to start she shepherded them to the door, where good-night was said:

"Well, good-night, Aunt Kate, and thanks for the pleasant evening."

"Good-night, Gabriel. Good-night, Gretta!"

"Good-night, Aunt Kate, and thanks ever so much. Good-night, Aunt Julia."

"O, good-night, Gretta, I didn't see you."

"Good-night, Mr D'Arcy. Good-night, Miss O'Callaghan."

"Good-night, Miss Morkan."

"Good-night, again."

"Good-night, all. Safe home."

"Good-night. Good-night."

The morning was still dark. A dull yellow light brooded over the houses and the river; and the sky seemed to be descending. It was slushy underfoot; and only streaks and patches of snow lay on the roofs, on the parapets of the quay and on the area railings. The lamps were still burning redly in the murky air and, across the river, the palace of the Four Courts stood out menacingly against the heavy sky.

She was walking on before him with Mr Bartell D'Arcy, her shoes in a brown parcel tucked under one arm and her hands holding her skirt up from the slush. She had no longer any grace of attitude but Gabriel's eyes were still bright with happiness. The blood went bounding along his veins; and the thoughts went rioting through his brain, proud, joyful, tender, valorous.

She was walking on before him so lightly and so erect that he longed to run after her noiselessly, catch her by the shoulders and say something foolish and affectionate into her ear. She seemed to him so frail that he longed to defend her against something and then to be alone with

her. Moments of their secret life together burst like stars upon his memory. A heliotrope
envelope was lying beside his breakfast-cup and he was caressing it with his hand. Birds
were twittering in the ivy and the sunny web of the curtain was shimmering along the floor:
he could not eat for happiness. They were standing on the crowded platform and he was
placing a ticket inside the warm palm of her glove. He was standing with her in the cold,
looking in through a grated window at a man making bottles in a roaring furnace. It was
very cold. Her face, fragrant in the cold air, was quite close to his; and suddenly he called
out to the man at the furnace:

"Is the fire hot, sir?"

But the man could not hear with the noise of the furnace. It was just as well. He might have
answered rudely.

A wave of yet more tender joy escaped from his heart and went coursing in warm flood along
his arteries. Like the tender fire of stars moments of their life together, that no one knew of or
would ever know of, broke upon and illumined his memory. He longed to recall to her those
moments, to make her forget the years of their dull existence together and remember only their
moments of ecstasy. For the years, he felt, had not quenched his soul or hers. Their children, his
writing, her household cares had not quenched all their souls' tender fire. In one letter that he had
written to her then he had said: "Why is it that words like these seem to me so dull and cold? Is it
because there is no word tender enough to be your name?"

Like distant music these words that he had written years before were borne towards him from
the past. He longed to be alone with her. When the others had gone away, when he and she were
in their room in the hotel, then they would be alone together. He would call her softly:

"Gretta!"

Perhaps she would not hear at once: she would be undressing. Then something in his voice
would strike her. She would turn and look at him....

At the corner of Winetavern Street they met a cab. He was glad of its rattling noise as it saved
him from conversation. She was looking out of the window and seemed tired. The others spoke
only a few words, pointing out some building or street. The horse galloped along wearily under
the murky morning sky, dragging his old rattling box after his heels, and Gabriel was again in a
cab with her, galloping to catch the boat, galloping to their honeymoon.

As the cab drove across O'Connell Bridge Miss O'Callaghan said:

"They say you never cross O'Connell Bridge without seeing a white horse."

"I see a white man this time," said Gabriel.

"Where?" asked Mr Bartell D'Arcy.

Gabriel pointed to the statue, on which lay patches of snow. Then he nodded familiarly to it
and waved his hand.

"Good-night, Dan," he said gaily.

When the cab drew up before the hotel, Gabriel jumped out and, in spite of Mr Bartell D'Arcy's
protest, paid the driver. He gave the man a shilling over his fare. The man saluted and said:

"A prosperous New Year to you, sir."

"The same to you," said Gabriel cordially.

She leaned for a moment on his arm in getting out of the cab and while standing at the
curbstone, bidding the others good-night. She leaned lightly on his arm, as lightly as when she had
danced with him a few hours before. He had felt proud and happy then, happy that she was his,
proud of her grace and wifely carriage. But now, after the kindling again of so many memories, the
first touch of her body, musical and strange and perfumed, sent through him a keen pang of lust.
Under cover of her silence he pressed her arm closely to his side; and, as they stood at the hotel

door, he felt that they had escaped from their lives and duties, escaped from home and friends and run away together with wild and radiant hearts to a new adventure.

An old man was dozing in a great hooded chair in the hall. He lit a candle in the office and went before them to the stairs. They followed him in silence, their feet falling in soft thuds on the thickly carpeted stairs. She mounted the stairs behind the porter, her head bowed in the ascent, her frail shoulders curved as with a burden, her skirt girt tightly about her. He could have flung his arms about her hips and held her still, for his arms were trembling with desire to seize her and only the stress of his nails against the palms of his hands held the wild impulse of his body in check. The porter halted on the stairs to settle his guttering candle. They halted too on the steps below him. In the silence Gabriel could hear the falling of the molten wax into the tray and the thumping of his own heart against his ribs.

The porter led them along a corridor and opened a door. Then he set his unstable candle down on a toilet-table and asked at what hour they were to be called in the morning.

"Eight," said Gabriel.

The porter pointed to the tap of the electric-light and began a muttered apology but Gabriel cut him short.

"We don't want any light. We have light enough from the street. And I say," he added, pointing to the candle, "you might remove that handsome article, like a good man."

The porter took up his candle again, but slowly for he was surprised by such a novel idea. Then he mumbled good-night and went out. Gabriel shot the lock to.

A ghostly light from the street lamp lay in a long shaft from one window to the door. Gabriel threw his overcoat and hat on a couch and crossed the room towards the window. He looked down into the street in order that his emotion might calm a little. Then he turned and leaned against a chest of drawers with his back to the light. She had taken off her hat and cloak and was standing before a large swinging mirror, unhooking her waist. Gabriel paused for a few moments, watching her, and then said:

"Gretta!"

She turned away from the mirror slowly and walked along the shaft of light towards him. Her face looked so serious and weary that the words would not pass Gabriel's lips. No, it was not the moment yet.

"You looked tired," he said.

"I am a little," she answered.

"You don't feel ill or weak?"

"No, tired: that's all."

She went on to the window and stood there, looking out. Gabriel waited again and then, fearing that diffidence was about to conquer him, he said abruptly:

"By the way, Gretta!"

"What is it?"

"You know that poor fellow Malins?" he said quickly.

"Yes. What about him?"

"Well, poor fellow, he's a decent sort of chap after all," continued Gabriel in a false voice. "He gave me back that sovereign I lent him, and I didn't expect it, really. It's a pity he wouldn't keep away from that Browne, because he's not a bad fellow, really."

He was trembling now with annoyance. Why did she seem so abstracted? He did not know how he could begin. Was she annoyed, too, about something? If she would only turn to him or come to him of her own accord! To take her as she was would be brutal. No, he must see some ardour in her eyes first. He longed to be master of her strange mood.

"When did you lend him the pound?" she asked, after a pause.

Gabriel strove to restrain himself from breaking out into brutal language about the sottish Malins and his pound. He longed to cry to her from his soul, to crush her body against his, to overmaster her. But he said:

"O, at Christmas, when he opened that little Christmas-card shop in Henry Street."

He was in such a fever of rage and desire that he did not hear her come from the window. She stood before him for an instant, looking at him strangely. Then, suddenly raising herself on tiptoe and resting her hands lightly on his shoulders, she kissed him.

"You are a very generous person, Gabriel," she said.

Gabriel, trembling with delight at her sudden kiss and at the quaintness of her phrase, put his hands on her hair and began smoothing it back, scarcely touching it with his fingers. The washing had made it fine and brilliant. His heart was brimming over with happiness. Just when he was wishing for it she had come to him of her own accord. Perhaps her thoughts had been running with his. Perhaps she had felt the impetuous desire that was in him, and then the yielding mood had come upon her. Now that she had fallen to him so easily, he wondered why he had been so diffident.

He stood, holding her head between his hands. Then, slipping one arm swiftly about her body and drawing her towards him, he said softly:

"Gretta, dear, what are you thinking about?"

She did not answer nor yield wholly to his arm. He said again, softly:

"Tell me what it is, Gretta. I think I know what is the matter. Do I know?"

She did not answer at once. Then she said in an outburst of tears:

"O, I am thinking about that song, *The Lass of Aughrim*."

She broke loose from him and ran to the bed and, throwing her arms across the bed-rail, hid her face. Gabriel stood stock-still for a moment in astonishment and then followed her. As he passed in the way of the cheval-glass he caught sight of himself in full length, his broad, well-filled shirt-front, the face whose expression always puzzled him when he saw it in a mirror and his glimmering gilt-rimmed eyeglasses. He halted a few paces from her and said:

"What about the song? Why does that make you cry?"

She raised her head from her arms and dried her eyes with the back of her hand like a child. A kinder note than he had intended went into his voice.

"Why, Gretta?" he asked.

"I am thinking about a person long ago who used to sing that song."

"And who was the person long ago?" asked Gabriel, smiling.

"It was a person I used to know in Galway when I was living with my grandmother," she said.

The smile passed away from Gabriel's face. A dull anger began to gather again at the back of his mind and the dull fires of his lust began to glow angrily in his veins.

"Someone you were in love with?" he asked ironically.

"It was a young boy I used to know," she answered, "named Michael Furey. He used to sing that song, *The Lass of Aughrim*. He was very delicate."

Gabriel was silent. He did not wish her to think that he was interested in this delicate boy.

"I can see him so plainly," she said after a moment. "Such eyes as he had: big, dark eyes! And such an expression in them – an expression!"

"O then, you were in love with him?" said Gabriel.

"I used to go out walking with him," she said, "when I was in Galway."

A thought flew across Gabriel's mind.

"Perhaps that was why you wanted to go to Galway with that Ivors girl?" he said coldly.

She looked at him and asked in surprise:

"What for?"

Her eyes made Gabriel feel awkward. He shrugged his shoulders and said:

"How do I know? To see him, perhaps."

She looked away from him along the shaft of light towards the window in silence.

"He is dead," she said at length. "He died when he was only seventeen. Isn't it a terrible thing to die so young as that?"

"What was he?" asked Gabriel, still ironically.

"He was in the gasworks," she said.

Gabriel felt humiliated by the failure of his irony and by the evocation of this figure from the dead, a boy in the gasworks. While he had been full of memories of their secret life together, full of tenderness and joy and desire, she had been comparing him in her mind with another. A shameful consciousness of his own person assailed him. He saw himself as a ludicrous figure, acting as a pennyboy for his aunts, a nervous, well-meaning sentimentalist, orating to vulgarians and idealising his own clownish lusts, the pitiable fatuous fellow he had caught a glimpse of in the mirror. Instinctively he turned his back more to the light lest she might see the shame that burned upon his forehead.

He tried to keep up his tone of cold interrogation, but his voice when he spoke was humble and indifferent.

"I suppose you were in love with this Michael Furey, Gretta," he said.

"I was great with him at that time," she said.

Her voice was veiled and sad. Gabriel, feeling now how vain it would be to try to lead her whither he had purposed, caressed one of her hands and said, also sadly:

"And what did he die of so young, Gretta? Consumption, was it?"

"I think he died for me," she answered.

A vague terror seized Gabriel at this answer as if, at that hour when he had hoped to triumph, some impalpable and vindictive being was coming against him, gathering forces against him in its vague world. But he shook himself free of it with an effort of reason and continued to caress her hand. He did not question her again for he felt that she would tell him of herself. Her hand was warm and moist: it did not respond to his touch but he continued to caress it just as he had caressed her first letter to him that spring morning.

"It was in the winter," she said, "about the beginning of the winter when I was going to leave my grandmother's and come up here to the convent. And he was ill at the time in his lodgings in Galway and wouldn't be let out and his people in Oughterard were written to. He was in decline, they said, or something like that. I never knew rightly."

She paused for a moment and sighed.

"Poor fellow," she said. "He was very fond of me and he was such a gentle boy. We used to go out together, walking, you know, Gabriel, like the way they do in the country. He was going to study singing only for his health. He had a very good voice, poor Michael Furey."

"Well; and then?" asked Gabriel.

"And then when it came to the time for me to leave Galway and come up to the convent he was much worse and I wouldn't be let see him so I wrote him a letter saying I was going up to Dublin and would be back in the summer and hoping he would be better then."

She paused for a moment to get her voice under control and then went on:

"Then the night before I left I was in my grandmother's house in Nuns' Island, packing up, and I heard gravel thrown up against the window. The window was so wet I couldn't see so I ran downstairs as I was and slipped out the back into the garden and there was the poor fellow at the end of the garden, shivering."

"And did you not tell him to go back?" asked Gabriel.

"I implored of him to go home at once and told him he would get his death in the rain. But he said he did not want to live. I can see his eyes as well as well! He was standing at the end of the wall where there was a tree."

"And did he go home?" asked Gabriel.

"Yes, he went home. And when I was only a week in the convent he died and he was buried in Oughterard where his people came from. O, the day I heard that, that he was dead!"

She stopped, choking with sobs and, overcome by emotion, flung herself face downward on the bed, sobbing in the quilt. Gabriel held her hand for a moment longer, irresolutely, and then, shy of intruding on her grief, let it fall gently and walked quietly to the window.

She was fast asleep.

Gabriel, leaning on his elbow, looked for a few moments unresentfully on her tangled hair and half-open mouth, listening to her deep-drawn breath. So she had had that romance in her life: a man had died for her sake. It hardly pained him now to think how poor a part he, her husband, had played in her life. He watched her while she slept as though he and she had never lived together as man and wife. His curious eyes rested long upon her face and on her hair: and, as he thought of what she must have been then, in that time of her first girlish beauty, a strange, friendly pity for her entered his soul. He did not like to say even to himself that her face was no longer beautiful but he knew that it was no longer the face for which Michael Furey had braved death.

Perhaps she had not told him all the story. His eyes moved to the chair over which she had thrown some of her clothes. A petticoat string dangled to the floor. One boot stood upright, its limp upper fallen down: the fellow of it lay upon its side. He wondered at his riot of emotions of an hour before. From what had it proceeded? From his aunt's supper, from his own foolish speech, from the wine and dancing, the merry-making when saying good-night in the hall, the pleasure of the walk along the river in the snow. Poor Aunt Julia! She, too, would soon be a shade with the shade of Patrick Morkan and his horse. He had caught that haggard look upon her face for a moment when she was singing *Arrayed for the Bridal*. Soon, perhaps, he would be sitting in that same drawing-room, dressed in black, his silk hat on his knees. The blinds would be drawn down and Aunt Kate would be sitting beside him, crying and blowing her nose and telling him how Julia had died. He would cast about in his mind for some words that might console her, and would find only lame and useless ones. Yes, yes: that would happen very soon.

The air of the room chilled his shoulders. He stretched himself cautiously along under the sheets and lay down beside his wife. One by one they were all becoming shades. Better pass boldly into that other world, in the full glory of some passion, than fade and wither dismally with age. He thought of how she who lay beside him had locked in her heart for so many years that image of her lover's eyes when he had told her that he did not wish to live.

Generous tears filled Gabriel's eyes. He had never felt like that himself towards any woman but he knew that such a feeling must be love. The tears gathered more thickly in his eyes and in the partial darkness he imagined he saw the form of a young man standing under a dripping tree. Other forms were near. His soul had approached that region where dwell the vast hosts of the dead. He was conscious of, but could not apprehend, their wayward and flickering existence. His own identity was fading out into a grey impalpable world: the solid world itself which these dead had one time reared and lived in was dissolving and dwindling.

A few light taps upon the pane made him turn to the window. It had begun to snow again. He watched sleepily the flakes, silver and dark, falling obliquely against the lamplight. The time had come for him to set out on his journey westward. Yes, the newspapers were right: snow was general all over Ireland. It was falling on every part of the dark central plain, on the treeless hills, falling softly upon the Bog of Allen and, farther westward, softly falling into the dark mutinous Shannon waves. It was falling, too, upon every part of the lonely churchyard on the hill where Michael Furey lay buried. It lay thickly drifted on the crooked crosses and headstones, on the spears of the little gate, on the barren thorns. His soul swooned slowly as he heard the snow falling faintly through the universe and faintly falling, like the descent of their last end, upon all the living and the dead.

Christmas at Trelawny

E.E. King

IT WAS A GRAND old place, all curving mahogany staircases and domed glass ceilings. I'd come at Christmas, come for peace – peace and time to breathe, think and finish the damn thesis dangling over my head like some literary sword of Damocles.

It was "perfectly normal," they'd said. "Many of our most brilliant students suffer issues of completion." But I could hear the whispers, or rather I could feel them, creeping out of night corners like phantom rats gnawing at my fragile sense of purpose and belief.

My mother had been haunted by similar demons, as had my aunts, grandmother and her sisters before her. My lineage reached backward into a pedigree of despair. They were all gone now. All dead by their own hand before age thirty, and all around Christmas.

My mother received her medical degree from Harvard. She only practised for a year, before going to Oxford to study history, where she'd met my father, who was finishing his doctorate in Physics. They had fallen madly in love, married and had me.

Two years later, on a Christmas trip to the Cornish coast, she had waded into the cold North Sea, never to return.

I thought I'd escaped. I'd been a quiet, calm, studious child, reaching for nothing more emotionally challenging than stones and bones. I had few friends. I was taunted for my thick, black eyebrows and unruly dark hair, though now I realize it was not so much my appearance, but my bookish introspection that made me an outcast.

At nineteen, I entered the Earth Sciences department at Oxford, and a year later, I waded into the pond at Island Wood, my pockets weighed down with fossils purloined from the lab.

My father, now a Physics professor at Oxford, was called. Rest and medication were prescribed. And so, I'd been sent to recuperate at Trelawny Manor, the oldest Estate in Cornwall.

I packed a sketch pad, charcoal and a panoply of medicines. Antidepressants that kept me from feeling joy. Mood stabilizers that fogged my brain, and painkillers to soothe my ankle, which I'd broken in my wade toward eternity. The grey cloud that had enveloped my world had lifted slightly, but only because I was too numb to feel anything as strong as despair.

During the summer, Trelawny Manor was a stop for scholars and tourists. In winter, it was mostly deserted.

I'd taken a train to Cornwall and a cab to the manor. The driver was a red-faced man with inquisitive blue eyes. My small bag, which he tossed in the trunk, was dwarfed by his huge, meaty hands. Would he speed away with my belongings, leaving me alone and without clothes, shoes or medication?

He slapped me on the shoulder, genially, but with such force as to propel me into the polished leather back seat. He was just being affable, but my spirit shrank from the contact.

"Welcome to Cornwall." His breath smelled of winter nights by ageing pub fires. "And Merry Christmas. You've come to the best little county in Great Britain, not that I'm prejudiced."

"Me name's Charlie. Lived here all me life I have, and I can tell you just about anything you want to know." He started the cab and peered at me, keen eyes curious.

"Well now, I haven't even asked where you'r headed? Me missus always said I talk more than I think."

"I'm going to Trelawny Manor," I whispered.

He made no sound. I looked up, fearful that a glance might unleash another torrent of unwanted chatter. All color had drained from his ruddy cheeks, leaving him pale as a peeled potato.

"Do you know it?" I asked.

"'Course I do," he said. "And a mighty fine place it is… in the summer… but at Christmas…" His voice drifted away like a fading wind.

I thought of asking what was wrong with the Manor at Christmas, but I dreaded conversation more than mystery.

Trelawny's roots reached back to the 1600s. Four stories of stone that coiled above the land like an enormous ammonite. The coast was miles away, but to my left it curved sharply inland and looked to be an easy walk from the Manor.

Charlie pulled up to a grand circular entrance and handed me my bag.

"If you don't like it here, miss," he said, pressing a card into my hand, "just give a call. There's many another place that'd be happy for lodgers."

I twisted my mouth into what I hoped was a smile. My face felt stiff, the muscles unused from staring into the void.

The large wooden doors opened surprisingly easily considering their mass. Behind a walnut desk sat a tight-lipped, doughy woman with an almost unruly halo of blueish-grey curls. It was the only free, even slightly wild, aspect of her person.

The corners of the woman's mouth turned upward as she handed me a key, but the smile didn't reach her cold blue eyes.

"I'm Mrs. Molchany," she said. "You're the only one here, and I'll be the one seeing to your needs.

"I serve breakfast at eight, elevenses at 11:30, luncheon at one, tea at four, and dinner at six, but I never stay overnight.

"There are many paths through the moorland, but don't use the track on the left. It leads most direct to the sea, but it's dangerous. Many a sheep and more than one child has been lost there. Once the black mud gets ahold of you, you'll never escape." She said this with an odd satisfaction.

"You'll be wanting to look at this," she said, pushing a faded, red-leather book toward me. "It's been our guest book since 1602, signed by each and every one of our guests." She said this smugly, as if she had personally supervised the inking of each and every signature. "And which part of our rich history will you be investigating while you're with us?"

"Ancient," I said. "Precambrian Serpentine."

She didn't reply, just stared at me out of those probing cool eyes, as if I were a not very interesting relic, which she needed to keep safe even if she doubted its value. Or perhaps it was me, floundering in a sea of suspicion, and finding it, even where there was none. I took the key and turned away.

My room had a large bay window that looked out over Cornwall's shaggy moorland and cold, raging sea. It smelled faintly, not unpleasantly, of lavender and slightly fermented kelp.

Despite my fatigue, I couldn't sleep. I took the one sleeping pill I was allowed and waited. Perhaps a tiny exploration would exhaust me?

The hall was like the inside of a giant, chambered nautilus, a creature whose relatives date back to the Early Pleistocene. Swirling mahogany balusters hung with Yuletide holly swept upward to a stained-glass crystal cupola. Beneath the dome stood a huge Christmas tree, hung with tinsel. What day was it? Boxing Day? Christmas Eve?

I smelled the library before I saw it. A fragrance of vanilla and almonds. Father said that the smell was caused by the breakdown of chemicals in the paper. Odd that decay should smell so sweet. Perhaps there is a heaven for books that people never dream of, where ideas live on.

The thought made me uncomfortable. I liked facts, fossils, the hard clarity of science. Not these fanciful notions drifting through my mind, obscuring the hard, unwavering light of reality. If I cut down on the mood stabilizers, would I be clearer?

A powdering of stars twinkled through the bay windows. Bookshelves lined the walls, but they were disappointingly bare. I turned to leave, finally wearied, when a slim leather volume caught my eye. It had no legible title, only the indentations of worn script and a flash of gold embedded in the vanished text.

Tragedy at Trelawny was inscribed in curling letters on the frontispiece. I took the book to bed, where I fell into a dark dream. Something wakened me.

Moonlight poured through my window. Every blade of grass seemed etched into the land. For the first time in months, my mind was equally clear.

To the left, where the coast bent closest toward Trelawny I could make out dark huddled figures around a small fire. Odd that anyone should venture there, where Mrs. Molchany had said the cliffs were the weakest, but perhaps my bearings were confused by the wandering clouds and flat light. Perhaps it was some local Christmas custom?

One of the figures straightened up and began walking toward my window. It was a woman, as small as I, but so slender and well-formed, she gave the impression of great height. There was something ominous about the intensity of her focus. She seemed so fixated on me, or at least on my lighted window, as to be ignoring her surroundings, though she walked along the very edge of the roaring waves.

* * *

I woke late, not leaving my room till 6:00 pm. Mrs. Molchany awaited me in a preposterously large dining room with overcooked greens, a desiccated turkey, Yorkshire pudding and a small mince pie. Was I feasting on the remains of some other, more festive Christmas?

"You must have needed your sleep?" She smiled, but there was a sharpness in those cold blue eyes.

"I—I've been ill," I stammered.

"So I've heard."

The blood rushed to my face. I tried not to think about what she'd heard.

"Depression was nothing to be ashamed of," they'd said.

"And—and the moon was so bright," I added.

"Moon?" she said. "You must'a been dreaming. T'was a new moon, black as a Newgate knocker."

* * *

I spent my days resting by the window, studying *Tragedy at Trelawny* and the venerated guest book. Both books were extraordinary. One for what it said, the other for what it implied.

Tragedy at Trelawny was an account of the trial of Truth Device, the first guest of the manor. Accused of witchcraft by her ten-year-old daughter Grace, Truth had been burned at the cliff's edge, on Christmas 1659. It was a list of dates, prosecution, and death, brutal and horrible.

The guest book was different. Its swirls of signature were open to interpretation. I liked tracing my fingers over the slightly indented curves, the pages filled before typewriters had destroyed the art of calligraphy. There was personality evident in each, essence in ink, a mirror of the soul.

I had never much been interested in souls, or philosophy either. Those things less real than science and mathematics. If you learned a formula or the properties of a stone, you had data that would never change. A plant that was edible was always edible, but a theory about the soul or God was as malleable as wet tissue. And history looked very different depending upon which version you read. Now though, sitting on the window seat, looking over the moors and the frothing sea below, I ran my finger over the old signatures, imagining the people who had written them. It may have been a lonely way to spend Christmas, but it was what my soul craved, as well as what the doctor ordered.

* * *

True to her word, Mrs. Molchany had a huge, largely indigestible breakfast on the sideboard at eight, which gave way to stale granola bars at 11:30, followed by tea, and dinner. Tea was the only meal I enjoyed, not the dry, hard scones, but the rich, slightly grainy clotted cream with strawberry jam that filled all the corners in my hungry heart.

I began to cut the dose of the antidepressants and mood stabilizers, trying to find the perfect balance. The painkillers didn't dull my perceptions but made them sharper, like bottled clarity.

I awoke early, avoiding the shale and serpentine cliffs that held both the fossil past and my own unfinished thesis. Instead, I tramped the narrow paths of mud and moss till I was tired, then returned to my window seat, running my hand over the rough penmanship of Truth Device. I couldn't say why her signature had such power over me, just that it drew me to wonder about its origin as before I had only wondered about fossils and bones.

Then the sky opened and poured for two days. I should have worked on my paper. I could have written letters detailing my progress and health. Instead I sat in my window, inhaling the fragrance of vanilla and almonds that drifted up from the guest book, until a signature caught my eye. Nicole Turner, December, 1998. It was my mother's; made the same year she had marched into the sea, never to return.

I closed my eyes, seeing in that inner darkness her leaving me, without a backward glance. What had driven her into the cold, unfeeling waters? What had driven me? Nothing solid, nothing specific, just an unbearable sadness, a dark, suffocating curtain I could not see beyond. It was written into my genes, engraved by maternal hands so deeply, there was no escape.

I began to leaf back through the pages. Each name a dark house, concealing lives behind ink walls. And there – fifteen years before my mother's visit, I found another familiar name: Alice Turner, my grandmother, which was as far back as I could trace. With a family like mine, you don't look for ancestors. You're afraid of what you might find.

The next day gave way to a sudden, unexpected burst of sun. The moors glittered. Steam rose from the grassland like departing spirits. There was something almost transcendent in their vast loneliness.

I packed a small bag with water, a few purloined granola bars, my sketch pad, my painkillers and a small spade and set out toward the cliff, where I had seen night fires burning.

I dared not take the most direct route. It looked an easy walk, but I remembered Mrs. Molchany's warning. Without trees as signposts, land and sea flattened into an endless perspectiveless swath of green and grey. It took me more than an hour, mud sucking at my shoes as if to pull me down beneath the emerald carpet. At the bluff's edge, the ground gave way.

The sun was bright, but winter brisk. I shivered. Still, having come this far and found this... whatever it was... I pulled out my spade and began to dig. Beneath the grass was a hole, almost a meter deep and about half as wide again.

The bottom of the hole was covered in black clay and lined with white feathers. It might have been a bird-plucking hollow; such pits were common at the turn of the nineteenth century. But no – what I had thought was dark clay was really a charred body. As my eyes grew accustomed to the dimness, I could just make out small, outstretched limbs, a long sinuous neck and a tiny, delicate head that was mostly orbital lobes. It was a carbonized swan, lacking only its beak.

There is a legend that swans were introduced to Britain in the twelfth century by Richard I, but the bird is native. Ownership was recorded by marks nicked into the beak. Any swan that didn't bear one was the property of the crown. The penalty for ignoring swan marks, or for killing birds, was a year's imprisonment.

On top of the swan nestled fifty-five eggs, seven of which contained chicks close to hatching. The shells of the eggs had mostly dissolved, but moisture had preserved the membranes. There was something unutterably sad about the dried, yellow embryos, curled in on themselves like pictures of despair. As little as I liked to admit it, this seemed like a witch pit.

Uncover a nest or discover a den, and there will be a reason for everything, every twig or dropping or bone. But witch pits were the product of delusion, the human drama I'd been trying to avoid my whole life.

The killing of swans has been illegal since the eleventh century, and the witchcraft laws were only scrapped in 1951. A shiver snaked up my spine as I imagined someone digging a hole, and carefully laying in these offerings. What had made them desperate enough to risk death if caught?

As I turned the bones over in my hands, I realized they were bound together with faded orange cord – a synthetic twine not manufactured till the 1960s. Stuck to the twine was a scrap of newsprint. I could just make out a faint headline. "Dr. Nicole Stevens to join History department at Oxford."

I imagined generations of women coming here to ask favors of their gods, devotees reaching back into the 1600s in an unbroken chain, but surely my doctor mother had not been among them? I leaned back, hoping for support, but as my sweater touched the wet mud, the anguish of the body superseded the torments of the heart.

I snipped the string on either side of the paper, not an approved collection practice, but I needed to get back, and I wanted – no needed – this paper. It was proof that I was not mad.

The sun had begun to sink into the waves. Gray clouds blew in like an advancing army, blotting out sea and shore, encasing me in pervasive twilight. My pocket flashlight was dead.

An ice-cold raindrop slapped my face. I didn't know how far I had gone, or even if I was headed in the right direction. I might be walking straight toward the cliff and the sea below. For the first time in for ever I didn't want that. No, I wanted to live, at least long enough to discover why my mother's name had been buried in a witch pit on the Cornish coast, and why my mother and grandmother had visited Trelawny Manor. But neither the yearning to live, nor the desire to die are enough to make it happen. I stumbled and lay on the wet grass, the rain driving me into the earth. I imagined my body dissolving in the bog, my bones turning to fossils for some later archeologist to discover.

When I awakened, Father was sitting by my bed. His pale grey eyes peered at me over wire reading glasses.

"You were found on the moors." His voice was as detached as if he were explaining a simple equation to a slow undergraduate.

I looked down at my hands. They were empty.

"Did you see the paper?"

He shook his head, "All they found on you was your pack, a dead flashlight and an empty bottle of pain pills. Your fist was closed, but nothing was in your hand."

My evidence, dissolved in the rain.

"Did you know Mother was here?" I asked. "I found her signature in the guest book."

He shook his head. "I didn't, but she was studying the history of Cornwall. It's logical she might have visited."

His face was proof against necromancy. I would not tell him that my grandmother had also been here. I would not tell him of the witch pit with my mother's name bound up in twine. He would have an explanation. As for the newspaper, he might believe it to be a delusion of my fevered mind. It sounded more reasonable than anything I could conjure.

Father had brought me a few sad Christmas presents; a tin of biscuits, and a book on Crowell's fossils. It was worse than being forgotten.

When I was well, or at least well enough to lie in bed and read, he left. He had classes to teach, and papers to write, a life outside of Trelawny and his crazy daughter.

"Be healthy," he said, his slightly chapped lips brushing against my cheek. "Finish your paper, but don't pressure yourself."

My father had made certain I followed the doctor's dosage. It made me foggy. I needed to think. I needed to work. I halved my dose of anti-depressants and quit the mood stabilizers altogether. But instead of studying the Precambrian shale, I delved into the witches of Cornwall.

The witch trials of Western Europe lasted three hundred years and killed more than eighty thousand witches. Orthodox wisdom attributed the hysteria to a slate of almost supernaturally bad weather, freak frosts, plagues of mice, even a couple of rains of frogs. But it wasn't just the ice age that caused the witch hunt. Protestantism had recently emerged. And what better way to make converts than to combat satanism? The hysteria began in Germany, with "The Hammer of Witches," a guide on how to identify and interrogate necromancers. It was ugly stuff. The reason I'd studied rocks and stones was to avoid these dramas. I had enough trouble with the demons in my DNA.

* * *

A man bends over me, head shrouded by a black hood. Piercing blue eyes stare out of the darkness. "Is it not true, Grace Device, that your mother, Truth, is a witch? Is it not true that her spirit can enter the likeness of a brown dog?"

He bends my small, pliable fingers back.

* * *

"Wake up, miss, wake up."

Someone was shaking me. Mrs. Molchany's chill blue eyes examined me.

"You were having a nightmare, miss."

I wanted to ask Mrs. Molchany if she'd seen *Tragedy at Trelawny,* but the words stuck in my throat.

"A history of Trelawny? I'm sure I don't know what you are referring to."

Had I spoken aloud?

"I don't know of any such history, miss."

Why was she lying?

* * *

It was almost two weeks before I felt well enough to leave Trelawny. Then, almost against my volition, I found myself wandering toward town and The Boswell Museum of Witchcraft.

As I reached up, the door opened. An old woman stood inside.

"I'm Mrs. Gypsy Evansleaver." She smiled, her skin crackling into a million welcoming folds. "Welcome to The Museum. Centuries have passed, yet in this wee, quiet corner of England, we are unchanged, perched right on the edge of the beyond."

She took my hand. A pulse of electricity raced up my arm.

"My mother was here once," It felt like a confession. "Not here-here, I mean," I stammered. "But in Cornwall."

"What was her name, dear?" She leafed backward through a guest book.

Nicole Turner, December, 1998.

"Did—did you know her?" I whispered.

She shook her head. "I fear there's things ye need ken to that only the dead may tell. Come to my house this Wednesnight. We will ask the coven. Mayhap it will put your soul at peace."

I shook my head, but even as I did, I knew I would go. I had never been to a séance. While my school mates clustered together in darkened rooms over Ouija boards, I read about rock substrates. My dead were already too close, woven into my genes like a warning.

* * *

I called Charlie to take me. He arrived in his old black cab, shiny as a hearse.

"How good it is to see ya, miss." His round, red face broke into a smile. "Where are you going?"

"To Mrs. Evansleaver's."

His lips tightened. He said not a word but sped through the night, stopping so suddenly I slammed into the rear of his seat. My door opened into darkness.

"It's thata way. Just follow your nose. When you see a slate path, take it."

He disappeared before I could ask how to reach him.

I stepped down, twisting my weak left ankle, and washed down a painkiller with a swig of the whiskey I'd begun carrying with me since the witch pit fiasco.

I found the turnoff, not by sight, but by the scent of moist earth and some odd sense of having turned this way before. It wasn't until I got close that I could see the house, a slender stream of smoke rising from the thatch like departing spirits.

The door opened before I could knock. Gypsy Evansleaver was bordered on each side by two old women, three plump, one thin, and all sharp-eyed. Wrinkled by years, yet somehow unfettered by time. Behind them, six wooden chairs formed a half circle. The fire in the large brick hearth cast their faces in an orange glow.

"Come in, me dear, come in," said Gypsy. She took me by the elbow. Again, I felt that strange flow of current.

The crones bent around me like an undiscovered country. They were made timeless by their obvious belonging. I coveted that sense of rightness. I was a stranger, born out of season, haunted by an idea called home.

Gypsy propelled me toward a chair. I wondered at the fortitude of such women who denied even the comfort of cushions to their old bones.

"Take a sip of this, dear." She poured me a shot of some golden liquid. It softened the edges, yet made the room somehow clearer.

* * *

Only the glinting of eyes beneath his hood shows me that this is a man and not Death himself.

"Confess," he says. "Confess and be saved."

A crowd surrounds me. Them I have known since I was but a wee tacker. Yet they gaze on me as if I am a stranger.

In the center my mother is chained to a pole, clothes torn, breasts bare for all to see. I point a small, trembling, white finger toward my mother. "I have heard her talking to a brown dog," I whisper.

"Louder," cries the man.

"She smears the fat of murdered babes on her broom-end!" I scream.

"Witch," says the man.

"Witch," echoes the crowd.

I hear her voice. The same that used to sing me lullabies, but it is harsh and raw.

"If my flesh and bone accuse me, so it be. And this same curse now be in the blood through the generations. Not one woman of my flesh shall live past my years of twenty-nine Christmas tides. As you have cursed me, I curse you."

* * *

"Are you all right, me dear?" Old faces bent over me. The same faces as were in the crowd.

"I must go!" Hands grabbed at me. I staggered into night. In the road, Charlie's cab was waiting. I was saved! I dove into the back seat.

In the mirror, his eyes met mine. They were the cool, blue of my inquisitor.

I rolled out into the damp grass. He would not trap me again. I had been given another chance. This time, I would not betray my mother. I could save her. I will save her. I head left, taking the shortest path toward the coast.

* * *

"Interesting reading material." My father nodded toward a pile on the bed. He leafed through *The Cornwall Witches.*

"The main witness against Truth Device was her daughter, Grace, who was but nine years old" he read. "And the tale continues." He picked up a newspaper.

Witches of Cornwall, 2010

"An archaeologist has unearthed three witch pits in Cornwall. One contained twenty-two eggs, all with chicks close to hatching. Another held a burnt swan. The egg pit dated to the eighteenth century, the swan pit to the 1980s.

"And it seems you haven't been taking your meds." My father's voice was as dry as Mrs. Molchany's scones. "We pulled you out of the bog on the edge of the cliff. It's a wonder you aren't dead. You will stay here for a while, where you can be…monitored. And no more reading about witchcraft. I know it's a sad place to spend Christmas, but next year will be better." He scooped up the books, kissed me on the forehead and left.

Christmas? It was not yet Christmas?

The door opened and a tight-lipped, doughy woman, face framed by an almost unruly halo of blueish-gray curls entered.

"I'm Nurse Molchany," she said. "I'll be the one seeing to your needs."

Tannenbaum

Jonathan Robbins Leon

VIOLET HATED THE tree the moment her father brought it home. "It's ugly," she said, but Mommy shushed her. It was almost black, only green in certain light. Its branches curled and twisted like fuzzy spider arms, and Violet doubted that even tinsel could make it merry.

"It was the last one on the lot," Daddy said. "The salesman thought he was out, but he found this one still on the truck."

Mommy kissed him on the cheek. "It's fine. Just needs a little trimming is all. Some ornaments and lights, and it'll be perfect."

There hadn't been money for a tree, not with Daddy furloughed, whatever that meant. But then Grandma Addie sent presents early, and there was a check for Mommy and Daddy, a doll for Violet.

They dragged the dusty box of ornaments out of the garage.

"Aren't you going to help me?" Mommy asked.

"I don't want to," Violet said. She felt sure that the tree's needles would be sharp, and anyway, it smelled. Their last Christmas tree had made the whole house smell like a forest. It was like having one of those fancy candles Mommy used to buy, only the scent stayed all December long.

This tree though? Its scent reminded Violet of the time she'd helped Grandma Addie clean her spice cabinet. Some of the jarred leaves and powders had gone bad, and the further back Violet had reached in the cabinet, the stickier the jars had become. When they were done, her fingers were gooey and smelled sweet. Not in a pleasant way, but like something syrupy you knew might be poison.

That's what this tree smelled like. Christmas was only three days away, but still Violet worried the smell would seep into the couch and curtains. Missy, her cat, hid behind Violet's legs and made a low noise in the back of her throat, apparently not liking the tree any more than Violet did.

"If you're not going to help, then you can go to your room," Mommy said.

The girl took her new doll and went upstairs. When Violet had called to thank her for the gift, Grandma Addie had said that, as a little girl, she'd had a doll just like it, with a little black and white swimsuit, her pouty mouth painted ruby red. It came with three dresses and little plastic shoes. Violet decided that her doll was going to a Christmas party, and she needed to look her best, because maybe she'd find a boyfriend. And maybe they'd kiss. And then he'd buy her presents and they'd get married, and she could be a doctor for animals, and she would make lots of money, and they wouldn't have any children, because children can be messy.

Of course, Violet didn't have a boy doll, so her doll did a lot of changing her mind about which of the dresses to wear, and by the time she'd chosen one, Violet had decided that now she was a model and wasn't going to a party after all.

She was so invested in her playing, she didn't realize it was almost bedtime until Mommy came to find her. "Would you like to come down for stories and eggnog?"

Violet nodded.

"Listen, be nice about the tree, okay? You'll hurt Daddy's feelings."

Mommy had a Zoom call for work, so it was Daddy's turn to read books. Violet climbed next to him on the couch, the tree directly across from them, partly blocking the TV in their too-small living room.

"Do you like the tree?" Daddy asked.

Violet held her mug of eggnog very carefully in her lap and nodded.

"I'm sorry Christmas isn't very big this year. Santa's going through a hard time."

"Daddy!" Violet rolled her eyes. "I'm too big for Santa anymore. I know it's you and Mommy who buy the presents and eat the cookies."

"Well, I hope you're not too big for stories, Miss Know-it-All."

Violet laughed and told him she wasn't. Daddy was better at reading than Mommy, because he used voices. Tonight though, Violet had trouble listening. The tree bothered her. Every time she looked somewhere else, the tree seemed to move. From the corner of her eye, she'd catch sight of its branches curling like tentacles. Only when she looked directly, it was still again, though an ornament or two might be swinging gently on their ribbons.

Daddy coughed, breaking off in the middle of a sentence. "Sorry," he said. "Tickle in my throat. I'll be right back." He left Violet alone with her eggnog.

She kept her eyes trained on the tree, trying to puzzle out exactly why she hated it so much. She wasn't being very nice, she thought. Daddy was trying to make the best of this Christmas, and it did look a little nicer with garlands and the little ornaments she and Mommy had made last year out of popsicle sticks and glitter. She closed her eyes and tried to remember the last tree.

A loud hiss and a scurrying of feet. Violet opened her eyes to see Missy jump away from the tree, as if something had spooked her. She hadn't even known the cat was in the room, but Missy used her back paws to scram fast as she could.

"Stupid cat," she said aloud, though she kept her eyes on the tree until Daddy came back.

* * *

The next morning, gifts had appeared under the tree.

"It's not Christmas Eve until tomorrow," Violet pointed out.

"Well, they had to be wrapped," Mommy said. "And your father told me you're too old for Santa this year."

Violet spent the morning drawing at the kitchen table.

"No cartoons today?" Mommy asked.

She shook her head. She didn't want to be alone in the living room. Even with presents, the tree looked out of place. Not like a Christmas tree at all. It was like having a lion in the home that pretended to be a housecat.

The cat. "Mommy, where's Missy?"

Her mother glanced down at the cat's food bowl by the fridge, still full. "I don't know. Must not be hungry today."

Violet went to check the usual places, under tables and behind curtains. Missy liked to nap in a pet bed in Mommy's office, but there was no sign of her there either. Only dark green needles. She brought them to her mother.

"Look."

"There you go," Mommy said, examining them. "Now we know why she's hiding. That naughty girl's been messing with the tree."

"But they feel funny. Kind of fuzzy."

Her mother took one and rubbed it between her index finger and thumb. "Huh. Leave it to your father to buy the wrong kind of tree."

"What kind of tree is it?"

"I don't know, baby. Why don't you go use your tablet and figure it out? Like a game. I have to get cooking. Grandma Addie's coming over. Aunt Darlene and the cousins might swing by on Christmas with presents, and Grandma can't be around that many people." There were all kinds of rules with the virus. "So we're going to do a big fancy dinner for just the four of us tonight."

"What will we do for Christmas?" Violet asked.

"I don't know. Maybe we'll order a pizza." Mommy meant it to be funny, but Violet stomped up the stairs feeling cheated. A pizza for Christmas, and an ugly octopus for a tree. What was next? A box of scabs for presents?

Dinner that night was boring. The grownups went on and on about how delicious it all was, but without her cousins running around or the pies and cakes her aunts always brought, Violet realized that most of the special dishes were yucky to her. Stuffing was just soggy bread, and every vegetable was made worse by being served as a casserole. Even turkey was just a dry version of chicken without the crunchy skin.

"Where's that cat of yours?" Grandma Addie asked. She'd saved the scraps from her portion of turkey and collected them on her dessert plate. "Will she eat the fat?"

"We haven't seen her all day," Violet said. "Something's happened to her."

Mommy told her not to be silly. "She's just hiding because she's worried I'll be mad at her for bothering the decorations."

Later they all collected in the living room to talk. Violet would have liked if the television was on, but Grandma Addie was very old and didn't like television. She'd had Daddy late and always called him her *surprise baby*. So they all sat around, and Violet tried not to look bored while they gossiped about other relatives.

"That's a strange tree," Grandma Addie said. "Is it one of those fake ones?"

"No," Daddy said.

Grandma Addie's mouth bulged as she pressed her tongue to the roof of her dentures. Her eyes narrowed as she stared at the tree. "Best thing to do with that is burn it."

Daddy laughed, but Violet could tell it had hurt his feelings. They bundled Grandma into her coat and scarf, and she promised to call when she got home.

"Are you sure you won't stay over?" Daddy asked. "I don't like you driving at night."

"I'll let you baby me when I'm eighty. Besides, I wouldn't stay in a house with that tree if you paid me."

Violet knew how she felt. She hoped Missy might be waiting for her in bed, but no such luck. Mommy kissed Violet goodnight and said they'd look for her tomorrow.

All night, Violet had trouble sleeping. She thought she heard Missy padding around, but when she opened her room and called, the cat ignored her and went still. Only when the door closed could she hear her scrabbling about, as if looking for food or a way out.

* * *

"Violet Anne Lewis!" her mother said. "You tell the truth right this minute. Why did you open these presents?"

"But I didn't!"

Shreds of paper were everywhere in the room, the gifts themselves discarded on the floor.

"Do you expect me to believe they opened themselves then?"

Mommy and Daddy were staring down at her, their arms folded across their chests.

"I didn't do it!" Violet shouted at them.

Daddy raised his voice to match hers. "Watch your tone, young lady!"

Mommy took a softer approach. "I know this Christmas hasn't been what any of us wanted. We can't have a big Christmas. We can't have everyone over at the same time."

"I didn't do it," Violet said.

"And you've made it perfectly clear how you feel about the tree."

"What about Grandma Addie?" Violet asked.

"Are you saying Grandma Addie came over here and opened all the presents?"

"No! I'm saying she didn't like the tree either. She said we should burn it."

But her parents didn't want to hear any more about the tree. She was sent upstairs for the morning, and when she came back down, the presents had been put away, the floor of the living room swept clean.

Violet knew it was best to give her parents some space, even if it was Christmas Eve. She spent the afternoon searching for Missy, inside and out, without turning up any clues.

By night, she'd hoped her parents would have cooled off, but Daddy asked if she was ready to apologize. When Violet said she had nothing to apologize for, she was sent to her room with a plateful of leftovers. Instead of eating the day-old mush, she crawled into bed with her doll, hoping that when she woke up it would be Christmas and her parents would have chosen to believe her.

She woke instead to scraping and tapping sounds coming from the first floor. "Missy?" she whispered. Maybe the cat had opened the presents. What had gotten into her? Throwing the blankets off, Violet crept out of bed and down the stairs.

She was careful not to make any noise, not wanting to spook the animal. She'd catch it in the act and then wake her parents. The mischief noises grew louder as she neared the living room, and Violet knew she'd have her cornered, the living room only having one entrance.

"Bad girl!" she said, standing on her tiptoes to hit the switch.

Only, in the flash of light, she saw, not the cat, but...something else. It scuttled up the wall, dozens of legs propelling it forward. Racing across the ceiling, the something attacked the light fixture, sending glass from the bulbs raining down on the hardwood below.

Violet screamed. The icicle lights outside provided just enough glow for her to see the creature aim its trunk, or what Violet had thought was its trunk, at her. A black hole appeared, and Violet realized, seeing a dozen rows of tiny, triangular teeth, that this was its mouth. Not a tree at all, but an animal. A monster.

Ornaments still clung to its limbs, and it stalked its way toward Violet, slowly, as if curious.

There was a thunder of feet, and then her parents were in the room. "Violet?" her mother asked. The room was mostly shadow, and Mommy didn't understand yet that something was wrong.

The little girl could only point, her finger trembling.

"What the hell is that?" Daddy asked, blinking as if his eyes might be playing tricks on him.

Still, the thing crept closer, a wet, sucking breath coming from its open orifice.

"Rob," Mommy said, her hands fumbling in the drawer of the TV stand behind her. "Get the gun, Rob!"

"There aren't any bullets," he told her, his voice shaky.

Within an arm's reach of the creature, Violet could see how they'd mistaken it for a tree, its branch-like appendages covered in tough bristles, its body tube-like. The smell was overwhelming now, coming from the mouth, which reminded Violet of the underside of a starfish. The eyes were imperceptible, though Violet knew they must be there, nestled in the dark of its body, for it watched them, carefully approaching.

It occurred to her that the animal was scared. Perhaps it had been trapped on the truck, and then trapped in their house. What else could it do but look for a way out and grab what food it could find?

Orange flared in the darkened room, Mommy having struck a match. The creature emitted a keening sound as she set fire to the matchbook. "Mommy, no!" Violet said, but it was too late. Her mother threw the flaming bundle, perhaps still believing the monster to be a tree.

In response, the creature lunged for her, knocking her hard to the floor, her head bouncing on the hardwood with a crack.

"You son of a bitch!" Daddy said, flinging himself at it, as if he could hope to overpower a monster. They collided together, beast and man, and Violet knelt down next to her mother to try and shake her awake. No sooner had Violet gotten to her knees, however, than the spiny tapered end of the creature's tail whipped her bodily to the nearest wall, plunging everything into darkness.

* * *

Violet woke to the soft golden hue of Christmas lights and the sharp pain of a dozen stab wounds. "Mommy?" she said, attempting to rub the sleep from her eyes. She couldn't move, and waking, she saw the immobile shape of her mother's body where she'd left it. "Mommy!"

A wet smacking from the corner of the room caught her attention. The tree, or whatever it was, was hunched over her father, eating his head like a bear devouring a watermelon. At her scream, it looked up from its midnight snack.

Violet tried to run, but her extremities were wrapped tight with garland. The oddity reached one bristling limb out and caressed her face. Looking down at her body, she saw the ornaments hooked into her flesh.

"Mommy!" she called again. The thing backed away, surveying its work, then reached down for the star dangling from its tail, approaching to place it just so on Violet's sweet head.

Time and Tide

Clare Marsh

March 19th 2019

I SMOOTH DOWN the trousers of my formal suit. I want to present myself as professional and competent but, at the end of today's ordeal, how will the public and press view me? Daniel will drive us to the inquest. My hands shake, palms sweaty. The memory of last Christmas hangs heavy as an anchor, dragging me into icy depths. During the journey, I'll mentally rehearse my story again. But I'm still undecided – when I testify, should I tell the truth? And, if so, would anyone believe me?

* * *

Christmas Eve 2018

I called at Daniel's cottage to pick up the British Legacy Land Rover. Normally he drove us over to the island, but he'd rung me earlier to say he was ill. I found him holed up on the sofa under a blanket, watching daytime TV, something he always said he despised.

'What's the matter?' I said. 'Is it man flu?'

He managed a grin. 'No, I feel like death warmed up. Have you rung our area director?'

'No need to trouble him. Marion and I can cover today as there won't be many visitors. Where is your aunt, by the way? We'd better make a move.'

'His aunt is here,' Marion sniffed pointedly as she emerged from the kitchen. 'I've left you bread and homemade soup for lunch, Danny dear, and here's a nice cup of hot lemon.'

'You're a treasure,' Daniel hugged her.

'Now dear, I don't want to be catching your nasty germs,' she pushed him away with a coy smile. 'Otherwise who'll cook Christmas dinner for us?'

Before shutting the front door I shouted, 'If we're not back by six, send out a search party!'

'I should hope we'd be back well before then. This is the first time British Legacy has made us open up on Christmas Eve.' Marion reverted to her usual grumpy self. It would be a long, long day without Daniel to lighten things between us.

Rounding the bend down to the harbour, then driving onto bright, wet sand, I felt exhilarated. The deserted island loomed half a mile ahead – the iconic outline of St Nectan's Abbey a fairy-tale silhouette against the ice-blue sky. The golden figure of the saint balanced on the spire glinting in the December sunshine. Jagged rocks surrounded the island and the walls around the tiny harbour over there were sheer. The only access was by the causeway up to two hours either side of high tide, or by boat across Saints Bay.

But there was a chalkboard notice that the ferry wouldn't be operating today. I spotted Tom and wound down my window. He called out from the deck of the 'Isle be back' (his little joke) which bobbed at her moorings. 'There'll be no grockles, I'm stayin' in port.' By that, of course, we knew he meant The Pilgrims' Inn.

'See you in there later for a Christmas drink,' I snorted.

Tom's tufted eyebrows furrowed as he squinted up at the mackerel clouds. 'Mind the weather, could turn nasty later, though it's not forecast.'

'Oh, we'll be back before it breaks,' I said with the complete confidence of the ignorant.

A stiff breeze topped the receding waves with white laced foam as I headed for the causeway, driving over the now drying cobbles. Although I tried hard not to jolt us, Marion tutted and clutched her battered handbag.

'It's a much smoother ride when my Daniel's at the wheel.'

I gritted my teeth, 'Of course Marion, but do you want to take over?'

'I've never had cause to drive.'

We went over in silence, until I pulled up the steep slope in front of the gift shop.

'I'll start stocktaking. Please give the rooms a Christmas treat, Marion.' She scowled at me. The café was her usual domain. It wasn't my fault we'd been instructed not to open it today. She resented me being appointed her manager, 'A graduate and not a local,' I'd overheard her complain to Daniel.

'Yes, Ms Webster.' Her lips curled as she emphasised the 'Ms'.

'Just call me Alice.' But I knew she never would.

Only a few hardy souls visited, all wearing hiking boots and expensive cagoules. They were generally self-sufficient once they'd shown their British Legacy membership cards and bought the guidebook. I worked my way through the 'Christmas Fare' which would rapidly lose its charm after the holidays, reducing sale items ready for our return after Boxing Day. Then a book caught my eye; *Legends of British Legacy Properties*. I'd only worked here for a couple of months and ought to know more of the island's history. I put it aside to browse through during my lunch break.

I already knew the basics – this was a holy island, a place of pilgrimage for centuries and the relics of St Nectan, in the abbey, were reputed to cure any disease. What I didn't know before was that in 1348, when the Black Death raged, a band of pilgrims sought sanctuary on the island on Christmas Eve. However, when they dropped their hoods the black marks of impending death scarred their faces. The Abbott, impervious to their desperate pleas, ordered his men to 'drive them back into the sea, to cleanse them of their sins'. The abbey servants obeyed, stoning the terrified pilgrims with rocks. Injured, they fled to the causeway, which was vanishing under the racing winter tide. Their screams were dreadful, and their leader cursed the Abbott and St Nectan's Isle with his dying breath.

The Abbott went ahead and celebrated Midnight Mass, as if that evening's events were of no consequence. He prematurely gave thanks for their deliverance from the pestilence, while a terrific storm raged around the Isle. But to no avail. The entire population of the island sickened and was ravaged by the end of January. The last surviving monk's written testimony was the only record of the catastrophic events. For many years it remained, like much of England, deserted after the Great Mortality.

'Remarkable, isn't it?' I could hear Marion telling the last visitors about our beautiful Tidal Clock. 'It was made in 1786 to help islanders plan their journeys to the mainland safely. Mind, sometimes the clock has played false, leading to drownin's.'

The visitors made their excuses and scurried back to the mainland. Her tale had the desired effect – she wanted them gone.

I walked to where the clock stood in the entrance hall. How archaic to trust in something so ancient. We always relied on Daniel's experience of the vagaries of local tides and weather.

'Shouldn't we be going?' Marion moaned. 'I've got so much to do for Christmas dinner; the sprouts won't prepare themselves.'

The walnut case of the Tidal Clock gleamed in the rays of the setting sun, the engravings of the moon's phases looked impassive on its face. On cue, it chimed three times and showed high water at 7pm. Then it hit me; surely the sun couldn't be setting at 3pm. I checked my watch. It read 16:00. Had Marion altered the clock to trick me into leaving earlier? With a jolt I realised if she'd done so she'd have moved the clock forward not back. I felt the first prickle of anxiety. I tried to ring Daniel for advice, but the signal was lost.

'Let's go right now.' I rapidly locked the shop, slipping the keys into my pocket, while Marion turned off the island's generator.

As we hurried to the harbour, I skidded on the stones, dropping the Land Rover keys and my phone into an unreachable cleft in the rocks. I swore. Marion was livid.

'Look what you've done, now we'll have to walk over fast before it gets dark.'

'Sorry Marion,' I said, and I meant it. 'It should only take us fifteen minutes to cross; it won't get dark for a while yet. I grabbed a torch from the office.'

While Marion as usual was dressed in her sensible flat shoes and stretch 'slacks', my heels and tight skirt soon became a liability as we were on the causeway.

Darkness was falling fast as we reached the halfway point and the biting wind became ferocious. The full moon rose with an oily halo; in its silver twilight the causeway became a patchwork pathway of iridescent cobbles leading us safely home.

A chain of swinging lights became visible, appearing to come towards us from the shore. I couldn't make sense of them. Even the usually opinionated Marion was stumped.

'Can't surely be fishing boats out tonight?' She sounded puzzled. We heard the growing sound of singing, soon drowned out by a terrific roaring noise. The sea appeared to rear up as the waves hurtled towards us across Saints Bay at the speed of a galloping horse.

I clutched Marion's arm. 'We've got to go back to the island.'

'Well, I'm going to the mainland, come hell or highwater,' Marion shouted. 'I've got Christmas to attend to, even if you haven't.'

A straggle of ragged, cloaked figures approached us carrying crucifixes, chanting, lanterns swaying frantically on poles in the wind. We stopped, trying to take this in.

'Maybe it's a historical re-enactment organised by the Legacy?' Marion said doubtfully.

I froze. Surely, I would have been informed if so? The men seemed unaware of us, just focused on reaching the island. The leader's hood slipped. Marion and I stared into the abyss of human misery in the eyes of this dying man. The hideous sores on his exposed arms and face were livid and smelt of putrefaction. I retched.

Marion screamed, running along the causeway, the waves now lapping at her feet. Arms flailing, she slipped backwards into the water. The lifebelt post was on the far side of the pilgrims. I wanted to help her, but nothing would induce me to pass through their midst. I kicked off my shoes and charged back to the Isle. My lungs burned, feet lacerated then stinging in the salt water. The edge of the causeway vanished under the encroaching tide. Somehow, I reached the shop, unlocked the door and bolted it behind me.

Collapsing behind the counter, I sobbed, struggling for each breath. The wind howled, trying the windows, rattling them, begging for admission. I remained in darkness apart from the torch. I couldn't contemplate going outside to the generator house. Cut off, no communication, I huddled wet and shivering under one of the Heritage Tartan Throws from the display. Would anyone on the mainland raise the alarm?

Suddenly there was shouting and running footsteps. Perhaps help had come? Or maybe, miraculously, Marion had risen like Poseidon from the heaving sea. I felt momentarily hopeful, then over the wind I could hear screams from the causeway. I'll never know whether they came from Marion or the Plague Pilgrims meeting their recurring fate.

I raided the shop for Legacy mulled wine and I gulped it down, trying to erase the images from my mind. I must have dozed for hours. I woke to distant chanting, surely the Legacy Plainsong CD which played on an endless loop in the abbey during opening hours? Then I remembered the generator was off.

Peering out of the window, I saw the impossible; flickering candlelight in the abbey, turning the stained glass into jewelled kaleidoscopes, belying the horror of the night's events. Midnight Mass was being sung.

Throughout the night, the chiming of the Tidal Clock woke me hourly and I cursed it, drunkenly blaming it for luring Marion to her death. I realised my encounter with the Plague Pilgrims had saved me from the lethal tide by driving me back to the island. And, had Marion not been so pig-headed about preparing her bloody Christmas dinner, she'd have survived too.

At dawn, I woke up to hammering on the door. Daniel and two police officers had crossed over with Tom in his boat. Their faces registered shock at my dishevelled condition. I tried to explain what had happened to Marion, but it was just slurred gibberish.

Marion's body washed up along the coast on Boxing Day, her bloated grey face contorted in agony. Or horror.

* * *

March 19th 2019

The jury returns a verdict of Accidental Death. I must have sounded deranged when questioned. British Legacy provided legal support, of course, covering their backs over their 'duty of care' towards Marion as their employee – and my perceived deficiencies as her manager in not saving her. The Coroner is compassionate about the terror I'd faced on the causeway with the unexpected storm-force wind and moon-fuelled tidal surge. However, she dismisses my account of the Plague Pilgrims as 'hallucinatory'.

But Daniel believes me, the only one whose opinion I really care about. He heard the fragmented story from me over Christmas and, seeing the traumatised state I was in, somehow knew I was telling the truth.

* * *

British Legacy has stated that it won't be opening St Nectan's Isle next Christmas Eve.

Workshop

Marshall J. Moore

ALL WAS NOISE and heat in the workshop foundry. The air was choked with smoke and fumes that made Wensley's eyes water behind his round-rimmed spectacles. His slender ears ached with the ceaseless groans of the great engines, the continual pounding and clanging and hammering of the assembly lines.

In summer the midnight sun would filter down through the layers of ice, bathing the chambers below in a bluish gloom. But now it was deep winter, the season of Night Unending, and the cavernous workshops were lit only by the harsh orange glow of the vast forges and furnaces.

"Automation," Wensley said, wiping at his sodden brow with the back of a red-stained hand. Liquid poured from the machine beside him into a mold on the conveyor belt. Wensley dutifully injected each mold with red pigment from a small hose. "That's one of the two devils that afflicts us, my friend. That damnable march of so-called progress."

His neighbor, a younger alf named Trescott, grunted to show he was listening but did not look up from his work.

"It was better in the old days," Wensley continued, pausing for a moment as the hydraulic piston between them smashed down upon the conveyer belt between the two alves, pressurizing the liquid plastic so that it emerged solid, perfectly contoured to its mold. "Back before all these machines came in to stink up the place."

Wensley was an old alf, old enough to remember the times before the great machines had overtaken the honest work of their hands. His face was lined but beardless; the alves were forbidden from growing facial hair of any kind. That was a privilege reserved for the Big Man alone.

"Back then," Wensley continued, coloring another mold, "you could take your time. It was all done by hand, with tools you could actually hold. And none of these plastics or electronics, either. Woodworks all. Beautiful toy soldiers, rocking horses—"

The piston came down again, interrupting the old alf's reminiscences. Before he could resume, Trescott interjected:

"What's the second?"

"Eh?" Wensley turned, adjusting his glasses to squint at the younger alf. Less than two centuries old, Trescott's face was smooth and unlined.

"The devils that afflicts us," Trescott repeated, picking up one of the molds and hammering the plastic bricks free from it with a small mallet. "You said there were two. Automation and what else?"

"Ah," Wensley nodded. "That damnable bastard Dickens. He's to blame for all this."

He gestured vaguely at the cacophonous workshop, an immense subterranean chamber of ceaseless industry. Hundreds of alves labored here, bent over the endless assembly lines or operating the complex machinery, sweat glistening on their bare shoulders. The heat of the workshop was too oppressive for any clothing heavier than sleeveless undershirts.

The piston smashed down between them again. As it lifted, Trescott asked, "Dickens?"

"Dickens," Wensley spat. "Was a writer from – oh, around the time you were born, I guess. Before him, the Holiday was a small affair. Matter of fact, it was outlawed in some places. Only the Germans really went in for it the way everyone seems to these days. But Dickens, he went and *publicized* the Holiday. Started a whole craze for it. And now everyone the world over is mad for it."

The old alf waved his arms, taking in the whole of the factory.

"Dickens created the demand for all of *this*. And with all the new machines, the Big Man could meet demand with supply." Wensley sighed and watched as the red plastic bricks swept down the conveyor belt, towards the crew of alves who would package and wrap them in brightly colored paper before the conveyor automatically loaded it into one of the chutes that led down into the dimensionless space of the Sack.

"You could add him to your list," Trescott suggested.

"Who?"

"The Big Man." Trescott grinned, rewarded by the look of horror on Wensley's face.

"Don't say that!" he hissed, glancing furtively around them. "You never know who might be listening."

The assembly lines of the workshop were patrolled by the Helpers, the spies and secret police of the Big Man. Even now Wensley could see one of them drawing near, the belled hat that was his badge of office jingling with each step.

The two workalves turned back to their assembly line, but it was too late. The Helper had caught them looking at him, and was detouring towards them.

"Coalstockings," Trescott swore under his breath. "It's Elcorn."

Though Wensley disapproved of his younger comrade's language, he echoed the sentiment behind it. Elcorn was one of the most interfering of the Big Man's Helpers, quick to root out any hint of dissension against his regime.

"Worker Wensley!" Elcorn snapped as he reached their assembly line. His red and green hat jingled above his pointed ears. "Worker Trescott!"

"Sir?" Wensley asked, bent over the assembly line, dutifully injecting pigment into the liquid plastic as quickly as he could.

"Your work product is down eight percent," Elcorn said, consulting the clipboard clutched in his good hand. His other hand was a bronze claw. Such prosthetics were common in the workshop, where output was everything and safety standards no more than a bitter joke. Wensley was one of the few alves to have reached a venerable age without losing a limb to the crushing jaws or merciless blades of the factory's endless industrial machines.

"Sorry, sir," Wensley said, his hand slipping from the pigment hose. A bead of sweat formed on his brow, but he dared not wipe it away while Elcorn stood looming over him, ready to report him.

"Getting a bit old to work the floor, aren't you, Worker?" Elcorn asked, looking pointedly at Wensley's shaking hands. "Perhaps it's time we found you a more suitable occupation, eh? Like wrangling the Big Man's reindeer, for example."

Wensley was unable to suppress the shudder that rocked his shoulders at the thought. The reindeer were monstrous creatures, brutish and foul-tempered, as old and cruel as sin itself. More than one alf's life had been cut short by their huge antlers or stomping hooves.

And the Big Man doted upon his pets like they were his own children. Any alf who failed to tend to them to their master's satisfaction was likely to end up as the beasts' next meal.

"No, sir," Wensley answered, fighting to keep the stammer from his voice. "I'm still fit to work the assembly line, honest."

"You do realize," Elcorn said, his voice as soft as it was dangerous, "that we are only a fortnight away from Night Unending, do you not?"

"I'll...I'll pick up the slack," Wensley said, his hands shaking so badly that he could barely hold the pigment hose. "I've worked here since the Big Man first moved us beneath the Pole—"

"Ah," Elcorn breathed. A wide, ugly smile twisted his face. "So it's seditious talk as well, then? You know better than to repeat the lies of envious minds, Worker Wensley."

It was no lie. In the days of Wensley's youth, better than twelve hundred years ago, the alves had been a free and proud people. They had labored in mines and forges of their own, devising wondrous crafts through the clever skill of their own hands. Owing allegiance to no master, they had lived in close-knit clans, dwelling deep in the mountains and beneath the earth where no mortal man dared tread.

Until the Big Man came.

"I...it just slipped out, sir." Wensley swallowed hard. "I didn't mean anything by it, honest."

Elcorn chuckled drily. "I'm sure you didn't, Worker Wensley. Although perhaps an alf with so loose a tongue should be transferred someplace where no one will hear him. The coal mines, for example."

Wensley's hose clattered to the assembly line, spraying red pigment everywhere. He tottered from his stool, landing painfully on his knees as he grasped Elcorn by the hem of his trousers.

"No," Wensley half-sobbed, half-moaned. Tears glistened in his wide round eyes as he stared up imploringly at the Helper. "Elcorn, sir, *please*, anything but that—"

"Get off me!" Elcorn snarled, shoving Wensley roughly off him. The older alf fell backwards, pain exploding behind his vision as his head collided with the hard metal edge of the conveyor belt.

"Leave him alone!" Trescott shouted. He was on his feet, mallet clenched in his fist.

Elcorn turned, face twisted in a scowl. "As for you—"

Trescott hit the him full in the face with the mallet.

The Helper spun in a pirouette so perfect it was almost comical, an arc of bloody spittle jetting from his mouth, following the trajectory of a tooth Trescott's mallet had knocked loose.

All noise in the cavernous workshop suddenly ceased, save for the groaning and creaking of the automated machines. Elcorn lay sprawled on the floor beside Wensley, his expression dazed. Trescott stood over him, his chest rising and falling in great breaths.

Slowly, Elcorn raised his prosthetic claw to his lip. When he pulled it away, blood glistened against the bronze. His eyes traveled from it to Trescott, the mallet still in his hand.

"Traitor," he hissed, a vicious light in his eyes.

Trescott raised the mallet.

The piston slammed against the conveyor belt behind them. As if in answer, a great *boom* reverberated through the workshop, shaking tiny flecks of ice loose from the icy ceiling far overhead.

Another *boom*, and another, a steady rhythm. One by one, every alf in the workshop stood from their workplaces, their tools and trade forgotten as they stared at the titanic door at the far end of the cavern.

It was more gate than door; twelve feet high and nearly as wide, wrought of the cold black iron whose very touch was anathema to the alves. Thick runes were carved across its face, though in this latter age not even old Wensley could recall what they meant.

As the booming sound grew closer, tools tumbled from worktables, half-finished presents clattered on their conveyor belts, and alves quaked in their boots. Even the light of the great furnaces seemed to dim in grim anticipation.

The huge doors burst open.

Grotesquely huge, more than twice the height of the tallest alf, his belly wobbling gelatinously beneath the layers of red furs. His face was crimson, round-cheeked and unwrinkled despite his immense age. The white beard fell long and tangled over his enormous barrel chest, and his eyes glimmered darkly in their deep sockets. His mouth was oddly small in his broad face, parted just enough to show the even rows of white teeth, straight and flat as tombstones.

The Big Man threw back his head and laughed.

"Ho, ho, *ho!*"

* * *

Wensley had been no more than a small alf-child, but he could well remember that day the blood-colored sledge had first dropped from the sky, drawn upon gale and lightning by the team of snorting, savage reindeer. The Big Man had driven them mercilessly, hurling dire invectives and cracking his long whip over the beasts' heads, driving them into frenzy.

The older alves whispered that he was the last of the Jotunn, the fearsome giants who had long prowled the cold wastes of the world. Others said he was one of the great heathen sorcerer-kings, fleeing north from the worshippers of the crucified god whose name would one day be given to the very Holiday for which the Big Man's alven slaves labored.

Whatever the truth behind these whispers, it was immaterial in the face of the Big Man's overwhelming presence. He landed in a flurry of snow and ice, laying into the cowering band of alves with his whip. Some of Wensley's clan attempted to flee, but already the Big Man had his Helpers —alves from other clans, bullied and cowed into the Big Man's service. These quislings set upon Wensley and his family with vicious glee, binding them with heavy chains and loading them onto the crimson sledge, bound for the Big Man's polar fortress.

Some brave but foolhardy alves attempted resistance, fighting back against their tormentors with no weapons but tooth and nail. The Big Man met them boisterously and brutally, wading in with his massive fists and the cruel thongs of his whip. Blood streaked the snow as more than one alf fell crushed beneath the soles of his heavy black boots.

And all the while, he laughed his booming laugh.

* * *

The Big Man stood framed in the massive doorway, his booted feet planted wide apart, his fists against his hips. His grin was wide and without warmth.

"Ho-ho!" he repeated, his deep basso voice reverberating off the workshop walls. "A Merry Christmas to you, my jollies!"

There was a chorus of echoing replies from the workalves, though the tension lingering in the air gave the lie to its forced sincerity. Only the Big Man ever referred to the Holiday by its proper name. Scuttlebutt on the workshop floor was that he took some sick pleasure in twisting the festival of the god who had driven him from his home into a mockery of itself, a monument to avarice over charity. But no one knew for certain.

The Big Man's beady black eyes scanned the workshop, tracking across the grimy, wary faces of the alves until his gaze alighted on Trescott, still standing over Elcorn with his mallet raised over his head.

"Oh ho ho!" the Big Man bellowed. His thick legs carried him across the factory floor in half a dozen titanic strides. He gripped Trescott by the shoulders with one huge hand and hauled the alf bodily off the floor, chortling all the while.

"What have we here, my jolly fellow?" he boomed, raising Trescott to his eye level. The alf's feet dangled beneath the Big Man's huge fist. "A friendly workplace tussle, eh?"

"He attacked me, Master!" Elcorn spat, wiping bloody from his mouth as he clambered to his feet. Beside him Wensley rose shakily, grasping the conveyor belt for support.

"Oh-ho!" the Big Man bellowed, pulling Trescott so close that the alf flinched away from the gobs of flying spittle. "Striking a Helper! Sounds like someone belongs on the List, eh?"

Trescott paled. The List of Naught was a compendium of those who had irrevocably earned the Big Man's enmity. Those upon it were stripped of all they had, then turned out into the Arctic cold. Their frozen forms could still be glimpsed through the sheets of ice that formed the workshop ceiling.

"Master," wheezed a creaking voice from below. "Please, kind Master..."

The Big Man peered down to see Wensley staring up at him, his round eyes wide behind his spectacles.

"Hmm?" the Big Man rumbled. "Something to add, my fine fellow?"

"He was only trying to protect me," Wensley said. His aged voice trembled but did not break. "Helper Elcorn and I had a misunderstanding—"

"The old one was speaking sedition," Elcorn spat. "Talking as though there were a time before we dwelled at the Pole—"

"*Ha!*" the Big Man chortled. The echo of his laugh rolled like thunder through the workshop, and his enormous belly shook as his beady eyes stared shrewdly down at Wensley. "We've never lived anyplace but here, old boy."

"Of course not," Wensley said quickly. "I just meant...it was a slip of the tongue, Master..."

"Well," the Big Man grinned, "that's easily dealt with."

He bent and hauled Wensley to his feet, Trescott still dangling from his other hand.

"Helper!" he said to Elcorn. "Lies are as quick a way as any to end up on the List of Naught. See that this old fellow's no longer tempted, will you?"

"As you command," Elcorn said, his own greasy grin nearly as vicious as his master's. "What's to be done with him?"

"Take his tongue," the Big Man said, his voice suddenly losing its jovial tone. Now it was as hard and dark as coal. "That'll stop any seditious talk."

A hastily stifled gasp rose from the crowd of watching alves. Wensley moaned. He began stammering apologies, promises, pleas, but Elcorn shook him roughly until he clammed up.

"And the other one?" Elcorn asked, glaring up at Trescott, swinging from the Big Man's hand and looking green in the gills. "He *struck* me, Master. With a weapon."

"It was just a mallet!" Trescott objected weakly. The Big Man had been slowly squeezing his fist shut the entire time he held him. By now Trescott felt like a grape about to pop.

"Hmm." The Big Man tugged at his long white beard, beady black eyes narrowing.

Abruptly, he released his grip on Trescott. The alf dropped to the factory floor, landing roughly on his rump. He sat up, breathing in deep, greedy gulps of air. Directly behind him the piston slammed against the conveyor belt.

"See," the Big Man said, lowering himself to a squat with his hands on his thighs. His voice was quiet now, so low that only Trescott could hear him properly. "Today, it's a mallet. Yesterday it was fists. Tomorrow – what? There's enough metal in this factory for you to make weapons. I won't have you come after m— after my Helpers with knives and axes."

For the first time, Trescott met the Big Man's gaze full on. There were wrinkles around those beady black eyes. Trescott realized abruptly that even the overlord who drove them cruelly was not immune to the ravages of time.

The Big Man was getting old.

"So," the Big Man said, straightening. His booming voice now carried throughout the factory, jovial once more. "My fine fellow. You know what happens to those who raise a hand against my Helpers?"

Quick as thought, he seized Trescott by the shoulders and spun the alf around, so that he was facing the assembly line. The strength in the Big Man's mammoth hands was inexorable as he placed both Trescott's hands onto the conveyor belt.

Directly beneath the piston.

"He loses the hand," the Big Man grinned.

Trescott began to thrash wildly against the vicelike grip holding him down.

"Save it," the Big Man told him. "If old Elcorn there can make do with one bronze hand, you'll get by with two."

"No," Trescott pleaded, his breath coming in rapid, panicked gasps as he kicked and struggled uselessly. "No, please no, Master—"

The piston came crashing down.

Trescott screamed.

The Big Man's deep laugh echoed through the factory.

"Ho, ho, *ho!*"

Gray Christmas

Templeton Moss

I'LL NEVER FORGET the first time I saw the Gray One. I had seen the stone cottage on the hill just outside of our village and had once asked my father who lived there, for I had seen a light in the window and knew someone must dwell inside.

"You mustn't ask about that cottage, Esther," is all my father said.

But I wondered about that cottage and who had lit the light I saw glowing from within.

Then, one day, when I was at the market with my mother, she suddenly gasped and pulled me away into an alley.

"What is it, Mother?" I asked but got no reply. All around, I saw the other villagers ducking into alleys or behind walls; grownups hiding like children.

I was about to ask my mother again what was going on…but then I saw him.

He walked with a limp. He leaned on a cane that looked like it was made of bone. He was hunched over and took very small steps. In his hand, he carried a burlap sack. He was thin. He was tall, even hunched over as he was. His head was bald and crisscrossed with scars. His left eye was pale blue, like it was dead. His nose was long and bent to one side. His mouth hung slightly open as though he could not close it all the way.

He was old. His long beard was gray. His skin was gray. Everything about him was gray.

"Who is he, Father?" I asked that evening as I was helping clear the dinner table.

"We call him the Gray One," said my father, with the reluctance of a parent who is forced to answer a question he wishes had never been asked. "He's the man who lives in that cottage on the hill."

"Mostly he stays up on his hill," added my mother. "But once a month he comes down to visit the market. I guess even monsters need to eat."

"Monster?" I said. I was surprised. He didn't look like a monster to me. He looked old. He looked strange. But he was nothing like the monsters in the stories I had heard.

"It is best that you put the Gray One from your mind, little one," my father said.

"Yes," my mother agreed. "Let's have no more talk of that terrible man."

I tried to do as my parents said and put the Gray One from my mind. But I found I couldn't. From my window, I could see the light in his cottage at night. Some nights, when I couldn't sleep, I looked up to see if the light was there. And, if it was, I talked to him. Told him about my day and why I couldn't sleep. I knew he couldn't hear me, of course. I may have been a child, but I understood that much. But it made me feel better to talk to him.

From then on, Mother was careful not to let me leave the house on the Gray One's market day. But every time we went, I looked around, wanting more than anything to see him once again. The weather got colder, the nights got longer, and soon a blanket of snow and ice covered our village. I thought of the Gray One often as the winter came on. Alone in his stone house. I never saw smoke from the cottage's small chimney. I worried he wasn't warm enough.

At last, it was Christmas Eve. I was so excited for the following morning that I knew I would never be able to sleep. Instead, I sat at my window and looked up at the Gray One's home. I saw the candle in the window go out. I had seen this many times before and thought that the Gray One had gone to bed.

I was wrong.

Just as I was turning away from my own window, I saw the door of the stone cottage open and the Gray One step outside. He locked the door to his cottage – though I couldn't think who would want to go inside – and began to walk, very slowly, down the hill.

I couldn't control myself. My curiosity took over. As quickly as I could without waking my mother and father, I pulled on my boots and my cloak and I went outside to follow the Gray One to wherever he was going. I crept out of my house as silently as I could. I didn't know what my parents would say or do if they saw me, but I knew they would be furious.

I followed the Gray One from a distance. It was difficult, because he moved so slowly and I didn't want him to know I was there. I tried to stay to his left, the side that had the dead eye so that, even if he did hear me and look around, he would not see me following him.

He led me to the graveyard.

Why wasn't I afraid? I should have been. I was alone, at night, in a graveyard with a man the whole village called a monster. My own mother and father had warned me to keep my distance from this man. Everyone I knew fled from him when he was doing nothing more dangerous than buying bread and cheese at the market.

But, as a child, in that graveyard, I felt no fear.

Not even when he spoke to me.

"It's awfully late for a little girl to be out on her own," he said. It was an old, raspy voice. A gray voice. Like an old gate, rusty from lack of use.

"I'm not on my own," I said. "You are here with me."

"The next time you want to follow someone, wear softer shoes. I heard your boots on the cobbles a while ago."

"My name is Esther," I said. "What may I call you?"

"What do your parents call me?"

"They...they call you the Gray One."

He didn't say anything. I moved closer to him. He was standing at a stone, looking down on it as though paying his respects to the occupant of the grave. I was standing right alongside him, now. His right side. The side with the good eye. I no longer needed to worry if he could see me or not.

"Who is it?" I asked. I thought perhaps it was his wife who had passed away. His father or mother. An old friend, perhaps.

"I don't know," he said in that gray voice. "No one does."

I looked down at the stone. It was old. Very old. Older, perhaps, than the village itself. Whoever was buried there had died long before anyone in town had been born. And time had worn away the writing on the stone so that it appeared small and blank.

"I don't understand," I said. "If you don't know who it is, why are you here?"

"*Because* I don't know," he said. "Because no one knows. I come here every Christmas Eve and I seek them out. The stones without names. The stones of those whose families are long gone. The stones no one comes to visit. I spend my Christmas with the nameless dead."

"But why?"

He pointed to the unmarked grave at our feet. "There," he said, "right down there, only six feet away from where we stand, is an old box full of bones. But those bones were once a man or a woman. Maybe even a child. Someone rejoiced when they were born. Someone sobbed when they died. In between, there was a life. Long? Short? Happy? Sad? We'll never know. But they were alive, Esther. As alive as you or I.

"And one day – a faraway day – they'll ring the bells and sing laments for you. People will weep as you are lowered into the ground. They'll cry for you and pray for your soul. And afterward, someone will come to visit your grave…for a while. Until they, too, are laid to rest. And time will wear away your stone, just as surely as it did to this one. The years will erase your name and there you'll be: another box of bones the living have forgotten."

He was talking about my death. As casually as if we were discussing the next day's weather. It's not the sort of thing one normally says to a child, but I don't believe I was shocked or horrified by what he said. I suppose, young though I was, that I understood I would meet death myself one day. I had seen the seasons come and go. Seen puppies grow into hounds. Seen flowers bloom and wither and bloom again. This was not even my first visit to the graveyard. So there must have been a time when I understood that death is the price we all pay for the privilege of living.

What must it be like? That moment when we, as young children, come to that haunting realization? Can any of us remember it? Or is it not something that we learn? Are we born with some quiet voice that reminds us that our days are numbered? Like the soft, almost imperceptible ticking of a clock in a distant room, never letting us forget that time moves in one direction and cannot be slowed nor stopped.

In any case, there I stood. A child, shivering in the cold of a bitter December night, standing next to a man my mother had called a monster and he was telling me that my body would die and decay and that I would one day be forgotten.

I tell you again, though I am sure you won't believe it: I was not afraid.

"That's why I seek them out," said the Gray One. "Why I come to see them every year on Christmas Eve. Because I can't bear the thought of them being alone. Not tonight, at least."

"But you are alone, are you not?" I said.

He nodded. "Your people…the villagers…they hate me. They fear me."

"They don't know you."

"They don't care to know me. They see my face…my eye…they see that I am not like them and they call me 'monster.' And that is why I don't care to know them. Why I keep to myself. Why I stay up on my hill and only come down to buy enough food to last another month. Why I prefer the company of the dead. It is only the living who are cruel, child."

"I am alive," I said. "And I don't hate you. I'm not afraid of you."

"No," he said, thoughtfully. "I suppose not."

Later, he walked me home. He stayed on the street outside my house until I was safe inside. Then he made his slow, steady way up the hill to his home.

It's funny. I remember so vividly what passed between myself and the Gray One that night, but I can recall practically nothing of the Christmas morning that followed. I must have been looking forward to that morning for weeks, perhaps even a full year, but it came and went like a flash of light from a flickering candle. Here for a fraction of a heartbeat, then gone forever.

But that night, after the presents had been opened and the songs sung and every last crumb of the pudding devoured, I was back in my room. And, again, I looked up the hill to see if there was a candle in the window of the stone cottage. When I saw that there was, I dressed hastily, as I had done the night before. I crept through the house and found a sack, which I filled with old blankets, a pair of my father's old stockings, a few candles, some kindling, a loaf of bread. Anything I could find that I thought he might need, but which my parents wouldn't miss.

I moved quickly but quietly. Then when the sack was full, I snuck out and climbed the hill. I knocked on the door. I waited. The Gray One opened the door.

"No one has knocked on my door in…what are you doing here?"

"I couldn't bear the thought of you being alone," I said. "Not tonight, at least."

The people of my village lived the rest of their lives secure in the knowledge that the Gray One was a monstrous old hermit who spoke to no one and lived his life in well deserved solitude. None of them, not even my own parents, knew that he had a friend. A friend who crept up to his cottage whenever she could. A friend who made his little stone house more comfortable. A friend who, every Christmas Eve thereafter, joined him on his visit to the forgotten dead of our little graveyard.

But the clock in that distant room never stopped ticking. I became a woman. Then a wife. And, soon, I will be a mother. But before I was any of those things, I was a little girl who followed a monster into a graveyard.

The cottage on the hill has stood empty for many years now. But I still visit him. Every Christmas Eve.

The Last Christmas Tree

Jane Nightshade

ANNA WAS LEFT alone at Gull Wing Farm three weeks before Christmas. The Simonsons, owners of the hulking coastal California estate, were needed in Reno, where Mrs. Simonson's sister was ailing. They drove off to Nevada in the 1938 Packard sedan, leaving Anna with Jandy the foreman and his horse-drawn wagon as her only reliable link to Carmel, the nearest town.

"I know you will handle everything!" Mrs. Simonson exclaimed upon leaving. "You are such a smart and capable girl, Anna."

It was a terrible time for Helen Simonson's sister to take ill. Not only were the holidays approaching, but visitors were scheduled to arrive from England on Christmas Eve. Anna was expecting three tots who had become recent orphans, the children of Mr. Simonson's late cousin from Surrey. They had been staying with an uncle since their parents' demise, and he had been pathetically eager to send them to America "for the duration of the war." The childless Helen Simonson frankly hoped that the uncle would let them stay forever.

An old-fashioned matron with pretensions of chatelainery, Mrs. Simonson had hired Anna to tutor the invited children. And so, Anna spent her first month at Gull Wing Farm preparing the children's bedrooms, schoolroom and lessons, and was looking forward to their arrival with great anticipation. However, two days before they were scheduled to come, Mr. Simonson called Anna with bad news: "Clara has died, regretfully, and we must stay in Reno past Christmas. You'll have to meet our visitors at the train station in Carmel by yourself and explain the situation as best you can."

On the early afternoon of Christmas Eve, Jandy drove her to Carmel in his cart, drawn by the foreman's beloved old draft horse, Gray Malkin. They got to the station just after the last train had pulled out for its next destination, as the tracks were bare when they arrived.

The children's names were Lettice, James, and Frederick – ages ten, nine, and six, respectively. Standing on the deserted platform with a stern-looking, middle-aged woman in black, they were instantly recognizable. They had a different air about them that was both more sophisticated and more innocent than their American counterparts. The woman in black was undoubtedly Miss Jessop, who'd been hired by the Simonsons to accompany them on the long trek from England by ship and train. The little group had taken the last leg of their trip down from San Francisco, where they had been staying with Mrs. Drake, another sister of Mrs. Simonson's.

"Miss Jessop, I assume?" Anna said, approaching the woman.

"Aye," she answered, in a thick Scottish brogue that was barely understandable to American ears. "'Tis me. The children you will know from their letters."

"Yes. Such charming letters they all wrote."

Anna moved to shake hands with each child, from eldest to youngest, favoring them with her warmest, most inviting smile.

"This must be Lettice. Welcome, dear."

Lettice made a little half-curtsy, spreading out her pleated woolen skirt. "Thank you, Miss," she said with a strange, grave air. She was a very pale girl with silvery blonde hair streaming out of a red crocheted cap. Her hand, through knitted gloves, felt cold.

"And you, James. Such a big, strong boy."

"Pleased to meet you, Miss," he replied, with a slight bow. James did not smile either, and his hands were also cold. He wore a flat tweed cap with a bill, and a matching suit with short pants and high woolen socks. His knees looked very white and frigid.

"And here is little Freddie," Anna greeted the third child.

Freddie also made a slight bow. Like his brother, he wore a suit with matching short pants and long, heavy socks. "I'll try to be on my best behavior, Miss," he vowed, with a solemnity that tugged at Anna's heart. His small hands were the iciest of all, which gave her a start.

"We must get you all home as soon as possible," she said. "We'll have hot cocoa near the fire that Mr. Jandy started before we came. That'll warm up those cold hands."

The skies were gray and ominous, and Anna feared that a proper Monterey torrent was on its way. She hoped to be home before they were all assaulted by the great, slashing, icy sheets of water that often came to the central coast in December. The little party hustled to the cart.

"Here's a-hopin' we get home afore the floodgates open," Jandy said, while affixing a heavy tarp over the cart.

A few drops had already started to splash down as they settled in behind Jandy. They drove on toward Gull Wing Farm in an embarrassed silence, as Anna's attempts at conversation were answered with polite, monosyllabic responses from the visitors.

Then Miss Jessop spoke unexpectedly, in her laconic brogue.

"Appears to be a wicked storm brewing up, Miss. I was led to believe that the American state of California was a balmy place. Mrs. Drake's in San Francisco was surpassing chilly – and now this."

"It *is* balmy – in most parts. The Monterey Peninsula and San Francisco have a climate all their own, alas. The north part of the Pacific Ocean is quite cold and the fog that comes from it follows suit. I'm from Chicago, and I too was disappointed to find it wasn't all the sun and sand you see in Hollywood postcards."

"Where is Hollywood?" asked Lettice, in a surprisingly animated tone. "May we visit it, please?"

"I'm afraid it's very far from here," said Anna. "But there is a movie palace in Carmel, and we can get Mr. Jandy to drive us there sometime. They play the *Our Gang* comedies. Do you know them?"

"Hmm." There was no real answer, and the children and Miss Jessop sank back into their customary taciturn manner.

They only jolted out of their silence when a car appeared on the dirt road leading to the house, speeding at them from the opposite direction. It swerved and went onto the rough shoulder and around them at the last possible minute, honking furiously. Gray Malkin bucked and whinnied, and the racket he made was joined by Jandy's angry loud cursing and Freddie's screams of terror.

"Oh! A motorcar!" Freddie shrieked. "I don't like motorcars!" Lettice and James had grabbed each other, and both were white-faced. Miss Jessop was holding on to the back of Jandy's seat, pale-knuckled, with a disturbed and unsettled expression on her face.

"Whew!" cried Anna. "Is everyone okay? That was a close one!"

"There appears to be no injury on our part," replied Miss Jessop. "But wee Master Frederick is quite shaken. There, there, Freddie, don't cry. There's a good boy."

"Inconsiderate sufferin' fool," barked Jandy, after bringing up Gray Malkin. "Oughtta get the sheriff after him, but I didn't see the plate number."

"We don't like motorcars," said Lettice, in a quiet, tremor-laden voice. "Are there many at the farm?"

"No, dear," said Anna. "The only one we have is currently away with the owners of the estate."

"Good," said James, and then at that moment, the skies opened wide, and a torrential rain knifed its way down on the cart, the tarp, and poor old Gray Malkin.

* * *

The tarp didn't do much to keep the little party dry, and they were all damp as Gull Wing House came into view.

"Don't worry, dear. We are quite used to a watery clime," said Miss Jessop to Anna. "Although the rain in England, while voluminous, is not so fierce."

Anna made a weak smile. "I'm sorry we do not have better weather to greet our visitors. We don't often get them here."

She thought back to the first day she'd spent at Gull Wing. She'd been shocked at the often foggy and windy climate of the Monterey Peninsula. In her opinion, Gull Wing House fit the climate perfectly: gloomy, under-heated, and full of promises that didn't quite pan out. She hoped the children would not be intimidated by the house. She'd worked hard to make their bedrooms, playroom, and schoolroom cheerful and bright, in contrast to the rest of the house.

Jandy drove the cart up to the front porch of the house and soon busied himself with unloading the visitors' luggage. Large and white, Gull Wing was built in the 1880s in the French Third Empire style, with mansard roofs, a tower, and hooded, deep-set windows. The interior featured odd nooks and crannies beneath stair-steps or hidden behind false doors, and the walls were lined with decades of taxidermied Simonson hunting trophies: deer, elk, mallard ducks, and even a great, glassy-eyed bear. The hooded windows overlooked the north Pacific Ocean from a wind-ravaged cliff. Behind the house and below it, spread out vast, verdant land, where the Simonson family had farmed tomatoes, lettuce, and table grapes for three generations.

Anna ushered Miss Jessop and the children into the reception hall, where a fire blazed in a large, baronial fireplace.

"Please sit down," Anna invited the visitors. "I'll get Mrs. Sanchez, our housekeeper, to bring cocoa. There's a powder room off the left hall if anyone needs freshening up."

"I would prefer tea, if it's not too much trouble," said Miss Jessop.

"No trouble at all."

A loud crack filled the room as the storm kicked into higher gear, and lightning and thunder made their appearance. Wind and rain lashed the house's windows and shook its great timbers.

"Oh!" Lettice cried, shivering. "This storm is so loud! I hope it lets up soon."

Her eyes settled upon the enormous spruce tree in the right corner of the vast room. "A tree for Christmas! Lovely! But it hasn't got any baubles or tinsel. It's *bare*."

Anna smiled. "That's because I was saving it for you and your brothers to help decorate. We've got ten trays of beautiful ornaments to hang and as much tinsel as you can imagine. Now, you can go to your rooms and rest after your cocoa, and then, when dinner is over, we can all trim the tree! Does that sound fun?"

"Oh yes, please!" Lettice's pale face lit up. "That would be ever so lovely."

Later, when Anna showed Miss Jessop and the children to their rooms, Lettice repeated the last phrase at every opportunity. She applied it to the boys' bedroom, decorated in cadet blue, and to her own lilac-and-white retreat. Only the playroom did not elicit an "ever so lovely" from Lettice – or any enthusiasm from her brothers.

Anna was puzzled.

"You don't like the playroom? I thought you'd love it. It's the sunniest room in the house, and I picked out the wallpaper myself."

"It's delightful," said Miss Jessop, in a tone that woefully contradicted her words.

"That's just it," blurted out James. "The wallpaper! We're grateful for the toys and the space but it's just that...you see, Miss...we don't like motorcars."

Anna understood then. The wallpaper she'd chosen sported a pattern of antique automobiles driven by jaunty Edwardian couples. The children said earlier that they didn't like "motorcars," but Anna had not realized how deep this strange phobia went – or that it was also shared by Miss Jessop. "That's... that's quite alright," stammered Anna, flushing. She ushered them all out of the playroom hastily. "We can find another place for you to play in. This is a very large house."

"That'd be best," said Miss Jessop, in her laconic way.

* * *

"Such a wonderful dinner, Mrs. Sanchez," said Anna. The visitors, however, had eaten little, although Mrs. Sanchez had labored long to make traditional English roast beef for them. Anna chalked it up to tiredness and unfamiliar surroundings.

"And now that we've finished our dinner, we may go into the great hall and trim the tree!" she announced grandly. The children exclaimed in turn:

"Lovely!"

"Oh, I do love a good tree-trimming on Christmas Eve!"

"Have you got an angel for the top?"

"Yes, dears!" cried Anna. "A great sparkling angel with fluffy golden wings!"

"If you don't mind, Miss, I'd rather retire for the evening," said Miss Jessop. "I've got a detective story to finish and I'm at the last chapter, where Monsieur Poirot is due to finger the murderer. The children are in good hands with you."

Mrs. Sanchez accompanied Miss Jessop to her room while Anna led the delighted children into the great hall. She took the trays of ornaments out of a cabinet and invited them to choose their first ones. Lettice opted for a red glass ball with a Santa painted on it. James picked a small wooden airplane. Little Freddie grabbed a ceramic candy cane. Outside, the wind slammed against one of the hall's huge windows, and rain beat furiously on the glass.

"Such beautiful baubles!" Freddie said in admiration. "May I be the one who places the angel at the top, when we come to the very end of all of them?"

"Well, I don't know," said Anna. "James or Lettice might want to have the honor."

"Oh, we must let Freddie do it!" cried Lettice. "Because he's never done it before, and now is his last chance."

"You silly goose!" replied Anna. "He is only six. There are years of Christmases ahead."

Lettice looked grave for a moment. Her pale face took on a solemn cast much too old for her. "Well, no one really knows how many Christmases are ahead of them, do they?" Then she brightened up, and sifted through another tray of ornaments, exclaiming "cunning" over a plaster Christ child in a manger.

What a morbid thing for a child to say, thought Anna, disturbed. Still, she supposed that Lettice was remembering her lost parents, poor thing. Anna had never been told exactly how they had died–she assumed it had something to do with the war.

But soon Lettice was arguing with James boisterously over a miniature train ornament, and then they were chasing each other around the Christmas tree while little Freddie laughed and clapped his hands, and Anna felt festive again. It really was quite fun having children running about in the gloomy vastness of Gull Wing House.

When every ornament and tinsel strand was hung, Anna helped Freddie climb a ladder to place the angel at the summit of the huge tree.

"She really is a brilliant angel," said Freddie, his face glowing with wonder. "With her golden wings and sparkly hair."

"Brilliant!" agreed Lettice and James in unison. They all stood before the tree after that, surveying the grand transformation of the humble spruce.

"I do believe it's the most splendid tree ever," said James, and the other children agreed, with shining eyes and flashing dimples.

The grandfather clock in the great hall chimed the ninth evening hour. "I'm tired now, Miss," added James.

"Yes, I suppose you are. It's been a long day. Does anybody want a bedtime story?"

"I do!"

"I do!"

"Me too!"

Anna opened a glass-fronted bookcase and chose a slender book. "It's up the staircase for you, and down the hall to the boys' room where we'll all gather for *The Velveteen Rabbit*. But first, you must brush your teeth and put on your pajamas."

* * *

But these things don't matter at all," read out Anna, in her best end-of-story voice, "because once you are real, you can't be ugly, except to people who don't understand." She closed *The Velveteen Rabbit* with a gentle whoosh! and smiled at the rapt children.

"It's quite a dear story," said Lettice, with glistening eyes. "It's sad to see it come to an end."

Anna gave a little laugh and hugged the child. "But never fear, it's just the first of many stories I plan to read to you...To all of you!"

There was a little pause, and James and Anna exchanged knowing glances. "I suppose," said James, with an authoritative air, "that anything's possible, if a stuffed cloth rabbit can become a real one."

"Absolutely," laughed Anna, "and now it is definitely time for bed. It's nearly ten."

She helped each pajama-clad boy climb under their covers and turned the light out. "Good-night, dear boys," she said softly. Then she led Lettice to her room and turned back the lilac quilt on the bed.

"Do you expect that Miss Jessop has by now finished her detective story?" asked the child, as she snuggled under her quilt.

"I expect so," replied Anna.

"Good. I wanted ever so much for her to know the murderer before—" Lettice paused as if catching herself.

"Before what, dear?" Anna puzzled, as she leaned over the bed.

"Tomorrow!" Lettice finished. "Before *tomorrow*. It'll be Christmas and she won't have time to read then..."

She was interrupted by a loud, shrieking whistle, sounds of furious honking, which were followed by a terrible cacophony of metals clashing, scraping and smashing. And then, cries of terror and anguish, and a great, ominous explosion.

Lettice sat up in bed and clutched Anna in horror. "It's beginning!" she cried, burying her face in Anna's bosom.

The door flung open, and in rushed James and Freddie. They clung to Anna's skirts fearfully, trembling and crying. "It's coming from the playroom," screamed Freddie. "The noise, the terrible noise. It's the motorcars. Oh, I don't like motorcars! Make them stop, Miss!"

Anna trembled also, shocked to the core. Where did they come from, those dreadful and impossible noises? It sounded like a multi-car accident on the stretch of road below, but that was unlikely. There were hardly two cars at a time on that road, even at the busiest hour of day. And all of it sounded as if in a near room, not down a high cliff a mile or more from the house.

The noises wore down to a cold and ominous silence after about five minutes. The children's hands continued clutching various parts of Anna's body until Miss Jessop appeared in the doorway of Lettice's bedroom, wearing a prim flannel nightgown, her face sheet-white under an old-fashioned ruffled cap.

"I expect there's been a large tree down and lightning caused the sap to explode," she said. "And poor animals nearby, screaming in fear. I've heard it before in Scotland. But there's no need to take fright now, children. Everything's over and done with now."

"It wasn't a tree!" cried Freddie. "It was a motorcar! In the playroom next door to us, and so very, very loud."

"Nonsense, Freddie," said Miss Jessop briskly. "I've been to the playroom and there is nothing. Stop squeezing our kind Miss and give the poor girl a chance to breathe. That goes for James and Lettice as well. Remember the wonderful time you all had tonight. Be glad for the good instead of crying when it's over."

The calming delivery of Miss Jessop's words had an effect on the three children. They slowly disengaged themselves from Anna's skirts and bosom, and obediently followed the dour Scotswoman's orders. Lettice lay down and pulled up her covers, and the boys straightened their pajamas and trotted meekly to Miss Jessop's side. As she shooed them into the hall and toward their own bedroom, she looked back at Anna and said, "Sometimes the bairns want a firm hand, Miss, as we say back in Glasgow."

Anna smiled weakly. "Thank you, Miss Jessop, for all of your help. And now, I must telephone someone and try to find out what caused that awful disturbance. There may be injuries that I could help with. Good night, children. Tomorrow will be Christmas and Christmas is always wonderful!."

"Indeed, Miss," said Miss Jessop. "Good night to you."

"Good night, Miss!" cried Lettice, as Anna exited the bedroom behind Miss Jessop. "It really is an ever so lovely last tree that you gave us."

Last tree? Anna was just starting to get used to Lettice's strange comments. She found Mrs Sanchez downstairs in the telephone alcove in the hall. The housekeeper, garbed in a striped robe, was trying unsuccessfully to make a call. "No dial tone!" she said in disgust, handing the receiver to Anna. "Been out most of the day!"

Anna tapped the receiver cradle several times but got only dead air. "What a time for the phone to go out! With animals or humans possibly injured from that awful crash a few minutes ago."

"Crash, Miss Anna?" Mrs. Sanchez sounded confused. "I didn't hear no crash."

"Surely you must have heard it? So loud and terrifying. Isn't that what you were trying to call on the phone about?"

"I didn't hear nothing. I wanted to call my brother and wish him a Merry Christmas Eve, that's all."

"But but…what about Jandy? I must go to him and seek his help…"

"In the kitchen for a nightcap with me all evening. We didn't hear nothing but the storm."

"But that's impossible! The children heard it and so did Miss Jessop!"

"Perhaps it was just the wind," said Mrs. Sanchez, turning back toward her kitchen. "Jandy wants another nightcap now, I suppose."

* * *

Anna woke up to a strange stillness permeating the second floor of the big house. The storm was over, and a few rays of chilly light were poking through the gloom of her bedroom window's blinds.

"Christmas morning!" she said aloud, as she sprang from bed and put on a quilted dressing gown. "Mrs. Sanchez will need help with breakfast."

She paused in the hall before Lettice's bedroom and debated waking the children up. She was surprised they weren't up early for the big day, like most children everywhere, but she supposed they were still very tired from traveling. She put her ear to Lettice's door, hoping to hear sounds of stirring, but there was only silence.

Downstairs, she could smell sweet rolls baking in the kitchen before she entered and likewise, she appreciated the comforting sound of bacon sizzling on the griddle. It was already nearly nine. Mrs. Sanchez was leaning over the huge wood-burning range, her back to the kitchen door.

"Merry Christmas, Mrs. Sanchez! Your breakfast smells delicious!"

"Never met a child who don't like gooey sweet rolls," she turned and grinned. "Englishes or no Englishes. By the way, there's a message from Mrs. Simonson's sister, Mrs. Drake in San Fran, for you. The phone is working again, and she sounded rattled. The number is on the fridge."

"Mrs. Drake? Oh dear, I'll take it in the hall."

The long-distance operator connected Anna to San Francisco. "Hello? San Francisco? Stand by for a call from Carmel."

"Yes, I've been expecting it," came a woman's thin voice, which did indeed sound "rattled."

"Mrs. Drake? It's Anna calling from Gull Wing Farm. I had a message and it sounded urgent."

"Yes, dear," said Mrs. Drake. "I'm afraid it's not a very Happy Christmas morning. I am sorry to say, but your visitors will not be arriving, today or any other day. I tried to call yesterday to tell you their train was delayed for hours because of the weather, but your phone was out. And then, this morning, a telegram came from the rail company with the most awful news."

Mrs. Drake made a small sobbing noise and then collected herself. "When the train got moving again, it somehow collided with an automobile, and was derailed, around ten o'clock last night. There was an explosion, and everyone in the first passenger car...they died. I regret to inform you that Miss Jessop and the children were in that car."

Anna felt her heart drop into her stomach. "That's impossible! Surely, there is some kind of mistake? Because they—"

"No mistake, dear," interrupted Mrs. Drake. "Their train never arrived in Carmel. And now if you will excuse me, I must make arrangements with my sister Helen...and...the family in England." With that, she rang off, leaving a shocked and confused Anna holding a dead receiver.

It must be a mistake, Anna's mind screamed at her frantically. There was likely another train, another group of children, and another nanny. That was the only explanation.

Dropping the receiver, Anna ran toward the stairs at the end of the hall and took them two-by-two. She ran to Lettice's room first, shouting the child's name, while banging against her bedroom door as loudly as she could. There was no answer. She pushed open the door and gave a little gasp.

The room was empty. The bed was tidily made. But there was no Lettice anywhere in the room. Her luggage and clothes were absent as well.

Anna whirled around and ran to the boys' room, calling their names at the top of her lungs. Again, no answer. She opened their door and saw that this bedroom, too, was empty, with beds neatly made, and with luggage, personal items, and clothes all missing.

Next, she ran to Miss Jessop's room. The room was also bereft of nanny, luggage, and clothes. She entered, closed the door behind her and leaned against it, bursting into anguished tears, her face buried in her hands.

But *where did they go?* she thought. *How did they leave with no transportation from the house? Am I mad? Did we all simply imagine them, Mrs. Sanchez, and Jandy and I? This nightmare can't be happening – it's all so unbelievable.*

She took her hands away and surveyed the empty room again. Then she saw it: a sealed envelope resting on top of the nightstand next to Miss Jessop's tidy bed. Quickly, she opened it and read the handwritten note inside:

> *Dear Miss Anna,*
>
> *I expect that you will be wanting an explanation. I wish I had one myself. What I know is that we were stranded on that train for hours, and then we went to sleep and woke up on the platform where you found us. There was an understanding somehow that we were being given a small Grace by Providence, but that it would end in the night with a terrible event. The children wanted their last Christmas tree, you see, and myself…well, my final wish was to get to the end of my detective story. A very silly thing, but there it was. Now, sadly, our Grace period has ended, and we must meet our assigned fate. Thank you for your warm hospitality and kindness. The children did love their last tree so very, very much.*
>
> *Kindest regards,*
> *Margaret Jessop.*

Anna dropped the letter and wept again, unashamed. Years later, when she was still not quite over the experience, she would tell her own children that Christmas miracles could indeed come true, and that sometimes, they were very strange.

In the Howling of the Wind

Marie O'Regan

THE OLD MAN watched as the child pressed close to the window, staring wide-eyed at the falling snow – flakes large and small dancing in the moonlight. He shivered as a sudden draught swept into the room; the door swinging inward as if presaging the arrival of something wondrous.

It was nothing. "Just the wind," he muttered to himself.

The child turned towards him, his eyes full of questions; and the old man felt his spine turn to ice.

"What is it, Grandpa?"

"Nothing…it's nothing, child. Just the wind."

The boy stared at the door, and sighed as it swung shut once more. "Do you think they'll come?"

The old man nodded, clearing his throat as he gestured at the room – the gifts under the tinsel-laden tree, the mantel groaning with cards and pine garlands, complete with golden bells and red velvet bows. "Of course. It's Christmas Eve. Why wouldn't they come?"

The boy said nothing, just stared at his grandfather with an intensity he found unnerving.

The old man leaned forward, tried again. "They're your parents, Matthew, of course they'll come."

This time the boy responded. "How can you be sure?"

"They love you. You are…" he hesitated, suddenly unsure, then continued, "…their flesh. Their blood." He reached out to the boy, who skirted his grasp and hovered just out of reach. "Trust me. They'll be here."

The wind howled as if the skies themselves were in pain, and the boy's gaze shifted to the fireplace, where the wind whispered in sympathy.

"I don't like the sound the wind makes in the chimney."

"What do you mean?"

The boy smiled briefly at him, nervous; aware of how fanciful his words sounded. "It *cries*."

The old man laughed heartily at that. A little *too* heartily. "It's just air, Matthew. Just air." He sat back in his armchair with a sigh and gripped the armrests tightly, taking comfort in feeling the worn fabric under his fingers. On nights like this he drew strength from the feel of the fire warming his skin, the grooves his weight had worn in the chair over the years, the touch of cloth against his body. *This* was what counted, what was real…he cared nothing for what lay beyond the confines of his refuge.

Lights swept across the window suddenly, then were gone. Matthew ran back to the window and pressed his face to the glass. "Grandpa! It's them!" The bell stayed silent, and there were no voices at the door. The boy's smile faded as he surveyed the empty street.

The old man watched as the child raised his hand and laid it flat against the icy pane as if he wanted to melt the ice with its warmth. He called the boy's name, softly, but he didn't answer. He almost didn't hear the boy's sob, muffled as it was by the sudden shriek of wind that battered the house, rattling the windows in their ageing frames.

"Matthew."

The boy said nothing.

"Matthew, come here... Please."

This time the boy came, reluctant, and the old man could see the pain etched on his face. He ached to stroke the child's cheek, hold him close – but that was impossible for a child like Matthew. All he could do was talk to him, and this he did willingly.

"You're a good boy, Matthew. And they love you, even now. If there's a way for them to get here – to get to you – they will."

The boy nodded, but his disbelief shone through. It was in the slump of his shoulders, the way his eyes slid away from his grandfather's, the sorrow on his face. He turned away, and went back to his puzzle, sitting hunched over it on the living room floor.

The old man loved his grandson, always had. Gazing at the forlorn figure bent over his jigsaw he offered up a silent prayer, *Please God, let them get through.*

* * *

The chiming of the clock on the mantel woke the old man up, and he heaved himself out of his chair, huffing. Moving around wasn't as easy as it used to be, he found. The clock said it was nine pm, and the shadows flickering on the walls confirmed the day's passing. The fire crackled in the hearth, and Matthew was still working on his puzzle, his little face solemn but determined. It wasn't natural for a child to be so quiet, he mused. It didn't seem right, although he knew Matthew was perfectly happy – lost in his own little world, where he had always been happiest; never more so than now.

Wandering over to the window, he stared out at the poorly-lit street. Snow had drifted against the walls and hedges, he saw, the parked cars buried almost to the tops of their wheels. The snow on the road itself was pristine, no traffic had disturbed it – and it would be morning, probably, before the gritters reached this far out from town. He sensed the boy's eyes on him and turned, forcing a smile. "The snow's deep, lad, do you think they'll make it?"

Matthew regarded him in silence for a moment. His answer, when it came, was terse. "You're the one who said they would."

"Well, yes, but the snow..."

"You promised." The boy's tone brooked no argument, and the old man sighed, then nodded. "I did, didn't I. And I meant it, Matthew. If they can make it, they will."

Matthew's smile was singularly humourless, and the old man flinched. "Remember what you said, Grandpa."

"About your parents?"

"About them...and about breaking promises."

The strength drained out of the old man's legs, and he fumbled himself back into his armchair. "What did I say, boy?"

Matthew's smile widened, baring his teeth; his eyes seemed to shine yellow in the firelight, and the old man cursed himself for a fool.

Matthew drew closer, his mouth close to the old man's ear. "You said you must never break a promise. You said God watches."

"God always watches, Matthew, you know that." His voice was thin, quavery, and the boy sniggered as he drew back.

"God's not the only one who watches, Grandpa."

He fought to quell the chill that rose in him at the boy's words. "What do you mean?"

"Others watch, too..." Matthew glanced around, nervous again. "Sometimes I can almost see..."

The wind moaned and whispered in the trees, and the boy's attention was broken. Restless, he returned to the window, and the old man sighed with relief. Matthew had always been such a sunny little child. When had this solemn creature taken his place?

The wind sobbed and moaned in the eaves; this old house was far from well insulated, and it found its way through numerous cracks and gaps with ease. The old man turned his head to the sound – it seemed deeper, somehow, more sonorous. Was that a voice he could hear? The wind seemed to whisper to him, and he fancied he could smell something – a scent that was tantalisingly familiar, but he couldn't place it.

Not yet.

Music wafted down the stairs, a piano tinkling somewhere close by. Matthew stood, and this time his smile was genuine. "Listen, Grandpa. Listen!"

The old man took a step closer to the closed door, flinching as a gust of wind blew it open. The hall was empty, no sign of trespass – just dust motes dancing in the chill night air. Turning back to the boy, he asked, "I almost recognise it, don't you?" He moved towards the door, but hesitated at the threshold to the hall. It was dark out there, the shadows thick and somehow glutinous.

He sensed Matthew, standing just behind him, and moved to take the boy's hand. The boy moved back once more, and the old man sighed. He should have known better. Matthew had never liked to be touched, even before…

"Who is it, Grandpa?" The boy was eager, but not so eager that he'd come close. The old man yearned for the warmth of a hug from his grandchild, but – as ever – he knew the child wouldn't allow it.

"I'm not sure, Matthew." He glanced back at the front door, dots of white peppering the blackened glass as the snow fell outside in the dark. It was firmly closed. "I didn't hear anyone come in, did you?"

Matthew looked at him strangely, and started up the stairs.

"Come back, boy!" His voice was harsher than he'd intended, and Matthew stopped at once.

The old man moved forward, climbed past Matthew slowly, then continued his ascent. The music faltered, just for a moment, and he froze; gesturing to Matthew to *be still*. He listened to his breath rasping in his throat, his heart stuttering in his chest – and finally the music began again. It was clearer now, and he thought he recognised it. *Für Elise*. His breath caught in his throat as the memories came thick and fast; how his daughter had loved that melody. One of the earliest tunes she had learnt when she was taking lessons, she had fallen in love with it and played it relentlessly, driving him to distraction even though he loved it. Now it floated down the stairs, bringing images of his beloved girl: Elise drawing, one foot curled beneath her as it always was; Elise at the piano, tongue poking between her lips as she concentrated on her lesson; Elise sleeping, hair spread across her pillow like a little angel…

He wiped a tear from his cheek, and took another step forward, only to freeze when the door at the top of the stairs opened and light spilled out, bathing him and Matthew in a golden glow.

A woman stood silhouetted in the doorway, her features indistinct in the light. Matthew made a move as if to step forward, arms outstretched…and the old man's heart leapt. "Matthew, no!"

Matthew turned to face him, his face wet with tears. "You said she wasn't here! You said we were waiting for them to come!"

"We are, boy, trust me!" Helpless in the face of the child's anger, he struggled for the words to make this right: a way to convince him of the truth.

Matthew's face was all the answer he needed, and it pained him to see so much anger on that sweet face.

The woman at the top of the stairs took a step forward, peering down the darkened hall. The old man stared at her, tears streaming down his face. Why wouldn't she look at them? What more did he have to do?

* * *

"Mark, is that you?"

As if summoned by his name, the front door blew open and snow blasted through the opening. A tall, dark-haired man rushed through and forced the door shut behind him. As the wind died he took his coat off, but first he shook the snow from his shoulders. He raised his eyes to the woman at the top of the stairs, and his face broke into a smile of such warmth that even the old man couldn't fail to be moved by it.

"Elise!" He stepped forward, raking a hand through the unruly mop that fell over his eyes. "Am I glad to be home! Have you seen the snow?"

The woman laughed, and started down the stairs towards him. "It's coming down fast now, isn't it."

As she reached the bottom he swept her into his arms, holding her tight. Her face was buried against his neck as he asked, "How is he? Is there any change?" Her body stiffened, and he knew the answer even before she shook her head

He held her tighter.

* * *

Matthew, sitting on a step about halfway up, turned to glare at his grandfather. "Who does he mean?"

The old man shook his head, unsure. "I...I don't know."

"You do, don't you! You *do* know who it is!" The boy ran down the stairs towards his parents, but stopped short of going to them. He turned to his grandfather suddenly, terrified. "But...when did she come in, Grandpa? I didn't hear her, did you?"

"No, Matthew, I didn't." He stared at the couple entwined in the hall, and gasped as the shadows grew deeper, swallowing them whole. They were alone once more. The boy whimpered and ran back to him, cowering by his side but not touching. "I didn't hear a thing."

"Where did they go? Did you see?" The old man could only shake his head – the house had changed, somehow; the wind carried voices and sounds from things unseen, and the night outside was fierce.

They couldn't leave.

* * *

Midnight, and the old man woke to find the fire sputtering. Matthew was asleep on the rug before it, curled up in a ball. His beloved puzzle was gone.

The old man stared around the familiar room, wondering how things had changed, and why. Shadows flickered in the dying firelight, and with them, the room...*altered*. There was a painting over on the far wall that he didn't remember, had certainly not bought – it was too modern for his tastes, too *bright*. The television (how he hated the things, had always kept it hidden in a unit that looked like a wooden chest) was displayed proudly, and it was huge – not the smaller model he remembered. The ticking seemed to grow louder, and he turned to stare at the clock on the mantel. It was still there, calling him, but some of the ornaments up there were new, weren't they? There was a photo frame that was unfamiliar, with a bud vase beside it, now empty. He went and stared at the photo, felt the chill of the room sink into him. The figure that stared back was his own, a photo taken by his daughter Elise, on his seventieth birthday. For the life of him he couldn't remember when that had been, and wondered anew if he was going senile. He moved to the window and looked out at a wonderland; the ground was thickly carpeted with fresh snow and the sky was midnight blue, starlight making the snow glow cobalt-white.

There was another photograph on the windowsill, and he traced the outlines of that familiar face – feeling the chill pervade his body. Matthew. A happy, cheeky Matthew – not the quiet, untouchable shadow he had become. Next to this was a photograph of Elise with her husband, Mark; as yet untouched by the world's harsh reality. These pictures spoke of happy times, and he struggled to remember them...to remember his place in all this. And Matthew's.

He looked back at his chair, and froze. His beloved chair was gone, replaced by something newer, sleeker. He didn't like it. Yet when he closed his eyes and touched this...the familiar cloth sprouted beneath his fingers, only to vanish when he looked again. The smell of smoke made him cough, and for just a moment the heat in the room was intense – then the chill settled in once more.

And what of Matthew? He stared at the sleeping boy, wondering whether to wake him; he knew the child wouldn't react well. He rubbed his eyes, unsure of his vision suddenly – the boy appeared *dimmer*, somehow. Less there. He wondered how many more of these tricks the house would play on him before the night was over.

He stumbled into the hall, lost in this space that, once so familiar, now felt so strange. Music floated downstairs again, and he cried out in fear. Where was she? He made his way quickly up the stairs, eager to see his daughter, have her tell him what was happening.

* * *

Elise sat on the bed, clasping a picture in her hands, her face wet with tears. A bedside lamp made the tear tracking down her cheek glisten. The old man hovered in the doorway, unwilling suddenly to intrude on this, his daughter's grief. A door on the other side of the bedroom opened, and Mark appeared.

"Elise?"

She smiled up at him, put the photo back on the bedside table. Matthew laughed at her from it, caught in delight at some past party. "I'm sorry. I'm okay, really."

Mark nodded, sympathy evident as he asked, "Can I get you anything?"

She thought for a moment. "A tea would be nice, if that's okay?"

He grinned at her, then. "Should have known." He crossed to the bed, kissed her on the forehead. "Of course it is. I'll be back in a minute."

He brushed past the old man without acknowledgement, his face set. The good humour was purely for his daughter's benefit. What was wrong, he wondered? Was she ill? He moved closer, silent, unwilling to disturb her now she seemed to be resting.

She lay on the bed, eyes closed, and the old man became aware of the plaintive strains of *Für Elise* once more, the CD player beside the bed set low. He had named her for this song, over her mother's wishes. She had thought it too fanciful, instead of beautiful. He supposed it was lucky she'd loved the tune as much as he did.

He sensed movement beside him, and realised Matthew had joined him at his mother's bedside. The boy stared forlornly, and the old man was saddened to see how pale he was. Elise rolled over, and before he could think what to do, he found himself and the boy back out in the hall, just in time to sink deeper into the shadows as Mark returned.

The hall brightened for a moment as Mark went into the bedroom, then darkened again. Matthew and his grandfather stood just outside the door, listening, a little ashamed of themselves. Elise and Mark thought they were alone, and perhaps that was best – though neither of them could have said why.

* * *

Mark sat on the edge of the bed, a steaming mug of tea in his hand. He shook his wife gently. "Elise, wake up. Your tea."

She opened her eyes and stared blankly at him for a moment, then smiled and sat up, taking the cup. "I must have drifted off."

"Not surprising, love. You must be exhausted."

Her smile faded as she tried not to cry. "I'll rest when he wakes up."

Mark opened his mouth as if to speak…and then closed it again. This was old ground, gone over too many times already. The wounds were fresh, just under the surface, and he had no wish to open them again.

The phone shrilled, and Elise dropped her cup.

* * *

Matthew sat on the hearth, his arms wrapped tightly around him. He stared up at his grandfather.

"Where did they go, Grandpa?"

"I don't know, boy." He was staring out of the window, at the tracks their car had left in the snow as it screeched out of the drive. "I don't know."

Matthew wasn't about to give up. "But it's late – the middle of the night. Why didn't they check I was alright, or take me with them?"

The old man could only shake his head. "I suppose because they knew I'd look after you." He sat down heavily, relieved to find the room back as he remembered. "But they should have told us, that's true."

The house was dark, and cold, but neither moved to turn a light on, or lay the fire.

Time passed, shadows fell. And the wind was screaming.

* * *

Elise stared at the shape in the bed before her, so pale and weak. She could barely take in the doctor's words. "He's been showing signs of waking, Mrs. Banks. Very slight…but definitely there." A monitor went off again, and nurses bustled, clustering around their patient. He still hadn't moved. She felt a hand rest on her shoulder, and another snake round her waist. She leaned back – grateful for Mark's warmth. He kissed her hair.

"What do you think, Mark? Will he wake up?"

He sighed. "I don't know, darling. But God, I hope so."

"It's been so long…" Elise's voice cracked, and she put a hand to her mouth; desperate to contain her grief.

Mark nodded. "I know."

They looked on, then, as the doctors worked; and they waited and watched, as they had for so long – forlorn in the hope that this time, maybe this time, hope would win.

* * *

Dawn was breaking through the living room window, its watery rays struggling to illuminate the cold and stark room, where Matthew and his grandfather sat waiting. As the room brightened, Matthew cried out – and his grandfather whirled towards him. The boy was...flickering. The old man watched in shock as the image of the lad faded out of sight. Then he was back, just for a moment...reaching out towards him. With a cry, he made a grab for his grandson's hand, desperate for the contact...and to keep Matthew with him.

Too late.

* * *

Elise was exhausted. Mark was by her side, and they leant on each other as they searched for some sign of the doctors' success. As dawn broke, Elise called her son's name, her voice shocked. Following the direction of her gaze, Mark saw his son open his eyes briefly, and smile at his mother.

* * *

"Matthew!" He was back, suddenly, and the old man slumped with relief. The boy was jittery, frightened...but he was here. "What happened, boy? Where did you go?"

"I don't know." The boy was staring around him, as if he were trying to fix his position, set it in stone. "It was bright...there was a bed...and my mother was there."

The old man wept. "Did she see you?"

"I think so." Matthew's voice shook with emotion, the first real feeling the old man had seen since...when, exactly? "She smiled...I *think* it was at me."

The boy began to fade again, and the old man moaned. "Don't leave me, Matthew. Don't leave me alone."

The boy flickered back into view and smiled. "Don't worry, Grandpa. I won't." He grasped his grandfather's wrist, and the old man cried out at the surge of feeling that shot up his arm.

* * *

They were back in that room, by the bed, but this time they were together. Matthew stared up at his grandfather, then at the figure in the bed, his face milk-white.

"Grandpa, look!"

The old man obeyed. "I don't understand, Matthew. How can this be?"

Matthew drew closer to the figure, traced the contours of its face, entranced. "I don't understand either. How can it be me, Grandpa?"

* * *

Back in the house. Alone. The old man groaned as he surveyed the living room he'd loved so much, and he remembered. The heat rose around him as he saw those flames lick the carpet and up the walls, the ember of coal that had caused this carnage glowing innocuously on the floor in the midst of it all.

He saw, again, the Christmas tree going up in flames, the smell of pine pervading the house as if it were no more than a scented candle. He groaned as he saw his beloved chair blacken, then burst into flames, the fumes causing the old man (he recognised himself, and started to cry) to scream in anguish as he rose to his feet and tried to put the flames out, calling out the name of the boy entrusted to his care while his parents were at a party. "Matthew! Matthew!"

He saw the child, huddled on the stairs, coughing; tears tracking through the grime on his face as he called in vain for his grandfather. He saw the hope in his eyes die as he realised no help was coming. Then he saw the boy slump to the floor as the smoke overcame him, eyes closed.

As he watched himself fall to the floor, flesh blackening as the flames licked at his body, he heard the front door as it broke under the force of the fireman's axe. He felt himself smothered – too late – by a blanket as he heard another man's voice call for oxygen: "There's a kid up here! Quick, bring oxygen – he's still alive!" He remembered the feeling of panic as he fought to stay alive. He'd been entrusted with the child, he had to look after his grandson!

Now, as the memories crashed in and he realised – too late – what had happened that fateful night, he heard Matthew calling him; and then he was back by the boy's bed, watching as he woke.

* * *

"Grandpa?"

Elise was crying, even as she smiled at the boy and shushed him, brushing his hair back off his face just like she had every night since the beginning. Mark watched his wife and son whilst trying not to show that he too wanted nothing more than to break down after the stress of the last months.

Matthew looked beyond them, his body frail and his face wan – but he saw his grandfather. And he smiled.

The doctors were checking the boy over, this child that had hovered for so long in the between spaces, neither dead nor alive. Matthew took no notice. He looked at his grandfather, and he reached out his hand.

The old man reached for the boy's fingers, clasped his hand in his own even though he knew neither of them could really feel it. He tried to explain, to make it right.

"I was supposed to look after you, Matthew."

"You did, Grandpa. It wasn't your fault."

Elise frowned, worried. "What wasn't Grandpa's fault, Matthew?"

"The fire. He thinks he didn't look after me."

Elise shook her head. "The fire was no one's fault, darling. A fluke, that's all. Your grandfather would never intentionally let you get hurt."

Matthew nodded. "I know, but he thinks it was."

"He does?" Mark drew closer, leant over his son. "Can you remember the fire, son? Can you remember anything?" He exchanged glances with his wife, fearful of the answer.

Matthew shook his head. "No, nothing. I was coughing, then it was dark." His face brightened as he did, indeed, remember something. "I remember Grandpa, he's been with me."

"He has?" Eager to soothe the child, and close this chapter, his parents played along. They had no wish to lose him again if he was stressed, they just wanted to forget – and move on.

"All the time," Matthew continued. "He helped me with my puzzle while we waited."

"Waited?"

"For you to come home from the party."

Elise felt Mark's hand tighten on her shoulder. In the months since the party, while they'd buried her father and watched their son as he lay comatose, she'd blamed herself again and again for leaving them; for being out of the house when disaster struck. For leaving them alone. Had her father somehow managed to stay with Matthew, through all this? Had he stayed by his side?

Matthew giggled, and Elise fought to stay calm. "What's funny, sweetheart?"

Matthew's smile was warm, his delight genuine. "Grandpa. He says thank you for not blaming him, now he can go – find peace." Matthew's face fell. "He's leaving."

Mark cleared his throat, amazed at Matthew's words. "He needs to go to Heaven, son. He needs to rest."

"He died?"

Matthew's voice shook, but then the smile returned as his grandfather spoke. "Your place is here, Matthew, with your parents. I can leave you now you're back with them; it's where you belong."

"But where will you go, Grandpa? When will I see you again?"

"I'm going home, son. And I'll always be watching you, never fear." The old man started to fade, and Matthew's face fell. He buried his face against his mother's chest, feeling her wrap her arms around him. His grandfather smiled, and nodded, and pointed out of the window, at the snow. "Go home, Matthew. It's Christmas, and your parents have everything ready, just waiting for you."

Matthew sniffed back a tear as his grandfather faded, and looked up at his parents. "It's Christmas?"

Elise nodded happily. "Yes, it is, Matthew. Tomorrow…" She looked at the clock on the wall, "no, today, in fact."

Matthew grinned, then, and waved at what seemed, to everyone else, to be thin air. "Bye, Grandpa. Bye…and Happy Christmas!"

Midnight for Clementine

Katherine Quevedo

SOME FOOL PLUGGED in the Christmas tree after midnight. From my spot on the sofa, I watched the ornaments blink around, confused by the eerie, unfamiliar glow. My seven sisters, the other Christmas dolls, scratched their yarn hair and rubbed their porcelain faces with porcelain hands. Cloth met cloth as Clementine's rag arm nudged my torso.

"Mariah."

"I'm already up, Clem. You don't need to whisper."

"I saw who did it."

She glanced toward the far arm of the sofa, where the nativity set rested on the end table. I spotted two of the three Magi, Melchior and Balthasar, dressed in their fineries and stirring next to their camels. Where was the third?

"Not Caspar," I gasped.

She glared at me. The reflections of Christmas tree lights in her eyes blazed at my implication. Whenever my sisters and I made our annual visit to the nativity set to pay our respects, Clementine always tossed her orange yarn braid with more gusto than usual while she and Caspar ogled each other for half the visit. When we'd finally head back to the sofa, her porcelain cheeks always looked rosier than usual.

I used to think them both silly, until the first time Rope Man appeared on our side of the tree. His slender twine body and round wooden head faced me that year and the next. He wore a red felt hat and matching boots. As an ornament, he wasn't free to move about as we were. How I longed to climb to his branch and unhook him from the tree so he could visit the hearth, the nativity set, and of course my sofa home.

That's when I first understood how Clementine felt. Caspar's entire body was porcelain, so he was breakable like us, but much firmer; and Rope Man's whole body was pliable like our rag limbs, but his wooden face and felt hands weren't brittle. His similarities assured me that we could talk as two kindred spirits, but his differences made him exotic and alluring.

Now at the nativity set, a third figure joined the other two Magi by their camels: Caspar. Clementine turned away quickly and gazed out past the fireplace toward the Christmas tree.

"So who did it?" I asked.

"It's hard to say. I just saw him drop from one of the stockings."

I eyed them, four giant flaps hanging from the mantel like battle flags.

"Actually, it might have been a her. They moved really fast from the plug."

I noticed Nutcracker standing in his usual spot in the corner of the brick hearth. "We could ask Nutcracker." I said it softly, but he must have heard his name, for he rolled his bug-eyes at us.

"No use," Clementine said a bit more loudly. "He wouldn't open his toothy mouth for anyone unless they were a nut to split." This time Nutcracker's eyes narrowed until they looked a normal size. "I saw the figure go up the tree," she finished, looking at me expectantly.

"Forget it," our sister Lorraine said on my other side. "We should just unplug the tree and leave it at that."

"We?" I said to her. "Coming, are you?"

"Unless I can trust you two to just unplug it."

"But what if it's plugged in for a reason?" Clementine said.

She had a point, even though I couldn't imagine what such a reason would be.

Lorraine shrugged, probably having reached the same conclusion, yet not wanting to admit her curiosity. After a moment, she said, "Fine. We climb."

* * *

We raced past the brick hearth. Familiar territory so far. Countless times Clementine and I would race to the tree skirt and back. She always won. Sure enough, she got to the tree skirt first again, but now she hopped onto a gift box, grabbed a low-hanging candy cane, and disappeared up into the branches. Lorraine took more time climbing up the box and pulling herself up by the same candy cane. I climbed up last. After slipping off the candy cane twice, I finally succeeded using a French horn ornament of gold wire.

I did my best to stand on the narrow branch. Needles poked through my wool dress and tugged at my yarn hair as though to throw me off. This was just the bottom layer, and already I longed for our sofa. I looked back. Our other sisters turned their shocked faces away and refused to watch our progress. After all, the nativity set was one thing, but who actually spent time up in the tree?

I took a step. The whole branch wobbled. I grabbed a Christmas tree light to steady myself and looked up. The prospect of climbing a 10-foot tree buckled my rag knees, and if Lorraine hadn't caught my arm, I would've slipped down into the gift pile.

Clementine loped up the branches with a certain grace, while Lorraine moved methodically from layer to layer. I clambered after them both. Next thing I knew, Clementine came racing down the tree. Had she already made it to the top? I heard her yell, "It matches! Quick!" Then suddenly, she used her speed to launch herself from the tree toward the nearest stocking. I gasped. She caught the toe and swung from it for a few seconds before lugging herself, hand over hand, up toward the mantel. One of her porcelain hands gripped the mantel's edge, then the second.

And then everything in my vision slowed.

I watched Clementine's porcelain head rush toward the hearth. I squeezed my eyes shut, but it only made the sound of her face shattering against the brick even louder. Why not over the carpet, my insides wailed? Why, why over the only hard surface of the entire living room floor? I opened my eyes. Christmas tree lights blurred everything in my vision. For a moment I thought I was falling from the branch.

I gripped the tree needles, took a deep breath, and dared to look down at Clementine's body. No more gracefulness. Her rag limbs stuck out haphazardly, one leg completely twisted around and her orange yarn braid drooping from one shoulder. Two small bits of porcelain peeked out from under the braid like scraps of peanut shell. Nutcracker stood near her in his usual corner of the hearth. His broad, stoic face stared straight ahead, hard as the rare shell he couldn't crack. He hadn't even tried to catch her or break her fall.

"You!" I screamed at him. The small ornaments around me turned to look. "You could have helped her. You could have saved her."

He stared straight ahead, desperate to ignore me, but hadn't he revealed earlier his exceptional hearing?

"Mariah," Lorraine called, trying to sound responsible even as her voice wavered with grief and fear. "We have to keep climbing."

But all I could see was an image of Nutcracker breaking Clementine's head in his toothy wooden jaws. I knew the fall had done it, the hearth's impact, but he may as well have murdered her. What difference did it make?

"Mariah! Climb!" Lorraine glared down from a branch several levels above me. Her braid was coming loose and her limbs quivered, although she'd regained control of her voice. "You're hopeless." She continued climbing.

I managed to pull myself up to the next layer and the one after that. The third one seemed impossibly high to reach, even where the branches met the trunk. The whole tree seemed to be growing, stretching out its layers even as I clung to it. I shook my head. Artificial trees don't grow.

I didn't realize I'd spoken aloud until a voice replied, "Nor do they wither, and neither should you."

I spun and saw Rope Man's slender profile. He'd turned toward me as far as the loop attached to his hat would allow. The top of his right eye had been ripped off at an angle, giving his otherwise cheerful smile a hint of menace from the side. I walked to the branch's edge to face him straight on. The reflection of a tree light below us made his black eyes glimmer, one with innocence, one with mischief.

"I'd like to help you," he said, "if I could." He shrugged helplessly.

All those times I'd envisioned unhooking him from the tree, and here I was with both a chance and a reason but none of the elation I'd always imagined.

"I am so sorry about your sister," he said. His left half looked condoling, his right half looked like he wanted to avenge her personally.

I wanted to take his felt hands in my porcelain ones and weep. Instead, I thanked him and extended one hand out for a handshake. "I'm Mariah."

"Rope Man," he replied, confirming what others had told me when I'd asked around about him. His hand was impossibly soft. I was sorry to let it go.

"My sister and I could really use your help."

His eyes shifted toward the hearth.

"My sister Lorraine," I said quickly, pointing upward. Again I felt an urge to grab him and weep, but it wouldn't do anyone any good, least of all Clementine. Enlisting his help, at least, would benefit all parties involved. "Wait right there." As soon as I said it, I realized it was foolish to say to a hanging ornament.

If Rope Man was offended, he hid it well. He looked at me with his sly profile and said, "Surely."

I hoisted myself onto the branch holding Rope Man's loop and crawled to where he hung. Why couldn't he just have had a simple hook? Sliding him off the branch required all my strength and balance. The other nearby ornaments – two hand-painted angels and a mouse holding an acorn – watched my progress and glowered at us with envy. Once freed, Rope Man helped me up to the next layer of branches before pulling himself up after me.

For the most part, we climbed quietly. My mind dwelt on memories of when Clementine and I had gone waltzing across the dining room table or played tag around the centerpiece, or the time she'd insisted that the crystal goblets in the china cabinet would look like a rainbow if we saw them cast in light. Of course we'd never bothered plugging in the tree to find out. Now I spied the goblets gleaming in their corner where the Christmas lights barely reached, but it was enough.

Wouldn't you know it, she was right.

After we had climbed up a few layers, Rope Man paused. "It's good to know your name finally, Mariah." He cleared his throat and looked at me with his innocent side. He looked cheerful, if self-conscious. "I noticed you right away when I first hung facing the sofa. When you went with your sisters to the nativity set, the other dolls trod right on through, but you always took great care to step around the raffia straw in the stable."

I worried that my cheeks were turning rosy under his gaze, like Clementine's after one of those stable visits. I glanced at his arms. Their fibers resembled the raffia straw I'd always tried so hard not to trample.

"Mariah," Lorraine called suddenly. "There you are." She hopped down from the branch above me and paused. "The rope man?" Her tone made it a description, not a name.

"Rope Man's willing to help us."

"Nice to meet you," he said.

"Likewise," she replied stiffly. I hoped it was out of preoccupation and grief.

"What did you discover up there?" I asked.

"It's a candle. A fairy, as far as I could tell. Her dress is glow-in-the-dark, and she's using the lights to charge it up."

As soon as she finished her sentence, a cry came from above and a blur of white crashed down past the branches where we stood.

"The Angel," Rope Man cried.

Yes, it had been too big to be anything other than the beautiful tree topper. We rushed to the outermost tip of the branches and looked down. The Angel lay on her side at the edge of the tree skirt, but unlike Clementine, her soft cone body – needlepoint on a plastic base – had landed unharmed. She thrashed about, trying to push herself up by her short arms, but succeeding only in rolling in a circle.

I turned to Lorraine. "You get the Angel back up the tree. Rope Man and I will go after the candle. That way at least there'll be two of us." I turned to Rope Man. "That is, if you don't mind."

"Of course not."

As Lorraine headed down, Rope Man and I pulled ourselves up to the next layer. An eerie green glow emitted from the top of the tree. Peering through the branches, we saw the Fairy Candle sitting, hugging her knees, head drooping.

"I still glow," she said to herself. "I still glow. Why, why if I still glow?"

I tried to hoist myself up closer to get a better look at her, but she heard me and jumped to her broad wax feet. "You'll burn, too," she spat. Then with grace befitting a fairy, grace that may have rivaled Clementine's, the Fairy Candle swung from the nearest ornament and soared over to the mantel. She landed squarely on her wax base.

Rope Man turned his left profile, the innocuous one, toward me. "Unravel me."

"What?"

"Unravel me. You need to get over there safely, before she gets away, and I'm made of enough strands for that. Tie one end to a branch so you can swing across." He grabbed his coiled torso, about to rend the glue holding him together.

"No!" I pressed his chest to keep him from pulling. Already I'd endured watching my sister fall and shatter; I wasn't going to lose anyone else tonight.

Rope Man's torn eye made him look unsatisfied, but his other eye looked grateful, unfulfilled in a different way, as if he longed to embrace me but dared not try. "We need a way to that mantel," he said. He spread his rope arms wide, and I knew it was a gesture of our lack of options, not an invitation for that embrace. "Do you have any other ideas?"

I studied the mantel, where the Fairy Candle hugged herself and rocked next to a berry-red pillar candle. Prickly evergreen branches covered the surface, dangling slightly over the edge and resembling the very tree bough we stood upon. "If only you had a proper hook."

Even his torn eye made him look taken aback at this comment.

"I'm so sorry, I didn't mean it like that."

He looked relieved.

"There must be something here we can latch onto the mantel display," I explained. I spotted a large candy cane. It was tall, heavy, and awkward, but I maneuvered it off its branch as best I could. "Take this. Go on, you're lighter than I am. Take it. I'll hold onto your feet and swing you toward the mantel. Can you hook this onto one of the branches and pull us up?"

He hesitated.

"It's much better than unraveling you," I said.

He nodded. He took the candy cane to the end of the branch, gripped it as tightly as his felt hands would allow, and allowed me to grab his ankles. I glanced at our destination. The Fairy Candle was glaring down at Nutcracker, pacing, plotting. Much as I despised his selfishness, her instability sickened me more. It frightened me. She'd shown she was capable of hurting another, hurling down the Angel.

Soon we both hung upside-down, Rope Man beneath me against the tips of lower branches with the candy cane, my feet clamped around the branch, my yarn flopping past the top of my head. I felt like an inverted ornament, dangling, in pain, and unsure how to get out of that position. I arched my back with all my might to try to lift Rope Man away from the branches toward the mantel. He and the candy cane rose slightly, then flopped back down. I used what little momentum I had to raise them higher. It took several tries, but we managed to hook the candy cane onto the lowest branch above the fireplace and create a bridge from tree to mantel.

I quickly unhooked my feet and held my breath as I swung toward the stockings. The lights of the tree shrank away, and I felt Rope Man struggle above me as the weight of my head, hands, and feet transferred to him and threatened to drag us both down to the cruel brick below. My sister's broken body lay beneath me. I squeezed my eyes shut. Eventually I felt long needles of evergreen poking my sleeves and the hard, flat surface of the mantel's edge pressing my chest. Rope Man pulled me to safety.

I stood on a stable surface for the first time since I'd left the tree skirt. We'd made it! I gazed at Rope Man, my eyes surely belying my own urge to embrace him. Unfortunately, my elation stopped short when I noticed the Fairy Candle leaning against the pillar candle, watching us.

I gasped. Her wick, short and black, stuck out the top of her head from a shallow crater ringed with wads of wax. She hadn't been lit for very long, but the effects made me want to both stare and look away simultaneously. For a moment I pitied her. It must've been difficult enough having a wick when everyone else in the living room had either a hook, a loop, or nothing at all protruding from their head. But to know she was the only one intended to burn, and not just be admired…

"Unbelievable," she said, staring at me. "It's as if you don't realize how breakable you are. Especially after that other pretty doll slipped on my wax earlier."

Had she smeared her wax on the edge that Clementine had grabbed as a trap, or was it a tragic accident? I didn't care. Rope Man had to wrap his arms completely around me to hold me back. My pity for her melted away like her head. My anger burned like her wick. I wanted to stick that wax head into Nutcracker's mouth and clack his jaws shut, then use whatever was left of her to set fire to him for his apathy.

"Calm yourself," Rope Man whispered.

It was a struggle to do so. I inhaled the mantel's sharp pine scent and tried to think of a way to reason with her.

She narrowed her eyes at Rope Man. "And you, teaming up with free-roamers. I'll bet all the other ornaments are ready to disown you."

"We haven't done anything wrong," he said, releasing me. "Unlike you."

"Why should I be the only one to burn? Why should I burn at all? I don't need to be set on fire to glow!" she wailed. "See?" She gave her bright green dress a flourish. "I had to turn on the tree lights to make sure. I thought I'd lost my glow. Why else would this happen to me?" She pointed at the concavity of her head.

Neither of us could offer her an answer.

Rope Man gestured at her dress. "You obviously haven't lost your glow. I'm sure whoever did this to you quickly realized it was a mistake. Maybe it won't happen again."

"And you," she yelled down at Nutcracker. "You did nothing. Nothing to help me. Not even comfort me."

"But why take it out on the Angel?" I asked. "She didn't do anything to you."

"Because she makes a lousy wick."

Wick? Did she intend to set the tree on fire? She pulled out a matchbox from behind the pillar candle and placed her foot atop it. So that must have been what Clementine was after when she'd rushed toward the mantel. She'd seen we were dealing with a renegade candle and figured there was only one way to deal with those. Clementine hadn't called out, "It matches," she had said, "*Get* matches"!

Rope Man inched back. If the Fairy Candle made good on her threat, she'd end up setting all of us on fire, the whole living room. She opened the matchbox and withdrew a match. Gripping it at the very bottom and holding it as far away from herself as she could, she lit it.

"No!" I yelled.

She raised it and lit the pillar candle. She took the still-burning match, gave us a wicked grin, and threw it at the tree. Luckily, mercifully, the flame blew out quickly in its trajectory. Rope Man and I leaned against each other in relief.

The Fairy Candle stamped her foot. Her gaze fell on Rope Man. "You'll do nicely." She reached for his loop.

He pounded and kicked at her, but his felt hands and boots couldn't even dent her wax. I lunged, hoping my porcelain would fare better. She threw Rope Man aside, subdued me, and tied my arms together, then my legs, in painful double knots.

"Watch this," she whispered to me.

She grabbed Rope Man and lifted him over her head to inch the tip of his hat toward the pillar candle. Half of his face looked terrified and desperate; the other half looked infuriated that she'd put him into such a position. He thrashed like a fish, giving me enough time to contort my wrists as best I could so my hands could pull at the knot in my arms. I tried to keep my shoulders still; each time they moved, the knot tightened and my shoulder seams ached.

The candle flame licked ever closer to Rope Man's hat. Hot beads of wax slid down the pillar. If only it could be her wax sliding down. The thought gave me an idea, if I could just untie myself in time. Little by little, the knot gave way. I freed my arms and kept my hands behind me so the Fairy Candle wouldn't notice me untying my legs. Rope Man struggled, but she continued lowering him gradually toward the flame, relishing the anticipation.

The instant all my limbs were free, I leapt up, pulled Rope Man from her, and wrapped my arms around hers. Pounding at her was no use, but she'd shown me how my own limbs made good bindings. And mine weren't the only ones. Rope Man coiled himself around her too. She thrashed as we lifted her off the mantel.

"Pillar," I managed to grunt.

Together, we positioned the bottom half of her body as close as we could to the pillar candle's flame. She shrieked as her base softened. We thrust her on top of the pillar candle. It extinguished the flame, but it also trapped her onto the other candle as their melty waxes fused.

She swung her arms to try to break the bond. It wouldn't hold for long. Rope Man pointed at the matches, but he dared not get any closer to them. I took a deep breath. My porcelain parts may be fragile, but they weren't flammable. I rolled my lace sleeves up as far back as they could go, grabbed a match, and lit it.

First I had to melt her arms into her body to keep her from lashing out at us. Then Rope Man hoisted me up so I could reach the wick. I squeezed my eyes shut to block out her contorting face, one side drooping while the other stirred like liquid. But my hard porcelain hands couldn't block out her screams. Time stretched out as it had when Clementine fell, until finally the screaming stopped.

Another noise emerged, a dull whirring sound. Rope Man nudged me, and I looked around to see that it was the clamor of ornaments and my sisters cheering for us on both sides of the room. Lorraine waved from the top of the tree, where she'd restored the Angel to her proper place. Two plush gingerbread ornaments, whom she must have unhooked to assist her, waved at her side. The Angel bowed her head to us.

The gingerbread men helped cushion our landing from the mantel. If only they could've been unhooked sooner. Though they probably couldn't have saved Clementine, it still stung to feel their fluffy arms lowering me near her body.

Lorraine unplugged the tree, bathing us all in delicious, soothing darkness at last. She agreed to help me carry Clementine's body to the end table – on the condition that I leave Nutcracker alone. I obliged. So much the better for all of us if he remained alone. Lorraine carried the shards of Clementine's face; I couldn't bear to, and Rope Man already had his hands full with Clementine's shoulders. I carried her ankles, trying to keep her body taut between Rope Man and me in our makeshift procession.

We arrived at the stable. Rope Man and I stepped softly around the raffia straw and lay Clementine down in the soft nest. My sisters trooped over from the sofa and joined the nativity figurines in a semicircle around her body.

Caspar stepped forward and knelt over her with his myrrh. He picked up a shard that had once been her rosy cheek, pressed it to his own, and closed his eyes for a moment. Then he laid the shard back down. He rose and studied Rope Man and me with his dark eyes. "Come with me," he said.

Caspar led Rope Man and me to the sofa arm. He faced us and put a hand on either of our shoulders. He said nothing, but his eyes revealed that he'd seen everything we'd endured that night. He knew that both of us would willingly unravel or burn for the other. He knew how long we'd spent gazing at each other from afar, just as he and Clementine had done, and that we had a chance to bring some purpose to her loss.

"Go be together," he said. That was all.

Rope Man and I immediately understood and believed him. We would've obeyed even if we didn't, if only for the regret in his eyes.

* * *

The next morning, while all the ornaments, dolls, and nativity figurines slept, a giant's voice echoed into my dreams: "How did one of the Christmas dolls end up in the tree?" How did I end up there, indeed. If only they knew how far the climb had truly been.

I felt my sleeping body float away from prickly needles, away from Rope Man's arms. But it was all right. I knew how to get back up there tonight, when we would all awaken to our gentle darkness, the quiet shadows of a mercifully quiet room. Our midnight.

A Strange Christmas Game

Charlotte Riddell

WHEN, THROUGH THE death of a distant relative, I, John Lester, succeeded to the Martingdale Estate, there could not have been found in the length and breadth of England a happier pair than myself and my only sister Clare.

We were not such utter hypocrites as to affect sorrow for the loss of our kinsman, Paul Lester, a man whom we had never seen, of whom we had heard but little, and that little unfavourable, at whose hands we had never received a single benefit – who was, in short, as great a stranger to us as the then Prime Minister, the Emperor of Russia, or any other human being utterly removed from our extremely humble sphere of life.

His loss was very certainly our gain. His death represented to us, not a dreary parting from one long loved and highly honoured, but the accession of lands, houses, consideration, wealth, to myself – John Lester, Esquire, Martingdale, Bedfordshire, whilom John Lester, artist and second-floor lodger at 32, Great Smith Street, Bloomsbury.

Not that Martingdale was much of an estate as country properties go. The Lesters who had succeeded to that domain from time to time during the course of a few hundred years, could by no stretch of courtesy have been called prudent men. In regard of their posterity they were, indeed, scarcely honest, for they parted with manors and farms, with common rights and advowsons, in a manner at once so baronial and so unbusiness-like, that Martingdale at length in the hands of Jeremy Lester, the last resident owner, melted to a mere little dot in the map of Bedfordshire.

Concerning this Jeremy Lester there was a mystery. No man could say what had become of him. He was in the oak parlour at Martingdale one Christmas Eve, and before the next morning he had disappeared – to reappear in the flesh no more.

Over night, one Mr Wharley, a great friend and boon companion of Jeremy's, had sat playing cards with him until after twelve o'clock chimes, then he took leave of his host and rode home under the moonlight. After that no person, as far as could be ascertained, ever saw Jeremy Lester alive.

His ways of life had not been either the most regular, or the most respectable, and it was not until a new year had come in without any tidings of his whereabouts reaching the house, that his servants became seriously alarmed concerning his absence.

Then enquiries were set on foot concerning him – enquiries which grew more urgent as weeks and months passed by without the slightest clue being obtained as to his whereabouts. Rewards were offered, advertisements inserted, but still Jeremy made no sign; and so in course of time the heir-at-law, Paul Lester, took possession of the house, and went down to spend the summer months at Martingdale with his rich wife, and her four children by a first husband. Paul Lester was a barrister – an over-worked barrister, who everyone supposed would be glad enough to leave the bar and settle at Martingdale, where his wife's money and the fortune he had accumulated could not have failed to give him a good standing even among the neighbouring country families; and perhaps it was with such intention that he went down into Bedfordshire.

If this were so, however, he speedily changed his mind, for with the January snows he returned to London, let off the land surrounding the house, shut up the Hall, put in a caretaker, and never troubled himself further about his ancestral seat.

Time went on, and people began to say the house was haunted, that Paul Lester had 'seen something', and so forth – all which stories were duly repeated for our benefit when, forty-one years after the disappearance of Jeremy Lester, Clare and I went down to inspect our inheritance.

I say 'our', because Clare had stuck bravely to me in poverty – grinding poverty, and prosperity was not going to part us now. What was mine was hers, and that she knew, God bless her, without my needing to tell her so.

The transition from rigid economy to comparative wealth was in our case the more delightful also, because we had not in the least degree anticipated it. We never expected Paul Lester's shoes to come to us, and accordingly it was not upon our consciences that we had ever in our dreariest moods wished him dead.

Had he made a will, no doubt we never should have gone to Martingdale, and I, consequently, never written this story; but, luckily for us, he died intestate, and the Bedfordshire property came to me.

As for the fortune, he had spent it in travelling, and in giving great entertainments at his grand house in Portman Square. Concerning his effects, Mrs Lester and I came to a very amicable arrangement, and she did me the honour of inviting me to call upon her occasionally, and, as I heard, spoke of me as a very worthy and presentable young man 'for my station', which, of course, coming from so good an authority, was gratifying. Moreover, she asked me if I intended residing at Martingdale, and on my replying in the affirmative, hoped I should like it.

It struck me at the time that there was a certain significance in her tone, and when I went down to Martingdale and heard the absurd stories which were afloat concerning the house being haunted, I felt confident that if Mrs Lester had hoped much, she had feared more.

People said Mr Jeremy 'walked' at Martingdale. He had been seen, it was averred, by poachers, by gamekeepers, by children who had come to use the park as a near cut to school, by lovers who kept their tryst under the elms and beeches.

As for the caretaker and his wife, the third in residence since Jeremy Lester's disappearance, the man gravely shook his head when questioned, while the woman stated that wild horses, or even wealth untold, should not draw her into the red bedroom, nor into the oak parlour, after dark.

'I have heard my mother tell, sir – it was her as followed old Mrs Reynolds, the first caretaker – how there were things went on in these self same rooms as might make any Christian's hair stand on end. Such stamping, and swearing, and knocking about on furniture; and then tramp, tramp, up the great staircase; and along the corridor and so into the red bedroom, and then bang, and tramp, tramp again. They do say, sir, Mr Paul Lester met him once, and from that time the oak parlour has never been opened. I never was inside it myself.'

Upon hearing which fact, the first thing I did was to proceed to the oak parlour, open the shutters, and let the August sun stream in upon the haunted chamber. It was an old-fashioned, plainly furnished apartment, with a large table in the centre, a smaller in a recess by the fire-place, chairs ranged against the walls, and a dusty moth-eaten carpet upon the floor. There were dogs on the hearth, broken and rusty; there was a brass fender, tarnished and battered; a picture of some sea-fight over the mantel-piece, while another work of art about equal in merit hung between the windows. Altogether, an utterly prosaic and yet not uncheerful apartment, from out of which the ghosts flitted as soon as daylight was let into it, and which I proposed, as soon as I 'felt my feet', to redecorate, refurnish, and convert into a pleasant morning-room. I was still under thirty, but I had learned prudence in that very good school, Necessity; and it was not my intention to spend much money until I had ascertained for certain what were the actual revenues derivable from the lands still belonging to the Martingdale estates, and the charges upon them. In fact, I wanted to know what I was worth before committing myself to any great extravagances, and the place had for so long been neglected, that I experienced some difficulty in arriving at the state of my real income.

But in the meanwhile, Clare and I found great enjoyment in exploring every nook and corner of our domain, in turning over the contents of old chests and cupboards, in examining the faces of our ancestors looking down on us from the walls, in walking through the neglected gardens, full of weeds, overgrown with shrubs and birdweed, where the boxwood was eighteen feet high, and the shoots of the rosetrees yards long. I have put the place in order since then; there is no grass on the paths, there are no trailing brambles over the ground, the hedges have been cut and trimmed, and the trees pruned and the boxwood clipped. But I often say nowadays that in spite of all my improvements, or rather, in consequence of them, Martingdale does not look one half so pretty as it did in its pristine state of uncivilised picturesqueness.

Although I determined not to commence repairing and decorating the house till better informed concerning the rental of Martingdale, still the state of my finances was so far satisfactory that Clare and I decided on going abroad to take our long-talked-of holiday before the fine weather was past. We could not tell what a year might bring forth, as Clare sagely remarked; it was wise to take our pleasure while we could; and accordingly, before the end of August arrived we were wandering about the continent, loitering at Rouen, visiting the galleries at Paris, and talking of extending our one month of enjoyment into three. What decided me on this course was the circumstance of our becoming acquainted with an English family who intended wintering in Rome. We met accidentally, but discovering that we were near neighbours in England – in fact that Mr Cronson's property lay close beside Martingdale – the slight acquaintance soon ripened into intimacy, and ere long we were travelling in company.

From the first, Clare did not much like this arrangement. There was 'a little girl' in England she wanted me to marry, and Mr Cronson had a daughter who certainly was both handsome and attractive. The little girl had not despised John Lester, artist, while Miss Cronson indisputably set her cap at John Lester of Martingdale, and would have turned away her pretty face from a poor man's admiring glance – all this I can see plainly enough now, but I was blind then and should have proposed for Maybel – that was her name – before the winter was over, had news not suddenly arrived of the illness of Mrs Cronson, senior. In a moment the programme was changed; our pleasant days of foreign travel were at an end. The Cronsons packed up and departed, while Clare and I returned more slowly to England, a little out of humour, it must be confessed, with each other.

It was the middle of November when we arrived at Martingdale, and found the place anything but romantic or pleasant. The walks were wet and sodden, the trees were leafless, there were no flowers save a few late pink roses blooming in the garden. It had been a wet season, and the place looked miserable. Clare would not ask Alice down to keep her company in the winter months, as she had intended; and for myself, the Cronsons were still absent in Norfolk, where they meant to spend Christmas with old Mrs. Cronson, now recovered.

Altogether, Martingdale seemed dreary enough, and the ghost stories we had laughed at while sunshine flooded the room, became less unreal,when we had nothing but blazing fires and wax candles to dispel the gloom. They became more real also when servant after servant left us to seek situations elsewhere; when "noises" grew frequent in the house; when we ourselves, Clare and I, with our own ears heard the tramp, tramp, the banging and the chattering which had been described to us.

My dear reader, you doubtless are free from superstitious fancies. You pooh- pooh the existence of ghosts, and "only wish you could find a haunted house in which to spend a night," which is all very brave and praiseworthy, but wait till you are left in a dreary, desolate old country mansion, filled with the most unaccountable sounds, without a servant, with none save an old care-taker and his wife, who, living at the extremest end of the building, heard nothing of the tramp, tramp, bang, bang, going on at all hours of the night. At first I imagined the noises were produced by some evil-disposed persons, who wished, for purposes of their own, to keep the house uninhabited; but by degrees Clare and I came to the conclusion the visitation must be supernatural, and Martingdale by consequence untenantable.

Still being practical people, and unlike our predecessors, not having money to live where and how we liked, we decided to watch and see whether we could trace any human influence in the matter. If not, it was agreed we were to pull down the right wing of the house and the principal staircase.

For nights and nights we sat up till two or three o'clock in the morning, Clare engaged in needlework, I reading, with a revolver lying on the table beside me; but nothing, neither sound nor appearance rewarded our vigil. This confirmed my first ideas that the sounds were not supernatural; but just to test the matter, I determined on Christmas-eve, the anniversary of Mr. Jeremy Lester's disappearance, to keep watch myself in the red bed-chamber. Even to Clare I never mentioned my intention.

About ten, tired out with our previous vigils, we each retired to rest. Somewhat ostentatiously, perhaps, I noisily shut the door of my room, and when I opened it half an hour afterwards, no mouse could have pursued its way along the corridor with greater silence and caution than myself. Quite in the dark I sat in the red room. For over an hour I might as well have been in my grave for anything I could see in the apartment; but at the end of that time the moon rose and cast strange lights across the floor and upon the wall of the haunted chamber.

Hitherto I had kept my watch opposite the window; now I changed my place to a corner near the door, where I was shaded from observation by the heavy hangings of the bed, and an antique wardrobe.

Still I sat on, but still no sound broke the silence. I was weary with many nights' watching; and tired of my solitary vigil, I dropped at last into a slumber from which I wakened by hearing the door softly opened.

"John," said my sister, almost in a whisper; "John, are you here?" "Yes, Clare," I answered; "but what are you doing up at this hour?" "Come downstairs," she replied; "*they* are in the oak parlor." I did not need any explanation as to whom she meant, but crept downstairs after her, warned by an uplifted hand of the necessity for silence and caution.

By the door – by the open door of the oak parlor, she paused, and we both looked in.

There was the room we left in darkness overnight, with a bright wood fire blazing on the hearth, candles on the chimney-piece, the small table pulled out from its accustomed corner, and two men seated beside it, playing at cribbage.

We could see the face of the younger player; it was that of a man about five- and-twenty, of a man who had lived hard and wickedly; who had wasted his substance and his health; who had been while in the flesh Jeremy Lester. It would be difficult for me to say how I knew this, how in a moment I identified the features of the player with those of the man who had been missing for forty-one years – forty-one years that very night. He was dressed in the costume of a bygone period; his hair was powdered, and round his wrists there were ruffles of lace.

He looked like one who, having come from some great party, had sat down after his return home to play cards with an intimate friend. On his little finger there sparkled a ring, in the front of his shirt there gleamed a valuable diamond. There were diamond buckles in his shoes, and, according to the fashion of his time, he wore knee breeches and silk stockings, which showed off advantageously the shape of a remarkably good leg and ankle.

He sat opposite the door, but never once lifted his eyes to it. His attention seemed concentrated on the cards.

For a time there was utter silence in the room, broken only by the momentous counting of the game. In the doorway we stood, holding our breath, terrified and yet fascinated by the scene which was being acted before us.

The ashes dropped on the hearth softly and like the snow; we could hear the rustle of the cards as they were dealt out and fell upon the table; we listened to the count – fifteen-one, fifteen-two, and so forth – but there was no other word spoken till at length the player whose face we could not see, exclaimed, "I win; the game is mine."

Then his opponent took up the cards, sorted them over negligently in his hand, put them close together, and flung the whole pack in his guest's face, exclaiming, "Cheat; liar; take that!"

There was a bustle and confusion – a flinging over of chairs, and fierce gesticulation, and such a noise of passionate voices mingling, that we could not hear a sentence which was uttered. All at once, however, Jeremy Lester strode out of the room in so great a hurry that he almost touched us where we stood; out of the room, and tramp, tramp up the staircase to the red room, whence he descended in a few minutes with a couple of rapiers under his arm.

When he re-entered the room he gave, as it seemed to us, the other man his choice of the weapons, and then he flung open the window, and after ceremoniously giving place for his opponent to pass out first, he walked forth into the night air, Clare and I following.

We went through the garden and down a narrow winding walk to a smooth piece of turf, sheltered from the north by a plantation of young fir trees. It was a bright moonlight night by this time, and we could distinctly see Jeremy Lester measuring off the ground.

"When you say 'three,'" he said at last to the man whose back was still towards us. They had drawn lots for the ground, and the lot had fallen against Mr. Lester. He stood thus with the moonbeams falling upon him, and a handsomer fellow I would never desire to behold.

"One," began the other; "two," and before our kinsman had the slightest suspicion of his design, he was upon him, and his rapier through Jeremy Lester's breast.

At the sight of that cowardly treachery, Clare screamed aloud. In a moment the combatants had disappeared, the moon was obscured behind a cloud, and we were standing in the shadow of the fir-plantation, shivering with cold and terror. But we knew at last what had become of the late owner of Martingdale, that he had fallen, not in fair fight, but foully murdered by a false friend.

When late on Christmas morning I awoke, it was to see a white world, to behold the ground, and trees, and shrubs all laden and covered with snow. There was snow everywhere, such snow as no person could remember having fallen for forty-one years.

"It was on just such a Christmas as this that Mr. Jeremy disappeared," remarked the old sexton to my sister, who had insisted on dragging me through the snow to church, whereupon Clare fainted away and was carried into the vestry, where I made a full confession to the Vicar of all we had beheld the previous night.

At first that worthy individual rather inclined to treat the matter lightly, but when a fortnight after, the snow melted away and the fir-plantation came to be examined, he confessed there might be more things in heaven and earth than his limited philosophy had dreamed of.

In a little clear space just within the plantation, Jeremy Lester's body was found. We knew it by the ring and the diamond buckles, and the sparkling breast- pin; and Mr. Cronson, who in his capacity as magistrate came over to inspect these relics, was visibly perturbed at my narrative.

"Pray, Mr. Lester, did you in your dream see the face of – of the gentleman – your kinsman's opponent?"

"No," I answered, "he sat and stood with his back to us all the time."

"There is nothing more, of course, to be done in the matter," observed Mr. Cronson.

"Nothing," I replied; and there the affair would doubtless have terminated, but that a few days afterwards, when we were dining at Cronson Park, Clare all of a sudden dropped the glass of water she was carrying to her lips, and exclaiming, "Look, John, there he is!" rose from her seat, and with a face as white as the table cloth, pointed to a portrait hanging on the wall. "I saw him for an instant when he turned his head towards the door as Jeremy Lester left it," she explained; "that is he."

Of what followed after this identification I have only the vaguest recollection. Servants rushed hither and thither; Mrs. Cronson dropped off her chair into hysterics; the young ladies gathered round their mamma; Mr. Cronson, trembling like one in an ague fit, attempted some kind of an explanation, while Clare kept praying to be taken away – only to be taken away.

I took her away, not merely from Cronson Park but from Martingdale. Before we left the latter place, however, I had an interview with Mr. Cronson, who said the portrait Clare had identified was that of his wife's father, the last person who saw Jeremy Lester alive.

"He is an old man now," finished Mr. Cronson, "a man of over eighty, who has confessed everything to me. You won't bring further sorrow and disgrace upon us by making this matter public?"

I promised him I would keep silence, but the story gradually oozed out, and the Cronsons left the country.

My sister never returned to Martingdale; she married and is living in London. Though I assure her there are no strange noises in my house, she will not visit Bedfordshire, where the "little girl" she wanted me so long ago to "think of seriously," is now my wife and the mother of my children.

The Dark-Eyed Boy

M.C. St. John

HE TOOK THE WRONG ONE.

This is what I want to say to Adam, because it's better than starting with *once upon a time*. But my son claims he is too old for fairy tales. I don't blame him. I thought I was too when I was eleven, when I thought I knew how the world worked.

Sitting by the fireplace, I glance over at him on the loveseat. His body is sprawled out across the cushions, his ankles hanging off the edge of the padded arm. Instead of the fire, it's the light of his iPhone cast upon his face as he scrolls through social media. He's a good kid, if only a little basic. He's a victim of his time, I suppose, like we all are. I still love him.

The last thing he wants to hear from me is some musty yarn. He doesn't have the attention span or the interest.

I don't have the courage.

If it's all a story, something I've confabulated over the years, it's not worth bringing up. But if what I remember is true – if somehow the intervening years have sharpened the truths to finer points – then it is too terrible to say aloud. A nightmare only becomes real, the old saying goes, if it's told to someone else.

A knot pops in the fire and embers stir in the hearth. The sound is loud enough for me to tense up, raising the hair on my arms.

"Dad, you okay?"

"I got caught drifting." I yawn as a cover. "It's getting late. You have to Zoom early for school tomorrow."

"I don't *have* to. It's practically winter break." Adam shuts off his phone and points to the window. Snow hits the glass, builds up on the sill, and falls off in mounting piles, as it has been for hours. "If this keeps up, we'll be quarantined *and* snowed in."

"No matter what happens," I say, "you have to finish what you started." Then I stand up to shepherd. "Come on, up you get. Check your window upstairs. Make sure it's shut and locked. We can't let anything get in."

"Like all them woodland varmints?"

"I didn't know you had a sense of humor."

"At least one of us does," he says, smirking.

He's a wise ass, just like me. He has to watch himself because of it. When he gets older, I tell myself, he will. When he gets older.

He's halfway up the steps when I call to him.

"Adam, I love you."

"Hallmark moment, Dad. *Yeesh.*" He doesn't break his stride while responding. "Love you too."

Then his footsteps creak along the ceiling above me. His bedroom door opens, shuts, and – like a true soon-to-be teenager – locks.

Rather than follow suit and get ready for sleep myself, I walk over to the corner of the living room. Adam and I set up the Christmas tree there, a fake spruce with old discount store baubles and lights. Like the tree, there is a fake floorboard nearby, right along the edge of the hearthstones, that I lift up. In that chilly hiding place, I have one of my deer hunting rifles and a box of shells. I take both back with me to the chair by the fire.

It will be a long night.

He took the wrong one. How easy that could have been to start things off.

Watching the darkness and snow swirl outside, I know it would have been too much for me. Too sharp. Too real.

Alone now, I start the other way.

* * *

Once upon a time, there were twin brothers who could only be told apart by the color of their eyes. One brother's eyes were pale blue, the other brother's dark brown. They lived in a log cabin at the edge of the woods. The cabin was built by their uncle, who was a very good carpenter. He also happened to be very German. His name was Otto.

The twin boys caused Otto a lot of grief. Not because either of the boys was bad – not at first – but because they reminded Otto of his sister. She and her husband, the boys' parents, died when their house caught fire the year before.

Otto took in the boys. He was happy to have more family in his log cabin, safe from harm. Otto was good at fixing things. It was his nature.

The boys were uneasy those first few weeks. They both were very quiet, and had a habit of echoing each other.

Sometimes, the boy with pale eyes pointed up to a bird in a tree, and the boy with dark eyes would then do the same, even when the bird had flown away. Other times, the boy with dark eyes crouched down to turn over stones and watch the bugs wriggle, and the boy with pale eyes would follow, even if the bugs were eating a dead thing, which was unpleasant to watch.

They were trying on more of each other and seeing what fit.

Uncle Otto thought of a way to help things along. One day, as autumn gave way to winter, he told his grand idea: to build something for the upcoming holidays. How about a sleigh for Saint Nicholas to put presents in?

The boys liked the idea of presents. They both smiled real smiles, their first since their parents died.

Excited, Otto went around the cabin to his small workshop. Inside, he talked of his cherished woodworking tools, and the lumber he had cut from the forest timber with them. Then he showed the boys how to use a saw, a hammer, a plane, a level, and all the other useful tools. Then they got to work to build a sleigh for Saint Nicholas.

The boys were quite good with their hands once they set their hearts to a task. And Otto, proud uncle that he was, enjoyed the work. He told stories while the snow fell outside. Stories about their family, and the old times in Kassel, where their family was from. As I said before, Otto was quite German. He knew all the branches of their family tree like he knew all the tributaries of the Fuld River. He also knew folklore.

Everyone in America knows of Saint Nicholas, he said, but do you know of Krampus?

The boy with pale eyes shook his head. His dark-eyed brother did the same.

It is good you do not. Krampus is a bad thing, a demon with a forked tongue. At the beginning of December, he visits the houses of misbehaving children. He beats some with his switch, rattling the heavy chains he wears with each swing. He also carries a basket on his back for the *very* bad children. He throws them in and carries them away. It is a hard lesson for misbehaving, but a fair one to learn before it is too late.

You do not want to be on the list for Krampus. You want to be on the list for Saint Nicholas, for good boys who deserve presents on a sleigh come Christmas morning.

There has to be a balance. It is what our stories tell us. Good and bad, Saint Nicholas and Krampus. They are brothers, in a way. Maybe not twins but close, close!

Uncle Otto laughed at his own joke, and got back to work.

The boys did too, though slowly at first. They both were thinking about all their uncle had told them. They had grown quiet, as they had when they first arrived.

By the next day, the sleigh was built. The boys had learned a great deal about woodworking, including how to prepare shellac to seal their work, which they did together. The boy with dark eyes mixed the shellac with mineral spirits, and the boy with pale eyes dipped clean rags in the mixture and carefully wiped the sleigh until it shined. With the project nearly done, Otto went to the log cabin to make coffee and grilled cheese sandwiches for lunch. He was a proud uncle.

But after he finished grilling the last cheese sandwich, Uncle Otto turned off his stove and sniffed. There was still smoke, but where was it coming from?

He ran outside.

There, in the falling snow, was his lovely workshop on fire.

The twins stood there, watching. One boy cried, his pale eyes glistening. The other boy simply watched, the fire glowing in his dark eyes.

After he put out the fire, Otto took his strap to the dark-eyed boy. After he got no answer as to how the lantern tipped over and burned the oily rags, Otto kept shining his strap.

May Krampus come for you, he said between blows. May Krampus come and take you away, you terrible child.

* * *

The storm has picked up, and the wind howls underneath the eaves. It moves the woods outside. The bare trees have been holding in their big, brittle hands mounds of snow and ice. Something outside snaps. Branch after branch, cracking and falling. The wind moans.

I sit and wait, the rifle lying across my lap. Listening.

I've waited this long. A few more hours to go.

* * *

Uncle Otto was a very different uncle after that. Gone were his smiling ways, his friendly nature. He had prided himself on fixing things. But seeing what happened proved that there were some things damaged beyond repair.

As Otto watched his workshop burn, he couldn't help but think of his sister's house suffering the same fate.

He took to speaking more German to himself. The boys listened to him as they cleaned up what remained after the fire, clearing burnt logs and sweeping away ash. They did not understand their uncle's harsh words, but they could gather their general meaning. He still held his strap.

There were other times that Uncle Otto turned away from the boys and spoke to the forest. His German words wandered into the woods. They sounded like both a confession and a prayer and possibly a plea. Perhaps something was listening.

Night came. Otto had a good meal for supper. The boy with pale eyes had leftovers, crying as he ate the scraps. The boy with dark eyes had nothing.

Let that be a lesson to you, Otto said in words they knew. Bad boys will have no comfort in this world. You are learning it the hard way tonight.

Then he sent them upstairs to bed.

It was deep into the night when the boy with pale eyes woke up. Outside his window he watched snow falling. He thought he had woken up from a bad dream. But when he heard more noises coming from the next room down the hall, he knew that the bad dream had not ended.

The boy slipped out of bed and nudged open his door.

Something was in the hallway. Something large.

By the moonlight the figure stood on two furry legs. As it took a few steps, the boy heard the light clomping noises from his bad dream. They sounded like the hooves of a restless horse.

The figure was adjusting something on its back. The boy dared to lean farther out of his doorway to see, and his heart turned to ice. It was a large wicker basket with broad leather straps. The figure had slipped the straps onto its shoulders. A heavy weight shifted in the basket, as if it were filled with potatoes.

The boy knew what was in the basket was not potatoes.

For when the figure turned toward the stairs, he saw the horns growing from its head, a bramble of sharp bones. He saw the moonlight glint off of its fangs, and the tongue that lolled from its open jaws.

It paused, listening. Waiting.

Deciding.

And the boy was afraid.

Then the figure turned away. Between the light clomps of its hooves came the muted clank of chains. Frozen, the boy stood listening to each footfall down the stairs. Only when the front door shut did the boy take a breath and rush back to their bedroom.

The bed was unmade and empty, the blankets rustling with the wind. The window was open, and the snow blew in from the winter's night.

* * *

The same wind is blowing now. The house trembles on its foundations. The strand of brightly-colored bulbs flickers on the fake Christmas tree and then gives up the ghost. The storm must have snapped the power lines. The only light comes from the dying fire, which brings me no comfort. It never has.

* * *

That Christmas, Uncle Otto treated his nephew to a few presents. These presents did not arrive on a sleigh as planned, but they were wrapped neatly in newspaper and placed under the tree. One was a wool sweater, another a cap pistol. The last was a large book.

This is a collection of stories from our homeland, Uncle Otto said. Fairy tales, ghost stories, legends. Read them to remember where you came from. To remember your mother. To remind you to stay good. Will you stay good?

The boy nodded, taking the book.

And every December after that first, they lived in the log cabin at the edge of the woods. The boy with pale eyes learned much more about carpentry. He helped his uncle build a new workshop. When he was older, he learned how to hunt deer in the woods. He only killed one each season, enough to make venison for the winter. He worked hard in school, and then at jobs in town. He tried to be a good person with everything he did, not only to make his uncle proud but also to make up for the bad things that happened when he was a young boy.

Mostly he succeeded. He grew up and fell in love with a beautiful woman. And though the marriage did not last, the man with pale eyes had a son, who was good, if only a little basic.

He also took care of his Uncle Otto until the carpenter was old and gray. And though Otto did finally pass away, he gave the log cabin to his nephew, so the man with pale eyes and his son could live there. They live there still.

Light and dark. Good and bad. Everything had a balance.

Everything except what happened to the dark-eyed boy.

Every year, when the snow began to fall, the man with pale eyes would bring out the large old book that was a beloved gift from his beloved uncle. He would read the stories of Saint Nicholas and his sleigh and remember the workshop that had burned down. He remembered how convincing he could look when he cried. He had practiced how to be sad. People believed him.

Then he would read the stories about Krampus and his wicker basket and recalled how he and his brother would imitate one another. They would wear each other's clothes and expressions.

It was a fun thing to do as children. They were twins who could only be told apart by the color of their eyes. When they were asleep, though, no one could tell them apart. Not their mother, not their uncle. And certainly not a stranger.

Reading the legend again, year after year, the man with pale eyes would remind himself on what night *Krampusnacht* fell. He would stay up then to see if this night was the night that the balance would be struck, that the debts would be repaid. He waited for the sound of cloven hooves on the cabin steps. He braced himself to see a shadow among the falling snow, one with tangled horns atop its head.

But at the end of each of those long nights, nothing came.

Though he had escaped an awful fate, he also learned the true meaning of punishment. It was a far cry from *happily ever after*, but he took cold solace in the lesson he had learned.

* * *

Tonight is different.

I look out the window and see my ghostly reflection staring back. In the dim light, my eyes are sockets, far darker than my brother's eyes once upon a time. The resemblance is uncanny. I force myself to keep staring, to see beyond myself to the deeper night.

The forest trees sway their naked branches, throwing shadows in the moonlight. They play across a huge, unbroken mound of snow. The rebuilt workshop, now decades old, lies beneath that mound, hidden under layers of cold, blank white.

My woodworking tools are buried there, along with my memories. No matter how much I've tried to fix myself over the years, I never could. Not really. I can make a beam level and a door true, like my uncle taught me. But there has always been something crooked inside me.

They were accidents, all of them. Honest.

I tried to be good. I *tried*.

Doesn't that count for something?

But now from the edge of the woods, another shadow arrives as my answer. It lumbers out from behind the buried workshop and heads towards the cabin. The wind ripples its fur. Its eyes shine like coins. They are pale and cold, those eyes. Like mine.

I leap up from the chair, lift the rifle to my shoulder. As I rush out of the living room, I stumble over a box at my feet. Rifle shells rattle along the floorboards. There will be no time to reload, to try again. I have to make do with what I have. What I am.

The wind moans and the house creaks. But I also hear the hooves on the porch steps, and the heavy clank of chains. The shadow moves across the sidelight window. It hunches down. Heavy breath fogs the panes.

The doorknob turns one way, then the other.

I stand on the other side, beading my shot, listening. Waiting. Deciding.

He took the wrong one.

But he discovered his mistake soon enough. I was a clever boy to fool him. Instead of returning to take me away, though, he waited for another boy to come around. One that could fit in his basket when the time was right. What better punishment than taking away my son?

The door strains against the frame, threatening to break.

I raise my rifle, steady my hands, and pray I am good enough now.

The Great Staircase at Landover Hall

Frank R. Stockton

I WAS SPENDING a few days in the little village of Landover, simply for the purpose of enjoying the beautiful scenery of the neighborhood. I had come up from Mexico because the weather was growing too warm in that region, and I was glad of the chance to vary my interesting and sometimes exciting travels with a little rest in the midst of this rural quiet.

It was early summer, and I had started out for an afternoon walk, when, just upon the outskirts of the village, my attention was attracted by a little group at a gateway which opened upon the road. There were two women and an elderly man. The women appeared to be taking leave of the man, and one of them frequently put her handkerchief to her eyes. I walked slowly, because I did not wish to intrude upon what seemed to be an affecting leave-taking; so when I reached the gate the women had gone, but the man was still standing there, looking after them.

Glancing over the low fence, I saw a very pretty grove, apparently not well kept, and some distance back, among the trees, a large, old house. The man was looking at me with a curiosity which country people naturally betray when they see a stranger, and, as I was glad to have someone to talk to, I stopped.

"Is this one of the old family mansions of Landover?" I asked. He was a good-looking man, with the air of a head gardener.

"It is not one of them, sir," he answered; "it is the only one in the village. It is called Landover Hall, and the other houses growed up around it."

"Who owns it?" I asked.

"That is hard to say, sir," he said, with a grim smile; "though perhaps I could tell you in the course of a couple of weeks. The family who lived there is dead and gone, and everything in it is to be sold at auction."

I became interested, and asked some questions, which the man was very willing to answer. It was an old couple who had owned it, he said. The husband had died the previous year, and the wife about ten days ago. The heirs were a brother and sister living out in Colorado, and, as they had never seen the house, and cared nothing about it, or about anything that was in it, they had written that they wished everything to be sold, and the money sent to them as soon as possible.

"And that is the way it stands," said the old man. "Next week there is to be a sale of the personal property – a 'vandoo' we call it out here – and every movable thing in the house and grounds is to be sold to the highest bidder; and mighty little the things will bring, it's my opinion. Then the house will be sold, as soon as anybody can be found who wants it."

"Then there is no one living in the house at present?" said I.

"Nobody but me," he answered. "That was the cook and her daughter, the chambermaid, who just left here. There is a black man who attends to the horses and cows, but he will go when they are sold; and very soon I will go too, I suppose."

"Have you lived here long?" I asked.

"Pretty near all my life," said he.

I was greatly interested in old houses, and I asked the man if I might look at the place.

"I have not had any orders to show it," he said; "but, as everything is for sale, I suppose the sooner people see the household goods the better; there's many a bit of old furniture, candlesticks, and all that sort of thing, which strangers might like to buy. Oh, yes; you can come in if you like."

I shall not attempt to describe the delightful hour I spent in that old house and in the surrounding grounds. There was a great piazza in front; a wide hall stretched into the interior of the mansion, with a large fireplace on one side and a noble staircase at the further end, a single flight of stairs running up to a platform, and then branching off on each side to the second floor.

On the landing stood one of the tallest clocks I have ever seen. There were portraits on the walls, and here and there a sporting picture, interspersed with antlers and foxes' heads mounted on panels, with the date of the hunt inscribed beneath. There was an air of largeness and gravity about the furniture in the hall, which was very pleasing to me, and when I entered the long drawing room I found it so filled with books and bric-à-brac of the olden days, with many quaint furnishings, that, had I been left to myself, even the long summer afternoon would not have sufficed for their examination. Upstairs was the same air of old-fashioned comfort. The grounds – the grass rather long, and the bushes untrimmed – were shaded by some grand old trees, and beyond there were gardens and some green pasture-fields.

I did not take the walk that I had proposed to myself. When I left the old house I inquired the name of the agent who had charge of the estate, and then I went back to the village inn, where I sat communing with myself for the rest of the afternoon and all the evening.

I was not yet thirty, I had a good fortune, and I had travelled until I was tired of moving about the world. Often I had had visions of a home, but they had been very vague and fanciful ones.

Now, for the first time in my life, I had seen a home for which I really might care; a house to which I might bring only my wearing apparel, and then sit down surrounded by everything I needed, not even excepting books.

Immediately after breakfast I repaired to the office of Mr. Marchmay, the lawyer who had charge of the property. I stayed there a long time. Mr. Marchmay took dinner with me at the inn, and in the evening we sent a telegram to Colorado. I made a proposition to buy everything for cash, and the price agreed upon between Mr. Marchmay and myself was considerably higher than could have been expected had the property been sold at auction. It is needless to say that my offer was quickly accepted, and in less than a week from the day I had first seen the old house I became its owner. The cook and the housemaid, who had retired in tears from its gateway, were sent for, and reinstalled in their offices; the black man who had charge of the horses and cows continued to take care of them, and old Robert Flake was retained in the position of head gardener and general caretaker, which he had held for so many years.

That summer was a season of delight to me, and even when autumn arrived, and there was a fire in the great hall, I could not say that I had fully explored and examined my home and its contents. I had had a few bachelor friends to visit me, but for the greater part of the time I had lived alone. I liked company, and expected to have people about me, but so long as the novelty of my new possessions and my new position continued I was company enough for myself.

At last the holiday season came around, and I was still alone. I had invited a family of old friends to come and make the house lively and joyous, but they had been prevented from doing so. I afterward thought of asking some of my neighbors to eat their Christmas dinner in the old house, but I found that they all had ties and obligations of their own with which I should not seek to interfere. And thus it happened that late on Christmas eve I sat by myself before a blazing fire in the hall, quietly smoking my pipe. The servants were all in bed, and the house was as quiet as if it contained no living being.

For the first time since I lived in that house I began to feel lonely, and I could not help smiling when I thought that there was no need of my feeling lonely if I wished it otherwise. For several years I had known that there were mothers in this country, and even in other countries, who had the welfare of their daughters at heart, and who had not failed to let me know the fact; I had also known that there were young women, without mothers, who had their own welfare at heart, and to whom a young man of fortune was an object of interest; but there was nothing in these recollections which interested me in these lonely moments.

The great clock on the landing-place began to strike, and I counted stroke after stroke; when there were twelve I turned to see whether I had made a mistake, and if it were now really Christmas day. But before my eyes had reached the face of the clock I saw that I was mistaken in supposing myself alone. At the top of the broad flight of stairs there stood a lady.

I pushed back my chair and started to my feet. I know my mouth was open and my eyes staring. I could not speak; I doubt if I breathed.

Slowly the lady descended the stairs. There were two tall lamps on the newel-posts, so that I could see her distinctly. She was young, and she moved with the grace of perfect health. Her gown was of an olden fashion, and her hair was dressed in the style of our ancestors. Her attire was simple and elegant, but it was evident that she was dressed for a festive occasion.

Down she came, step by step, and I stood gazing, not only with my eyes, but, I may say, with my whole heart. I had never seen such grace; I had never seen such beauty.

She reached the floor, and advanced a few steps toward me; then she stopped. She fixed her large eyes upon me for a moment, and then turned them away. She gazed at the fire, the walls, the ceiling, and the floor. There came upon her lovely features an almost imperceptible smile, as though it gave her pleasure thus to stand and look about her.

As for me, I was simply entranced. Vision or no vision, spirit from another world or simply a mist of fancy, it mattered not.

She approached a few steps nearer, and fixed her eyes upon mine. I trembled as I stood.

Involuntarily the wish of my heart came to my lips. "If—" I exclaimed.

"If what?" she asked, quickly.

I was startled by the voice. It was rich, it was sweet, but there was something in its intonation which suggested the olden time. I cannot explain it. It was like the perfume from an ancient wardrobe opened a hundred years after a great-grandmother had closed and locked it, when even the scent of rose and lavender was only the spirit of something gone.

"Oh, if you were but real!" I said.

She smiled, but made no reply. Slowly she passed around the great hall, coming so near me at one time that I could almost have touched her. She looked up at the portraits, stopping before some old candlesticks upon a bracket, apparently examining everything with as much pleasure as I had looked upon them when first they became mine.

When she had made the circuit of the hall, she stood as if reflecting. Fearful that she might disappear, and knowing that a spirit must be addressed if one would hear it speak, I stepped toward her. I had intended to ask her if she were, or rather ever had been, the lady of this house, why she came, and if she bore a message, but in my excitement and infatuation I forgot my purpose; I simply repeated my former words – "Oh, if you were but real!"

"Why do you say that?" she asked, with a little gentle petulance. "I am not real, as you must know. Shall I tell you who I was, and why I am here?".I implored her to do so. She drew a little nearer the fire. "It is so bright and cheerful," she said.

"It is many, many years since I have seen a fire in this hall. The old people who lived in this house so long never built a fire here – at least on Christmas eve."

I felt inclined to draw up a chair and ask her to sit down, but why need a ghost sit? I was afraid of making some mistake. I stood as near her as I dared, eagerly ready to listen.

"I was mistress of this house," she said. "That was a long, long time ago. You can see my portrait hanging there."

I bowed. I could not say that it was her portrait. An hour before, I had looked upon it as a fine picture; now it seemed to be the travesty of a woman beyond the reach of pigments and canvas.

"I died," she continued, "when I was but twenty-five, and but four years married. I had a little girl three years old, and the very day before I left this world I led her around this hail and tried to make her understand the pictures. That is her portrait on this other wall."

I turned, and following the direction of her graceful hand my eyes fell upon the picture of an elderly lady with silvered hair and benignant countenance.

"Your daughter?" I gasped.

"Yes," she answered; "she lived many years after my death. Over there, nearer the door, you may see the picture of her daughter – the plump young girl with the plumed hat."

Now, to my great surprise, she asked me to take a seat. "It seems ungracious," she remarked, "that in my own house I should be so inhospitable as to keep you standing. And yet it is not my house; it is yours."

Obedient to her command, for such I felt it to be, I resumed my seat, and to my delight she took a chair not far from me. Seated, she seemed more graceful and lovely than when she stood.

Her shapely hands lay in her lap; soft lace fell over them, like tender mist upon a cloud. As she looked at me her eyes were raised.

"Does it distress you that this house should now be mine?" I asked.

"Oh, no, no," she answered, with animation; "I am very glad of it. The elderly couple who lived here before you were not to my liking. Once a year, on Christmas eve, I am privileged to spend one hour in this house, and, although I have never failed to be here at the appointed time, it has been years, as I told you, since I saw a fire on that hearth and a living being in this hail. I knew you were here, and I am very glad of it. It pleases me greatly that one is living here who prizes this old place as I once prized it. This mansion was built for me by my husband, upon the site of a smaller house, which he removed. The grounds about it, which I thought so lovely, are far more lovely now. For four years I lived here in perfect happiness, and now one hour each year something of that happiness is renewed."

Ordinarily I have good control of my actions and of my emotions, but at this moment I seemed to have lost all power over myself; my thoughts ran wild. To my amazement, I became conscious that I was falling in love – in love with something which did not exist; in love with a woman who once had been. It was absurd; it was ridiculous, but there was no power within me which could prevent it.

After all, this rapidly growing passion was not altogether absurd. She was an ideal which far surpassed any ideal I had ever formed for the mistress of my home. More than that, she had really been the mistress of this house, which was now my home. Here was a vision of the past, fully revealed to my eyes. As the sweet voice fell upon my ears, how could I help looking upon it as something real, listening to it as something real, and loving it as something real.

I think she perceived my agitation; she looked upon me wonderingly.

"I hoped very much," she said, "that you would be in this hail when I should come down tonight, but I feared that I should disturb you, that perhaps I might startle or—"

I could not restrain myself. I rose and interrupted her with passionate earnestness.

"Startle or trouble me!" I exclaimed. "Oh, gracious lady, you have done but one thing to me tonight – you have made me love you! Pardon me; I cannot help it. Do not speak of impossibilities, of passionate ravings, of unmeaning words. Lady, I love you; I may not love you as you are, but I love you as you were. No happiness on earth could equal that of seeing you real – the mistress of this house, and myself the master."

She rose, drew back a little, and stood looking at me. If she had been true flesh and blood she could not have acted more naturally.

For some moments there was silence, and then a terrible thought came into my head. Had I a right to speak to her thus, even if she were but the vision of something that had been? She had told me of her husband; she had spoken of her daughter; but she had said no word which would give me reason to believe that little girl was fatherless when her mother led her around the hall and explained to her the family portraits. Had I been addressing my wild words of passion to one whose beauty and grace, when they were real and true, belonged to another? Had I spoken as I should not have spoken, even to the vision of a well-loved wife? I trembled with apprehension.

"Pardon me," I said, "if I have been imprudent. Remember that I know so little about you, even as you were."

When she answered there was nothing of anger in her tone, but she spoke softly, and with, I thought, a shade of pity.

"You have said nothing to offend me, but every word you have spoken has been so wild and so far removed from sense and reason that I am unable to comprehend your feelings."

"They are easy to understand!" I exclaimed. "I have seen my ideal of the woman I could love. I love you; that is all! Again I say it, and I say it with all my heart: Would you were real! Would you were real!"

She smiled. I am sure now she understood my passion. I am sure she expected it. I am sure that she pitied me.

Suddenly a change of expression came over her face; a beaming interest shone from her eyes; she took some steps toward me.

"I told you," said she, speaking quickly, "that what you have said seems to be without sense or reason, and yet it may mean something. I assure you that your words have been appreciated. I know that each one of them is true and comes from your heart. And now listen to me while I tell you—" At that moment the infernal clock upon the landing-place struck one. It was like the crash of doom. I stood alone in the great hall.

The domestics in that old house supposed that I spent Christmas day alone; but they were mistaken, for wherever I went my fancy pictured near me the beautiful vision of the night before.

She walked with me in the crisp morning air; I led her through the quiet old rooms, and together we went up the great staircase and stood before the clock – the clock that I had blessed for striking twelve and cursed for striking one. At dinner she sat opposite me in a great chair which I had had placed there—"for the sake of symmetry," as I told my servants. After what had happened, it was impossible for me to be alone.

The day after Christmas old Mr. Marchmay came to call upon me. He was so sorry that I had been obliged to spend Christmas day all by myself. I fairly laughed as I listened to him.

There were things I wanted him to tell me if he could, and I plied him with questions. I pointed to the portrait of the lady near the chimney-piece, and asked him who she was.

"That is Mrs. Evelyn Heatherton, first mistress of this house; I have heard a good deal about her. She was very unfortunate. She lost her life here in this hall on Christmas eve. She was young and beautiful, and must have looked a good deal like that picture."

I forgot myself. "I don't believe it," I said. "It does not seem to me that that portrait could have been a good likeness of the real woman."

"You may know more about art than I do, sir," said he. "It has always been considered a fine picture; but of course she lived before my time. As I was saying, she died here in this hall. She was coming downstairs on Christmas eve; there were a lot of people here in the hall waiting to meet her. She stepped on something on one of the top steps – a child's toy, perhaps – and lost her footing. She fell to the bottom and was instantly killed – killed in the midst of youth, health, and beauty."

"And her husband," I remarked, "was he—"

"Oh, he was dead!" interrupted Mr. Marchmay. "He died when his daughter was but a mere baby. By the way," said the old gentleman, "it seems rather funny that the painting over there – that old lady with the gray hair – is the portrait of that child. It is the only one there is, I suppose."

I did not attend to these last words. My face must have glowed with delight as I thought that I had not spoken to her as I should not. If I had known her to be real, I might have said everything which I had said to the vision of what she had been.

The old man went on talking about the family. That sort of thing interested him very much, and he said that, as I owned the house, I ought to know everything about the people who formerly lived there. The Heathertons had not been fortunate. They had lost a great deal of money, and, some thirty years before, the estate had passed out of their hands and had been bought by a Mr. Kennard, a distant connection of the family, who, with his wife, had lived there until very recently. It was to a nephew and niece of old Mr. Kennard that the property had descended. The Heathertons had nothing more to do with it.

"Are there any members of the family left?" I asked.

"Oh yes!" said Mr. Marchmay. "Do you see that portrait of a girl with a feather in her hat? She is a granddaughter of that Evelyn Heatherton up there. She is an old woman now and a widow, and she it was who sold the place to the Kennards. When the mortgages were paid she did not have much left, but she manages to live on it. But I tell you what you ought to do, sir: you ought to go to see her. She can tell you lots of stories of this place, for she knows more about the Heathertons than anyone living. She married a distant cousin, who had the family name; but he was a poor sort of a fellow, and he died some fifteen years ago. She has talked to me about your having the old house, and she said that she hoped you would not make changes and tear down things. But of course she would not say anything like that to you; she is a lady who attends to her own business."

"Where does she live?" I asked. "I should like, above all things, to go and talk to her."

"It is the third house beyond the church," said Mr. Marchmay. "I am sure she will be glad to see you. If you can make up your mind to listen to long stories about the Heathertons you will give her pleasure."

The next day I made the call. The house was neat, but small and unpretentious – a great drop from the fine hall I now possessed.

The servant informed me that Mrs. Heatherton was at home, and I was shown into the little parlor – light, warm, and pleasantly furnished. In a few minutes the door opened, and I rose, but no old lady entered.

Struck dumb by breathless amazement, I beheld Evelyn Heatherton coming into the room!

I could not understand; my thoughts ran wild. Had someone been masquerading? Had I dreamed on Christmas eve, or was I dreaming now? Had my passionate desire been granted?

Had that vision become real? I was instantly convinced that what I saw before me was true and real, for the lady advanced toward me and held out her hand. I took it, and it was the hand of an actual woman.

Her mother, she said, begged that I would excuse her; she was not well and was lying down.

Mr. Marchmay had told them that I was coming, and that I wanted to know something about the old house; perhaps she might be able to give me a little information.

Almost speechless, I sat down, and she took a chair not far from me. Her position was exactly that which had been taken by the vision of her great-grandmother on Christmas eve. Her hands were crossed in her lap, and her large blue eyes were slightly upraised to mine. She was not dressed in a robe of olden days, nor was her hair piled up high on her head in bygone fashion, but she was Evelyn Heatherton, in form and feature and in quiet grace. She was some years younger, and she lacked the dignity of a woman who had been married, but she was no stranger to me; I had seen her before.

Encouraged by my rapt attention, she told me stories of the old house where her mother had been born, and all that she knew of her great-grandmother she related with an interest that was almost akin to mine. "People tell me," she said, "that I am growing to look like her, and I am glad of it, for my mother gave me her name."

I sat and listened to the voice of this beautiful girl, as I had listened to the words which had been spoken to me by the vision of her ancestress. If I had not known that she was real, and that there was no reason why she should vanish when the clock should strike, I might have spoken as I spoke to her great-grandmother. I remained entranced, enraptured, and it was only when the room began to grow dark that I was reminded that it was incumbent upon me to go.

But I went again, again, and again, and after a time it so happened that I was in that cottage at least once every day. The old lady was very gracious; it was plain enough that her soul was greatly gratified to know that the present owner of her old home – the house in which she had been born – was one who delighted to hear the family stories, and who respected all their traditions.

I need not tell the story of Evelyn and myself. My heart had been filled with a vision of her personality before I had seen her. At the first moment of our meeting my love for her sprung into existence as the flame bursts from a match. And she could not help but love me. Few women, certainly not Evelyn Heatherton, could resist the passionate affection I offered her. She did not tell me this in words, but it was not long before I came to believe it.

It was one afternoon in spring that old Mrs. Heatherton and her daughter came to visit me in my house – the home of their ancestors. As I walked with them through the halls and rooms I felt as if they were the ladies of the manor, and that I was the recipient of their kind hospitality.

Mrs. Heatherton was in the dining room, earnestly examining some of the ancestral china and glass, and Evelyn and I stood together in the hall, almost under the portrait which hung near the chimney-piece. She had been talking of the love and reverence she felt for this old house.

"Evelyn," said I, "if you love this house and all that is in it, will you not take it, and have it for your own? And will you not take me and love me, and have me for your own?"

I had my answer before the old lady came out of the dining-room. She was reading the inscription on an old silver loving-cup when we went in to her and told her that again Evelyn Heatherton was to be the mistress of the old mansion.

We were married in the early winter, and after a journey in the South we came back to the old house, for I had a great desire that we should spend the holidays under its roof.

It was Christmas eve, and we stood together in the great hall, with a fire burning upon the hearth as it had glowed and crackled a year before. It was some minutes before twelve, and, purposely, I threw my arms around my dear wife and turned her so that she stood with her back to the great staircase. I had never told her of the vision I had seen; I feared to do so; I did not know what effect it might have upon her. I cared for her so earnestly and tenderly that I would risk nothing, but I felt that I must stand with her in that hall on that Christmas eve, and I believed that I could do so without fear or self-reproach.

The clock struck twelve. "Look up at your great-grandmother, Evelyn," I said; "it is fit that you should do so at this time." In obedience to my wishes her eyes were fixed upon the old portrait, and, at the same time, looking over her shoulder, my eyes fell upon the vision of the first Evelyn Heatherton descending the stairs. Upon her features was a gentle smile of welcome and of pleasure. So she must have looked when she went out of this world in health and strength and womanly bloom.

The vision reached the bottom of the stairs and came toward us. I stood expectant, my eyes fixed upon her noble countenance.

"It seems to me," said my Evelyn, "as if my great-grandmother really looked down upon us; as if it made her happy to think that—"

"Is this what you meant?" said I, speaking to the lovely vision, now so near us.

"Yes," was the answer; "it is what I meant, and I am rejoiced. I bless you and I love you both. " and as she spoke two fair and shadowy hands were extended over our heads. No one can hear the voice of a spirit except those to whom it speaks, and my wife thought that my words had been addressed to her.

"Yes," said my Evelyn; "I mean that we should be standing here in her old home, and that your arm should be around me."

I looked again. There was no one in the hall, except my Evelyn and myself.

Snowman

Lamont A. Turner

LUKE PATTED a wad of snow onto the belly of the snowman in the front yard, smoothing it out so it blended in.

"Fixed it," he said, stepping back to admire his work.

"The final touch," Mike announced, adjusting their father's fedora on the snow man's round head.

"He looks mad," Luke said: "Maybe we should have given him a smile."

"Wouldn't have been right," Mike said, putting an arm around Luke's shoulder. "He never smiled unless he was hurting one of us. I like him better like this."

The boys headed to the porch of the house where they shook the snow out of their hair and slipped out of their galoshes, lining them up against the wall by the door. Inside, Alice, their mother sat at the kitchen table, gazing out the window at the snow man.

"Why you sitting here in the dark, ma?" Luke asked, switching on the overhead light. Their mother didn't answer. She didn't move at all. Mike found a paper towel and dabbed away the tear running down her swollen cheek, taking care not to press too hard.

"It's all over now," Mike said. "He can't hit you anymore. He's gone now. We just have to put up a good front for Uncle Bill when he gets here, then we're home free."

She stiffened at the mention of Uncle Bill. "Bill can't come here," she whispered. "Not now."

"It's okay," Mike said. "Luke and me took care of it. You know Uncle Bill always stops by on Christmas Eve. If we told him he couldn't come over, he might get suspicious."

"What about my eye?" she asked, running a finger along the purple bruise that had spread to the side of her nose.

"That actually helps us," Luke said, pouring himself a glass of eggnog from the fifth in the refrigerator. It had alcohol in it, but his mother didn't object. "We say dad hit you and then ran off. You tell Uncle Bill you threatened to press charges this time, so dad has a good excuse to stay away."

"It's not like anybody would be surprised he would run out on his family," Mike added. "After Uncle Bill leaves, we find a more permanent place to hide the body. Nobody will even give the matter another thought."

"What about the rifle?" the mother asked.

"Buried in the snow by the bushes," Luke said. "Stop worrying. We got this."

Mike patted his mother's hand as the sound of Uncle Bill's truck churning up the gravel in the drive drew Luke to the window.

"Looks like Uncle Bill has problems," Luke said, prompting Mike to join him. Smoke was seeping from under the hood of Bill's truck. They watched Uncle Bill climb out and lift the hood, staggering back as a white plume of steam enveloped him.

A few minutes later, Bill was standing in the kitchen, cursing his bad luck.

"Ten to one, the engine is shot," he said. "It's my own damn dumb fault. I should have pulled over as soon as it started overheating. Now I'm going to end up spending a grand instead of the twenty bucks it would have cost me for a new radiator hose. Where's Rob? He might be able to tell."

"Rob's gone, Bill," Alice said, raising her head to reveal her swollen face. "I don't think he's coming back."

"What the hell happened to you?" Bill asked, grabbing her by the shoulders and pulling her into the light. "Rob do that?" Alice nodded.

"That bastard!" Bill exclaimed. "My brother never was worth a shit, especially when he was hitting the sauce. What're you going to do?"

"We'll make it," Alice said. "My job at the diner pays the bills. Rob hasn't worked in months. I can't even remember the last time he was sober."

"Well, you can count on me to do what I can, Alice," Bill said. "You know how I feel about you and the boys. I guess Rob took the car?" Mike shot Luke a furtive glance, and Luke nodded, signaling the car was well hidden.

"He did," Alice said. "I'll be able to use my father's to get to work and back until I can save up to get a new one. He's out of town right now though."

"Looks like you're stuck with me for a few days then," Bill said. "No way I'm going to find a mechanic on Christmas Eve. I hope that won't be a problem. Hell, it might even be good having me around in case Rob comes back and tries to start something."

"You're always welcome here, Bill," Alice said, and she meant it. She had always liked Bill, and probably would have married him instead of his brother if she hadn't met Rob first, and if Rob hadn't gotten her pregnant.

"I got something for you boys in the truck," Bill said, trying to sound cheerful. "Why don't' you go have a look while I help myself to some of this eggnog? There's something out there for your mother too, if you'll be good enough to fetch it."

On the way out to the truck, Luke regarded the snow man, studying it for signs of blood seeping through its icy façade. Thinking Luke was being too obvious, Mike nudged him with his elbow.

"It'll be alright," Mike said.

"What's the weather supposed to be like tomorrow?" Luke asked. "What if it warms up? What if Uncle Bill stays past Christmas?"

"I've been thinking about that," Mike said, opening the door of the truck to discover two new hunting rifles next to a large gift-wrapped box on the back seat. Afraid of the memories they might dredge up, Mike let Luke carry the rifles while he toted the box, being sure not to crush the ribbons his Uncle had taped all down the front.

They left Uncle Bill in the kitchen with the eggnog, a fifth of whisky, and their mother, who insisted on wearing the fur coat Bill had given her. The plan had been to let Bill have Luke's room in the back of the house, but, to the boy's surprise, after a few hours Alice led Bill to her room and closed the door behind them. While neither boy thought it justified what their father had done to them and their mother, it made him seem a little less like a madman to see the accusations he'd made had some merit. It was obvious their mother and uncle had been in love for some time, though they doubted if either of them had ever acted on it before that night.

"Think they'll come back out tonight?" Luke asked.

"Nope," Mike said. "Not till morning, after they've sobered up. You stay here just in case though."

"What're you going to do? The ground's still too hard for digging."

"I'm going out into the woods to look around," Mike said. We might be able to hide him in the gully if we can figure out how to keep the critters off of him."

Luke handed him the rifle his uncle had bought him.

"What's this for?" Mike asked.

"If they wake up and notice you're gone, I'll say you snuck out to do some shooting," Luke said, though Mike suspected that had been an afterthought. He punched Luke on the shoulder, and set out with the rifle.

Passing the snowman, Mike noticed the wind had elongated the mouth he'd etched with his finger, giving the snowman a smirk. His hands tightened around the rifle. He could almost feel the sting of his father's belt and hear him chuckling as he brought his arm down again and again. His father's mirth had always increased in proportion to the pain he inflicted. It had been the sound of his father's laughter, mingled with his mother's screams, that had made it possible for him to pull the trigger. Even with half his face blown off, the man had managed to grin up at him as he dragged him out to the yard and encased him in snow.

It didn't take Mike long to find a hollow tree in a gully that was large enough to accommodate the corpse. He could topple the snowman into the wheelbarrow, haul it to the gully, then pack the opening with dead leaves and branches until the ground thawed and Bill was gone, though he was starting to think Bill might be around a good deal longer than expected.

On the way back, Mike imagined going to live with Uncle Bill at his house in the suburbs. It would be the best thing for all of them, especially his mother. She wouldn't have to slave away at that dingy diner, begging for tips, her bruises covered with mascara. Let his father rot alone out here in the sticks. After a while, they might even forget what he did to them. Mike might even forget what he'd made him do.

Coming to the edge of the woods, Mike noticed the porch light was off, and he fell back behind the line of trees. It could be a sign from Luke that Uncle Bill or their mother was up, and to proceed with caution. He strained his eyes, focusing on the kitchen window. For a moment he thought he'd seen a figure flit past, too tall to be Luke or his mother. Something wasn't right. What was it that was making his heart beat so fast? The snowman! The snowman was gone!

Mike ran to the spot where the snowman had stood to find a set of tracks leading up to the house. How? There was no way his father was alive, not with half his head gone. Had Luke broke down and confessed? Did Uncle Bill have the body up at the house, staring down at it while he phoned the police? Running as best he could in his galoshes over the icy ground, Mike reached the porch steps as the wind caught the storm door and battered it against the wall. Why was the door open? He stumbled up the stairs and into the house to the sound of whimpering.

Luke huddled in the corner before their father, who was slowly slipping his belt out of his pants loops.

"How?" Mike said, the word dying on his lips as his father turned around to reveal the frozen snow and lumps of coal Mike had used for the snowman's eyes still clinging to the face beneath the battered fedora. The belt whipped out and snapped at the air. Suddenly remembering the rifle in his hand, Mike raised it, but the thing with the snowman's face grabbed the barrel, yanking it from him and raising it like a club. Luke screamed. Mike threw his hands up over his head. The Snowman laughed.

A series of shots rang out, causing Mike to drop to the floor and scamper off on his hands and knees. When he finally peered out from behind the sofa, he saw Bill, poking at a shape on the floor with Luke's rifle.

"I had to do it," he said. "He was going to bash Mike's brains in."

Mike stood and looked down at the man on the floor. The shot had dislodged the remaining snow to reveal a face missing both eyes and most of the nose. Luke was giggling. He hunched over, clutching his stomach as his laughter reached a manic crescendo.

"The shot knocked his hat off!" Luke shouted as his mother draped a blanket over his shoulders and helped him to his feet. "Just like the song! Just like Frosty!"

Mike knew his brother would be alright. He was a tough kid. They would both be alright now. No one would ever suspect or believe their father had already been killed once before. It would be assumed he died as a result of the shots Bill fired, and that those shots had been justified. Mike got a dish towel from the kitchen and dropped it on his father's face, blotting out the sight of the grin that still lingered there

And a Piece of Coal Where Her Heart Once Beat

Suzanne J. Willis

NOTHING LASTS forever. Not Christmas, with its bright lights and spangled promises of good things that never quite come to pass. Not the dreams of magic that it conjures for children everywhere. Not even Krampus, with his sack of coal and his cold heart. Even villains grow old and achy, age softening their sharp edges, allowing things akin to nostalgia and loneliness to seep to the surface.

It made him wish that the mountain had not been hollowed out, like a sponge, full of tunnels and caves and oubliettes, designed to deter or trap any intruders. Designed to keep Krampus hidden, deep inside the mountain, where he could keep his lists of naughty children and plan his cruelty for the year to come. For if there was someone to seek him, they would never, ever find their way.

And if they did, what would they find? He asked himself, stroking his whitened beard and staring into the fire. *Nothing but a sad old bovine, hiding himself away from the world.* Disgust welled up inside him like bile. How was it that age had snuck up on him? He could not remember ever having been anything like a child... Then again, his type – oh, yes, there were others like him, though they went by different names, in different forms – lived a long, long time.

But nothing lasts forever. Castles crumble, wishes fade, even the oldest of the trees in the woods on the mountain above die after thousands of years.

"Then you must make it last!" he said to himself, rising from his chair and ignoring the knotty pains in his back. He took to pondering how he might do so while wandering the passages that curled around on themselves. Occasionally he stumbled across the remains of young daemons who liked to climb up from the deep fire pits to try to fight him. Even they could not find their way out into the world or back to Hell, once they were lost in Krampus's labyrinth.

He also stumbled on other things, too, the sort that he had thought hidden for all time. Long-lost memories of a young boy, trying desperately hard to hide his hoofed feet from the other boys in the town. A broken silver fob-watch, its face studded with tiny rubies like drops of blood, lid carved with words in an old language he could not understand. And, in the darkest, farthest corner, where he could not remember having been before, a cloche jar that covered something shrivelled and desiccated. In the candlelight, he thought it looked a bit like a heart. As the flame flickered, he could have sworn that it gave a one feeble beat, then another.

Without knowing why, he lifted the glass gently and picked up the heart. It was warm. He lifted it to his lips, and swallowed it whole. A baby's cry, thin and hollow, echoed through the hallway, dying away as a bitter wind blew through behind it. And, with that, Krampus knew what he must do – how he could indeed make his story go on forever. He walked through the tunnels, up the thousands of ancient stone steps, exiting through the huge fireplace of the abandoned castle topping the mountain in which he lived. Slowly, as the snow fell and winter bit the air with its sharp teeth, he set out, stumping across the late winter lands in search of his successor.

Hundreds of miles away, the girl Lulah, only ten years old and small for her age at that, set out in her mother's only winter coat and shoes stolen from the general store in the raggedy strip of shops that had once been a village. She would need them, she knew, but it also didn't hurt to have added another crime to her short list. Theft, though, was a small thing compared to what she had come to think of as *the necessary mischief.* Lulah had had to do something impressive to show Krampus she was capable of more than plain disobedience.

The stories her mother had told her about him were supposed to scare her, she knew. Instead, they had left her with a little kernel of hope that warmed her, despite the old shack they called home, the pinching hunger, the grey march of poverty. Hope that there was a strange justice at work in the world and that she could use that to her advantage.

Lulah breathed deeply, pushing away the sick feeling twisting inside her as she thought of her mother. The freezing air kissed her cheeks red and the wind, she thought, fair whistled through her bones. But she didn't look back. Not once.

Lulah and Krampus each walked through the deepest winter, never quite meeting up, although there were near misses in the bare forests, where the only company was the howling of wolves and the thunder of the hooves of wild horses, and in the abandoned village that stood at the juncture of the two frozen rivers. It wasn't until the springmelt had begun that they met on the Devil's Bridge, a stone arch that stretched over the still water. Twinned with its reflection, it formed a perfect circle. One through which, it was said, Krampus rode to collect souls.

Lulah and Krampus each stood at either end of the bridge, looking at one another. Both thin and exhausted, as though winter had eaten them up and left behind husks.

Surely not this one, he thought as the urchin walk towards him, chin held up defiantly.

Though she didn't show it, Lulah was shaking in her shoes. He was so much bigger than she imagined; though his back was stooped and his fur matted, the huge horns on his head looked sharp enough to cut glass. His hooves clattered on the stone as he walked toward her. They met at the halfway point.

"You?" he asked.

Lulah pointed to the water below. It reflected the trees as they opened up to spring, the curve of the bridge, the swallows darting above. But neither Lulah nor Krampus appeared there. The reflected bridge was empty.

She smiled up at him. "Me."

* * *

Krampus took a Christmas wish from the string garlanding the mantelpiece. In the firelight, the beads glowed vermillion, emerald, indigo. He rolled it between his gnarled fingers before handing it to Lulah.

The girl smiled at him. "This one will taste like apples," she said, biting into the scarlet wish. It popped between her teeth, making her skin blush. She had already learnt so much, in the nine short months since Krampus had led her back to the ruined castle, down through the labyrinth, into his lair. It was the only place that had ever felt like home to Lulah.

Krampus smiled, pointing to the Christmas tree hung with glass baubles. The children inside them, made miniature by his magic, cried and shook the glass. Krampus and Lulah laughed.

"You are the naughtiest of them all, Lulah! Daughter of Krampus, who will take children to hell long after I'm gone."

Krampus hooked his horns under the string, flinging the wishes into the air. They landed on the long table, turning to a feast of blueberries, sugared violets, crispy goose, steaming pudding.

Not quite daughter *yet,* she thought. Lulah lifted her hands to her head, where the beginnings of her own horns sprouted, glossy and dark. Pity flared inside her. For the children in glass cages. For her parents. Had she truly broken their silly hearts by leaving baby Tom in the woods?

The cold must have made his ending quick. And she had had to be sure, hadn't she? No ordinary wickedness would have called Krampus to take her away. Her pity faded as she remembered winters with no food, and spindly trees against the snow whispering *sorrow, sorrow.* Better to let the winter creep through her bones, to freeze away any goodness that could make her weak.

Curving her mouth into a smile, Lulah reached across and tapped one of the glass baubles. Coal showered the little boy inside, until his tears ran black. Krampus lifted her up, and spun her about, almost like a parent would do on Christmas morning. Although no parent dug their claws into the soft flesh of their child's arms or grinned through sharp yellow teeth. If they had, no child would have remained bright-eyed and giggled back, as Lulah did.

Face to face, each monster and child both.

On cloven hooves, Lulah and Krampus danced in the firelight, delighting in Christmas misery, then ate their feast of stolen wishes. With each bite pieces of Lulah's heart turned to black, hard coal. For so long as it beat coldly inside her chest, she would scribe her own Krampus tale from the shadowy dreams of a darkling once-child. She would forget that she had been a girl called Lulah, and all that that had cost her. Her reign as Krampus would last forever.

Ashes at Midnight

Cassondra Windwalker

I KNEW HE only loved me because he dreamed of her every night.

I was twelve years old the first time I saw her, hollow-eyed and sooty-faced, her singed hair hanging lank down her grimy nightgown as she glared at me from the mirror, a sprig of holly clenched in her fist. She kept close in those early days. I learned to swallow my fear when I caught a glimpse of her reflection in a glass of water or gazing back at me from a foggy window. Harder to ignore was her rasping cough or the smell of burning flesh, but I managed.

She wasn't always so ethereal in her hatred, though. More than once she set the bees on me. I begged Father Ryan to box them up, send the hives to some happy beekeeper, but he refused. Heirloom honey, he called it, a legacy from my parents to the church. And she had a way with water, ironically enough. Other kids could be tempted into the woods, where swamp and sinkholes gaped beneath curtains of Spanish moss, but not me. It only took one slip, one sucking pit of slime with her cold, bony hand closing over my ankle, pulling me down, to keep me out of the forest for good.

Fin saved me that time, just like he had the night of the fire. I'd screamed, panic-stricken, clutching desperately at the vines that gave way as soon as I touched them, and he leapt across the knob-kneed mangrove roots to grab my arms and pull me bodily from the mire. I collapsed into his arms in tears, sobbing gibberish, inconsolable till he half-carried me safely back to his house. That was what Fin always did: he saved me.

Growing up next-door to each other, we'd sidestepped the boy versus girl conflict that consumed our classmates. We'd been best friends, like our moms, since before we could talk. So on that terrible Christmas Eve, when Fin had seen the flames leaping from our house, he'd rushed over without even waking his parents first. He climbed up the trellis my father had deliberately built extra-strong, a silent paternal nod to a friendship he knew, even then, would challenge every law of heaven and earth, and found me unconscious in a locked room.

My poor parents died on the other side of that door. They certainly could have escaped had they only gone down the stairs, but they wouldn't leave me. Fire investigators were baffled by my locked door, and I had nothing to offer them by way of explanation. Events were too traumatic, my memory was scrambled, and no-one wanted to push a twelve-year-old orphan with smoke inhalation too far. Even Fin didn't ask, though his silence was louder than any question: he knew as well as his parents did that I wasn't allowed to lock my door at night. My dad was a cop, for Pete's sake. He knew better.

Fin hadn't known my parents were coughing out their last breaths on the other side of that door. He never talked about that night, either, but I have an impression of all the sensations he carried with him: crashing timbers, roaring flames, billowing smoke, the percussion of his own heart in his veins, the sound of his voice screaming my name, over and over.

Brigid. Brigid. Brigid.

That's my first clear, unshadowed memory: Fin's voice, saying my name. It was as if he spoke me into life.

And ever since, she's been trying to unspeak me.

She was strongest in the beginning. Now, twenty-one years later, I hardly ever see her. I've grown so much more powerful than her over the years, I can't resist the urge to taunt her sometimes. I'll linger beneath Fin's shoulder in the mirror, cupping his scruffy jaw in my palm or pulling him down for a kiss while she watches. I set fresh flowers on the graves every week. I even planted honeysuckle for the bees along the fence where our yard bounds the cemetery.

After the fire, Father Ryan persuaded one of the families in town to foster me so I wouldn't disappear into the system. The church purchased what was left of my home, and the good father ensured the funds went to pay for my college. Meanwhile, the burned skeleton was razed and the small acreage added to the churchyard, so my former backyard was now peppered with gravestones. All that remained of my childhood home were the bee-boxes and the huge old oak trees that had survived the flames.

If Fin and I had loved each other with all the unquestioning, innocent passion of childhood before the fire, we were inseparable after. I was troubled, of course: inexpressibly but undeniably altered, and still Fin's constancy was unchanged. Neither of us ever had eyes for anyone else, and as soon as we both graduated from the state college, we married. I rather think his parents secretly hoped he would at least experiment first, date a few other people, but there was no chance of that. I could never have borne it.

And with her nocturnal visits, neither could he. It was a beautiful, wicked irony that her steadfast refusal to give up was almost certainly what bound him to me so tightly. I could only pretend in the daylight at what she gave him in the darkness, but to him, we were one and the same. His madness for her was too great to ever allow him to see me with sane eyes.

She was not content with our happy little symbiosis, though. I knew, beyond a doubt, she'd do anything to destroy me, and I lived in continual terror at first. My foster-family, Father Ryan, and even Fin put my sleeplessness, my staring eyes, and my cold skin down to trauma. If I jumped out of my skin at every little noise or started horribly at a passing shadow, they soothed and consoled me. I couldn't tell them about her, how she'd appeared right after the fire and how she dogged my every step. They'd have thought me completely insane.

As her strength waned, I grew lax in my vigilance against her incursions. On the first cycle, the seventh anniversary of the fire, I was entirely unprepared for her sudden surge in power.

Nineteen years old, Fin and I were both staying at his parents' house for the Christmas holidays. We walked together to the churchyard, red-ribboned wreaths whose golden bells gently rung with every step dangling from our hands. The ritual was only just that for me: all my thoughts, my longings, were consumed with Fin. I've loved him as long as I can remember, you see.

When we arrived at the gravestones, I did the appropriate obeisance, placing the wreaths on their iron holders and resting my hand on each frosty stone in silent prayer. Fin had loved my parents too: they'd been more aunt and uncle to him than neighbors, and he'd always been haunted by the knowledge they'd been right on the other side of my bedroom door, frantically trying to reach me, to save me from the fire that claimed their lives. He blamed himself for not crossing the room, not opening the door and pulling them through the same window he used to save me. He couldn't have known, of course, and he'd only been a child at the time anyway. But Fin is like that – too good for his mortal bones.

When we stood back up, the cold wind came shrieking around us through the old oak trees, but still I didn't realize my danger. I wrapped my arms around him, distracting him from grief with the warmth of my mouth, and that was more than she could bear.

It sounded like a scream, like the shout of the earth being broken open, when the oak tree shook loose its mighty limb and felled me where I stood. Somehow, impossibly, it pulled me clean out of Fin's arms and left him standing, showered in cold rain and broad, wet, spine-fingered leaves that covered his eyes and resisted his efforts to tear them away. I couldn't speak, could barely make a sound – she'd impaled me into the soggy cemetery ground with a broken branch.

They saved my life, but the damage to my organs was catastrophic. I would never have been able to bear Fin's children anyway, but no-one knew that then, and they broke the news to me as gently as they could. Another man might have quailed at the thought of staying with a woman who couldn't give him children of his own, but Fin never hesitated. I think he might have even loved me more. A hero complex, has my Fin. The more I needed him, the more he loved me. I think that's what makes him such a good high school teacher. All those little lost souls in need of saving. Where lesser men get burned out, he gets inspired.

At any rate, I learned my lesson. I should have known that she'd gain strength in the seventh year. When the next seven-year cycle came around, I was prepared. Or so I thought. It was easy to beg off the customary Christmas pilgrimage that year – a little eggnog, a few tears, and Fin was all too understanding. He insisted on drawing me one of my favorite baths, steaming hot with aromatic salts. I'd first begun the indulgence when her powers began waning, delighting in the torment they allowed me as she came so close but couldn't hurt me. Eventually I became so accustomed to her silent petulance, I practically forgot she was there. Except on those occasions when Fin joined me – I know I should be the bigger person, since I have everything she longs for, but sometimes the urge to provoke her is just so strong. And how she suffered when he loved me with that beautiful body of his.

It's the strangest communion, when the only person who really, truly knows you is the person intent on your destruction.

But that night, I wasn't thinking about her at all when I slipped into the scalding hot water. I was distracted, caught up in all the ordinary, mundane, harried hustle of human holidays. I could hear Fin's sister and her husband arriving downstairs, Fin had Christmas carols playing over the house stereo system, I needed to pull the goose out of the oven in twenty-five minutes. A few moments of peace was all I needed.

She pulled me under.

I still gasp for air thinking about it. I can feel the porcelain lip of the tub slipping under my frantic hands, feel her implacable iron hands holding me beneath the water. In a panic, I sucked in a breath as soon as the water closed over my head, and the water hitting my lungs only made me panic further. My eyes stung in the hot salted water, but I couldn't look away from her gaze burning into my own, afire with fierce triumph as my vision began to darken. It was sheer chance when my foot, sliding fruitlessly for purchase along the bottom of the tub, knocked loose the drain plug. I didn't even realize what I'd done until the water receded from my face and her hold vanished.

The bathroom was a wreck, water everywhere. Bright red handprints on my bare chest were sure to bruise. I remember the tiles cold and hard under my knees as I frantically sopped up the water while trying to quiet the sobbing that bubbled up from my aching throat. I wore a high-necked sweater and kept the lights dim in our bedroom for the next two weeks, waiting for her gruesome caresses to fade. Fin already thought me delicate. I couldn't risk him going back to Father Ryan with his concerns.

The good father had eyed me askance for a while now. I couldn't say what tipped him off, but not long after the fire, while everyone else was still cosseting me and making excuses, Father Ryan grew oddly cold. He was still carefully charitable, still checked up on me with my new foster-family, still made sure I filled out my college applications when the time came and helped me get my first job, but something in him had withdrawn. And Fin had gone to him several times over the years, although he thought I didn't know.

Poor Fin.

But my sympathy didn't extend to Father Ryan. I remember how cool his eyes had been, even though his hands were tender, when he treated my bee-stings after that first attack. And he'd been the one tasked with breaking the news to me about my torn womb after the oak tree pierced me through. Even then, his compassion had worn the trapping of a dress rehearsal. He'd tried to give me a silver crucifix at my Confirmation, but I'd told him I preferred to wear the gold one that had been my mother's. How could he argue with that?

It wasn't that I thought he could ever convince Fin of his suspicions, even if he dared to breathe them aloud. Fin had loved me, loved this body, too well and too completely for too long to ever be persuaded otherwise. But he already insisted I see a psychologist once a week. I didn't want him to add drugs to my repertoire of interventions.

This year – this year might be the end of it all. The third seven-year cycle. I believed she would be more powerful than she'd ever been, and if I could defeat her one more time, perhaps she'd finally be banished forever. Freed of her dark shadow, I could be the woman I was meant to be. Fin and I would become the magic he always said we were. The fear, the tension that strung my sinew like catgut on a fiddle, the smell of smoke and scorched flesh that never left my nostrils, would vanish along with that creature in my mirror.

All I had to do was survive Christmas Eve.

Fin's sister Rachel, her husband Lake, and their baby girl Rowan would be here soon, along with Fin's parents Patrick and Kate. When Patrick and Kate had moved to Florida, they'd sold us the home Fin had grown up in. It might seem odd to some that Fin and I lived next door not only to a churchyard, but to a churchyard built on the ashes of the home where my parents had died, but in the South, the living and the dead have always walked close. So a Christmas dinner shared over gravestones wouldn't have raised an eyebrow.

In fact, my married family would no doubt be dismayed that this year, I was going to skip the traditional cemetery side of the festivities. I'd already told Fin, who as was his nature, easily assented to whatever I told him made me feel better. I expected Father Ryan would raise an objection, but with Fin on my side, I had no worries on that score.

Still, I would have to remain vigilant. I didn't intend to be alone till the night was over. And I definitely wouldn't be taking a bath. Thank God for dry shampoo.

Is there anything more enchanting than Christmas Eve? Snow in Louisiana would be too much to ask, but the night was cold and so clear, stars twinkling above the spreading black limbs of the old oaks trees like so many Christmas lights. Our warm, cozy home was redolent with the scents of cinnamon and rum, crispy buttered goose skin and yeast bread, sugar cookies and baked cheese. Fin had carols playing, and Rowan's infectious baby giggles pealed out like Bing Crosby's silver bells. The dinner table was hardly visible beneath the platters and plates piled high with food, and red wine gleamed like blood in crystal glasses. Even Father Ryan's steady gaze on my shaking hands couldn't dim my joy. At last, at long last, I would be free of her. Fin would be mine, and only mine. I would be safe.

Midnight. The fire had started at midnight, all those years ago, and now midnight would again bring me life.

She'd been oddly quiet all day. I was beginning to wonder if I was wrong after all, and there would be no final surge of power, no last confrontation. Perhaps she would only fade into the darkness in the end. Even the smell of smoke had faded, and I no longer tasted ash in the back of my throat.

Tossing back the last of my third glass of wine, I headed down the hall for a quick trip to the bathroom. It was nearly midnight now. Like an addict hunting a fix, I needed to check the mirror one more time.

Cold air gusted over me, and the pleasantly heady warmth of the wine drained away, leaving me terribly sober. The front door stood wide open. A soft laugh, wracked with coughing, drifted in. I felt my eyes stretching wide, my nostrils flaring, as my heart ratcheted painfully against my breastbone. I knew already what I would find as I stepped to the threshold, my legs shaking so hard I could barely stand.

One of Rowan's tiny shoes rested on the stone step. Acorns spilled everywhere across the lawn, forming a path that inevitably led to the churchyard. A vicious wind whipped the trees into impossible shapes, a macabre dance of bark-boned skeletons worshipping the moon. The stars had vanished. Piles of dead leaves leapt and swirled, rushing into the house and tearing at my face.

"Fin!" I cried. "Rachel!"

Chairs scraped and footsteps sounded behind me, but I couldn't wait. I cast one glance behind me before I stepped out into the night and saw Father Ryan was the first to reach the hallway.

"Rowan," I gasped urgently, her shoe clutched in my hand. His eyes met mine, and I saw his hand go reflexively to his own crucifix. I turned and ran, acorns slipping and rolling under my feet, the sound of flames roaring in my ears.

I loved that baby. She was everything I could never have, and her perfect innocence, her sheer and uncomplicated delight in being alive, enchanted me. She wasn't even two years old yet. Maybe once upon a time, hurting a child would have been inconceivable to my double, but she was desperate now. No doubt mad with her confinement in a world that wasn't hers, not to mention the torment she inflicted on herself by clinging to a lover she had long lost.

Every night Fin said her name in his sleep.

My name now. My name for the last twenty-one years.

I hadn't wanted to kill her parents, not exactly. You're familiar with the phrases *scared out of her skin* or *she was beside herself with fear,* aren't you? Modern people forget those aren't metaphors. A big enough emotional shock can send a soul wandering. I'd watched her for years. She was my double, after all, my human twin on the other side of the fae. All I needed was a scant second, and I could drive her into my place and steal hers for myself.

For Fin. I'd done it all for him.

Killing her parents had simply been an unfortunate side effect. Although it had worked out well for me – two fewer people to dissect and doubt my reactions. Not to mention my status as a grieving orphan made me absolutely irresistible to the boy who already adored her. That damn priest with one foot in heaven and one foot in hell saw way too much, but we weren't in the Old Country, after all. Americans are far too prosaic to fall under any spell he might try to cast.

I wasn't, though. So I preferred to keep my distance when I could.

Behind me, Rachel and Lake and Fin were screaming Rowan's name, though the wind all but snatched their voices away. I knew Rachel and Patrick wouldn't be far behind. My straining ears caught the barest echo of a baby's giggle. I vaulted over the dried honeysuckle clinging to the low fence. The moment my feet landed on the spongy cemetery earth, everything fell silent.

The wind stopped blowing around me, though when I looked back, the trees on the other side of the fence were bent nearly double in some terrific gale. The dead honeysuckle flowered, ghastly corpse-white blooms and black leaves springing up and forming a wall between me and my family. Between me and Fin.

The bees awoke and rose, adding their buzzing black mass to the boundary.

"Fin!" I screamed uselessly. Somehow I knew the others saw none of this. On the other side of midnight, they searched for Rowan, never sensing how their paths tangled.

Hollow with horror, I spun slowly to face her.

She stood between her parents' graves, bouncing the baby on one sooty hip. She'd aged along with me, of course, but still she wore that same ragged white gown. Ashes gusted around her, though the air was painfully still. She coughed, then smiled at me, her lips gaping slowly as the lips of a rotting corpse might slide open in the sun.

Rowan laughed and clutched at her long dark hair, fearless and stupid. Stupid baby. Why did I love the creature so much?

"Let her go," I growled.

Her dark eyes, so much like mine and so different, sparkled. With a nod, she bent and set the child in the frost-caged grass on her mother's grave. Rowan laughed again, peering at me from behind the headstone as if we played peek-a-boo.

"But you must stay," she said and came at me then, drawing from her skirts a sharpened wooden stake I knew instinctively to be made of ash.

She was desperate and hungry, a mortal creature trapped in an immortal realm. The only magic she possessed was that of love. Love had enabled her to haunt Fin's dreams all these years and bind his heart faster and faster to her own, but it could hardly defeat one such as me. As soon as I felt her skin under my hand when I seized her arm, twisting it, I knew she'd never even tasted the food of the fae, so intent had she been on escaping that land. More fool her. She had no hope of defeating me without the strength it might have given her. And to be sure, she was right that eating it would have kept her forever from the mortal world into which she'd been born, but she could always have carried Fin with her into that netherland, had she undone me.

But with a speed that surprised even me, I undid her instead.

She'd crafted a beautiful weapon, no doubt. I pictured her, all those dark days she'd spent banished from the sunlight, carving and shaping and sanding, praying Fin's name into every knot and curl. It was pure poetry when that wooden shaft sank through her flesh and bone and pierced her heart.

To my sorrow, my sorrow, it was not her voice crying out I heard as the ash sing its way home but Fin's, a wild, animal shout of grief and horror rising over the howl of the wind tearing at the honeysuckle.

I caught her in my arms as she fell, watched the darkness in her eyes become light till even her bones caught fire with that heat and she was gone.

In that instant, a torrent of wind and rain shattered over Rowan and me, sweeping away the bees and the wall of honeysuckle in an icy gust. Rowan burst into tears, and I snatched her to me, trying vainly to shelter her from the onslaught of the storm as I stumbled and ran back to the shelter of the house. I had nearly reached the front porch when Rachel appeared, her eyes frantic beneath her rain-slicked hair.

"Rowan!" she cried on a half-sob, seizing her from my arms. "Oh, thank you, Brigid. Thank you."

"Get inside," I told her, wiping uselessly at the rain on my own face. "I'll find Fin and Lake. Your parents."

"And Father Ryan," she said, diving into the warmth and safety of the house without wasting another breath.

I found Lake and Father Ryan together, attempting a sort of side-by-side grid search where the swampy forest met the edge of the lawn. Lake, a big man who rarely interested me, nearly crumpled into himself when I told him the baby was safe with her mother in the house. Father Ryan took one look at my eyes, no doubt hoping to see Brigid there, and made the sign of the cross as a grey sort of grief overtook the lines in his face and turned them to granite. He didn't say a word, only trudged wearily behind the jubilant father as he hurried back toward the house.

Kate and Patrick were in the rose garden, calling their granddaughter's name forlornly into the storm. Their old bones were only too glad to return to warmth and shelter once they learned the baby was safe and sound.

Fin, I found back where it all began. He stood in the center of the churchyard, rain and darkness streaming down his body, his face raised to the starless sky as if he could see her ascending there. I almost believed it was his voice I heard raging in the storm. I touched his arm gently.

"We found her," I said. "She's in the house with your sister."

He started horribly at my touch, his eyes rolling like a wild horse's as his gaze met mine, danced away, and returned.

"I thought—" I had to lean close to catch his voice. "I thought—"

He seized me then, his fingers biting into my arms so tightly I had to fight not to cry out. He searched my face, frantic. "I thought you were dead.

"I almost – I almost thought you'd *been* dead, ever since that night, and this whole life had all been a dream."

He stood in the sodden grass that had once been the footprint of a house where he had snatched a girl from an inferno, as if he could save her again.

He couldn't, though.

I wrapped my arms around his trembling body, held him as fiercely as I could, willed all my life and heat into his icy limbs. "Come on," I urged him. "I'm okay. Rowan's okay. Everything is going to be all right. Let's get you warmed up before you catch your death of cold. We have presents to open. It's Christmas Day."

He withdrew, looking at me with dazed eyes. "Midnight," he murmured. "It's past midnight."

"Yes." I pulled him down, kissed his unresponsive lips. "Come on."

He followed me docilely enough. And he still holds me close in the wee hours of the morning, still makes me coffee in the mornings, still draws me hot baths on long days. He could never believe his Brigid isn't in this body he has known so long.

But he doesn't dream of her anymore. He doesn't say her name in his sleep. And day by day, his eyes grow colder, his heart stonier. My tongue always tastes of smoke now, and I pull ash splinters from my palms. I tore out the honeysuckle, but it comes back every year.

Biographies & Sources

Grant Allen
Wolverden Tower
(First Published in 1896)
A man of letters noted for his staunch advocacy for Darwin's theory of evolution, Charles Grant Blairfindie Allen (1848–99) was a prolific Canadian novelist and science writer. Born on Wolfe Island in Lake Ontario, Allen eventually emigrated to the United States, then France and England, studying at Oxford. While his first works, such a *Flowers and Their Pedigrees* (1886), were on science, fiction eventually became his primary focus. He produced over 30 novels and numerous short stories in his lifetime, exploring genres such as mystery, science fiction and romance.

John Kendrick Bangs
Thurlow's Christmas Story
(First Published in *Harper's Weekly Magazine*, 1894)
The Mystery of My Grandmother's Hair Sofa
(First Published in *Ghosts I Have Met and Some Others*, 1898)
Author, editor and humourist John Kendrick Bangs (1862–1922) contributed to some of the most notable publications of his time, working as Associate Editor for *Life* magazine, before serving as Editor of the Departments of Humor for *Harper's Magazine*, *Harper's Bazaar*, and *Harper's Young People*, then moving on to *Munsey's Magazine*, *Literature* and *New Metropolitan* before being appointed editor of *Puck*, the era's leading American humour magazine. He authored many novels and short stories, and inspired the term 'Bangsian fantasy' to describe fantasies which explore the afterlife, and historical characters residing in it, as their setting.

S. Baring-Gould
Mustapha
(Originally Published in *A Book of Ghosts*, 1904)
The Devon-born clergyman S. Baring Gould (1834–1924) is most famous as author of the hymn 'Onward Christian Soldiers' (1865). (Arthur 'Gilbert &' Sullivan wrote the famous tune.) But, along with more ambitious religious works, including a sixteen-volume study of *The Lives of the Saints* (1872–77), Baring-Gould was a keen collector of folk songs. His folkloric interests inspired a major work on *Curious Myths of the Middle Ages* (1866–68) and a *Book of Werewolves* (1865). It's no surprise, then, that his short stories should so often have taken a supernatural or macabre theme: *A Book of Ghosts* appeared in 1904.

J.M. Barrie
The Ghost of Christmas Eve
(Originally Published in *My Lady Nicotine*, 1896)
James Matthew Barrie (1860–1937) was a weaver's son from Kirriemur, Angus, Scotland. Under the protection of his oldest brother and sister (qualified teachers), Barrie went to school, first in Glasgow and later in Dumfries. In the grounds of Moat Brae House, Dumfries, Barrie and his classmates played the pirate games that would later be the basis for *Peter Pan*. Barrie later studied Literature at Edinburgh University, and eventually moved to London to pursue his ambition to

write for the theatre. A chance encounter in Kensington Gardens led to a lengthy friendship with the boys of the Llewelyn-Davies family. More immediately, it completed the creative jigsaw that produced the play of *Peter Pan* (1904).

E.F. Benson

Between the Lights
(Originally Published in *The Room in the Tower, and Other Stories,*1912)
The Gardener
(Originally Published in *Visible and Invisible*, 1923)
The Horror-Horn
(Originally Published in *Visible and Invisible*, 1923)
The Other Bed
(Originally Published in *The Room in the Tower, and Other Stories,*1912)
Edward Frederic ('E.F.') Benson (1867–1940) was born at Wellington College in Berkshire, England, where his father, the future Archbishop of Canterbury Edward White Benson, was headmaster. Benson is widely known for being a writer of reminiscences, fiction, satirical novels, biographies and autobiographical studies. His first published novel, *Dodo*, initiated his success, followed by a series of comic novels such as *Queen Lucia* and *Trouble for Lucia*. Later in life, Benson moved to Rye where he was elected mayor. It was here that he was inspired to write several macabre ghost story and supernatural collections and novels, including *Paying Guests* and *Mrs. Ames*.

Algernon Blackwood

The Kit-Bag
(Originally Published in *Pall Mall Magazine*, 1908)
Algernon Henry Blackwood (1869–1951) was a writer who crafted his tales with extraordinary vision. Born in Kent but working at numerous careers in America and Canada in his youth, he eventually settled back in England in his thirties. He wrote many novels and short stories including 'The Willows', which was rated by Lovecraft as one of his favourite stories, and he is credited by many scholars as a real master of imagery who wrote at a consistently high standard.

Sir Andrew Caldecott

Christmas Re-Union
(First Published in *Not Exactly Ghosts*, 1947)
British writer Sir Andrew Caldecott (1884–1951) is best known for his career as a British colonial administrator. Born in Kent, he joined the Colonial Office in 1907, after graduating from Exeter College of the University of Oxford. He was first posted to British Malaya, now Malaysia and Singapore, where he lived until the 1930s, briefly returning to England in 1922 to serve as Malayan Commissioner at the British Empire Exhibition. In 1935 he was appointed Governor of Hong Kong, but left just over a year later to serve as Governor of Ceylon, now Sri Lanka, where the political independence movement was rapidly gaining pace.

Ramsey Campbell

Calling Card
(Originally Published in *Dark Companions*, 1982. © 1982 by Ramsey Campbell.)
Ramsey Campbell has been given more awards than any other writer in the field, including the Grand Master Award of the World Horror Convention, the Lifetime Achievement Award of the Horror Writers Association, the Living Legend Award of the International Horror Guild and the

World Fantasy Lifetime Achievement Award. In 2015 he was made an Honorary Fellow of Liverpool John Moores University for outstanding services to literature. Among his novels available from Flame Tree Press are *Thirteen Days by Sunset Beach*, *The Wise Friend*, *Somebody's Voice*, *Fellstones*, and his *Three Births of Daoloth* trilogy: *The Searching Dead*, *Born to the Dark* and *The Way of the Worm*.

Donna Cuttress
The Shallows
(First Publication)
Donna Cuttress is from Liverpool, UK. Her work has been published by Crooked Cat, Celestial Press, Firbolg, Flame Tree Publishing, Nocturnal Sirens Publishing and Black Hare Press. Her work for The Patchwork Raven's 'Twelve Days' is available as an artbook. She is a reviewer for the Spooky Isles site and has had work in Darkstroke Publishing's *Dark Anthologies* series. She has also been a speaker at the London Book Fair, and has previously been published by Sirens Call as part of Women in Horror Month. Her work with Red Cape publishing is now available on Audible.

Charles Dickens
The Story of the Goblins Who Stole a Sexton
(Originally Published in *The Pickwick Papers*, 1836)
The Haunted Man and the Ghost's Bargain
(Originally Published by Bradbury & Evans, 1848)
The iconic and much-loved Charles Dickens (1812–1870) was born in Portsmouth, England, though he spent much of his life in Kent and London. At the age of 12 Charles was forced into working in a factory for a couple of months to support his family. He never forgot his harrowing experience there, and his novels always reflected the plight of the working class. A prolific writer, Dickens kept up a career in journalism as well as writing short stories and novels, with much of his work being serialized before being published as books. He gave a view of contemporary England with a strong sense of realism, yet incorporated the occasional ghost and horror elements. He continued to work hard until his death in 1870, leaving *The Mystery of Edwin Drood* unfinished.

James Dodds
Elvis Saves Christmas
(First Publication)
James Dodds is a recovering technical writer. During his working life, he produced a small library of books that, happily, went unread by everyone. Upon retirement, he got serious about writing fiction. His work has appeared in *2100: A Health Odyssey*, *The Avenue* and *Enchanted Conversation*, among other publications. He lives the quiet life out in the country west of Spokane, Washington with his wife (and primary editor) and his dog (a secondary editor who pulls story drafts from the waste basket and rips them to shreds).

JG Faherty
Yule Cat
(Originally Published in *Appalachian Winter Hauntings*, 2009)
A life-long resident of New York's haunted Hudson Valley, JG Faherty has been a finalist for both the Bram Stoker Award (2x) and ITW Thriller Award, and he is the author of 9 novels, 11 novellas, and more than 80 short stories. He writes adult and YA horror, science fiction, paranormal romance,

and urban fantasy. He grew up enthralled with the horror movies and books of the 50s, 60s, 70s, and 80s, and as a child his favorite playground was a 17th-century cemetery. (Which explains a lot.) His latest novels are *Sins of the Father* and *The Wakening*. Follow him at twitter.com/jgfaherty, facebook.com/jgfaherty, and jgfaherty.com.

Marina Favila
Mr. Anders Meets a Stranger
(First Publication)
Marina Favila's short stories appear in *Weirdbook, Wraparound South,* Harvardwood's *Seven Deadly Sins,* and Flame Tree Publishing's *Haunted House Short Stories,* among others. Her audio piece, 'Holy, Holy', is a 2021 humour finalist for *The Missouri Review*'s Miller Prize. Scholarship includes essays on Shakespeare, poetry, and film in academic journals, such as *Modern Philology, Cahiers Élisabéthains, Spiritus,* and *Texas Studies in Literature and Language.* She is professor emerita at James Madison University, where she taught Shakespeare for twenty-five years.

Kevin M. Folliard
Bone Chill
(Originally Published in *More Christmas Terror Tales: Spine-Tingling Holiday Chillers,* 2016)
Kevin M. Folliard is a Chicagoland writer whose fiction has been collected by The Horror Tree, The Dread Machine, Demain Publishing, and more. His recent publications include his horror anthology *The Misery King's Closet,* his YA fantasy adventure novel *Grayson North: Frost-Keeper of the Windy City,* and his 2022 dinosaur adventure novel *Carnivore Keepers.* Kevin currently resides in the western suburbs of Chicago, IL, where he enjoys his day job in academia and membership in the La Grange Writers Group.

Elizabeth Gaskell
The Old Nurse's Story
(Originally Published in
Elizabeth Gaskell (1810–65) was born in London and is widely known for her biography of her friend Charlotte Brontë. In a family of eight children, only Elizabeth and her brother John survived past childhood. Her mother's early death caused her to be raised by her aunt in Knutsford, Cheshire, a place that inspired her to later write her most famous work, *Cranford.* Tragedy struck again when Gaskell's only son died, and it was then that she began to write. All the misfortune in her life led her to write her many gothic and horror tales.

John Linwood Grant
Aunt Hetty
(First Publication)
John Linwood Grant is an author/editor from Yorkshire with some eighty short stories and novelettes published in venues such as *Lackington's, Vastarien, Weirdbook,* and *Space & Time,* and in several award-winning anthologies. He writes dark contemporary fiction and late Victorian/Edwardian supernatural tales, and edits anthologies of period-set supernatural fiction. His novel *The Assassin's Coin* features the meticulous Edwardian assassin Mr Dry, and his second collection *Where All is Night, and Starless* – weird fiction and Folk Horror – came out in 2021 from Trepidatio, with a third collection under construction. He can be found on Facebook, and at his eclectic website greydogtales.com/blog.

John Berwick Harwood
Horror: A True Tale
(First Published Anonymously in *Blackwood's Magazine*, 1861)
Kent-born author John Berwick Harwood (1828–99) often published his stories anonymously, contributing stories to *Once A Week*, *Blackwood's Magazine* and more. He remains best known for his tales of ghosts and the supernatural, including several eerie Christmas stories, and also wrote numerous novels, as well as articles chronicling his travels to China.

Nathaniel Hawthorne
The Christmas Banquet
(Originally Published in *Mosses from an Old Manse*, 1846)
The prominent American writer Nathaniel Hawthorne (1804–64) was born in Salem, Massachusetts. His most famous novel *The Scarlet Letter* helped him become established as a writer in the 1850s. Most of his works were influenced by his friends Ralph Waldo Emerson and Herman Melville, as well as by his extended financial struggles. Hawthorne's works often incorporated a dark romanticism that focused on the evil and sin of humanity. Some of his most famous works detailed supernatural presences or occurrences.

K.M. Hazel
The Unforgiven
(First Publication)
K.M. Hazel resides in the 'Black Country', a post-industrial area of the English Midlands which features prominently in many of his stories. His fascination with ghosts and the supernatural is largely a consequence of attending a school that was so haunted it had its own 'ghost club', which met at lunchtimes to discuss all things spooky. He is currently working on the first series of a podcast that will blend the modern phenomena of Creepypasta with the classical English ghost story. A previous Christmas ghost story appeared in Book 12 of *The Ghastling*.

Larry Hodges
Christmas Interrupted
(First Publication)
Larry Hodges has over 125 short story sales and four SF novels, including *Campaign 2100: Game of Scorpions* and *When Parallel Lines Meet*, which he co-wrote with Mike Resnick and Lezli Robyn. He's a member of Codexwriters, and a graduate of the Odyssey and Taos Toolbox Writers Workshops. He's a professional writer with 17 books and over 2000 published articles in 170+ different publications. He's also a professional table tennis coach, and claims to be the best science-fiction writer in USA Table Tennis, and the best table-tennis player in Science Fiction Writers of America! Visit him at larryhodges.com.

Dr. Jerrold E. Hogle
Foreword
Jerrold E. Hogle is Professor Emeritus of English and University Distinguished Professor at the University of Arizona. The recipient of many teaching awards and research fellowships, he has published widely on nineteenth-century literature and the Gothic. His books range from *The Undergrounds of The Phantom of the Opera* and the *Cambridge Companions* to both *Gothic Fiction* and the *Modern Gothic* to *The Gothic and Theory* volume in the Edinburgh Companions to the Gothic series.

Jane Margaret Hooper

Bring Me a Light!
(First Published in *Once A Week*, Series I Volume IV, 1860–61)
As is the case for many other women of her time, there is little record of the life of British author Jane Margaret Hooper (1818–1907), who was often credited under her husband's name as Mrs. George Hooper. In addition to 'Bring Me a Light!', a classic Victorian ghost story, she also penned several novels, including *The House of Raby: or, Our Lady of Darkness* (1854), and was mother to several children.

M.R. James

Oh, Whistle, and I'll Come to You, My Lad
(Originally Published in *Ghost Stories of an Antiquary*, 1904)
The Story of a Disappearance and an Appearance
(Originally Published in *Ghost Stories of an Antiquary*, 1904)
Montague Rhodes James (1862–1936), whose works are regarded as being at the forefront of the ghost story genre, was born in Kent, England. James dispensed with the traditional, predictable techniques of ghost story construction, instead using realistic contemporary settings for his works. He was also a British medieval scholar, so his stories tended to incorporate antiquarian elements. His stories often reflect his childhood in Suffolk and his talented acting career, which both seem to have assisted in the build-up of tension and horror in his works.

Jerome K. Jerome

Told After Supper
(Originally Published by Leadenhall Press, 1891)
Jerome Klapka Jerome (1859–1927) was born in Staffordshire, England. A novelist, playwright and editor, his humour secured his popularity. Inspired by his sister Blandina's love for the theatre, a young Jerome tried his hand at acting under the name of 'Harold Crichton'. After three difficult years, Jerome departed from the stage and pursued a number of odd jobs as a teacher, journalist and essayist – to no avail. However, success eventually arrived through his memoir, On the Stage – and Off. Building upon the strength of his writing, Jerome's best-known novel, Three Men in a Boat (1889) exemplified his comic talent. However he also delved into more genre tales, like the chilling ghost story 'The Man of Science' or the early robotic story 'The Dancing Partner'.

James Joyce

The Dead
(Originally Published in *Dubliners*, 1914)
James Joyce (1882–1941) is the epitome of the avant-garde literary modernist. Born into a middle-class family in Dublin, he attended various Catholic schools before enrolling at University College Dublin, where he studied French, English and Italian from 1898 to 1902. During this time, he published his first piece, a glowing review of Ibsen's *When We Dead Awaken*. On graduation, he went to study medicine in Paris, but dropped out claiming ill health. He published his collections of naturalistic short stories, *Dubliners*, in 1914, followed by his long-awaited first novel, *A Portrait of the Artist as a Young Man*, in 1916. The literary techniques – parody, puns, stream of consciousness, internal monologues – employed in this latter and developed in his most famous work, *Ulysses* (1922), were groundbreaking.

CHRISTMAS GOTHIC SHORT STORIES

E.E. King
Christmas at Trelawny
(First Publication)
E.E. King is an award-winning painter, performer, writer, and naturalist – she'll do anything that won't pay the bills, especially if it involves animals. Ray Bradbury called her stories, "marvelously inventive, wildly funny and deeply thought-provoking." She's been published widely, including by *Clarkesworld* and Flame Tree. She's currently painting a science museum in San Paula, CA and also co-hosts The Long Lost Friends Show on Metastellar YouTube. Check out paintings, writing, musings, and books at: elizabeteveking.com and amazon.com/author/eeking.

Jonathan Robbins Leon
Tannenbaum
(First Publication)
Jonathan Robbins Leon identifies as a queer author of memoir and fiction. His work has been published by Flame Tree Press, Dark Moon Digest, and Distant Shore Publishing. He resides in Historic Kissimmee, where he and his husband act as caretakers to a haunted house and fathers to a super villain. In addition to writing, Jonathan's endeavours include serving as a library cataloguer and geeking out with his bestie on their podcast book club 'They're Coming to Read You, Barbara!'.

Clare Marsh
Time and Tide
(Originally Published in *Spiriting Through Christmas*, Crowvus Press, 2019)
Clare Marsh lives in Kent, UK and is an international adoption social worker. She writes poetry, flash fiction and short stories. A previous winner of the Sentinel Annual Short Story Competition, her writing has appeared in *Lighthouse, Ink, Sweat and Tears, Flash Flood, Pure Slush, Places of Poetry, Rebel Talk* and *Acropolis* anthologies. She won the 2020 Olga Sinclair Short Story Prize. She was awarded M.A. Creative Writing (University of Kent) in 2018 and nominated for a Pushcart Prize for a poem in *The Binnacle* in 2017.

Marshall J. Moore
Workshop
(Originally Published in *Death Throes Webzine: Horrific Holiday Issue*, December 2020)
Marshall J. Moore is a writer, filmmaker, and martial artist from Kwajalein, a tiny Pacific island. He has trained a professional mercenary in unarmed combat, once sold a thousand dollars' worth of teapots to Jackie Chan, and was once tracked down by a bounty hunter for owing $300 in library late fees. His short stories have appeared in publications from Flame Tree Publishing, Mysterion, Air and Nothingness Press, and many others. A member of the SFWA, he lives in Atlanta, Georgia with his wife Megan and their two cats. Find him on Twitter at @Kwaj14 or on Instagram at @kwajmarshall.

Templeton Moss
Gray Christmas
(First Publication)
Templeton Moss started writing in high school as part of a hopelessly misguided attempt to get girls to like him. Since then, he has written plays, short stories, novels, poems and angry social media posts about movies (he cannot believe Lin-Manuel Miranda still hasn't won an Oscar!). His

hobbies include naps, pizza and cartoons and his turnoffs include manual labour and the music of ABBA. He currently lives and (when he has to) works in Louisville, Kentucky.

Jane Nightshade
The Last Christmas Tree
(First Publication)
A native Californian, Jane Nightshade is a former corporate writer turned horror, sci-fi, and crime writer. Her non-fiction writing about horror and crime film/television has appeared online at Horrornews.net, *Horrified Magazine* (horrifiedmagazine.co.uk), *Ghouls Magazine* (ghoulsmagazine.com), and *Mandatory Midnight* (davidpaulharris.com). Her fiction has appeared in several anthologies and has been dramatised by NoSleep Podcast and Octoberpod. She is the author of *The Drowning Game, A Novella of the Supernatural*, available in digital form on Amazon, and of an upcoming collection of ghost stories from Dark Ink Publishing. Online, Jane mostly hangs out on Twitter at @JaneNightshade. She also blogs at hive.blog/@janenightshade.

Marie O'Regan
In the Howling of the Wind
(Originally Published in *Estronomicon* Christmas Issue, 2008)
Marie O'Regan is a Shirley Jackson and British Fantasy award-nominated writer and editor based in Derbyshire. She is co-editor of *The Mammoth Book of Body Horror, Exit Wounds, Wonderland, Cursed* and *Trickster's Treats #3*, and sole editor of *The Mammoth Book of Ghost Stories by Women and Phantoms*. She is also the author of the collections *Mirror Mere, In Times of Want and Other Stories, The Last Ghost and Other Stories*, the novella *Bury them Deep* and the novel *Celeste*. Marie is the co-chair of the Horror Writers Association UK Chapter and ChillerCon UK, which took place earlier this year. Find out more at marieoregan.net.

Katherine Quevedo
Midnight for Clementine
(First Publication)
Katherine Quevedo was born and raised just outside of Portland, Oregon, where she works as an analyst and lives with her husband and two sons. Her fiction has appeared or is forthcoming in *Nightmare, Fireside Magazine, Best Indie Speculative Fiction Vol. III* and *IV, Triangulation: Habitats, Last Girls Club*, Short Édition's *Short Circuit, Factor Four Magazine, Apparition Literary Magazine, Myriad Lands Vol. 2*, and elsewhere. When she isn't writing, she enjoys watching movies, singing, playing old-school video games, belly dancing, and making spreadsheets. Find her at katherinequevedo.com.

Charlotte Ridell
A Strange Christmas Game
(Originally Published in *The Broadway Annual*, 1898)
Charlotte Riddell (1832–1906) was born in County Antrim, Ireland. After the death of her father she moved with her mother to London in 1855. She is best known for her ghost stories with their atmospheric settings, which Riddell drew from her own experiences in Ireland and London. Riddell struggled to earn a living from her writing, despite being a highly popular author, and due to her poor circumstances became the first pensioner of the Society of Authors in 1901.

M.C. St. John
The Dark-Eyed Boy
(Originally Published in *Gothic Blue Book Volume VI: A Krampus Carol*, 2020)
M.C. St. John is a writer living in Chicago. He is the author of the short story collection *Other Music*. His stories have appeared, as if by luck or magic, in *Burial Day Books*, *Dark Ink Books*, *Nightscript*, *Oddity Prodigy Productions*, and *Wyldblood Press*. He is also a member of the Great Lakes Association of Horror Writers, serving as co-editor for the horror anthology Recurring Nightmares. See what he's writing next at mcstjohn.com.

Frank Stockton
The Great Staircase at Landover Hall
(First Published in *Afield and Afloat*, 1900)
Discouraged by his father from pursuing a career as writer, Frank Richard Stockton (1834–1902) worked for years as a wood engraver. After the death of his father, he eventually took a position at a newspaper in 1867, publishing the fairy tale 'Ting-a-ling' later that year. It was children's stories such as this that would be Stockton's legacy, as he broke with the moralizing tradition of the time, instead writing witty and charming tales of adventure, which gently mocked human faults and eccentricities.

Lamont A. Turner
Snowman
(First Publication)
Lamont A Turner's tales of mystery and horror have appeared in numerous print and online publications, such as *Mystery Weekly*, *Mystery Tribune*, *Cosmic Horror Monthly*, *Frontier Tales*, *Schlock*, *Dream of Shadows*, *Jitter*, *Little Demon Digest*, *ParABnormal*, *Crimeucopia*, *Lovecraftiana*, *Stranger with Friction*, *Terror House*, *Dark Dossier*, *Black Petals*, *Dissections*, *Yellow Momma*, *Bewildering Stories*, *Serial*, and *Wicked Library Podcast*. His stories have also appeared in over 30 anthologies. *Souls in a Blender*, his first collection of short tales, is available from St. Rooster Books on Amazon and Godless Horrors.

Suzanne J. Willis
And a Piece of Coal Where Her Heart Once Beat
(Originally Published in *The Dark*, December 2021)
Suzanne J. Willis is a Melbourne, Australia-based writer, a graduate of Clarion South and an Aurealis Awards finalist. Her stories have appeared in anthologies by PS Publishing and Prime Books, and in *Mythic Delirium*, *Lackington's*, and *The Dark*, among others. Her debut short story collection, *Of Starfish Tides and Other Tales*, is due for release by Trepidatio Publishing in 2022. Suzanne's tales are inspired by fairytales, ghost stories and all things strange, and she can be found online at suzannejwillis.webs.com.

Cassondra Windwalker
Ashes at Midnight
(First Publication)
Cassondra Windwalker is a poet, essayist, and novelist presently writing full-time from the southern coast of Alaska. She enjoys long walks on abandoned volcanic beaches, collecting otter skeletons, and drinking the tears of critics. Her most recent gothic horror, *Hold My Place*, was published January 2022 by Black Spot Books. Her other novels and full-length

poetry collections are available in bookstores and online. You can reach her via social media on Twitter @WindwalkerWrite, on Instagram @CassondraWindwalker, and on Facebook @ CassondraWindwalkerWrites.

FLAME TREE PUBLISHING
Epic, Dark, Thrilling & Gothic
New & Classic Writing

Flame Tree's Gothic Fantasy books offer a carefully curated series of new titles, each with combinations of original and classic writing:

*Chilling Horror • Chilling Ghost • Asian Ghost • Science Fiction • Murder Mayhem
Crime & Mystery • Swords & Steam • Dystopia Utopia • Supernatural Horror
Lost Worlds • Time Travel • Heroic Fantasy • Pirates & Ghosts • Agents & Spies
Endless Apocalypse • Alien Invasion • Robots & AI • Lost Souls • Haunted House
Cosy Crime • American Gothic • Urban Crime • Epic Fantasy • Detective Mysteries
Detective Thrillers • A Dying Planet • Footsteps in the Dark
Bodies in the Library • Strange Lands • Weird Horror
Lovecraft Mythos • Terrifying Ghosts • Black Sci-Fi • Chilling Crime
Compelling Science Fiction • Christmas Gothic*

**Also, new companion titles offer rich collections of
classic fiction, myths and tales in the gothic fantasy tradition:**

*Charles Dickens Supernatural • George Orwell Visions of Dystopia • H.G. Wells
Lovecraft • Sherlock Holmes • Edgar Allan Poe • Bram Stoker Horror • Mary Shelley Horror
M.R. James Ghost Stories • The Divine Comedy • The Age of Queen Victoria
Brothers Grimm Fairy Tales • Hans Christian Andersen Fairy Tales
Alice's Adventures in Wonderland • King Arthur & The Knights of the Round Table
The Wonderful Wizard of Oz • Ramayana • The Odyssey and the Iliad
One Thousand and One Arabian Nights • Persian Myths & Tales • African Myths & Tales
Celtic Myths & Tales • Greek Myths & Tales • Norse Myths & Tales • Chinese Myths & Tales
Japanese Myths & Tales • Native American Myths & Tales • Irish Fairy Tales
Heroes & Heroines Myths & Tales • Gods & Monsters Myths & Tales • Beasts & Creatures
Myths & Tales • Witches, Wizards, Seers & Healers Myths & Tales • Paradise Lost*

Available from all good bookstores, worldwide, and online at
flametreepublishing.com

See our new fiction imprint
FLAME TREE PRESS | FICTION WITHOUT FRONTIERS
New and original writing in Horror, Crime, SF and Fantasy

And join our monthly newsletter with offers and more stories:
FLAME TREE FICTION NEWSLETTER
flametreepress.com

GOTHIC FANTASY

For our books, calendars, blog
and latest special offers please see:
flametreepublishing.com